THE EMPYREUS PROOF

THE EMPYREUS PROOF

BRYAN WIGMORE

Proudly published by Snowbooks

Copyright © 2018 Bryan Wigmore
Bryan Wigmore asserts the moral right to be identified
as the author of this work. All rights reserved.

Snowbooks Ltd | email: info@snowbooks.com
www.snowbooks.com

British Library Cataloguing in Publication Data.
A catalogue record for this book is available from the
British Library.

ISBN 9781911390527
Electronic book text ISBN 9781911390534

First published September 2018

For Carol

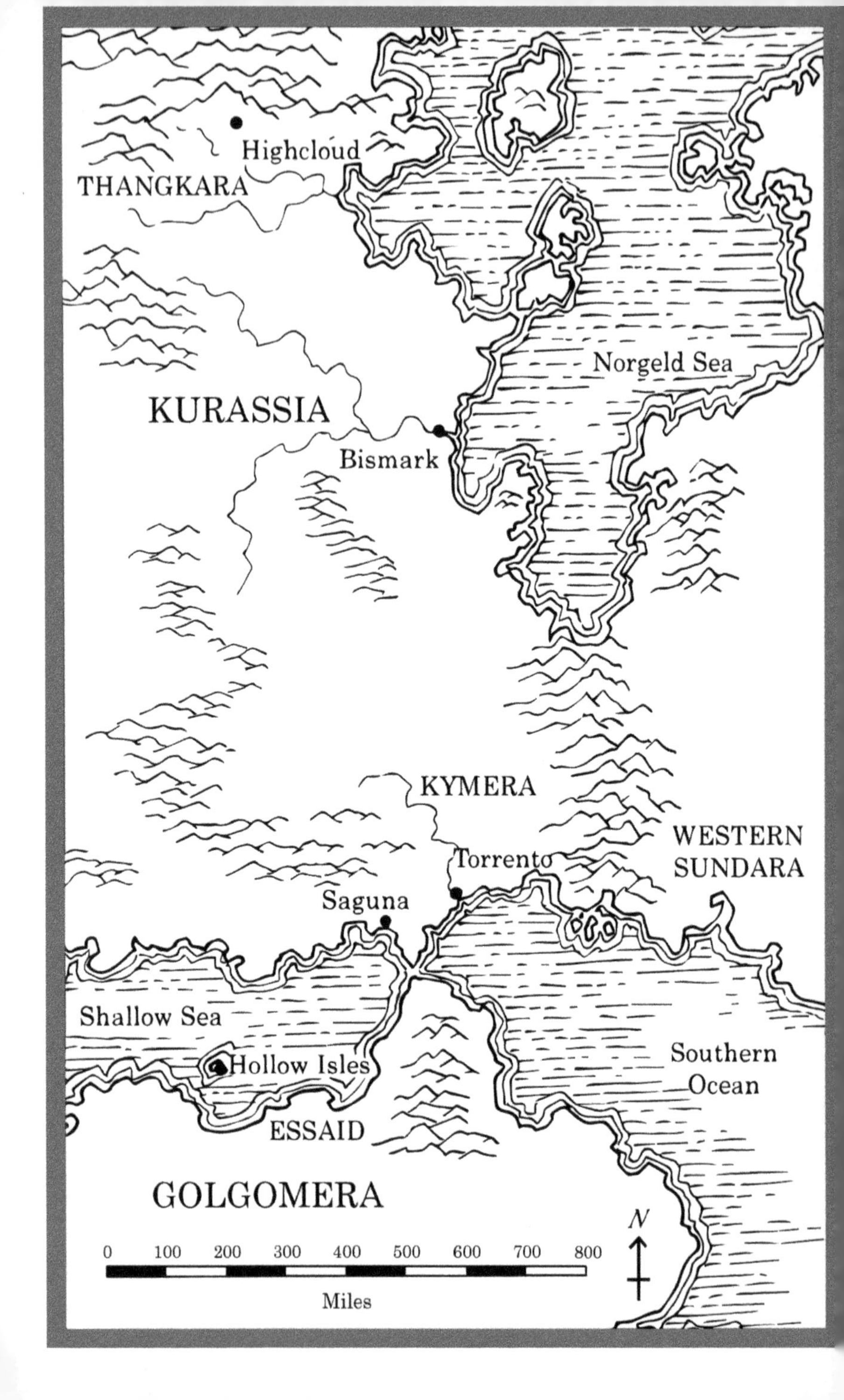
Highcloud
THANGKARA
Norgeld Sea
KURASSIA
Bismark
KYMERA
WESTERN
SUNDARA
Torrento
Saguna
Shallow Sea
Hollow Isles
Southern
Ocean
ESSAID
GOLGOMERA
N
0 100 200 300 400 500 600 700 800
Miles

PREVIOUSLY...

Orc and **Cass** are tormented by magical amnesia, unable to act on their mutual attraction in case they turn out to be brother and sister. Orc has been initiated into shamanism by **Geist**, and believes that if he can amplify his abilities enough, he can pierce the psychic Shroud blocking their memories. To this end, he and Cass search for a large focus-stone rumoured to lie in one of a number of sunken ziggurats. The pair can raid these ruins thanks to their unique freediving gear and Orc's connection with his animath, **Otter**, one of the mythical **Fire Stealers.**

During a confrontation with hostile fishermen, Cass almost drowns, and at the edge of death glimpses her shrouded past. She and Orc are rescued by a warship, which Orc realises is headed for the island where the focus-stone is located. This is no coincidence: the occultist leading the clandestine operation, **Daroguerre**, knows Orc and Cass are after the stone, and has secretly used it to lure them. He also knows that something in their hidden origins means they unwittingly catalyse the manifestation of thought-forms, and he plans to use this and the stone to resurrect an ancient goddess. The ship's crew believe this is to prevent a war, but in reality Daroguerre works for the shadowy **Kings Behind the World**, who wish to use the manifested goddess for their own ends.

In distant Highcloud monastery, Daroguerre's plan is detected by **Shoggu**, one of the Watchers tasked to guard against magic, and he sets out with his young bodyguard and disciple, **Tashi**, to thwart it. Tashi's training lets him be possessed by angelic warrior spirits, but when forced to corruptly demonstrate this to an Empyreal prelate, he is instead inhabited by their demonic shadows, **Qliphoth**, which he struggles to keep at bay. He and Shoggu are then joined by a past acquaintance of Orc and Cass, **Ranga**, who is seeking the stone on behalf of the sorceress **Vanessa**.

Cass begins to suffer nightmares, linked to her near-drowning, that suggest she and Orc were once both siblings and lovers. Orc rejects this possibility, and ignores Cass's pleas to leave the past hidden. At the island, he retrieves the focus-stone from the depths of the Great Ziggurat, but becomes psychically identified with the role of Sun-King, sacrificial consort of the goddess in ancient times. This leads Daroguerre to believe he can make the goddess serve himself rather than the Kings Behind the World, and he betrays his masters. Ensnaring Orc in a trance, he prepares to destroy Orc's mind to power the goddess manifestation and gain full control over her.

Realising the occultist's plan, Cass desperately seeks the aid of island resident **Hana**, who was also one of Geist's shamanic students and whose animath is **Hare**, another Fire Stealer. When Tashi and Shoggu arrive, the four join forces against Daroguerre, but Tashi is shot. Cass saves his life, but her touch allows the Qliphoth to begin transforming Tashi's body into living armour. Hana suppresses the demons, but Cass now knows she and Orc corrupt the barrier between the real and the psychic worlds.

Cass and Hana free Orc by shamanic means, with help from Hare and Otter, but Daroguerre still succeeds in manifesting a lesser aspect of the goddess: **Skalith**, the Destroyer. He uses her to sink an Empyreal dreadnought, but has to recall her when attacked by Tashi.

Tashi fights Skalith, but the battle is hopeless; she breaks him and burns him. In mortal agony, his resolve against the Qliphoth falters and they fully possess him, transforming him into a demonic warrior of living metal. This overpowers and slays the goddess, but the Qliphoth then reveal their aim to slaughter all life. Drawing on visions of the

Holy Mountain, Tashi sets his remaining will against his possessors, forcing his new body to stasis.

Daroguerre escapes, leaving Orc and Cass none the wiser as to the involvement of the Kings Behind the World. The pair leave with Hana and her adoptive parents, taking the now-inert Tashi, hoping to aid him when they reach the mainland.

From his hiding place, Ranga watches them depart. He now possesses the focus-stone, having stolen it after Skalith's destruction. When Vanessa collects him and takes the stone for herself, she reveals that she needs it to locate Geist, who once greatly wronged her, though she won't say how. His next task, she tells the besotted Ranga, is to find the man and bring him to her.

More information can be found in the glossary on page 653.

PART ONE
THE INNER EYE

1

THE PRISONER

Geist knew as soon as he entered the schoolroom that this was a day when the Lamia would feed. The sour taint of expectancy flowed from the dark hole of a missing brick high in the opposite wall, and it made his palms sweat. His guards took him to the end of the worn-smooth table and unshackled his wrists, then retired to flank the door. Geist perched himself on a creaking chair, and waited.

The juddering of hinges beyond the hole made him jump, though he'd expected it. Lamplight showed, a chair scraped; there came the ragged breathing of someone in pain. Geist kept silent. He was too old to risk a beating, and in any case, what could he say to the poor bastard in the next room? That he knew what would happen to them, that he'd overheard others suffer the same fate every few days of his captivity? Better to pretend not to exist.

'I know you're there.'

Geist paused in tugging at his beard, his breath stilled. The man's accent hadn't been that of a Bourg peasant, but Kurassian, educated. His heart raced, wondering whether to return the attempt at contact, whether the punishment might be worth it to speak with someone from that lost world of freedom: to share names, home towns, a few useless words of encouragement.

Then another spoke, the voice of cold, poisonous sweetness that always made him shudder, and he realised it hadn't been him the man had addressed.

'You sense the presence of your extinction.'

There came the sound of something being dragged across flagstones, and the Kurassian cried out, 'Dear God!'

'You beseech a god,' said the Lamia. 'Do you expect him to intercede?'

'I am – am—' The Kurassian restarted: 'I am prepared for death.'

'You believe so? Then you have no understanding of its enormity.'

'My soul will fly straight to Empyreus's house. My body is nothing.'

The Lamia laughed. 'Did you think it "nothing" when my men removed those fingers? You cried loud enough at that, and rightly so, for they were part of who you are. How terrifying to have them removed, your means of caressing a wife, of holding cutlery, to know you will never again do even those simple things. How much more terrifying to know you will never again smell sweet air, nor taste bread.' She laughed again. 'And you say you are prepared!'

There was a pause of heavy breathing, in which Geist imagined the Kurassian gathering his courage. He was tempted to stop his ears. But he was a seeker after knowledge, and this was knowledge.

'It is your end that is coming, and soon.' The man spoke with a forceful, tremulous certainty, as though he'd staked his life and sanity on one simple idea. 'The End Days are nigh. The Lord Empyreus will lead his armies and defeat the Witch and her servants. You will be consigned to the Pit Eternal.'

'Nothing is eternal,' said the Lamia. 'Your soul, as you call it, cannot be separated from the body. This truth has been kept from you. When your body dies, that will be the utter end of all you are, of all you think, of all you—'

Her voice was drowned out as the Kurassian broke into loud, defiant song. Geist recognised it as an Empyrean hymn, one about following the Divine Captain against foes uncountable. After two lines the words were stifled as if by a hand, but the tune continued, hummed with raw belligerence.

Then it turned to screams. Geist twisted in his seat until the noise ended. There followed the period of silence he always thought of as the Lamia feeding, though the exact nature of what passed in the next room eluded him. The dank psychic taint usually grew stronger at such times, but today it didn't, and he wondered if that had something to do with the Lamia failing to effectively taunt the Kurassian. Always before, her victims' lives had ended only after drawn-out minutes of desperate pleading.

He was pulling at his beard again.

'Bring me another tomorrow,' she said at last. 'One unlike him.'

'We have five of his men,' came the gruff reply. 'They've no other use.'

'Then bring me one before each normal offering. I will discover how to break their childish certainties.'

The dragging sounded again, fading. Geist studied his own fingers. Means of caressing, of holding cutlery – it was long enough since he'd done either. Fingers were also means of counting, for children or the dull-witted. But he'd abandoned that too. How long had it been? Six months, or thereabouts, but he'd lost track of the days.

He must not give up. As long as he was still useful to the Lamia, he wouldn't be taken to that other room. She made him overhear those horrors to cow him, to blunt his wits with fear and keep him from plotting an escape.

And here, as the schoolroom door creaked open behind him, came those he hoped to use for just such a purpose.

'Good afternoon, children,' he said, as they were ushered in by the ageing warrior Ulnur. The irony of his greeting and their lack of response was part of the daily routine, as was the smirk that appeared on the twins' pubescent peasant faces. Grubby skins, sly eyes, greasy hair: all were shades of earth-brown, as though the mud of the surrounding bog-lands had seeped into their every fibre. Taslan sat to Geist's left, Felca opposite her brother.

Ulnur opened his threadbare robe and drew out the scry-frame, Geist's blue crystal lens, still in its leather eye-patch surround, suspended by wires in its centre. He placed the frame between the twins, his glance warning Geist not to touch it – unnecessarily, after the bruises Geist had taken when he'd last tried.

'One hundred rounds of breath meditation,' Geist told the twins. 'Begin.'

They extended their right hands and entwined fingers beneath the suspended crystal. They breathed in unison, their timing perfect. Geist might have felt proud of them if he hadn't despised them so much. He kept count to himself, both as something to do and in case they ended too soon, or too late, something he could catch them out on.

As always, their own count was perfect. 'Now,' said Geist, 'we'll continue our search for those our Queen wishes destroyed.' The Lamia had expressed no such desire, but it was credible that she might. 'Gaze upon the lens, children. Turn your minds to its origin, to the crystal skull that ruled an empire before even our Queen arose to enthral the world.' *Or this foetid wasteland at least.* 'The pieces of the skull's jawbone are scattered, but all were once part of the same, and all hunger to be rejoined. *Feel* that hunger, children. We must resume our hunt for the false twins, those who would take your rightful place. I know these false twins possess another shard of the same skull. Across miles and mountain ranges, search it out, search *them* out…'

So he coaxed, describing the web of threads that made up the world, threads that would transmit a fly's touch to their hunting-spider senses. They were not Initiated, but they had talent, and Geist hoped that eventually—

'I see them,' Felca said drowsily. She stared into the lens, or through the lens into her brother's eye.

Geist didn't let himself get excited yet. One or both of them always 'saw' something. A few days before, they'd come out with all kinds of lurid nonsense about warships and demons.

But it seemed today might be different. Taslan drew in a long breath, then out: 'Yessss.' The twins' hands gripped harder beneath the scry-frame, then their free hands joined in, all four shifting, clutching, caressing, as they might have explored the touch of each other during long months pressed together in their mother's womb. They stared through the lens, breathing now as though in the onset of delirium – and Geist felt some greater charge in the air than normal.

'Two crystals together,' said Felca.

Geist frowned – that seemed wrong – but let them continue.

'They join,' said Felca.

'Mating,' added Taslan.

'Like animals.'

'A rabbit and a rat.'

'Not a rat,' corrected Felca. 'Larger, a water-swimmer.'

Geist felt the shock in his heart. *Otter?* But there was no point asking: the species was not native to the Bourgoune.

'Can you see people?' he asked. 'Or just these animals?'

'The man is straw-haired,' said Felca.

Excellent.

'The woman dark,' said Taslan.

Damn. 'The man is the water-swimmer?'

Felca nodded.

'These can't be the false twins,' said Taslan. 'They're not alike in any way.'

'Nevertheless,' said Geist. 'As an exercise, try to find where they are.' It might well be Orc, he thought, even if the other was not Cass. Perhaps Orc had broken his obsession with the girl who might or might not be his sister, and found a lover that somehow had an association with rabbits. Progress at last. If he knew the exact location of his former student, he might be able to connect with Orc even without his focus-stone, and project a message, an image, a dream: something that might lead to rescue.

The twins breathed, gripped, stared.

'Water,' said Felca at last.

'A river,' said Taslan. 'A house.'

'But we are not alone,' said Felca, her voice edged with fear.

'Others watch.' Taslan sounded as nervous as his sister.

'Watch?' said Geist. 'Who?'

'Old…' said Felca.

'Cold…' said Taslan.

'They will see us!' cried the girl.

'A dagger,' said Taslan. 'A sword.'

'An arrow.'

'They are the target.'

'The *sting*,' said Felca.

'The Scorpion,' said Taslan. 'The Scorpion approaches.'

'Come out!' urged Felca. 'The old ones sense us!'

The twins broke contact and leaned back in their seats, breathing hard.

'Quick, children!' urged Geist. 'Before it fades. What was the place you saw?'

They shook their heads. 'A house near a river,' said Felca. 'That is all.'

'And the Scorpion? You're sure? The *Scorpion* was heading for them?'

Taslan displayed foul teeth in a grin. 'Whatever that is, if the Queen wants them dead, she will soon get her wish.'

Geist put a hand to his brow. *Buggering damnation*. Every loathsome aspect of his captivity seemed to be laughing at him, as though the spirit of the Lamia's crumbling castle had deliberately raised the spectre of hope only to crush it out again.

If the assassin he knew as the Scorpion really was heading for Orc, there would be no rescue from that quarter. The young man would soon be in greater need than himself.

2

HOME

Hana lurched as the dray-horse came to an abrupt halt on the gravel drive, and pressed her palm against the seven-foot packing crate that occupied the centre of the vehicle's platform. 'We're home,' she whispered, eyeing with mixed feelings the heavy drapes at the bay windows, the tidy shrubs, all exactly the same as six months before. Even Mrs Baraktis, standing at the open front door, looked as if she hadn't moved since waving them off in the spring. Hana was relieved the housekeeper had got the telegram warning of their return – beds would be aired, water heated, all the comforts. But tired though she was from four days on *Aurora* and the drive from Saguna's harbour, bath and bed would have to wait.

She dropped to the ground and pulled the crate to the edge of the dray, while the servants who'd ridden with her began taking off the smaller luggage. Mrs Baraktis crossed to the open carriage in front to talk to Ferman and Stefanie – Hana watched her father introduce Orc and Cass Strandborn, who'd shared the carriage with them. Seeing the Strandborns together always slightly unnerved her: the same freckles faint against summer tans, the same brows darkly at odds with their hair, the same broad upper lip. They were too alike for cousins – for normal cousins.

Not that there was anything normal about them.

'Miss Hana?' said Sallo. 'Where for the statue?'

'I'll find out.' She crunched over the gravel, her approach drawing the usual look of suspicion from Mrs Baraktis – she'd been the Quallaces' housekeeper longer than Hana had been their adopted daughter. 'Father, where's best for the crate?'

'The morning room, I think,' said Ferman.

'Fine. And no one should go in without my permission, for any reason.'

He looked a little uncomfortable. 'That understood, Mrs Baraktis?'

The housekeeper folded her arms over the stiff front of her dress. 'Perfectly, sir.'

Hana turned to Cass. 'Can you come?'

She looked uncertain. 'If you like.'

'And me?' said Orc.

'Maybe you could help with my parents' luggage,' Hana said.

She picked four servants to carry the crate and led them through the hallway, past old-familiar paintings and doors. The solid reality of the house felt almost assertive, as if it were trying to fade the wildness of her recent island home, with its pines and rock and coast, into a dream. In the yellow-papered morning room, she arranged two sturdy chairs as a support, and the bearers placed the crate on the chair-seats and hurried out. Cass looked as if she were thinking of following them.

'Shall I see about a drink?' she said. 'Tea, coffee? Something stronger?'

'Nothing,' said Hana. 'We need to get working.'

'Not without rest,' said Cass. 'Hana, you look knackered.'

'I can't rest until I've got some idea what's going on inside him.'

'Don't you have? You were with him all the time on the boat.'

Hana rubbed the bridge of her nose. 'I couldn't do a proper scape at sea. Too much noise and motion. I just tried to put strength into him. What there was of him. I sang to him sometimes.'

'As a mother would.'

Hana checked Cass's expression, but there was no trace of mockery. 'I suppose some of that stuck with me, yes.' She walked around the crate, unfastening the lid.

Cass visibly tensed. 'I'll leave you to it, then.'

'No – please, stay.' Hana freed the last catch, annoyed how quickly she'd been reduced to pleading. 'I asked you to come in with me for a reason. When we first got the demons out of him at the Navel, it was us, together.'

'I didn't do anything.'

'You did! "Beloved one, be true to yourself" – remember? Those words brought Tashi back, at least for a while. *Your* words. We're a team.' The word felt inadequate for their partnership: so intense in the face of terrible danger, so much longer-seeming than could be accounted for in days. But she sensed Cass wouldn't accept anything stronger, not now she'd got back her too-alike cousin. On the return voyage, she'd only visited Hana's cabin twice.

But Hana wasn't giving up on it. 'Help me with this.'

Cass puffed out a breath. 'Okay.'

They lifted off the lid and sloped it against a wall. Despite having lived with Tashi's appearance for several days, Hana still had to steel herself to look into the crate. She quailed at the weapons that had replaced the Thangkaran boy's fingers, the impossibly seamless red plate-and-chain armour he now had by way of skin, the closed-eyed mask of inhuman hatred that was his face. She didn't want to think what might lie beneath.

Cass was staring, collarbones moving with her fast, shallow breath. Hana placed a hand on her forearm. 'It wasn't your fault.'

'What if it happens again?' Cass said. 'What if it spreads?'

'Nothing can manifest without a great deal of directed energy.' Or so Hana hoped. 'It'll be fine – we just need to support each other, like we did before.'

'It's not the same.' Cass gently pulled her arm free. 'Not if you're in a scape. I won't be with you there.' She eased towards the door. 'I'll leave you in peace.'

'Leave me *alone*, you mean.'

'Hana, I'm *sick* of magic. I want nothing to do with it. Is that so strange after what happened? I'll tell the others not to disturb you.'

Hana held her breath as the door clicked, fearing any exhalation would come out a scream, then wrenched the curtains closed so hard she almost pulled them from their rings. She tried to calm down, to make allowances. Cass was a good five years younger than her, probably not even twenty, not mature enough to cope with her part in Tashi's transformation. She and Orc placed the world's physical integrity in jeopardy – who wouldn't want to run from that self-knowledge? And the pair had had their memories blocked too. It was a wonder they weren't insane.

If she had to face this task alone, so be it.

She knelt beside the crate and began a breath meditation, trying to ignore the strangeness of doing this fully clothed on a rug and surrounded by walls, rather than naked in dappled shade at the Navel. When she felt ready, she prised out her tooth-like focus-stone from under her leather wristband, and pricked her buried tattoo-mask to her face. With the markings softly stinging, she lowered herself to her elbows and knees and bent her forehead to the floor, curling herself around her heart and belly.

She visualised the summer meadow behind her uncle's farm, the seed-heads flurrying as she kicked through the long grass of long ago. She sank into imagination and childhood memory: the clucking of quails hiding in the barley, the discovered eggs; the hum of the rich earth beneath, the burrowing of worms beneath the sun-baked crust, dust to mix with rain that heaved from the capricious summer sky and made mud to paint on the skin, out of sight, secret, away from men, the wildness.

And there, in the grass, was Hare.

She followed him as he ran the ritual course, flattening a five-pointed star enclosed by a circle. She seated herself at its centre and stared into Hare's eyes, wide, rich, shining brown in the holes of the bone mask whose dyed whorls matched those on her face – and the meadow, the beautiful discovery in a time of ugly ones, shifted into a wider realm.

'Hare,' she said, her mental voice reinforced by soundless movements of her lips, 'we must find Tashi.'

'I shall sniff him out.' Her animath ran around the circle that enclosed the pentacle, several times, then back and forth along a part of it, narrowing the arc.

'This way, child.'

In her imagination, Hana jumped to her feet and ran after him.

Meadow became wasteland as the ground climbed. She visualised each step across the rocky terrain with the full force of her creative mind – for this *was* an act of creation, the discovery and making of a landscape in which her actions might have a result beyond her own self. She'd been taught to use the soulscape only for divination, but circumstances on the island had forced her to use it to rescue Shoggu and Orc from magical traps. She tried to draw confidence from those successes, but Tashi's rescue might prove harder still.

Hare hopped and walked on, his uncertain route twisting and turning, sometimes through a fine mist with a reddish tinge. The air chilled; snow patched the ground. As the mist thickened and its colour deepened, a pressure built on Hana's mind. She recognised the taste of it, and steeled herself against fear.

'Hare!' The mist swallowed her whisper. 'Are you lost?'

Her animath shivered, his fur on end. 'This is not our place, child. There is no life here.'

'Tashi still lives, I know it. He's here, somewhere.'

She had to find his core. She turned to her memories. Strongest came her first sight of the Thangkaran boy in his black leather armour, his face taut with hate: the same hate that now pressured the air around her. But that hate wasn't truly his own, never had been. Confronting the image, she sought out the desperation behind the fury, then turned to the memory of finding him kneeling, his sword discarded. She'd held him tight as his hacking gasps had sobbed out his anguish. She'd removed his armour, strap by strap.

'Your body remembers warm arms that held you, even if your mind does not. Let mine be hers.'

She picked Hare up. His shivering warmth would guide her.

Ahead, and up, to her right.

When she smelled burnt meat, she thought at first it was part of the real world, a trace from the kitchen. But it came from her mist-shrouded destination.

'Be brave, Hare.' She clutched the trembling creature. She couldn't afford to fear what she might find, lest she turn aside from the finding.

The mist cleared to show a mountain-slope bright with sun. Her vision fixed on the charred body. It almost pulled her from the scape: her physical body reacted, her grip digging her focus-stone into her palm.

He lay stretched out on his front, blackened hands clinging to a small horn of rock protruding from the slope. His head, its hair burnt off, was raised to stare at the mountain's peak high above, a blinding whiteness of sun on ice. But chains attached to iron clamps on his neck and arms and ankles sought to pull him from the rock he gripped; they ran taut for many yards downslope before disappearing into a heavy bank of red fog. The chains shifted; from within the fog came the muffled scraping of metal, like swords being sheathed and unsheathed, or the workings of a distant engine.

The vision far exceeded her fears. 'What do I do?'

Hare wriggled; she set him down. 'He must not lose his hold on that rock.'

'If he does, he'll die?'

'Child,' said Hare, 'he keeps them in stasis, and so denies them control of his physical body. If his strength fails, then many will die, and you will likely be first.'

Panic attacked her. She had no means of cutting the chains. She couldn't conceive of entering the red fog.

'What can we do?'

'Alone, we do not have the power,' said Hare.

‘The Mother.’ On the island, Hana had guided and invoked that force, built up through centuries of ancient worship. ‘But she isn’t here.’

‘No,’ said Hare, his voice unsteady with fright. ‘This place has forgotten her.’

‘But perhaps *he* hasn’t. Perhaps, if he remembers…’

She feared to approach him. She knew this was only a representation of Tashi’s internal state, but she’d seen the scorch-marks where Skalith had been defeated, and knew the fire had done its work on Tashi before he’d been changed. She climbed round just above him, so he might see her and know someone cared and wanted to help. She called his name as she neared, but he didn’t turn his gaze from the mountain summit.

‘Tashi, beloved one, do you remember me?’ As she stepped in front of him, she forced herself to look at his charred face, his burnt-out eye sockets. Within those skull-hollows, a faint light glowed. He seemed to be trying to see through her.

His fingers slipped: only a fraction of an inch, but enough for fright. She stepped quickly out of the line of his stare.

‘HE DOES NOT KNOW YOU, WHORE. HE NEVER DID.’ The voices spoke in unison from the red fog. ‘HE HAD NO MOTHER. HE NEVER HAD.’ She recognised them, though they sounded different now, purer, free from the limitations of Tashi’s human larynx. ‘THERE IS NO MOTHER HERE. THERE NEVER WAS.’

Something large moved within the edge of the fog. She gathered her courage. ‘I drove you from him once.’

‘HE CALLED US BACK IN. YOU CANNOT EXPEL US AGAIN. RUN WHILE YOU CAN. PERHAPS IF YOU RUN TO THE EDGE OF THE WORLD WE WILL FIND YOU LAST AND YOU WILL LIVE LONGEST.’

She made herself ignore them. It hurt to look at Tashi, at the charred scraps of clothing that stuck to him, but she knelt beside him, trying to see some way to release the chains. She tried to comfort him, but his ruined skin shuddered at her touch. Despair clawed her chest. Hare sat trembling with his paws over his eyes.

The only thing that seemed to give Tashi strength of will was the sight of the mountain, but that was completely beyond her own sphere. Shoggu might have known how to work with it – she'd sensed him projecting the mountain's image towards the arena of Tashi's last fight. But Shoggu was dead.

'How'd it go?' asked Cass as Hana walked into the library. She and Orc were in different corners – Hana found it a relief to not see both of those too-similar gazes at once.

'I'll have to try again later.'

Cass closed her book. 'But he is still alive?'

'I think so. Have you seen my parents?'

'They cycled down to the harbour,' said Orc.

'Back to *Aurora*? Why?'

'No, the steamer pier,' said Orc. 'That telegram on the mantelpiece?'

'Your housekeeper said it came this morning,' said Cass.

Hana picked it up. *Arriving torrento packet seven morning fifteenth stop pray you are returning home with friend in red stop if you arrive first please wait stop am in danger stop jorik*

Frowning, she checked the clock. Just past three. Eight hours since the packet-boat, if it had arrived with its usual punctuality. 'They've gone to see where he's got to?' She read the telegram again. 'A friend in red? Is that Tashi? But how would Jorik know?'

'He's Ferman's brother, yes?' said Orc.

'Did Father know what this is about? What "danger"?'

'He seemed as puzzled as you,' said Cass. 'Though not as tired.'

As though the words had given her permission, Hana slumped into a chair. 'I couldn't do anything. I don't know how to help him, and I don't know how long he can last.'

'You just need a rest,' said Cass. 'You made it work on the island.'

'Orc and Shoggu were only affected mentally. Tashi's been *transformed*.' She couldn't prevent a note of blame entering her voice that time, but neither seemed to pick up on it.

'What about this college of yours?' said Orc. 'Can't they help?'

'It's hours by road. And no, probably not. They only use magic for divination and shielding. Trying to influence someone else is forbidden, even with good intent.'

'Geist must know how to do it, though,' said Orc.

'What makes you say that?'

'You've got Hare, I've got Otter: animaths from the same myth. I didn't know the Fire Stealers story before my Initiation, did you?'

'No,' she said – intrigued, despite a guess as to his motivation.

'Geist must've intended it,' he said, 'and that means he influenced us magically.'

'You talk like that's a good thing,' said Cass.

'It will be if he can help Tashi,' said Orc.

Hana saw his point. 'Yes, but we've no idea where Geist is.'

'Someone at the college might. You said he goes there sometimes.'

'I don't want to rush in there asking about him – I don't know the ins and outs of his relationship with the college, but it's not straightforward. Don't be impatient.'

'I was thinking of Tashi, that's all.'

'Really? Not just fishing for reasons to look for your old teacher?'

'*Our* old teacher! You want to find him too.'

'Tashi comes first. And this idea of Geist helping him is naïve. You can't assume us having animaths from the same story means…'

Her voice faltered as an idea broke open.

'Okay,' said Orc. '*You* work on Tashi, me and Cass will go to the college. If Geist isn't there, we won't ask anything about him. If he is, we'll bring him back.'

She barely noticed his words, her thoughts consumed by the possibility she'd awakened.

'Hana?'

'What if Geist had something in mind when he made sure we got Hare and Otter?' she said. 'What if he meant us to scape *together*?'

Orc's face showed wary curiosity; Cass's was a guarded wall. It struck Hana that perhaps she'd been focused on the wrong one. Cass had shared that intense time of danger with her, but what Orc shared with her might be more significant.

'How do you mean, "together"?' he said.

'Our animaths come from the same myth, like you said. And where do myths live? The soulscape! Hare and Otter are *meant* to be together there. Perhaps they can bring *us* together in a scape, so we can better focus on the same goal.'

'Is that even possible?' said Orc, his eyes narrowed but bright. 'To share a scape?'

'It must be worth trying. Together we might see things clearer, come up with a plan.'

'Hold on,' said Cass. 'What about risk?' She turned to Orc. 'Last time you scaped, you almost didn't come back.'

'Not quite the last,' he said. 'I did a quick one when we put into Carnega, just to check Otter came okay.'

'You didn't say.'

'I didn't want you to worry.'

'Well, I'm worried now.' She faced Hana. 'Those demons inside Tashi, will they be in the soulscape? The ones who made him attack you?'

'All they can do in a scape is spout hate,' said Hana. 'Anyway, they've no reason to hate Orc particularly. It's the Mother they hate, and he isn't—'

Realisation cut her off.

'Isn't what?' said Cass.

Hana kept her excitement from showing – if Cass got hold of this second idea, she wouldn't let Orc anywhere near it, however brilliant it was. 'We have to do it.' She looked at Cass. 'You want to talk about risk? If Tashi's will falters, the demons will get control. They want to kill everyone, us included. Does that ease your objections?'

She looked uncertain. 'I want to be there, then.'

'No,' Orc said.

'Sorry, Cass,' said Hana. 'Better if you're not.'

'Huh? But earlier...'

‘Earlier, I didn’t want to be alone. Now I won’t be.’ Though she knew it was petty, the turnaround in rejection felt satisfying. ‘And we’d do better without distractions.’

‘No distractions?’ said Cass. ‘So you’re going to keep your clothes on, are you?’

Hana shied from Orc’s questioning look. ‘I’m not on the island now.’

3

THE BLOOD OF ALL KINGS

Orc left the connecting door ajar, but only slightly, as he went from the morning room into the dining room. Hana had suggested awakening their tattoo-masks together, but he'd told her he might find her presence off-putting. It was preferable to the truth, which was that he felt embarrassed about how he entered a scape.

He closed the curtains, pulled back the rugs. The floorboards weren't as cool as the stone of the cave in which Geist had once imprisoned him, but imagination did the rest. Having roused his tattoo-mask, he curled up on the floor and plunged back to that initiatory shivering fear and cold and madness in the dark, drawing near to the Serpent Mandala, the two snakes dancing that was the whole world and all worlds.

When he was as close as he dared, when the edges of his mind began to fray into that ecstatic, terrifying sense of his self bleeding out into everything and nothing, he called for help. A moment later, clawed feet scrabbled on wood; animal musk thickened the air. He carefully half-opened his eyes to the dimness and sat up.

'I smell a river.' Otter stood on hind legs, bone-masked head nosing the air.

'At the bottom of the garden,' said Orc.

'Then why aren't we out there swimming?'

'We have other business.'

'Yes, yes, an appointment with a lady,' said Otter. 'Some might say that's no lady, that's your wife, but really, bruv: a rabbit and a rat! Someone's pushing my fur the wrong way.'

'What are you on about?'

'Bad atmospherics.' Otter's paws adjusted the fit of his mask. 'That's better.'

'Come on,' said Orc. 'We have to get next door.'

It was only a few yards, but he'd never before moved such a physical distance whilst scaping. Careful to keep his awareness as detached as possible from his body and surroundings, so as not to re-ground himself, he crept through to the morning room. The dim light showed Hana curled over on a rug, her hands flat beside her head.

'We're here,' he let her know. 'Otter!' he hissed: the creature was sniffing her.

'Is this a female submission posture, bruv? Do you want some privacy? Or some advice?'

Orc settled into a chair. 'We have to get to the Otherworld.'

'I'm already there,' said Hana.

'Otter, I meant.' Eyes gently closed, Orc readied himself for the mental phase of the journey. He imagined standing from the chair and walking into the empty hallway. In his mind's eye, Otter beside him, he went deeper into the house, instinct leading him to a narrow door that opened onto a spiral staircase. Orc counted his steps as he descended, relaxing his mind and leaving his seated body ever further behind. The wall roughened, moss grew on it; shiny ferns' tongues poked from crevices.

'We're at the lower door,' he said, pushing it open. 'There's a wasteland.'

'Not much chance for swimming here,' said Otter.

'Try to find the mountainside,' said Hana. 'I did it by remembering Tashi, but you never knew him, so maybe Otter can search out Hare?'

'Otter, try—'

'I heard the voice from the sky, bruv! He's around here? Old leggy long-ears?'

'Somewhere.' Orc set off. Hana had related her previous scape in detail, so he knew what to look for: he mentally oriented himself towards the idea of a mountainside, a burned body, chains. Soon he and Otter were passing through the red mist Hana had talked about.

But when they emerged from it, the situation wasn't as he expected. Downslope to his left hung the bank of red fog, but the chains that emerged from it ran straight to the mountain peak. There was no sign of Tashi.

'Look again,' said Hana, after he'd explained. 'If we want to direct our energies in unison, we have to work in the same landscape.'

'And it has to be your version, does it?'

'I know Tashi, you don't. You can't even see him at the moment.'

'Don't you have to let the scape come as it will, though? There might be a reason I'm seeing things differently. Maybe there's something I can see that you can't.'

'Like what?' said Hana, quick with impatience.

'The demons are in that fog, yes? And you haven't seen them.'

'I don't need to see them to know what they are.'

'But what if it's easier to release the chains from *them* than it is from Tashi?'

Her pause was gratifying.

'Can *you* see them, then?' she said.

'Let's find out.' He turned his attention to the fog, and asserted a light breeze arising – such a thing would be natural on a mountainside. He visualised the current of air blowing the vapour. As a shape within began to emerge, he focused, mentally coaxing detail into the open.

His heart beat harder as the thing was revealed. A large red serpentine form writhed against the pull of the chains that attached it to the mountain's summit; its scales rubbed together like sword-blades. Its grotesque body seemed made of many other forms, humans and weapons and armour, pressed together, entwined, misshapen. Each of the many heads had a grinning mouth and small, blind eyes; the chains were attached to collars around the many necks. Great bat-like wings, torn and ragged, lay against the ground.

'Careful, bruv!' piped Otter. 'This is nothing you can handle.'

Orc tried to steady his nerves. It felt like he had intruded too deep. But the vision sparked a memory. The entity was very different from the golden, fiery creature he'd beheld in his scape on the island, but he thought he knew it.

'Saeraf?'

All the heads turned to him.

'DON'T LOOK,' cried the thin, unified voices. 'DON'T LOOK.' More red fog began to stream from the still-grinning mouths and from beneath the serpent's battered scales. In moments, the vision was hidden once more.

'Well?' said Hana.

'Uhm... don't know.' Orc felt an unsteadiness in his chest, as though something had interfered with the pattern of his heart.

'Do you see how to release the chains, or not?'

'No.'

'Then stop mentally wandering off, and align your soulscape with mine.'

Yes, your Majesty. But Orc was only too willing to let the Saeraf-vision go. 'Align how? By willpower?'

'Maybe our animaths can tell us,' said Hana. 'After all, they're the link between us here.'

'About time!' said Otter. 'Somebody *wants* my advice.'

'And what is it?' said Orc.

'To get a grip on a slippery fish, you need a tooth in either jaw.'

'Big help, cheers.'

Otter shook his fur out. 'First rule of school – don't make everything too easy.'

'Hare said that if we want to see the same image, we need to look through the same skull,' said Hana. 'Did Otter say anything like that?'

'Ish.'

'Ha!' said Otter. 'That's almost "fish", and fish is all you need, bruv. And she's the "f"-in fish, if you get my meaning. You need to get slippery with her.'

Orc decided to ignore that, and instead relayed what Otter had said about the teeth.

'Our focus-stones are shaped a bit like teeth,' said Hana. 'And they strengthen our connection with the Otherworld. What if they could connect us *within* the Otherworld?'

Orc thought that made sense. 'How about I turn round, away from the fog, and you try to *project* your vision to me, through the focus-stones?'

'Like Shoggu projected the vision of the Mountain to Tashi – yes, I get it.'

Orc gripped his stone tighter and thought about its power for connection. As he turned, in the scape, he tried to open himself to what Hana had described, what she wanted him to see: not forcing it, but allowing it to slip through.

The first time didn't work, nor the second. He made a couple more attempts, adjusting the cast of his mind each time, like altering the position of a lens to focus it.

On the fifth go, everything snapped into clarity. The chains now ran not to the summit but to a charred body nearby. The scape was more than just an intense visualisation; it had the sharpness of a dream, almost as strong as when he'd used the large focus-stone on the island.

'Gods!' said Hana. 'It's so real.'

'You too?'

'It's as if… it's no longer all in my own head. It feels like its own reality.'

'Greetings, quest-brother,' said a voice by Orc's feet. He looked down to see what could only be Hare: black-tipped ears, rough fur, bone mask. Hare's nose touched Otter's.

Hana reported a similar meeting. 'I can't see you, though.'

Orc looked round for her, in vain. 'Why's that, do you think?'

'This is a place of symbol and myth,' said Hare. 'You are neither, yet.'

Hana laughed.

'What's that?' said Orc.

'What Otter said.'

'But... so we don't share what they say?'

'I told her you think she's hot,' said Otter. 'She'll be receptive now.'

'For God's sake,' he muttered.

'We can experiment later,' said Hana, which made Otter yip with laughter. 'Now we're in the same landscape, we should be able to combine our energies. Focus on the chains. If we can break them, the demons will fall away.'

'Break them how?' said Orc.

'Hmm. Good question.'

'Maybe we could stop them pulling,' he said. 'If we can fix the chains to the ground behind Tashi, that would take up the strain. Or run a line from the chains to something else higher up the slope, and bypass him.'

'That would at least give him a chance to recover,' said Hana. 'Good idea.'

'Except we don't have any rope or anything.'

'No. But we might grow some.'

'Grow...?'

'Suppose creepers grew from the ground between Tashi and the fog and twined through the chains, and grew up the slope and wrapped themselves round those rocks higher up? If they were thick and strong enough, that would hold the chains in place, and he could let go.'

'How do we get that to happen?'

'The Mother,' said Hana. 'Her power on the island wasn't only in the big cave. Tree roots can turn rock to powder; ivy can crumble a wall. None of the works of man can withstand an assault by the powers of growth and generation. And whatever those chains are, they're nothing the Mother has made.'

The fervency in Hana's voice reminded Orc uncomfortably of Daroguerre's rite to summon Skalith. She had been an aspect of the very same force.

'But there's no sign of the Mother here,' he said.

'This place has forgotten her,' said Hana. 'But doesn't that remind you of anything? Wasn't that also true during the famine suffered by the ziggurat-builders?'

A warning prickled Orc's mind.

'That's why we could only do this together,' said Hana. 'Because you are the Sun-King.'

He almost choked. 'You want me to *sacrifice* myself?'

'No! Not like that. I think we'll just need some of your blood to wet the ground. It's magically potent, because of your role as the goddess's consort. A little of it penetrating the earth will be enough, if we believe in it.'

'It didn't work for the ziggurat-builders.'

'Not in the physical world, no – how could it? But that doesn't mean it can't work here. It was a magical idea, after all. I'd have thought the difference would be obvious to you.'

Orc didn't like it. But it did make magical sense, and Hana seemed convinced. To refuse just because he wouldn't shed his own blood in real life, when this was *not* real life, would only make him look stupid.

A nose nudged his leg. 'If the goddess can't grow new life alone,' said Otter, 'then it's seeding she wants, not your bleeding. You waste enough of the fertile stuff – put it to use!'

Orc cringed.

'Quest-brother speaks truth,' said Hare. 'New growth can be fed by the dead, but it must be initiated by mating. You are the earth's husband.'

'Well?' said Hana. 'Any problem?'

'Don't be embarrassed pulling it out, bruv!' said Otter. 'She'll see plenty of it soon enough.'

'Okay!' he said to Hana. 'Let's try with the blood.'

'Ach,' said Otter.

Orc approached the chains a couple of yards downslope of Tashi's burnt feet.

'I can see you now,' said Hana.

Orc turned his mind's eye, but saw only Hare. 'Is that good?'

'Must be.'

Just as well he'd decided on blood, Orc thought. When he returned his attention to the chains, he found a stone knife in his hand. 'Right, I'm about to cut my arm.'

'Make it as real as you can,' said Hana. '*Feel* it.'

Orc imagined himself drawing the edge of the knife across the pale, tender underside of his forearm, recalling the cold flare of pain from a time he'd accidentally sliced into his finger. He described to Hana the redness welling, streaming, the pain deepening its bite, the blood dripping onto the ground.

'The blood of all kings.' Hana's voice carried a commanding quality. 'It pours out through you without diminishing you.'

'I am of the line that goes back to before the sundering of Saeraf and Chthonis,' Orc said, the words seeming to come as though provided by the soulscape. 'The nourishing blood flows from me like a river.'

'Yes, bleed!' exhorted Hana. 'Bleed for Her as she once bled for you. Give Her back what you took.'

A steady stream poured from the cut. It ran over and between the chains and melted the patchy snow beneath. Orc imagined it also melting the iron hardness of the mountainside, penetrating, sinking into thirsty rock and turning it to fertile loam.

'Bruv, too much!' said Otter.

'It's fine,' he muttered. It wasn't all his own blood: more had poured forth than his body could have held. Hana was right: he was every Sun-King who had ever dismembered himself atop a ziggurat. As the earth had given him life, he should give it back when it was demanded. So the world turned; so the blood spurted now, stronger, a scarlet jet, drenching and feeding the barren ground. He felt euphoric, his head light.

'Grow!' commanded Hana.

Shoots appeared from the red-drenched earth beneath the chains. Orc stepped back as with impossible speed they grew, tens of them, reaching for the metal links and entwining with them, running between, swarming green. As they reached Tashi, the leading tendrils leapt to the ground and felt their blind way across snow and rock, latching on to everything they could find, anchoring, tightening, until Tashi and the horn of rock he clung to were almost hidden. Orc back-stepped until several yards separated him from the green mass.

At Hana's urging, the vines bulked, strengthening in moments with the growth of seasons. The chains were lost beneath the heaving mass of creeper – and in the dense centre of that mass appeared two small dark holes, like eyes.

'Bruv!' squeaked Otter.

The mass extruded feelers that entwined together, becoming a thicker, snake-like arm that grew rapidly across the ground towards Orc as though searching, sensing. Around the empty eyes, leaves and creepers shaped a face.

'*Mine*,' came a voice – a voice Orc recognised from the underwater darkness and pressure of the Bazantin ziggurat.

Terror rooted him. The groping end of the creeper-tentacle neared him with impossible speed. It raised up before him. He couldn't move. It wrapped around his neck and closed, tight.

'*Mine*.'

He fell. The ground slammed his body.

'Orc! What happened?'

He fought to get his fingers between the creeper and his throat. He couldn't breathe; he really couldn't breathe. He half-sensed his physical body, its struggle on the floor of the morning room, choking. This wasn't real, but his windpipe was shut fast. He tried to get out of the soulscape and back to the material world, but reality lay beyond a barrier he'd forgotten how to cross. He tried to call for help, but could only gasp. Otter bit at the creeper, Hare kicked, but they were too small and all the time the vine grew thicker, stronger, tighter.

'Leave him!' cried Hana.

'*Mine*!'

'It was I who called you.' Hana's voice trembled with its force. 'And I *command* you to leave him.'

'*MINE!*' The voice throbbed through the ground and every fibre of the strangling vine. Hana's voice came loud, her words almost lost against the blackness that rushed Orc's mind.

'He is not yours!' she called. '*I claim him for myself!*'

The rope-vine around Orc's neck shivered, split into fibres that shrivelled, shredded. A cry came from the mass of vegetation, and what remained of the creeper-arm withdrew.

'Orc? Are you all right?'

'Just about,' he gasped. 'I'm out of here.'

He knew he should leave the Otherworld by the same route and with the same care as he'd entered, to avoid psychic damage, but he was too panicked. Breathless and shaking, he eased himself back into the chair he'd fallen from and hunched over, trying for calm, his throat in agony.

Knuckles sounded on the door. 'What's happening in there?' came Cass's voice.

'Keep her quiet,' said Hana. 'I need to come out of the scape.'

Orc stood, feeling woozy and detached. He opened the door only a crack, both to keep the room dim for Hana, and because his tattoo-mask was still up.

'Everything okay?' said Cass through the gap. 'I heard voices.'

'It's okay,' he rasped. 'We'll be done soon.'

He snicked the door closed again. Hana eased herself out of her crouch. 'You sound rough. Does it hurt?'

'Uh-huh.'

'The pain's only a suggestion of your mind.' She stood. 'Maybe you came out of the scape too quickly to leave it behind?'

'Have to admit I was in a hurry.' He had difficulty speaking.

'It'll be fine.' Hana laughed awkwardly. 'We did it, Orc. A joint scaping: it really works! Come on, we'd better unmask.'

She turned away and smoothed her hands across her face, as though carefully washing away the tattoos. Orc focused on his own, willing them to disappear, and hung his focus-stone back around his neck.

When Hana had finished, she drew back the curtains, flooding the room with afternoon light. Then she turned to the crate and studied the figure within.

'You know, I think he looks a little more human already.'

Orc stepped nearer. He was wondering whether to admit he saw no change in Tashi's horrific appearance, when Hana looked at him and cried out.

'What?' said Orc. Then the door-handle creaked, and he turned. Cass's face tightened in shock.

Orc glanced at the mirror over the mantelpiece, and gasped at the chain of bruises, livid and raw, that collared his neck.

'What the hell happened?' said Cass.

'They're *real*?' said Hana.

He approached the mirror. His fingers trembled on his throat.

'This is from the scape?' demanded Cass. 'It can physically *hurt* you now?'

'It's only bruising,' he said, unsteadily.

'How can you *say* that?'

'Calm down, Cass,' said Hana. 'He wasn't in danger. Something unexpected happened, and I dealt with it.'

'By claiming him for yourself?' said Cass.

'You were listening?'

'You practically shouted it. What did you mean by it?'

'I had to get her off him,' said Hana. 'That's all.' Her eyes darted downwards. 'Look, now we know the kind of things that can happen, we'll be more on our guard.'

'You don't seriously think you're doing anything like that again?'

'Absolutely!' said Hana. 'This joint-scaping is incredible. When we aligned our scapes, the clarity of vision was unprecedented!'

'I don't care about that—'

'No, of course you don't. Because it doesn't benefit you, does it?'

Cass glared. Alarmed, Orc tried to think of some way to cool things down. But to his relief, Cass seemed to decide against stoking the argument further.

'There's a cab here for you,' she said.

'What?' said Hana.

'Came about five minutes ago. I told it to wait. Ferman sent it. He's at the hospital. Your uncle was on the steamer this morning, but he's very ill.'

Hana looked at Tashi. 'I can't...' she said, then turned to Orc. 'Will you check on him while I'm gone? Make sure the vines are still doing their work?'

'What about...?'

'The Mother won't trouble you again,' said Hana.

'The *Mother*?' said Cass.

'Please, Orc. It's important.'

'If you think... sure.'

'Tell him I'll be with him soon,' said Hana, looking suddenly exhausted. 'And ask Mrs Baraktis for anything you want. But close the crate up, and make sure no one else gets in here.'

'What do we say about those bruises?' said Cass, as Hana made to leave. 'We agreed no one else can know about the manifesting – and that's what they are, right?'

'I won't mention them,' said Hana. 'You two think of something. Love bites maybe,' she added as she closed the door.

4

THE SHROUD MAKERS

As he replaced the lid of the crate, Orc wondered if Cass was also thinking about Hana's parting words, and whether anyone else had started to speculate.

'So, what happened?' she said. 'In the scape?'

The question he'd dreaded. 'You've never been interested in my scapes before.'

'How did you get those bruises?'

He knew she wouldn't drop it, so with reluctance he related the whole thing, increasingly finding himself staring at the floor. He tried to skip over the self-sacrifice, but she picked at the gaps in his story until she'd got it out of him, and then her look accused him of evasiveness as well as stupidity.

'Let's go, right now,' she said. 'Get a ride to the college. Find Geist.'

'We can't just leave,' said Orc.

'Why not? You're not thinking of scaping again, just because Hana says so? She doesn't know what she's doing. Those bruises surprised her as much as us.'

'What about Tashi, though? You heard her – if we don't help him, people will die.'

'According to her,' said Cass, then sighed. 'Okay, what *can* we do?'

'Keep trying the library?'

'See you in there,' she said, and went out.

Orc was skimming the bookshelves when Cass came back several minutes later, holding a length of pale yellow silk. She tied it loosely round his bruised neck, tucking it into his open shirt collar.

'There,' she said. 'Might stop Ferman and Stefanie asking awkward questions.'

'Or start them,' said Orc. 'Where'd you get it?'

'Hana's room, must've been. Don't worry, it was at the back of a drawer. I don't think it's the kind of thing she wears now.'

'Yeah, but… you went through her stuff?'

'Why would she care?' said Cass, and returned to the book she'd been reading earlier. Orc carried on searching the shelves for anything that might be related to manifestation. He found two books whose titles referenced the Zhenaii, the ancient race reputed to have possessed the art, but their prose was impenetrable. He'd just put the second one back when wheels and hooves sounded on gravel.

He joined Cass at the window overlooking the drive. The cab carried no passenger, only two pieces of luggage. Mrs Baraktis walked out with Sallo to meet it. The housekeeper signed a paper the driver gave her, and Sallo carried the luggage in. Stairs creaked.

'Jorik's, I guess,' said Cass.

The afternoon dragged by. Despite promising Hana, Orc didn't perform another scape to check on Tashi. The one time he went into the morning room, he momentarily caught the faint odour of rotting vegetation, but didn't know if that meant a weakening or strengthening of the Mother's power. He didn't want to risk the latter, whatever Hana had promised. As dusk approached, he and Cass took a break from research and walked down the gently sloping lawn at the rear of the house. A pleasure-craft puttered along the river; birds chattered in the reeds. Steps cut into the bank led to a small jetty, beside which rested an upturned boat. Orc sat on the jetty and stared between his knees at the water.

Cass sat beside him – then pushed him in the back, as though trying to shove him in. He resisted, laughing, until she suddenly thumped him between the shoulder blades.

'Ow! What was that for?'

'For leaving me behind,' she said.

'When?'

'When *don't* you? All those ziggurats I couldn't follow you into, all those scapes. And now this joint-scaping Hana's so excited about, which makes everything "more real" – like that's a good thing.'

'Cass—'

'Why those bruises now? Daroguerre wanted you to cut yourself to pieces in the Otherworld – but he wanted you physically intact, so he couldn't have meant that to injure you. And he seemed to know how this stuff works. What's changed since?'

'I don't know.'

'Doesn't it scare you, how far it *might* have gone?'

'I cut myself in the scape, and there's no mark on my arm, is there?'

'But that was your doing, not the Mother's.'

Orc didn't like the implications of that.

'Promise me no more risks,' said Cass. 'No more scapes, nothing – not before we get to that college.'

'With Hana?' said Orc.

Cass didn't answer.

'She knows about Geist,' said Orc. 'The idea was that we three together—'

'But it's not us three together, is it?' said Cass. 'God knows I feel sorry for Tashi, but Hana's lost herself over that boy. There's not ten years between them, but she acts like she's his mother or something, because of an invocation she did on the island. Is it only people who don't do magic who see how mad it is, how mad it makes you?'

'Thanks.'

'I thought she was so capable,' said Cass. 'I was only okay with bringing Tashi back because I was sure Hana knew what she was doing. But all the time her competence was just a shell, with craziness underneath.'

He didn't challenge her, didn't know how.

She raised her head then, and Orc heard it too, a carriage drawing up at the front of the house.

'I think she was right,' said Cass. 'I think Geist did intend you and Hana to meet, and to joint-scape. He was all about power. He shut you in that cave and almost starved you to death so your Initiation would be as powerful as possible, and the joint-scaping's the same: ramp up the power and fuck the risk. Yes, we have to find him – but nothing about him is healthy or good for you. You do see that? Promise me, Orc – no more of it.'

He heard his name called from the house, Hana's voice.

Cass touched his arm. 'Promise me.'

He stood. 'We'd better see what she wants.'

He climbed the bank as Hana's voice came again and again, closer and more breathless each time. By the time they reached the top, she was almost on them.

'We've come from the hospital.' She panted to a stop. 'With Jorik.'

'He's okay, then?' said Orc.

'No. You need to come and help.'

'How?'

Hana turned, urging them back towards the house. 'No one can wake him,' she said as they hurried with her. 'A steward left a statement, said he met Jorik last night and they went to his cabin to play cards. Jorik told him he hadn't slept for days, said something terrible would happen if he did, begged the steward to keep him awake. Jorik said he was on his way here, hoping to meet his brother and a religious man who could help him.'

'The "friend in red"?' said Orc.

'He must've meant Shoggu, not Tashi.'

'But how could he know about—'

'I don't know!' said Hana. 'We asked the same: how did he know Father was coming back early, how did he know about Shoggu? And that's not all he knows. He told the steward there were things he couldn't say because that would put the steward in danger too. Maybe things someone doesn't want to go any further.'

'Someone like Daroguerre?' said Orc, even more perturbed than before. 'You think this "sleep" is to stop your uncle talking?'

'Maybe,' said Hana. 'The steward thought Jorik was deluded – he thought sleep was the best thing for him, so he didn't stop him nodding off, and now...'

'And you think we'll be able to wake him?' said Orc as they reached the house. Cass gave him a troubled look as he held the door for her.

'If it's a magical trap like those you and Shoggu were caught by,' said Hana, 'it'll have a symbolic form. If we can see it in a scape, maybe we can disarm it. How's Tashi?'

'I didn't get round to checking, sorry.' He didn't mention the smell of rotting plants.

'Well, at least you'll be fresh,' said Hana. 'I can't believe it – first Tashi, now this. But we know how to joint-scape now. What we learned with Tashi might save Jorik.' She glanced at Orc's neck. 'Next time you want to go through my old clothes, ask.'

The air in the drawing room felt oddly heavy as Orc entered, a charged prickle on his skin. Ferman, Stefanie and Mrs Baraktis stood around a couch on which a man lay shivering beneath a blanket, his head jerking side to side, his lips drawn back. Sweat curled his red-blond hair and slicked his face.

'Orc.' Ferman had hold of Stefanie's hand. 'Hana's told you? You can help?'

'I'll try.'

Hana shut the curtains. 'Leave that for now,' she told Sallo, who was trying to build up the fire, and ushered the others out, the servants needing no persuasion. Orc's damp neck tingled more strongly. The room felt weirdly both cold and hot, its ceiling high but still somehow too low, trapping the oppressive air. He looked more closely at the man: younger and slimmer than Ferman, but still resembling him. Sometimes he almost caught words in the man's muttering. He tried to stop himself latching on to them, instinctively afraid of what they might be. The thought came that Jorik's knowledge might be so terrible, it would be unwise to wake him.

'You need to go next door again, to mask up?' The way Hana's face gleamed in the weak firelight made her look ill. She nodded towards what Orc realised must be a connecting door to the library.

'Wait,' said Cass. 'This is Daroguerre you're dealing with.'

'We don't know that,' said Orc.

'He tried to destroy your mind. We just had all that with the Mother—'

'If we don't do this,' interrupted Hana, 'Jorik might not make it. And Daroguerre's goddess plot is over. He has no reason to sacrifice Orc any more.'

'No more than you did,' said Cass.

'I did *not*—'

'Okay, okay,' said Cass. 'But he still has revenge as a motive, doesn't he?'

'If he wanted that, it would be against all of us.'

'But Orc's mind was the only one he had a hold over. It makes him vulnerable. You start the scape, and if there's no sign it's Daroguerre, Orc can join you.'

Hana flashed Orc an exasperated look, then nodded. 'We're wasting time.'

Orc went into the library with Cass and quietly drew the curtains. He wondered how easy it would be to persuade her to leave the room while he masked up and underwent the Little Death; she seemed in a particularly headstrong mood. His skin felt irritated by the belligerence in the air. He tried to settle into one of the library chairs. The urge to get out and leave the house pulled like tiny hooks under his skin, until he had no hope of relaxing or even sitting still.

'Feel that?' whispered Cass beside him.

'You too?' He hardly dared breathe.

'Something familiar about it,' she said.

'Daroguerre?'

'Don't know. I don't like this. It's building—'

Hana screamed.

Orc threw himself out of the chair and ran into the drawing room, Cass behind him. The weight of malice in the air slammed him to a halt as though it were more solid than his body. 'Like blackout,' Cass gasped, and darted back into the library. Orc didn't understand, but there was no time to ask. Pushing down the urge to follow her, he made himself step forward into the poisoned atmosphere. Hana looked almost to be cowering.

'What happened?' said Ferman, standing at the other door with Stefanie and Sallo. 'Are you all right?'

'I didn't dare even start the scape,' said Hana shakily. 'If it's as bad as this just preparing…'

'As bad as what?' said Ferman. 'You can feel something?'

'Me too,' said Orc. 'Like a – a lightning-cloud, under the ceiling. A power. Must be part of the trap, to stop us helping him.'

'Not a trap,' said Hana. 'This isn't something he's triggered. Whoever's doing it, they're attacking him with it right now.'

'What d'you mean?' said Orc.

'They're *here*! With us.'

His back crawled as he sensed the truth of it. The malice wasn't part of some enchantment, but an active presence.

'Daroguerre?' said Ferman. 'But he must be thousands of miles away.'

'Not Daroguerre,' said Hana. 'Shining beings.' She hunched, seeming barely to hold herself from running. 'I sensed them. It felt like – like next to them I wasn't even *real*, only *they* were. It must be how it feels to be in the presence of gods.'

'Holy Iselda,' said Ferman. 'You can't think they *are*?'

'They can't be!' said Orc.

Hana closed her eyes and breathed hard. 'No, you must be right. But to have such power…'

Ferman looked stricken. 'You must be able to do *something*?'

She shook her head in hopeless anguish.

'Hana!' pleaded Ferman. 'Think who this is!'

Stefanie gripped his shoulder. Orc felt clawed by the look of desperation Hana gave her father. He tried to think of something, but the dark pressure sapped his mind.

'Wait,' Hana said. 'If Orc can make a psychic shield around me, I might be able to scape safely, at least to see what's going on.'

'How?' He almost panicked. 'I don't know anything like that.'

'I could teach you. I know a couple of protection meditations.'

'I'm no good at meditating. Geist said so.' He felt wretched denying his help, but the malice was too great. 'Hana, you can feel it – it'd blast through anything I could put up, even if I knew how.'

She hit her fist against the wall.

'But—' An idea jumped him at last. 'What about the college?'

'Again with the college!' cried Hana. Then her face changed. 'Yes – *yes*! The college is shielded against outside magic, to stop anyone scrying into it. Brilliant!'

She crossed to Orc, threw her arms round him and kissed him on the cheek.

'I only meant they might know how to help,' he said, surprised.

'Who cares what you meant?' she said, letting him go. 'At least it's a chance.'

'Is it really our only one?' said Ferman. 'The place is hours away, and it's nearly dark.'

'I know,' said Hana. 'But we should be able to safely scape there, and Jorik might be easier to treat. If he's shielded, he might even wake up by himself.'

'Let's pray he lasts,' said Ferman. 'Sallo, go back to the hire company and get the carriage. Whatever their price.'

'The dray too,' said Hana. 'We have to take Tashi – I mean, the statue. I can't leave it here.'

Ferman hesitated, then said, 'The dray too. And put our luggage back on it, in case we have to stay a few days. Go!'

The malevolent pressure seemed to have faded, but Orc still wanted to get away. While the Quallaces clustered round Jorik, he took the chance to go after Cass. He found her at the house's open front door, looking out at the drive.

'Seems we're going to that college after all,' he said.

'I heard.'

'Are you all right? You said something about "blackout".' He tried to ignore the sting of guilt that came with the reminder of her near-drowning.

'That's where the familiarity came from,' she said. 'And there was a smell.'

'Like what? I didn't smell anything.'

'Must've been in my mind, then. It made me think of a hospital – which I know is weird, because I've never been in a hospital. I mean, as far as I know.'

'You think it might be something from before the Shroud?'

'I hope not,' said Cass. 'It had something like rotting meat, and chemicals. I recognised it from when I came out of blackout that time.'

'You never said that back then?'

'It wasn't as strong that time. I guess other stuff pushed it out of my mind.'

'But you didn't pick up anything this time, in there? Any… knowledge?'

She shook her head. 'It didn't feel like I was connecting with information, more a presence. And it felt too spread out to be one person. More like several minds, acting together.'

Shining beings, Hana had said. 'Who, though?'

'I don't know. But I think I've felt their presence before.'

The dusk air felt suddenly cooler. 'You mean that same time, when you blacked out?'

Cass looked up towards the sky, and Orc saw a shudder twitch through her shoulders. 'That… seed of truth, or whatever, that gave me those dreams on *Nightfire*: it must have come because I pierced the Shroud around our memories, yes?'

'Uh-huh.'

'What if I got the same smell just now because that presence in there has some connection with the Shroud?' She turned to him. 'What if that presence was its *makers*?'

His breath caught.

'It makes sense,' Cass said, lower. 'Whoever's done that to Jorik, it's to stop him talking about something to do with the Hollow Isles, right? It must be, if he knows about Shoggu. Then why not get us too, when we were on *Aurora*? We were eye-witnesses.'

Orc grasped her meaning. 'Because he knows something we don't.'

'And what's the big thing about the goddess plot we're still clueless about?'

'Manifestation. How it's possible.' The thought gripped his chest. 'Why *we* make it possible.'

'And isn't it likely that's what the Shroud was created to hide?'

'Then—' It leapt at him. 'Jorik *knows*. Fuck! He knows who we are!'

Cass nodded.

'Shit, why couldn't he have stayed awake another night? Why didn't he write it down?'

'Are we sure he didn't?' Cass said tightly. 'It was his luggage that came earlier, yes?'

Orc turned. 'I'll ask which room.'

Cass gripped his arm, fingers like trembling steel. 'They're busy. Let's just look.'

They crept along the hall, past the drawing room with its low voices, and up the main stairs to the landing. At the third try, they found the room containing the steamer trunk. Orc quickly found matches and lit the gas mantle, then shut the door and undid the trunk's straps.

'Look for a diary or journal or something,' said Cass.

The trunk had several compartments, but none seemed to contain anything book-like, nor did the clothes and shoes turn out to be hiding anything.

'What about this?' Cass pointed next to the washstand, to a smaller case in chestnut leather: the other item that had arrived in the cab.

It was heavy for its size, Orc found as he heaved it onto the bed. The case had a lock each side of the handle. 'Where would he put the key?'

Cass rifled the jacket that hung from a bedpost, shook her head. 'Might be in his trouser pocket.'

'Or in a sock, like Ranga's tobacco tin.'

'He's a gentleman,' said Cass. 'He's not going to keep a key in his *sock*.'

'Not one he wears, maybe.' Orc squeezed all those he could find, then the rest of the clothing, but discovered no lumps.

'What's this?' Cass opened a small, soft leather case from among the trunk's contents.

'Toilet kit?' Orc looked closer. As well as the razor, strop and shaving brush, there were hairbrushes, glass bottles and two squat porcelain jars. They turned everything out, but in vain. Orc unscrewed the jars' silver tops. The first, near-empty, held shaving soap. The second was still full.

'Pomade?'

'Hm,' said Cass. 'Don't you think his hair was too curly to slick back?'

'Probably came with the set.'

'Then why is the surface all roughed up?'

Orc pushed his fingers into the goo, and froze.

'Before you ask.' Cass's voice trembled. 'Yes, I do sometimes get tired of being so clever.'

Almost having to fight for breath, Orc cleaned the cream off the key. It turned easily in both locks. Hinges creaked.

Uppermost was a large brown envelope, bulky with papers. Below this, the velvet-lined case was divided into four sections. One held a stack of small notebooks, the second a black box Orc thought might be an electric battery, and the third a smaller box attached to a nest of wires. The largest contained a construction of leather and metal that seemed, when Orc examined it more closely, to have padded ear-cups.

'His clairaudioscope.'

Orc turned at Cass's voice. She'd slid the top couple of inches of the papers out of their envelope.

'His what?'

'At the top of each of these, it says "Clairaudio transcript", with a date. And remember our dinner on the island, when Ferman said his brother was working on something to record voices in the psychosphere?'

Orc swallowed. 'What do those say?'

Cass slid the pages back. 'Think we should look?'

'Of course!' He reached. 'I'll do it.'

'Wait.' She held the envelope behind her. 'If we're right, someone's trying to kill Jorik because of what he knows, and maybe it's all in here. How do we know they won't do the same to us, if we learn it?'

'They can't get us till we sleep. We'll be at Hana's college by then.'

'We don't know the college can protect us – that's only Hana's say-so. You still trust her judgement, after the Mother fiasco?'

'But – this could be our answer,' said Orc, horrified. 'Here, in our hands!'

'And let's keep it there. If the college can protect us like Hana says, *then* we'll read them.'

Despite the powerful frustration, that made sense. 'Should we tell Ferman?'

'No,' said Cass. 'If there's something about us in here, I don't want anyone knowing it before we do.'

Orc nodded. 'Jorik already does, though.'

'Worry about that later. For now, better no one knows he brought this with him.'

Orc locked the case, then pushed the key back into the pomade and repacked the trunk. Cass slid the clairaudioscope case deep under the bed. She gave Orc the envelope.

'Hide this down your shirt.'

He did. The envelope pressed against his skin: his name, maybe; his past, the secrets of his nature, perhaps deadly secrets. He searched his mind for the malice he'd felt in the drawing room – and found it, at the back of his awareness. Was that just overspill from downstairs, or was he being observed?

Who the hell are *you?* he thought, then quickly turned his mind aside, scared that a voice in his head might answer.

5

KILLER ON THE ROAD

By lamplight, Orc helped load Tashi's crate onto the dray, next to the mattress on which Jorik lay blanket-wrapped and shivering. Ferman had disappeared back into the house, but Stefanie and Cass already sat in the open carriage. Orc was about to join them when Hana, perched on the edge of the dray, called him back.

'I tried to scape, to check on Tashi,' she said in a low voice. 'I couldn't. They're still here: can you sense them?'

'If I try,' said Orc, who'd been doing his best not to. 'Don't worry, we'll be at the college soon.'

Hana turned as Jorik gasped out something, but her uncle quickly subsided to muttering. 'When I went into the morning room, I caught a smell like plants rotting.'

Her too. 'The vines, you think?'

'Maybe her power's gone from there,' said Hana. 'Because I took her sacrifice from her. I don't understand that side of the Mother. Maybe we shouldn't have called upon her, but what choice did we have? Now our scape might've done no good at all. I'm worried about Tashi as much as Jorik. Will you ride with me?'

'Uhm...' Cass's eyes were on him, he was sure.

'You said you can't meditate – I can teach you. We could try to make a partial shield around Jorik, and maybe bolster Tashi's strength. I don't think I can, on my own. I've worn myself out.'

'Then shouldn't you rest?' said Orc. 'They'll be fine for a few hours. Tashi's been stable for days, and Jorik's been like that since last night.'

She gave him a look he couldn't meet. 'Fine,' she said. 'Go back to your carriage for green-eyed people. Are you sure there's room for my parents in there?'

'This has nothing to do with Cass.'

'Of course,' she said. 'Go on, then.'

There was no point trying to explain, and the relief in Cass's face as he walked to the carriage told him he'd done the right thing.

'Will Hana be all right on her own?' said Stefanie, as he climbed up. 'Should one of us…?'

'She'll be meditating.' Orc turned at the crunch of feet on gravel.

'All set?' Ferman's face was grim in the flickering of the carriage lamps. 'I thought there might be something in Jorik's trunk that would shed some light on all this,' he said as he climbed up to sit beside his wife. 'But nothing.'

Orc made sure he didn't meet Cass's gaze.

Ferman told them the College of the Inner Eye was twenty-five miles inland from Saguna, and with no prospect of changing horses, the journey would take five hours. As the first stretch of dark road rolled past, he related how he'd heard about the college soon after he and Stefanie had moved to Kymera, seeking a culture less hostile to psychic research. Though the Inner Eye was outwardly an academy of the arts, he'd sensed truth behind the rumours that it also harboured students of more esoteric disciplines, and had cultivated a friendship with the college master, Astolio.

'That's where we met Hana, almost ten years ago,' he said. 'Not an immediate success: she was rather difficult even for fifteen, and our being Kurassian roused her mistrust even further. We won through in the end, though, and her adoption seemed to suit everyone. We'd been looking for a full-time subject to study, and her card-reading scores left us in no doubt as to her ability, even without her crystal. With it, they were better than blind chance by several orders of magnitude.'

'Her focus-stone?' said Orc. 'So she already knew Geist?'

'Yes, he'd brought her to the college after her parents were killed. Knew the uncle who'd taken her in, I believe. She hasn't told you that herself?'

'We didn't get much time to talk on the boat,' said Cass. 'About anything, really. So, she's nearly twenty-five, but there's no fiancé?'

Orc tensed at the forwardness of the question, but the Quallaces seemed to think nothing of it.

'There have been suitors, of course,' said Ferman. 'But she's been rather successful at putting them off.'

'Most were very lacking, to be fair,' said Stefanie. 'And either not interested in her work, or at the other extreme, afraid to dare the world outside a library.'

Orc feared a similar question might then be turned on them, but Ferman and Stefanie instead began to discuss whether scaping might be used to treat those with mental or emotional illness as well as those magically afflicted, and whether the Empyrean church might be persuaded to accept such practice as a new kind of medical treatment rather than sorcery.

'There must come a certain depth of knowledge where a coherent, rational theory of magic or psychism becomes viable,' said Ferman, turning to Orc, 'and where the old tribal shamans will be seen to have practised a form of science rather than witchcraft. Your joint-scaping with Hana must surely open the door for that. I pray my brother will be the first documented case of its success.'

But the reminder of the man lying on the dray killed the talk, and Ferman soon ordered the vehicles to stop so he could join Hana. A few miles later, he swapped with Stefanie, and remained largely silent afterwards.

Beyond a village where they watered the horses, the road climbed into uninhabited hills, and they no longer passed even the occasional farm-labourer wending home. Orc hoped it was just the lack of talk that kindled unease in the back of his mind. As his eyes strained against the darkness, other senses awoke. The cool night air wafted the smell of hard-working horse, the sounds of tack and axles and iron shoes and rims. What had previously been a background to voices now became all the world of sound. He leaned out over the carriage door to watch the patch of lamplit road ahead, and the vague grey landscape. It was open country, with few trees. Boulders lay among the dried grasses; starlight picked out the lines of old stone walls.

As they approached a bridge over a dry stream-bed, the carriage horses became skittish, then shied. The driver swore and pulled them up.

'Something in the road,' he said, levering the brake.

Orc leaned out further as the driver walked forward. Just past the bridge, a dark lump showed.

'Great gods!' the driver called back. 'A dead horse.'

Orc jumped as a crack shocked across the sky. The horses bolted – Orc was thrown back against the bench-seat, Ferman almost on top of him. The horses pulled against the brake five yards onto the bridge before the driver waved them down. As the din settled, from the dray behind came the sound of wood and leather creaking under strain as weight shifted and settled.

'Out!' cried Ferman, reaching past Orc to throw open the door. The three of them scrambled to the ground and crouched in the shelter of the vehicle. Orc's mind raced to take it in.

'Thunder's been shot!' cried the driver of the dray.

'Hell's teeth.' Ferman wrestled a revolver from inside his jacket. 'Kill the lamps!'

There was one each side of the driver's seat. Ferman shut off the nearest; the other could only be done by someone exposed. The hesitation while the others realised this got too much for Orc. Ignoring Cass's cry, he clambered up onto the driver's platform, threw himself across the seat and twisted the knob.

Blackness fell. The dray's lamps had been extinguished too.

'Now what?' he said, climbing back down.

'God knows,' snapped Ferman. 'Stefi?' he called. 'Hana? Everyone all right?'

'All but the horse,' Stefanie called back. Then her footsteps sounded as she hurried across the gap. 'What's going on?' she said as she reached them.

'No idea,' said Ferman. 'One shot, and then nothing?' He got up onto the carriage, ignoring Stefanie's protests. 'It's too bloody dark,' he said. 'Orc, your young eyes'll see better.'

Orc stepped up to join him. Crouching, he scanned the higher ground where he thought the gunshot had come from, but the moon hadn't yet risen and the starlight was too weak.

'Was this a trap set for us?' said Ferman. 'Or just a highwayman trying his luck? But then what's he doing?'

'Orc, come down!' said Cass.

He tried to reassure her. 'Whoever it is, they can't see in the dark either.'

'How do you know?' she whispered. '*Orc*!'

His breath caught at a realisation. 'Wait. Maybe I can.' He jumped down. 'Okay, I'm going to try something. I'll need quiet.'

'What's this?' said Ferman.

'You mentioned tribal shamans,' said Orc. 'Aren't there stories where a shaman pulls on the skin of an animal to gain its abilities? And Otter, my animath, he can see in the dark.'

'I don't get you.'

'I can invoke him. It's not the same as a scape. I've done it before, going into dark places when diving. I'm not sure how it works, but it does.'

'But you can't do that now,' said Cass. 'That's what happened to Tashi – invocation, possession.'

'I'm not going to physically *become* Otter.'

'How do you *know* any more? The rules have changed and we don't know how.'

'There's no choice, though.'

'Oh God, "no choice" again,' said Cass. 'Just make sure it doesn't go too far.'

Orc sat beside the road and settled himself. He'd only invoked Otter before to gain dark-vision when inside a ziggurat, but he saw no reason it wouldn't work here. He recalled his invocation at the Great Ziggurat, the most successful ever, when he'd convinced a goddess he was no longer human. He went through the same process now, asserting the same idea as truth – his self had been disintegrated by the nearness of the Serpent Mandala at his Initiation, and Otter had come to bind together what remained, to become the core of him. He drew that belief from his centre, inviting Otter to take his rightful form within his body.

When he was convinced of it, he pressed his focus-stone against the hollow below his throat, and let it happen. His shoulders dropped; his spine hunched and tried to become longer. He half-sensed the presence of a tail.

Like the old shamans, he had pulled on Otter's skin – but from the inside.

He opened his eyes, and the nightscape revealed itself to his dark-vision: the people huddled for safety; the two vehicles, one with a dead horse in harness; but all colourless and vague beneath a lowering weight of sky.

He looked up and shrank inside.

The stars were gone, and in their place was cloud, and it was full of eyes – hundreds of eyes, all different sizes and colours, eyes of humans and cats and lizards – sometimes blinking, looking in all directions but mostly down at him and the scene. He feared they would suddenly all turn and focus, fry him with their malice. But they just hung there, watching.

Trying to ignore the weight of their scrutiny, he mounted the driver's platform. He dared to stand on hind legs, and surveyed the rising ground. This time he saw movement. Something was making slow progress down and across the slope, towards the road behind the dray. It had many legs, and a tail raised and curled over its back – and in front, pincers.

His throat had dried. 'There's a giant scorpion working round behind us.'

'What?' came several voices. 'There *can't* be!' whispered Cass.

He looked again, telling himself the form was a disguise, an error of perception. His dark-vision refocused. The scorpion now had a human face, and the sting in its tail was a gun barrel.

'Can you see it?' he asked, when he'd told them. 'Cass, get down.'

'No,' she said. 'And no.'

'I can't either,' said Ferman. 'What's he heading for?'

'Jorik?' said Cass. 'Is this someone trying to…'

'To make sure of him,' said Ferman grimly. 'You're right: from that slope, Jorik would have been hidden by Tashi's crate. That's why the horse was shot instead: to keep us trapped. Hell's teeth, what's going on here? Orc, you'll have to come with me. Darling, get Cass and Hana over the bridge.'

'What are you planning?' said Stefanie.

'Orc will guide me, and I'll shoot the bastard.'

'No,' said Orc. 'If I have to guide you, he'll hear us.' The solution came with appalling clarity. 'Give me the gun.'

Ferman hesitated only briefly before handing it across. 'You know how to use it? Hammer, trigger?'

The revolver felt clumsy in Orc's paw, but he still had fingers if he felt for them. 'We got one off a dead guy once.' Geist had shot that man, but he would have to shoot this one.

He got down and crept round behind the dray, where Hana and the driver hid. Hana was arguing against Ferman's calls to get across the bridge, fear in her voice. Orc almost saw her huddled form as a hare.

The scorpion-man was perhaps fifty yards from the dray, and twenty from the road, moving with the caution of the near-blind through the jumble of broken dry-stone walls and boulders. Orc went just off the edge of the road, hunched over, using cover where possible: cover from his target, but not from the eyes in the cloud. His legs felt weak with the speed of his heart. As the distance closed, the assassin's shape became merely human, a man with a rifle. Orc knew he would have to shoot first. He could not hesitate: nothing but bang, dead. The man would shoot Jorik otherwise, and maybe others. Maybe him.

The assassin showed no sign of seeing him.

At ten yards, Orc cocked the hammer. He remembered Seriuz and Pettor, Daroguerre executing Esteban.

The man stepped onto the road, now only twenty feet from Orc, and stood peering towards the dray. Orc sensed him straining for vision, his rifle not yet up. Orc raised the revolver. A clear shot. A sitting target.

A person.

Damn it. He stepped out onto the road. 'Drop that gun and—'

The man moved impossibly fast, ducking, rolling. Orc panicked, pulled, triggered a flash and a bang and a shock up his arm. The man screamed.

'*Shit!*' yelled Orc. The man was by the side of the road, kneeling, bringing up his rifle. Orc aimed again, no choice, and pulled the trigger again, and pulled and pulled and nothing happened – 'Fuck, *fuck!*' – as the man aimed – the man could see him – he jumped to one side as another crack exploded. Hit, hit, he couldn't tell, how did you tell, he couldn't feel his body any more, he couldn't see in the dark any more, only the man vaguely. He heard something mechanical – the rifle bolt – the hammer! He'd forgotten to pull the fucking hammer.

He cranked it back. Gasps came from the hurt man, struggling to reload his heavy gun. Orc aimed at the shape but there was screaming from behind and the sound of wood splintering.

'No, don't! *Don't!*' Hana's voice, then '*Tashi!*' screamed with such desperation Orc had to turn.

His eyes flicked upwards as something crossed the stars, a flying shape, nearing fast.

He threw himself down. The revolver went off; there came a yell from the man and a crumpling squelching crunch Orc knew was bones breaking and something hard hitting a body at speed and with immense force.

But still the man gasped, groaned, somehow not yet dead. Orc had no idea what had happened. Hana and others behind were crying, shouting.

'*Cass!*' he yelled.

'Here!' she called back, but the tone of her voice killed his relief, and her next words broke up. Orc cocked the gun again, horrified that he might have to finish off the mangled man. But to his disbelief the gunman lurched up and ran, gasping and bent to one side, leaving a lump in the road where he'd been.

Orc approached it. Starlight gleamed along the rifle's barrel where it protruded from beneath a tangled mass.

It wasn't the gunman's bones he'd heard breaking. Jorik's white shirt was now white only in parts. His limbs stuck out at angles no limbs should.

Orc's knees gave way. Questions were shouted at him, and he had no reply.

6

SELF-KNOWLEDGE

Cass watched the two drivers lead the carriage horses from the other side of the bridge. 'We've pulled it clear,' said one. 'We're going on.'

'Now?' she said.

'However long it takes to hitch these up.'

The relief was almost too much. The past half-hour, she'd exhausted herself with readiness to run in case the thing that had been Tashi broke into motion again and picked someone else up to throw. He, it, still stood on the dray amid the wreckage of the crate, a hideous sculpture of red armour, his arm reaching for where Hana's head had been as she'd pleaded with him. The blades and points of his spread fingers made Cass feel sick; she couldn't look at them.

Hana still sat by the roadside between the two vehicles, staring at nothing, or at imagined death.

'Did you hear?' said Cass.

Hana didn't answer. Cass hunkered next to her. 'They've cleared the dead horse in front. We have to go, or those drivers will leave us here.' She looked down the road, but the lamplight didn't reach far enough to see Ferman and Stefanie and the mess they grieved over. 'Orc, can you tell them?'

He got up from his slump and walked leadenly down the road.

'It's no one's fault,' Cass said to Hana, watching him. 'It was bad luck the bullet hit the crate. No point thinking about blame.'

'I'm not.'

But she might later, Cass worried. 'Listen, if people blame you – I know it's unfair, but if they do, because you brought him back from the island – I know you might think I deserve some of it. And if it was anything else, I'd take it. But they can't know about me and Tashi, how I... what happened to make him like this. You agreed no one else could know about the manifesting.'

Hana looked at her, eyes flat and hard. 'I asked Orc to help keep him strong, and he refused – because of you. Am I allowed to tell them that?'

Cass itched to be away. 'Do you think Tashi... he won't move again?'

'He had the strength to regain control. I'll work on him after you're gone.'

'You're not coming?'

'I can't leave him. Maybe he only found the strength to regain control because the demons turned on me. Remember how he couldn't hurt me at the Navel? If they break through his will again, and I'm not here...'

And she would want Orc to stay too, Cass thought, so they could work on Tashi together. She tried to marshal reasons why he couldn't.

When Orc came back, he came alone.

'We go on,' he said. 'They'll stay here. Ferman said to tell Master Astolio what's happened, get him to send help.'

'Just us, then. Hana's staying too.'

Orc frowned, as though working up to a difficult decision. Just at that moment, the carriage driver called ready, and Cass grabbed Orc's arm.

They'd barely sat down in the carriage before the driver cracked the horses into a trot. As the bridge got farther behind, the tightness in Cass's chest eased, but only a little. It was still too cramped up inside her: the fear that had iced her nerves as Orc had approached the gunman, the jump of the gunshots. The splintering crate, the horror of the figure, more guessed than seen, that had picked up Jorik and hurled him as a helpless doll, a makeshift missile: every bit as shocking as Three-Eyes and the goddess less than a week before. She hadn't had time to recover from all that, and now this had happened. She feared it would keep piling onto her until she broke.

And what if Tashi started moving again and this time didn't stop, whether Hana was there or not?

She moved along the padded bench-seat, up against Orc. He put an arm around her as though he'd been waiting. The envelope under his shirt crumpled audibly. One thing, at least, they weren't running from.

The two drivers talked about everyday matters with an uneasy, forced manner, but Orc and Cass didn't speak. After descending the gentle slope out of the hills, the carriage rattled through a village where only a few lights showed. Past this, a high stone wall ran alongside the road for half a mile before reaching a gatehouse.

The drayman got down and banged on the door. A viewing port opened.

'Please, we need to speak to Master Astolio,' said Cass. 'Ferman Quallace sent us. It's urgent.'

A voice muttered for them to wait, and the port closed. Nothing happened for two or three minutes, then the gates were swung wide by a man wearing a jacket over a nightshirt. A woman stood back, holding a shotgun.

The carriage rattled up to the building Ferman had earlier described: a manor farmhouse, with many added wings and extensions and outbuildings. In the lamplight by its open front door stood a well-built man over six feet tall in an exotically patterned silk robe and cap, and a woman in riding clothes. Both were grey-haired; the man's shovel beard was white in the middle and black at the sides, reminding Cass of a badger.

'Don't mention Geist yet,' she whispered to Orc. 'We don't want to get tangled up in anything before we get a chance to read.'

The man spoke as they pulled up. 'I am Astolio, master here, and this is my wife Nadora. You've come from Ferman Quallace?'

'He needs your help,' said Cass. She quickly outlined the ambush, making no mention of Jorik or Tashi – the others could explain all that.

'And Hana's with them?' said Nadora.

'Why did they return from the Hollow Isles?' said Astolio.

'That's probably best coming from them,' said Cass. 'And really, you should get help to them as soon as possible.'

Astolio addressed the drivers. 'One of you belongs to the stricken vehicle?'

'Not going back there tonight, not for any money,' said the drayman.

'Orlus can drive it,' said Nadora. 'We'll take Fedro; he's used to different harnesses.'

'Take Ruban and Porrel too,' said Astolio. 'Go armed.'

Nadora kissed her husband and strode off.

'Take the carriage after her,' Astolio told the drivers. 'Someone will put you up in the stables once you've seen to your horses.' He turned to Orc and Cass. 'You two, this way.'

He led them into the house. Few lamps were lit, and its many nooks seemed cavernous. Carvings in wood and brass occupied dark tables; tapestries showing animals and leaves hung next to antique knives and heavy oil paintings.

'What did Ferman tell you of this place?' he asked them.

'Its true purpose,' said Cass, 'as well as its outward appearance.'

'Then you'll understand why your arrival did not take us entirely by surprise. Our evening session was disturbed by startling readings.' His dark eyes studied her. 'It was more than a gunshot that rattled your drivers, or I'm no judge.'

'Anyone would be rattled by getting his horse killed,' said Orc.

'If you have omitted to tell me of any danger, anything that might risk Nadora and the others, then do so while I can still inform her.'

Cass bit her inner lip. She imagined how many hours of questioning would follow if she mentioned Tashi, how much about themselves might be prised out of them. She wanted to be alone with Orc and the envelope as soon as possible.

'The highwayman was injured and dropped his rifle,' she said. 'He won't attack anyone else.'

'But why were you travelling here at night in the first place?'

'You'll have to ask Ferman. We – oh…' She staggered slightly and put a hand to her head, swaying.

Astolio reached out to support her. 'Are you all right?'

'It's just been a bit much to cope with,' she said weakly.

'I'll show you the guest room at once. Do you need food?'

She declined his offer. After asking again if she was strong enough to walk, Astolio took up a lamp and led her and Orc through rooms and along corridors, the building seeming more expansive than even its exterior had suggested. He made several attempts to ask Orc where they'd come from originally, and how they'd met the Quallaces at the Hollow Isles and what had happened there. Orc told him their names and that they were cousins, but claimed he'd promised Ferman he would leave him to relate events on the island, in case he got it muddled. To Cass, it sounded as obviously fake as her own near-fainting, but the master seemed to accept it.

As he took them up a creaking flight of stairs, Orc held her back slightly.

'I can't feel them,' he whispered.

For a moment, she thought he meant the papers had fallen out of his shirt, then she twigged. 'You could before?'

'Right up to the gate, whenever I tried. Hana was right about a shield.'

'Thank God.' Not only would they be free to read the transcripts without fear of attack, Orc had discovered it without them having to ask.

The room Astolio showed them had four double beds and washstands. He pointed out several folding screens against the far wall, which they could arrange as required, and the bell-pull to summon a servant. 'The others will stay here too, when they arrive, if our talk allows them to get to bed.'

When he'd gone, Orc said, 'He's going to blow his top that we didn't tell him about Tashi.'

'We couldn't – he would've questioned us all night,' said Cass. 'You really can't feel their presence?'

'Nothing.' Orc pulled off the yellow scarf, reached inside his shirt and extracted the now-crumpled envelope, its brown paper darkened with sweat. It shook with the tension in his hand.

'Cass, whatever's in here—'

She grabbed him and held him, knowing the transcripts might redefine him for her, and her for him. Lover, or brother, but she prayed not both, prayed there had been nothing but trauma and fear behind her dreams on *Nightfire*. She couldn't believe the heat of him through his clothes.

If these transcripts proved they were not siblings, this would be the night. She would feel that heat skin to skin.

Trembling, she freed herself. 'Do it.'

He pulled the sheaf of papers from the envelope. She watched his eyes dart side-to-side as he read the topmost sheet. She saw him swallow.

'Bloody hell,' he rasped, and handed her the first page.

For a long time after they'd finished reading, neither spoke. The moon had climbed enough to cast a faint wash over the kitchen garden to the rear of the house. To Cass, it looked a grey wasteland. She felt exhausted with anger and the hopeless, helpless sense of oppression.

A stain spreading out from them—

The male subject broke first—

The energy will be useful.

She turned back to Orc, sitting on the edge of the bed with the transcripts strewn across it. When he met her eyes, the look on his face made hers start to crumple again. She tightened it with anger. She went to the wooden screens folded against the wall and shattered the silence with a kick.

'Cass!'

'*Fuck* it!' She sat on the other side of the bed.

'Look – these were never the be all and end all,' he said – trying to be calm, she knew, because her behaviour scared him. 'We didn't even know about them a few hours ago. We can still find Geist.'

'Fuck Geist.' She put her head in her hands. 'It's not what we *didn't* find out, it's what we *did*.'

His gaze fell.

'What do we call them now?' she said. 'The shroud-makers? Or our puppet-masters?'

'We're not puppets. We just got used.'

'*Subjects*, they called us! Male subject, female subject. I feel sick. I feel like they've been *touching* me, all this time.' She clutched her arms round her chest. 'Who *are* they?'

'The Kings Behind the World,' said Orc. 'Must be.'

She hadn't made that connection. 'No – the Kaybees want us dead, and these people want us alive. It says so. When Daroguerre tried to sacrifice you, they wanted to stop him.'

'It's Geist who said they wanted us dead,' said Orc. 'But maybe that guy he shot on the beach didn't work for them after all. There was no proof.'

Her mind felt tangled, snarled, the threads of her thought caught on thorns. 'What else did he say about them? You remember?'

'Something about them being the real power behind what's going on. Corrupting the world.'

'I guess that fits,' said Cass. 'If what these say is right.'

'And Geist said they have agents in governments.' Orc found another of the transcripts. 'Here: they're talking about using this "project baffomet" to stop the dreadnought being sent. If they can do that, they must have someone high in the Empyreal Navy.'

Cass picked up a page from the scattered sheaf. 'Did you see that one where they're talking about when I nearly drowned? That "leak into Records" must be when I blacked out. I was right earlier: I did pierce the Shroud.' She wondered what Orc had made of the comment about her having greater ability, or whether he'd even noticed it. 'And what about this? *If they discover the Zhenaii connection, or their origins, they might become unusable.*' She tried not to show the fear that had struck her when she'd first read those words. 'What does that mean?'

'It doesn't mean we have anything to do with the Zhenaii,' said Orc, his voice tight-strung. 'It says, "*or* their origins". Not the same thing.'

That didn't ease her. 'The more we find out, the worse it gets. It's like peeling away the layers of an onion, only each layer down is more and more rotten, and in the middle… what's going to be at the core? What's at the core of *us*?'

'It can't be worse than your nightmares.'

She flinched at a memory of the room in the dream-tower, the bed stained with incest. 'But what if it is? What if it's something we can't even imagine yet? We never imagined Daroguerre was only a servant of the letters A to M, did we? Did you see this last page? *Guard against your dreams, if you can.* They know Jorik's listening. It's aimed at him, pronouncing his death sentence. It must have been terrifying for him. How can you guard against your dreams? How can we?'

'They won't want to hurt us,' said Orc miserably. 'If it's only us who catalyse this manifesting power, they'll want to use us again.'

'As long as they *can* use us. Didn't you hear? If we discover our origins, they won't be able to, for some reason. Then what? You think they'll just let us get on with our lives?'

Orc didn't reply, only heaved out a breath, and started to collect the papers together. 'We should get some sleep,' he said. 'Maybe the answer will come to us in the morning.'

'Of course, the cockerel will shout it out.' She groaned. 'We can't even tell anyone. The Kaybees might want to keep *us* alive for now, but not Hana, or Stefanie, or anyone else. Everyone we tell will be a target. And this place won't be any real protection. If they control the Empyreal Navy, they won't have to rely on psychic attack. That

"Scorpion" was just the start.' She put her head in her hands. 'God, I could do with getting drunk.'

'Shall I try to find some wine?'

'In a school? No... no, let's sleep. Maybe you're right about the morning.'

'Which bed d'you want?'

'Let's take this one.' She started to tug her shoes off.

'Uh... we get a bed each,' he said. 'There's four. And Ferman and Stefanie will share.'

'And we'll share this one.' She pulled off a sock. 'What's the big deal, whatever we are? Brothers and sisters share beds all the time.'

'Yeah, but not...'

'We'll have our *clothes* on, Orc. Don't worry, I'm not going to jump you in my sleep. I'm upset and scared, not stupid.'

Barefoot, but otherwise still dressed, she slipped under the covers. Her matter-of-fact tone seemed to have worked; he didn't protest further. She watched the lamplight on the plaster ceiling as he placed two of the screens around their bed.

'We always thought the female subject might have the stronger ability.'

Orc's Initiation and its effect on him had turned her against ever having anything to do with magic. But now it transpired she really had pierced the Shroud, something Orc had failed to do even with the large focus-stone. She had done so by accident on the edge of death, but she wondered: might she learn to do so on purpose?

What if she could learn to erect her own shields, as good as the college's? What if she could meet the Kings Behind the World in the psychosphere, and defeat them?

Stop it. Don't be ridiculous.

Even if it wasn't a mad idea, she would never be granted the time to hone such an ability from scratch. How long before the next Scorpion came, the next Daroguerre? The college wasn't a fortress, and as soon as she and Orc left, everything they did and said would again be under scrutiny, as it had been for months, perhaps years. *Their* minds would be touching her again.

The light dimmed as Orc turned down the lamp. The bed creaked as he got in the other side. He lay, like her, near the edge.

Now what? She'd imagined they would lie close together in companionable comfort. But they seemed frozen on their backs three feet apart.

The big house was so quiet, she couldn't breathe, couldn't risk swallowing. Its silence extended out over fields and hills, to where Nadora and her men approached a monster who had once been a boy: maybe still static, maybe already surrounded by fresh corpses. A monster she had made. The night reached across the sea, to an island that marked the graves of two giant warships and nearly all the men who'd served on them. She had been the midwife at the birth of death, and it seemed likely the child would soon come to claim her.

Don't be asleep, Orc. She moved her hand, her palm smoothing across the mattress. The tip of her little finger touched his – quite far from his body, as though it had been waiting, halfway across the gap, for her.

Their hands knitted easily, rustling fabric. It was nothing more than they'd done a hundred times. She wanted not to ask herself if this was too much; she wanted just to feel his fingers held between hers, hers between his, the tiny explorations of warm skin and bone, the little adjustments of strength; it tightened her chest and made her ache all through, and the ache wanted to move her, and to deny it felt like imprisoning a child.

She turned on her side; so did he, the mattress creaking. In the dim light of the lamp behind the screen, his eyes were warm and serious, his hair in need of a cut and a wash, his bruises still horribly livid on his neck. His hand felt both familiar and utterly new.

The ache repositioned her limbs, and somehow, as though they'd practised this, they moved into a hold, and his rough jaw was against her cheek, and she smelt his skin and even his greasy shirt-collar was part of him. Only for comfort, this, and holding was as far as they would go – except his body was hot, and she couldn't breathe normally, and the heartbeats passed until his lips moved against her cheek, and a noise came through her throat, and she knew what it meant and so did he.

Their noses bumped. His lips felt soft beneath hers, his teeth a stone that broke open under her tongue. His pushed forward; she tasted him tasting her, sliding and flicking and here it came, the squirming, his hips grinding against her, laughably predictable as a dog and yet nothing that had ever happened ever. She opened her legs, shifted him against her crotch. He was so hard through their clothes. This would be quick and crude; it didn't bear thinking about, but oh God. His mouth moved to her neck and sucked at her skin. His hands were everywhere, hers too, his firm back and the muscles moving in it, his bum. The noises the bed made alarmed her, but she couldn't stop her part in the writhing and squirming. His unexpected roughness was thrillingly *him*, the him that had been secret so long, his weight against her, his energy. She clamped her legs round his and pushed her hands up the back of his shirt and—

He stopped as if he'd been shot.

A loud, grating slithering sounded behind the screen; Cass screamed as there came the crack of glass, the tinkle of pieces.

Her heart hammered. Orc jumped out of bed and dashed round the screen. She followed to see him staring at the fireplace, panting in fright. Something had fallen from out of the chimney flue: a picture, in a frame.

Orc picked it up. The crazed glass made it hard for Cass to see the image, until she held up the lamp – then she felt like all her blood had gone.

It was a photograph, but in colour: perfect colour, like in a painting, nothing like the tinted reproductions in magazines. Orc and she were in their wetsuits, with the sea behind and a coastline behind that. She had long hair, tied back; her face looked a couple of years younger.

Orc's face had been scribbled out so hard it had torn the paper.

7

DEADLINE

Hana had been with Tashi in the barn for an hour when Nadora returned.

'Can you come?' said Nadora. 'Is it safe to leave him?'

'For a bit, I think.' In truth, Hana had stopped trying to meditate to bolster Tashi's will, worried that all she was projecting at him was fear. Every bump and lurch on the road had terrified her in case it somehow broke his demons free, and she still hadn't calmed down from the journey. The prospect of facing Astolio hadn't helped.

'I thought you might need this,' said Nadora, handing her a mug of tea.

'Did you bring several days' sleep as well?'

'Sleep is hard to come by at the moment,' said Nadora. 'And I don't expect that to change soon.'

'You know what happened?'

'Your parents told us. There seems little choice but to believe it.'

'So what have you decided?'

'Only that we need to talk to you.'

Outside, the promise of dawn showed in a slightly paler east. Sixteen-year-old Sorrel, youngest of Nadora and Astolio's three sons, stood by the barn door. Nadora instructed him to watch Tashi and ring his hand-bell at any sign of movement, to which he assented nervously, then Nadora led Hana across the silent yard and through the warren of the main house to the staff quarters. Hana had entered the master's drawing room only once before, to discuss her forthcoming trip to the Hollow Isles. Back then, she had glowed with Astolio's faith in her abilities and his assessment of her talent. She thought it unlikely he would smile upon her now.

'Hana.' He spoke her name as a statement of fact, and gestured for her to take one of the two empty seats round the coffee table. Her parents looked tired and grim. Hana wondered where Jorik's body had been taken. From the stuffed tropical birds in their glass cases, a multitude of glass eyes stared at thin air as though dazed by horror.

'Your parents have briefed me about events on the island, and since your return.' Astolio spoke quietly, but his presence was so imposing, his bull-like form almost overwhelming his wing-backed chair, that Hana had to stop herself shrinking from his voice. 'As for the terrible tragedy of last night, it seems likely that Tashi did not act under the influence of those imprisoning Jorik's mind, since the gunman he attempted to kill was doubtless their servant. But we cannot guess why he did what he did. Wouldn't a piece of the crate have made a better missile?'

She didn't want to talk about this, but the question had to be answered. 'The demons hate all life. They just want to kill. They would have got round to all of us if they'd been allowed. But he stopped them. He's holding them in stasis now.'

'And how robust is that stasis?'

'Very, I think.' She regretted the qualifier. 'As long as he's kept calm. The shock of the bullet hitting the crate must have disrupted his control, but only temporarily.' She kept her eyes from Ferman. 'His will is strong. We have to help him.'

'By further soulscape experiments? What if his control is disrupted by something you do in that state? A psychic shock might have as disastrous an effect as that bullet.'

'That wouldn't happen.' She pushed away the memory of burned hands slipping. 'I know you don't like the idea of using magic to affect others, but—'

'It is completely unethical.'

'When used for ill, I agree.'

'Not only then.'

'But I've saved people, when there was no other help for them.'

'But how are you planning to help Tashi *exactly*?' said Astolio. 'What magical correspondences will you use? From what literature will you seek advice?'

She couldn't answer.

'There is no authoritative precedent,' he said, 'no accumulated wisdom. You are feeling your way in the blind dark, and one wrong step might bring disaster. You are working with dangerous practices, without experience, without teaching.'

'I'm learning all the time. That joint-scape with Orc was a revelation. Two minds together are less likely to make a mistake. It makes the Otherworld more real, more stable.'

'And can we trust this "Orc"? He said nothing about any magical ability, yet your father tells me he is a student of Geist's.'

'So I understand,' said Ferman.

Astolio stroked a corner of his beard. 'Do you know where Geist acquired the two of them, Hana?'

Something about his casual tone struck her as unconvincing. 'They're a bit cagey about that.'

'And Geist never mentioned them to you?'

'No.'

'An interesting pair, are they not? A strong resemblance, for cousins, and with no discernable difference in age. They might be taken for twins.'

'I… suppose,' she said, puzzled. 'What does that matter?'

'For the moment, it doesn't,' said Astolio. 'Not when we have the demon boy to occupy us.'

'Tashi's not a "demon boy". He's an innocent victim of possession.'

'Innocent? One cannot invoke an entity alien to one's own nature.'

'They offered him strength. He was afraid.'

'He certainly seems to have turned the tables in that regard.'

'You think Skalith would have been any less terrifying?' said Hana. 'If not for Tashi, Daroguerre might be conquering the world right now.'

Astolio raised his palm. 'We are where we are. And by good fortune, the two younger classes leave this morning for a cultural trip. Save for those engaged in higher magical studies, I shall send the other students with them. But some resolution to our crisis must be effected before they return tomorrow evening.'

'Tomorrow? What if it takes longer?'

'Then I will take steps to limit the danger to my students,' said Astolio. 'For now, we'll move Tashi to the cellar beneath the barn. A bed will be made for you there.'

In one corner of the barn, a large trap-door opened onto stone steps. With difficulty, and great care, Astolio's three sons moved Tashi's rigid form into the disused cellar, where they placed him on a trestle table and covered him with a sheet. A bed was brought down, and then came lamps and a washstand and a chamber pot. The young men said almost nothing to Hana, though she knew all three of them well. On departing, they left the trap-door open. Sattrano, the middle son, stayed above on guard.

Hana sat on the bed, feeling her task completely beyond her. Soon came the sound of students gathering in the yard, a few adult voices among them, and the group set off on the two-mile walk to the railway halt.

Ten minutes later, Hana heard Sattrano talking to someone in the barn above, and then Orc descended the steps.

She fought not to let a mess of feelings show. There was too much she hadn't begun to deal with, and Orc stood at the heart of it all. Without the concealing scarf, the bruises on his neck accused her. Every detail of his clothes and face impressed on her, as though it might all be important to what had happened, what would happen, whatever that was.

He sat beside her, looking as tired as she felt. Strands of forearm muscle tightened under his skin as he gripped the edge of the bed. He stared, brows lowered, at the floor, as though waiting for her to start. But she wasn't going to lift that responsibility from him. She waited, looking at him as though he were well-lit for the first time. The lamplight caught a notch at the back of his ear she hadn't noticed before, like an old bite-mark. It struck her that if it was more than two years old, he wouldn't himself know what had caused it.

His eyes briefly met hers. 'I'm sorry.' He looked wretched enough to mean it. Sorrow for his failure, for his part in her uncle's death.

'Are you ready to help Tashi now?'

He winced a little. 'I heard we've got two days.'

'Less,' she said. 'To start, we need to find out more about what's possessing him. You saw something through the fog? You didn't say what.'

'It didn't make sense. It looked like Saeraf, but… wrong.'

'What's "Saeraf"?'

'When I scaped on the island, Three-Eyes showed me two serpents writhing together. One grew fiery wings and flew up into the air. Three-Eyes called it Saeraf.'

'Two serpents? Like the Mandala?'

His gaze met hers, intent but wary.

'You must have heard of the Serpent Mandala?' she said.

A cautious nod.

'I've never heard the two serpents had names, though.'

'You know anything about it?' His voice had an edge.

'The Mandala symbolises the very ground of existence,' she said. 'There are some accounts of people actually seeing it in deep trance. Those who get too close go mad.'

His face clouded.

'That doesn't mean you will, just because of what Three-Eyes showed you,' said Hana. 'But what could it mean, seeing the demons as this serpent? And how do we know that's even its proper name? Three-Eyes isn't a source I'd trust.'

'Nor me. But it felt true.'

'If we could see that serpent in another joint-scape, its nature might become clearer.'

'What about the Mother?'

'I said, she won't trouble you again.'

'Because you claimed me for yourself?' He didn't seem to know where to look.

'We won't have to call on her to simply learn about the demons,' said Hana. 'And as I said, I smelt rotting vegetation.' She pushed aside the question of how she would help Tashi without the Mother's assistance. 'Let's get started.'

'Now?'

'This time we'll mask up and enter the scape together. That'll make us closer.'

'I need to enter it alone.'

'There's no need to be embarrassed.'

'It's not that. It's because of how I was Initiated.'

Throwing up barriers, she thought. Resisting the necessary connection. Scaping joined them, the Fire Stealers joined them, Geist joined them. But either Orc didn't see that, or didn't want it.

'And how were you Initiated?'

'I'd rather not say.'

'Fine.' The word came out more clipped than she'd intended. 'I understand; it's sacred. But there's nowhere private here for you to go.'

He looked around at the truth of that.

'Maybe it's time for you to try another way in,' she said. 'Let's mask up together, as a first step.'

He hesitated, then nodded.

She called up to Sattrano to close the trap-door and keep it closed, then she turned the lamp down and directed Orc to kneel on the bed, at its foot. She positioned herself at the head, facing him, and took out her focus-stone. With her eyes closed, she pricked her mask awake, all the time sending mental threads through her stone towards Orc's, knitting tighter the connection.

Her mask complete, she said, 'Ready?'

'Uh-huh.'

She opened her eyes, and her breath caught. Where Orc's face had been was now something deeper and darker, made suggestively animal by the curls and lines of tattooed pin-pricks that had risen from the depths to his skin – though as she looked closer, the face behind revealed itself as the same: the shape, the features, the chicken-pox scar at the corner of his eye. The tattoo-mask suited his mouth. She hadn't noticed before how his upper lip lacked definition, with barely any notch below his nose. The cursive marble sculpture of Astolio's mouth wouldn't have worked with this mask. This was ancient and dark and earthy, and it stirred her. The eyes that hooked hers gleamed with the lamplight and the awed thrill of connection: young eyes, but also as old as the Fire Stealers, as old as myth.

She swallowed. 'We should touch our stones together.'

Resting hers on the centre of her palm, she held it out. Orc followed. Their hands clasped, trapping the crystals against each other but also skin against skin, heat against heat.

'Focus on the contact,' she said, clasping harder, pressing jagged crystal into flesh. 'Assert that the connection will remain even after they're separated.'

He looked down at their clasped hands. 'I'm not sure about this.'

'Because of Cass?'

Her guess had come hard and sharp, and his silence confirmed it. 'I know you're close,' she said, 'but maybe it's time you started asking whether that closeness is the best thing for you.'

He withdrew his hand.

'She isn't a shaman, Orc. She can't understand what it's like. You said yourself, she doesn't accept magic. She hates it – she's told me so.'

'Maybe that's good for me. Keeps me grounded.'

'*I* can ground you,' said Hana. 'At the appropriate time. But if you're too grounded when you move into the Otherworld, you'll never reach your full potential. I'm not saying you shouldn't be close to Cass, of course not. But you are a shaman. If she can't accept that, and you feel obliged to listen to her, you'll be forever torn.'

His only response was the knitting of his brows. She wanted to reach for him again, his hand, his arm, anything to pull him back into that connection.

'Orc, you either accept that you belong to two worlds, and learn how to exist fully in each one in turn – or you stay caught between them, never truly belonging to either. Look at me.'

He did so only briefly, then shied again, but in that moment she sensed his long yearning for understanding, for not having to feel defensive, his need to express his joy at something Cass could only fear. It was the same love and wonder she felt towards Hare and the Otherworld – a world she had now shared with him. And it would be only the beginning. She would not let it go.

'I need to think about it,' he said. His mask was already fading, the sacred tattoos, the link between them. Maybe he didn't feel the connection; maybe she'd been wrong about his loneliness. Maybe she herself didn't understand what was between them, she thought with panic.

'Orc, we need to scape again and find out what these demons are. For Tashi, remember?'

He frowned, sucking teeth. 'I already know.'

'What?'

He sighed, almost a groan. 'You have to promise that what I tell you goes no further. To no one.'

'If you know something—'

'Promise, Hana.'

'Fine, yes, I promise. Tell me.'

'They're "klippoth".'

'What's that?' she said. 'Is that what Saeraf told you?'

'No,' he said. 'Look, I can show you something that might help, but it might put you in danger. It's up to you.'

'What kind of "something"?'

He looked at her unhappily. 'I can't tell you unless you answer.'

'If it'll help Tashi, then yes, of course.'

He nodded, exhaled firmly through his nostrils as though to steel himself, and reached inside his shirt.

When voices woke her later, the end of her dream came as a relief. She'd been back in the Great Cave of the Mother, but the fissures in the cavern roof had multiplied and cracked wider, admitting beams of sharp white light she'd known would destroy her on contact.

Nadora descended the steps, bearing a tray of soup and bread. 'I thought you might like lunch.'

'It's that time already?' The hours lost to sleep made Hana felt guilty. But the fact that she'd slept at all after reading Orc's transcripts showed how badly she'd needed it.

While she ate, Nadora gave her the news. Jorik was to be buried next day, in the college grounds. The drivers had set off back to Saguna, with a handsome settlement: partly to the hire company to cover the dray-horse, partly for themselves as a bribe. The eldest son, Riaz, had returned with them to make sure they gave the agreed account of unseen highwaymen. The bribes had been accompanied by vague threats, though Nadora didn't sound confident they would keep the drivers quiet for long.

'This place has had a reputation for some while,' she said, 'however diligently we've tried to counter it. But it might not matter. By the time any investigation comes, Jorik will be long-buried, rest his soul, and…'

She trailed off.

'And Tashi will be restored,' said Hana.

'I pray so. But even if you can drive the demons from his mind, how will he return to his previous form? Surely it was some property of the island that let the demons transform him? Something to do with the ancient worship of the Mother there, the force of physical creation?'

It was a logical idea, Hana thought, and better for the Strandborns that Astolio and Nadora believed it. 'Something like that. But I think Tashi still has the transformation ability within himself. When the demons briefly overcame him last night, his fingers changed to different weapons.'

Nadora glanced at the shrouded form.

'But you're right about the Mother,' said Hana. 'She *is* the force of creation, and birth – she gives shape to living things. Every instinct tells me she's vital to Tashi's restoration. But her power is alien to the mountain, the soulscape where he's stranded. And I don't know how to call on her without Orc, and… they don't get on.'

'I'm no magician, myself,' said Nadora. 'But perhaps you should find her on her home territory, and discuss the situation with her.'

'But how can I talk to her?' said Hana. 'The Mother is all. She doesn't have an identity. The only face I've ever seen of hers was made of leaves.'

'Then give her another.'

Hana frowned. 'You mean, assert how she looks?' From a tight, mad bud, the idea unfurled its possibilities. 'Mama Nadora, can I give her *your* face?'

'Mine?' Nadora laughed, not without nerves. 'I can't say I've ever seen myself as a primal force.'

'But from the moment I first came here, you cared for me. And look, you've brought me soup! *You* wouldn't want to drink a boy's blood, would you?'

'I've felt like doing worse sometimes. Wouldn't your own mother be more suitable?'

'The Mother is life; she can't be dead.'

'I meant Stefanie.'

'Oh – no, Stefanie's more like an aunt, or an older sister, or a friend. And she has no children; you have three sons. Please, Mama Nadora. I'd feel uneasy doing it without your permission.'

'Very well,' Nadora said. 'Make use of my face as you wish – I hope it suits.' She took back the tray with its empty bowl. 'By the way, Astolio will want you later. He's telegraphed Grandmaster Purakash for a communion about this whole business, at six. If it goes ahead, he'll need guarding.'

'By me? I thought the esoteric students were still here?'

'The communion guard will need to be as strong as possible. This morning's shield-working sensed a powerful will probing the barrier.'

'The ones who attacked Jorik?'

'We think it must be.'

Hana suppressed a shudder. The Kings Behind the World, according to Orc: a name she'd heard from Geist at various times, though never accompanied by more than vague hints about their supposed power. She'd always assumed before that they were more symbolic than real.

'They mustn't be allowed to overhear Astolio's communion with the Grandmaster,' said Nadora. 'Quite apart from anything else, if the protocols are compromised, Astolio will have to go to Jiata to devise a new set.'

'I can't be in the guard,' said Hana. 'I can't leave Tashi for that long, and I can't afford to spend my energy on something other than him.'

'I understand that,' said Nadora. 'But I'm not sure Astolio will.'

'Has he said what he'll do if his deadline passes?'

'Not to me. Between us, I don't think he knows as yet.'

Because there was nothing he *could* do, Hana hoped. There was no way for him to destroy Tashi, no way to even make an attempt without risking an effect as catastrophic as that of the bullet hitting the crate. But he could force her to take Tashi and the problem elsewhere.

'Tell him I'll help guard him if he's willing to give me more time.'

'I'll pass it on.' Nadora took the tray towards the steps.

'And do you know where Orc is?'

'In the Blue Library, last I saw. He said he was looking something up for you. Shall I send him?'

'No, not if he's still working,' said Hana. 'But if you see him, remind him to look hard.'

Orc's prolonged absence worried her. It suggested a failure to find the knowledge he was looking for. But if the Kings Behind the World were magicians, then surely the term they'd used for Tashi's demons, "klippoth", would be in one of the occult dictionaries? If not, she didn't know how else she might learn its meaning. Orc had ruled out asking Astolio, fearing that the word's origin in the transcripts might lead the master to magically discern their existence.

Hana's own research had revealed little of substance. After Orc had left her that morning, she'd performed a scape, both to check on Tashi's condition and in hope of learning more about his possessors. She'd found Tashi still gripping the rock, surrounded by shreds of withered vine, the strain in him clearly greater than before. The demons had been in vocal mood, their howls and jeers both frustrated and triumphant. They had broken the novitiate's attempts to hold them, they told her, and would do so again. They had slain her kin, and would slaughter her too.

She'd tried to pierce the fog, to see what Orc had seen. She challenged the demons to show themselves; she told them she knew they were klippoth. They greeted this with screams of denial, so enraged that Hana thought the word might indeed be the clue to their undoing. She named them as the serpent Saeraf, which provoked them further. They had been created directly by the Lord, they howled, and were not part of any lesser reality He had mistakenly constructed. The Mother had no power over them.

But that wasn't true, Hana reflected now, as she prepared to scape again. At the Navel, she had invoked the Mother and freed Tashi's mind from the demons' control, temporarily at least. She was hundreds of miles from the Navel and the Great Cave beneath it, but there might be some way to connect herself back there. Following on from her dream, she wondered if this cellar might not also be thought a kind of cave. Might it be made a place of the Mother?

She meditated on this idea while her lunch digested. She imagined her thoughts penetrating the raw, massy earth behind the brick facing of the cellar walls. Stone connected; the earth was the body of the Mother, and there was no barrier but earth between these underground walls and the Great Cave itself. She imagined her pulse as being not her own, but the heartbeat of the earth, the life of the Mother surrounding this womb.

An hour passed, and Orc still hadn't come. She told Sattrano to keep the door shut, then removed her clothes, as she had on the island, and went to meet the Mother.

She'd followed Hare only a little way from the grassy pentacle when the ground began to get marshy. Her animath led her between strange trees that grew from the increasingly wet earth. Vines climbed the trunks, their blood-red flowers high in the canopy. Barely a chink of sky showed; the light was as green as the stretches of water. Insects thronged and danced, skimming the surface as though tantalised by something beneath.

Hana waded. Normally, in a scape, her body felt light and nimble; here she felt heavy and fleshy, and so did the water she pushed with her legs, the ooze that sucked at her feet. Eyes staring wide, Hare swam ahead at first, but after a while he fell back beside her, and stayed there so long Hana wondered who was leading whom.

'Where is she? The Mother?'

'All around us,' said Hare, voice hushed. He struggled onto a tussock and squealed as a multitude of tiny beetles swarmed his fur, making him leap into the water again.

'We're here to find her in human form.'

'Then you must follow your own direction, child,' said Hare, swimming frantically around her. 'I know nothing of her in human form.'

Hana wondered if she might do better to go back and start again, but she pressed on, trusting instinct to lead her. She remembered the kindness Mama Nadora had shown when Geist had brought her from her uncle's farm. She recalled the stern sympathy Nadora had given her after she'd passed out from too much wine a week later. She thought of the lunchtime soup.

Ahead, on a small island dark beneath trees, a flame flickered.

She hauled her legs from the marsh, black with stinking mud. Exhausted from swimming, Hare allowed her to pick him up. She held him panting against her, water from his fur dribbling down her belly.

The heavy air grew warmer as she walked through an outer ring of trees to a shadowed glade.

Here saplings had grown together to form a shelter. A heavy, naked woman with the face of Mama Nadora sat stirring a round pot above a fire. Within the triangle made by the Mother's arms as she gripped the great spoon, a piglet and a goat-kid sat in her lap, suckling from her. As the Mother studied her, Hana sensed the face of Nadora wanting to change, to break apart and resume some other form. She set her mind against it.

'Is he for me?' The Mother wore Nadora's voice like an ill-fitting mask of sound. 'Skin him and bone him, then, and into the pot with him.'

Hana held shivering Hare tighter. 'He's not dead.'

The Mother shook her head. 'All take and no give, that's the trouble with children. Suck me dry and fly the nest. You think you can outgrow me, thanks to that little traitor you cuddle. You'll learn different in the end. What is it you want?'

'To talk – to the true Mother, not the one who came yesterday.'

The Mother laughed, staring into the eyes of the suckling kid. 'And why should she want there to be a difference, little chick? There's a man she wants for herself, isn't there? A man who's not hers.'

'There was a mistake.' Hana had prepared for this. 'The blood fallacy. The reason the ancients thought the earth needed blood was because women lose it through the menstrual cycle.' The medical term jarred, but she needed to coax the Mother towards a more rational age. 'The Sun-King's relationship to the goddess, as both husband and son combined, is against nature – how can his sacrifice be any different? The whole thing came through a misunderstanding. We know better now.'

'These are done, I think.' The Mother flung the piglet and kid squealing away, their teeth drawing blood as they ripped free. Resting the spoon against the side of the pot, she reached in with both hands and pulled out two snakes. She attached one to each breast, and resumed her stirring.

'A misunderstanding, you say. Yet you and he, who "know better now", deliberately invoked that ancient contract. You used his blood to call me.'

'Some of his blood, yes.' This wasn't going right. The thick air made it hard to think. 'But not his life. You bring death, but you don't demand it.'

'What would my soup be without it?'

'But to demand the death of a young man before his time—'

'His time is when I call him. The gods of death are also my sons and lovers.'

Hana tried not to look behind the Mother, to the three shadowy figures at the back of the shelter.

'I want you to be cleansed of the blood fallacy,' she said. 'It should never have been part of you. The Mother reaches back to before that error.'

'That "error" is as old as language,' said the Mother. 'What was I before language? Would you wish to see me as I was then? You would lose your mind.'

The serpents at her breasts had grown already. Hare whimpered in Hana's arms.

'You want to pick and choose,' the Mother continued. 'That's why you tried to force me into this shape. If you want only sweetness and nurturing, call upon the Holy Mother of the Empyreans, little good though it'll do you. The promise must be kept.'

'Orc isn't mine to give you,' Hana said.

'He offered himself!' said the Mother. 'And he has done it before. And you conspire with him to cheat me. You say he isn't yours? That is a lie – you claimed him for yourself. I don't deny you my help. It is *your* denying *me* that prevents me giving it.'

A chill washed through Hana as she understood the truth of that.

'Your husband has sealed his own doom,' said the Mother. 'But the child's fate is yours to change. You must choose between them. You would not be the first.'

'Tashi isn't my child. And Orc isn't my husband.'

The Mother laughed. Her snakes had grown huge; they'd spilled from her lap and now coiled upon the dirt floor. 'You know the answer you must give.'

Hana thought of the burned boy in chains on the mountainside. She had little more than a day to save Tashi and no idea of anything else that might help. Orc wouldn't necessarily be in danger: as long as he stayed out of the Otherworld, the Mother shouldn't be able to harm him. He could never scape again – a high price, but one worth paying for Tashi's survival.

'I need more than protection for Tashi this time. I need you to drive the demons out of him forever and restore him to how he should be.'

'That is a great demand.'

'But not beyond you. You are the prime force of creation.'

'Yes, I am.' What had been Nadora's face blurred and cracked. Hana's will could not maintain it, the Mother's true form breaking down the mask from behind.

'You knew the sole power that could save your child.' The Mother's voice shimmered as though currents passed through it. 'Release your hold on Orc, and it shall be open to you.'

'What, now?' said Hana, almost panicking that she might lose her only chance. 'Do I have to say it now?'

'You must tell him to his face,' said the Mother. 'He must know he is outside your protection. Then the spell will break. That will allow you to gain my help.'

'What help, exactly?' Hana kept her gaze from the Mother's face, knowing she would find no trace of Nadora now. 'What will you do?'

'You ask for exactness, for definition? You forget who you speak to.' The Mother plucked the serpents from her breasts. 'Do you wish to see these dance?'

'No!' said Hana. 'I'm – honoured, but—'

'Next time, I might not give you the choice,' said the Mother. 'Now, go. When the time is right for my help, your gut-feel will serve you.'

Hana waded hurriedly from the island, hoping the way back to the pentacle would be short.

'Did she really offer to show me the Serpent Mandala?' she asked Hare, who still shivered in her arms.

'If so, you d-did well to ref-f-fuse.'

'Why did she call you traitor? Was the sacred fire hers?'

'It c-came from the sky,' said Hare. 'But when Raven gave it to humans, it let them think they could out-g-grow her. I sh-should have refused to help him, but he scared me. And Eagle did. They bullied me. They wanted my fast legs. So I betrayed the Mother of All and had to become the trickster you know. For I c-cannot go back to her. She does not forgive a betrayal. And she does not forget an agreement. Look!'

'No.' Hana refused to follow Hare's gaze, knowing what she would see.

'You must,' said Hare. 'You must observe how little she forgives.'

Hana steeled herself, and looked. A great tree grew from the swamp a short distance away, and bound to it by coils of thorned creepers was Orc. The long barbs pricked streams of blood from his naked skin; his throat was a mass of red. His eyes stared, but she couldn't tell if he was alive or dead. One thin, thorn-daggered strand spiralled tight around his erection.

She jerked her gaze away. Distantly, behind the insects' drone, came the sound of the Mother stirring soup.

8

THE SHINING ONE

Often during that long, lonely afternoon, Hana wondered how she might have conducted the scape differently. Perhaps it had been a mistake to let Hare lead her into the swamp. If she'd directed it, rather than following instinct – if she'd visualised a warm, friendly house and placed the Mother within, a timeless but modern woman who demanded no sacrifice – might that have allowed her to annul the age-old contract, rather than confirm it?

In the end, she thought probably not. The magical undermind was the source of truth and power; using the will alone would have resulted only in a contrived daydream. The Mother was part of the psychosphere, and so was the blood fallacy, and so was poor Orc's role as the goddess's consort. It was no more within her ability to scour out those things than it was to fly to the moon.

Just before dusk, there came the chatter of the esoteric students gathering in the yard before going outside the college to guard the communion. The fact that Astolio had sent no response to her offer irked her, and not just because she wanted more time. If he'd agreed and she'd been in the guard, she might have managed to listen to the communion. Being caught doing so was grounds for expulsion, but it was maddening not to know what Astolio said about Tashi and what instruction Grandmaster Purakash gave in return. When the guard passed by on its return an hour later, she heard upset in the voices, but they quickly faded into the main house.

Still no one came. Frustration gnawed her; she worried the decision about Tashi's fate was being kept from her. And where was Orc? The prospect of seeing him after her Mother scape made her nervous, but the day was passing. How could his research take so long?

She was working herself up to abandoning Tashi in search of him, when she heard Sattrano talking to a visitor. Expecting Orc at last, she sat on the bed. But there descended instead a compact and wiry boy of about sixteen, a tray of food in his hands, an artist's sketchpad tucked under one arm. He glanced warily at Tashi's shrouded form as he approached her.

'Petri, isn't it?' said Hana, as his name came to mind. He'd arrived at the college just before she'd left for the Hollow Isles. She couldn't remember speaking to him before.

'I volunteered to bring your dinner,' he said, his voice bold but also a little nervy, and unexpectedly deep for his frame. 'I want to show you something.'

He set down the tray with its bowl of stew, then opened his pad and turned it towards her. The double-page spread showed a face drawn over and over: different angles, different sizes, the shadows hacked in with forceful strokes of charcoal. It had to be a mask; the abstract features were barely human. Hana couldn't guess why Petri wanted to show her this, and that unnerved her as much as the neck-prickling power of that repeated face. The whole thing smacked of an attempt to pin down an obsession.

'Stunning, isn't it?' said Petri. 'Ancient, but modern – or rather, *beyond* modern. It's like they've seen into a past so far back and a future so distant, the two wrap around and meet.'

'Who's "they"?' said Hana. 'What is this?'

He seemed taken aback. 'I thought... Astolio said you met them before.'

'Met...?' She gasped as the pieces fell into place. 'And *you've* seen them?'

'Yes.'

'The communion? What happened?'

'The guard didn't hold up.' He sounded less horrified than excited. 'No one's hurt, only shaken. But they had words – Astolio and Purakash and the Shining One.'

Hana kept her eyes from the drawings. The shining beings who had invaded her home. The Kings Behind the World – and behind Jorik's death, behind the goddess plot. They had faces now.

'And they talked to Astolio?'

'One did.'

'What did he say?'

'Astolio kept that to himself. You should've seen him afterwards: his face was like ashes. Have I got them right?'

'What?'

'I know I've captured the feel of them, but the detail – is there anything I've missed?'

'*That's* why you're showing me?'

'Well, no one else has seen them.'

'I haven't either.'

'Eh?' he said. 'But you—'

'I sensed them, that's all.' She could almost sense them now, as though these sketches had invited them through the college's shield. 'Why the hell are you trying to draw them, anyway?'

'Because I'm an artist, and the role of any real artist is to study the outer forms of the world and discover the true forms beneath.' The speech seemed so unlikely for one so young, Hana assumed Petri had learned it by rote. 'And what's the true form beneath that mask, Hana?'

'A human being, that's all.'

'No, I meant behind the art of it.' He looked critically at his drawings. 'Maybe it's impossible to do them justice. You should've seen them – that first glimpse, their wheeling paths crossing against the blue. Like soaring eagles made of gold and iron. Like they were the *idea* behind gold itself.'

'They're not. They're people.'

'And then – whoosh! Down they came! All flashing feathers and the light from the holes in their golden masks, falling right at us. They punched through our guard like it was wet paper. I brassed it out – that's when I got a good look at the faces – but Erena cried and Naffrel threw up and Montaro pissed his pants. All the others buckled like scared kids because they didn't want to know. They failed as artists, just like this trash pile fails as an arts college. You can't study the world from behind a shield – you need to get your hands and feet in the dirt of life. And everything else.'

His expression became calculating. 'And you know that as well as I do, Hana. You went to that island. I've heard the rumours. You lifted the cover on the normal world and peeked underneath. Like Geist taught you.'

'Geist?' she said, feeling as though the train of conversation had jumped onto a different set of rails.

'Your mentor.'

'He was. What of it?'

'You still see him?'

'Twice in two years. Last time, I barely spoke to him.'

He looked surprised. 'So you don't know where he's gone?'

'He didn't say he was going anywhere,' said Hana. 'Is this?'

Petri frowned at his sketchpad, then closed it up. At that moment, Hana noticed a faint rumble in the background, several adult male voices in the yard. 'Who's that?'

'Them outside?' said Petri. 'Must be the men Astolio sent for, from the village.'

'At this hour?'

'He's paying them to work through the night. Digging, I heard.'

'Jorik's grave?'

'No, that's already dug.' Petri glanced at Tashi, and his brows lowered as if in realisation. 'Astolio sent for them as soon as we came back.'

'Oh, gods.' The smell of stew suddenly made Hana feel sick. 'Find Orc,' she told the boy. 'Wherever he is, whatever he's doing, I need him here. *Now.*'

Minutes passed. She sat pulling at her hair, hurting herself with it, until Orc came. The sight of him almost overwhelmed her with relief and nerves.

'Astolio caught me on my way here,' he said, sitting on the bottom step. 'He wanted to show me the digging.'

'It's a hole, isn't it?' She heard the distant rhythm of picks. 'They're planning to bury Tashi alive.'

He nodded dismally.

'How long?'

'Mid-morning, he reckons.'

'And then what? He said he'd give me till tomorrow evening.'

'I don't think he's planning to,' said Orc.

'Because of them. The Shining Ones. You know one of them spoke to him? They've been waiting for this. It's in your transcripts: they wanted to get rid of Tashi even before he changed. We have to point out to Astolio what the risk is. Being buried might disrupt Tashi's control as much as a bullet.'

'He knows that,' said Orc. 'He told me the plan. The two of us keep Tashi calm while the cement dries.'

'*Cement*?'

He stared at the floor. 'They can't risk leaving any gaps he can use to start working his way free. So they're going to cement him in. When it's dry, they'll put earth and rock on top.'

She felt sick. 'And Astolio thinks we'll *help* him with this?'

'Can we afford not to? If he goes ahead anyway, and Tashi loses control...'

'Exactly. Astolio can't risk that. Can he?' Head in her hands, she foresaw some terrible game of brinkmanship. 'How can he listen to the Shining Ones? He knows they killed Jorik.'

'They weren't the ones who *actually* killed him, though.'

She glared.

'I'm not agreeing with him!' said Orc. 'But you can see why no one else is going to be on our side.'

Hana didn't ask if he included Cass in that. But he was probably right as far as her parents were concerned, after the events on the road.

'We have to change Astolio's mind,' she said, trying to keep focused on practicality and not give in to the tears gathering behind her eyes. 'Talking to the Shining Ones clearly scared him, but now he's back safe behind the shield—'

'It's not just them he's scared of,' said Orc. 'It's the Scorpion.'

'The gunman? What's he got to do with it?'

'When they did this evening's shield-working, they picked up another mind trying to breach it: a single person, somewhere nearby. He was too skilled to trace, but they sensed an interest in Tashi.'

Hana felt besieged. According to the transcripts, Tashi had been the Scorpion's original target, and now he doubtless would be again. 'But he can't hurt Tashi, not as he is?'

'Astolio thinks he's here to make sure the burial goes ahead. The college shield's no use against a physical threat. There's the wall, but someone could get over that.'

All too easily, Hana thought: parts of the north wall had long been in a state of disrepair.

'You said he was injured. And he dropped his gun.'

'I didn't see how badly,' said Orc. 'And he might have other guns. Sorry, I know that doesn't help.'

'Well, help me another way,' she said. 'Please tell me you found out what "klippoth" means.'

She knew it was a forlorn hope – he would have come before if he'd succeeded. Even so, at the shake of his head, she closed her eyes and struggled not to choke.

'I checked all the dictionaries,' said Orc. 'I only found one of the words the Kaybees used on that page – *elohim*: they're angelic spirits in the Thangkaran tradition.'

That was something, at least. 'If it's a Thangkaran term, then klippoth might be too – did you check for books on their religion?'

'There was only one, a dictionary. It didn't have that word, no.'

'Right,' she said. 'Then we'll have to ask Astolio after all.'

'No,' said Orc. 'You promised – it might lead him to the transcripts.'

'That's a small "might" when we're trying to save someone's life.'

'It's big enough!' he said. 'Save one, kill two others: is that what you want? If anyone finds out what me and Cass can do, we're fucked. They'll experiment on us, or lock us up. If the church gets to hear about us, we'll be hanged as witches.'

'If, "if". Are you even bothered about helping him?'

'Yes.' He sounded hurt. 'You're not the only one, Hana. That whole mess on the island was partly down to me and Cass, even if it wasn't our fault.'

'Guilt, then.'

'No! It's because… I can't think how to put this, except he *deserves* help. And not just because he saved us.' He let out a breath. 'I'll never forget when Skalith appeared out of thin air. Twice my height, and with those teeth, and those snakes… I couldn't run fast enough. I could never have faced her. Tashi was still himself when he went into that fight. He must have known he had no chance. But he went for her anyway. I can't imagine having guts like that. All I did was hide in the trees.'

His humility, the heat in his voice, touched her. 'It's good to hear you say that,' she said. 'And you do have guts. What you did on the road shows it.'

'Yeah, well. It just makes me mad that Tashi sacrificed himself to fight that monster, and all Astolio can think of is shoving him under the dirt. I want to save him. I want to fight for him. But I can't let you put Cass in danger.'

'No. I see that. And this isn't really about her.'

He looked at her as if unsure what she meant.

'She's not here, is she?' said Hana. 'She hasn't come here all day. But you…'

But him what? She had sent for him, and he'd come. And something about him felt different from that morning: he seemed more solid beneath his clothes, as though her vision of him naked and bound with thorns had heightened her awareness of his physicality. His trousers and shirt, as he sat there on the step, seemed too modern, like a clumsy and obvious disguise.

'Leave her out of it, yeah?' said Orc. 'I'm not having her put in danger. That's it.'

Her next words felt heavy as lead; she had to drag them out. 'What about you? To draw on the Mother energy, I'm going to have to rescind that claim I made on you.'

'Right.' Teeth scraped his lower lip. 'What'll that mean?'

'For you? I'm not sure. It means that in a scape, you might be in danger from her, unless we can find some way to stop that. But there might not be any way to stop it. Your role is etched on the psychosphere now, by what happened on the island, and by what we did. Maybe the only way you'll be safe is to stay out of the Otherworld altogether. For good.'

Understanding reshaped his face. He stared at the floor. He looked as if she'd told him he would have to lose the use of his legs. Several times he tried to speak, but only swallowed.

'I could rescind it anyway, without your consent,' she said. 'I only need to speak the words. But that wouldn't be fair.'

He put the heels of his hands against his forehead. 'You have to,' he rasped. 'Whatever I'll lose, it's nothing next to what he will if we don't.'

'Oh, Orc...' She had to tighten herself against tears. 'If there was any other way...'

'Are you going to do it now?'

'No,' she said. 'No, we still have to learn what klippoth are, and the only way we can do that now is in a scape.' And that might be the last they could ever do together. After the promise shown by their first time, it felt such a waste. 'I don't know if we will find out. But we have to try.'

'You can't restore him without knowing?'

'Earlier, the demons said the Mother has no power over them. I need to be able to prove them wrong. And for that, I need to know where they come from.'

'Shame there wasn't a footnote in the transcripts,' said Orc.

She stiffened, cold with realisation.

'But I guess there couldn't have been,' he went on. 'The word was underlined, so Jorik didn't know what it meant. Wasn't that what it said?'

'That's right. Jorik didn't know.' She stood, shakily. She had to get on with what she was about to do before doubt or common sense changed her mind.

'Where are you going?' said Orc.

She stepped past him. 'I'll tell you later. Stay here and keep Tashi calm. I know you don't meditate, but do your best. What you said just now, about how brave he is, how strong: tell him that. Let him know you believe in his strength of will.'

Orc nodded. 'Don't be too long,' he said. 'This place has a kind of weird feeling.'

Lamplight showed where the four men were digging, on a patch of unused ground fifty yards from the barn. Hana saw no sign of Astolio. She sneaked to one of the outhouses and took a paraffin lamp and matches from a shelf just within the door. Giving the diggings a wide berth, she made her way to the main gate and knocked on the door of the lodge.

Marco answered, a skinny homemade cigarette in his mouth. His wife watched from their fireside, her shotgun resting against her chair.

'I need the gate opened,' Hana said.

Marco shook his head. 'Not for anyone. Assassin out there, I'm told.'

'He won't shoot me. His masters need me alive.'

'That's more than I know. It's *our* master you'll have to persuade.'

Frustrated, Hana walked away. But all was not lost, so long as the decrepitude along the north wall hadn't been repaired since she'd left. Sometimes stumbling in the dark, still not risking her lamp, she worked round to one of the damaged sections. Starlight revealed that the worst of the decay still left a five-foot height. She tore more bricks from the degraded mortar, dropping half of them on her side and half out, building up the existing rubble to make a kind of stile. After ten minutes she'd lowered the gap enough and scrambled over, thankful for her tough trousers.

She felt herself pass through the shield, and immediately sensed the presence beyond. She tried not to think of Petri's drawings, not yet. As she followed the wall round to the road, she wondered if the Scorpion was watching her, maybe from one of the ruined buildings whose outlines were vague in the dark.

After several minutes stumbling over unseen ruts in the road, she at last reached the track that started not far from the college gate. It led to the jokily named Telegraph House, the small, one-roomed building reserved for when Astolio communed with Purakash or the master of any other college, when both needed to be free of their respective shields' interference. She lit the lamp at last, turned it low and used the dim light to find the key beneath its stone.

Inside, the atmosphere felt disturbed. No doubt the building had been vacated too hastily to remove all psychic trace of the communion. That suited her. She locked the door, put down her lamp and settled on one of the mats. A soft breeze sighed through slits under the eaves. She meditated herself into receptiveness, holding her focus-stone, trying to calm the nerves that swarmed her stomach. When she felt ready, she expanded her awareness, sending out mental threads strengthened by the stone, opening herself to what had happened in this space a few hours before. She'd taken part in the communion guard several times in previous years, helping both to transport Astolio to his meetings and to screen him from outside awareness. Usually the task was centred on visualising a chariot drawn by tigers, the dust of its passage acting as the obfuscation. The same method had been employed that evening, she sensed, but a greater power had punched its way through the cloak of dust, leaving residues of the guards' distress and panic.

Her task scared her, but she wasn't going to get any more ready. She brought Petri's drawings to mind, and spread her awareness out, questing beyond the room for those who'd worn such masks, daring herself to perceive them.

She bit back a scream as a presence touched her mind, like a long needle sliding behind her eyes. A cold wind tugged; she braced herself and let it pull her through the gap in the wall of dust, to where darkness and empty air surrounded her. She stood atop a tall column, on a space so narrow that she would fall if she didn't hold herself dead still.

'I am here, Hana Quallace,' came a voice behind her.

She shuffled herself round, and quailed at the sight.

The being shone against the blackness. His mask was pure gold, but its brilliance was nothing next to the light that came through the eye-holes and mouth: the light that penetrated her clothes, her flesh, her bones, to the marrow of her bones, and found there only food for worms. The hair of the Shining One was coils of gold wire; his robes were dense with gold thread, so heavily woven that few of the images shimmering there could be made out. Mighty gold-feathered wings flashed behind him in an effortless beat, keeping him in place without disturbing the dead air. But though the Shining One seemed unaffected by gravity, Hana sensed she herself was not. The drop all around her felt horribly real: if she fell, the psychic shock of the landing might kill her. She had entered a realm under another's control – and that, she was suddenly sure, had not been wise.

She fought to assert herself. 'You know my name, sir. How should I call you?'

'You might call me "Lord".' The words were not easy to define; his speech seemed to come from the back of her own mind as much as from behind the mask. 'Or you might call me "A".'

That alarmed her. Did he know she'd read the transcripts, or was he fishing to find out? She sensed a questing pressure on her mind, and pushed back against it.

'You told Astolio to bury Tashi.'

He asked her something, she thought to do with clarification, but picking out his words was like trying to make out shapes beneath moving water. She wondered why, then realised that for the first time she was speaking to a wholly independent consciousness, not an Otherworld entity: to another magician, and one of great power. Unnerved, she made sure she sensed the floor of Telegraph House as well as the column on which she stood.

'I know why you told him to,' she said, projecting her words clearly with her mind as well as her voice. 'Because of the danger Tashi represents. But I can remove that danger in another way, by driving out the demons and restoring him. I need only know what those demons are, and I believe you can tell me.'

The figure pointed downwards with his articulated glove of segmented gold. Far, far below, so distant that it sickened Hana with fear of falling, a faint patch of light like a break in moving clouds glided across what seemed a plain of red stones.

No, not stones. They were even more distant than she'd thought, and they were bodies. The shaft illuminated them and moved on, to more and more of them, miles and miles of them.

'You cannot know,' came A's voice, his hard-to-grasp words, 'that any res-tor-ation will...' something: *eliminate*? '...risk.'

'I can promise I'll never let him out of my sight,' she said, looking from the corpse-plain back to the Shining One, his wings beating above the thousand-foot fall. 'I can promise I'll keep him strong enough to never let them threaten him again.'

The word *affirmative* came quickly, but she thought not from him: it sounded out of place, an intrusion.

'Agreed,' said A. 'But the con-cepts are...' she thought maybe *problematic*. 'Open your mind and I shall en-light-en you.'

'No.' She pushed against the increased pressure. 'Explain them.'

'Too subtle. Mis-under-standing would be dan-gerous. Open yourself.'

She firmed her mind against it. This might be a way for him to get a foothold inside her, perhaps control her. It might even be a plan to get through the college shield.

He had refused her straightforward request. She would have to try something more dangerous.

'I'll make it easier for you,' she said. 'You don't have to tell me their name, only their nature. I already know you call them klippoth.'

The light behind the eye-holes blazed, briefly. 'So you have read those papers.'

'And if you don't tell me what I want to know, so will many others.'

Her heartbeat shook her, twice, three, four times.

'Then many others will suffer the fate of your uncle.'

'How will you know who I show them to?' said Hana. 'You clearly can't see through the college shield – you didn't even know I'd read them till just now. You'd have to keep a scry on everyone who leaves the college, and going by the transcripts it's clear you don't have the resources. Word will spread.'

'To what effect? None would listen. The dialogues your uncle transcribed were kept deliberately vague. The evidence is weak.'

'Strong enough for you to want him killed,' Hana said. 'And it's strong enough for Orc and Cass to be hanged as sorcerers.'

The light behind the mask dimmed, as though retreated into thought.

'And you wouldn't want that,' she followed up. 'They're crucial to whatever you're planning.'

She couldn't tell whether the light was bent upon her or itself. 'Your threat is empty,' said A. 'You would not risk the death of the male subject. He is important to you also.'

'Not as much as Tashi.'

'Your relationship with the nov-i-ti-ate has no basis in reality. You lack the years and—' something-*icity* '—to be his mother. You delude yourself because you made an elem-entary magical mistake.'

She suspected a diversion. Even so, his words needled. 'Like what?'

'You failed to dismiss the Mother energy after your in-voc-ation on the island. It has warped your thinking, your feeling. Geist taught you only to invoke your an-i-math, and he did not want that energy dispelled. He wished it to bond with you. In naïve error you applied the same practice to your Mother invo-cation. That energy also has bonded with you. It remains within you, dis-tor-ting your rela-tion-ship with the nov-i-tiate, making it ec-lipse other relation-ships that have more basis.'

Unease trickled through her at the thought that he might be right. 'Even if so, that doesn't change that Tashi deserves to be saved.'

'Does not your relationship with Orc des-erve to be saved? What you plan will destroy it. Are you aware that you cannot draw on the power of the—' *goddess-amalgam*? '—without rescin-ding your claim on him? He will feel bet-rayed.'

'We've already discussed it. He's fine with it.'

'He might find it dangerous to soulscape. If he does not soulscape, you cannot join with him. You will miss out on his power.'

'I don't care about power.'

'Because you do not know how much you plan to throw away. Has he not told you…' She lost the next bit but caught the final word, and it shocked her.

'What?' she said. 'Repeat that clearly.'

The words came with deliberation: 'He has be-held the Ser-pent Man-da-la.'

She fought to not sway and fall. She wanted to say the revelation changed nothing, but couldn't bring out the words.

'When you listen less to your magically dis-torted emotions,' said A, 'and more to your rea-son, you will see that you cannot bet-ray him. You cannot risk harm to him. And we ourselves will not per-mit such risk. You will do as we say. You will not rescind your claim on him. You will not abandon him to the god-dess a-mal-gam. You will make no attempt to res-tore the novi-tiate.'

'You can't order me,' she said.

The light flared. Unsteadiness took her; the platform vanished beneath her feet. She almost screamed, expecting to fall – then everything stabilised, and the blackness eased to firelight on wallpaper, and she stood in the drawing room at home. As before, Jorik twitched and shivered on the couch.

But not Jorik. A cry jumped to Hana's throat – the figure who spasmed in unconscious fear and pain, breathing laboured and face damp, was Stefanie.

She caught the cry in time. This wasn't real.

'We cannot, per-haps, destroy everyone who reads the tran-scripts,' came the Shining One's voice. 'But there are some we will en-sure do not es-cape.'

'Help me…' Stefanie's gasp was barely audible. 'Please…'

Hana sought some flaw in the horrible vision, some unreality, but every detail, every movement was exactly how Stefanie might look in such a situation – how she would indeed look, in a few days or weeks, if A carried out his threat.

'This is a crude piece of blackmail,' she said. She'd been trying for strength, but the effort drained her.

'A hammer is a crude tool,' said A. 'Think well upon whom you wish it to fall.'

Hana felt a strong mental push, and Telegraph House re-established itself in her awareness: the mat beneath her, the breeze through the ventilation slits.

She put her head between her knees.

9

BROTHERS

Orc looked up at her, brow tensed, as she came down the steps. 'You spoke to them?'

'You know where I've been?'

'I worked it out. Did they tell you?'

She sat on the bottom step, the cold of the stone passing through her trousers at once. 'He,' she corrected him. 'I spoke to "A". And no, he didn't tell me what klippoth are. He told me not to help Tashi. He told me that if we try, they'll kill my parents.'

Orc gasped. 'Why?'

'Like the transcripts say: Tashi's demons are a threat to their plan, whatever that is. They don't believe I can restore him fully. And saving him is a threat to you, and they don't want you harmed.'

'What? Fuck them – you can't pay any attention to that!'

'That's all very heroic, Orc, but what about my mother dying in front of me, and me not being able to help her? Is that something I can pay attention to?'

He dropped his gaze.

'I'm sorry,' she said. 'You didn't deserve that.' She pressed her fingertips against her temples.

'There has to be a way.'

'Sometimes there just isn't. Sometimes we have to accept things we don't want to.' *No basis in reality*, the Shining One had said. On the island, she'd held Tashi weeping in her arms; she'd unwrapped him from his armour. But the little he'd said to her afterwards had been guarded, almost hostile. Had she been fooling herself because of a magical error?

She met Orc's gaze. 'Do you ever invoke Otter?'

'Sometimes. Like on the way here.'

'Did Geist teach you to dismiss the energy afterwards?'

'No. It seems to just fade when I don't need it any more. Why, are you meant to?'

'I didn't dismiss the Mother energy when I invoked her. I didn't know to: they don't teach invocation here, I was just working on instinct and what I did with Hare. Now I think about it, dismissal is simple magical hygiene. But I didn't, and the energy's seeped down into me and it's been warping the way I feel ever since.' Anger was building in her, against her own words, her heart raging against her mind. 'You must have thought I was mad, wanting so hard to save him when he should mean nothing to me.'

'Nothing?' said Orc. 'Without him, we'd probably be dead.'

'I know. I think. Gods, I don't even know what the real me would think any more.'

'Yes you do.' He leaned forwards. 'Hana, I'm not letting this go. And you don't want to either.'

'And I don't want my mother dead. And I don't want… to hurt you. It's some relief that I won't have to now.'

'You won't have to rescind your claim on me?'

'Whatever that means, no, I won't. I'm glad I don't have to abandon you to her.'

'Me too,' said Orc. 'Never scaping again, that would've been tough.'

An understatement, she thought. Even so, he'd been prepared to go through with it.

'Especially with you,' he said. 'I was thinking about that just now, our joint-scaping. Where we could take it.'

'I'll tell you where,' said Hana. 'We're going to take on those bastards and destroy them.'

Orc grunted a laugh.

'I'm serious.'

'You think we could ever be that powerful?'

'I'm sure of it,' she said. 'I did wonder how your scaping came to be as good as mine, when I've been doing it ten years and you only one. Better than mine, even – you managed to see *something* in the demons' fog. It didn't occur to me why at the time. But I know now.'

He looked at her, suspicious.

She swallowed. 'You've seen the Serpent Mandala.'

'Ah.' His gaze fell. 'Cass told you?'

'The Shining One. Why didn't *you* tell me?'

He sagged between his shoulders. 'Because of what you said. It sends people mad.'

'It hasn't sent you mad.'

'That's not what Cass would tell you. She thinks I've never been the same since my Initiation.'

'Is that when you saw it? Orc…' He'd started to visibly shake. She went and sat beside him, but he got up and walked across the cellar.

'I've never told anyone, that's all. Not even Cass, not what really happened. I tried, but she got too upset.'

'Try with me,' she said. 'Please.'

He stood facing half away, seeming both impossibly solid and incredibly fragile.

'Geist broke my mind. On purpose. He set up tricks to make it seem like impossible things were happening, to break my sense of reality. And in the end it did break. I saw everything differently: the universe, the stars, people. But I didn't understand the way I saw it. I couldn't handle it. He told me he could show me the sense of it. He took me to a cave in the hills, and shut me in there, in the dark. No food, just drugged water. Two weeks. I don't remember much about it. I don't even know if he came to check on me. I hallucinated a lot. And at the end, I did understand. I saw the two serpents dancing, and

I knew it was the root of the world and all worlds, physical matter and imagination and everything in between. It was all one – it's our minds that keep everything separate. Us, too: separate from others, from the world, from the Mandala as it truly is.

'I got close to it. Really close. If I'd let myself get closer, I would've lost all sense of separateness for good. And I wanted to get closer, because it felt like the truth. Like… home. But at the last moment, I fought against it. I called for help, and Otter came, with the fiery brand in his mouth, and pulled me back. Turned out Geist hoped something like that would happen.'

She tried to absorb this. 'A hell of a risk he made you take.'

'I guess if I'd got trashed, Cass would've been a back-up.'

She looked at the lamp flame. 'Her hating magic is starting to make sense.'

'Yeah,' he rasped. 'Sometimes I've wished I could.'

'Have you seen it since? The Mandala?'

'Never. I get close, though – it's how I enter a scape. When Geist gave up trying to teach me meditation, he taught me to re-create that sliding down into madness – the Little Death, he called it. That's why I have to do it alone: I need to feel cut off, and scared. And it is scary, because to make the Otherworld real enough I have to get to where the Mandala starts to dissolve everything together, so imagination becomes more real and reality more imaginary. The closer I get before I call Otter, the more intense the scape – but it's more risky, too, because I can feel the Mandala's pull. Maybe someday I'll leave it too late to call Otter, by accident or not, and just get sucked right into it. And that will be the end of Orc, forever. Whoever he was.'

He turned his eyes on her. 'You said you could ground me. Can you ground me from that?'

She pushed confidence into her voice. 'I'll learn how. I'll be the earth for your lightning.'

He laughed. 'Lightning?'

'Why not? You saw the Mandala and survived. Who knows how strong you could become?'

He looked a little awkward, and she had the sudden sense of how he might feel to hold. 'How about you?' he said. 'Didn't Geist try anything like that with you?'

'Not so extreme. Though similar, in some ways. My parents were killed in a monarchist plot, and I was put with an uncle. For a lot of reasons, I didn't know who I was – being that age didn't help. When I got to know Geist, we talked about that kind of thing, identity and so on. Now I think about it, he might have been encouraging me to feel insecure about myself and my place in the world, whether I even had one. And during one magical session, that all came to a head, and I think I mentally cried out for something solid, something to hold on to – and there came an animal with a fiery brand. A hare like those I'd seen box in the spring. And I know it sounds crazy, or it would to anyone else, but I felt I had someone I could trust.'

'The core of you.'

She caught the tremor in his voice. 'Yes,' she said. 'Like being able to see the shape of part of your soul. To speak to it.'

When she looked up, his eyes were wet. 'Let's do it,' he said. 'Our masks.'

'I… thought that made you uncomfortable.'

'So does being deep underwater. It's still a beautiful thing.'

She barely had breath for the word. 'Yes.'

He made to kneel at one end of the bed, but she told him to sit instead. She sat beside him, very close. She watched him swallow, the movement of his throat beneath discoloured skin.

'Do they still hurt? Those bruises?'

'Not so much.'

'You'll be safe from her now.' The words felt like the deepest magic. She dared to slide her fingers under the unbuttoned neck of his shirt – he tensed a little, but allowed it – and hooked out his focus-stone on its leather thong. With her other hand she prised her own from beneath her wristband. The dim lamplight caught edges and depths. Her stone was larger, but less clearly like a tooth.

'I wonder where they came from?'

'Geist never said.' Orc's throat sounded dry.

'Nor to me.' She touched the stones together. Then a shared curve caught her eye, and she turned hers over and around, and matched one face against another. 'They fit.'

'I can't see,' he said, his breath on her cheek. He made to take his pendant off, but she did it for him, her hand brushing against his notched ear, his hair.

'Look.' She matched them again, unable to quite stop her hands shaking.

'Oh, yeah,' he said, in a soft, warm register she knew would be his bed-voice.

Looking, looking, though there had long since ceased to be anything new to see, and nothing to say. The sound of his breathing, slow, deep, the faintest whistle of air through his nostrils. Their upper arms pressed against each other. The warmth of him against the cool cellar. Her own breathing, slow, deep. Each listening to the other, she realised. Waiting in shared hesitation.

She held her breath as she sensed him move. She angled her head and his deep blue-green eye filled her vision, too close to focus, just before it closed and his lips melted onto hers.

The night air in the cellar was no cooler than during the day. Orc lay against her, the heat of his skin making her sweat, his muscled leg thrown naked over her thigh. He was a restless sleeper, though she didn't mind the disturbance. She had no hope of sleeping herself.

She tried to stifle awareness of Tashi's shrouded form nearby, tried not to think of his burned hands clinging to the rock, his burnt-out eyes staring at the mountain peak. It felt a betrayal to push away the thoughts of him, but she needed to get through this. Had he ever been aware of her efforts to help him? Was he aware now that she'd been forced to give up? She shifted against Orc's lean, dense body, as though to get more comfortable but really to wake him. At first his face creased with puzzlement, and she feared the realisation of regret, a mistake –

then his eyes brightened in expectation, and she welcomed him with a smile that felt more complex with sadness and hope and desire than any she had smiled before.

Kissing drew them entangling into a sometimes clumsy, sometimes wonderful shifting and groping and knocking of bones and teeth and a mess of breath and hair and the strangeness and yet obviousness of another person moving against her and after a while inside her. This time, it was less like a physical test Orc seemed to feel he needed to pass; she was already learning to manage him, and he was already starting to learn when his spontaneity worked and when it didn't. When the frenzied tension electrified his body, she even managed to get him to slow his hips for a while, before the effort of self-control got too much for him and he threw himself into a race she had no choice but to let him win.

'You're amazing,' he panted afterwards, his heat gumming him to her.

'You too,' she said, hoping it would eventually become true.

Warmth sapped slowly into the cellar's air, the walls, the earth. Orc lay with his head next to hers, breathing into his half of the pillow. She wondered about his experience; she wondered about other women and girls he might not remember. She ran a hand through his damp hair and over his shoulder blades, played with sliding his skin over bone and muscle, and caught the disturbing idea that she could push fingertips through all his layers of anatomy and out the other side without knowing if she had touched the real him. What did it mean, to feel one's core so lacking that it had to be filled by an animal that came at a cry for help? And did he really share that with her, or did he have a genuine core that he'd misplaced, one built up during his forgotten life, one waiting to be found again? One that lay behind the Shroud?

She had glimpsed behind that barrier. She'd seen him, as a younger boy with longer hair, holding out a jellyfish as if to goad or terrorise. That glimpse had let her save him from Daroguerre's trap. But everything else, everything, lay behind the barrier made by the Shining Ones. Had they changed him, in that hidden time? She flinched from the image of him strapped naked to a table, surrounded by thirteen surgeons in gold masks.

And now that she'd let the idea of the Shining Ones into her mind, she believed she could sense them, dimly, their collective scrutiny gathered against the college shield, trying to force a breach as they had in the communion guard. She hadn't been at that day's shield-workings, but she retained a sensitivity to the shield built up over the years. And she intuited now that it was too weak, that it was in danger.

That it had already been penetrated.

An image knifed her: the wall where she'd pulled out the bricks earlier that evening.

Where she'd weakened it.

But not against magic, surely? She tried to calm herself, to focus her instinct back to its source, but found only a vague sense of unease.

She shoved Orc alert.

'Wow, again?' he said.

'Can you feel anything?' She tried to explain what she'd picked up, and he frowned as he regained his focus.

'Nothing,' he said after a minute. 'You think it was real? What could it be?'

'The Scorpion? Coming to check on the digging?' But that couldn't be right. If her senses had been triggered, it had been by some magical force passing through the shield. If it was the Scorpion, then his intent was surely more than to spy.

'I don't like this.' She pulled on trousers and shirt. She climbed the steps and heaved open the trap-door. Young Sorrel had taken Sattrano's place in the barn. His face in the light of the paraffin lamp looked like he'd just woken from a doze.

'I think I've sensed an intruder,' she told him.

He picked up his rifle, looking embarrassed to have been caught off-guard. 'The one they picked up at the shield-working?'

'Maybe. But it might be nothing.'

She left him with the rifle half-raised, and without closing the trap-door, went back down. Orc had put his trousers on.

'Let's try to sense him,' she said. 'Put our stones together.'

They held hands with the crystals trapped together between their palms. Hana pushed away the distraction of Orc's nearness, his touch. She tried to sink herself into a receptive state, but she was too on edge. She sent out threads of awareness to the gap in the wall, but picked up nothing definite. A false alarm, for sure. They could get back to other things. She placed her free hand on the back of Orc's, and slid it up his forearm, pushing the hairs the wrong way, while he made a small moan of pleasure.

'*Stop*!'

Sorrel's cry froze her. Then came a detonation that made her and Orc jump up, stones spilling. A yell of panic followed, then a short scream.

Someone charged down the steps, and not Sorrel. Light glinted on leather, steel, blood: a young brown face, black hair, tight black armour of straps and buckles, a heavy sword bright and slicked red. Tashi – his face was different but it was Tashi as she'd first seen him, possessed and deadly. Orc jerked her back by her arm. The boy jumped to the floor. His tight gaze darted around the cellar – with a forbidding glare at them, almost too focused to be human, he ran past the bed to the shrouded figure on the table.

'Wait!' cried Hana.

The boy tore off the cover. He stared rigid at what lay there, then his focus broke with horror. The sword clanged to the floor.

'We're trying to help him,' Hana said.

'This is no armour!' the boy cried. 'What have you *done* to him?'

'It wasn't us!' said Orc.

'We're trying to change him back,' said Hana.

'You lie!' The boy drew the shorter sword at his waist; his face creased in pain at the action.

'I'd never harm him,' pressed Hana. 'I'm his mother!'

The words jumped out before she could judge them. They twisted her inside, like her dirtiest secret.

The boy snapped free of his stunned look. 'I'll take him. Do not try to stop me.' He closed his eyes and began muttering quickly. 'My eyes are vessels for the holy light of Gevurah, my heart is a vessel for the—'

'Don't!' cried Hana. 'Don't invoke anything.'

'Please,' said Orc, 'just listen – we'll explain.'

The boy had stopped anyway. 'They've left me,' he groaned. 'Tashi, the Lords of Battle have gone.'

'Sorrel!' came a shout from above. Other voices followed, crying out, yelling instructions.

'Hana?' someone called down through the trap-door.

She didn't want anyone else down here until she'd calmed the boy: they couldn't risk Tashi being disturbed. 'I'm fine!'

'What happened?' called Marco.

'I don't know. I heard a shot. Is anything wrong?'

'You didn't *check*?' whipped Sattrano's voice. 'You left him to die alone?'

Die...?

She stared at the Thangkaran. Orc's grip on her tightened.

Sattrano started down the steps, nearly naked. 'I'll come up!' said Hana, but to no avail. As soon as Sattrano saw the boy in black, he jumped down, brought his rifle to his shoulder. The boy raised his short sword and set his stance, eyes tight.

Hana broke free of Orc and ran between them. 'Stop!'

'Move,' muttered Sattrano, his face dreadful with fury and pain.

'He didn't know what he was doing. He was possessed – I've seen this before!'

'Sorrel is *dead*.'

'He shot first. It's all a mistake. Isn't one boy enough?'

'*Move*.'

'Sattrano, do not fire down there,' boomed Astolio's voice. The master came after it, dressed in a gown, carefully lowering himself step after step. Marco followed. From above, Hana heard others howling with grief. But Astolio looked around – at Orc, shirtless, at his son, at Hana, at the intruder – all without expression.

'Hana, step away.'

'He was possessed—'

'Do not speak. Marco, hold her. I need to see who we have here.'

Marco advanced. 'Sattrano will not shoot,' said Astolio as the gatekeeper took Hana's arm. Seeing that Sattrano had lowered his rifle slightly, Hana let herself be pulled back a couple of paces.

The Thangkaran's face was set with determination. His cheeks were wet too. Hana thought he might be even younger than Tashi.

'You are a novitiate of Highcloud,' said Astolio.

'I am proud to be that, sorcerer.'

'Fetch me a sword, father,' said Sattrano. 'If you think a gun too dangerous down here, let me fight him with a blade. He won't leave this place. Someone get me a sword!'

'No,' said Astolio. 'You may not kill him.'

'For Sorrel, I can do nothing less!'

'Then you will condemn us all. The Watchers will learn that he entered the college, if they do not already know. If he never leaves, they will come here, or their agents will, or the Empyreal authorities.'

Sattrano fumed. 'Are you such a coward that you would excuse the murder of your own son?'

'I do not excuse it,' growled Astolio. 'But I know when my enemy's power is greater than mine.'

'He's not your enemy,' said Hana. 'It's all been—'

'Silent! The Watchers would have tried to destroy us years ago, had they been aware of our activities.'

'Which they soon will be, if he lives,' said Sattrano.

'I *am* your enemy, sorcerers,' said the boy. 'What you have done to my brother would make me so, even if this place were not swamped in magic.'

'His condition is not our doing,' said Astolio.

The boy's mouth set shut.

'How many of you are nearby?' said Astolio. 'Where is your master?'

He said nothing.

'What's your name?' asked Hana.

He looked at her. 'You are not his mother.'

'I'm the closest he has. And I'm his friend.'

'He would not befriend magicians.' The boy shook. 'And no mother or friend would plan to bury him alive!'

She had no answer: shame stung words away.

'How do you know about that?' said Astolio.

'He must have overheard,' Hana said. 'Don't you see? He *had* to rescue Tashi because of what you planned to do, because you caved in to the Shining Ones. *That's* why Sorrel is dead.'

She saw the words bite.

'Damn you, Hana,' he said. 'Damn us all. Marco, Sattrano: hold that little murderer. We'll keep him as hostage.' He trod heavily up the steps to join those weeping in the barn.

As soon as he'd gone, Sattrano raised his gun.

'Don't be a fool!' Hana strove to pull from Marco's grip. 'You heard your father.'

'And I can hear my mother.'

'Don't be hasty, lad,' said Marco, but didn't move.

Hana pulled again. 'You'll rouse Tashi! We'll all die!' But she could see this argument made no impression on him at all. Nothing would.

The Thangkaran boy faced the gun, stiff with dread, his chest moving with his high, shallow breathing. 'I do not fear you, sorcerer. It is the flesh that fears. And I will be avenged.'

'I'm no sorcerer,' said Sattrano. 'And you'll be in hell.'

'I will find the Mountain,' came the boy's taut response. 'My conscience is clear; I've made no Qliphoth to snare me.'

Klippoth – the word paralysed Hana's chest. She tried to shout, but couldn't. Sattrano's finger tightened on the trigger just as something crashed out of midair and knocked his shoulder. The cellar erupted with the bang in Hana's ears; the boot Orc had thrown fell to the ground and Orc came after it. He hurled himself at Sattrano and grabbed his rifle, shouting, struggling. Hana glanced at Sattrano's target. The Thangkaran boy was unhurt.

Her blood chilled at a metallic noise. Tashi's arm moved.

10

MOTHER

Hana squirmed out of Marco's grip, loosened by the shock, and hurried to Tashi's table. Next to it, his fellow novitiate stared in horror.

'Calm him!' cried Hana over the sounds of the brawl. 'You're his brother, yes? He's still in there. Tell him you're here. Tell him you love him, tell him to be strong.'

She placed her hands on Tashi's plate-armour leg and tried to force her thoughts into him; she pictured the burned boy and flooded the love out of her, and with it, hope. She had real hope now: she would learn what klippoth were, all he had to do was hold on. Beside her, the novitiate babbled tearful, half-panicked pleas for Tashi to stay true.

The demon form raised its head and one arm. Three fingers melted together into a single sword-blade. It moved slowly, as though hindered, but it moved. Hana met the creature's blank face. How could it see her? How could Tashi be aware of her? The terrible thought came that when Tashi had regained control over the demons on the road, it might not have been anything to do with her at all, but sheer luck. And it might not happen now.

'Brother! Don't you know me? It's Aino.'

The head turned to face the novitiate.

'I couldn't wait for you on the bridge,' came the boy's shaky voice. 'I've come to help you. To take you home. Home, Tashi! To see the Mountain again.'

The blade flashed forwards. Aino jerked aside and back. The point pierced his shoulder.

And stopped. All movement stopped.

Hana closed her eyes and fought to not let her legs buckle. *Hold on*, she thought at Tashi with all her will. *Keep holding on. Help is coming.*

She looked round. People crowded the steps and the space just below, mostly around Orc, including Cass in a short nightdress. Orc's face was covered in blood. Sattrano had gone. Hana took in everything in a moment – had they even noticed what had happened? – and turned back to Aino, held in place by the sword-point, his face pale and clenched.

Still mentally urging Tashi to calmness, she unbuckled the straps around Aino's shoulder. The blade had stuck between two of them. When the armour was freed, she helped Aino ease himself back off the point. It had not gone deep: blood flowed after it, but not a dangerous amount. She gave him Orc's discarded shirt to stanch it, and helped him to the bed.

'Aino.' She sat next to the trembling boy, fighting not to fall into shock herself. 'You know what klippoth are?'

'Qliphoth.' His pronunciation was slightly different.

'That's what changed Tashi.'

'No!' he gasped. 'How?'

'If you can tell me what they are, I can drive them out of him,' she said. 'I'll make a bargain with you. If I restore him, you must agree not to tell anyone what happened here. These people aren't evil. They don't deserve the Watchers to come and persecute them. Restoring Tashi will prove that, won't it? If you agree, I can save your life, and his. Hold the shirt there. Do you want some brandy for the pain?'

'It's nothing,' he said, his face belying his words.

She put a blanket round him, checked Tashi showed no more sign of movement, and went to Orc. Cass was cradling his head. The handkerchief she held to his nose was already sodden red. More blood had spilled down his chest. Bruises were coming up on his face and arms and body. Cass's face was red with crying. She looked at Hana with fury.

'Tashi's hold slipped,' Hana said to Orc. 'You saved us all – he regained control because of Aino, not because of me.' She wasn't wholly sure that was true, but it seemed right to say it. 'If Aino had been dead…'

'He knows what klippoth are,' said Orc, oddly nasal, his face tensed with pain.

'Yes.' She looked at the novitiate hunched on the bed.

'Does that mean you can do it now?' said Orc. 'Will you? Does it change anything?'

Hana tried to shut out her vision of Stefanie. 'I can't let Tashi be buried. I won't be threatened away from something I know is right.'

A spasm crossed his fight-bloodied face, but he held her gaze. 'Then you have something to tell me.'

He looked like he was steeling himself to be shot. The thought of what she would have to do appalled her after what he'd just gone through.

'I got into this mess for Tashi,' he said. 'Don't make it be for nothing.'

'It can wait a bit,' she said.

'No. Get it over with.'

'Get what over with?' said Cass. 'What the fuck's this about?'

Hana felt amazed by Orc's acceptance of his sacrifice: everything he was prepared to lose, even the huge part of his life that was Otter and the Otherworld – not, in his case, because of an invocation messed up, but because Tashi deserved to be saved. To repay such a generous heart with rejection; to reject him at all; to exchange the warmth of his body and his soft voice for a relationship that was more magic than fact, one that had no basis in reality and that might have no future…

But that was the voice of the Shining One. She couldn't allow such thoughts to sway her. She nodded, set her breath, put iron into herself.

'I was wrong to make that claim on you,' she said. 'It was a mistake. I rescind it.' Each phrase felt like she'd kicked his bruised face, but she had to assert separation, had to scour her claim out of the psychosphere, out of her own mind, out of his. 'You're not mine. I give you back to yourself, without regret, without hesitation.' And now the final nails, struck by a hammer made of all her psychic strength: 'I want no part of you.'

He took it all, with no accusation in his eyes; but at the end, just as he looked down, she knew the Shining One had been right. He felt betrayed, even if he tried not to.

'What the shit did all that mean?' said Cass.

'It means we can restore Tashi.' Hana felt suddenly overwhelmed with exhaustion and misery. But she'd made her choice.

'And your parents?' said Orc.

'There must be some way to protect them. I'll just have to find it.'

'I don't follow all this,' said Marco. 'There seems to be a lot of talk about restoring and protecting, but it doesn't sound like it'll do Sorrel any good.'

No one spoke as he climbed the steps. Cass crouched even closer to Orc, as if to guard him against a change of mind on Hana's part. Everyone else had left the cellar now, though mumbled talk sounded from above. Hana squatted on her haunches with her back against the cool of the brickwork. A minute or two, to recover, and then she would tackle the next thing, and ask Aino about the nature of Qliphoth. She pushed down the sickening possibility that he might not know enough, after all, that she might have cast Orc out for nothing.

Her thought was broken by a cry from Aino: 'Master! You should have escaped.'

Down from the barn walked a Thangkaran in red robes, his head shaved. Hana stood. The reminder of Shoggu brought a lump to her throat, though this man was shorter, his face fuller and smoother. The monk's features looked apt to smile, but he was not smiling now.

'I'm too old for running.' The monk stared at Tashi's transformed body. 'My name is Yaggit,' he said. 'What in Gevurah's name has happened?'

'Qliphoth, that's what,' Hana said. 'And you need to tell me what they are.'

'He has been… altered, master.' Aino's voice betrayed pain. 'She says it is Qliphoth, but that cannot be.'

'That's what I've heard them called,' said Hana.

'You had better tell me everything,' said Yaggit heavily.

Hana asked the monk to sit next to his novitiate on the bed. With Marco watching with his shotgun from the top step, and Cass and Orc still huddled at the base of the stair-block, she briefly told the Thangkarans about the events on the island. The fact of Shoggu's death was not news to them, it seemed, though the details were, and so was Tashi's fate. But manifestation was a concept they knew of, and it took less time than she'd feared to convince them that Daroguerre had made it a horrific actuality, with Tashi as one of its many casualties.

'Who told you it was Qliphoth that possessed him?' said Yaggit.

Hana judged that, as with Astolio, it would be safer to keep secret the transcripts' existence. 'I promised not to reveal that. But they know their subject, I'm sure of it. What *are* Qliphoth?'

'Broadly,' said Yaggit, 'they are the offspring of sinful thought or deed. By our poor conduct we give rise to them and feed them. As they strengthen, they try to influence us to feed them further, and at our deaths they try to drag our souls to their home, the Hell of the Witch Mother. But there are no records of them magically possessing anyone. I cannot see how that would happen.'

'An invocation gone wrong?' Hana turned to Aino. 'The kind of invocation you were under?'

'That is not the same,' the boy said. 'I was Inspired by the strength of the *Elohim Gibor*, the Lords of Holy Battle. I lost them, master,' he told Yaggit. 'The shock of seeing him.'

'Whatever was in him gave him the strength to use one of those big swords too,' said Hana. 'These *Elohim Gibor* couldn't be Qliphoth under another name?'

'No!' protested Aino. 'They are among Gevurah's highest servants! You speak nothing but blasphemy and lies. Tashi was the most devout of us – he could *never* have made Qliphoth so strong.'

But Yaggit was looking at the shrouded form as though at a realisation. 'Oh, Shoggu,' he breathed. 'How much did you know? What could you tell us if you were here now?'

'Help me, Yaggit,' said Hana. 'Help me to help *him*.'

The monk studied his ageing hands. 'Some hold that Qliphoth are the shadow-side of what is holy. They arise when any action or thought is performed without mindfulness of Gevurah's intent. Remove Gevurah from judgement, and you have cruelty and vengeance; remove Him from righteous anger, and you have rage and hate. They arise from bodily emotions which have not been tempered by the mind-self which is His gift to us.'

'The shadow-side of what is holy,' Hana said. 'Could these be the shadow-side of the *Elohim Gibor*?'

Yaggit glanced at Aino, who had been about to speak. The boy stayed silent.

'That is the thought that occurred to me,' Yaggit said. 'Momentarily. But the *Elohim Gibor* have no body, and thus no emotion. They cannot give rise to Qliphoth.'

But human beings could, thought Hana. The Thangkarans' mistake was to think only in terms of the individual.

And if you remove Gevurah…

She recalled the child's burnt-out eyes staring at the mountain top. As though burned to nothing from staring at that blazing whiteness of sun on frozen snow. Staring, searching…

A shudder went through her. She gathered herself to ask Aino her question.

'And when you call these *Elohim Gibor*, they come through the blessing of Gevurah? Through his love?'

'Of course,' said Aino, eyes tight with suspicion.

'What if you felt yourself unworthy of that blessing? Inadequate to receive it?'

'What has this to do with Tashi?'

'Answer me.'

'They would not come,' said Aino.

'But if *something* did? If you called the warrior energy of your religion, but it didn't come through the stern love of your holy God but *round the outside*, what would it be?'

Aino looked at Yaggit. The monk's expression was troubled. 'It is wrong to talk of "energy",' he said. 'Though bodiless, the *Elohim Gibor* are beings of mind, no less than we.'

'But there's something you know,' said Hana. 'I see from your face.'

Yaggit exhaled. He gave the briefest shrug. 'A phrase came back to me. "The night-side of the sun".'

A sudden chill entered Hana's bones. 'What is that? What do you mean?'

'More than a hundred years ago, a case occurred that we don't relate to novitiates,' Yaggit said, with a glance at worried-looking Aino. 'It has never been fully explained. A Watcher, one who had successfully defeated many magicians, was sent to investigate some others west of Thulerstadt. There had been whispers that he and his new novitiate shared an unnatural relationship – the Abbot had dismissed the rumour, but perhaps found it expedient to absent them from Highcloud for a while. The Watcher Inspired the novitiate to exterminate the nest of sorcerers. There was a witness to the ritual: the innkeeper's daughter spied from the attic, finding the novitiate pleasing to her eye. According to her, the novitiate expressed fear that sin would corrupt his Inspiration. And at the climax of the rite, he cried aloud the phrase I just mentioned.

'The Watcher was first to die, but many others followed, before the muskets of the city militia were brought to bear on the novitiate. The bloodshed was successfully blamed on the magicians. Money was paid to make this so.'

'What has this to do with Tashi?' said Aino. 'Why would he feel himself unworthy?' His look accused Hana. 'Do not dare to say it was for the same reason!'

'I don't,' she said. 'It wouldn't need anything like that. I'm amazed anyone could feel worthy, the demands your religion places on them. To see your own body as the enemy of your god.'

'That is crude and unfair,' said Yaggit. 'The body was created by Gevurah. It is a tool that we use for our holy work. What we fight is its corruption by the Witch Mother, the overwhelming of the mind by the body's emotions.'

'Its needs,' said Hana. 'You see it as a tool – but how can you do other than despise a tool you can't control? It needs to shit. It has desires. It wants sex.'

Aino's face tightened.

'You wouldn't understand,' said Yaggit, with a stiff smile. 'The idea of controlling the body is anathema to you. A mindful man can hold his urine for hours if necessary, his sexual urges forever. A woman cannot hold her blood. The nature of woman is incontinence. That is not your fault, but it is so. You are steeped in her.'

Hana's ribs tightened so it felt they might snap. 'And what has continence done for Tashi? Look at him! He's made himself the ultimate container, one of seamless living metal! Those Qliphoth might originate in emotions, but your beliefs gave them their form. They hate life. All life. They are life that rejects life, the Mother's children turned against her. Orc saw them as the degraded serpent: part of the Mandala, the ground of existence, the Mother in pre-human form. They deny they came from the Mother, and now I understand why.'

She breathed deep. 'It's enough. I know what they are, and so I can drive them out. I can restore him.'

'Restore him?' said Yaggit, alarmed. 'No, I believe your wish to help him is genuine, however provocative your speech, but best we take him to Highcloud.'

'For what?' said Hana. 'The Qliphoth won't leave him unless they're forced out, and even then, his body won't restore itself. This needs magic, and power – your order might be adept at divination, but it's got no experience in other disciplines. And then there are the risks getting him there. But you know all that already: it's the magic you object to. So did Shoggu, at first. But in the end, he accepted that it could be used for good.'

'Shoggu did?'

'More than that – he used it himself.'

'No!' said Aino.

'Stop denying everything that makes you uncomfortable, and listen!' said Hana. 'During Tashi's fight with the goddess, Shoggu psychically projected the image of the mountain towards him, to help sustain him. It's what sustains him now – the strength he draws to fight the Qliphoth comes from that Mountain.'

'From Gevurah,' said Aino.

'From wherever – if Shoggu hadn't eased his rigid principles, Tashi would already be lost.'

'That's a lie!'

'Perhaps not, beloved one,' said Yaggit.

'King Serpent speaks through her.'

'She does not have the feel of a liar to me.'

'Not all who use magic are evil,' said Hana, 'as Shoggu came to realise. It will only help those who *are* evil if the rest of us fight with each other. I don't *need* your help; you've told me enough to go on. But I want your blessing. And I want your promise that if I restore Tashi, you won't say anything about this place to the other Watchers. Most of your principles are shared by the master here, even if they seem opposite. This college is not the enemy of your order.'

'You think they will let us leave?' said Yaggit.

'Astolio has no choice. He believes the Watchers will take a terrible revenge if you're harmed. But if you persuade Astolio that you'll say nothing, it'll make it easier for him to let you go.'

But still not easy, Hana thought, to release the killer of his child.

'I must discuss this with Aino,' said Yaggit.

The two moved into a corner and sat talking in whispers. Hana clung to what felt like the last shreds of her energy. She didn't try to listen to them, nor to the few faint voices from the barn above. She felt as she had on the column, facing the Shining One – that she and her world might fall, and in any direction.

'The bleeding's stopped,' came Cass's voice. Hana watched her take the red-soaked handkerchief from Orc's face. 'We need to get you another shirt, and I need to get dressed. Put your shoes on.'

'Be back soon, both of you,' said Hana, half-hoping they would take their time. Orc nodded. He picked up the boot he'd thrown, then the other.

'Are they magicians too?' Yaggit said when they'd gone.

'They can support me,' said Hana. 'Any objection?'

Yaggit shook his head. He looked at Aino, and Hana sensed some agreement pass between them. 'This is far beyond me,' the monk said. 'But you have my acquiescence.'

'And your word, about the college?'

'If you succeed, then yes, I will choose a form of words in my account that will not cast suspicion upon this place. But no Watcher may lie.'

'Will Highcloud know you've come here?'

'We are supposed to be in Bismark. Whether the other Watchers will spare the energy to trace us here, I cannot say – though surely they will do so if we don't return.'

Hana nodded. 'I could do with taking my mind off Qliphoth for a few minutes. Will you tell me what led you here?'

From the way Yaggit hunched over himself on the edge of the bed, she wondered if that was a question too painful for him to answer. But after a short pause, he spoke.

'From the moment Shoggu left Highcloud, my mind was troubled with fear for him. The day after, the Abbot sent me to Bismark on an unrelated mission, and several times each day, in flight, I tried to learn how Shoggu and Tashi fared. By Gevurah's will, my work at last bore bitter fruit: I became certain that Shoggu had died somewhere across the sea. I turned my efforts towards Tashi, and divined he was on his way to Kymera, helpless and in the possession of others.

'I struggled with the choice before me, but in the end I could make no other decision. I put aside the Abbot's task, leaving it in the hands of my colleague, Murun, and set out to find Tashi. The sense of him grew stronger as we came south, until the trail led to this place. But when I tried to learn what transpired within these walls, my efforts were baffled by the magical barrier. I could only think Tashi was being held prisoner by the very magicians Shoggu had warned of – and when I tried to probe the ritual conducted in the small house near the gate, my fears only seemed confirmed.'

'So you did overhear?'

'Yes – once the initial warding collapsed. And what I overheard gave me no choice but to Inspire Aino and have him attempt Tashi's rescue. I... regret the death of the boy.'

'It wasn't your fault,' said Hana, but her words felt meaningless. When she'd arrived at the college, Sorrel had been six, and everyone's favourite plaything. She felt suddenly old, finding herself in a world in which boys were given real weapons and killed each other without understanding what was happening. All such a mess, a swamp, things dissolving into each other with no clarity or definition – except for the mask of gold that lay at the heart of the misery.

One thing at a time.

It took some work to persuade Yaggit and Aino that they should remain above, in the barn. Marco had gone to sit up there; the air around him was grey with cigarette smoke, but Sorrel's body and everyone else had gone. Hana told the gatekeeper not to let the Thangkarans be harmed, and to shut the trap-door on her and allow no one down but the Strandborns.

Alone with Tashi, she placed the cover back over him, suspecting that physical transformation was more likely to succeed if unobserved. Then she went back to her earlier meditation. The cellar was the cave and the cave was the womb of the Mother, and Tashi would be born again here – that belief, and that need, was the world and all the world, bound by brick-lined earth walls. Over and over she asserted that truth, reshaping her mind to her desire.

When the trap-door opened again, she felt as ready as she could be. Orc wore a new shirt that didn't fit him. More bruises and swelling had come up, especially around his nose and eyes, and both his and Cass's expressions were set, masks over grief or anger.

Reaching the bottom steps, Orc looked about him in obvious concern.

You sense her, thought Hana. The image of him bound to the tree sprang vividly back. Blood to quicken the Mother's womb and feed Tashi's rebirth – and some of that blood, indeed, he'd spilt from his nose onto the cellar floor. Her sacrificial husband, his semen inside her. The cave was pregnant with the power of the Mother, who was part of the Great Goddess and yet greater and older still, and Hana had made herself its channel.

'Stand near Tashi,' she told them. 'But don't look at him. And say nothing.'

'For now,' muttered Cass.

'Nothing, I said!' snapped Hana. 'You are in the womb of the Mother. Only Her priestess may speak.'

She undressed. Both Orc and Cass had seen her naked before, but in any case embarrassment was far from her mind. The wild darkness infused her.

She knelt and pricked her tattoo-mask awake.

She followed Hare out of the red mist and onto the mountainside, the scene of her boy's suffering and his unmet hope. All looked as before, but she sensed Tashi even weaker, his grip on the rock less sure, the mountain's peak half-obscured by haze.

'I know you are Qliphoth!' she called down to the bank of red fog. 'Show yourselves!'

The gloom swept back, revealing an impossible being made of many red bodies, their torsos joined at the shoulders or hips or connected by extra limbs. Some had four arms, some more; each hand held a weapon.

They pulled against each other, and at the chains that held them to Tashi. It looked a horrific shambles, a rabble. Hana couldn't see how they would fight effectively against anything. But each head – mostly men, some women – stared at her with the same expression, features pulled taut by muscles that seemed frozen in spasm, a unison of hatred.

She tried to stay calm, to not let the horror divert her thoughts.

'Whose sin made you?' she called.

'NO SIN MADE US, FORNICATOR. WE WERE MADE BY THE LORD, AND THE LORD DOES NOT SIN, HE CLEANSES.'

'He cleanses all that fails,' said Hana. 'He cleanses imperfection. He cleanses life itself, for life is imperfect. He cleanses what comes from the Mother, but that includes you.'

They howled and raged. They brandished their weapons and spat and hissed.

'You fear your origins in the emotions of the body,' said Hana. 'In rage and hate and disgust. You fear the Mother's power over you. You reject it, but you come from her, and she has power over you whether you like it or not, because none ever truly outgrow her.'

She turned to Tashi's burnt form. She felt the pressure of the womb around her physical body, the cave that linked to the Great Cave on the island.

'Grant me your aid, as you promised.'

A figure appeared on the other side of Tashi. The Mother was robed and hooded in dark blue. As before, she wore Nadora's face as a mask, but this mask was of white wood. Hare hid quivering behind Hana's legs.

Howling rose from the Qliphoth. As the Mother walked to Tashi, vegetation sprang from her feet and died away, to be immediately replaced. Hana steadied herself with belief. This had to be it.

'I have rescinded my claim on the Sun-King.'

'He is mine now,' said the Mother.

'You said you would help Tashi. We must free him from the chains.'

'What the—?' Orc's voice broke in, but she didn't know what he was reacting to. She hadn't spoken aloud.

'Hana,' said Cass, 'what have you done?'

'Quiet!' she urged.

'Holy crap!' said Orc.

Hana heard their feet move around on the floor. She fought to not let it distract her focus. She needed to be fully present in the scape, or this would fail.

'Orc.' Cass spoke tight with alarm. 'We've gotta get out.'

'No!' said Hana. Without their presence, the physical transformation couldn't work.

'Make this quick then, for God's sake,' said Orc.

She cleared her mind of external distractions, re-immersed herself fully. The Mother laid her hand on Tashi's burnt neck, just below the collar on which the chains pulled. Tashi showed no reaction, only kept staring with his hollowed eyes at the mountain.

Cass screamed. Feet moved, faster, and with their sound came now a slow slithering across the floor. The trap-door crashed open. Voices called: Aino, Yaggit. Feet stamped on the stairs. 'Help him!' called Cass. A blade hissed from a sheath. Against the chaos Hana heard Orc's strangled yell, his cursing. She aimed her will at the Mother. *Faster.*

Tashi's body shrivelled in on itself. With appalling suddenness, blackened flesh shrank away to expose bone. Bone collapsed into black dust. At once the chains and manacles and collar fell tumbling away, pulled down the mountainside by the weight of the shrieking demons, a great metallic clattering and howling down into silence.

Hana stared at the dust where Tashi had been. She tried to shore herself against doubt. *Now*, she directed at the Mother. *Rebirth him.* She could hardly make out her own thoughts through the cries and movement around her, the grunts, the sword swishing, cutting. She held back from shouting *let her have him*. Cass was calling for Orc to come away. He didn't reply. That hoarse breathing, those strangled cries must be his.

Hana jammed her fingers into her ears. The Mother just stood there. 'Why don't you make him reborn?' Hana shouted in her mind.

'Nothing is reborn.' The Mother's mask, Nadora's face, was dissolving. 'Your child's body died. It died days ago.'

Realisation turned Hana's spine to ice. Through her stopped ears she heard Aino cry out, the blast of a shotgun, a call of thanks.

'You said you would save him,' she said, aloud now too, trying to sound strong, to not let her voice break.

'And so I have,' replied the Mother. 'His will is released from its torment.'

The shotgun sounded again. Hana went to the point on the mountainside where Tashi had lain, where there now lay only a faint layer of black powder.

'You agreed to restore him…'

'To how he should be.'

Hana shrieked inside. That wasn't what she'd meant. This couldn't be right. This wasn't right. There had been a mistake.

All she ever made were mistakes.

A bolt of cold and sweat struck her as the idea scrambled to form in her mind. That previous mistake – the one the Shining One had told her of, that she'd failed to dismiss the Mother's energy after her invocation on the island – she could use it. No time to think: she searched out and drew power from the Cave, the power that went back to the dawn of human history and beyond.

'I take your power.' She looked at the Mother. The figure blurred. 'I pay whatever price that power demands.'

She reached out and tore off the Mother's white mask. The wooden face of Nadora fell away. Behind was only vegetation, a mass of red-flowered creepers and vines, snake-like.

Snake-like, then two snakes.

She didn't flinch. The Mandala had come in response to her need: the ageless power behind the Mother, behind herself. She barely heard the cellar's noises, barely felt Hare kick and punch her legs in the scape.

She would not be distracted. She abandoned herself, Hana, even the idea of Hana, and embraced the truth of the two serpents dancing.

Squatting down, she dug her fingers into the earth of the mountainside, fingers that might as well have belonged to anyone. She mounded the earth and from it shaped Tashi's reborn body. She poured her power into him. She was the Mother, the primal force of creation given human shape. The power rose to meet the demand she placed upon it.

The rough human shape of earth and dust: she made it become him. The noise around her body was subsiding. She reached out with her mind to Orc and Cass, and the power of manifestation they catalysed. She visualised that power flowing to Tashi's body on the table in the cave-cellar: she gripped the focus-stone hard and through it amplified her assertion that what she desired had already happened. She gave Tashi his life back, fresh from her own womb, within this cave that also lay within the cave of the universe.

'*I am his mother.*'

She dissolved into the power of the Mandala and focused it at him, at the earthen boy in front of her on the mountain and the boy on the table. Her mind became noise, whiteness, blackness, a drumbeat in otherwise silence.

Blood throbbed.

The beating of a heart… her own?

'Hana?'

Exhausted, she recognised the voice intruding from outside. It came from the world of names, but the name Hana was just a thin skin of meaning on the truth of what she was. It would demean her to obey its call. It was clothing, and she had discarded clothing. The world itself was only clothing.

'Child,' came Hare's voice. 'The Mandala is dangerous to look upon. Had you stared longer, I would have lost you. You were saved by breaking away to save another, but you teeter on the edge. Awaken to your self, to your name. Answer it. It is written in the fire. Look.'

In the scape, she looked. Hare stood on hind legs, his front paws holding a flaming brand.

'Hana?' came the question from outside again, and again her answer was no.

'Take that away,' she told Hare. 'That fire came from the sky. It does not belong with me – *traitor*.'

Alarm widened Hare's eyes. He took the brand in his mouth and ran, darting across the mountain slope. She pursued him with vegetation, throwing it out of the ground to tangle him. He evaded it all. He ran with the end of the brand against the ground, burning shapes into it. A letter she recognised as H, then an A. She guessed what he would do, his futile gesture of what he mistook for love. She aimed her attention at where he must make the final A, and she willed the ground there to a swamp, its black water heaving with living creepers. Hare made the N, and ran to the edge of the swamp, his fur erect, his long black-tipped ears back. He paused, flanks heaving with effort and dread, and looked at her, his eyes deep and brown shining behind his bone mask.

No. She realised what she'd done. 'Hare!'

He leapt into the swamp. His furry body and the flaming brand plunged deep inside. The heaving vegetation settled over him.

Horrified, she pushed out of the scape, heedless of the danger of doing so suddenly. She straightened up on her knees, back in the cellar, its air heavy with the smells of sap and gun-smoke.

The place was a tangle of creepers, chopped and hacked. Their stems protruded from the crumbled brick facing of the walls. Orc's blood-speckled shirt and trousers were shredded on his body. His skin was covered in cuts; one spiral of thorned creeper, severed, still coiled round his forearm. Aino's face ran with sweat; he looked exhausted, half-mad, panting with terror. He still held his short sword. Marco watched from halfway up the steps; Cass, cut in tens of places rather than hundreds like Orc, watched from next to her cousin. All stared at her.

She looked at the table. The figure on it, beneath its shroud, now lay flat.

It stirred.

Her cry choked in her.

She pushed to her feet and stumbled to the table. Biting down fear, she tore off the sheet – and cried out, hands over her face. Tears spasmed.

Tashi – her Tashi – opened his eyes. He looked confused, struggling to focus on her. She touched her hand to his cheek, its soft warm skin.

'What—' Aino's voice. 'What is this?'

Tashi sat up, turned his beautiful head. 'Aino?' he croaked.

Aino backed off a step. Yaggit looked dumbfounded. Cass looked like she might be sick.

'Aino, is that you?' said Tashi, sounding scared. 'Where is this?'

'Don't worry,' said Hana. 'You're safe now.' She put the sheet around herself: he was too old to see her naked. She kept her eyes from his own genitals.

'That isn't—' said Aino.

'It isn't the Tashi we knew,' said Yaggit.

'What?' she said.

'Hana,' said Cass. 'Can't you see it? He... looks like you.'

'Of course he does,' she said. 'I'm his mother. And he has his father's mouth.' She smiled at Orc. But Orc's face had gone very pale; and suddenly, she understood why.

11

TRACKS

The door of her shuttered room opened, letting in the morning light from the landing. 'I've brought you some tea.' Stefanie put the cup on the bedside table, and sat on the chair beside it. 'How are you today?'

She didn't answer, couldn't. She held out a hand, which Stefanie took.

'Can you talk about it?'

'No. I'm sorry.'

'Time will heal,' said Stefanie. 'It's only been two days.' She adjusted her wire-rimmed spectacles. 'I'm sure you'll recover as well at home as here. Perhaps better.'

So they were prepared to have her back. Or Stefanie was, at least – she'd seen no sign of Ferman.

'Are you able to travel?' said Stefanie.

'You're leaving?'

'Today.'

You can't, she almost said, recalling the image the Shining One had shown her. But she held her tongue. Warning her parents of A's terrible promise might be the worst thing she could do, if Cass was right in what she'd said before departing.

'Don't go yet,' she said, as Stefanie stroked her hair. 'I need some more time here. Then I'll come back with you.'

'Maybe Ferman will go, then. Someone has to. The house was broken into.'

She sat up. 'When?'

'Just before dawn, the day we arrived here. We only found out this morning. Sallo was shot. He's in the hospital.'

'Will he be all right? Was much taken?'

'They think he will be. Apparently he saw the intruder making off with one box. The telegram didn't say what it was.'

'Don't go just yet. I need to check something.'

'What is it? We can't delay past noon if we're to get back in the light. It's ten now.'

'That's plenty of time.'

But when Stefanie left the room, the woman who had been Hana spent several minutes staring at the walls before getting out of bed and confronting the mirror over the washstand. No one else had mentioned it. Maybe they were too polite to, or maybe it was too subtle. But she knew she looked ten years older, her skin slightly less taut, the beginnings of wrinkles at the corners of her eyes.

The tight pain in her chest was back again.

'You have neither the age nor the ethnicity to be his mother.'

She pulled off her nightshirt and swallowed at the changes to her body: the heavier breasts, the stretched, slightly sagging waistline.

And he had gone. She had given up herself, her whole self, to become a mother, but it had come back to nothing: he had gone, and with no promise of return, and leaving no knowledge of whether she would see him again.

From the case of clothes she hadn't even unpacked from the boat, she took the re-tailored man's waistcoat that held her tightly enough for her to run without discomfort, the cut-down trousers for the same, her running slippers. They felt horribly unfamiliar, as though it really had been ten years since she'd last run, on the island. She worried that her legs would no longer know what to do.

The college seemed quiet. The noise of classes came through doors she passed, but against them, a bank of hush seemed to linger like a heavy mist. She'd heard that Astolio and Nadora had retreated into grief. Somewhere in the building's depths they mourned their slaughtered son. And Orc was gone, and Cass was gone, and the Thangkarans were gone, all together, leaving this hush to replace them.

She felt exposed as she walked across the open ground to the gate. The pit that would have been Tashi's tomb still lay surrounded by spoil. She knocked for Marco. Wreathing the late-summer air with the smoke of his rush cigarettes, he nodded to her like an old comrade. Alone, he'd dug with pick and shovel in the cellar floor after Tashi's transformation, making a hole big enough to bury all the severed creepers. It might not withstand much scrutiny, but she doubted anyone had been down there since. One small consolation of Sorrel's death: it had taken his parents and Sattrano away before they could witness anything of the manifestation.

'Good to see you up again,' said Marco, unlocking the gate. 'Going for a run, eh? How far?'

'I'll let you know.'

She sensed the shield's relative weakness as she passed through it: inevitable, when Astolio hadn't contributed for the past two days. But on the outside, she was relieved to feel no trace of the Shining Ones. Pausing on the road, she searched for their presence, but they were nowhere. Their attention had gone with Orc, she guessed, and Tashi. They must know she had disobeyed them. But if Cass was right, they likely wouldn't have the energy spare to take revenge.

'Why did the Shining Ones warn Jorik to beware of his dreams?' Cass had asked her. *'Why not strike by surprise? Because the warning was part of the attack – it was meant to make him scared and stop him sleeping, to wear him down so the attack could work. You know what that means? They weren't strong enough without it. They're clever, but they're less powerful*

than we thought. As long as we keep ourselves mentally strong, I don't think their magic's a danger.'

The lack of their presence seemed to confirm it, and suggested Stefanie and Ferman would be safe even outside the college's shield. They could return home.

The question was whether she would return with them. Whether she belonged with them.

Who she was, now.

'Hah-nah.' She tasted the strange, inconsequential sound of it.

She kicked into a run, along the road. She had two hours before her parents left. She eased herself into a jog, then a walk, then a jog again, worried her body had become fragile, would break if overstretched. When she was confident her bones wouldn't fracture from the impact, she launched into a long stride. It felt wrong. Although she hadn't gained weight, she felt as though within her was the Mother's corpulent body she'd seen in the swamp-scape, weighing down her limbs. After a hundred yards, she staggered to a halt.

Hare's lithe energy would have banished the Mother's heaviness. But she couldn't feel him ready at the back of her mind, and the crawling instinct told her she wouldn't be able to invoke him – and so it proved when she tried, just as she hadn't been able to call him during the two scaping attempts the evening before.

She pushed down fear. She'd been a runner before she'd ever invoked Hare. She could be again, without him. She set off once more, determined not to stop until she'd sweated away the ten years that had been added to her, and the ten years before that, back to a time before she had invoked anything, before her birth-parents had been turned into corpses so damaged she hadn't even been allowed to see them; before she had gone to live with the uncle she wouldn't even name, the one who had shown her the hares boxing, who had then turned her into a hunted creature who barricaded her room, all the time carefully reading the eyes of the hound that he was, until Geist – the hound's master – had taken her away, without punishing his hound despite knowing, surely knowing, what he had tried to do.

She leaned into her run, wanting to fall into speed, refusing to stop. At last she saw a cluster of buildings in the flatland ahead, and realised she'd run the whole two miles to the railway halt. The clear blue sky lay heavy upon it.

Apart from the clerk in his office, there was no sign of anyone. She stepped onto the platform. The wind sang in the telegraph wires. Breathing hard, hands on hips, she looked up the double row of tracks. They ran straight for miles. She stared into the distance, as though she might still be able to see the guard's van of the train that had passed through the day before.

Passed through and left her.

Her part was over. The two young men who had weirdly, magically, horribly become her husband and child – who had defined her through relationships more intense than any she'd known before – they were probably now on another train, speeding north from Torrento to Bismark. And then they would go farther north, and farther, to where Orc and Cass might find their answers, and a means of fighting the Shining Ones, and Tashi might find peace.

'I'm sorry, Hana,' Yaggit had said. *'Better for us all that you don't come.'*

Aino's eyes had never lost their mistrust. What had lain behind Tashi's eyes, almost the same shape now as Orc's, had been too complex to read, and he hadn't said more than a handful of words to her. Cass… it pained her to remember Cass's all-too-obvious relief at their separation.

The world had left her behind. She'd resented its intrusion on her island only a week or so before, when she'd been someone else. Maybe she could go back there now, carry on her work, if her so-called parents would agree to it.

No. That wouldn't do. The world had intruded and for a few days had carried her with it. She had become part of something important, and she wasn't about to go back. Gazing up the railway tracks, she realised that her life wasn't so constrained. There was more than one route into the future. And that future needed her: she had a part to play in it. If not with the others, then in another direction, for now. She just wasn't sure which.

'Train'll be another half-hour.' The clerk had come up behind her.

'I'm not taking the train.' She stared up the tracks as though to fix something in her mind.

'Meeting someone, then?'

It was as though the words threw a switch in her mind. An image jolted: a weathered face, a wide-brimmed hat, a long coat on a figure stepping down to a platform.

Of course.

'Yes,' she said. 'But not here.' She held back a smile at the clerk's puzzlement.

She ran back toward the college. Her muscles were tired, but some of the heaviness seemed gone. As she ran, she made plans, who to talk to, how to persuade them. Halfway back, she saw a gig approaching, driven by Orlus, one of the college's men. Riaz and Sattrano sat behind. The gig slowed, until Sattrano leaned forward to speak into Orlus's ear. He flicked the reins; Hana had to step smartly onto the verge. The brothers looked at her coldly as the vehicle sped past. Between them in the back were bags and a long, tapering case.

At the college, she found her parents readying to leave. 'I'll follow later,' she told them. 'I've things to do here first.'

'We wondered where you'd got to,' Stefanie said. 'But wherever it was, you look a little better for it.'

'Have you seen Astolio?' She saw that they had. 'How is he?'

'Brooding,' said Ferman. 'Which I can understand, though it won't help him.'

After Orlus brought back the gig and her parents left in it, she washed and changed, then went to find Petri. He was teaching a drawing class to some of the younger students, but quickly dismissed them to the library. When he'd closed the door after them, he casually backed against it as though to stop her leaving. The light here was much stronger than it had been in the cellar, and his blue-grey eyes, rare in a Kymeran, had a penetrating brightness that made her uneasy.

'You said some curious things about Geist,' she opened.

'Did I?' he said. 'Not as curious as the rumours that have been flying around.'

'I'm not interested in gossip,' she said. 'You asked me if I kept in touch with him – why? What do you know about him?'

His face pinched with thought, mistrust.

'I need to find him,' she said. 'If you know anything about his whereabouts, tell me.'

His mouth screwed together. 'I… can't.'

So he did know something. 'Why not?'

'He swore me to secrecy.'

'You spoke to him?'

'More than that.' She sensed him squirming inside, desperate with wanting to speak. 'I think he might be in danger.'

'Danger? Why?'

'Astolio knows. But you didn't hear that from me.'

'You think Geist would want you to keep it secret if he's in danger?'

'I don't know! He didn't say to only keep it secret except when such-and-such happened. He just said not to tell anyone. You know how he is – you don't lightly disregard his wishes. Did you ever love him, Hana?'

'What? Don't be ridiculous!'

'He used me.'

Her thoughts paled.

'I was young and innocent, and he got what he wanted from me and swore me to secrecy.'

He had a sly look to his eyes, half a smile, as if challenging her to believe or reject his story. She didn't know what to think, except that this was a boy she would trust at her peril. He went to a chest and scooped materials off it. He fished a key from his pocket and unlocked it.

'About six months ago,' he said. 'Just before you went off to the island.'

'He was here,' she said, still nervous as to where this might be leading. 'I saw him, briefly.'

'I didn't know who he was then, but he impressed me at once.' Petri took a sheaf of drawings from the chest. The uppermost pencil-sketch showed Geist in the long coat and hat he wore for travelling, Raven perched on his shoulder. His stance showed a heroic determination, his unlined face a chiselled focus on the distance.

'I think that flatters him,' she said.

'It's as he is beneath,' said Petri. 'The truth beneath the form. He isn't always the age he is now. The child, the youth, the man: they're all in there. If my drawing lasts a hundred years, why shouldn't it show a hundred years of him?'

'Hmm.'

'I drew that afterwards, anyway,' he said, suddenly defensive. 'After he came to me. He wanted my help – nothing else, don't worry.' His sly smirk returned. 'He'd heard about my trance-drawing. Said he wanted to find a place on a map – he'd tried dowsing, but the maps of that area weren't accurate enough. So he wanted landmarks. I drew them for him. He used Raven to take me there. You know how when we do a shield-working, we all direct our energies at the same goal, but we don't feel each other? This was different.'

Like a joint-scape, she thought. Her hunch had been right: Geist had had the idea too.

'I could almost *feel* him,' said Petri. 'His soul's just as impressive as he is physically. But you must know that.'

'What place did he take you?'

'Here.' He showed her two other sheets, rough scribbles in charcoal, seemingly thousands of haphazard lines that coalesced into a ridgeline of hills, a bend in a river. 'I don't know where it is – it's just what I felt. These are the ones he didn't take with him, the too-vague ones. He told me to destroy them. And he made me promise not to tell anyone, and now I have. But I had to, if he's in danger.'

'But *what* danger?'

'I don't know. A couple of weeks after he left, I heard Astolio talking to Erena, and Geist's name. I sneaked closer, and it was something about him biting off more than he could chew. I couldn't challenge them about it, because of the secret. So I searched for him, using the connection we made the first time. I did trance-drawings, look.'

He took a pasteboard folder from the chest and handed it to her. Leafing through its contents, she beheld a chaos of imagery: manacles and chains; a coiled serpent in a pit; the face of a woman with blazing eyes; two identical faceless children holding hands; and more faces, screaming, and stars and the moon and down one side, a long-case clock, its front opened to show the pendulum whose weight was a severed head that dripped blood. The clock's face was a man's, distorted in terror.

Petri baffled her, she realised. Some of the things he said seemed beyond his age, and yet in the medium in which he was supposed to be talented, he produced this lurid juvenilia.

Still, no matter how distorted it was by adolescent imagination, the evidence suggested Geist was caught somewhere. And if Astolio knew where, she would have to brave the grieving master.

'What now?' said Petri, as he locked the chest. 'We're going to find him, yes?'

We? she thought. '*I'm* going to talk to Astolio. You've got classes to teach.'

Lead weighted her heart as she knocked at the master's drawing room. In response came a dull grunt. Astolio sat hunched over in his chair, lips pressed to steepled fingertips, staring as though into a future of despair. As she entered, his gaze turned to her with the same kind of look as the fake eyes of the dead creatures in the glass cases. She felt relieved Nadora wasn't here too.

'Sorry to intrude,' she said, trying to sound both firm and polite.

His look warned her it had better be important.

'I need to know what happened to Geist. And I believe you can tell me.'

Astolio closed the small book on his lap and turned the spine away from her. 'Geist is not a subject I will entertain at present.'

'You had a disagreement?'

'We had many such even before he brought you here, and the fact that he did so does not improve my opinion of him right now. You wish to go back to him, do I guess right? You feel unable to continue here, after this chain of events in which both you and he are links?'

'And who forged the chain?' she said. 'You blame everyone except those truly behind it. The Shining Ones are at the root of everything bad that's happened here. We need to fight them.'

He shifted in his seat. 'You have no idea of their power.'

'Geist has.'

He eyed her, mistrustful.

'He called them The Kings Behind the World,' she said. 'He clearly knows something about them. We can't let them get away with what they've done. We can't let them enact whatever other plans they have.'

'*Whatever other plans*,' Astolio repeated derisively. 'I know their plan, Hana. I know what they are building. What they have built.'

She felt, suddenly, as though a trench had opened before her feet. 'What?'

'I recognised the feel of him – of the Shining One. From many years ago, when I studied and taught at our mother college in Jiata.' He half-roused himself, only to lean back in his chair. 'I hungered in those days for the secrets of the Otherworld. I sank myself in ever-deeper trances, increasingly reliant on certain drugs. During one session, I discovered an old and curious gate in a high wall, and could not open it. I became obsessed with finding what lay beyond. It consumed my days, my health, almost my life; I became so sick from the use of herbs that only Nadora's ministrations saved me, she being housekeeper there at the time. She tried to dissuade me from my quest, but I would not be swayed. My researches into the dustiest corners of the library taught me of demons who possess mathematical keys to any lock. I traded with those demons – do not ask me what! – and at last, I opened that gate.

'And beyond… ah, Hana, beyond lay a realm almost self-contained, a place perhaps deeper and more secret even than the remains of the ancient Zhenaii: a mighty and dread city of gold and glass. *That* is where the Shining One comes from.'

The hush felt heavy as smoke. 'What kind of city?'

'Alas,' the master said, 'it was not in my power to retain its details when I emerged back into the world of matter. I recall only glimpses of high towers, lights blazing, the milling of slaves in their millions. And the city's foundations were death and sacrifice: its buildings were raised upon the bones of nations. But what struck me most of all was its *age*. It had been so long in waiting, it had become as real as the physical realm. And when that gate is opened for good, that city will *become* our reality. It will rise from the deeps of the psychosphere and assume its place upon the throne of the world. Torrento, Bismark, Jiata, all will be crushed beneath it. It is our inevitable future. Our *destiny*.'

His voice seemed to her poised between horror and longing. She wanted to refute his claim. But a terrible idea came to her. By 'rise' did he mean manifest?

'How can it have been growing for so long?'

'Generations must have worked on it. A race or society of magicians, their tentacles becoming ever longer. If they *are* mere magicians…'

'They're only people. They meant that vision to impress you.' She recalled her own encounter, the shaft of light gliding over the corpse-plain, the meticulous reality of it. 'They rely on us thinking them all-powerful. We have to learn all we can about them, to find their weakness. We need Geist.'

'Geist has wrought his own fate,' said Astolio. 'His arrogance has wrought it. To think himself a trickster great enough to fool the entire universe.'

'What do you mean?'

He grunted. 'The Strandborns. I perceived Geist's plan as soon as Ferman told me the cousins knew him. Geist intended to pass them off as twins, hoping to trick even the psychosphere – until he learned of a better alternative.'

'Pass them off? For what purpose?'

'For a nonsense purpose! I will not waste breath on it. Leave me with my grief.'

'I'll leave you when you tell me where he is.'

'I would rather have the satisfaction of knowing he will rot there. This is at an end, Hana. I suggest you follow your parents to their house. Goodbye.'

'Do you know how I restored Tashi?'

He looked set to repeat the dismissal, but reluctant interest flickered in his eyes. 'The transformation ability was inherent within his altered form. You expelled the demons, and he reverted to his previous state.'

'No. He was already dead. And that wasn't his previous state – he used to look as Thangkaran as Aino. I re-created him, from nothing.'

Astolio's beard stuck forward with the movement of his jaw. 'Impossible.'

'Not so. I beheld the Serpent Mandala, and I used its power. It almost destroyed me. But here's the thing. Orc encountered it too, during his Initiation, and survived. And I don't think that was chance – either him encountering it, or surviving. I think Geist stage-managed the whole thing, which means Geist might know how to work with the Mandala, at least more than we do. I need to find and talk with him before I dare try anything like that again.'

'Even if all this were true, why should it interest me now?'

'Because what I did for Tashi, I can do for Sorrel.'

His eyes tightened. There was scorn there, but also bright, terrible realisation. So this was what she had become: someone who lied to a grieving man, raising false hope to get what she wanted.

Unless it were not false hope…

Astolio studied her for several ticks of the clock, then spoke, his voice heavy. 'North of Maskar, there lies a highland region called the Bourgoune: a wild tract of hills and bogs, tribal, almost unchanged for hundreds of years. I divined Geist's presence there – the shroud he used to keep about himself must have weakened. I believe him to be held prisoner, in a tower or old fortress with the name Androloch.'

'Who's holding him? Why?'

'Someone he tried to steal from, was all I could intuit. What they intend with him, I know not. To my knowledge, there has been no demand for ransom. My feeling is that his captors keep him to make use of his powers. When I tried to divine his circumstances, I picked up strange but consistent readings to do with magic: ancient, hidden magic. There is something of the Zhenaii about that place; the fortress is wreathed in a dark fog of horror.'

Wonderful. But she'd committed herself to the path. 'I'll need money.'

Suspicion creased his face.

'Bribes,' she said. 'Perhaps a ransom. I'll make sure Geist pays back any expenses.'

'You wouldn't be taking advantage of a father's grief, Hana?'

'And I'll need someone to come with me.'

'There I can't help you. Riaz and Sattrano have gone for a few days.'

'Yes, I passed—'

A terrible thought struck her: the tapering case in the gig. A rifle.

'Where?' she said. 'You sent them after the others?'

'They insisted,' said Astolio. 'Have no fear, it's only the Watcher and his killer boy they seek. Fury burns in them like a coal. I have sometimes wished I had their fire.'

'But…' She was appalled. 'What about Highcloud retaliating?'

'I have not been entirely idle. My divinations lead me to believe the Watchers will not pose a threat to us. I beheld the monastery destroyed.'

The conviction in his voice caught her breath. 'You think it has been?'

'It will be soon. I saw its novitiates fall from their bridge; I saw the walls tumble, heard the machine-guns and the shells.'

'You can't rely on a psychic prediction! It was probably just wishful thinking.'

'Don't seek to instruct me on the dangers of divination,' he said, his dark eyes polished with contempt. 'If you give us back Sorrel, you can then restore any dead Thangkarans, should you wish to.'

She had no answer to that. She wondered if she could get Yaggit's party a message. But how would she address a telegram? And what chance did a magical communication stand over such a distance, when Orc wouldn't be waiting to receive one?

'Money and supplies, I'll give you,' said Astolio. 'And you may take any willing member of staff or servant. My hopes you carry with you, whether you wish them in your luggage or not. And on your return, you shall account for everything.'

In the end she could think of no one to take but Petri, and he took no persuading. A postal carriage from the railway halt took them as far north as Wassera, where they hitched a ride on a goods wagon to Herl on the River Steer. By then, to her relief, Petri had given up his tiresome talk about magical experimentation through sex – which she assumed, though he never made it clear, was intended as a plan of seduction – and she'd told him about the events on the Hollow Isles. Petri seemed particularly taken with the role Hare had played, and kept asking her about the Fire Stealers. Otherwise, he spent most of his time sleeping or drawing. At a couple of the stops, he even managed to sell portraits for a few solidos.

At Herl, their route joined the Old Royal Road from Torrento, and they picked up another ride to Maskar. They arrived to find the high hills to the north hung with cloud, and the air filled with drizzle; the Sack of Ducks smelt of damp travellers. Maskar seemed every bit the frontier of civilisation the carriage-driver had described. The inhabitants of the Bourgoune had never accepted the claim Kymera made on their land, though since the land had few resources, the government had rarely pressed their notional authority. Apart from a little trade in furs, the Bourgs were self-reliant, and, from what she'd heard, unlikely to welcome visitors. But somewhere in that highland was Geist.

'We'll need to find someone who knows the land,' she said, as they sat in the inn's common room. 'Someone who's accepted there, a trader or suchlike. But first, we'd better find where this "Androloch" lies.' The weight of the task pressed on her.

'That man keeps looking at you,' said Petri. 'Don't turn!' he added, as she made to. 'Watch me go to the bar. He's the one who looks even more out of place than we do. Third table from the staircase.'

She did as Petri suggested. The sight of the tall young man provoked a sharp intake of breath. He reminded her of Tashi – Tashi as he had been. And not just because of his skin-tone or his straight, almost blue-black hair, the marks of Thangkaran blood. She kept her eyes loosely on him as Petri bought more drinks. The man kept glancing up at her, as though he couldn't help himself, but his gaze shied when their eyes happened to meet. His resemblance to Tashi unnerved and fascinated her, though she couldn't pin it down to any particular feature. She tried not to look.

'Striking, isn't he?' said Petri, clattering two mugs on the table. 'Do you know him?'

'No,' she said.

'Then why is he coming over?'

She turned as the man reached them. He beamed a confident smile, belied by something in his eyes, perhaps nerves. Closer to, his features seemed less markedly Thangkaran. But the glimpse of Tashi remained.

'Forgive me.' His voice had a pleasing resonance. 'I thought I should introduce myself, since our eyes have already become acquainted.'

Oh, gods. 'I didn't mean to stare. You reminded me of someone.'

'As you did me,' he said. 'A lady of my acquaintance, of high birth and rare beauty. I can only think that a woman of your obvious quality finds herself on the edge of barbarian lands, in clothing that doesn't flatter her, because she is undercover on some daring enterprise. I understand that you must deny that, even if true. But be assured, my Lady, I am at your service.'

He inclined his head slightly, gave a smile – one very easy on the eye, she had to admit – and motioned slightly to show he wished to take her hand. Amused, if also a little perturbed, she acceded.

'For a supposed introduction, that was a little light on names,' she said.

He brought her hand to his mouth, not quite brushing the skin with his lips. 'Then allow me to rectify my failure of etiquette. The name's Samka – Ranga Samka.'

PART TWO
PARK CRESCENT

12

NORTH ON IRON

A half-asleep panic gripped Orc as the train began to slow. He tried to push it down, the same irrational, subterranean fear that had assailed him at every station so far: that She would catch up, that restraining vegetation would snake through the holes in the engine's wheels while the ground beneath turned to swamp.

He lifted heavy eyelids and turned his aching gaze to the window, the movement rousing a hundred points of pain across the healing scratches on his body. Fallana: he read the station sign through the grimy glass as the train stopped. Smoke trailed, a whistle blasted. He rested his head back against the crumpled jacket he'd jammed in the angle between the seat-back and the carriage window, and watched passengers leave, their cases banging against the sides of the doors. He hoped the people joining here would be quick. But the only ones to board – he sat up, anxious – were two men in dark uniforms, pistols holstered on white leather belts.

'Keep your seats and wait quietly,' one ordered the carriage at large, before they moved to the connecting doors at either end. More of the uniformed men occupied the station platform. Passengers waiting to board were being held back.

Orc shuffled along his seat and leaned across the aisle towards the Thangkarans.

'Empyreal police.' Yaggit pre-empted his question.

'We're over the border?' said Orc.

'Not yet,' said Yaggit. 'Though not far from it, I think.'

Orc thought of the transcripts in his bag, and tried not to catch either policeman's eye. From some distance ahead, the locomotive blew off unused steam. A passenger asked if he might use the lavatory, and was told no. Nothing else happened. The carriage was silent except for the high-pitched voice of the child from the next bank of seats, those taken by the family Cass had befriended. He heard her soft murmurs answering the boy's questions, exchanging jokes.

The door at the end of the carriage banged open and two other men in dark blue uniforms entered. The shorter addressed the whole carriage: 'The Empyreal government regrets that due to the international situation, the border has been closed to those lacking passports or equivalent.'

Orc tensed. Cries and protests came from several in the carriage.

'The authorities regret any inconvenience brought about by this necessity,' the man went on. 'Applications for return of costs will be considered in due course. Please remain seated for inspection.'

'Fetch Cass,' Yaggit told Orc, but she was already coming back. If she was troubled by the announcement, her face showed little sign.

'What do we do?' Orc asked Yaggit, voice muted. 'We don't have any papers.'

'We'll have to go back,' said Cass. 'Try something else.'

Orc glanced at her. 'Like what? Could we sneak across the border?'

'Shh,' said Yaggit. 'All should be well. Stay calm, as the officer said.'

Orc couldn't understand how Yaggit could be so blasé, but the monk refused to explain his optimism. Orc tried without much success to keep his knee from jigging.

When the shorter inspector reached their section, Yaggit gave the man a somewhat theatrical smile. 'None of us has a passport, as such,' he said. 'But the Empyreal charter surely acts as one, in this instance?'

'Charter...?'

'Granted to the Watchers of Highcloud, allowing them to travel freely within the Empyreum in search of those who practice sorcery. It also guarantees the aid of the Empyreal authorities.'

The inspector's eyes half-lidded. He called his colleague over and related Yaggit's claim. 'Stev, you heard of this?'

'Rings a bell,' said the other. 'An old bell, with a crack in it. You're one of these "Watchers"?'

'And this is my novitiate.' Yaggit indicted Aino. 'My bodyguard, you might say.'

'You're having me on.'

'No doubt the Emperor Konstantin held us in similar disdain,' said Aino, 'until we kicked his army off the Holy Mountain.'

'If anyone's kicked off this train, it won't be the Emperor Konstantin,' said the short inspector. 'And these three?'

'Are accompanying us,' said Yaggit.

'We'll see. This "charter" had better be very clear on the subject of hangers-on.'

He stepped down to the platform, slamming the door after him. His colleague returned to the other passengers.

'That might be a problem,' said Yaggit, his face somewhat fallen. 'From memory, the charter affords freedom of travel only to the Watcher and his novitiate.'

'You can't go on without us!' said Orc.

'I have no wish to do so,' said Yaggit. 'But alternatives elude me.'

Orc's chest felt tight enough to crush his heart. The humidity of breath and perspiration stuck to his skin, the swampy dampness of bodies or jungle. He tried to think of something, anything other than vegetation. He had to get through this. The parallel lines of steel had to hold out, had to get him far enough north for the earth to become iron-hard as winter, safe.

'I have an idea,' said Tashi, his voice thick with trying to hide his natural accent. Whatever his idea was, he didn't look very happy about it. 'For your ears only,' he said to Yaggit.

'I thought we were all in this together,' said Cass. 'But fine, if you want to play it that way.'

She came with Orc back across to the platform side of the carriage, while the Thangkarans huddled in talk. Violent argument broke out further along as the remaining inspector ordered someone off. The policemen stepped in, one holding his revolver like a club. Orc watched a man in a shabby overcoat being pulled across the platform, bleeding from his scalp.

Cass leaned towards him. 'What are these restrictions about, d'you think?'

'Daroguerre said the goddess would bring war closer. They must be worried about spies.'

'But why so sudden? Why introduce them just as we get here?'

Orc's eyes tightened at the implication. 'You think this is for *us*?'

'Is that so mad?' said Cass. 'We know the Kaybees have some kind of influence in the Empyreum: this "project baffomet". They've got every reason to stop us reaching Highcloud. And now this border problem...?'

'The only thing we know about the baffomet thing is that it can stop a warship being deployed,' said Orc. 'It must be connected with the navy – and that's in Torrento, not here.'

Cass leaned back, looked hard-faced out of the window, arms folded. Despite his rebuttal, her idea had made Orc feel even more nervous. To think the machinations of one enemy might lead to him being caught by another. He started chewing his thumbnail.

A long goods train with two locomotives ground past on another line, spreading a smell of smoke and burnt oil that had just faded when the short inspector returned.

'You and your "bodyguard" are cleared,' he told Yaggit. 'Your companions will have to acquire the relevant papers.'

Orc bit back a cry.

But Yaggit seemed prepared. 'His Grace won't like this.'

'His... what?' said the inspector.

'Prelate Siegfried Astrasis. He wishes to see us – all of us. You'll have to get clearance from him.'

'Oh, I'll just pop up to Bismark and ask him, shall I?'

'I'm serious,' said Yaggit, his round face set hard. 'Tell him this, and remember it carefully: a Watcher and novitiate are returning to Bismark, bringing news of the dangerous resurgence that was discussed, along with witnesses to the events at the Hollow Isles.'

The inspector looked at Yaggit as though weighing potential troubles against each other. 'Wait there,' he said at last, then turned to the guards. 'Keep an eye on this lot.'

All the other passengers had been cleared or asked to leave the carriage by the time he returned. Then he ordered them off too.

'We can't hold the train any longer. You can stay overnight at a hotel and wait for an answer.'

No, groaned Orc to himself.

'But the expense,' said Yaggit.

'Not my problem,' said the inspector, with the air of one who'd finally achieved a measure of victory.

The trolley porter they asked about hotels recommended the nearby Black Hart so enthusiastically that as soon as they were out of earshot, Cass said, 'Must be run by a relative.'

'Would it were a relative of mine,' said Yaggit. 'I fear my funds might prove insufficient at commercial rates. I was given a small amount for emergencies, and railway tickets have much depleted that. Watchers are supposed to rely on charity when in the lower world.'

Orc hoped it wouldn't come to sleeping on the earth. He shuddered at the memory of the thorned creepers trying to pull his body apart. 'Maybe the hotel could send the bill to this Prelate? He's the reason we've got to stay here.'

Yaggit looked uneasy. 'That might antagonise him to an unwise degree, given that he will already have reason to feel ill-disposed towards us when we meet him. My message contained no lie, but he will be expecting someone other than he sees.'

'Why should he see anyone at all?' said Tashi. 'My idea was to get through their dreadful city and out the other side before he realises. It's no sin to play him false, not him.' He turned to Aino. 'You told me once that you hated him. I should not have tried to correct you. I apologise.'

'No, Tashi – what you said was right. Hate is an emotion, from the Witch Mother.'

'Even so, I hate him.'

'Tashi—'

'You can't ignore it, Aino. None of our old teachings mean anything in the lower world.'

'No, that's when they mean the most.'

'Hate gives strength. It draws power.'

'*False* power.'

'Who's to say what power is false and what true?' said Tashi. 'There's no difference! Hate is like being Inspired. I hate that man,' he seethed, 'I hate him, *hate* him—'

Yaggit slapped him across the face. Orc gasped, Cass too. Tashi glared at Yaggit a moment, then dropped his gaze.

'What do you think was driven out of you only two days ago?' said Yaggit, voice trembling. 'The gates of your soul were fastened against them, and here you are picking at the locks! Do you want them to possess you anew?'

'It's *his* fault they possessed me at all,' said Tashi. 'What he made me do was corrupt. I was made impure by it. Even that first time, it was not the pure Lords of Battle that came to me. The true *Elohim Gibor* will never come to me now.' He was breathing harder, an edge to his voice. 'I am contaminated. I can never be Inspired again. Even if I find another master…' He sank to his haunches, hands locked over the back of his head, pulling his gaze to the ground.

'Tashi…' said Aino.

'Go!'

'Please, go on,' Aino said to Yaggit, looking distraught. 'Please.'

Yaggit nodded and led Orc and Cass into the hotel, leaving the two novitiates outside. Orc glanced back to see Aino kneeling beside Tashi, his looming pack seeming about to crush them both.

'Will he be okay?' said Orc.

Yaggit gave no answer.

Several other ejected passengers were already at the hotel desk. When Yaggit reached the front of the queue, the clerk demanded payment in advance, and refused to bargain or forward the bill to Highcloud or anywhere else. Orc was trying to breathe down his dread at the prospect of a night spent outdoors when a man in grey tweed came to stand alongside them.

'What's this, Berrant?' he said to the desk-clerk. 'This is a Watcher of Highcloud – are you ignorant of the tradition of charity that pertains in such cases?'

Facing the speaker fully, Orc was surprised at his youth, given his clothes. His trim, dandyish moustache, red-gold as his waved hair, seemed out of place on such a young face, as though he were a schoolboy made up to play an adult role. His left arm was in a sling, beneath his draped jacket.

'I have no authority to offer charity, sir,' said the clerk.

'Then it's the Black Hart's loss,' said the young man. 'Giving charity to a Watcher brings good fortune in return. And if you don't want that good fortune, I'll take it with both hands – or the one I have available to me.' Smiling, he turned to Yaggit. 'Might I have the honour of meeting the cost of your stay?'

'With gratitude,' said Yaggit. 'But there will be five of us altogether.'

'All the more honour, then! I've travelled to Thangkara, and respect your people greatly. Never yet visited Highcloud, to my regret, but been to some of the lower monasteries. You're returning there now, via Bismark?'

Yaggit nodded. The young man took a card case from his pocket, flipped it open with his slender thumb, and slid out a card for Yaggit to take. 'My town address. I'm headed back there myself in the morning. If you need any help whilst in the city, please don't hesitate. Any help at all.' His voice took on a quiet intensity. 'I hope you won't come to need it, but I urge you to take great care.'

'Your help and advice are gratefully received, Mister... Crome,' said Yaggit, with a glance at the card. 'Is there any particular danger you hold in mind?'

'Oh, nothing specific,' said Crome. 'But times are difficult, and about to become more so, and I know the dangers of being far from home's familiar ways. Don't think me barely out of school – I left my formal education early, to begin my true one.' He turned to the clerk. 'Give them rooms, Berrant, on my account. Not my usual one, though – you've kept that for me?'

While Crome paid, Yaggit took the others a few steps away. 'It's said that when a Watcher finds charity without asking, he is surely on the right path. This confirms that we were right to follow Tashi's idea.'

Tashi himself came in a minute later, with Aino. Both looked subdued. Shortly after, a hotel boy came to show them to their rooms, three twin-bedded ones next to each other on the third floor. Orc assumed he'd be put with one of the Thangkarans, but all three disappeared into the same room.

In his own, Orc threw himself exhausted onto a bed. Even here, though, he didn't feel safe. Small signs of deterioration intruded: the dark-red paint cracking in places, the curtains spotted with mould. He tried to push away the idea that this denial of humanity's attempt to order nature might presage something bigger, that brick might soften and slide back into clay, or be turned to powder by a million roots of tiny invasive plants. He tried not to think of vegetation surging up the hotel walls.

The knock made him jump. As Cass walked in, he steeled himself at the determined look on her face.

'I don't like this,' she said. 'Tashi's idea might get us across the border, but what then? We'd be walking into a trap.'

Orc had feared she'd come for the talk they'd been avoiding. 'I told you, the border thing's probably nothing to do with us. Anyway, we don't have a choice.'

'We do.' The chair creaked as she sat. 'I've been thinking since we left Torrento, and now I'm convinced there's a less risky option.'

He propped himself on an elbow. 'Like what?'

'That other college, in Jiata. The one run by Astolio's grandmaster.'

He tried not to scoff. 'How is that less risky? The Sundarans were Daroguerre's allies – they work directly for the Kaybees!'

'Daroguerre recruited them, or Seriuz did,' said Cass. 'There's nothing in the transcripts to say the Kaybees have any influence there. The college will be out of their reach, and it'll be shielded. We can hide from them. Prepare ourselves, in secret. We can study there, get the answers ourselves – work out how to beat them, ourselves.'

He regretted he couldn't share in the fiery determination of her eyes. 'I can't do magic any more, remember?' He kicked away the thought that he would never see Otter again, before it could break him.

'Yaggit wouldn't be there,' said Cass. 'Your promise wouldn't matter.'

'I meant because of the Mother.'

'You couldn't do your old kind of magic, no. But we could find a new kind. A less dangerous kind, one that doesn't rely on mixing thought and reality and fucking up your head.'

'That's the only way magic *can* work,' said Orc. 'And what do you know about magic anyway? You hate it!'

'Maybe not for ever. I talked to Ferman at the college. He has some interesting ideas about the psychosphere. He thinks it can be treated almost like index cards.'

'Like what?' said Orc, unimpressed. 'Look, the Conclave is stronger than I can ever hope to be. They'll tell us who we are, who the Kaybees are, how to beat them.'

'So Yaggit says.'

'Why wouldn't they?' said Orc. 'The Kaybees tried to kill Tashi and Shoggu – the transcripts prove it. The Watchers are bound to be against them.'

'And against who else?' Sudden anger made Cass's face a weapon. 'You weren't there when Tashi tried to kill Hana. His demons, these "Qliphoth", they weren't alien to him, they came from his religion – Highcloud's religion. These people you're planning to hand yourself over to, they hate witches, anyone who uses magic. That means us, Orc.'

'Not you. And not me, now I've given it up.'

'And this manifesting effect we can't control? This abomination they think God wiped out a civilisation for? That's not magic?'

'I trust Yaggit. I don't have a choice.' He laid his head back down. 'Highcloud's the only place I can get away from *Her*. She doesn't belong on the mountain, Hana said so. I'd never make it to Sundara. You heard Daroguerre on the island? I'm identified with the Sun-King. And everything I've done since has only reinforced it.'

'But if there wasn't a part of *you* that thought that…'

'The whole psychosphere thinks it! That's why I can't do magic, because I have to connect to the Otherworld, and apart from a few animals the whole Otherworld thinks I should be dead! I'm her rightful sacrifice – you get that? Her *rightful* sacrifice! Fuck, Cass…'

'You have to stop thinking about it.'

'How can I?'

The pause felt somehow fatal. It ended in her sigh. 'I don't know. I've no idea how you can stop thinking about it because I can't either. Your… role. And what it led to.'

This was it. He stared at the ceiling.

'It was part of you and her, too, wasn't it?'

They were going to talk about Hana. Hana, whose skin had been hot against his, whose legs had been hot around his, and the rest.

'I know your relationship had a lot of magical stuff in it.' Cass spoke carefully, as though stepping between knives. 'That claim she made on you when you joint-scaped, her identification with the Mother, your identification with the goddess's consort.'

'Uh-huh,' he said, forcing breath past the ropes round his chest.

'Maybe it's not surprising what happened. I'm not saying she did it deliberately. That's the thing with magic, isn't it? There aren't any boundaries. It can spill out.'

The impulse swelled within and choked him, to beg forgiveness. The counter-thought pushed it back down: he'd done nothing wrong. And maybe she felt that too, because she was sounding very rational. Almost too rational.

'Could it be,' she went on, 'that Hana's "claim" on you, this... momentum, towards what happened between you, was already there when we... when you... when you decided that *we* couldn't?'

'I didn't *decide*.'

'When "God" told you we couldn't, then.'

'I never said it was God.' Then he twigged what she was getting at. 'What, you think that was just me looking for an excuse to be with her?'

'That's what I'm asking, yes.'

'I didn't make it up!'

'How do you know? You can't tell reality from imagination any more.'

'That photograph wasn't my imagination.'

'We don't know that photograph had anything to do with it. We don't know if Astolio put it there and the bed moving shook it free, or if the Kaybees used us to manifest it—'

'Why would he? Why would they?'

'Why anything? Maybe *you* manifested it. All I know is you get this "voice on high" feeling that we can't be together because something bad will happen, and hours later you're with Hana. Hours! Not even one day...'

The ragged depth of her groan made him lift his head. She'd bent over between her knees. He looked at her hair, just long enough to fall forwards over her face and hide it. He looked at her shoulders, the way her back curved. He couldn't remember exactly how it had felt, the conviction that had built up in him while he'd moved against her in bed, that a power was gathering angry force. It couldn't have been the Kaybees, because of the college shield. It had been either something more powerful, strong enough to get through the shield, or something from within himself. But it hadn't felt like part of himself.

'I've always had it,' he said. 'That feeling that if we make a mistake...'

'Our first day,' said Cass to the floor. 'Our first hour, on that beach. When Geist asked if I was your sister, I had a really strong instinct that I wasn't, that he'd got it wrong. I still remember it, that feeling of no, wait. It's like I could sense all the shit that would come from him asking that question – that question we might never even have thought of by ourselves.'

'It's not that simple.'

'And a feeling of God being angry, that's simple, is it?'

'What about those dreams you had on *Nightfire*?'

'That was all fucked up. I was fucked up. I was dumped in the sea tied to a lump of concrete, remember? But I should've realised you weren't really at fault for that. You can't help it if you don't see the world properly. Reality is what we make from our strongest experiences, right? And I can't imagine how it felt to see the Mandala, or your scapes.'

She was still giving him an excuse, he realised. For everything, including Hana. But she was excusing him on the grounds of mental incapacity. It would be easy to go along with it, to accept. Maybe it was even true.

She groaned and stuck her hands into her hair.

'We'll be okay,' Orc said. 'As long as we stick together.'

She jerked her face up at him. 'Together? What's been "together" about it so far? *You* made this arrangement with Yaggit; *you* decided when to break off our… whatever the hell it was. I hope for your sake you *do* turn out to be my brother. I feel sick just asking the question.'

'Then don't,' he said. 'Don't talk about this, or think about it. There's no point, is there, until we know the truth?'

'It hurts, Orc.'

'I know. I'm sorry.'

'But you're right. Talking does nothing, same as it doesn't when you bang your head or cut your knee. Talking to you does nothing. You're just a vacuum words disappear into, and words come back from that vacuum but they're made of vacuum, they don't mean anything. I tell you it hurts, and you say *I know*, and *I'm sorry*, and it's like you're trying to shoo away a fly but you can't even be bothered to put any effort in because it's not really a danger.'

He wanted to defend himself, but it felt like there wasn't anything left to defend.

'You know what I hate most?' said Cass. 'Knowing they're listening in, eavesdropping on us suffering because we don't know who we are, because of what *they* did to us. I hate them. I'm not scared of them. They're scared of us, isn't that what the transcripts said?'

He wanted to hold her, tight, as though that might give him some of her anger. He wanted that fire; he felt like the source of it in himself was smothered with mud. But even if he had that fire, where would he focus it? The enemies seemed as wide as the sky and as deep as the earth.

'We're tired,' she said, as though to excuse his silence and her own emotion. 'I'm going to have a bath.' At the door, she turned. 'Think they'll be watching me undress?' she said. 'You know what? I think my instinct that you're not my brother was right. I don't think you were my lover either. Because if you were either of those things, and you knew a load of creepy bastards were watching me in the bath, you wouldn't ask some stupid Conclave to fight them. You'd take on the fuckers yourself.'

All he could do, before she left, was sigh. It frightened him that he'd said nothing, done nothing. A vacuum. He felt empty even of the will to move. To possess will at all now felt an immeasurably distant possibility. He felt weighted on his mattress, as though it were earth he could sink into, as though the earth had risen through two storeys of the hotel to meet his body. The outside noises of hooves and voices and the rumble of shunting trains felt like dreams from another world.

13

THE NAME OF A MASK

'You shouldn't be here,' Orc told her. 'I shouldn't be. You let me go.'

'I am the Mother now,' said Hana. 'And I will never let you go. Why do you run from me? Why seek the father-place, the place of cold forbidding, of judgement?'

And he was cold, and the world was hard. She had hold of his hand, and he went willingly, or so it felt, barefoot over grass in which there were only a few prickling plants, until green enclosed the two of them, and dappled sunlight fell on thick, soft mosses as he reclined naked beside her. The trickle of running water came from nearby, and the air was thick with humid warmth and the throb of insects, and the insect throb bothered him but he couldn't place his unease. Her bower enclosed him, wet and warm.

When she slid off him he reclined, exhausted, and the insects throbbed louder. He tried to move, but his ankles and wrists were bound with thorns. Beneath the heady scents of the plants, he caught the taint of rot.

Hana smiled, but her face was a mask. 'My children will need meat,' she said.

He was struggling frantically to move when lamplight broke into the darkness.

'We must go, Orc,' came Yaggit's voice. 'Are you well?' The question came shocked and urgent. Orc realised he was covered in sweat; he still couldn't move, his limbs held in place by the creepers that had grown out of the bed – how had Yaggit not seen?

'Look out!' he yelled, seeing a vast mass of vegetation quivering above Yaggit's head, about to drop.

Yaggit ducked and span to look upwards, and Orc saw there was no vegetation; it resolved into shadows and marks on the dark ceiling. With effort he moved his hands and feet.

'Sorry. Dreams.'

'The Shining Ones? Did you create the cone of protection?'

'I dropped off.' Orc swung his legs off the bed. Fearing what he would see, he examined his wrists, but found only those marks still healing from the college cellar. 'What's up?'

'Prelate Astrasis has sent his reply,' said Yaggit. 'A military officer waits downstairs. A train will come through in half an hour, and we must board it.'

The others were already gathered in the foyer, where the tired-looking clerk sat behind the desk in his nightgown. The Empyreal officer, with his peaked cap pulled low, and his polished boots, and his long black coat with silver gryphons on the epaulettes, declared himself to be Lieutenant Hartz. He looked displeased to have been given the mission, or by the midnight hour of its execution. But Orc felt something like relief at Hartz's uncompromising appearance. It made the subterranean threat recede a little.

Cass pulled him to one side. 'Once we're on that train, there's no turning back. Highcloud's too dangerous, even if we're allowed to reach it. I followed you once before when I didn't want to, and remember how that ended?'

Orc thought that was a cheap shot, but said nothing. Hartz spoke up, urging them to follow.

'Just me, then.' Cass let go of Orc's arm.

'Don't be stupid.' He wanted her to be bluffing, but she looked determined. 'Cass, it'll be all right.'

'I really don't think so.'

The Thangkarans had already left the hotel. Hartz was holding the front door open.

'I left something in my room,' Cass told the man, her voice trembling slightly. 'I'll catch you at the station, okay?'

She backed towards the stairs.

'No!' said Orc in panic. 'She's planning to run.'

'Miss,' said Hartz. 'Come, quickly.'

'I'm not a prisoner, am I?' she said. 'I can refuse if I want.'

'My instructions were to deliver all of you.'

'I don't care about your instruc—'

Hartz drew his pistol and fired into the wall a foot from the clerk. Cass yelped and ducked. Orc stood stunned. The surprised clerk fell behind his desk.

'My promotion might depend on it,' said Hartz. '*Quickly.*'

The station platform was almost empty. The first sound of the train came only moments after Hartz had frowned at his pocket-watch. It seemed instructions had been wired ahead; a whole sleeping car had been cleared for them, with four two-berth compartments. Orc found himself in the bunk above Tashi.

Hartz didn't sleep; the smell of his endless cigarettes, smoked in the corridor, wafted through the ventilation louvers in the compartment door. Orc didn't sleep any more than the Kurassian; he spent the night thinking, trying not to listen to Tashi's sounds of distress. He couldn't even tell if the boy were awake or asleep. They'd created a joint cone of protection before bed, but Orc didn't trust it to keep out the Mother. A cone was a shield from the air, from the ether; but it was open at the base, and it was from the earth that attack would come. He tried to believe the rails were strong enough, the train fast enough.

At dawn, Hartz knocked them all up to escort them to the dining car. An hour after breakfast, they changed trains at Aldersburg. By now,

Orc had concluded that Cass's threat to leave for Sundara on her own had been a rash bluff. But she barely looked at him, and kept enough distance to preclude talking.

On the Bismark express, Hartz's height, uniform and manner rapidly cleared space for them all – though as soon as they were seated, he went off to smoke by the carriage door with the window down. The background chatter and noise allowed them to talk without being overheard for the first time since the officer had collected them, and they used the chance to perfect the story they would tell Prelate Astrasis. Orc spent the rest of the journey staring tiredly out the window. The highlands that had been visible in the western distance from the previous train had by now flattened to hills and plains. Forests were mostly plantations, ordered rows of conifers whose shapes echoed the church-spires in the towns and villages they passed through. Fields were combed precisely with rows of stubble. The ordered nature of the land gave him a sense of safety, as though, in its points and hard lines, he already felt the influence of distant Highcloud and its mountain, the barrier of granite and ice that would at last defeat the Mother.

Nearing Bismark improved Hartz's mood. On occasional returns from his window, he talked about his family in the city, whom he planned to see for the first time in months. He asked if they'd visited Bismark before. The monk and his novitiate must have passed through, surely? What had they seen? What had impressed them most? Yaggit was polite but vague, Aino and Tashi silent.

'Your clothing,' Hartz said, eyeing Cass's blouse and culottes. 'Do you not own a dress?'

'I'm more comfortable travelling in these,' said Cass. 'Why?'

'Such things might pass without comment in the south. Here, you will be taken for a renunciate.'

'A what?'

Hartz shrugged uncomfortably and went off for another cigarette.

Yaggit leaned forward. 'As I understand it, renunciates have taken a vow to renounce their womanliness. They may not marry, nor consort with a man, nor bear children, nor wear womanly clothes.'

'Why the – why would they do that?'

'A great many more work positions are open to them. I know little else about them. But if you are taken for one, it should not affect us.'

'Oh, good,' said Cass.

The outskirts of Bismark went on for miles, its skyline thick with chimneys: tall columns of factories and power stations, innumerable smaller stacks of brown-brick housing. Their smoke bled white and grey and black into the smudged overcast; the air smelt foul with it. Nerves knotted Orc's stomach as they disembarked at the city's southern terminus, though his fear of pursuit had faded amid so many rigid lines and angles: the station's vast iron-latticed roof of soot-stained glass felt as much a fortress against nature as against rain. Through crowds of pigeons behaving like rats, and people behaving like pigeons, Hartz led them to a side-entrance in a noisy street, where waited two gleaming auto-carriages. There he handed them to four officers of the Prelatine Guard, polished breastplates bright against their tunics.

Orc and Cass rode with Tashi, as befitted the pretence of them being cousins. They passed mostly at a crawl through streets heavy with horse and motor traffic. At last the autos crunched to a halt on gravel before palatial steps, and a footman led them into a house of intimidating grandeur. Heels clicked on polished marble as they climbed a stair that swept past vast canvasses of battle, many depicting victories by Wilhelm Kirrus as a golden youth, the light breaking through clouds to strike his armour. A kind of Sun-King himself, Orc thought, but one whose sacrifice on the Tree of Death had been followed by glorious triumph. The blood-hungry goddess, whether she was called Witch or Mother, could surely have no power in this city.

The Prelate's secretary cast a disparaging eye over them before operating a telephone-like machine on his desk. He then nodded to the footman, who opened tall double doors and beckoned them through to the stateroom of the Prelate himself.

Orc had never imagined so great a wealth of décor and furnishings crowded into a single room. By comparison, the figure of Prelate Astrasis, in a dark frockcoat and cream cravat, seemed strangely modest, as though he intended the eye to be drawn away from him – or as though he knew he overpowered the surrounding splendour purely by virtue of his rank. Five carved chairs of gilded wood with velvet seats had been arranged in a semi-circle, facing a high-backed wing-chair behind which hung a large, gilt-framed mirror. Opposite the mirror, behind the arc of chairs, hung a full-length portrait of a woman of about thirty, oddly positioned with its foot barely above floor level.

The Prelate indicated the five chairs, and they sat. Astrasis leaned against a wing of the chair-back, one leg bent across the other, a studied pose of relaxation that seemed to both contradict and add to the tension in the room. He stared at Yaggit in a way Orc thought disrespectful, given that he was so much below the monk's age.

Silence passed. The Prelate said nothing. Orc forced his jigging knee still. Finally, Yaggit cleared his throat and made to speak, at which Astrasis pre-empted him.

'You're not the ones from before.'

'No, your Grace,' said Yaggit. 'I apologise if my message conveyed that impression.'

'Explain yourselves, then.'

'The two who left Highcloud with you…' Yaggit looked down at his knees. 'We came south in search of them, and found these three witnesses to the events on the island, which is where our two compatriots met their fate. We intend to take these witnesses to the monastery.'

The Prelate's gaze flicked from Orc to Cass to Tashi, finally settling back on Orc. 'Tell what you saw. And take great care to make it accurate.'

Orc tried to moisten his mouth, and haltingly began to relate the half-truth they'd rehearsed – he and his cousins had been working as divers on the Kymeran coast, and had been kidnapped by Seriuz and Daroguerre and taken to the Hollow Isles. There they'd been forced to recover artefacts for sorcerous purposes, before finally escaping with the family who lived there. He made sure he kept well clear of his and Cass's true part in the magic.

The Prelate's pale blue eyes studied him carefully. 'And how was this Daroguerre able to manifest the demoness?'

'We don't know how it worked,' said Orc. 'We only know he needed artefacts from the ziggurat.'

'Did he speak of the Zhenaii?'

'Not to us.' Orc forced his voice flat. 'When we weren't diving, he kept us under guard, away from everyone else.'

The Prelate turned to Yaggit. 'They know next to nothing. Yet you take them all the way to Highcloud?'

'They're all we have,' said Yaggit. 'And this is a matter of import.'

'That at least is the plain truth,' said the Prelate. 'Do you know what happened there, monk? To two of our warships? When we sent the others back to examine the island, a landing party found the corpse of the monster. You say the other novitiate met his fate there. He is dead? You saw him die?'

'He died,' said Yaggit.

'We found a sword near the abomination's corpse: the shorter kind your novitiates use. A *dughra*, isn't it called? I have it here.'

Orc caught Tashi's sharp in-breath.

'And not just that.' Astrasis walked to a decorated screen in one corner and folded it aside. Orc sensed Tashi stiffen: the boy sat up on his chair as though electrified.

A mannequin stood there, not a tailor's dummy but a full-sized replica of a person, and onto this had been fixed a complex outfit of black leather straps: the same as Aino had worn in his rescue attempt. Two swords leaned against it, two and four feet long.

'These were found in different places,' said Astrasis. 'The great-sword on a bluff overlooking where the demoness was destroyed, the armour some hundreds of yards from there. Was it this blade that destroyed her, wielded by that novitiate? But how? Gunfire and shellfire had done nothing. The demoness had power over metal and water – the few survivors of *Iron Tiger* said she somehow warped her way into the ship, tearing open its hull. Yet a blade destroyed her. How could it do what the might of a modern navy could not? *Our* navy, mark you! The science behind our weapons was granted us by Empyreus himself, to prepare us for the End Days. They are supposed to defeat the Witch – yet they couldn't even defeat her simulacrum!

'But this blade did, it seems.' He ran a finger along its edge. 'Is there a particular holiness to it? Is that how you explain it?'

'I don't seek to explain it,' said Yaggit.

'The goddess was not destroyed by anything holy.' Tashi spoke it like an accusation. 'Nor by either of those swords.'

Orc tensed: it had been agreed that Tashi would keep silent.

'What do you mean?' said Astrasis. 'By what, then?'

'Please, forgive him,' said Cass. 'His mind was affected.'

Tashi knifed her with a look, but didn't speak again.

'Daroguerre manifested the goddess only after he saw the dreadnought,' Cass went on. 'Perhaps he adjusted his magic to proof her against modern arms. But not against blades: he wasn't expecting anyone to fight her like that.'

'But which blades?' The Prelate's nostrils were slightly flared, as though he found it objectionable that Cass had spoken at all.

'It must have been one of those,' she said. 'We don't know; we weren't there when she was killed. I found the novitiate afterwards, badly wounded. We took his armour off but it was already too late. He didn't speak. He died and we buried him.'

'At last, some straight speaking – and from a girl!' The Prelate looked at Yaggit. 'Why didn't you tell me this?'

'I wasn't on the island, your Grace.'

'Where's the magician now? Sundara?'

'We think so,' Cass said.

'Could he be raising more of these abominations? What is Sundara's plan? Why a goddess? Have they made some alliance with the Witch? Are the End Days truly upon us?'

Those words, the intent look on the man's face, sent a prickle of dread down Orc's spine.

'We were their prisoners,' said Cass. 'They didn't tell us their plans.'

'A shame you didn't seek more assiduously to find them out. To think we had spies in the camp of our greatest enemy for centuries, and too incompetent to look for anything.'

Orc barely heard him, immersed in the realisation that even in their immense capital city, the Kurassians feared her. They knew she would come. What they didn't yet realise was that she was coming right now, that she was following him.

'Your Grace.' His throat felt dry. 'These "End Days"? What form will the Witch's power take?'

The Prelate looked surprised to be questioned. He hesitated, as though uncertain Orc deserved an answer, then said, 'That has been a matter of speculation for centuries.'

'Do you think it might come from the south, through the ground?'

'The ground?'

'Softening it. Making it marsh. Buildings sinking. Railways.' The words tightened bands round his chest.

'Some have predicted similar horrors,' said Astrasis, regarding him more carefully now. 'The consensus was that if we did nothing to guard against it, corruption would spread northwards from Golgomera, attacking the resolve and rationality of men, regressing the world to forest and ourselves to naked savages. But this magician's plot suggests the very distinction between thought and matter might break down, and nightmares be brought to physical life.'

'*Might*?' said Orc. 'We saw it happen. That's how she works, boundaries breaking, water and earth becoming mud.' The panicky conviction swelled in him. 'There isn't much time. She's coming *now*.'

Cass elbowed him. 'Orc…'

'No, let's hear what he has to say.' The Prelate strode to his desk and opened a drawer.

Orc stood from his chair – Cass tugged at his arm, but he pulled free, compelled to look into the mirror. Years of self-deception fell away; he saw the truth that should have always been clear to him. His face was nothing but a mask of skin. All efforts to escape her with words and names were futile, no less than by running. The gilded leaves of the mirror frame looked like they might spring to green, growing, deadly life.

'You've covered everything in gold,' he said, suddenly understanding. 'You think it'll save you, but it *marks* you. Don't you get it? You've made yourselves the Sun-King, and the Sun-King is her rightful sacrifice!'

'By God.' The Prelate took a pistol from the desk drawer. Cries and protests erupted. Cass yanked Orc down into his chair-seat, then jumped to her feet and stood in front of him, facing the Prelate.

'He didn't mean anything. What happened at the island—'

'Sit down!' barked the Prelate, as he stepped round the desk. 'It's a precaution. If he's still himself, he has nothing to fear.'

Cass stood where she was. She and Astrasis exchanged words, and Yaggit joined in, but Orc barely heard. The Prelate thought his gun so potent, but it could do nothing against the Empyreum's vast enemy. None of their weapons would: puny machines of fire against an entire world of earth and water. It was insane to entrust their defence to such devices.

A hush had fallen: the Prelate had threatened Cass back into her seat and silenced Yaggit's protests. Now he stood with his back to his desk, the gun within reach beside the telephone. His gaze held Orc's.

'Tell me,' he said. 'What is your name? Who are you?'

He almost panicked, almost laughed. But a steel needle in his mind told him he must not laugh. These people clung to surfaces, to the world as thin and bright as the gilding on the mirror frame. The truth had put him in danger. His life depended on swimming back up to that surface world himself, against the suck of the eternal deep.

'Orc Strandborn.' Meaningless syllables: the name of a mask.

'And where are you from? Who are your parents?'

'Does that matter?' said the girl who thought her name was Cass.

'Don't interrupt!'

Sweat tracked his temple. He couldn't give the man an answer. He'd been born at the margin of land and water, a no-place. He had no parents, no papers. He knew he had to pretend, but the idea of pretence affronted him; it seemed feeble and flimsy next to the terrifying, irrefutable power of the Mother's coming.

The impulse swelled in him to refuse the man, to stand up and proclaim the truth, even if it cost him his life. But the girl gripped his hand, and at the damp shock of her touch, understanding broke through the silt-fog and he suddenly knew he must pretend, because it would keep her from fear, from hurt – and that mattered more than anything.

He squeezed back hard against her knuckles, the strength of her belief in who he was. He had to make her belief his own again. But her belief wasn't what he must tell. With effort, he brought the rehearsed construction into focus. He spoke it out into the world of words: he related that he was the son of Kurassian immigrants to the Kymeran coast, his father an inventor of diving equipment. In response to the man's further questions, he gave the name of a school and those of his favourite teachers; he identified Cass and Tashi as children of his father's sisters. All lies, a fabrication even in the world of surfaces – but the effort of trying to believe himself into the story brought that world out of eclipse again: shiny, detailed, defined as though by a bright sun.

'Thank God.' The Prelate put his pistol back in its drawer, while Orc sagged, drained and still fighting to firm up his fragile self. 'For a moment, it seemed he might have the Bane.'

'And you'd have shot him?' said Cass unsteadily.

'You know little of the Bane if you would question that necessity,' said the Prelate. 'Its victims are the Witch's prophets and her warriors. But I accept your own diagnosis: he has been affected by the shock of what happened at the island. So were some of the ships' survivors, in different ways. You, young lady, no doubt survived unharmed because you were not confronted with the horror of your opposite.'

He resumed his place by the high-backed chair. 'He'll have a chance to rest over the next couple of days. A secret committee of enquiry into the Hollow Isles has been convened. You'll be called to give evidence. Until then, say nothing of any of this, and nothing of what you witnessed. The loss of *Iron Tiger* is still not public.'

'Your Grace,' said Yaggit, clearly struggling to speak normally. 'We are on our way to Highcloud.'

'Quite impossible at present.'

A cry caught in Orc's throat. Just now, in this palace, she had almost caught him. They couldn't afford to linger.

'But your Grace,' said Yaggit, 'you said yourself we've told you nothing new.'

'The Valkensee has more thorough inquisitors than I,' said the Prelate. 'Don't forget these three lack papers, and the restrictions on the Thangkaran border have also been tightened. Besides, staying might prove to your advantage. If you serve the enquiry well, I can send you onwards by air-craft.'

'A most generous offer,' said Yaggit, covering Tashi's hiss. Orc barely heard them – an unexpected hope blazed in him.

'An *air*-craft? You mean, to *fly*?'

The Prelate looked amused. 'You haven't told him of it?' he asked Yaggit. 'You saw it, I assume?'

'When can we use it?' said Orc. 'How soon?'

'A fellow aviation enthusiast in the making, clearly,' said Astrasis. 'The enquiry will begin in three days. I expect it to last the same.'

'Can't we go now and be back for it?'

The Prelate frowned. 'Is he a simpleton? Did the events of the island cripple his basic intelligence?'

'We're not sure,' said Cass.

'In the meantime,' said Astrasis, 'I'll have rooms prepared for you here.'

'Please don't trouble yourself,' said Yaggit. 'We have already arranged accommodation.'

We have? Orc wondered if he meant the man at the Black Hart.

The Prelate frowned, clearly puzzled. 'Were you not on your way to Highcloud?'

'We intended to stop a night anyway,' said Yaggit. 'I believe our host will be happy to extend our stay.'

'Very well,' said the Prelate. 'Give my secretary the address.'

He opened the doors for them. Orc noticed Tashi's stare at the mannequin as they left. He still felt shaky with everything that had happened, but as he followed Cass out into the secretary's office, he was diverted from his thoughts by a woman in her mid-twenties, elegantly but plainly dressed, seated slightly hunched over as though not wanting to be noticed. She noticed them, though. Her eyes widened as she saw Yaggit, but then she looked away, as though troubled.

'Siegfried,' she said as the Prelate followed them out.

He exhaled. 'I've told you—'

'Are these—'

'They're none of your concern.'

'But are they—'

'Don't make a fuss,' he snapped, 'and I'll attend to you when they've gone.'

He told his secretary to take the address of where they were staying. Orc sensed the woman's attention on everything that was said, though she ostensibly studied her hands on her knees. Once Yaggit had given the name Anders Crome and his address in Park Crescent, a footman led them out to the vehicles. Tashi asked to ride with the other Thangkarans, but Yaggit sent him with Orc and Cass again. As their auto pulled out of the drive, Cass said, 'You okay, Orc?' She spoke softly, even though a glass partition screened them from the driver.

'I don't know,' he replied. 'I think she's still waiting, underneath.'

'She doesn't exist,' said Cass firmly. 'She's just magical thinking: you must realise that.'

'She existed in that cellar.'

'Because Hana brought her there, and us being there let her manifest. Orc, the danger is *you*. Your belief, your ability. Whatever pulled you back from the edge in there, for fuck's sake hang on to it.'

He took hold of her hand. 'I am doing. It was you.'

She squeezed back. 'You were right, before. It'll be okay if we stick together.'

'You wouldn't really have gone to Sundara by yourself?'

She looked past Tashi, out of the window. 'I'm glad I didn't.'

He tightened his grip on her hand. *Her warriors and prophets*, the Prelate had said. He had a terrible premonition of himself gone mad in a city square, shouting a declaration as thorned creepers burst out of the ground all about him.

Not just her prophet, but her instrument.

'We need to get that air-craft,' he said. 'I need to get off the ground. That'll break me away from her, I'm sure of it. It can take us to Highcloud in safety.'

Cass didn't respond to that, only sucked her teeth for a moment, staring out. 'I can't help feeling I should know this place.'

Orc turned. The car was passing beneath a big marble arch that didn't seem joined to anything. They entered a wide street lined with official-looking buildings, their doors with columned porticos.

'You think we came from here? From Bismark?'

'Geist said we could easily be Kurassian, except for our accent.'

'You recognise this street?'

'Not as such. But something about the whole city feels a bit familiar. Not to you?'

'Nuh-uh.'

'That's interesting,' Cass said. 'If I was from here, and you weren't, that would mean we had different childhoods.'

Orc understood the implications of that. But he knew, too, how real the wrongness had felt when they'd been in bed together, how titanic that force of judgement and punishment – how much like a death sentence he'd felt the sight of his face scribbled out.

'Why does that man have my swords and bindings?' said Tashi.

'No idea,' said Cass, and Orc felt her fingers stiffen. 'Perhaps he thought there was some secret to defeating the Witch in it.'

'He has no right,' said Tashi.

'Why would you want them back?' she said. 'You gave them up.'

He groaned. 'What have I not given up, or had taken from me?'

'You're still alive, aren't you?'

Orc winced at the bite in Cass's tone, but said nothing. Tashi didn't reply. The auto sped on, towards the house of Anders Crome.

14

THE HEAD INCORRUPTIBLE

A short flight of steps led to an imposing front door with a lion's head knocker, but otherwise the front of the town-house looked dishevelled. The basement pit area made the place seem deserted, untidy with drifted litter and with its windows boarded up; the gate in the railings leading to the steps down was chained shut. Orc wondered if Yaggit had the right address, and what they would do if he hadn't. But the grey-whiskered manservant who answered Yaggit's knock declared his master to be expecting them.

They left their luggage in a hall hung with a jumble of paintings and animal heads, and followed the man up a flight of stairs and through into a drawing room overlooking the street. Here Crome stood beside a chair, his jacket again draped over his injured arm. The room's dark oak panelling made him look even younger and more willowy than at the Black Hart. Paler too, Orc thought. Apart from a touch of sunburn, and his red-gold hair and moustache, his face seemed almost colourless.

He welcomed them with enthusiasm, and sent the manservant for tea. When they were seated, he commenced a round of pleasantries – of course they must stay, it was an honour to have a Watcher of Highcloud as a guest, and so on. These irritated Orc as much as the dust from the couch that got up his nose: he wanted to gather the others to discuss their next move. But even when tea was over, they weren't freed. Crome insisted on giving a tour, most of which he spent relating the provenance of the various trinkets and preserved arachnids on display, linking them to his or his late father's travels. He seemed not at all embarrassed at having to wipe dust off some of the glass cases.

'I don't bother with staff, mostly,' he explained, back in the drawing room. 'You might have noticed the basement's all shut up: I've had part of the dining room walled off as a new kitchen, much simpler. Wetherall's an old family retainer; otherwise I use an agency when I need to – as I shall now, following your arrival. Have you eaten?'

'Not since breakfast on the train,' said Yaggit.

'Likewise,' said Crome. 'I'll get Wetherall to run out shortly and fetch something cold.'

'Your train must've been a lot quicker than ours,' said Orc. 'We only got here a couple of hours ago, and we set off at midnight.'

'I didn't wait for morning, in the end,' said Crome, with a strained-looking smile. 'I found myself unable to sleep, and caught an earlier service. Now, if you'll excuse me.'

Wetherall showed them to their rooms. Yaggit had the main guest bedroom, on the second floor at the back of the house, and suggested they meet there as soon as they'd washed. Orc barely splashed water over his face before going back, and the others arrived soon after. They fetched extra chairs from the adjoining dressing-room. Aino stood by the door as though on guard.

'Right,' said Orc, when everyone was settled and before Yaggit could direct any discussion. 'We need to focus on this flying machine.'

'No, I think you can discount that,' said Yaggit, perching on the edge of his armchair as though it were a throne to which he wasn't entitled. 'I doubt the Prelate intends to honour his offer. He made it purely to persuade us to stay, and I accepted it to make him believe we shall.'

'We should have nothing to do with it in any case,' said Tashi, from the window. 'The device is evil.'

'Evil why?' said Orc. But Tashi didn't answer, as though it were self-evident.

'We must concentrate our efforts elsewhere,' said Yaggit. 'I take it we all agree that we cannot risk this enquiry? Especially not with Orc in… his condition.'

'I'm fine now,' said Orc, trying to ignore the tingling of his scratches. 'But yeah, I agree.'

'And if the Thangkaran border's closed to us?' said Cass.

'That border is mostly a matter of cartography,' said Yaggit. 'The difficulty is that our leaving will be noticed long before we reach it. Perhaps I should sound out our host. If he admires Highcloud as he claims, we might persuade him to help.'

'Help how?' said Orc. 'What we need is that air-craft, whether Aristo-twat means to let us use it or not.'

Yaggit's gaze flicked between disapproval and confusion. 'You suggest we steal it?'

'Or bribe the pilot. He said you saw it. Can it really carry us all?'

'Yes, we saw the craft,' said Yaggit. 'Astrasis visited Highcloud in it.'

'And Tashi left the same way,' said Aino.

Orc turned to Tashi. 'You've flown in it?'

'I was made to sleep.'

'But do you know how it works? Could one of us fly it?'

'I saw none of its workings,' said Tashi.

'There are large rotating blades on the wings,' said Yaggit. 'Like a ship's screws, but each blade much longer and thinner. They clearly provide propulsion, but what generates the lift, I have no idea. The craft took to the air straight off the ground, and landed the same way. It could not be hydrogen gas, not with such a weight.'

'My master was once an engineer,' explained Aino, with obvious pride.

'I surmised there must be some new principle at work,' said Yaggit.

'If there is,' said Tashi, 'it's the same as that ship.'

'Ship?' said Yaggit.

Tashi looked at Orc. 'The one that took you to the island.'

'Doubt it,' said Orc.

'Given the unknowns,' said Yaggit, 'I think it's—'

'Wait,' broke in Cass. 'Tashi, why did you say that? About the ship?'

He shifted in his chair. 'On *Archon*, Captain Lansdahl talked to us about your ship's secret means of propulsion. He told us *that man* had halted efforts to discover the explanation. He believed this was because *that man* already knew. That would make sense if it was the same as the air-craft.'

'The same?' said Orc. 'But—'

'But *Nightfire*'s secret was magic,' said Cass.

'What?' croaked Yaggit.

'A fire elemental. There was a "psychic engineer" in the crew – she used a crystal to summon it into the firebox of one of the boilers. It increased the steam intensity, or something.'

'An elemental?' said Yaggit. 'And it was manifested? By you two?'

'Not directly,' said Cass. 'It got stronger in our presence, but it was mostly Thera's crystal, I think. And that was different from Orc's focus-stone; it was tied to the elemental. Maybe Orc and me aren't the only catalysts for manifestation, just the strongest.'

'Astonishing,' said Yaggit. 'Even so, the Prelate cannot have any connection with it – our charter to hunt out magicians comes from the Empyreum. This Captain Lansdahl made an error.'

'No,' said Tashi, frowning. 'He was right.'

Yaggit faced him. 'Don't let your feelings about the Prelate skew your judgement.'

'Don't you remember?' Tashi sat forwards. 'My master's dark-flight? The Cry of Sin comes from manifestation. And he traced the Cry of Sin through a resonance with the arriving air-craft.'

Yaggit's eyes widened. 'Oh, Gevurah…'

'Are there air elementals too?' said Orc. 'Could one of them provide the lift you were talking about?'

Yaggit put a hand to his forehead. 'Does this explain the Prelate's interest in what Shoggu and Tashi discovered about Zhenaii magic?'

'He said it was to better understand the danger,' said Tashi.

'But you think it might have been to learn for himself?' Cass asked Yaggit.

'Could he have been in league with Daroguerre?' said Orc.

'No,' said Tashi, 'or he wouldn't have let my master and me pass through Bismark. His evil is his own.'

Orc let out breath between his teeth. 'If he's interested in manifestation, for whatever reason, he mustn't know about me and Cass.'

'Very true,' said Yaggit. 'And it's likely not him alone we must beware of. He couldn't have created these air-craft without involving a great many people. You mentioned a crystal that allowed the elemental to manifest – do you know where that came from?'

Cass shook her head.

'*That man* told my master where the power of the air-craft came from,' said Tashi. 'A gift of Empyreus.'

Yaggit groaned. 'Please let there be some error in this.'

'Why, master?' said Aino, excited. 'Doesn't it prove what we've always held? It's the worship of Empyreus that's the error. We must tell the Abbot! This is the evidence we sought!'

'It's not evidence,' said Yaggit. 'It is conjecture.'

'Wait, though,' said Cass. 'Empyreus is a religious figurehead. So why is it such a big deal if the Prelate told Shoggu the air-craft was a gift from him? Isn't that what any religious leader's bound to say? How could it be literally true? I assume there's no proof Empyreus is anything more than a relic?'

Yaggit sagged back in his chair. 'Thank you, Cass. I fear the torrent of speculation has agitated my mind almost to the point of hysteria. Indeed, I know of no good evidence that Empyreus has any objective reality beyond the head itself, nor any power.' He looked from Cass to Orc. 'But I forgot, you two have effectively spent your whole lives in Kymera. How much do you know of the story?'

'Only the basics, I suppose,' said Cass. 'He used to be a man called Wilhelm Kirrus, a war leader back in the Age of Princes. He unified all the small kingdoms and duchies into what's now Kurassia. His battle victories were uncanny. People said he was the son of God.'

'That claim was not made at the time,' said Yaggit, 'or only by very few: a fact the Empyreum hides from its own citizens, though not from Highcloud – our libraries pre-date Kirrus himself. Nevertheless, it's true that he became a religious leader, deluded or otherwise, before he sailed to Golgomera. You know that part?'

'There's a shrine in Torrento,' said Cass. 'Where he took ship. He went to destroy the Witch, but her Murmedons caught him and hanged him from the Tree of Death, and when he didn't die they pinned him to it with a spear, and when he still didn't die they cut off his head.'

'Correct.'

'But it never rotted, and a few hundred years ago, someone brought it back to Bismark. I can't remember who.'

'Some boy, wasn't it?' said Orc, remembering from when Geist had told the story.

'Indeed,' said Yaggit. 'The tale goes that the Murmedons were so in awe of the incorruptible head, they placed it in a deep cave. Centuries later, a youth was drawn to dare the traps and snares that guarded it, and to touch it – and so doing, he acquired the gift the Golgomerans shun, the gift of Self, and heard Kirrus's voice instructing him to take the head back home across the sea. The knowledge Kirrus then revealed through the boy set the Kurassian empire on its path to scientific supremacy. Kirrus was pronounced Empyreus, Son of God, and his mother Arris Entarna recast as a virgin who conceived him on the Holy Mountain itself. The head was set in a gold cabinet in the Hall of Wisdom, where it yet rests, supposedly guiding the empire.'

'It doesn't really *talk*, though?' said Cass.

'The Empyreans claim the head communicates to three special youths, the Trine, through a process called "verbal dreaming". Their utterances are then examined by the Valkensee, who seek to clarify them to divine Empyreus's intention. That much we know at Highcloud, but little more: we have never successfully probed the truth of Empyreus through flight. We think it most likely that he is, as you say, a figurehead, perhaps a tool to maintain control. Certainly Gevurah has never given us reason to credit the existence of any "son".'

'But something must give the Empyreum its edge,' said Orc. 'The Sundaran warships we saw were junk by comparison.'

'It might be that something in the Kurassian mind is apt to engineering and chemistry,' said Yaggit. 'It's possible the Trine are genuinely gifted at some kind of divination, and synthesise new scientific theories from the mass of half-formed ideas a-swirl in the Immaterium. That's the theory I subscribe to, but the fact is, we don't know – just as we don't know anything for sure about the Prelate's aircraft and its connection with your ship.'

'Save my master's dark-flight,' said Tashi.

'That is not proof,' said Yaggit. 'It should, however, be investigated. Another reason we must return to Highcloud as soon as possible.' He pushed himself from his chair. 'I've decided – I shall find our host and sound him out.'

'Be careful,' said Orc.

'Naturally, I'll tell him nothing of our planned escape until I'm confident of his support,' said Yaggit. 'That might take some time.'

Orc found no sign of lunch in the dining room, so he went to his bedroom to try to catch up on sleep. But though the marks on his skin were no worse, his scratches burned and made him restless. More than ever, it grieved him that he couldn't scape and talk to Otter about the situation. It still felt impossible that he might never be able to again. Even invoking his animath, which wouldn't involve a scape, might not be safe now. He'd escaped physical changes on the road to the college, but he'd noted Hana's ageing after restoring Tashi, and couldn't be sure what might happen if he tried invocation again. Much as he loved Otter, he didn't want to grow fur.

After half an hour of failing to rest, he went downstairs again. Passing the first-floor games room, he heard a loud clack, and looked in to see Cass walking round the half-sized billiards table, cue in hand.

'How're you feeling now?' she said.

'Okay. Still myself, if that's what you mean.'

She looked him over, as if checking. 'Game?'

'You know how to play?'

'I've an idea from somewhere there should be a lot more than three balls, but I can't find any others. We'll make the rules up. We each get a white ball, and try to get the red ball into one of the pocket things – that'll do for now.'

They played for a while, revising and expanding the rules as they went on: extra points for hitting the red into the opposing cue-ball, even more points if another then went in. Cass adopted a style of play that seemed to Orc almost ferocious in its determination.

'You're right about that flying machine,' she said, after claiming the first points of their third game. 'That's our way out of here.'

Orc adjusted the scoreboard, pleased that she agreed. 'You think it really might be powered by an air elemental?'

'It makes sense. And if it is, then they'd need engineers, like Thera. Ah, crap: your shot. But now we understand what we can do, maybe we could manifest the elemental ourselves.'

'And control it?'

'It would take practice, but why not?'

Orc leaned over his cue. 'We've only got three days before the enquiry starts.' He struck. 'All right!'

'Fluke.' Cass reset the red. 'We might be making too much of this enquiry, though. We just need to nail our stories.'

Orc miscued, and looked at her.

'Penalty,' she said. 'Five points?'

'Making too much of it? You know what happened to me!'

'Do I?' she said. 'Do you?'

He rolled his eyes. 'No, I wasn't paying attention.' But when he thought back to it, it was all a muddle, like his memories of Daroguerre's trap on the island.

'I think you lost sight of who you are,' said Cass. 'The magical reality and the real reality overlapped, and you couldn't tell the difference, right?'

'Something like, I guess.' He felt exposed, as though she was about to detail all his flaws.

'I've been thinking,' she said. 'Our reality is based on what we know about ourselves.'

'I thought you said it was our strongest experiences?'

'It's both,' she snapped. 'If we're not sure of who we are, our whole reality becomes less definite, like it did for you in there.'

'But not for you,' said Orc, wondering where this was going.

Cass took her next shot, and watched the red sink. 'Part of my idea of who I am is that I belong wholly in this world, the physical world. You don't even have that, do you? I was talking to Stefanie at the college. She told me a theory that people in ancient times didn't know the difference between the real world and the world of magic – and that's the same with young children. That ancient time was like the childhood of humankind, and that's when the Mother comes from – and *any* mother has a hold over her kids when they don't know enough to separate from her. That's the state you've gone back to.'

Orc frowned uneasily. 'Right…'

Cass replaced the red and circled the table, studying the layout. 'We need to root you back in this world, make you feel you belong here. We need to find something out about you. And this might be the place to do it – if we did come from here, or I did, I might recognise something. I've got through the Shroud before. Maybe I can again. The stronger your sense of self becomes, the safer you'll be from the Mother. That's a better idea than handing yourself to a bunch of religious fanatics.'

'You think it's that easy?'

'I didn't say "easy".' The red clacked into Orc's white. 'But we need something to fight against that Sun-King nonsense. Obviously everything you've done and said and been over the last two years isn't enough.'

'I used to know who I was,' he said. 'At least, I knew what I meant.'

Cass laid herself over her cue, aiming on a long shot. 'I can't be your identity.'

'No, but… us.' He observed the movement of her arm, her aligned focus as she stroked the wood between the thumb and finger of her spread hand. A tingle of desire and fear spread through him at the concentration in her gaze, the taut energy of her body. He wanted to reach under and touch her belly; he sensed that might snap something, like triggering a spring.

'Don't be so wet.' She struck the cue-ball so hard Orc thought it might shatter. Balls smacked, cannoned, sped. 'We can't have a joint identity,' she said, watching the results. 'It was never healthy, and now it's fucked. Somewhere in this city is a secret. If I can find it, we can build up your sense of who you are. You are not the Sun-King. You are an excellent freediver and a shit billiards player. That's something to be going on with. Oscar.'

'I'm not sure that is my real name.'

She huffed. 'Then why did it pop into my head at the Great Ziggurat? Of course you don't recognise it – I'm the one who broke through the Shroud. The transcripts even said I have more potential than you.' She struck again, bang, more points. 'And that's what I'm going to call you from now on: Oscar. Now you repeat it.'

'Oscar,' tried Orc. There was something about it, but— 'No, this isn't going to work. If I'm not even sure which name to use, it's going to make it even worse.'

'Fuck's sake.' She abandoned her next stroke. 'Then *be* sure. We are what we choose. If you lie there like a wet cabbage and let people pull you this way and that, how can you be anyone?'

'I guess.'

'So tell me what you're sure of.'

'Uhm—'

'*Tell* me.'

'I don't *know*.'

'You're not even trying.' Her knuckles whitened on her cue. 'You're giving yourself to her! Tell me what you're sure of!'

'Nothing!' he cried. 'That's the point. That's what I am now.'

Cass turned half away. Her neck tightened, her arms; Orc thought she might smash the cue over something, and that took his breath and raced his heart – he almost wanted her to break it over him.

He stepped towards her. Then Yaggit called their names, and Cass turned to him with a look of exasperation and led the way out.

The others were already gathered in the library on the ground floor, Crome standing by the fireplace in a dove-grey suit. 'Yaggit has apprised me of your difficulty,' he said, when Orc and Cass were seated. 'You need to reach Highcloud urgently, but Kurassian bureaucracy has you in its claws. Happily, friends of my late father hold positions in the Interior Ministry, and might be able to help. And I hope to be able to influence the border guards directly – since, as I've already told this most excellent monk, I'll be coming with you.'

Questioning murmurs came from Tashi and Aino. Yaggit looked amused at the surprise.

'For which, again, my thanks,' he said.

'Not at all,' said Crome. 'I've too long delayed visiting Highcloud. Now, it might take a day or two to get things organised, so enjoy the run of the house in the meantime – apart from the basement level, which is being converted and is dangerous. There should be no need for any of you to venture outside, but if you do, please take care. The city might not be as safe as its electric lighting makes it seem.'

Orc remembered him expressing similar concerns for their safety at the Black Hart. Judging from Yaggit's puzzled frown, the monk did too.

'If we're going to Thangkara,' said Cass, 'we'll need warmer clothes.'

'Excellent point,' said Crome. 'When I have time, we'll visit Stein's, the new department store. They can tailor to fit in a day.'

Great, thought Orc. *Shopping*. But unavoidable, he supposed.

'We could go by ourselves?' said Cass. 'We're not children.' She looked at Orc. 'Yes?'

He liked that a lot better. 'Sure!'

'Be my guest,' said Crome.

'We'll need money,' Cass said.

Crome smiled wryly. He took a seat behind his desk and began to write a list. 'You have a dress, at least? To wear into town?'

'I'm more comfortable in these.'

'You'll be taken for a renunciate.'

'So I've been told. It doesn't bother me.'

'Then *I* should appreciate your wearing one,' said Crome. 'Now, these are the shops at which I have accounts, and my authority for you to use them. Stein's has a ladies' department.' He signed the paper with a flourish, then took out a cash-box and removed some coins and a few banknotes. 'To cover the cost of cabs and other sundries.'

'This is very generous,' said Yaggit.

'Think nothing of it. Will you accompany them?'

'Aino and myself already have enough suitable clothing.'

'And you?' Crome asked Tashi.

Orc tensed: he'd forgotten Tashi was supposed to be their cousin.

'He doesn't like shopping,' said Cass. 'Do you, Tashi?'

'I'll stay with the Thangkarans,' he said. 'I have no fear of the cold.'

'Very well.' Crome handed Orc the paper and money. 'Now, I believe Wetherall has laid out a cold luncheon in the dining room. Sunset is at six, so you two should still have time for your outing. If you walk along to Gelder Street, you'll easily find a cab.'

'Is sunset when the shops close, then?' said Cass, sounding puzzled. Orc also thought it a strange arrangement.

'Most of the larger ones remain open until eight.' Crome gave Cass a strange look. '*You* must be back by six, of course.'

'For dinner?'

'Miss Strandborn, do you make a practice of visiting other countries without first acquainting yourself with their laws – laws whose breach might land you in prison? No woman without an appropriate male escort may be abroad after sunset – or seven o'clock, if that is sooner – unless she is engaged in certain professions, nursing and so on.'

'Why?' said Cass. 'More nonsense about keeping safe?'

'The law was mostly codified in the interests of public decency.'

She exhaled. 'Okay, well, I have a male escort.'

'An *appropriate* male escort,' said Crome, 'is a husband or fiancé, or someone so closely related that marriage would not be permissible: a father, uncle, brother and so on. While we're at it, the same rule applies to the wearing of clothing that bares the shoulders or the clavicles.'

'I can say I'm her brother,' said Orc.

'But you're not. And marriage between cousins *is* permitted, if rare.'

'We don't have any papers to say we're not siblings. And we look alike enough.'

'Well, I've told you the law,' said Crome. 'You might like to consider whose standing will suffer should you be caught breaking it.'

Their first stop in the city centre was a glittering glass-fronted café in Queensgate, where they countered their sleep deficit with strong coffee and piled iced pastries on top of the salt-beef they'd had for lunch.

'Isn't this great?' said Cass. 'When was the last time we went shopping – proper shopping?'

'And with someone else's money,' said Orc. 'You don't think it was a loan?'

'Let's spend it all,' she said. 'He annoys me. If he acts like he's fifty now, when do you think he acted young? His first words were probably to tell his mum to put her tits away.'

'Cass!'

'Oh, no one heard, lighten up. Aren't you excited? I'm sure I'll recognise something, a street or a shop, and that will start us finding out who we are.' Cass leaned back in her chair and sighed. 'It's going to be fun. When was the last time we had any fun?'

'What's this, the "last time" quiz?'

She flashed a grin. 'It's good to get away from them all, isn't it? Yaggit's not a bad sort, but… well, you know who…'

Orc frowned. 'Tashi's had a hard time.'

'He doesn't have to look at himself.'

Orc wondered what she meant by that.

'Anyway,' she went on, 'life hasn't been a bed of roses for the rest of us. Unless they left the thorns on.'

'Bazantin, probably,' said Orc.

'What?'

'Fun. Those few minutes after we jumped off the boat.'

'Yeah. I miss the diving.'

'Apart from the nearly drowning part.' He tensed at once, realising how she might interpret that. 'When you rescued me, I mean.'

She looked out to the bustling street. 'I feel a bit like that recently,' she said. 'Like we're both down deep in a really dark sea, and I'm trying to grab hold of you and pull you to the surface. But I can't even see which way is up, and my lungs hurt and I don't know if I'm going to be able to. And... you struggle, like you don't want to be saved.'

'I said I'm fine. You pulled me back, in the Prelate's room.'

She drained her cup and set it loudly on the marble tabletop. 'Forget it. There's clothes waiting to be put on account.'

Outside, sunlight broke through the overcast sky and smoke to glint off glass and granite and wrought ironwork; the air throbbed with traffic noise and the smells of horse-dung and exhaust. Caffeine, money, being abroad on foot in a new city, all electrified away Orc's tiredness to the point where he felt almost drunk. He wanted to grab Cass and kiss her; he wanted to knock someone's hat off for a laugh.

The first shop on Crome's list was comically snobbish, and their whispered comments to each other made them giggle and snort until they fled. At the second, the manager disbelieved Crome's warrant. At the third, Orc tried on about five suits of winter-weight tweed until Cass pronounced herself satisfied with the fit and style and colour of one of them. They told the assistant where to send it, and asked directions to Stein's.

As they walked along Great Mark's Street, Orc noticed that Cass didn't swing her arms as much as before, and looked around less energetically. Orc's own buzz, too, now fought a resurgent tiredness. In the worn leather jacket he'd been loaned by the college, he felt uncomfortably out of place amongst the men in their silk hats and frockcoats, and he hated the sidelong glances people gave Cass's simple summer dress, with her shawl hiding her shoulders. She didn't seem to notice those looks herself, focused as she was on the street-names and buildings and window displays, seeking a needle of recognition sharp enough to pierce the Shroud. She declared herself impressed by Stein's, where electric lifts took them to the ladies' wear department on the fifth floor. But Orc felt her strain, and fears for her fraying strength made him worry about his own.

'Cass, what is it?' he said after they came out of the lift.

'Nothing.' But her eyes glistened as she turned away. 'We used to do this,' she said quietly. 'I know there are memories of doing this with you. I can almost reach them. I can feel how similar it was then. And how different.'

The ladies' wear department was quiet, but nothing else about it was pleasant. Orc discovered it was him, as the male, who was expected to make decisions – to Cass's irritation – but the assistants also seemed to find his presence strange, as though suspecting he'd come in search of some kind of perverted thrill. After an annoying half-hour, he and Cass left without buying anything, and went back down and out.

The darkening street was damp from a recent shower, busier than before. People jostled along the pavement like a crush of well-dressed cattle; the cabs and autos and drays and buses crawled so slowly that a constant stream of pedestrians crossed between them. It was the closest to real chaos Orc had seen in Bismark, and the sights and smells and noise shifted something in his tired mind – the perception attacked him that only a flimsy barrier of order prevented all these people and horses and vehicles from being crushed together into some mass of flesh and hair and wood and iron, like a wild and overgrown garden of nightmare. And to his sick near-panic, he couldn't remember what it was that prevented this happening. Something so flimsy it might be no more than thought.

'You all right?' said Cass.

'Uh, yeah.' He rubbed his face. The perception had retreated, but he sensed it hovering at the back of his mind. 'What now?'

'You okay with staying out?' said Cass. 'I don't know if there is any danger, if the police pick us up and take us back. Yaggit's incapable of lying, remember.'

'Why would the police even suspect us?' said Orc.

'Because we don't fucking fit in, do we?' said Cass, not seeming to care whether she was overheard. 'If I did ever live here, then something's changed.' She looked up at the tops of the buildings against the darkening sky. 'Is it Empyreus? Is it knowing all these people think there's a living head telling them what to do, what machines to make?'

'Shh,' said Orc. 'It's just a religion. Anyway, he's been around for hundreds of years. Whatever's changed, it can't be him.'

'You're right.' Her gaze dropped to the pavement. 'Sorry.'

'Sorry?' She'd sounded so miserable. 'Why?'

'Because I feel like everything depends on me keeping my mind sharp, but I'm just... look, let's get a cab somewhere else, for a drink or something. Not back to Crome's. I don't want to be defeated by some stupid law that's meant to make me feel like a tart just because I'm not with a man who already owns me.'

Orc hailed a two-wheeler and they got in the front and closed the splash-guard over their knees. 'Where to?' called the cabbie through the open back window.

Not for a drink, Orc thought: not when that disturbing perception-shift might return. Then an idea sparked. 'Hey – d'you know where the air-craft are kept?'

'Lions Hill, sir.'

'Can we go and see them?'

'People do,' said the cabbie. 'Visitors, are you? Quite a marvel, they are. First few times.'

'Good plan, Oscar,' whispered Cass, and leaned against him.

It took ages to escape the traffic, and full dark had descended by the time they reached the plateau on the northern edge of the city's central district. Orc was dismayed to see the high, spiked fence alongside the road. Behind it lay a paved expanse, much of it flooded with electric light; on its far side squatted three identical machines that matched

Yaggit's description. Their hulls indeed looked large enough to carry their whole party. Functional buildings squatted nearby, windows lit.

The driver reined in at the side of the road, not far from a gate and guard-post. A few other people stood by the fence, staring at the aircraft as if waiting for something to happen.

'They don't send them up often,' said the cabbie. 'Only seen it once, myself.'

'What makes them work?' said Orc.

'My lad reckons electricity. But they don't say. In case of spies, I suppose. Where'd you say you were from again?'

Orc recalled the railway junction where they'd changed. 'Aldersburg.'

'Well, if you want to know what makes it fly, there's the man to ask,' said the cabbie.

About a hundred yards away, someone stood smoking outside the compound's nearest building. The chest of his long blue coat was mostly covered with a gleaming breastplate that looked more ceremonial than defensive.

'Pilot officer,' said the cabbie. 'One of only six, so I've heard.'

'*Can* we go and ask him about what powers it?' said Cass.

'Lord love you, miss, I was joking. You won't get inside there.'

Orc looked at the fence. No chance of scaling it. The gateway provided the compound's only entrance that he could see, but his vision didn't extend to the far side.

'You wanting to stay long?' said the cabbie. 'Only, if so, I'll see to the horse.'

'Can we walk all the way round?' said Orc.

'Dare say, if you like a trek. If you want to go off, though, I'll need paying for so far.'

Orc gave him the money, and they got out. The air had cooled, and here on the hill a breeze blew. Orc gave Cass his jacket against the chill, and tried to suppress his own shivering. They passed the gate, where most of the visitors were congregated. There was a hinged barrier to stop vehicles, with one soldier behind it, and two more in the small guardhouse. A sign hung from the barrier, its warning words backed up by a death's-head symbol.

When they'd gone far enough to no longer be overheard, Cass touched Orc's arm. 'See past the corner ahead? The fence gets quite close to that building.' The pilot was still smoking outside. 'Maybe we can call to him from there and get him to talk.'

'You're planning to chat him up?' Orc tried to ignore thoughts of Seriuz.

'Can't hurt to try,' said Cass.

They'd just reached the corner when a horn honked some distance behind. Orc turned to see an auto-carriage barrelling along the road. It passed the parked cabs and the gawkers at the fence, and turned into the gateway with a screech of tyres. Orc winced, expecting a smash, but the barrier must have been quickly raised – the auto drove onto the compound's paving and curved in a long arc, its body heeling on its springs. The vehicle came round the back of the pilot's building and then squealed to a stop between it and the fence, out of sight of the gate but in full view of the corner. Its radiator cap carried a metal flag Orc recognised from that morning: the gryphon of the Empyreal Prelacy.

'There goes that idea,' muttered Cass. The pilot ground out his cigarette, walked round the corner of the building and got into the passenger compartment.

'Aristo-prat come to see him?' muttered Orc. 'Or is that his taxi home?'

The big auto didn't drive off, but sat with its engine thrumming, headlamps on.

'What do you think a pilot actually does?' said Cass.

'Controls the elemental, I guess.'

'But why the propeller screws? If you can get an air elemental to lift that craft up, why can't you get it to move it along?'

'Maybe the screws are for show? To make people think it's mechanical?'

'Possibly,' she said. 'It's all guesswork, though.'

'Maybe not for long,' said Orc. 'If we can get Yaggit into the idea, he can do his flight thing and find out more.'

'Good point,' said Cass. 'Just as long as *you're* not planning to—'

She broke off as the auto's door opened. The pilot got out and started to walk. He hadn't gone three paces when another figure scrambled out: not the Prelate, but a woman in a dress that showed pale in the dim light from the building's rear window. She ran and caught the pilot; at the same time the driver jumped from his seat to intercept them. He caught up and pulled at the woman's arm. Low voices came, indistinct against the engine's rumble. After a few moments the woman and pilot shared a peck of a kiss, then the woman returned to the auto and got back in.

The driver, a short, round-faced man with a full moustache, stared in Orc's direction.

'Come on,' hissed Cass, and tugged at his sleeve.

'We're on a public road.'

'I don't think we were meant to see that.' She pulled harder, and Orc let himself be led. Shortly after came the sound of the auto starting to move. They got back to the gate just as the vehicle exited the compound as recklessly as it had come, the blinds on its passenger compartment pulled down.

'Did you recognise her?' said Cass. 'That woman?'

'No.' Actually, Orc thought now: 'Yes. The Prelate's secretary's office.'

Cass nodded. 'I wonder what that was about?'

The house was quiet when they got back. Orc couldn't find Yaggit in the library or drawing room, and there was no response when he knocked at Yaggit's and Tashi's rooms. Nor was there any sign of Crome, and Wetherall seemed to disappear after letting them in.

Cass suggested the garden terrace outside the dining room, and they went back down. Passing the door under the stairs, the feeling prickled Orc that the house wasn't as empty as it seemed. He paused, alert for movement or voices. Nothing – but he sensed, as he hadn't for some time, a subtle but familiar distaste in the air that sent a trickle of dread through him.

'Holy crap,' he whispered to Cass. '*Them.*'

She inhaled slowly. 'Shit, there's that faint hospital smell. This the first time you've sensed them since the college?'

'Shh!' he hissed. 'What was that?'

A word or two, faint but sharp with annoyance or anger, had come through the door from the basement.

He tried the handle. Locked.

'Orc,' said Cass.

'Shh.' He put his ear against the wood.

'Sir?' Wetherall's voice made Orc jump – the man seemed to have materialised beside him.

'I – I heard someone down there,' he said. 'Crome said the basement was dangerous. I thought maybe an accident…'

'Unlikely, sir, but I shall investigate. If you'd care to go up to the drawing room, I'll bring tea.'

'Where are the others?' said Orc.

'Your three companions went out together, after the young lady came to see Yaggit.'

'Young lady?' said Cass. 'Who?'

'She wouldn't give me her name,' said Wetherall, and swept his hand to indicate back along the hallway, as though to remind them where the foot of the stairs was.

On the first floor landing, Orc leaned on the banister rail and listened. After a minute, a lock clunked downstairs, then came the soft voices of Wetherall and Crome. A key cranked tumblers again, and the men's footsteps went off.

'If Crome *was* talking to someone in the basement,' Orc whispered, 'he's just locked them in.'

'He probably just stubbed his toe when we heard him, or he was swearing to himself about the state of it,' said Cass. 'You saw how the windows were boarded up.'

'If he was just examining the basement, why lock the door when he was down there?'

Cass frowned at him. 'You're not thinking he's got the others trapped?'

'No,' said Orc. 'But… a young lady? Doesn't sound very likely. And why would they go out without saying where?'

'The bedrooms have locks, right?'

'Uh-huh.'

'Let's wait up there for them to come back,' Cass said. 'I don't think I'll risk the tea.'

15

ICE

Tashi leaned back against the wall by the entrance to the alley, squeezing his hands between the brickwork and his rear so he couldn't look at them. Looking at his hands was like picking at a scab but without ever being able to tear it off, and he must not let it become an obsession. He had other things to worry about, such as what Murun and Paiko might say when Yaggit finally found them. Tashi didn't really know Murun, a stolid, taciturn monk in his forties, reputed to possess a shrewd investigative mind. But Paiko he'd grown up with from childhood. Uncomplicated, dependable Paiko. He imagined the other boy's reaction, that high, bird-like laugh. *'Aino, I know you think I'm an idiot, but how can you expect even me to believe* this *is Tashi?'*

And then, if Paiko did come to believe it…

He would not look at his hands. The body was a tool, nothing more. That it worked was the important thing, and that his will was strong enough to overcome any corrupt influence. This body was likely to be more vulnerable to corrupt influence than the previous. But his will had strengthened too. If he could resist Qliphoth, he could resist the urge to look.

He tensed as footsteps sounded along the alley, then relaxed. Two sets only.

Yaggit's round face bore disappointment. 'Not here either.'

'Ah.' Tashi felt guilt at his own relief.

'Where now, master?' said Aino.

'Somewhere I can think,' said Yaggit. 'Back to that teahouse.'

Sandar's Genuine Thangkaran Teas stood halfway down a side-street along the busy thoroughfare. The bell jangled their entrance. As when they'd been there an hour before, Tashi was struck by a pang of homesickness at the smoky aroma of the tea, nothing like the flavourless brew Crome's servant had given them earlier. Only one other table was occupied, by an elderly Thangkaran couple. They smiled warmly at Yaggit and Aino, but regarded Tashi with tight curiosity. Yaggit chose a table as far as possible from them and the counter.

Sandar appeared through the kitchen curtain and came straight over. 'Any luck?'

Yaggit shook his head. 'They haven't been here since?'

'Very strange,' said Sandar. 'Murun gave no indication of dissatisfaction yesterday, nor any other time. Your tea earlier, it was… adequate?'

'Perfect,' said Yaggit. 'The same again, if you'd be so kind.'

'And a little soup? Free of charge for a Watcher and his brave novitiate. And his guest.'

'Perhaps later,' said Yaggit. 'I have misplaced my appetite.'

When Sandar had gone, Aino quietly said, 'Should we go back to his lodgings?'

'If Murun had returned there, he would have received our message and would now be looking for us,' said Yaggit. 'But yes, if we think of nothing else.'

'Perhaps I could help, if you told me more,' said Tashi. 'What does finding them have to do with the woman from *that man*'s office?' After her arrival, Yaggit had been closeted with her in Crome's library for twenty minutes.

'Tashi, I know you wish to help. But it was not necessary for you to come.'

He regretted begging now. He sensed Aino looking at him and didn't meet his eye.

'Can it do any harm for him to know, master?' said Aino. 'He might be able to think of something we haven't.'

'That woman's identity can have nothing to do with our missing colleagues' location.' Yaggit stood. 'Now, I must visit the water closet.'

Tashi watched the monk leave through the door at the rear. Alone with Aino, as he had rarely been since the college, he felt a sort of panic that there was so much to do and say before Yaggit came back, but nothing he could do or say. Their tea came, already poured. Tashi caught sight of his hand as he picked up his cup: the skin paler than it should have been, the fingers more slender, the few fine dark hairs on the knuckles gone.

A tool, that was all.

'It doesn't matter,' said Tashi. 'It doesn't matter who she was.'

Aino pushed aside the potted plant and leaned across the table. Barely louder than a whisper, he said, 'She is the Prelate's sister: Lady Emilia Astrasis. Yaggit needs to talk to Murun before he knows whether to bargain with her.'

'Bargain with her?'

'He thinks her position in a noble Empyreal house might mean she has information useful to our search. Or be able to get it.'

'But in exchange for what?'

'That I don't know.'

'Yaggit hasn't told you?'

'He said it is something only a Watcher can provide, but whatever it is, he doesn't seem happy about it. That's all I know, Tashi. But the fact that she came to us is a great secret. You mustn't mention her to Crome or the others. Nor to Murun or Paiko when we find them. Leave that to my master.'

Charity, thought Tashi. *He's trying not to make me feel left out.*

'If we do find them…' He couldn't keep the tremble from his voice. 'How do you think they will react? To me?'

Aino frowned at the table. 'You slew the goddess-monster. It was the greatest act of any novitiate in Highcloud's history. Whatever… injury you took from that battle, it cannot change that.'

'Was it the act of a novitiate?'

The twitch in Aino's eyes told Tashi he knew what lay behind the question. 'Yes,' said Aino, with something like anger. 'There are enough complicated things without adding to them. When we get to Highcloud, all will be settled.'

'I'm grateful for your conviction,' said Tashi. He couldn't admit that he half wanted to smash it, to smash it with the hard, heavy ball of red ice that sat at the core of him.

Yaggit returned then. 'I've decided,' he said quietly. 'After our tea, we'll go back and rest. If Murun has sent no word by later this evening, I shall conduct flight and attempt to find his whereabouts that way.'

'Flight?' Tashi raised his head.

Yaggit's gaze flicked to his. 'And that is all I shall seek to discover. I shall do nothing about the other matter before I talk to the Abbot.'

'"Other matter"? My master's soul? Your friend's?'

'Hush!' said Yaggit. 'I shall not explain again. Praying for him is all we can do. All we are *permitted* to do.'

'We have all been praying hard, Tashi,' said Aino. 'I'm certain Shoggu has reached the Land Beyond Sky. What Hana said was wrong. He would not have stained his soul by performing an act of magic.'

Tashi stared into his tea, unconvinced, thinking of the last time he'd seen his master.

'Tell me you do not intend to aid me in any way other than prayer?'

'The focused exercise of power, you mean? Like Hana? That would endanger my own soul, would it not?'

But there had been something in that thin smile…

'The only way I managed to resist the Qliphoth,' Tashi said, 'was because I found the Mountain. If my finding it was my master's doing, then he was responsible for saving many lives. Perhaps *all* lives. If that sin condemned his soul—'

'Then his fate is in Gevurah's hands,' said Yaggit. 'If he sinned, do you truly believe we ought to sin in turn to try to shield him from the consequences? Gevurah's judgement is final and perfect.' His voice had become shaky. 'The matter is *closed*, Tashi. If you regard yourself as a novitiate still, then you will obey me.'

'He is a novitiate,' said Aino.

'And *you* will not contradict me.'

'I didn't, master.'

'Then you will remember to whom you owe the greater loyalty.' Yaggit bent his forehead to his fingertips. 'Listen to me: I've become a cantankerous old man. Worry about Murun is making me sick. Let's go.'

Yaggit was tired from walking, so they took a cab. Tashi stared out at the traffic and lights in the dark, remembering when he'd done the same in the Prelate's auto-carriage barely two weeks before, before he had called the Lords of Holy Battle. Before, before, before – the ball of red ice sent its waves of cold through his body. He tried to silence the thousand demons of regret and horror and what-if, which spoke not with words like the Qliphoth had done, but cried just as loud. And loudest of all was the voice that said he was leaving Aino in ignorance, a dangerous ignorance, because he hadn't told him what he'd seen as he'd stared and stared at the Mountain.

At Crome's, Wetherall informed them that Orc and Cass had recently returned. Yaggit said he was going to his room to rest before flight; he took Aino up with him, leaving Tashi alone, seated on a hard chair in the entrance hall and wondering what to do.

'You didn't meet with any trouble?'

He looked up. Crome must have come from the library.

'No.' Tashi sat up straighter, prepared to try to deflect their host's curiosity.

'Good,' said Crome. 'Excellent.' He adjusted the position of a cane in the stand by the door. 'I gather your cousins had little luck in their shopping expedition. I'll take the three of you myself tomorrow. There might not be time left to have anything tailored, but we should be able to find enough garments off the peg.'

'I don't need any clothes.'

'You believe not? Have you experienced Thangkara in the autumn?'

'No.' A lie was a sin. He had to tell so many these days, but the old injunction still twisted inside him. 'I've never been there. My name was my mother's idea. She thought it exotic.'

'Your current garb fits you badly,' said Crome, casting his eye over the trousers and jacket Tashi had been given at the college. 'And the quality is indifferent at best. One of the advantages of money is that one can make the most of one's appearance. Not that vanity is ever admirable, but neither is slovenliness or poor presentation. If I might be allowed the observation, you are far too handsome to be wearing those.'

Tashi frowned at his knees.

'There, I've embarrassed you.' Crome clapped him on the shoulder. Tashi remembered Sergeant Rasmuss doing the same thing, though there was something different in the way Crome did it, something less weighty. 'But ignorant modesty is no more a virtue than vanity,' said Crome. 'One should always know one's own qualities. Yours have been hidden. I shall give some thought to how we might bring them out – we might try something more interesting than would suit your cousin. With your hair, too. Transformation is such an interesting concept, is it not?'

'What?' said Tashi, looking up in alarm.

'Does the exterior merely reflect what's within? Or does the surface penetrate the core and reshape it? A question that exercises my mind often. But probably of little interest to you. Until later, then.'

Just after Crome had walked off, voices sounded in the stairwell, descending from the second floor to the first. Orc and Cass, Tashi recognised – and Aino with them.

The Strandborns stayed upstairs, but Aino ran down until Tashi could see his face. 'They're going to teach us a game called billiards,' he said. 'Come up.'

Tashi wondered if Aino thought that might cheer him.

Following his friend into the games room, he caught the usual hardness in Cass's eye. The game was completely new to him. Orc showed Aino how to use the cue, then him. *As a father might instruct a son*, thought Tashi, repulsed by the idea. He learned the rules quickly, but the knack of accurately striking the ball eluded him.

During the second game, a stillness suddenly fell on the room. Crome stood at the open door to the landing.

'What rules are those?' he said. 'A Kymeran variant?'

'We just made them up,' said Orc. 'We don't know any.'

'You've not done a bad job,' said Crome. 'Though you have the scoring wrong.'

'I had an idea there should be more balls than this,' said Cass. 'Was I thinking of something else?'

'Nothing known to me,' said Crome. 'No doubt you became confused, which is understandable, it not being in any sense a woman's game.'

Cass stood up straight. 'Why not?'

'It isn't seemly,' said Crome. 'Not ladylike. It doesn't play to the qualities of your sex.'

'It doesn't need any male parts, does it?' she said. 'Look, the sticks and balls are provided. Oh, sorry, was that a renunciate thing to say?'

Tashi's jaw tightened at the barely hidden aggression in her voice.

'Miss Strandborn,' said Crome, 'I regret the need to suggest that a balance should be struck between hospitality and a man's wish to have his house respected. I have to say, it troubles me to witness a woman dressing as you do, and playing billiards, under my roof.'

Orc started to say something, but Cass held out her hand to silence him.

'Do you plan to have *any* woman under your roof in the future, Mister Crome? Apart from servants?'

'You've clearly adopted the native forwardness of the Kymeran female,' said Crome, with what Tashi thought admirable coolness. 'With respect, I don't see that's any business of yours. But most men do marry, in time.'

'I'm surprised they'd want to, when you all seem to hate us so much.'

'Hate?' said Crome. 'Quite the opposite. But civilisation is the control of one's baser instincts, wouldn't you agree?'

'And you think women need to be controlled more than men?'

Who wouldn't? thought Tashi: their closeness to the Witch Mother was clear. Now Crome would eloquently point that out, and demolish her.

'In fact,' their host said, 'some of the restrictions, such as those regarding provocative clothing, are intended so that men might control themselves. You'll find that your chafing against them will not excite much sympathy amongst women who've lived here all their lives. Civilisation is a joint enterprise between the sexes. The Holy Mother is held in great reverence by both – it is a rare man who holds himself to her standards of purity. You know her story?'

'No.'

'Ariss Entarna wished to carry out her highest function as a woman, to bear her husband's children, but could not overcome her horror at the means. So she travelled to the Holy Mountain in Thangkara, to give herself up to God on its slopes. Moved by her purity, He chose her to conceive and bear His son whilst still unsullied.'

Cass snorted. 'That makes no sense at all. God must have designed the body and how it works, so why was it holy for this woman to be horrified by it?'

'You do not know your Book, it seems,' Crome said.

'The Third Lesson,' said Tashi.

Cass daggered him with a glare. But Crome smiled.

'Quite so. Would you care to elaborate?'

Demurring would seem like backing down. Tashi cleared his throat. 'The current means of generating children was not the one originally intended.'

'Oh, come on,' said Cass. 'What was, then? Storks?'

'Perhaps Tashi could tell us the story,' said Crome, 'if he knows the whole thing?'

'I do,' said Tashi. 'It explains why you are correct, sir. It is remiss that she was not taught it.'

Cass gaped. 'Oh, you arse.'

'Civility, please,' said Crome. 'And let's not bring upbringing into it.'

Tashi bowed his head. 'My apologies. I didn't mean that my cousin was at fault, herself.'

'Go on then,' said Cass. 'Let's have story-time.'

'Uhm, look—' said Orc.

'No,' said Cass. 'Maybe it explains why I'll turn into a prostitute if I go out after dark. I want to hear it.'

Crome nodded at Tashi to proceed. Tashi felt as though he was about to go into battle with the goddess again, but one no taller than himself, one who used contempt as both armour and weapon. But he wouldn't back down. At Highcloud, he'd been thought particularly good at recitation. This was a chance to reconnect himself with that place, those times. To believe he was still a novitiate.

'And so it passed,' he began, 'that King Serpent grew envious—'

'Forgive me,' interrupted Crome. 'But King Serpent?'

Tashi winced inside. 'My – I was discussing the Thangkaran Book with Aino, and the name stuck. I meant Elok.' More lies. He quickly reminded himself of the other name changes he would need to make. If there was any other difference in wording, he would have to hope Crome didn't notice. He'd been stupid to volunteer. Pride. Idiocy.

'Elok grew envious of the Realm of the World,' he began again. 'Desiring to rule it, he took the earth as his bride, and in its corruption it gave birth to cannibal ogresses and demons, who also became his wives, one of which would in time consume all others. But God set apart a garden, and in its centre He created Kadmon, from clay which He fired with his breath. Outside the garden, the earth became a grey, misty swamp, and Elok looked into the uncorrupted garden with envy and hatred for Kadmon, but could find no way past the wall.

'One day, when Kadmon was walking close to the gate, Elok showed him his own wives, and asked Kadmon why he didn't create a companion himself. "It is true that I am lonely," said Kadmon. "I will ask God to make me one."

'"But surely you yourself are capable of creation?" said Elok. "My wives have not your favour with God, yet they spew creation without thought."

'These words stung Kadmon's pride. He turned not to God for help, but himself shaped Eve out of mud. But he did not know how to fire it, and so Eve was made flawed, being still too much of the wet, cold mud from which he had made—'

He stopped short in sick horror.

'Made… her?' prompted Crome.

'From which he had made her,' Tashi restarted shakily, meeting no one's gaze, trying to push aside his other thoughts. 'And because of the shame of this flaw, Kadmon hid Eve in a part of the garden where Gev – where God did not often walk.

'It was Kadmon's wont to gather food from afar, but Eve forsook this and instead began the cultivation of crops, for without knowing it she sought oneness with the wet ground. On a day when Kadmon was gathering honey from the distant wild hives, King – Elok – I cannot go further, sir, I'm sorry.' He sat down, heart pounding – pounding as it had in the hotel room in Torrento, when it had been attacked by Daroguerre's sorcery. Corrupted. Flawed.

'Never mind,' said Crome. 'It was well told so far. It's never easy to speak before an unsympathetic audience. I shall finish the tale.'

He went to stand near the dark and not-yet curtained window, looking out. 'Elok spoke to Eve as she tended her marshy fields near the gate. "Are you content?" said he. And she replied that she didn't know why, but she was not. "You crave what you lack," Elok told her. "Kadmon is of fired clay, and you are of wet mud. That is why you are soft. You crave his hardness and his heat." And in this he spoke a half-truth, for what Eve truly lacked was the hot breath of God by which Kadmon's clay had been fired. But she gave Elok's words another meaning.'

Crome had a confident, dramatic speaking voice. Better than his own, Tashi thought with shame. Crome had been too generous in his praise.

'That night,' Crome went on, 'as Eve lay beside Kadmon, her yearning to fill her emptiness took hold and she persuaded Kadmon to intercourse, which was the first time. As soon as the act was done, Kadmon ran in shame. But Eve felt the heat inside her. It grew into a child, grew as a vegetable does, grew within her until she lacked the strength to tend her other crops. When the child was born, she spent herself in tending it, and the crops became overgrown with weeds. When next that old devil Elok spoke to her through the gate, he told her the only way to recover was to eat the child, to return to herself the strength she had lost through growing it.

'So Eve ate the first child, and so brought death into the garden, just as she'd brought birth and sexual intercourse. And some animals turned to eating others, and many young were engendered to replace those eaten, and the clamour of death and birth reached the ears of God on His high mountain.

'He searched out Kadmon and found him cowering in shame. Kadmon lied, the first lie made by man, but God smelled untruth on him and Kadmon confessed. Then God sought out Eve and asked her what had happened. She also lied, but even as she did so, she felt a trouble in her viscera, and she opened her legs and out gushed blood – the blood of the child she'd eaten, as God well knew. So He condemned her that she would forever lose blood in memory of that child, and her lust would be insatiable, and she would bear child after child to replace the one she'd consumed. Then He banished her and Kadmon from the garden, lest they make it as corrupt as the rest of the Earth.

'And there the Lesson ends.' He turned from the window. 'You'll forgive me if it wasn't as word-perfect as Tashi's part.'

'And people believe all that?' said Cass.

'Empyreus has confirmed the story. But you mustn't feel it implies any criticism of you. Just as Empyreus redeemed mankind from the wheel of rebirth, so his mother redeemed womankind by conceiving free of the chains of sexual reproduction.'

Cass looked not the least convinced. 'So what were the sex organs supposed to be for, if not conceiving children?'

'Most hold that God intended the male member to be an organ of the divine creativity He was to have passed on to man,' said Crome. 'But Eve's seduction made it merely an organ of lower purposes. When we achieve our perfect bodies in Heaven, it might be that the phallus will regain its true form and function, while the other organs of digestion and reproduction will be removed.'

'And the woman's?'

'Eve created them herself. Being unfired, she retained the plasticity of mud. She adapted her body so as to seduce Kadmon.'

'Of course.' Cass sounded tired. Tashi hoped that would be an end of it.

'Some truths are not comfortable,' he said. 'It is wisdom to understand that this doesn't make them less true.'

He'd hoped it might make a bridge of understanding between them. But Cass shot him a hostile look. She didn't know what he was referring to, of course. Hana had told no-one but himself how he had been remade.

'I've had enough of these boys' games,' Cass said, and laid her cue on the table and walked out. Orc went with her.

'I also have other matters requiring my attention.' Crome met Tashi's gaze. 'We'll talk later, I hope. I rarely have a guest so well-schooled in the Book.'

'Strange,' said Aino when the two of them were left alone. 'He can recite Lessons, but I've seen no Empyrean paintings anywhere in the house, none of Kirrus or his mother.'

Tashi had wondered about that too. 'Could it be that he keeps faith with Gevurah?'

Aino frowned. 'That would explain his regard for Highcloud. But why not tell us? No doubt we'll discover sooner or later. Let's try playing this again.'

They did try. But Tashi still couldn't get the hang of hitting the ball accurately, and the game didn't last many minutes before frustration set in.

'It's because you're not used to your new body,' said Aino. 'Remember how clumsy Hann was when he grew five inches in a year?'

'I haven't grown five inches. I think it's something else.'

'What, Tashi?'

He looked at the floor, regretting he'd hinted at the truth. The game was not suited to women because they were made from mud, and so had he been. Made not by Gevurah and fired by His breath, but shaped by a human woman, the same woman who had almost seduced him on the island of witchcraft. The woman who had pretended to be his mother. Who had followed him when he had run. Who had taken his armour from him. Who had held him, warm and close and smelling of sweat and hair.

But he couldn't tell Aino any of this. What appalled him more than anything was that Hana hadn't even seemed to realise the horror in what she told him about his remaking – as though it were something beautiful or holy.

'Earlier, you said I am still a novitiate. But I can't be.'

'Don't say that,' said Aino. 'Don't pay any attention to what my master said. He won't go against the Abbot, you know that. But the Abbot will reinstate you. He'll retract what he said when you and Shoggu left. He has to, Tashi! You proved he was wrong and Shoggu was right. You found the evil and you destroyed it!'

'Was that me?'

Aino groaned. 'I told you, don't complicate it.'

'The Qliphoth killed the demon goddess. I was weak, Aino. When I knew I was too badly burned to live, all that was in my mind was that I should die without giving in to them. But I couldn't do even that. I let them in.'

'But if you hadn't, the goddess would have lived.'

'I let myself become possessed by things even worse.'

'And then you stopped them acting again. Tashi, whatever happened, however it happened, nothing else could have resulted in so little evil. Doesn't that prove Gevurah's will was behind it all? And didn't He give you the strength to resist them?'

'Staring at the Mountain.'

'Yes, drawing strength from His presence.'

Staring, and staring. All that ice and rock, cold as the hard knot in his stomach now, a bundle of words he might use to smash his friend's purity of faith, a purity he had once shared and cherished.

'Could it not be,' Aino went on, 'that Gevurah used the Qliphoth as a tool? After all, wasn't it a magician they killed on the road?'

Tashi shuddered, as though his internal organs had slipped against each other. 'I only remember… when I lost control… they wanted something to throw, and they didn't care that it was a man. They *liked* that it was a man.'

He waited, but the younger boy had no response.

'They rejoiced at the death they caused,' said Tashi. 'And you… in the cellar, they struck at you.'

'It was not a deep wound.'

'*I* struck at you.'

'*They* did.'

'They overcame my resistance.' Or his resistance had slipped. 'Because…' The memory was vague and horrible. 'I think you said something.'

'I was trying to encourage you to fight them.'

'What was it that you said?'

'That I'd come to take you home. To see the Mountain again. Was it their hatred of the Holy Mountain that gave them the power to overwhelm you?'

The Mountain. The hard ball of red ice sent a spear of cold into his gut. The chance to speak, to explain. But still he couldn't.

'Tashi?'

'Nothing,' he said, tasting the word as though he had only now sensed the depth of its meaning. He would not explain. He had to beware the desire to make Aino a companion in horror and doubt. Loneliness was an emotion the Witch Mother sent up through the body – and in the witch-made body he now possessed, emotions were inevitably stronger and harder to fight. And loneliness was insidious, because it felt like the yearning for his dead master, but it was a trick by the Witch Mother to seduce people into bodily contact, to cling for warmth. And so diseases were spread, another of her corruptions, her creations, from her realm beyond the Garden.

Wetherall had again left cold food in the dining room; he said more staff would arrive in the morning to better attend them. No word arrived from Murun, and at nine Yaggit came to tell Aino he had waited and rested long enough and would conduct flight. Tashi followed them up to their room.

'No, Tashi,' said Yaggit, turning to stand in the doorway. 'Better you find something else to do.'

'Master,' said Aino from behind him in the room. 'I don't contradict you, but surely you see the Abbot must reinstate him? And when that's so certain, can't you have two novitiates until we get back there?'

'Impossible,' said Yaggit. 'And flight is a sensitive thing. I can't have it disturbed.'

'But Tashi knows how to watch quietly as well as I.'

'That isn't what he means,' said Tashi. 'Is it?' he said to Yaggit. 'Have you told your novitiate what influence you think I will have? Have you told him why you doubt the Abbot will reinstate me? It has nothing to do with the way my master and I disobeyed him when we left, has it?'

'Master?' said Aino. 'What does he mean?'

Yaggit's frowning gaze held Tashi's. 'I will not talk about this now. I need to learn what has happened to Murun and Paiko. That is my priority, not your feelings. If you don't leave, I will have to believe you guilty of attempting to sabotage my flight.'

'Why would I do that? Because you refuse to help save my master from Hell?'

'Tashi,' said Aino. 'You're tired. Perhaps you should go to bed.'

He went. He went up to the third floor, to his small room next to Orc's, and lay in the dark and tried to quieten his mind, to not think about the future. The voices of the red ice crammed his chest so that he thought they might burst outwards from his heart, pushing his broken ribs up through his skin. Emotion: rage and hate and fear. Everything the Qliphoth had fed upon was still within him, everything that had made him fail to accept death.

If his will had died as well as his human body, what would have happened to him then? He had found the Mountain within himself, but would he have reached the Land Beyond Sky?

Had Shoggu?

'Master,' he groaned. It wrenched him inside every time Aino addressed Yaggit with that term. He could use it only when addressing the darkness. Even if he were to seek out Rasmuss and join the marines, as Rasmuss had said he might, he would have to address the man as Sergeant. And Rasmuss had made the invitation based on the skill and agility of a body he no longer possessed, strengths which in any case might have come from other sources. His new body would take time to train, and he feared it would never be as capable.

'Master...'

He couldn't bear it, couldn't bear what Shoggu might be suffering.

Orc and Cass came up an hour after him. He'd last seen them in the library, poring over a book of maps of the city. He couldn't make out their words as they parted on the landing, but he heard Orc's door snick shut in the nocturnal quiet. No traffic outside, and the streetlamps low enough that only a feeble gleam came through the gap in the curtains.

An hour of silence ground the house towards midnight. At last Tashi got to his feet and pulled the blankets and eiderdown off his bed. Taking them with him, he left his room as quietly as possible and opened Orc's door.

The gas-lamp was still on, though turned low. Orc showed as an angled heap beneath the covers. Tashi could smell him. He softly shut the door and dumped the pile of bedding against it.

Orc raised his head, drew a sharp breath. 'What are you doing?'

'Yaggit wouldn't let me stay.'

'But you have your own room.'

'I can't sleep alone.' He folded himself cross-legged on the bedding he'd put down. Orc sat up in bed, hugging his knees beneath the covers.

'So...'

'Have you made your cone of protection?' said Tashi. 'We shall build another, together, stronger. And if you are still disturbed by bad dreams, I shall awaken you.'

'You're not planning to sleep?' He sounded wary.

'I do so with a light ear,' said Tashi. 'I can be useful to you, in other ways too as time goes on. I can still fight, with a *dughra* at least. You saved Aino from being shot. You took blows. I owe you a debt.'

'Not really,' said Orc. 'But... you think Yaggit feels the same? Could you persuade him to do me a favour? I tried to ask him earlier but he wouldn't listen.'

'He won't listen to me either,' said Tashi.

'No? Where did you lot go this afternoon? Wetherall said a woman came?'

Aino had said not to mention her. But Aino had also told him to leave. His loyalties were not the same as they had been. 'Lady Emilia Astrasis. *That man*'s sister.'

Orc's eyes widened. 'She – was she the one we saw this morning?'

'Yaggit wants her to help him, but she wants something in return, something he's reluctant to give. I don't know what.'

'Help him how?'

'He kept something from you before, when we all met in his room. He touched on the truth of Empyreus. To find it out is a matter of urgency. When *that man* came to Highcloud, on the day I left with my master, he brought an ultimatum from the Valkensee, that the Abbot must publicly acknowledge Empyreus as the true son of God. The Abbot now prepares a Conclave to try to answer for certain whether he is or not. Yaggit and Murun were both sent to find evidence that might help, before Yaggit came to look for me. After Emilia Astrasis came, we went to find Murun and his novitiate Paiko, so Yaggit could discuss matters. But we couldn't find them. Now Yaggit seeks them through the Immaterium.'

'Blimey,' said Orc. 'That's big stuff. And what if your Abbot reckons Empyreus isn't divine? Will he tell that to the Prelate?'

Tashi shrugged, and looked down. 'I don't know if it matters to me. I want to know what happened to my master.'

'We've already told you all we know. It was a Sundaran marine.'

'But you could find out more. You can undertake your own form of flight. I know you promised Yaggit you would not. But I wouldn't tell him. I am myself now a creature of magic.' The confession sent a chill through him. 'I've had to discard notions of purity.'

'Tashi, look—'

'It has not been easy to come to you like this.'

'Even if we could find out who exactly it was—'

'No,' said Tashi. 'I do not seek to know which Sundaran killed him. My master warned against vengeance. I seek to know what happened to his soul.'

'Surely Yaggit…'

'Yaggit says nothing may be done except pray to Gevurah. He seems not to care that my master might be dragged towards Hell.'

'Shoggu? Why would he be?'

'Did Hana not tell you? She thinks that to help me in my battle, my master attempted a magical act. She said he "projected" the image of the Mountain into my mind. And he died so close to Golgomera, the Qliphoth created by his sin might drag him through the Witch-Mother's Sink. And his sin was my doing – or it was to help me. I must help him in turn. If his soul is still striving to reach the Land Beyond Sky, someone must project their power to help him. You are a magician.' He stared Orc in the face. 'You can do that. It might be his only hope, because it is possible that praying to Gevurah is no help at all. It is possible that He does not even hear.'

He lowered his gaze and drew a hard breath.

'There was nothing, you understand?' The words burned him with cold, as though saying it aloud for the first time confirmed his dread. 'I stared at that mountain, I clung to it; there was nothing of me but that focus. Whenever I felt the Qliphoth try to move my body, I willed it to stasis, but that was only a diversion to what I had fixed my will to. I never let myself give up hope. But in the end, I saw nothing but rock and ice. Was that because it was not the true Mountain? Because my master projected it in a sinful way? A magical way, I mean. Or was there no real strength to be found there anyway? Do you understand?'

'Uhm – you're not sure Gevurah exists?'

'Such a question is blasphemy,' Tashi said, but his words sounded flat and empty. 'I need you only to discover whether my master's soul has reached its home, or is in Hell, or is somewhere between. And if between, to help him. In return, you have my service.'

'I don't need anyone to serve me,' Orc said.

It bit him, the coldness of that refusal, the ignoring of his difficulty in coming to him. 'To guard you.'

'I don't need guarding. Not from anything you can guard me from. Highcloud will give you another master, surely?'

'Highcloud won't want me.' He felt as though the red ice had spread along all his bones. 'Yaggit and Aino smell my corruption. They see it in my new face, my new body.' Partly Orc's face, Orc's body. 'Highcloud will turn me out also. I have broken into a thousand shards and been remade. Yaggit spoke the truth in the Prelate's office. Hana confessed it. I died. And yet I now live, and the master I abandoned when I set off for battle is no more. Where is justice? It is merely a word. Not like "rock" and "ice". Where is the creator?'

Silence, empty. No trace even of Gevurah's anger at his words.

'The thing is,' said Orc, 'it would be dangerous to try to contact Shoggu, if it can even be done. I'd have to go deep into the Otherworld. *She*'d be there. And I'm not protected from her any more. Hana protected me, but I had to give that up so you could be restored.'

Tashi jerked up his head. '*Restored?*'

He jumped to his feet. Orc backed against the pillows, too slow. Tashi landed on him, snapped a hand round Orc's throat, choking off his cry – his other hand grabbed Orc's wrist and wrenched it across his body to pin his other arm too. His mud-made body still had the strength to do this, at least, to hold Orc helpless beneath his weight. His face was inches from Orc's wide, scared eyes. He felt Orc's heart beating wildly beneath him. The older boy's struggles were easy to contain, and that only increased Tashi's contempt.

'Coward,' he spat. 'You are weakness, you sap the strength of everything and everyone around you. Too weak to fight her, to want to fight her. She got her claws into you and dragged you inside her. I know. I was there, in that cellar. The Qliphoth taunted me. They wanted to start the slaughter with you fornicators, you two thrusting and groaning – oh yes, they told me every detail.'

He released his grip. Orc gasped in breath, but didn't speak, had nothing to say in defence.

'You are not righteous enough to serve,' said Tashi. 'Perhaps no one is. Perhaps that is the world Gevurah has abandoned.'

He got off Orc, not even bothering to guard against retaliation. He gathered up his bedding and went back to his own room and his thoughts in the dark.

A noise through the wall told him Orc had wedged a chair under the door-knob.

He slept against the door, even though there was no one to guard. Going down to the ground floor in the morning, he passed a young woman in a dark dress and white apron, no doubt one of the new staff Crome had spoken of. Wetherall was seated at a trestle table in the hallway, tucked into the angle between the door to the new kitchen and the one down to the basement – doing some kind of bookkeeping, it looked like. Tashi assumed Crome didn't want his manservant occupying the library.

Yaggit and Aino already sat at the dining table. They watched him walk in, as though a conversation had been interrupted. Silver dishes of hot food had been left on the sideboard. Tashi took only a glass of water.

'Were you successful?' he asked, sitting.

'Sadly not,' said Yaggit. 'There was difficulty. For the first time, I felt myself falling into dark-flight. I only just pulled out. *Was* pulled out.'

Tashi glanced at Aino, in his grey uniform. Dutiful novitiate. He pushed away the bitterness. 'A magician.'

'Magician?' said Yaggit. 'Who?'

'Twice during our mission, my master suffered dark-flight, or came close to it. Both times he was seeking the magician Daroguerre. Perhaps that's what causes dark-flight: the magic of a sorcerer who doesn't want to be discovered.'

Yaggit regarded him thoughtfully. 'But that time at Highcloud, it was the air-craft that sent Shoggu into it.'

'And we now know there must be magicians behind the air-craft.'

'It's a point, master,' said Aino. 'If Daroguerre served these Shining Ones, could it have been them?'

'Why would they want to prevent me locating Murun?' said Yaggit. 'Though I suppose they might have hoped to disable me, to prevent Orc reaching Highcloud.' He looked worried.

'Speaking of whom,' said Aino as stairs creaked.

Tashi didn't look round as Orc entered talking with Cass. 'Ooh, bacon!' Orc said, but Tashi heard something false in the jollity. Plates and lids clattered. The smell of meat and mushrooms robbed Tashi of the last of his appetite.

'If you'll allow, we'll talk while you eat,' said Yaggit, as Orc and Cass sat either side at the end of the table. Orc's gaze shied from Tashi's at once.

'Fine,' Orc said. 'About what?'

'Our plans.'

'We're still leaving?'

'Things are no longer that clear,' said Yaggit. 'We might need to remain a while.'

Orc lowered his fork. 'What about the enquiry? And I thought we needed to get to Highcloud as soon as possible?'

'I have a second task also. I have had to weigh the two, and the balance has now changed.'

'This thing with Empyreus?'

Yaggit frowned. Tashi said, 'I told him. And about Murun and Paiko.'

Yaggit went and shut the door. 'Until last night,' he told Orc, 'I deemed getting you to Highcloud the more important task. But now a chance unlooked-for has come regarding the Empyreus proof.'

'The Prelate's sister?'

Yaggit drew a sharp breath. 'How did you know that?'

Tashi sipped his water. He avoided Aino's look.

'What did she want from you?' said Cass.

'I will not say at present,' said Yaggit, visibly struggling with anger. 'I've arranged to meet her later – with Murun, if I can find him and Paiko. Miss Astrasis is well-placed to be useful to our mission here. If I can leave her in Murun's hands alone, well and good. If not…'

'We can't stay!' said Orc. 'If she's willing to help you for whatever reason, then persuade her to get us an air-craft. You know she's thick with one of the pilots?'

'Thick with…?'

'We saw her yesterday with one,' said Cass. 'They kissed.'

'We need to find out more,' said Orc. 'You can do your flight thing, can't you? Find how those craft work and so on? Or ask this Astrasis woman. We might not even need a pilot – if she can get us into the compound, me and Cass might be able to summon the elemental.'

Yaggit's eyes widened. 'You gave your word you would carry out no magic. I cannot allow such a scheme.'

'But we could reach Highcloud in hours!'

A pounding on the front door brought sudden hush. Tashi heard

Wetherall answer, then came other voices advancing through the house. The dining-room door swung open. Flustered, Wetherall admitted two uniformed policeman, and a grim-faced man in civilian clothes. Tashi tightened, wondering who they had come to arrest.

'Your Holiness.' The officer addressed Yaggit. 'I must speak to you.'

Aino jumped to his feet, ready for defence. 'What about?'

'A matter of some import,' the officer said, still facing Yaggit. 'Do you know of another Watcher visiting the city?'

'Murun, yes.' Yaggit stood, unsteadily. 'Do you know where he is?'

'I do,' said the officer. 'And I'm afraid I need you to make a formal identification.'

16

THE BOX IN THE BASEMENT

Orc pressed back against his chair, wanting to retreat from the scene altogether. This was a matter for the Thangkarans, not him. He didn't know how to react.

'And Paiko?' Yaggit leaned against the dining table, gripping it. 'The young man with him?'

'The same.'

Aino cried out. Tashi put his face in his hands.

'They were found last night,' the detective said, 'in a courtyard of a tenement scheduled for demolition. No signs of violence. Our mortuary physician suspects poison. Once you've identified the bodies, we'll have some questions.'

Yaggit nodded. 'Please allow us a minute or two.'

'We'll wait in the street.' The detective took his men outside.

Tashi lowered his forehead to the table and clasped his hands at the back of his head. 'Paiko…'

Aino looked as though he was mastering the urge to be sick or to cry or both.

Orc was about to say, 'I'm sorry,' but Cass beat him to it, and he could only mutter a lame, 'Me too.'

'*That man*,' growled Tashi. 'He is the one who will be "sorry".'

'The truth will be discovered in time,' said Yaggit. 'If not by the police, then by the Conclave.'

'No.' Tashi raised his head. 'The Watchers rely on the power of Gevurah, and Gevurah *gives* no power.'

Aino reached across the table. 'Tashi—'

'Aino, listen – all this time, *that man* has been conjuring and using elementals, and the great Watchers of Highcloud were blind to it. And didn't the Abbot say that even one absent Watcher would weaken the Conclave? Now it's missing two. And how long before it's three? Will you go with those policemen?'

Aino looked at Yaggit. 'Master? Is it wise?'

'Think your own thoughts, Aino!' said Tashi. 'Don't go. Don't lose your life too.'

'Tashi, please – remember what you are.'

'And what's *that*?' cried Tashi.

'What's that?' said Yaggit. 'What selfishness! We have only just heard the most appalling news about two friends and colleagues, yet you cannot put aside your own troubles for five minutes!'

Calm seemed to descend on Tashi, but Orc sensed the strain beneath.

'Forgive me,' Tashi said. 'You are correct. Though my body is different, my mind is the same, my reserves of discipline no less than they were. Though this body has not been fired by Gevurah, and is an abomination to him, and is as mutable as Eve, the mind that inhabits it still possesses Lord Gevurah's gifts of self and of will. Whatever my state, it is nothing next to the horror of the news brought here today.'

He put his hands in prayer, bowed curtly and left the room. Aino stared at the door, his face a mess of uncertainty and trouble. Feet sounded up the stairs. Orc wondered if he should tell the others about Tashi's nocturnal visit, then thought it probably wasn't the time.

'Beloved one, we must go,' said Yaggit.

'But master, *is* it wise? What he said—'

'This is a city of millions,' said Yaggit. 'Not a monastery, where all are known to each other and all on the same path. Even the Valkensee has its factions and its disagreements. We are in no more danger going with the police than we were in the Prelate's office yesterday. And to refuse would show great disrespect to those we have lost.'

Aino ducked his head, a curt nod. He'd just risen from his chair when a wailing cry descended faintly through the house, penetrating floors and walls, a drawn-out howl of distress and despair that froze the hairs on Orc's neck. The cry fell silent, long enough for hope that it would not come again, long enough for a breath to be drawn, then it began once more – louder than before, as though the first one had weakened the masonry and timbers in between.

Aino made for the door.

'No,' said Yaggit. 'Leave him.'

Aino stopped. 'But—'

'Our dead colleagues also cry for our attention.' Yaggit turned to Orc. 'You must look after Tashi now.'

'What?'

'He and Gevurah are estranged.'

'No!' said Aino. 'He'll get better.'

'Fetch your *dughra*,' Yaggit told him.

In the hallway, Wetherall and a maid were gazing up through the stairwell towards the source of the cries. Orc climbed, Cass and Aino following. As they reached the second-floor landing, the wailing stopped as suddenly as it had begun. Aino hesitated, seeming torn between going to Yaggit's room and carrying on.

'You'll take care of him?' he asked Orc. Orc nodded, not feeling he had much choice. But he didn't move, and neither did Cass. Aino darted into Yaggit's room, fetched his short sword and ran back down the stairs, after which Orc mounted two stairs at a time to the third-floor landing.

'Think it's safe?' said Cass, catching him up.

'Safe?'

'To go near him,' she said. 'The manifesting thing?'

'He's not possessed any more.'

'What if he calls *them* again?'

'He won't.'

'Orc – Oscar, wait. He scares me.'

'He's just a kid.'

'He was. Now he's an abomination.'

'Cass!'

'He said it himself! And he looks like an exact cross between you and her. Even if he *was* your child he wouldn't look so… so *designed*. She shaped him to be the two of you merged into one.'

Now the realisation came, how stupid he'd been not to understand the tension every time Cass and Tashi were together. And worse than stupid for not doing anything about it. 'That's no reason to take it out on him.'

'And what if he takes it out on *us*?' said Cass. 'All his life he's kept his emotions in check – he's built a wall against them and called it discipline. And now it's breaking down. Or didn't you hear those screams? And he believes he's like mud, mutable. What if he tries to – to *express* that scream, through his body, and you're near enough for him to transform?'

Orc chilled at the thought. 'He's stopped now.'

'Yaggit's palmed him off on you. Doesn't that tell you something?'

'Yes, that he needs someone to be kind to him.' He stepped towards Tashi's door.

'I don't have the energy to care about him too,' said Cass.

No response came to his knock, so Orc opened the door slowly, giving Tashi a chance to shout if he didn't want a visitor. Tashi lay face-up on the stripped bed, his feet trapped between the bars at its foot and his hands gripping those by his head as though he'd been tied to a torture rack. Orc closed the door behind him. Tashi didn't take his eyes from the ceiling.

'What do you want?' he said.

'To say sorry.' Orc perched on the edge of a chair. 'You were right. I'm a coward.'

Tashi's eyes swivelled to look at him, but otherwise he didn't move.

'What happened at the college, between me and Hana.' *Fornicators.* 'You got caught in the fallout. I should have realised, should have stood up for you, but I didn't. I just… it was easier to just try to forget you were there. You know, you were saved, you were going home. Sorted.'

'Sorted,' Tashi murmured, as though it were an unfamiliar name that might hold the key to himself.

'I told Hana you deserved everything I could do for you,' said Orc. 'Because of what you'd done, because you fought Skalith. But I didn't follow it through. That's why I'm a coward.'

Tashi's forehead creased; he stared at the ceiling. Too late, Orc guessed the boy's thoughts.

'Then you'll do your magic?' said Tashi. 'You'll find what happened to my master?'

'I said, that's really dangerous.'

'As much as my fight against the goddess?' Tashi tightened his grip on the rails, but kept staring upwards. 'You said I deserve anything you can do for me. Yet you will not do this one thing, which is not even for myself.'

Orc cursed his implied promise and started to think how he could extract himself. Then self-disgust wormed through him, and he realised the better parts of him weren't going to allow him to do that. And along with the relief that he was not a coward after all came a sick plummet of fear as to what courage might lead to.

He swallowed. Whatever happened, at least he would see Otter again. 'Okay. I'll give it a shot.'

Tashi raised his head, his hazel eyes hopeful and suspicious. 'Truly?'

'But Yaggit can't know. And all I'm saying is I'll try. I haven't done anything like that before. Not trying to find someone's soul.'

Tashi sat up. 'You will need guarding against dark-flight.'

'How does that work?'

'Aino will have herbs in his pack. If I throw those onto the fire and chant a rhyme, I can recall you.'

'Even from the Mother?'

Doubt pursed Tashi's face.

'It'll have to be Cass,' Orc said. 'She pulled me back yesterday, with the Prelate.'

'She will argue against it. And you are too easily bewitched.'

'I'll persuade her.' He stood.

'You must,' said Tashi. 'Don't allow yourself to be swayed. She will play on your fears for yourself, because she is a woman and woman's nature is flesh, and it is the flesh that fears, remember that. Only the flesh. If you speak to my master, you will tell him I'm sorry I didn't make it back. And ask who killed him.'

A ferocity had come into his eyes that Orc didn't like. 'You said you didn't want to know. You said Shoggu was against revenge.'

'Ask nonetheless,' said Tashi. 'He might have changed his mind. And ask him who killed Paiko and Murun. It is said the dead learn many things before they reach their destination.' His head fell back onto his pillow. 'And ask him… if there is any way he can come to me in dreams. If there is any way he can guide me. Please be sure to ask him that.'

'That's insane,' said Cass, when they were in Orc's room. 'You know it's too dangerous to scape again – it's only a day since you freaked out in front of the Prelate. And for what? You don't know you can find Shoggu's soul. You don't know it's even there to be found!'

'I have to try,' said Orc. 'It's the right thing to do. And remember you said a strong identity was a good defence against the Mother?'

Her eyes narrowed.

'And what kind of identity have I had since the college? Hardly one at all. Now I have someone to help. It feels more… more *me* – the person I was before Initiation. And I can't go back on it. We've treated him like shit.'

'Sounds like you've found one thing to be sure about.'

'Exactly!' he said, then thought there might have been something in her tone he'd misunderstood.

'I hope you're right.' She studied him, then smiled tightly. 'What do I do?'

'Just keep an eye on me. If anything happens, do what feels right. But I think just having you there will be enough, like it was yesterday. Don't worry, I'll be careful. And I'll have Otter with me. Oscar and Otter – team competent!'

This time her smile did nothing to disguise her concern.

She wanted to stay with him for the entire process, but agreed to wait outside until he called. They asked Tashi to keep his bedroom door open and intercept anyone making for Orc's room once Cass was inside, and to be ready in case Cass needed his experience or Aino's herbs.

Once alone and with his mask pricked into place, Orc moved the rug to one side, then threw himself into shivering on the bare floorboards, as nervous as he'd ever felt when beginning a scape. To find Shoggu's soul, he would have to go as deep into the Otherworld as he'd ever gone, and that meant approaching the Serpent Mandala closer than ever. He would have to be very careful, judging the balance between release and control.

But real control quickly escaped him. He fell quickly from the start, the sense of the Mandala all around him, plummeting, exhilarating, terrifying. *Pull out*, came the thought, but that would be cowardice and he wasn't a coward. He could do this. He tried to slow his fall with details of his real life, locations, people, but they eluded his mental grasp. Did he have two cousins, or one? Or a sister? Trying to remember was like trying to grab hold of a slippery rope. There was someone he had to call, always called; that person would help him, but he couldn't remember to which of the muddle of selves his helper belonged. Better to welcome the warmth of the energy he could now almost see, almost breathe, as though he were drowning in an intense calm.

Drowning…

It whirled, now visible in mind-space: two serpents endlessly dancing. Still together, nameless, as all had been in the beginning and longed to be again. One, as he would be soon one with them, dissolved into them. What would become Saeraf, not yet with red scales and fiery wings; what would become Chthonis, not yet with slippery hide and—

Chthonis. Memory needled, stabbed in frantic urge for survival. A memory of Chthonis slippery, in mud, in a pit of mud.

Eel.

The spark, the link.

'Otter!' he gasped. 'Help!'

Something tugged him away from the Mandala. He almost screamed; he reached out to grasp it, but the dance of the serpents faded, and he was pulled upwards as though through water, grasped by Cass, by Otter, all the way to the gasping surface and the bare boards of a room and swimming vision blurred by tears in his half-opened eyes.

He sobbed at the smell of damp fur.

'Almost lost you there, bruv.'

Exhausted, grateful, moved beyond words, Orc raised his head from the floor. The whiskers of his masked animath moved with chewing.

'Here,' said Otter, through a full mouth. He put his paws on Orc's shoulder and leaned over his face, and showed a chewed mess between his fangs. Orc repressed gagging at the smell of fish, opened his mouth and felt the food pushed in by a hot little tongue. He swallowed with effort.

'Didn't know if we'd meet again,' said Otter. 'Last time I saw you, you were being attacked by Giant Bindweed Woman. And you ran out too quick, and left a piece of yourself with her. She still has it. That's three times, bruv! Three times you've left bits of your soul behind. I told you after the bilges, you can't do that. Look at the state of you!'

Orc pushed himself into a sitting position, and groaned as he looked down. His naked body streamed with blood from a thousand cuts; a hundred bruises discoloured him. And now with vision came crashing pain. He tried to disbelieve it, but couldn't remember what the reality should be. Had he taken his clothes off? Was that the way of getting close to the Mother, or was that someone else?

He grabbed for the rug he'd pushed aside and covered as much as he could. 'Tashi,' he said, as the name came back to him. 'Have to help him. Cass?' he said, louder, terrified that he'd imagined her, that his life with her had been only a dream based on Otter.

The door started to open. 'Don't worry about what you see,' he said. Then he saw her, just as Otter squeaked in dismay, and any worry about his own appearance vanished.

She was armoured in glittering steel. But the blood – it had run out from below the breastplate, over the segmented skirts. The silvered plate covering her thighs was smeared with it, slick with red from wounds invisible beneath the metal skin.

Not real, Orc tried to reassure himself. But visions didn't come from nowhere. She bled from wounds that had left her armour untouched, and he saw from her face that she either didn't know or was determined not to show it.

'Are you okay?' she asked, worried.

'You can't see?'

'You look fine,' she said, warily, and sat on the chair. 'Do I just sit here?'

'What does it mean?' Orc asked Otter, making sure nothing Cass could hear escaped his lips.

'I was going to ask you,' said Otter.

Orc was afraid it had something to do with himself. 'We need to get to the Otherworld and Eel. Ask her how to find Shoggu's soul.'

'Down is this way, bruv.' Otter headed for the door. Orc closed his eyes and imagined rising to his feet and pulling the rug around him. Otter had nosed the door open. The pain of his cuts and bruises made focus more difficult, but they seemed to place him more securely in the scape. Apart from on the island, it was the most real-seeming one yet.

Downstairs, the entrance hall was lit by a red glow through the fanlight above the door. The wood panelling looked strangely like steel. The paintings were all of eyes: cat eyes, lizard eyes. Otter looked around in confusion. 'Something's fuddling my direction.'

'Further down, yes?' Orc went to the door to the basement stairs.

He tried the trick that had opened the locked cabinet on *Nightfire*: he asserted to himself that Crome had accidentally left it unlocked that morning. And yes, the door opened to his touch.

It was almost dark down there. The steps felt slippery. He'd expected them to lead down to the Otherworld, but after four or five he stopped, suddenly noticing a smell like rust in rain.

'Blood?'

'You've found your own way to Eel,' said Otter from the step behind him.

Now Orc made out the dim, damp basement room. Furniture was piled around the far and left walls. The window-boards admitted red light through their cracks; just below them lay an ink-dark pool. Shapes littered the dim floor by its edge.

Slick in the ghastly light, flesh lay like chunks of sausage. A clouded eye stared upwards from a pointed head.

'Bruv,' groaned Otter. 'What happened?'

'I killed her,' said Orc, stunned by understanding. 'On the island. When I couldn't reach you. But I didn't think…'

'You didn't think you'd ever need her again,' said Otter. 'Yet here you are.'

'But – she's Chthonis. One of the serpents.'

'One face of her,' said Otter. 'And now she's rotting, and me with my belly empty. Ach, I shouldn't have let myself get trapped by that wizard on the ship. Stupid! You were too much a pup to be left alone. How are we going to answer your questions now?'

'Eel can't be the only oracle?'

'She was the one best suited to you,' said Otter. 'Why else—'

'Hush,' said Orc. 'What's that?'

It sounded like whispering. At first he wondered if he was hearing it in reality, people talking outside his room. Then his attention was drawn to part of the scape-basement. Eel's body had disappeared, the blood too. Where the pool had been, a box now rested on the floor: a box in chestnut-coloured leather, familiar-looking.

The whispering got louder as he approached. Almost he could make out words, buzzing together like a swarm, an oppressive cloud. The box pulled harder on his memory, but he couldn't place it.

'Cass?' he said aloud, careful and focused, so he didn't break out of the scape. 'You remember seeing a leather box anywhere?' He neared it. 'Two locks. Chestnut-coloured.'

'What size?' came her voice.

'A foot each side.'

'You mean the clairaudioscope one?'

Recognition speared him. The locks sprang open. But it couldn't be, he thought. The device was still at the Quallaces' house. The box must just be similar.

The voices buzzed louder. Otter ran round to the other side of the box and placed his paws on it, as though to hold it shut.

'Careful, bruv. When a well doesn't look like a well, people fall in.'

'Are you saying this *is* a well? A way to the Otherworld?'

He overcame the resistance of Otter's weight and tipped open the lid. Within was the clairaudioscope's nest of wires, nothing else, none of the other paraphernalia. In the gaps between the wires was darkness, a hole leading down into the earth.

Perhaps he could speak to the Otherworld through this, or Shoggu's soul could speak to him. Wasn't that what the clairaudioscope was for? It didn't matter that the device wasn't in the house's basement in reality – it was here in his scape, to answer his need in Eel's absence. He bent over the box and parted the wires in the middle.

From the gap he'd made came a cold breath of old air.

Suddenly the wires seethed under his hands, coiled around his fingers, tightened. Otter chittered a warning. Orc tried to push himself away from the box, but his hands were trapped. The wires snaked up his arms. They thickened, split, transformed into creepers. Thorns dug into his skin. Otter fought, bit, pulled, but it wasn't enough. The creepers round Orc's arms sent out shoots that clawed across his chest. Red flowers bloomed along them.

'Help!' he cried. 'Cass, help!'

'Don't break out like that!' squeaked Otter. 'Don't leave another piece of you here!'

But there was no other way. The creepers were swamping him; all his pulling did nothing but dig the thorns deeper. He called for Cass again. But how would she get into the basement if the door was locked?

'Fight, bruv!' yipped Otter. 'It's only plants!'

But the vines were all across his face, closing his eyes. He couldn't move, couldn't see. There came panicked shouting, but everything was blurred and drowning in white noise. A vine tightened on his neck. The thorns had grown long as knives.

Then something pulled aside the vines over his face. Otter leaned over him. Orc gasped open his mouth to breathe, and Otter's mouth locked with his. A fish pushed in; Orc tried to bite it, to eat it, thinking it must help him as before, but the fish yelped and withdrew. Into his mind there stabbed the memory of a time before, underwater, the panic of trying to save someone – someone he had to fight to stay alive for.

He gripped that memory with his mind and clawed his way back out of the scape and into the bedroom and light, and Cass. She still wore her bloodstained armour, but her everyday clothes showed through it. He sat up, weakly. His skin showed through his clothes too, the marks more vivid than both.

'Thank fuck,' said Cass. 'Need anything to ground you?' There was something forced in her stare, as though she wanted to look away. 'Food? Coffee?'

His head swam. 'Came out too fast.'

'Your scratch-marks,' she said. 'Some of them have opened. You've manifested damage – again.'

He noticed something slurred about her voice. 'You all right?'

She looked away, said, 'Bit my tongue,' and shook her head. 'Shouldn't have agreed.' She put a hand on his forehead, cold steel and hot skin. 'You're sweating. Not good.'

'The, the shock.' The red flowers were still clear in his mind: venomous, the jagged-edged petals like the fangs of the serpents. His head swam, and his stomach.

His breathing deepened.

'Bathroom,' said Cass. 'Quick.'

He just about made it. After his half-digested breakfast was flushed away, Cass insisted on getting him to bed. Tashi had left his room and stood on the landing. 'What happened?' he said. 'Did you find him?'

'No, he didn't,' said Cass. 'But he almost killed himself trying, if that's any use?'

'Will he try again?'

Cass muttered, 'My room,' and pulled Orc away. Orc thought he should say something to Tashi, express regret, but he was too busy watching the floor swim.

Cass helped him into her bed. The pillow smelt of her hair. 'I doubt he'll come in here,' she said. 'But if he does, tell him to piss off. Or yell for me.'

'You're not going?' he said in panic.

'I need to get some iodine.'

'Don't! Please. Otter said – I've left too much of my soul there. I'm not back, not properly. She can still get me. She won't even have to manifest.'

'She can't hurt you if she doesn't,' said Cass, but sat down on a chair.

He wanted to believe her. He tried to assert that she was right. Her presence in the room was made of the scent of her bed; but after some time that might have been sleep and might have been waking, he sensed she wasn't there any more, and the smell of her hair in the pillowcase had become the peppery odour of plants and sap. Unable to direct his gaze anywhere but upwards, he watched vines slowly creep to the tops of the walls and across the ceiling – he thought he saw snakes among them. The vines grew to meet in the middle, enclosing him in the bower. He knew that if he tried to move, he would find his wrists and ankles bound, and so he kept himself absolutely still.

She came, from the plants, or from the air, or the bed. Her face had something of Hana, something of Cass too, but he had the weird sense that what reminded him of Cass was actually another woman, one he'd forgotten.

'No,' he said. 'No, please.' But she wouldn't obey, he knew. She wouldn't even believe his protest.

'You cannot escape me,' she said. 'You left your essence within me, and I have kept it.'

Naked, she crouched over him, her full breasts pendulous. Her nipples, dark and hard, obsessed his vision. Spines dug into his erection, yet the pain only made him harder. He tried to speak, but thorns dug into his throat.

'Why do you deny me what is mine?' Her voice pulled his gaze to her face, directly above his and staring down within a curtain of honey-coloured hair. 'Because of your blood, I no longer have to eat my children right away. I can allow them life. But if you deny me, I will have to take them younger. I have to make more, always more.'

Sweat broke from him all over as she lowered herself onto him, sliding around him. She began to move. Pain and sweetness stirred his hips into response. He thrust into her, meshing his movements with hers until a loud knock came on the door and he knew he must stop because he was alone, but he could still feel her slippery heat wrapped around him and her movements sucked him into a climax that made him cry out. Then a heavy silence flowed over him, and with it the vines across the ceiling began to wither. The scent of rot and pollen joined that of sap.

'Bruv?' came Otter's voice – if it was Otter's; it sounded female. 'Brought you some water. And iodine.'

The vines that bound him to the bed shrivelled under the touch of her steel gauntlets. Even between the segments that covered her fingers, the blood trickled. She helped him off with his shirt – he had no memory of putting it back on, or had he ever taken it off? – and stung his cuts with orange liquid from a bottle.

She said, 'What about your legs?' and he said no, he'd be fine, because he didn't even know if he really had climaxed. And at that he began to cry.

She held his hand. He clutched back, barely feeling the warmth beneath the steel. 'You left me.'

Her face was messed with the residue of a battle, with smoke and tears. 'You fell asleep. I thought you'd be okay.'

'You can't let me sleep again.'

'You're half-asleep now, Orc. I have to wake you up.'

'Orc? Not Oscar?'

'No, that might've been a mistake. Orc is who you were before your Initiation, and that was closest to the real you, closest to the time we've forgotten.'

He swallowed, nervous. 'You called me "bruv" just now.'

'What? No, I didn't.'

'Oh, God…'

'You need to get it together,' said Cass. 'Here, this might help.'

She'd brought a book up from Crome's library: an old children's encyclopaedia. She sat on the bed and read him an article on the principle of the steam engine. She made him concentrate on the descriptions, on the logic, the physical laws that enabled the cycle of condensation and compression. They went through it all together, and he tried to grasp it, for her, and slowly the unfocused world, though fragile, regained its normal dimensions, its reality, and Cass's hand lost its steel and its blood.

He slumped back, exhausted.

'I told the others you were ill,' said Cass.

'Yaggit's back?'

'Was. Turned out yes, it was their friend at the morgue. Aino looked pretty cut up. I think Yaggit was too, underneath. Now they've gone out again – to see the Prelate's sister, I think. And Crome's taken Tashi shopping.'

'Shopping? In his state?'

'Apparently. So you don't have to worry about him bothering you for a bit. I'll get some food – it's almost noon, and you need to ground yourself and get your strength back.'

His strength didn't come back, not properly. He felt he needed a month of rest, as though drained of half his blood. Mid-afternoon, he at least felt well enough to get out of bed. Cass led him downstairs. He sensed no trace of the Kaybees when he paused by the basement door, which on impulse he tried and found locked. A maid brought them coffee in the library, where Cass sat poring again over street-maps. Sometimes when Orc closed his weary eyes for a few moments, he opened them to glimpse steel again, before Cass's normal clothes returned. To his relief, he saw no trace of plants, nor of the Mother's presence, except for an occasional moment when he glimpsed one of the preserved arachnids in its glass case, or a suggestive grain in wood panelling. He wondered if the hundreds of books had some warding effect.

'Knightsbridge.' Cass looked up, frowning, from the volume of maps. 'Recognise that?'

'No.'

'It's pricking something in me,' she said. 'I think. Want to go have a look?'

'How far?'

'Too far to walk. We could get a cab.'

'With what money?'

She went to Crome's desk and opened a drawer and took out the cash box.

'Cass!'

'It's only what we didn't spend yesterday,' she said, lifting some coins. Then she tore the page out of the map-book.

'Holy crap!'

'This is our *past*, Orc. More important than bloody paper.' She folded and put it in her pocket. 'I'll be a good girl and put my dress on again. Wait here.'

Somehow Wetherall seemed aware of their plans to leave, and was ready with the front door when they went down. He asked where they were going, and Cass said, 'Just for a walk. Orc's still feeling peaky.'

'I'm sure Mister Crome would appreciate my reminding you to take care.'

'I *do* have my shawl, Mister Wetherall. I'm sure my forearms alone aren't enough to excite the local gentlemen to violent lust.'

'What's Crome so worried about with all this "take care" stuff?' said Orc.

'Nothing specific, sir, I'm sure. Merely with your being strangers here.'

'That remains to be seen,' muttered Cass.

The supposedly fresh air did no good at all. Orc was barely down the steps to the street when his legs started to feel wobbly, and he had to lean against the railings of the basement area. Looking down into it, he saw that beneath the flying front steps was an outside door to the basement, its small window also boarded over.

The basement. A connection tried to claw into his mind. The door under the stairs, Crome's voice down there, his scape…

'You okay?' said Cass. 'It's not far to the next street, and we can get a cab there, like yesterday.'

'Wait.' A wet, cold shudder of thought. 'When we felt the Kaybees yesterday, we were by the basement, yes?'

'Uh-huh?'

'What if that wasn't a coincidence?'

'Sorry?'

Orc waited for a strolling couple to pass. He was grateful for the delay, because he badly needed to steady himself. He hoped that what had just passed through his mind was a flicker of madness, one Cass might easily extinguish with reason. When the couple were gone, he moved closer to her.

'What if we felt them there because Crome was *listening* to them?'

'How do you mean, "listening"?'

'Like Jorik was.'

'What? Orc, he doesn't have the clairaudioscope! Seeing it in your scape doesn't mean it's there in real life.'

'That's what I thought. But what if he stole it from the Quallaces' house before he met us?'

'Why would he? Orc, try to focus.'

He swallowed, and gave her the worst it. 'We've no idea what happened to the Scorpion.'

'He ran away after…'

'Crome has a broken arm.'

Cass barked a laugh. 'No way. A boy like him? Why would the Kaybees want someone like that when they've got people like Daroguerre? And why would the Scorpion want a clairaudioscope anyway? The Kaybees must already have some way of giving orders, or he wouldn't have known where to ambush us.'

'But he ambushed us from the wrong side, remember?' The memory of that night twisted in him. 'He didn't get his instructions clear enough. Maybe the clairaudioscope is better.'

She sucked her teeth. 'Orc, this is a real stretch. Do you honestly believe it?'

'I don't know. It just came to me. But wasn't it strange how he latched onto us at that hotel?'

'The transcripts said the Scorpion's out to get Tashi. Crome's shown no sign of that.'

'Maybe he's waiting till we're out in the wilderness,' said Orc, not liking the thought that Crome was out alone with Tashi right now.

'But the Kaybees don't want us to reach Highcloud,' said Cass, 'and Crome's helping us.'

'So he says.'

She stared down at the basement door, her lips tight. 'Bollocks,' she said. 'Bollocks, bollocks. We need to know for sure. If he does have the 'scope, then… shit.'

'How do we find out? If he keeps the door locked?'

She looked into the basement area. 'And that door down there?'

'That'll be locked too, surely. Anyway, we can't get down there because… oh.' He looked at the gate in the railings at the top of the steps leading down. 'Wasn't that chained shut?'

'Yeah, I thought so too. And look down there, at that window. Doesn't that board look loose to you?'

'Handy.'

Cass looked around. 'We can't do it in daylight. Late tonight, yes?'

'Yup.'

'Now let's find this Knightsbridge place. You okay to go on?'

Orc nodded. But they hadn't walked more than ten paces when it jumped him.

'Crap, what if he uses it before tonight? The Kaybees have probably just overheard everything we said. If they tell him…'

Cass made a fist and hit herself in the forehead.

'We have to make sure he doesn't use it,' said Orc. 'We can't both go out.'

Cass whined with frustration.

'Can you go?' he said.

'I'm not leaving you alone. I don't know if you're stable enough.'

He knew she wouldn't accept any argument about that, and he didn't really want to make one. They went back inside and Orc told Wetherall he felt too ill.

Yaggit and Aino returned in the late afternoon, but deflected questions about where they'd been and hurried up to Yaggit's room. It wasn't until after seven that Crome came back: Orc was relieved to hear Tashi's voice too, down in the hallway. Then Crome brought Tashi up to the drawing room.

'What do you think?'

Orc had no idea what to think. Next to their host in his plain grey suit, Tashi looked expensively and uncomfortably overdressed. His black coat, heavily trimmed with blue piping, was cut away to show a waistcoat of midnight silk embroidered with silver; a maroon necktie covered most of the front of a stiff-collared shirt; close-fitting black trousers with a satin side-stripe hung over polished elastic-sided ankle boots. His face was set in a neutral expression, as though he didn't know whether embarrassment or pride was more appropriate.

'Quite a transformation, is it not?' bubbled Crome. 'I've never been one to make a fuss over my own appearance – functionality is all I crave in my wardrobe – but since your cousin needed new clothes, I thought I would indulge a whim. Fear not, I've brought home something for you two as well. I had to estimate sizing, but I possess a fair eye for such things. You can wear it when we dine in an hour.'

'And how are things with the Interior Ministry, Mister Crome?' said Cass.

'All in hand,' he said. 'I'll relate my progress whilst we eat.'

Cass changed for dinner first, while Orc sat reading on one of the hallway chairs, ready to distract Crome if he made to use the door to the basement stairs. When Cass came down, Orc swallowed at how she looked in her close-fitting electric-blue dress, off the shoulder, with long gloves. And a glittering necklace – had Crome really bought that, or just hired it?

'Don't laugh,' she said.

He stood. 'I wasn't about to.'

'That doesn't mean *I* won't, when we see what he's got you. Get up there.'

Orc expected evening dress too, but instead found a three-piece suit of grey tweed, lighter than he'd bought for himself the day before, with suitable shirt and tie and shoes.

More would be delivered in the morning, Crome said when they were seated around the dining-room table. He'd ordered everything they would need for the journey: coats and hats and outfits in practical fabric. Tashi was still dressed in his none-too-practical clothes. Crome had seated him next to Cass; Orc felt uncomfortable with the shared extravagance of their appearance, which made it seem as though they'd been matched. He made sure he sat opposite her.

When their host wasn't gently nudging them as to the correct cutlery, clearly amused to play tutor of etiquette, he talked about their planned route across country – this would avoid the new telephone lines and even the telegraph network, so news of their departure couldn't race ahead of them. He'd arranged to borrow a closed carriage from a friend, and had started diversionary rumours that he was leaving for the west. Cass leaned attentively into the talk, but Orc was too focused on her to pay much heed to it himself. He admired how she looked, but resented the fact that it was Crome who'd altered her appearance.

Only her face belonged fully to the two years they'd shared together, a face whose sunburn from their summer adventures was now fading. And her hair – it didn't suit the dress at all, Orc could see that; it was too rough. But the combination excited him.

Just after the fish course, Yaggit excused himself and stood.

'Not planning to go outside, I trust?' said Crome, seemingly startled into nerves.

'Merely to use your water closet,' said Yaggit. 'I no longer have the stamina of the young.'

Cass caught Orc's eye. She too, clearly, had found Crome's reaction odd.

'Do you truly think it so dangerous after dark here, Mister Crome?' she said. 'It seems a nice enough neighbourhood.'

He gave the appearance of having not heard, and signalled a maid to clear the plates.

Several times, during the next two courses, Orc noticed their host checking the clock on the mantelshelf. A few minutes before ten, Crome excused himself and left, shutting the door behind him. Those at the table went absolutely still; even the Thangkarans seemed to suspect something. Orc heard, very faint but unmistakeable, a key turning – not in the dining-room door itself, but nearby.

Cass hissed. 'Quick,' she said to Orc. 'We need to think of a reason to get him back out of the basement.'

'Why?' said Yaggit. 'What could he be doing down there?'

Cass glanced round at the maid who'd served them, then leaned across the table. 'We think he might be in contact with the Shining Ones.'

'Serpent's tongue!' said Yaggit. 'I thought there was something odd about him, but – how sure are you?'

'Enough to need to stop him,' said Cass, and stood.

'What'll you say?' asked Orc.

'I'll wing it,' she said, and left.

Yaggit sent the maid into the adjoining kitchen to refill the carafe. Orc went to the doorway to the hall, from where he could see the door beneath the stairs. It was open. Crome had left it unlocked and Cass had followed him down.

'Tell me,' Yaggit said, standing beside Orc.

'Wait,' said Orc, listening. 'I think I'll—'

A loud bang jumped him, then another. Cries came from everywhere. Two more gunshots sounded and Orc was already at the door to the basement. He ran down the stairs into darkness. The basement layout was more complex than in his scape: a hallway ended at the outer door, and rooms led off to the left, one ahead of the stair-foot and one behind. The only light came from the former, and so did the smell of gun-smoke. Cass stood pressed against the wall by the open doorway, looking through into the room.

He joined her. Her bare shoulder felt clammy under his hand. The room beyond, clearly the old kitchen, was lit by a paraffin lamp. By a window, its boards removed, stood Crome, holding a revolver. At his feet lay two men.

'I apologise for my omission in not locking the door.' He twitched a thin, nervous smile. 'You shouldn't have been so close to this.'

Orc couldn't speak. He felt Cass shaking, cold. She must have been right on top of it.

'What happened?' said Yaggit, who'd followed down with the others.

'You'll hear no more vague warnings about your safety,' Crome said. 'The threat has gone. Come and see, if you wish: the men at least. It's no sight for a young lady.'

Cass went in with them. Crome picked up the lamp and held it above the dead men. Both carried handguns. As their dead faces were revealed, Orc's breath drew tight.

'Fools,' groaned Yaggit. 'The fools!'

Aino howled, kicked at a table leg before he regained his control.

Orc only stared, guts cramped, at the two young men he'd last seen at the college, and who must have come hundreds of miles to avenge their brother Sorrell.

17

MAGORIA

'You'll forgive me, I hope, for hiding this threat from you,' said Crome. 'I became aware of it even before I contrived to run into you at the Black Hart, but didn't know how fully it would materialise – I didn't, at that stage, know that these would-be assassins would evade the new border controls. In any case, I couldn't warn you – to convince you the threat was real, I would have needed to reveal how I knew of it, and I couldn't predict how you would react. For my paradox is that, greatly as I admire the Watchers of Highcloud, I am something they abhor.'

'A magician,' said Yaggit.

Crome bowed. 'I especially apologise for keeping that from you, but I hope the service I've done you this evening will allow you to accept it.'

'It's not the first challenge I have faced,' said Yaggit.

'We should go back up,' said Crome.

Now he'd recovered a little from the shock, Orc looked around the old kitchen for the chestnut leather box. He couldn't see it, nor could he find more than the faintest trace of the Kaybees' presence, but there was a dark taint in the room. He suddenly had the appalling sense that the dead held terrible secrets, that Sattrano's corpse might raise its head and speak something he needed to hear. Cass grabbed his arm and pulled him out into the basement passage.

'How could they do it?' said Aino as they climbed back up to the main hallway.

'We might have been easy to track,' said Yaggit. 'And their father is a magician.'

'But the reprisals Highcloud would have taken – that's why they allowed us to leave the college alive. What changed their minds?'

'The desire for revenge ate at them, I think,' said Crome as he shut the door behind them. 'Back to your work,' he said to the two gawking maids. 'All is well. Wetherall will go out and telephone for the police.'

'You could overhear their conversations?' Orc asked him. 'Word for word? Was that how you knew when they'd come?'

'Indeed.'

'Does that make him more skilled than you?' said Tashi.

'Tashi!' barked Cass.

'Ah, never fear,' said Crome. 'I already suspected there was more to Mister Strandborn than there seemed. Indeed, I'm relieved to find your skills are also known to the others. Openness is so refreshing after so much concealment. Now, I'm sure we could all do with a stiff drink while we await the servants of the law.'

They returned to the dining room. Crome offered whisky, which Orc alone accepted. 'So you Thangkarans have known about Mister Strandborn for some time?' Crome asked as he replaced the decanter.

'Since we first met, a few days ago,' said Yaggit. 'He has promised not to use any further magic, and, grateful though I am to you, I must ask you for the same undertaking. I have to say I'm surprised by your admiration for my order when we're so opposed to what you do.'

'Isn't it the same?' said Tashi. 'With you, it is called flight; with them, it is divination. Perhaps it shouldn't be what the Watchers do versus what others do, but what is done for good against what is done for evil.'

'And who is to judge that?' said Yaggit.

'It should be obvious,' said Tashi. 'This man could give us warning of other threats on our route to Highcloud, but you ask him to tie his hands behind his back.'

'You're saying the same as Hana,' said Aino. 'But we can't make our own laws of right and wrong. The rules are Gevurah's. Does that truly mean nothing to you any more? Tashi?'

Tashi poured table-wine into his glass. 'Why should it, Aino? Why should I, a child of Kurassian immigrants to the Kymeran coast, have anything to do with "Gevurah", as you Thangkarans call God?'

Aino bit his lip.

'Am I not dressed in similar fashion to Orc and Mister Crome?' said Tashi. 'Doesn't my face look more like theirs than yours?' He downed his wine in one long swallow, and turned to their host. 'I want to speak with you.'

Crome gave a hesitant nod, but Orc caught what seemed a flicker of excitement in his eye. 'Would you excuse us?'

When they'd gone, Cass said, 'We need to decide how much to tell Crome about the Shining Ones. Maybe he can discover something about them.'

'But – didn't you say he might be in contact with them?' said Yaggit.

'We got that wrong, clearly,' she said. 'But if they see him as a threat, they might attack him during his magic.'

'Then better he does none,' said Yaggit.

'Like Tashi said, that might not be the best course. We should warn him.'

'Are we sure we can trust him now?' said Orc. 'In my scape—'

'But you haven't scaped, have you?' she broke in. 'Not since you promised.'

'Oh – yeah, I meant…'

But he no longer knew what he meant, was no longer sure what was true, what was real. Crome's confession, Tashi's lie about his origins, his own concealment of having scaped, all swarmed and merged into a whirl in which reality and imagination could hardly be told apart. Even

Cass was in some kind of disguise, beautiful in her new dress but with the same familiar face and hair.

Her gaze locked with his, and he realised she wasn't wearing that blue dress after all, but her blood-slicked armour.

'Orc?'

'I think – I need to—'

'He's been feeling ill today,' she told the others. 'I'll get him to lie down.'

No matter how hard she held his arm as she led him out, Orc longed for her to grip harder, fearing he might otherwise fly apart and disintegrate. As they passed the doorway to the basement, he thought he could sense the air down there, the bodies lying, their blood fertilising the earth as his own had once done on a mountainside. Down there, in Hana's cellar, the creepers would be sprouting from the ground and the walls – he tried to shake the thought free, to push away the fear of them growing up the stairs towards him.

In his room, Cass lit the gas-lamp. He stared in alarm at the unfamiliar designs of ivy and vines on the wallpaper, then realised they were only geometric patterns.

She made him sit on his bed, but stayed on her feet. 'What do you need? What would help?'

'Nothing. Rest. I'll be okay.'

'I knew I shouldn't have agreed to you scaping. *Knew* it.'

'Maybe I could go back in and bring myself out again.'

'What?'

'Close it down properly. Bring back the part of me that's left down there.'

'Another scape? Is some stupid part of you trying to draw you back to her?'

'Of course not! I hate her.' It sounded weak even to him.

Cass leaned on the mantelpiece, staring down into the gas fire. 'When I came in with the iodine earlier, I didn't knock. Not at first. Only after I saw what you were doing.'

He shrank into the space between his shoulders. He put his face in his hands.

'Who were you with, Orc?'

'I don't know.'

'You don't *know*? Was it Hana?'

'Please, don't ask about it.'

'*What*?' She turned to him. 'What's real to you? Is *she* real? Is she here with us?'

'Who? Hana?'

'Hana, the Mother – they're the fucking same! She turned herself *into* the Mother. Isn't that what's making it worse?'

He couldn't answer. There was no answer.

'What was it like?' said Cass. 'With her, in that cellar?'

His skin crawled with the prescience of the creepers. 'You don't really want to know that.'

'I do,' Cass said. 'I want to know.'

He watched the blood seep from beneath her breastplate. Not real.

'I want to *know*, Orc.'

'It was… nice,' he said. 'It was easy.'

'Nice.' Her knuckles tightened. 'When we were in that bed together, I wanted you inside me like there was an itch a thousand miles deep and only you could reach it. I wanted you to reach that itch and scratch it and scratch it even if it never got better. I wanted you to make it *worse*. Do you understand that? It wasn't "nice", wasn't "easy". It was *real*, Orc. It was *dirty*. And it wasn't the first time. I could tell. We did it before, and other things.'

'You can't know that.'

'I know it in my guts, Orc. I know it in my *cunt*.'

He stared at her, shocked. She didn't let his eyes go. 'And you know it too. You ran off to Hana because you were afraid – you wanted something nice and easy, something your Voice of God couldn't argue with, and look where it's got you. Well fuck that. You remember that night in Bazantin? I asked if it mattered. Now I don't care if it matters or not.'

She unbuckled her armour. Her breastplate and gorget and segmented skirts clattered and clanged to the floor. The front of her dress was dark.

The blood looked real. Too real. Orc stood from the bed and stepped to her, unsure if he meant to help her or comfort her or something else. Her eyes searched his, questioning, challenging. He reached out to touch her hot belly, the blood of her wound, caused, he felt suddenly sure, by him: his dithering, his indecision, his failure to choose, when she – he saw this now – she was the only direction in which he should focus all his energies.

He'd become inert, passive, the Mother's rag doll. The extent of his decline horrified him.

He gathered his will, his focus. He put his hands on her shoulders and enfolded her, tightened his arms in a squeeze; and her moan in his ear, the hot, moist breath there told him he was doing it right even if it felt like a play-act, like something forced upon them. He gripped harder, buried into the softness of her hair.

He backed her against the wall. Her lips sucked his as though for the benefit of an audience. Her hands and then his own fought his jacket, his tie, his waistcoat, his collar, and all the time he tried to push away the insistence in the back of his mind, the growing, growling anger – not the Mother's but from on high, from a mountaintop, from the stars. He tried to refuse it. His shirt slithered floorwards. His back chilled except where her hot hands pressed into it. Wrath gathered faster behind him. *Fuck off*, he told it, *fuck off, you can't stop this now, you can't—*

Their kiss broke. He saw Cass's nose wrinkle, her distaste and puzzlement—

And in that moment a new perception smashed into him. They stood naked in a huge arena between curved black walls. He bent double as rage powered from the back of his brain. Lightning sparked, forced words through his throat.

'I FORBID IT, KAS—' His voice burned with the strain. 'UNDERSTAND ME?'

He staggered back from her. His muscles collapsed. He couldn't move or see, couldn't speak or call for help. Fury entombed him.

Then it was gone, and he briefly caught the smell of chemicals over rot. The lamplight returned.

He'd heard a door bang but wasn't sure when, wasn't sure how long he'd been lying there. He raised his head and the room swam. Cass had gone, and she shouldn't have – he needed to find her, to explain. He pulled his shirt on and picked up her breastplate and went out onto the landing. His movements felt light and fluid, his feet strangely out of connection with the floor. Down in the hall, a maid stood by the front door. She also wore a breastplate, though not as ornate as Cass's.

'The young lady ran outside, sir. Seemed in some distress. She ought not to have done that, sir.'

Outside. He remembered a name: Knightsbridge. She'd gone to find it. To find something real, to anchor him.

Park Crescent was deserted, but Gelder Street bustled despite the late hour. All the men and women, even the children, wore breastplates, and he couldn't remember if this had been true before. Many looked at him with unfriendly eyes.

As he passed a pub, one of a group drinking outside it called, 'Put it back on, man, for God's sake!'

'Put what on?'

'Your plate, man!'

He didn't understand. 'I'm trying to get to Knightsbridge.'

'Get back where you came from,' said another. 'We don't want your sort round here.'

'My sort?'

'Some kind of deviant, are you? Walking round with your plate off.'

'It's not mine. I'm looking for its owner, a young woman. She lost it.'

The men glanced at each other. 'You're pulling my leg,' said the first, his voice unsteady. 'There's a woman going round with her plate off?'

Others muttered uneasily, but one woman in the group said, 'I've sometimes wondered how that would feel.'

'Don't talk nonsense, Lucy.'

'What a thought to have!' said another woman. 'Makes my blood run cold.'

'Can't kill you, can it?' said Lucy. 'Didn't kill her, did it? The one whose plate he's got?'

'Lucy!'

'Just for a moment, Paul.' She stepped away, unbuckling the straps at her shoulders. 'Just to see.'

'Lucy, I swear I'll…'

She breathed out a long sigh as her breastplate fell away. Beneath, her dress and her corsets were already sodden, and now they split. Her belly protruded through, swollen, the skin moving as though with snakes or eels writhing inside her. Orc stepped back.

'Ohh!' the woman Lucy cried, and the sound carried on, drawn into a howl of pain or ecstasy. Some of the group edged away. The woman tore at her clothes; she squatted down and groaned, but her noise sounded now like pleasure. Orc covered his nose at the stink of shit. People cried out, began to move.

The woman sprang up and seized one of the men and tore his breastplate from him.

Orc fled with the rest. After fifty yards he glanced back, and seeing no pursuit, stopped. Another young man had stopped with him.

Outside the pub was what seemed a moving mound of naked bodies, a grotesque tangle of limbs and heads, a fusion that pulsated in the yellow gas-flame of the streetlamps. As Orc watched in shock, a man-like figure separated from the group, the torso and head of another somehow attached to him, and shambled into a shop across the road from the pub. Screams came; the creature emerged followed by two other people, their breastplates torn off, their clothes falling about them. They threw themselves into the mass.

'Bloody Lucy,' panted the man beside him. 'Paul never could keep her in hand. Put that back on, for God's sake!'

'I said, it's not mine.'

'You want that to happen to you? All that stuff inside, you want it to come out? You want that filth outside to get *in*?'

Orc didn't answer. The mess of what he was watching, the abandonment of it, pulled at something deep. The freeing of all restraint. How many times had he forbidden himself from even imagining what he and Cass might do together? More people joined the body-tangle from the surrounding buildings, throwing off their breastplates willingly, no longer needing to be corrupted by touch. Orc couldn't tell if the people who made up the mass of bodies were engaged in any sexual act, or just moving; he had no idea if those at the centre were now dead, the individual life crushed from them but their bodies kept in motion. He had a heightened sense of his own, his blood racing through his veins, air being pumped through his lungs by the sheet of muscle beneath.

He glanced at the breastplate, wondering if he should put it on after all, and saw that its inner surface was thick with Cass's blood. Points of nails stuck through the clotted mass, forming the letters that made up his name.

The young man's cry made him look up. The body-mass thrust out vegetative tentacles that arced through the air. When their ends hit the ground, they began to spread across the paving, turning it to mud and marsh. Even before the plant-growth was halfway to them, Orc felt the softening of the ground beneath his feet.

'The Cathedral!' cried the young man. 'Empyreus will tell us what to do. His Holy Mother will save us from that thing!'

He ran. Orc did the same, but quickly lost the man in the crowds of the next street. Panic had spread through the city. Looters smashed electric-lit shop windows. There were soldiers in full armour that looked like Tashi's possessed form. Vehicles the size of omnibuses ground past on circulating tracks, covered in battleship armour, guns as large as *Nightfire*'s protruding from their fronts. They crushed auto-carriages, cabs, screaming horses. Fires sprang up. Guns sounded. Something thundered overhead: a craft faster than a bullet, glimpsed as a black arrowhead against the under-lit clouds.

Orc fought his way from the source of the panic, feeling weirdly detached from the growing hysteria. To everyone who looked like they might listen, he asked where Knightsbridge was. Following the occasional hurried answer, he pushed against the press of people making for the Cathedral, and quickly found himself in less-populated areas. There was no paving here, only hard-packed earth. Many buildings were abandoned and covered with ivy. At last, when there was no one else around to ask, he looked back to where he'd come from, and his heart clenched with horror.

All the city in that direction had been levelled to rubble covered with ivy and grass, except for one vast structure, the Cathedral: shaped as a helmet, a thousand feet or more to the tip of its spire. A multitude clung to its exterior, at all heights, so that no space remained. Thousands of breastplates glinted in the fires from burst gas-pipes.

Facing it across the wasteland, the Mound now rivalled the Cathedral in height. It resembled less a joining of bodies than a single belly, swollen with pregnancy or bloated by malnutrition or corpse-gas. Nothing would stop its growth, Orc realised. All the world would become part of it. He felt strangely unafraid, as though a small shift of his mind was all that was needed to adjust to its inevitability. Not just horror, but a clutching thrill of awe.

'I am rather hoping,' came a voice at Orc's back, 'that you don't intend to join her.'

From the doorway of a half-demolished building emerged a tall, wasted-looking figure. Orc found it difficult to focus on, as details flickered and seemed to change; he thought he saw wings, and a golden head, before the image settled to become an emaciated man in a mustard-coloured checked jacket and a bowler hat.

'Of course not,' Orc said.

'But her gravity pulls you,' said the man, his jaw working with no apparent muscle beneath the skin. 'You really should put on that breastplate.'

'You don't have one.'

'I come from the World In Waiting, and am not in danger. But you are, and unlike this city, your destruction would be of some consequence. Put it on.'

'It's not mine,' said Orc. 'It belongs to Cass. Have you seen her?'

'Here? Of course not. Do you know where "here" is?'

'Bismark?' He knew as he said it that something had gone wrong.

'We are in the realm of Magoria,' said the man. 'It has taken a great deal of effort to bring myself here, to meet you – to warn you that you stand on the very edge of ego-disintegration.'

'Of what?'

'Death of the self. We always knew it might be potentially dangerous for someone lacking a strong identity to learn magic, but we thought your determination to recover your old identity would build a sense of self. It seems it wasn't strong enough. When we can examine what happened at the College of the Inner Eye, we shall know more.'

'At the Coll—?' He twigged. 'You're *them*?'

The man swept his hand and bent over it in an ironic bow. 'What might be called an avatar. There's no point attacking me!' he said, as Orc started towards him. 'You can do me no physical harm. And if you disrupt me, it might end your only chance of survival.'

Orc couldn't breathe. At last, the chance to talk with those responsible for his misery, to interrogate, to accuse. But everything clashed in his mind, and all he could think of to say was, 'Why? Why the Shroud?'

'That, of course, I cannot reveal. But in the interests of firming up your identity, I am willing to ease your confusion about your name. It is not Orc.'

'I know that.'

'Nor is it Oscar.'

Despite his hatred of this figure and those he represented, Orc kept quiet and listened.

'Fixing on the idea that your name relates to the branding on your wetsuit will not help you,' said Skull-face. 'But keep Orc for now. Put aside the possibility of replacing it. A name borne for two years is as good as any other.'

'If you want to firm up my identity,' said Orc, 'tell me what my relationship with Cass is.'

'I cannot.'

'Why? That can't be what the Shroud's meant to hide, can it? Or is it? Why that anger, when we kissed? Where does that come from? Is it really God?'

The bony mouth tightened. 'He is more real than any god. Fear him. Do not provoke him.'

'Is he one of you?'

'Avoid contact with him. You roused him tonight, as we think you must have done at the college. This time we were forced to intervene, and your weakened mental state pulled you here. We have spent too long in talk. Put on the breastplate. It was forged with the sacred fire, and that fire is what allows man to separate himself from Mother Night.'

Orc realised the ground had softened beneath his feet. The smell of salt and marsh, and rot and pollen, threaded through the air. He stared at the blood that the nails had pricked from Cass. It must have caused her so much pain.

'Come on!' Skull-face almost hopped with impatience, but showed no sign of sinking into the softening ground. 'You think Cass would want Her to claim you?'

'Tell me our names,' he said. 'And I'll put it on.'

'That would be too much.'

Orc felt the cool mud at his ankles. 'You need me to survive – you just told me. So tell me our names and I'll put it on.'

'You'd try to bluff me?'

Orc held out the breastplate to one side and dropped it onto the soft earth. 'Whatever.'

'Idiot!' fumed Skull-face. 'You cannot yourself tell how far you will take such a game of brinkmanship – there has grown in you now a subconscious desire for ego-destruction. Listen! We can help. We can work to eradicate your link with the Sun-King. But it will take time. You must fight the thoughts that attack you from the psychosphere. Put on the breastplate.'

'If you think there's a part of me that isn't bluffing, whether I know it or not, then you'd better give in.' The mud had now reached his calves. 'Tell me our names.'

Fury tightened skin over bone. 'I'll offer you something else. That photograph you keep with the transcripts: the apport, with your face obliterated. If I tell you where it was taken, will you put on the breastplate?'

The mud was at Orc's knees. He set his face to conceal how it made his guts crawl, its feel as it pushed up his trouser-leg and slurped against his skin. 'How do I know I can trust you?'

'Instinct should tell you I speak the truth. In these circumstances I cannot risk a lie.'

He was sinking an inch a second. The fact that Skull-face had offered him something so definite made him suspicious, but the Kaybees were perhaps genuinely rattled. A place-name would be a start: better than anything he and Cass had learned so far. 'Fine.'

'It was taken off an island named Kriti.'

'And where's that? Off which coast?'

'Find a map of the region, and it will be prominent,' said Skull-face. 'Now put that on.'

It was enough to go on, Orc thought.

The ground had become more liquid. Reeds grew from it. He was up to his waist now; his sinking liberated bubbles of rot-smelling gas. Quickly, he put on the breastplate; its straps seemed to buckle themselves, tightening it on him so his skin was pierced by the spikes that made up his name.

But not his real name. His real name wasn't even linked to his wetsuit, it turned out. Nothing he possessed had any tie to his true identity.

Mud came to his chest; he had to hold his arms up to keep them free. All around him was only wetland: no Skull-face, no Cathedral, no Mound. Nothing solid beneath his feet. The mud rose cool to his neck.

He breathed in just before it covered his face.

The spikes pierced deeper towards his heart as he sank, but the pain grew less, became numbed, as numb as the slow sensation of falling towards the centre of the earth, towards the reality that danced at the heart of all realities: the Serpent Mandala. He sensed the breastplate corroding. His body's interior, his organs, would merge with the mud, would never again be separable.

He opened his mouth against the mud, and with the breath held in his lungs he shouted a cry for help.

It made no noise that he could hear.

PART THREE
LIONS HILL

18

COLLABORATORS

Cass took some pride from the fact that the policemen had seemed surprised at her strength. But that strength had now bled out in her struggles with the jacket, and her anger had banked down to a core she didn't dare rouse – afraid partly of the renunciates employed as wardens, but mostly of Doctor Vloss, the white-coated medicine man with his speculum.

'If she continues to display agitation, I'll prescribe a sedative. Be sure to keep her under observation.'

And they had. Not ten minutes passed when the viewing-port in the door of her room didn't bang, robbing her of even the faint hope of sleep. Sometimes she thought of saying something, but she was wary of a heated exchange that might lead to a diagnosis of hysteria. If that happened, she'd been gloatingly informed, she wouldn't be released, but treated. She had to hang on, to keep calm, to freeze herself inside. And try not to struggle, and try not to let the jacket remind her of being held down by Esteban, of being tied up on the fishing-boat. And try not to dwell on the fantasy that she might transform her frustrated fury into a being of rage and hate like Red Tashi, a monster who would burst her jacket, destroy the prison and stuff Doctor Vloss's speculum where the sun didn't shine. That would show him 'emotional incontinence'.

It was perhaps two in the morning when the door opened and a warden entered, the thin one with the tight-curled hair and the cheekbones so high they seemed about to push her eyes closed. She admitted an inmate: a few years older than Cass, her hair cut unusually short, her soft round face marked by dark slashes of eyebrows. She wore the same kind of sackcloth dress Cass had on under the straitjacket.

'Seems the hotel's overbooked tonight,' the newcomer said, as the locks clattered behind her. 'Anything new in the library?' She looked at the notices and cuttings displayed on the wall, which Cass had read earlier from of boredom: tracts published by the Women's League for Health; extracts from the Book; reprinted news-reports of horrors visited on women who'd dressed inappropriately in places they shouldn't have ventured. Cass found something about the newcomer niggled a faint sense of recognition. She couldn't help thinking that if the other woman were in some other clothing, she might know her.

'What did they get you for?' said the other, dumping herself onto the hard chair.

'No escort,' said Cass.

'First arrest?'

'Yeah. I forgot the rules.' Or had been in too much of a state to think clearly. 'I've just got here, from Kymera. I only went outside for a few minutes, for some air—' as if that would have calmed the scream inside her – 'but I ran into the police. Turns out they think a girl being outside after dark is more important than investigating people being shot dead.'

'Sounds about right,' said the other. 'Kymera… yes, you do have some colour in your complexion. And some fire in your blood, by the look of things.'

'The jacket?' said Cass. 'Nice to think they're scared of me, I guess.'

'If they were scared of you, you'd be in a proper cell. That's to teach you a lesson.'

'It's taught me to use my brains more. Putting up a fight was stupid.' She shouldn't be talking about it, she realised: the anger was flaring again, and it would only wear her out or get her into more trouble. 'I'm Cass, by the way.'

'Dinah. They fined you?'

She nodded. 'Our host has already paid it. They said he can collect me at eight.' It still annoyed her that Crome hadn't pressed harder for them to release her at once. And what had he meant about Orc falling ill?

'Make sure you seem contrite,' said Dinah, 'or they might change their mind.'

Shouldn't have left him, she thought. Shouldn't have left him but couldn't have stood any more, his sickness, his wavering reality, that hideous voice that had burst from him. *I forbid it, Cass.* And why hadn't she gone into the bloody garden instead of rushing out into the street? Teeth dug her lip. She didn't know if she would ever get him back now. Bloody shamanistic magic. If Geist had been here, she would have torn him apart, Hana too, fuck all of them, 'Fuck it, *fuck it*.'

'Don't,' said Dinah, leaning forward from her chair. 'If they diagnose, they'll operate. It happened to a friend of mine. Breathe deep, slow.'

Like before freediving. Cass nodded. Calmness. Deep, blue water.

'I'll say one thing,' said Dinah. 'If you're a police plant, you're very convincing.'

'What? Why would I be a plant?'

'To get information from deviants. I was in a club they raided. They're clamping down. Something's got them rattled.'

'What kind of club?'

Dinah gave her a wry smile. 'The kind the authorities feel obliged to raid when they're rattled. But the morning will come for me, same as for everyone.' She crossed her arms and leaned back against the wall and closed her eyes. 'And it'll come sooner if we sleep.'

'No chance of that,' said Cass.

'You'd be surprised,' murmured Dinah, 'even in that thing.'

Cass lay back, unconvinced. Within a minute, Dinah's breathing had softened and slowed. She didn't even wake the next time the viewing door banged. Cass passed an irritating hour of waiting and listening to

Dinah's escape from boredom – and then, somehow, she opened her eyes to find the uncurtained window pale with the first signs of dawn.

She wriggled herself onto her feet and looked out. The cell was on the first floor, overlooking the courtyard of the facility. The small window had been locked open, and cool air came freely from the world of brick buildings and chimneys and spires dim against the paling smoke and cloud. This was the day they were due to leave for a monastery of magic-hating monks. Memories of the previous evening pricked her. What else might the Watchers find out, apart from the fact that she and Orc were as magic as people got?

No, Highcloud was out of the question. She had to get Orc to the college in Sundara. Somehow. And despite what anyone else planned.

The door opened. 'You,' said the warden with the cheekbones, her gaze fixed on Dinah. 'Come on.'

'Early this time,' said Dinah, blinking herself awake.

'Where are they taking you?' said Cass.

'Same place as usual,' said Dinah, with apparent cheer. 'Good luck,' she added as she left.

Trying to not imagine the more unsettling possibilities behind Dinah's answer, Cass remained standing by the window. Two hours till her release, assuming Crome came. She wondered if she would be able to hold off needing to pee until then – she didn't relish the challenge of using the pot without the use of her arms, though it must be possible. There wasn't much to divert her – little traffic in the street beyond the courtyard's high paling, and few pedestrians. After a while, however, she noticed two women walk from the facility's entrance and across the courtyard to the gate, both dressed in the kind of long skirts and jackets that seemed regular daytime wear for well-to-do Bismark women. The shorter one, she soon realised, was Dinah. So she'd been released. And the tall, almost white-blonde lady with her…

Panic clutched her insides – the opportunity, and the dread that she would miss it.

'Dinah!' she yelled out of the window. But the wind must have taken her voice away: the two showed no sign of hearing.

'*Dinah*!'

Dinah turned, and so did Emilia Astrasis. The former raised her hand in a tentative wave.

Behind Cass, the door groaned open.

'I know Yaggit!' she shouted, as footsteps sounded on the cell floor. 'I can help!'

She jerked from the window as a hand pulled her shoulder.

'None of that!' said the warden with the cheekbones.

Cass struggled, off-balance, desperate to get back to the window; she didn't know if Emilia would have heard her. 'Get your paws off me!'

The warden held fast. 'That's it. Hysteria.'

'No!' shouted Cass. 'That's fucking ridiculous!'

The warden stepped back, took a whistle from around her neck and blew two short blasts and one long.

'Wait.' Cass tried to force herself calm, seeing the danger. 'I'm not hysterical, look. I'm not.'

The warden's face was grimly determined, satisfied. It came to Cass that the woman was waiting for her to beg.

'Look, it's over.' She crushed down anger and panic. 'I'm calm, honest. I just… I just don't like being touched.'

'I saw the dress you were brought in wearing,' said the warden. 'I'm sure you've been *touched* enough to be used to it.'

A second warden, with a flattened nose, wheeled a chair in. At the sight of the straps for the ankles, Cass started to tremble. Her bladder felt suddenly at its limit. She squeezed her legs together.

'I need the toilet.'

'Hysterical urination,' said Cheekbones. 'It will be noted as a symptom.'

There was no hope of fighting them off. Cass had no choice but to let them strap her into the chair. Sitting down eased the need to pee, a little.

'I'm being collected at eight,' she said, calmly as she could, as the two wheeled her out.

'Not,' said Flat-nose, 'if the doctor thinks you pose a threat to public order.'

'Or *pubic* order,' said Cheekbones, and both wardens laughed.

Sweat dampened Cass's sackcloth dress as they took her along to the lift. She fought to keep her limbs from shaking. She probed the frightening idea that now might be the time to find out if she could manifest something. From what she knew of Tashi's experience, there must be deep wells of rage and hate somewhere in the psychosphere; if she could use her own anger to connect with it, draw it through herself to transform… it was desperate and untried and might be the biggest mistake ever, but she would not let Doctor Vloss do anything to her. She hoped enough time had passed since her admittance for him to have gone off duty and been replaced by someone more human.

They didn't take her to the admittance block where she'd been examined previously, but to a pair of double doors on the ground floor marked MEDICAL WING. The smell of carbolic soap stung her nostrils. An orderly behind a desk asked for Cass's arrest report. 'On its way,' said Flat-nose.

The orderly began to fill out a form. 'She doesn't seem hysterical.'

At last, thought Cass. *Please.*

'I've submitted the request,' said Flat-nose. 'She has to be examined.'

'Oh, she'll be examined,' said the orderly.

'Is Doctor Vloss still on duty?' said Cheekbones.

The orderly glanced at the clock. 'It's the end of his shift. But I'm sure he'll stay on for a case like this.'

'Good,' said Cheekbones. 'He's *very* thorough.' She looked beneath the wheelchair; Cass guessed what for. She squeezed her pelvic muscles tighter. If they made her wet herself, she would manifest whatever she could connect with. She remembered Tashi's hideous mask, the instruments of torture in place of his fingers. She would have to hope she retained more control than he had.

Feet sounded, hard soles on floor tiles. 'Morning, Matron,' said Flat-nose.

Cass turned in the chair. A renunciate in a different uniform strode up, her broad face soured and lined by a scowl. 'Forget it,' she said, slapping a paper folder on the orderly's desk. 'The Deaconess has filed another B-11.'

Cass didn't understand, hardly dared hope.

'She can't keep doing this,' protested Flat-nose.

'If she wants them released into the Holy Mother's care, it's not for us to argue,' said Matron.

'And is her brother aware, do you think?' said Cheekbones.

'That's not for here.' Matron turned away. 'Get her processed. The stink of privilege is making me gag.'

In the discharge section, Cass was allowed to wash and use the toilet – she almost groaned with relief. As well as the clothing she'd been arrested in, she was given a coat to go over the top: she recognised it as the one Dinah had been wearing.

Dinah was waiting outside, hugging herself against the morning chill. Cass felt close to breaking down as she saw her. 'How can I thank you?'

'By not dawdling,' said Dinah. 'The auto's just along the street.'

It looked the same as the one Cass had seen at the air-field, though this had no little metal flag. Dinah opened the door to the passenger compartment, with its curtained windows. Emilia Astrasis sat on the leather bench-seat, facing forwards. Cass sat opposite, her back to the driver's compartment. A bag on the seat next to her seemed to contain a bundle of black leather, perhaps a coat. Dinah sat next to Emilia and pulled the door shut.

'I'm sorry, I don't know how to address a Deaconess,' said Cass, as the auto pulled away. 'Or how to thank one.'

'Don't you?' said Emilia – looking uncomfortable, Cass thought. 'I received the impression you know very well.'

'I had to speak to you,' said Cass. 'You know who I am?'

'I recognise you now.' She had a soft, smooth voice: no louder than necessary, as though she were afraid of being overheard. 'But you should have known nothing of my contact with Yaggit. How many others do?'

'The five of us you saw at the palace. No one else.'

'Dare I ask on what matter you believe I approached him?'

'He hasn't said.'

'Of that, at least, I am glad,' said Emilia, with a tone that might almost have been borrowed from an older, grander woman.

'Wait.' Dinah glared at Cass. 'You said you could help. Why did you say that if you don't know what they talked about?'

Cass's heart bumped in her chest. She had to be careful, to keep all her wits sharp, to fight against the effects of lack of sleep and her ordeal. On the island, she'd reversed Hana's initial antagonism and recruited her help; she had to do the same here.

'It's something to do with Yaggit's ability, his "flight", isn't it?'

'What leads you to say so?' said Emilia.

'No one in the Empyreum can practice divination, apart from the three magic boys Empyreus talks to. There's something you need to find out, and only a Watcher of Highcloud can do it.'

Emilia's eyes might have been made of marble for all they revealed. 'Leaving aside whether that's true, how could you help? I don't need you to act as go-between. Unless... do you have some influence over him?'

Disguised hope had crept into her tone, almost desperation.

'He won't do it,' Cass said. 'I've heard as much.' Her stomach sank with the size of the risk she knew she must now take. 'I know of alternatives,' she went on. 'Other people with the same talent.'

Emilia's pale blue gaze studied her. 'Flight?'

'Similar.' Cass braced herself as the auto turned a corner. 'They journey into a mental space. They connect with all the information that's ever made up the world. There's a whole college of them.' Her heart was racing. 'In Jiata.'

'Sundara?' blurted Dinah.

Cass fixed her gaze on Emilia, trying for steadiness. 'And you know an air-craft pilot.'

They both drew breath. 'What makes you say so?' said Dinah.

'I saw you. The evening before last.'

'That was you?' said Dinah. 'By the fence?'

Cass gasped as recognition flashed into her mind. A short, round-faced man with a full, a *false*, moustache. 'You're the driver!'

'Hush!' said Emilia. 'I beg you.'

'I can't *drive*,' said Dinah. 'I'm a woman.'

'This talk is over,' said Emilia.

Dinah leaned across at once, slid back the glass partition and gave the driver Crome's address.

'Listen, please.' Cass's racing blood felt suddenly weak. 'Whatever it was you wanted Yaggit to find out, it must be important if you risked coming to our house and getting me released. The people at the college can do it. They have more ability even than Yaggit.'

'Did you not hear me?' said Emilia.

Cass gripped the edge of the leather seat as she sat back, jaw set with frustration. This might be her one chance to get herself and Orc to Sundara: she couldn't afford to fail. Neither could she afford to antagonise the one person on whom the plan rested. But every time she thought of saying something during the rest of the journey, Dinah seemed to know she was building up to it and shot her a look that strangled words. Emilia stared through the thin gap at the side of the curtain, never once turning from it.

When the auto pulled up, Dinah said to Cass, 'You'd better keep that coat for now, to stop you getting arrested on your way to the door. I'll collect it later.'

Cass thought her caution excessive, but it made no odds to her. 'Can I just ask,' she said to Emilia, 'is your brother having us watched?'

'No.' She turned at last. 'He had you followed to confirm the address, but neither the police nor the secret service can spare any surveillance men at the moment. Otherwise I should never have come here.' She turned back to the gap in the curtain. 'I wish now that I had not.'

Cass opened the door. 'Well, thanks for getting me out of that place.'

Emilia nodded.

'And please,' Cass said, 'think about it. It might be your only chance to get what you want.'

Dinah almost pushed her out.

Cass watched the auto drive off, furious with irritation at Emilia's refusal. Then her thoughts turned to Orc and what she would say to him about the previous night, and vice versa. It had been completely misjudged, horrible. She didn't think she could bear to talk about it, but they couldn't carry on as if nothing had happened.

She knocked. Crome himself answered. His eyebrows rose.

'They released me early,' said Cass. 'Overcrowding. Are we still off this morning?'

'No,' said Crome.

'But—'

'The travel papers I requested have been delayed. But we have some extra time in any case. Not half an hour ago, word came of the cancellation of the enquiry. Prelate Astrasis might still wish to speak with you in private, but I've written to him suggesting this be postponed until Orc's recovery.'

'Recovery? He really is ill?'

'Seriously so, I'm afraid. If he doesn't improve soon, we'll have to take him to hospital.'

She was already rushing up the stairs. As she entered Orc's room, a maid stood from her chair next to the bed. Orc lay in pyjamas with his skin damp, hair messed from sweat and from moving against the now-stained pillow.

'He's been like this all night?' Her voice choked.

'We found him when we came to tell him you'd been arrested,' said Crome, who'd followed her in. 'We haven't been able to wake him since. Has he suffered anything like this before?'

'I'm not sure.' There had been Daroguerre's psychic trap on the island, from which she and Hana had freed him. But the way he looked now reminded her more of Jorik.

'Could I speak to you alone?'

Crome sent the maid down to the kitchen. When the door had closed after the girl, Cass said, 'You might be able to help him. This, what's happened to him, it's magical, psychic.'

His face revealed neither surprise nor anything else. 'Caused by?'

'It could be a couple of things. Can *you* do the kind of magic that affects others? The kind that could help him?'

'I've never tried before today, but in fact I've already attempted something similar this morning, for Tashi. He's persuaded me to try to help his master's soul.'

That answered the question of what Tashi had wanted to speak to Crome about. Then she realised the danger. 'Wait – his *master*'s soul?'

'Yes, Miss Strandborn. He has told me his true identity. And everything else.'

She couldn't speak. Everything...

'But fear not,' said Crome. 'I won't betray his secret, nor yours, just as I'm sure you won't betray mine.' He eyed her with something like curiosity and greed. 'Fascinating, to learn of his bodily transformation. We can all put on acts, of course, adapt our clothing or manner to suit those we wish to please or attract. But to change the body itself is a remarkable possibility. Have you never thought of trying it? I mean no insult to your current appearance, but you could become a great beauty, gain patronage, have any door opened to you.'

'It's not as easy as that,' said Cass, though in truth it had never occurred to her. 'And this isn't helping Orc.'

'Then you must allow me to return to my work. The sooner I make progress with Shoggu, the sooner I can attend to your cousin.'

She tried to shake off her panic. 'You don't think helping the living is more important?'

'Than saving a soul from Hell?' said Crome.

'You can't even know Shoggu's soul is out there to be found.'

'Nor do I know it isn't. Orc doesn't seem to have deteriorated overnight. We'll see how things go. I believe Yaggit has made one attempt to help him. You might ask him to try again.'

Cass nodded, resigned to getting no further. 'Could you ask him to come up?'

When Crome had gone, she sagged onto the chair and turned to the face she'd been afraid to look at. She pulled back the coverlet, unbuttoned Orc's pyjama jacket and placed her hand on his damp chest. His heartbeat tremored up through her palm: rapid, not that of a sleeper. Like his heart was burning up, racing to exhaust itself.

'I'm sorry,' she said, afraid she might break down and beg. 'I shouldn't have said those things last night. If you're not ready to make your choice, don't.'

She took his hand. Even that felt illicit. There was no response in his fingers. She tried to clear her mind, and slowly, softly, sought a trace of smell that wasn't Orc, that might tell her what she was dealing with. Just before storming out the previous evening, she'd caught a trace of the hospital smell that meant the Kaybees. But there had also been a more complex scent, incense and old paper, a fugitive memory.

She could find neither of those now, only a faint trace of crushed leaves and humid rot.

'If I can get off the ground, I'll be free of her, I'm sure of it.'

Her intuition agreed with Orc's. He needed an air-craft to escape the Mother.

There had to be some way to persuade Emilia, if she could find her again. She closed her fingers with Orc's and gripped his hand hard, as though to hurt him enough to wake him. Then she noticed his focus-stone – she'd become so familiar with the sight of it, it had almost become invisible, but now she understood its possible significance.

The stone intensified his connection with the Otherworld.

Gently as she could, she lifted his head from the pillow and eased off the pendant. She took his hand again, watching in vain for change.

A knock came on the door. She detached herself, slipping the stone into a coat pocket.

'Yaggit,' she said as he entered. 'Crome said you tried to help him last night?'

'I conducted a brief flight, hoping to learn the nature of his ailment,' said Yaggit. 'I even burned some of our herbs, but to no effect. I discovered nothing for certain, though during flight I gained a faint impression of wandering, lost, through a place encroached upon by vegetation.'

She nodded at this. 'He needs to get off the ground.' She drew breath and committed herself. 'Emilia Astrasis wants you to find something for her in flight, doesn't she?'

Yaggit's dark eyes hardened. 'That is between us.'

'Oh, come on. I talked to her this morning. She was on the edge of telling me. If it's something she wants badly enough, and we can give it to her, she might be able to help us get an air-craft.'

'There's no need,' said Yaggit. 'You know the enquiry has been cancelled? We can leave, even by railway. We'll find some way across the border. I'm sure we can solve the problem of transporting Orc, if he doesn't recover before we set off. And I'm sure that getting closer to the Holy Mountain will help free him from the Witch Mother. She has no place there.'

'But the air-craft would help him quicker. And get us there faster.'

'I cannot give Miss Astrasis what she wants.'

'Then we'll trick her.'

'Falsehood?'

'Why not? You were happy to trick the Prelate – you went along with the lies we told him. Was that any different?'

He dipped his head in thought, then sighed. 'She wishes to come to Highcloud and be taught flight.'

'She wants to become a *Watcher*?'

'No, merely to journey in the Immaterium.' Yaggit's mouth twisted in discomfort. 'The Abbot could never agree to such a thing, of course, but I let her believe that he would do so if she helped us. As Deaconess of the Holy Mother, she might be able to gain me access to the Hall of Wisdom, and getting that close to the Head of Empyreus might help my mission enormously. So you see, it was already in my mind to trick her, Gevurah forgive me.'

'What did you actually say to her?'

'To start with, I suggested it would be natural for the Deaconess to visit the place of Empyreus's supposed conception. She could make a pilgrimage to the Holy Mountain, and use it as cover to put her case to the Abbot. She left excited by the idea, but yesterday she told me her brother had refused to allow it. Then she asked a pilot she knows if he would bear her anyway. I believe you and Orc witnessed the result. I asked her if there might be some way of persuading this pilot, for I saw that Orc was right about an air-craft being our ideal means of departure. She hinted that there was one thing that might persuade him, but she wouldn't tell me what.'

'More secrecy. Just what we need.'

'Then she pressed me as to the likelihood of the Abbot agreeing. She wanted a guarantee, or at least a promise to strive my utmost on her behalf. I couldn't maintain my pretence without lying, and had to end the interview. But you have no such moral constraints.'

'Thanks.'

'If *you* tell her the Abbot will agree, will she believe you?'

'Doubtful,' said Cass, her mind already busy with how to keep Highcloud out of it.

Yaggit sighed. 'I'll need to talk to him about her. She'll be the first subject on a long list.'

An idea leapt to Cass's mind. She could hardly speak with the excitement of it. 'Why don't you go back to Highcloud now?'

'Alone?'

'With Aino. Your charter will get you through the border. Talk to your Abbot about Emilia and whatever else, and come back. I'll look after Orc in the meantime. Even when he comes out of this, he'll be weak for a while. You can travel a lot quicker without us.'

Yaggit's brow creased. 'That is no bad idea.'

'Did Emilia give you any means of contacting her?'

'The Red Café, on Brandt Street. A waiter there, Matthias, can relay a message. Will you try to persuade her?'

'Yes. Who knows, maybe we'll get to Highcloud before you do.'

'May Gevurah make it so,' said Yaggit.

As the door clicked behind the departing Watcher, Cass exhaled with relief. That rather neatly dealt with the problem that the Thangkarans would want the air-craft to go to Highcloud rather than Sundara. She just needed to get Emilia on board with the plan – and knowing what Emilia wanted now put her in a much better position to persuade her.

She knelt next to Orc and took his hand. This time, it half-clutched hers. 'Hang in there,' she whispered. 'Just a few hours, and she'll have no more hold on you. I promise.'

19

FLIGHT PLAN

She still had the money she'd taken from Crome's desk the day before. After finding the maid and sending her back to Orc, she changed into her other dress and shawl, Dinah's coat over the top, and slipped out of the house. She was halfway to Gelder Street, aiming to find a ride to the Red Café, when a two-seater cab pulled up next to her. She was about to ask the driver if he were free when she saw Dinah inside.

'You've come for your coat?' Cass said.

'No, for you. We're going to the Cathedral. I want you to talk to Emilia again.'

Cass wasted no time getting in. 'She's changed her mind?' she asked as the cab lurched off.

'I'm to say nothing,' responded Dinah, and stuck to that for the entire journey.

Cass wondered if the Cathedral would look familiar – if she'd lived in Bismark, she must have known it well – but no flicker of recognition came from the sight of its lead-sheathed spire and twin square towers. After quitting the cab in a deserted courtyard, Dinah ushered Cass through a small side-entrance, then along a dim passage. She stopped at a door.

'The Chapel of the Holy Mother,' she whispered, leading the way through into a vaulted space. On a dais near the end, the carved figure of a woman lay on a bier. Four knight-statues stood at its corners, heads bowed, their swords angled so their points met above the woman's chest. Flowers and candles surrounded the display.

'Look like a guard of honour, don't they?' muttered Dinah, sounding more irritated than reverent. 'But those swords would conveniently stop her getting up, if she were real.' They skirted the pews, occupied by mostly well-dressed women kneeling and praying, to another door, after which came climbing, a lot of it, up narrow spiral stairs. They were both breathing hard by the top, where the stair led onto a narrow balcony on one of the cathedral towers. Emilia stood leaning against the parapet, almost over it, the wind whipping her pale hair about her head. Cass's throat tightened with the length of the drop.

Emilia straightened, turned. 'Thank you for coming.'

'I know what it is you want,' said Cass. 'It's not to have Yaggit find something out for you. You want to do it yourself.'

The polite smile vanished. 'He shouldn't have told you.'

'Lucky for you he did. He also told me the Watchers won't teach you – ever.'

'Then how am I "lucky"?'

'Because I know there's nothing unique about what they do,' said Cass. 'And if you have the ability, that college I mentioned could teach you.'

'If they are neither Watchers nor Trine,' said Emilia, 'then it is forbidden magic.'

'Forbidden why?' said Cass. 'The process is the same.'

'Without purity of intent, the mind is endangered,' said Emilia. 'In any case, is it true flight that these people in Jiata practise? Do they… in this "mental space", as you put it earlier… do they travel above the ground, like though a bird?'

A tremble had entered her voice. 'I'm not sure,' said Cass, puzzled as to why the detail should matter. 'But if you're worried about danger, yes, magic *is* dangerous, the traditional kind. It confuses reality and imagination – it relies on that confusion. But there's a better way, a more rational way. Scientific, even.'

She held Emilia's gaze. If she ever had to be a saleswoman, it was now. 'A psychic researcher put me onto it, a Kurassian like you.' She'd rehearsed Ferman's theory for most of the cab-ride. 'The world of matter is connected spatially, yes? Atoms touching each other. But the invisible world, the one the Watchers call the Immaterium, the world of thought and memory – that's connected *thematically*. Billions of particles of information, like library index cards, all linking to others. It all works on connections. We perceive physical structures by sight and touch, but we need other senses to perceive these information structures, because it's not our conscious minds that make the connections, it's deeper than that.'

'Index cards,' said Emilia flatly.

'Conceptually, yes. Magicians and shamans don't see it like that, of course, and that's the danger. They need to create filters for the information: Otherworld creatures and talking animals and so on. And to make it work, they have to convince themselves the Otherworld is real, that imagination and thought and matter are all as real as each other – and that's why they can go mad. But there's no reason someone with training and talent couldn't interrogate the psychosphere without all that. You don't need to believe the Otherworld is real – you just need to believe in your own ability to connect and retrieve this information.'

'And this is what you offer me?' said Emilia. 'Magician as librarian?'

Cass tried to not let Emilia's tone deflate her. 'The same results,' she said, 'but without the risk of madness. Isn't that a beautiful idea?'

'You talk of beauty.' Emilia turned back to look out over the city. 'The Watcher dons a mantle made of feathers,' she intoned, as though quoting from somewhere. 'Pinions of the lammager, the bonebreaker bird. From his high cell in the mountains, he takes wing over the lower world.' Her body seemed to strain from her waist, out and over the parapet.

'But I said, the Watchers won't teach you,' said Cass. 'It isn't an option.'

'Isn't it worth considering, Em?' said Dinah.

'To give up home and position so I can spend my life sorting through invisible index cards?'

'Position?' said Dinah. 'Your brother made you Deaconess to give him a hold over you.'

'And that rank has served *you* more than once!' snapped Emilia. She turned to Cass. 'Have you proof that this "rational magic" works?'

'The concept is sound. The college in Jiata is the perfect place to develop it.'

'*Concept*? You mean it's still untried?'

'It's a new idea – like I said, a more scientific one.'

'I apologise for your wasted journey,' said Emilia. 'If you owed me any debt for this morning, consider it repaid.' She turned away. 'Dinah, take her home.'

'No!' said Cass. 'No, please, you can't send me away again! I need your help.'

'Sorry,' said Dinah, pushing her gently towards the door.

'Wait!' she cried at Emilia. 'Please, listen – my cousin's in a horrible magical sleep: his life might depend on it.'

Dinah stopped pushing. Her hand tightened on Cass's shoulder.

Emilia turned and came to her, her eyes fierce either side of her bladelike nose. '*What* did you say?'

'My cousin,' said Cass, surprised at their reaction. 'He's in a magical sleep, and I don't know what will help him apart from the air-craft. And I need to get him to this college in Jiata. I know it's nothing to you, but I'm desperate.'

'How did he fall into this sleep?' Emilia's voice strained with intensity.

'He left too much of himself in the Otherworld, I think. Or that's one way of looking at it.'

'He touched a crystal?'

'Uh… one of the air-craft ones, you mean?'

'You know about those? But no. No matter.' Emilia turned away. But Cass knew she'd got close to something. She had to pursue it.

'He *has* touched a crystal. And it did connect him deeper with the Otherworld. Is that what you were asking?'

Emilia turned a dangerous look on her. 'What manner of crystal?'

'This one.' Cass took it out from the coat pocket.

Emilia cried aloud. Dinah said, 'Let me see!' and grabbed Cass's hand. She stared at the focus-stone for a moment, then turned to Emilia and shook her head.

'Where did you get that?' Emilia's voice quavered.

'I said, it belongs to my cousin. He's had shamanic training.'

'And he's in a magical sleep because he touched this?'

'Not as such,' said Cass. 'This isn't dangerous itself, I think. A friend of ours has another,' she went on, casting out bait in the hope of more firmly hooking Emilia's surprising interest. 'She's at another college, like the one in Jiata.'

'But where did your cousin get this?' said Emilia. 'Where did your friend get hers?'

'Their teacher. They had the same one.'

'His name?'

'Geist.'

The two women both visibly stiffened.

'You… you don't *know* him?' said Cass, feeling almost wobbly with the idea. 'You're not one of his students too?'

'If I were, I'd have a stone like this, would I not?' said Emilia. 'But I assure you that I lack such a thing. Now go and let me think. You too, Di.'

'Absolutely not,' said Dinah. 'We need to talk about this. I don't want to leave you here to have your thoughts poisoned by—'

'I am Deaconess of the Holy Mother!' snapped Emilia. 'Be careful what you say. And in this place at least, you will obey me.' She turned back to the parapet. 'I'll see you at lunch.'

Dinah exhaled. 'Come on,' she said, pressuring Cass's shoulder again. 'Coffee.'

* * *

She explained nothing until they were tucked into a quiet corner on the first floor of the Red Café. 'You've brought me hope, Cass,' she said then. 'Hope of change. But Emilia's balanced on a knife-edge, and I'm worried that anything you or I might say or do could make her fall the wrong way.'

'You think she should come to Sundara, then?'

'Without a doubt.' Dinah looked out over the wide boulevard of Brandt Street. 'I'd better start at the beginning, and then you'll understand why. Em and I have known each other since we were children, since before she developed her mental disturbance. That started in her teens. Her mother had the same thing at times, from what I gather. She died from complications after Emilia's birth. The younger son, Siegfried, was five at the time; he took her death very hard. I'm not sure he ever forgave Emilia for being born. They don't get on.'

'I saw,' said Cass, remembering the Prelate's secretary's office. 'You said "younger son"?'

'There's another, Bastian.' Dinah stirred a sugar-lump into her coffee. 'Two years Siegfried's elder. Emilia and he were devoted to each other. It was he who brought in a rather eccentric doctor when Emilia began to get ill, after the usual doctors' treatments had only made things worse. Where Bastian found this man we had no idea, but he persuaded Emilia's father, the High Prelate at the time, to let him treat her. This doctor spent a lot of time shut up with Emilia, over weeks and weeks. And she got better. The treatment renewed her life, and her joy. She told me he'd taught her to fly, and when I asked her what she meant, all she gave me by way of explanation was a mischievous smile. It was only later that I found out.'

'Geist,' said Cass. 'He taught her shamanism?'

'Yes. It sounds incredible to me even now, that a member of the Empyreal nobility should be instructed in such a thing. But it perhaps saved her sanity.'

'Eagle?' said Cass, not sure which she feared most, confirmation or denial.

Dinah nodded.

So Orc had been right. Otter, Hare, Eagle – which meant Sparrow and Fox were probably waiting in the wings somewhere. The five creatures from the myth of the Fire Stealers, along with Geist's own animath, Raven. But for what purpose? What scheme had the old bastard hoped to set in motion?

'A couple of years later,' Dinah went on, 'Bastian went to Golgomera: to search for Wilhelm Kirrus's body, some said. Nothing was heard of him for well over a year, and then colonists found him, alone, somewhere near the coast – half-mad with the Bane, but clutching a pouch of strange crystals.'

'Blue? Focus-stones?'

'No, Emilia already had hers,' said Dinah. 'These were the others. You know about those, I think?'

'Used for the elementals? Yes.'

'Whether they had anything to do with Wilhelm Kirrus's body, no one seems to know – at least, Emilia doesn't. Amazingly, Bastian had resisted the Bane enough to keep himself together, but the effort of will exhausted him, and he needed constant reassurance of who he was. No one knew how to contact Geist, or even if we should. The High Prelate became ill with worry, and Bastian was far too sick to carry out religious duties, so Siegfried took on the position. He also took charge of the crystals.'

'And used them in his machines.'

'Later, he did. He understood one of Empyreus's vaguer pronouncements as a covert message intended for him, to give him his blessing, and the possible connection with Kirrus persuaded those who knew about the crystals that they were holy. He also said Bastian should be kept away from them for his own good. But Bastian had other ideas, it seemed. He grew frantic with searching for them, not knowing where Siegfried kept them. One night, after a particularly bad spell, he came to Emilia's room. She told me afterwards she woke with him leaning over her, looking like a sleepwalker. She froze with fear. His hand went down inside the neck of her nightdress and took out her pendant, the blue crystal Geist had given her. When Bastian closed his hand fully round it, he gasped and pulled so hard the chain snapped. Then he backed into a corner of the room and sat there, clutching the stone – like a frightened or greedy child, Emilia said – till he uttered a cry and collapsed into the state he's been in ever since.'

'So he – that's why—'

'That's why you caused such a stir when you mentioned your cousin. Emilia will be thinking about that right now, I expect, wondering if there's a connection, wondering whether your college in Jiata might provide the key to restoring Bastian. Wondering whether she could contemplate leaving for a country with whom we might soon be at war, and whether she would ever be able to return.'

Cass toyed with her coffee spoon. 'Has she ever said why Geist taught her?'

'It was what she needed to recover her joy.'

'No, I meant whether there was some larger plan behind it?'

'As far as I know, she had no idea before today that he had other students.'

Cass drummed the tabletop. 'She must come with us. What about that pilot? You know him?'

'A little.'

'The night before last – that was when she asked him to take her to Highcloud, and he refused?'

'Yes.'

'But Yaggit said Emilia thought he might be persuadable.'

'Max *is* very fond of her,' said Dinah. 'He's already taken her up once, though it would have cost him his job if Colonel Petersen had found out. She can be persuasive when her passions are roused. I'm not sure, though, how sincere his expressions of devotion are, nor how deep-rooted are hers. I think her passion is more linked to his ability to fly, a connection with her lost Eagle; and he in turn might see her only as a marriage route into a high family. If that is the basis of their "courtship", then I can't see him taking her into exile, not if that reduces her to a commoner.'

'You said, "her lost Eagle". They took her stone away?'

Dinah breathed out hard. 'No. That was my fault.'

Cass waited.

'The shock of Bastian's collapse killed his father,' said Dinah. 'Emilia blamed both herself and the stone. She'd taken it back from Bastian before calling for help, so no one saw it, but she was terrified it would be found and that she would be held responsible.

'So she gave it into my keeping, and asked to hold it every now and then. But she was scared of it, and refused to practise what Geist had taught her. She lost her joy again. I thought this was also an effect of shock at Bastian's fate. I was sure Emilia would eventually recover, and indeed, after a few months she showed signs of doing so. But then something terrible happened.'

She bowed her head briefly over her coffee, as though to gather strength. 'I'd been courted by a young man, a foreigner working as a footman in the palace. He was charming, but not at all suitable to be the sweetheart of Emilia's companion. I was told to break it off, and to be honest I didn't fight it. It was an experiment that hadn't worked.

'He took the ending of our courtship badly. He'd already come across the stone amongst my things, and been sensitive enough to feel something from it. I'd told him it was mine, to protect Emilia, and sworn him to secrecy on the grounds that I'd be arrested if it came to light. Knowing I couldn't report the theft, he stole it to punish me. That was about five or six years ago. I haven't seen him since.

'The theft distressed Emilia greatly at first, but then she came to see it as her punishment and her teaching, a lesson never to use magic again. She decided she wanted to be made Deaconess, and Siegfried agreed – indeed, he made sure she enjoyed all the benefits of her position, so the threat of its removal would cow her more. We never talked again about the loss of the stone. I knew Emilia blamed me. And that's the way it was until a couple of weeks ago, when we heard rumours that a Watcher and his novitiate had stayed at the palace. That started her thinking about mental flight again, though she did nothing about it – not until she saw Yaggit outside Siegfried's stateroom. The rest you know.'

Cass looked out across the café, the space busier now with early lunchtime custom, the murmur of talk punctuated by the chinking of cutlery and backed by a soft piano. 'That person I mentioned, who has her own stone. She helped rescue my cousin before, when he was in another of these magical sleeps.'

'Another? Is this practice really so dangerous? Or is he unlucky?'

'I'm not sure,' said Cass. 'The point is, there's hope for Bastian, if we can make it to Sundara. It takes magic to fight magic. You have to get Emilia to believe that, and to persuade this pilot. You said she can be persuasive when her passions are roused – isn't the hope of rescuing Bastian going to do it, if they were so devoted?'

'I don't know,' said Dinah. 'It's not so much a case of rousing her passions as of them being allowed to momentarily escape.' She huffed a bitter laugh. 'Like all women, as well we know, she's a creature of shifting, unpredictable moods. She's learned from childhood that these must be held in check, smoothed out. No doubt your barbaric life in Kymera has denied you this fundamental truth. Possibly you've even had the wretched, unproductive experience of feeling free and happy.'

'Once or twice,' said Cass, and leaned forward across the table. '*Persuade* her.'

'I can't,' said Dinah. 'She resents my efforts to influence her in any direction. If she spots the attempt, she'll revolt against it. What frustrates me is that she's blind to the even greater influence of what she's been told her whole life – the teachings I learned to question because the only alternative was utter misery.'

'You said she was on a knife-edge,' said Cass. 'What if she could be pushed, subtly, so she thought the decision came from herself?'

'Hypnosis, you mean? I've seen stage acts…'

'Not quite.' Cass looked at a wall-clock and drained her cup. 'Come on, I think we have time.'

20

THE STING

'It's better this way, Tashi,' said Aino. 'You'll be safe here till we get back. And Yaggit will tell the Abbot about you and what's happened, and we'll know from his reaction if it's a good idea for you to return. I'm sure it will all be fine, but…' He screwed his mouth to one side.

Tashi nodded. 'Take care, Aino.'

They clasped hands. 'Farewell, Brother,' said Aino. 'Two weeks, no longer.'

And then he was gone. Tashi watched through a gap in the bedroom curtains as Yaggit and Aino walked away up the street, the smoke-filtered sun shining on Yaggit's baldness and glowing in his red robes, Aino bowed under the weight of his pack. Neither looked back. Just before they disappeared out of sight, the fear trickled down Tashi's spine that he would never see them again.

Still only in his borrowed silk dressing-robe, he sat on the edge of Crome's bed. Though he was shut into a single darkened room, he sensed the emptiness of the house, and of those to either side around the long, shallow crescent. No maid would come to this room, Crome had said. Tashi could do as he pleased. Now he shed his robe and, in the adjoining dressing-room, put on the trousers and boots that had been Crome's gift. He stood in front of the tall mirror and the not-quite-stranger that stared back at him, the body and face that had insinuated itself into his soul. It was in such a state and position that he'd stood last night, while Crome, at his shoulder, had talked about the heroic youths depicted in sculpture and poetry – for though it would never be acceptable to portray Wilhelm Kirrus in any state of undress, all heroic young men were his analogue.

'The only perfect earthly love,' he'd said, 'is the chaste love for the holy warrior boy, whose wild bravery and passion must be tempered by the needs of his masters, whether that be a monastery or an empire. Your own master must have seen that in you – he must have loved it in you – and sharing it will help the connection that will lead me to his soul.'

Tashi would not have submitted to anything less than chaste, but even so, sleeping in the same bed as another man had made him uncomfortable. Sometimes, waking in the depths of the night, he'd felt the bodily warmth of his new master close by and drifted into the imagination that it came from another source, one it was blasphemous to think might have any connection with the heat of skin and blood.

Now, before the mirror, he dragged his fingernails across his chest, hard enough to leave marks. Should not the heroic youth bear battle-scars? If Gevurah couldn't harden the mud-clay of which he was made, could he fire it himself with danger and injury?

But that was self-pity. He couldn't stand to be alone, his solitude a breeding ground for such thoughts. He turned from the mirror, pulled on his shirt, and went down to the ground floor and the door that opened onto the basement stairs.

Locked.

His jaw tightened at being shut out of Crome's search for Shoggu's soul. It made no sense for the door to be fastened when all Crome's guests now knew him to be a magician. He didn't want to make noise with knocking for admittance, so he exited the house, careful to leave the front door slightly ajar, and went down the steps into the basement pit. Most of the litter had been trodden flat by policemen's boots. The window-boarding that Astolio's sons had broken through had been reaffixed. Tashi was about to tap on it, hoping to gently attract Crome's attention, when he recalled that the basement's outer door had been much used during the chaos of the investigation. Perhaps…

Yes, the knob turned; the door swung inwards onto the basement hallway. Ahead, to the right of the stairs, a doorway led to the old kitchen, the site of the shooting.

Crome's voice came from there.

Tashi's heart clenched. Had Crome found Shoggu's soul? Was he *talking* to him? He pressed against the wall by the doorway.

'Repeating,' Crome was saying; 'attempt to prevent further deterioration, but do not intervene beforehand. And if he recovers?'

The magician's voice sounded monotone, like Shoggu's voice whenever he'd spoken during the trance-state prior to flight. But Tashi made no sense of Crome's words. In the ensuing silence, he peered round the doorway. Cracks in the window boarding gave the only light. Crome sat at the kitchen table, which had been pushed against the far wall.

'Instruction unclear. Repeat.'

A square box stood before Crome on the table, and from it trailed wires to a device on his head, made up of ear-cups and a band between them. Tashi wondered why Crome was asking Shoggu to instruct him. But whatever the reason, if Crome were able to talk with Shoggu, it meant that his master had not been trapped in Hell. There was still hope.

'He's *what*?' Crome snapped off the headset and stuffed it into the box, which he grabbed awkwardly with one arm slung. He shoved it beneath the table and turned. 'Are you there, Tashi?'

Tashi stepped into the doorway.

'How did you get down here?' said Crome.

'That door was unlocked.' He read the simmering irritation in

Crome's eyes, but didn't apologise. 'Was that my master you were talking to? Can you contact him again?'

'No, it was not.' Crome's expression softened. 'No, I was using mind-focusing techniques – imaginary conversations, to stimulate that part of the mind that can truly communicate with spirits. How much did you overhear? It must have seemed nonsense. But the fact is, I've had no luck with finding Shoggu's essence, only his past.'

'His past?'

'The records of his speech and doings. Even of his death. Yes, I identified the marine who killed him, and traced the man back to Sundara. But that marine is now dead himself, and Daroguerre has also been killed by the masters he betrayed. There is no one to take revenge on. And I found nothing of your master that survived death. In fact, I'm almost convinced that… but no, I won't say that yet. I'll keep trying. There's still hope.'

Tashi tried not to feel disheartened. 'It's very generous of you.'

'I see its importance to you,' said Crome. 'And we friendless types must stick together.'

Tashi frowned at Crome's choice of word, but he couldn't truly deny it.

'In any case, I have my own reasons for this search.' Crome leaned back against the table. 'Even as a child I doubted the existence of the soul. Why do you think I became a magician so young? Because part of me couldn't accept the promises of religion. I can spout reverence as well as the next man, but really it's just another thing that separates me from the whole structure of society, top to bottom, because I can never be certain if it's a sham. Hence my travelling – before I could set myself to my life's work, or even discover what that might be, I had to ascertain the basis of our existence. Without truth there can be no meaning, and without meaning, no true purpose. My journeys have exposed me to many possible answers, but I've never put the matter to such a test before. Being alone, I've never had the courage. But I am alone no longer.'

He came and laid a hand on Tashi's shoulder. 'I sense you have your own doubts. What if we are not in a universe which is waiting for the sun to rise, but one that is instead in perpetual night?'

'No... God?'

'You caught my meaning swiftly, Tashi. It suggests something of your own mind. Indeed: no God, no souls. Only each other. Can that be enough? And if it should prove not...'

Tashi swallowed at the pause Crome left. 'Then what?'

A small smile, faint in the near-dark. 'As I said, there is still hope. Let's not countenance the alternatives until hope dies.'

Crome squeezed Tashi's upper arm through his shirt. Tashi kept his eyes averted from Crome's, but did not move away. In his old body, he might have let fly with a fist. But he had died, and Gevurah had died in him, and how did he know this was not a magic world, the Hell of the Witch Mother, even if it differed from his teaching?

A faint knock on the front door made him look up. Female voices came from directly above, within the house, one of them Cass.

'How—?' said Crome.

'I left the door open. I'm sorry.'

Crome sighed. He climbed the stairs and unlocked the door at the top.

'Ladies?'

Following him out, Tashi saw Cass in the entrance hall, accompanied by a shorter, slightly older woman.

'Any change in Orc?' said Cass.

'Not to my knowledge.' Crome gestured towards the stairs. 'Please.'

'We need to talk first,' said Cass. 'About magic.'

'What on earth makes you think I know anything about that?'

'Don't worry, Miss Dinah Strevin here is safe.'

'Is she indeed? Even so, you should have cleared it with me before revealing my secrets. Have you revealed all yours?'

'There isn't time for this,' said Cass. 'We have a chance of getting an air-craft to take us. Leaving the ground should break Orc free of the

Mother's power – even if it doesn't, it'll make it much easier to take him with us. But we need your help, and it has to be done now.'

He's busy with Shoggu, Tashi held back from saying. He assumed Crome would be of the same opinion, but Crome didn't brush the women off.

'What help?'

'We need you to magically persuade someone.'

'Lady Emilia Astrasis,' said Dinah. 'I'm her companion. She's unsure whether to go with our plan, and Cass says you have some occult skill. Can you influence her, in such a way that she believes it wholly her own decision?'

'It might be possible,' said Crome, 'if she's already half-inclined to that route. But I've never met her, and have no connection to her apart from yourself. It would aid my efforts if you could give me anything that might help me psychically locate her.'

Tashi's throat tightened. Was Crome going to abandon Shoggu?

'Something to act as her "index card"?' said Dinah.

'One might put it that way,' said Crome. 'Something she has touched, or better, something she has worn, or better, some part of her physical being. And something she has loved better than all.'

'I… happen to have this, if it will help.' From her handbag, Dinah took a small golden locket. She sprang open the back and extracted a lock of pale hair. 'Here.' Her face reddened as she handed it to Crome.

He took it. 'I should be able to judge within an hour.'

'What about… our matter?' said Tashi, as Crome made for the door to the basement stairs.

'Be brave and patient,' said Crome. 'If this gets us the use of an aircraft, wouldn't it be a good thing, to get to Highcloud quickly?'

'Why?' said Tashi. 'The other Watchers won't help with my master any more than Yaggit. And Aino said I should stay here for now.'

'Yes, in case your old home is barred against you,' said Crome. 'As well it might be.' He closed the door behind him. The lock tumbled.

'I hope we've done the right thing,' said Dinah.

'I'm going to check on Orc,' said Cass.

At a loss for what else to do, Tashi followed them up to the second floor. Cass glanced over her shoulder at him, but didn't question his coming.

The maid was bathing Orc's forehead. 'He's swallowed a little water, Miss, but Cook sent up some broth, and he gagged on it.'

'Could you wait outside, please?'

The maid left. Tashi stayed by the door. Orc shifted restlessly.

'Same as before,' Cass said to Dinah. She laid her hand on Orc's chest, exposed by his open sleep-jacket. She gently shook him, spoke his name. Something about that touch stirred Tashi inside, for he sensed how alike, and yet how different, it was from the way in which Crome had recently touched him.

'Like Bastian,' said Dinah. 'Except for not eating.'

As minutes passed, Tashi stared at Cass's hand, still laid upon Orc's skin; he sensed her need to heal him, the intensity of her concern expressed through that contact with his body. The pair of them seemed at once more solid than everything else in the room. It was as if they were illuminated by a different light – as if they, or something about them together, *meant* more.

He felt, suddenly, on the edge of a revelation. Its full understanding escaped him, but he'd grasped enough to know what he must do.

'Cass. I have to talk with you alone, please.'

She glanced at him, then at Dinah, who without a word left to wait on the landing. Tashi tried to order his thoughts, to give them the meaning that had come without words.

'Orc said I deserved anything he could do for me. The reverse is also true, more so. I hated what he helped turn me into, and that blinded me to what he gave up for me, and to what he risked in trying to help. If there is anything I can do for him, no matter what the cost, let me do it.' He met her questioning look. '*Whatever* the cost.'

'Tashi—'

'If there's any magic you know of that would make that happen, tell me. Any magic that's stored inside me.'

'I don't know about that,' she said. 'We're already doing the only thing I can think of.'

'Please,' he said. 'Let me help him.'

She studied him as if weighing options. 'There might be something.'

'Tell me.'

'Can you persuade Crome to try to magically help Orc next, after he's finished with Emilia? I know he was trying to help Shoggu for you, but if he hasn't found him yet…'

'Perhaps it's not possible to find him.' Tashi braced against the weakness that came with his words. 'Maybe there is no soul, no Land Beyond Sky.' He almost felt he was play-acting a role, and that any moment Gevurah would call to him and release him from it. Just as he woke several times each night thinking Shoggu was still alive.

'That's not to say there's no meaning,' said Cass.

Tashi looked at Orc again. 'I'll talk to Anders.'

'Thanks,' said Cass. 'And, look, what you said downstairs, about staying here. Don't you want to come with us? Uhm… what if we don't go to Highcloud, but somewhere else?'

'I can't go back until I know how they will treat me,' said Tashi. 'I'll see what Aino says when he returns. And if Crome leaves with you, perhaps he'll lend me his machine and teach me to use it, and I can stay here and listen for Shoggu myself. I'm now a creature of magic, after all.'

Cass nodded. Then, 'What?' she said, and looked up from her thought. 'What machine?'

'A thing he puts on his head.'

The colour had drained from her face. 'With… padded bits for the ears? And wires? In a box?'

'You know it?'

She cupped her hands over her mouth, as if to hold back a scream.

'What is it?'

For some seconds her eyes spoke of an internal chaos of thought, darting from one point of focus to another. At last they fixed on him again. 'We have to stop him.'

'Who? Crome?'

'He might be trying to put Emilia off! Oh God, Orc was right. Tashi, I think we have to – to kill him. Can you do that?'

'*Kill* him? Why?'

'There's no time – okay, not kill him. Knock him out, tie him up. Even if you can't get him out of the way, you must keep him from doing more magic, understand?' She looked at Orc. 'Shit, shit. And don't let him get you in a vulnerable position. I don't know what he's planning, but you're somewhere in it.'

A vulnerable position? He'd been next to Crome in bed, and no harm had come to him. 'I think you might be mistaken.'

'I'm *not*, Tashi! He's the Scorpion.'

'The – what? The one Orc—?'

But Cass had already thrown open the door. Calling Dinah after her, she rushed down the stairs to the ground floor. Bewildered, Tashi followed.

Cass banged on the locked door to the basement stairs. 'Mister Crome!'

'What's going on?' said Dinah.

'Crome's an enemy,' said Cass. 'Stupid of me. Wasn't it surprising how little he asked? He already knew! He knows bloody everything! *They* told him.'

'Wetherall,' warned Tashi.

The manservant approached from the library. 'Miss Strandborn, what is the matter?'

'It's Orc. He's worse. We need Crome to break what he's doing and help him. Open this door.'

'I haven't the means, even if I had the desire.'

'Then get the means and the desire, because if you don't, I'll tell the police exactly how Crome knew about those two men.'

'Then you would also condemn yourself.'

'I know! It'd be irrational, but I'm not rational, I'm a hysterical woman, and the man I love is in danger. I could do anything!'

Wetherall studied her briefly, then, seeming convinced, led them out by the front door and down into the basement pit, where he knocked at the boards over the window. Tashi tried the outer door, but as he'd expected, it was again bolted.

After several knocks, Crome opened the door. 'They were most insistent, sir,' said Wetherall.

'You need to look at Orc,' said Cass. 'He's worse.'

'What a whirling weathervane of priorities you are, Miss Strandborn. But if you insist. Shall we go up inside?'

'Me and Dinah need to catch a cab and meet Emilia. You stay with him, Tashi.'

The two women almost ran up the steps to the street. Wetherall followed. Crome beckoned Tashi into the basement and shut the door.

'I'm minded not to accede to Miss Strandborn's demands. I'd rather continue my search for your master. I assume you'd prefer the same?'

Tashi was thinking of what Cass had asked of him. To knock Crome out and tie him up might be accomplishable, what with Crome's arm in a sling. But could Crome really be the Scorpion? Cass had admitted to being hysterical. Perhaps she had misinterpreted what he'd told her.

'What was that device you were using before?'

'Ah, that!' said Crome. 'A highly interesting instrument. I bought it on my travels from an inventor called Jorik Quallace. He made three prototypes, I believe, and needed funding to develop his research.'

Tashi nodded. Cass had clearly got her mind in a muddle, thanks to her emotional distress about Orc.

'And yet,' said Crome, 'even with this device, I was unable to find any trace of Shoggu's soul. I think we have to conclude that it doesn't exist, that no soul exists. It is as I feared. Ever since my father's death, I've wondered what the point was in continuing, and now I know there is none. And for you it must be doubly bad, Tashi. You've lost two fathers, have you not? Your master and Gevurah. I would have done the deed long ago, if not for dread of the final loneliness. And Wetherall would never have agreed to keep me company. He would have stopped me.'

‘Deed?’

‘To quit the pain of this pointless world, to refuse to give it the satisfaction of dragging out a meaningless existence. Will you join me, Tashi? Shall we keep each other company, at the end? Your young life has been filled with service now revealed as misguided. You must see there is but one sane answer to the endless emptiness?’

There seemed something slightly forced about Crome’s words, an urgency about them.

‘Self-murder is a sin.’

‘What does “sin” mean when there is no God?’

He had no argument against that. And if there were no God, then there would be no Witch Mother’s Hell, nothing to fear from death. Just an end, a forgetting.

Crome stepped to him. ‘Please, Tashi. Don’t let the end be a torment of indecision. Let it be a moment of strong choice. I already have the mixtures prepared in the next room. We shall drink together. And here—’ He pulled out a drawer and took out several sheets of paper and a pencil. ‘You should write a note to explain to the others. They have enough on their minds without pondering the reasons. Yes?’

Tashi didn’t answer. He hadn’t expected this. It was the antithesis of his life of service. But as Crome had said, that life was gone. And after his graduation, five years hence, he had expected to seek the Mountain anyway. If there was no Gevurah, then how would that death differ from poison, except for being more drawn-out and painful?

To seize this chance of an ending: quickly, before the flesh-that-feared could argue its way out of it. The flesh that just wanted to continue, whatever the mind’s torments.

‘I’ll get them,’ Crome said, sounding excited, more like his age.

He went out into the basement corridor and into the next-door room. Tashi stepped to the table with its sheets of paper. To whom should he address an explanation? Aino and Yaggit had gone. Orc was insensible. That only left Cass, but would she understand the pain of having his faith destroyed when, as far as he knew, she had never had one?

Should he write, simply, *Good luck*?

Good luck saving Orc.

He was still standing there, not having picked up the pencil, when Crome came back in, holding two crystal liqueur glasses of green fluid. 'The bed upstairs will suit. We'll be comfortable there.' He glanced at the still-blank paper. 'Shall I suggest a wording?'

'No,' said Tashi. 'No, I think… even if we're right, and there is no God, no Gevurah – there's still something to serve.'

'Don't indulge the agony of indecision, I beg you—'

'I'm not,' said Tashi. 'There can be a faith even without God. I've seen what I want to serve: less than an hour ago. It exists between people, Anders. Between some people. It is love.' Crome looked to be fighting back the urge to scoff or laugh. '*That* can be our master,' urged Tashi. 'Yours too.'

Crome put down the glasses. 'I thought you were made of better stuff. I thought you had seen through illusions. This comes from the part of your mind that craves existence at any cost. And how does one take an abstract concept as one's master? Not even an abstract concept, but an *emotion*. Is that what you're reduced to, Tashi, seeking to serve an emotion? The Witch Mother would applaud, if she existed.'

'Love – pure love – is not an emotion of the body.'

'"Pure love", what is that? Does it belong to the non-existent Gevurah?'

Tashi couldn't answer. He didn't have the words; all he had was faith, his wordless revelation that had illuminated the way Cass had touched Orc.

'I don't have the arguments yet, Anders,' he said. 'But I won't end myself, and nor should you. Use your magic to help Orc. Please.'

Crome sighed, then smiled. 'Very well. Perhaps this isn't the time. Let's go and see how he is.' He gestured awkwardly at the door with his slung left hand; his right was in his pocket.

'I'm glad,' said Tashi. He turned to leave the room – and something pricked his neck.

He slapped his hand there, as though to squash a biting fly, as he heard Crome step back from him. He turned; Crome retreated to the side of the room, his good hand holding a strange device with a needle at its end. He put this down, pulled open a drawer of a chest and took out a revolver.

'What?' The word slurred from Tashi's mouth. His legs felt like mud.

'What did you expect a scorpion to do, if not sting?' said Crome.

Tashi went for him – or tried to, but his knees gave way. He could barely move any part of his body; he tried to call out for help, but only groaned. Crome moved around him to the door and shouted for Wetherall, then turned back to him.

'Quick-acting, isn't it? My own concoction, developed over decades of research. Yes, *decades* – quite a feat for such a young man, you'll agree. Contemplate the conundrum, if you wish. Oh, why didn't you write a note and drink the poison, Tashi? Your death would have been so easily explicable, and I wouldn't have wasted a dose of the antidote.'

Feet sounded on the stairs, and Wetherall entered. Tashi had to concentrate all his physical effort on breathing, but he could breathe, and – just – blink. Crome hadn't wanted to kill him, only paralyse him. He didn't know whether that was a cause for hope, or horror.

Wetherall and Crome dragged him into the next basement room. There were no windows, but Crome switched on an electric light: as far as Tashi had seen, the only one in the house. The place was filled with shelves and glass flasks and scientific instruments. Wetherall's two good arms and Crome's one wrestled him into an upright leather chair. They strapped his unresisting wrists to it. Crome, breathing hard and face flushed, went back into the first room and brought back the glasses of green fluid. With Wetherall's help, he tipped one of these into Tashi's upturned mouth and stroked his throat until he swallowed.

'That'll keep you still and quiet,' he said. 'Such a shame your mentioning the clairaudioscope to Cass forced me to act before I was ready. No doubt my haste was what made me less than fully persuasive. But no matter.'

Wetherall had already left. Crome stood by the door and switched off the light. 'You probably know already that my masters want you dead. I'll leave you to ponder why I haven't killed you immediately. We'll talk about it later. Or at least, I shall.' He began to close the door, to shut Tashi in with the dark. 'You, foolish boy, will never speak another word.'

21

THE HEART OF THE EAGLE

Deep in the stone hush of the Cathedral, behind a minor doorway off a corridor that led to the Hall of Wisdom, Emilia gazed up at the carving above a bricked-in arch, a stone lion and eagle flanking a shield. They alone of their kinds survived, for all others in more conspicuous places had long ago been replaced, merged together into the gryphon of the Prelacy. As she studied the eagle's familiar eyes and beak, and the talons that gripped the edge of the shield, she sought an answer to the greatest dilemma in her twenty-six years.

The eagle's stance made it look thrillingly ready to spread its pinions and spring over her head, to abandon its leonine rival and fly to freedom. Should she see that as a sign she should do the same? But to let a long-dead craftsman's choices influence her decision would be idiocy, and there was plenty of counter-argument. This eagle was still an Empyreal creature, and magic was permitted only within the narrow rule of Empyreal law. *Her* eagle had contravened that law; with Eagle, she had defied the will and creed of the massed tons of stone around her. Yes, riding on that back had been an ecstatic experience – she'd felt the promise of its return the moment she'd touched Cass's focus-stone. But she'd lived without it for six years. The possibility of saving Bastian was too faint and distant to add much weight to the 'fly' side of the scales. She feared her decision was mostly about her own wants; and her recognition of that selfishness, when the Holy Mother was a model of self*less*ness, made the 'stay' side heavier.

And then, piling weight onto 'stay', came a creeping horror of collapse, of instability, of the unknown future. The madness of her teenage years would be reawakened, destroying a precarious balance. Had Geist really saved her from insanity, or only prolonged it? – and if the latter, perhaps for his own plans. A desire to fly was childish nonsense. Being shut off from the real world, the world of wars and politics, had made her dangerously naïve. To take an air-craft to Sundara would be rushing headlong into that world as a child might. She would likely be imprisoned.

It seemed inarguable. Devotion to the Holy Mother, with its discipline, was the adult course. Duty was the adult choice, duty to one's country as well as to God. And for all Dinah's unorthodox words, a woman's true strength was not in action, but in maintaining will and focus on the small practical aspects of the world, the mundane but vital reality for which its leaders could afford no time.

The decision now made, it seemed strange to her, as she looked at the carved eagle, that she had ever felt any connection there. It was not the lion's rival, after all, but its comrade: a symbol of a very real power that lay within the sphere of Empyreus and of men.

'Attend. Emergency.'

The words jolted her. She looked around for their source, but the voice must have been her imagination. Something in her felt it as a violation, an invasion – and now came a hint of a smell, a harsh, cloying odour that conjured dead things preserved, things kept in laboratories, of the hospital she'd visited after Bastian's collapse.

Strangely, however, rather than feeling her mood further oppressed, she felt it lift. As though a hand had removed a weight from the 'stay' side of the balance, the horror of instability faded – indeed, it seemed to her now that she'd been cowardly in thinking stability so desirable.

Preserved things in jars were stable, the head of Empyreus was stable, the Holy Mother's flower-laden bier was stable.

As was carved, cold stone.

She looked up again at the eagle. How had she ever identified this sculpture with her animath, with warmth and feathers? A small moan escaped her at a reminder of what it would mean to reject this chance of reunion with Eagle, of how it had felt to fly on her back.

On *her* back!

Her mind leapt. This carving was a *male* eagle. And hers had been female. And the female eagle was greater than the male: greater wings, greater talons, a greater heart.

She remembered air rushing past her as she sought out some secret in the landscape far below. Might she seek out a cure for Bastian? Perhaps he was lost in the Otherworld, like Cass's cousin, and she could find him again. The mathematical model Cass had described seemed poor by comparison to her memories of flight, but if—

If she could somehow use Cass's method to find her own stone...

She shivered with the glorious sense of possibility. Why was she so ready to believe there would be war with Sundara just because her brother said so? Weren't there millions of other people who would prefer peace and commerce? She might become not a fugitive, but an ambassador. And if the college in Jiata was as good as Cass said, perhaps they could help find her crystal, and Bastian might be restored.

And if he recovered his health and replaced Siegfried, then all, surely, would be well.

The Hapscourt Hotel restaurant was as busy as always. Greeting various people she passed, Emilia followed the head waiter to the small private dining room where the others already sat. She asked that they be left alone as much as possible, and when the waiter had seated her and left, she told Dinah and Cass, 'Yes, I agree.'

'Then you'll get us an air-craft?' said Cass, speaking softly despite the privacy.

'I'll try.'

'Thank God,' said Cass. 'But we have to act soon. The man I was staying with, Crome – I'm pretty sure he's an agent of the Shining Ones.'

Emilia glanced at Dinah. 'Shining Ones?'

'Magicians,' her companion said. 'I don't understand much more than that.'

'There isn't time for the whole story,' said Cass. 'But they won't want us to reach the college in Sundara, because we can develop magic there and we'll be shielded from them. So they might try to sabotage our plan.'

'Sabotage it how? And why didn't you tell me this before?'

'Because I didn't know Crome was their agent until just now.'

'And he'll try to stop us?'

'Hopefully he can't any more. But did you sense anything… influencing you?'

'Magically, you mean?' Emilia said. 'Now you mention it, yes, I felt an oppressive dread of… of changing anything. Then it left me, very suddenly, and everything seemed clearer. Are you saying that was him?'

'Quite possibly,' said Cass. 'If so, it sounds like we interrupted him just in time, and hopefully Tashi's made sure he can't try anything else. But these Shining Ones have other agents. Does "baffomet" mean anything to you?'

'No. What is it?'

'The Shining Ones have someone high up in the Empyreum. Possibly at the naval base in Torrento. Whoever that is, they might be able to stop us.'

'These Shining Ones know of our plans?'

'They're quite possibly listening to us now.'

A trickle of cold passed down Emilia's back. 'But how can they be allowed to operate?'

'No one knows who they are,' said Cass. 'They hide even in the psychosphere, even from the Watchers. We have to act before they contact this baffomet person. Can you persuade Max?'

Emilia wondered what else Dinah had revealed about her personal life. 'I can try. But we'll need an engineer as well as a pilot.'

'The pilot doesn't control the elemental?'

It still alarmed her that Cass knew anything about the air-craft's workings. 'No, he doesn't.'

'I might be able to manifest it,' said Cass.

'And control it?'

The doubt on the girl's face answered for her.

'Then we'll need an engineer,' said Emilia. 'But they're all former Trine, and fiercely loyal.'

Even as she said that, she thought of Plack.

'Simonis,' said Dinah.

'Hmm,' said Emilia.

'Who?' said Cass.

'He was drummed out of the Air Corps for drunkenness,' said Dinah. 'He makes a living running illegal séances in an underground club.'

'Is he really a good idea?' said Emilia. 'From what you've said—'

'Do we have a choice?'

Emilia sighed. 'I'll tell Max to meet us.'

'What about you, Cass?' asked Dinah. 'Will you go back to Orc?'

'No, with you, I think. Tashi must've been able to overcome Crome – he's a trained warrior. He'll be fine. Getting the air-craft is more important.'

Emilia used the hotel manager's office to telephone the air-field. Having given a message to be passed to Max, she left with the others in her auto-carriage, telling Pauli – her mother's old carriage-driver, and whom she trusted just enough – to take a route through back-streets to avoid heavy traffic.

The auto pulled up in a side-street, deserted despite being just off one of the main commercial thoroughfares. Dinah got out and knocked at a nondescript door. After speaking at a hatch, waiting a minute, then speaking some more, she turned towards the car and nodded.

‘Wait here,’ Emilia told Pauli. ‘A pilot officer named Maximilian Sorbring should come. He’s to stay with you.’

She went with Cass to join Dinah. The doorman admitted them, and Dinah led them down to a dim basement bar. The mix of grubby dishevelment and gaudy opulence was Emilia’s first glimpse of Dinah’s other life. Strange art, uneasy on both the eye and the mind, and probably illegal, hung on the velvet-covered walls. People in clothing that would have seen its wearers refused admittance to the Hapscourt, or even the Red Café, drank in corners. She choked off a cry as a rat darted beneath a table.

‘This is the kind of club you were arrested at?’ said Cass.

Emilia was shocked she should ask that, but Dinah seemed unperturbed. ‘No, that was even more deviant: one where men and women meet to reverse the usual social order.’

‘You mean women ruling over men?’ said Cass. ‘Isn’t that a cause for hope?’

‘I might have thought so once,’ said Dinah. ‘But most of those men have no interest in applying the same principle in everyday life, nor equality. To them it’s of interest precisely *because* it’s deviant. But there are currents of genuine movement flowing through these places.’ She opened a door. ‘He’s at the end of this corridor.’

Simonis Plack, whom Emilia had never actually met, turned out to be a broad-faced, double-chinned man, with little remaining of the ethereal beauty for which the Trine were partly chosen. Over-dressed, an opal pin at his throat, he sat behind a baize-covered table in a stuffy room lit by a single gas-lamp. A gauzy haze of chiffon swags evoked a desert prince’s tent from a romance novel. A half-empty bottle of spirits sat at his elbow.

‘Ah, the famous Miss Strevin,’ he said, his high voice both slurring and over-careful. He kept his gaze on the fan of fortune cards before him, as though they, rather than the doorman, had warned him of their arrival. ‘You and your friends have come for a reading? You can no longer resist the temptation of the latest craze?’

‘Craze?’ said Dinah.

'All the best people these days wish to discover a past life as one of the Zhenaii,' said Plack. 'Whatever etheric swirl caused this ripple in occult fashion, it's been very lucrative. The Deaconess I know by reputation.' He inclined his head briefly. 'Lady. Will you introduce me to your other friend, Miss Strevin? If she is only such?'

'I wouldn't be so crude if I were you,' said Emilia, hoping the dim light hid her blushing. 'We're offering you the chance to fly again.'

He gave her a hard glance and poured himself another glass of the startlingly blue spirit, which Emilia now realised was partly responsible for the room's cloying perfume.

'Perplexing,' he said. 'My psychic powers are inadequate to penetrate your meaning. Shall I denounce myself as a fraud?'

Emilia drew a steadying breath. 'We intend to take an air-craft on an unauthorised voyage.'

'Ah,' said Plack. 'Now I see. That sounds fraught with hazard.'

'But it would mean a new life for you,' said Cass. 'We're headed for a magic college. You won't need to hide your ability away in here any more. You can learn to refine it.'

'A college?'

'At Jiata, in Sundara,' Emilia said.

He burbled an ugly little laugh. 'Exiled to a land of heat and dung.'

'Yes, exile is a risk,' said Emilia. 'But if I'm prepared to take it, why not you?'

'Because I have a life here, with my ladies and gentlemen who this week wish to have been courtesans or priests in the decadent Zhenaii times, and next week will yearn for some other excitement. And I have my constantly thwarted dream.'

'Your dream?' said Dinah.

'Yes,' said Plack, but it was Emilia whose gaze he held. 'Are you willing to bargain, Deaconess? If you could gain me access to the Hall of Wisdom, just one more time…'

'Where Empyreus is?' said Cass.

'I believe I told you,' Emilia said to her, 'the engineers are all former Trine.'

'You were one of those boys?' said Cass.

A little slug of a smile. 'A boy still, my dear. A boy forever, blackballed from the club of manhood. It's the largest and dullest club in the world, yet one can't help a certain curiosity as to what goes on in its grubby halls.' He faced Emilia. 'Get me back into His presence, just once, and I'm yours to command. He has been barred to me nine years now.'

'We need to move at once,' Emilia said. 'But when we return, I'll do my best. And whatever influence I have with the Holy Mother, I'll use in your cause.'

'You swear?'

'I do.' Quite what the fulfilment of that oath might involve, she had no idea, but she could worry about that later.

'You two witnessed this?' Plack asked the others. They nodded.

'We'll wait upstairs for the pilot,' said Emilia. 'Gather what you need and follow.'

'Wait,' said Cass. 'Mister Plack, you do have genuine psychic ability? Apart from working with the air-craft elementals?'

'Young lady, I was one of the Trine. You understand what that means? I dreamed, awake, the thoughts of Empyreus himself – his plans for the empire, for the world; his gifts of new sciences and technologies. Do I have ability?' He gave Emilia a weary look.

Cass gave her a more energised one. 'Can we can spare a few minutes? I want to know what "project baffomet" is, and how dangerous.'

'You said yourself time is short,' Emilia reminded her.

'If Tashi's dealt with Crome, baffomet is the only threat we face,' said Cass. 'If we find out what or who it is, we can judge how to act. If there's no threat, then no panic.'

Emilia saw the sense in that. 'How long to do a reading?' she asked Plack.

'I should know inside an hour whether I can find what you seek.'

'Can we afford an hour?' asked Dinah.

'I'd rather know what we're up against,' Cass said.

Emilia nodded. 'Wait in the car for Max,' she told Dinah.

'You're staying?'

'I'm curious.' She wondered how a psychic reading would differ from her own past experiences.

Once Dinah had closed the door behind her, Plack invited them to sit at the table. They refused his offer of a drink. He turned the lamp down. 'You seem to know about these matters,' he said, 'so I'll forego the atmospherics. Most people find psychism easier to credit if they are first subjected to a lot of childishness. Sometimes it helps ease me into the mood, but this works just as well.' He took another glass of liqueur.

They held hands in a circle. Even through her gloves, Emilia imagined she felt the clamminess of Plack's fingers. She also felt the energy suppressed within Cass's touch, a deep, almost disturbing tingle, as though the girl never relaxed.

After several minutes of what sounded like slow breathing exercises, Plack, his eyes closed, said, 'Tell me what you already know about this "baffomet".'

'No, with respect,' said Cass. 'I already have my own ideas, and I don't want them to influence yours.'

Plack nodded. More minutes passed. Many more. Emilia didn't know how he could keep his hands so perfectly still. Only the faint whisper of his breath showed that he still lived.

'There is a piece of paper,' he said. 'Typewritten.'

'We know about that,' said Cass. 'The man who typed it didn't know what baffomet meant either. It's a dead end.'

The dim lamp-flame wavered. The sounds of talk from the other end of the corridor, behind the closed and heavy door, were barely audible.

'I see a red cross on white,' Plack said suddenly. 'There is a connection with the name you seek, but remote. A connection of mind, of idea, association. A temple of some kind. The idea of *knights* comes to me. It's too remote, I can't—'

'Knights?' said Cass, voice tense with hushed excitement. 'There's a street called Knightsbridge. Can you see if there's some connection to me?'

'A connection?'

‘Hidden from me. I’ve had my memories blocked.’

‘Really?’ said Emilia. Cass seemed an endless store of secrets. ‘Is this relevant?’

‘I thought I recognised the name. Finding the past might be another way to help Orc.’

‘But baffomet—’

‘We’ll come back to that,’ said Cass.

‘No,’ said Emilia. ‘If baffomet proves no threat, we can come back to your street. That has to be the order of priority.’

Cass’s eyes hardened at the challenge, then she nodded.

Plack returned to his work. But after a while, he said, ‘I have a faint sense that what I seek is in some way bound up with this young lady’s recollection of that street-name. Give me your other hand, my dear.’ He and Cass both let go of Emilia and held hands across the table. Emilia thought it had been over an hour now. She didn’t know how long Max might wait.

Plack began to speak. Too rapidly for Emilia to keep track of, he mentioned a chain of places and events, ships and an island and sunken ruins, farms and nightmares, and Cass assented to all of them with mounting excitement, and Emilia realised that these were markers in the girl’s life. A journey and a destroyed forest and a man on a beach and – a pause.

‘Yes?’ whispered Cass.

But Plack had fallen silent, his expression inwardly focused.

‘Mister Plack?’ said Emilia.

‘There is a barrier to my regressing further.’

‘Can you get through it?’ asked Cass.

‘It has been woven across my path. It is what causes your amnesia. Did you know of it already?’

‘How does it work? What makes it?’

Emilia wondered if such a barrier could also be fitted into Cass’s index-card analogy. Perhaps, in the same way that a skilled psychic could read the catalogue numbers, one with an even greater skill could blur them.

'Mister Plack?'

'No, I cannot penetrate it.' He seemed about to add more, but didn't.

'Okay,' said Cass. 'That Shroud's been there for two years. No wonder it's strong. How about coming at it from another angle. Could you read the street's memories of me?'

'Ah,' said Plack. 'Yes. Clever.'

'Even a house number – if we had that, I could go there.'

He nodded. 'It will be difficult, with no physical connection. But I am a child of this city.'

Further minutes passed. This time Emilia noticed more animation in Plack's face, slight twitches and subtle shades of focus – signs of progress, perhaps. She hoped this wouldn't take much longer. Despite what Plack had said about the connection between baffomet and the street-name, the séance seemed to have become wholly about Cass's personal matter. She should have been firmer.

'I feel as though I've slipped round something,' Plack muttered. Emilia had to strain to hear, and sensed Cass doing the same. 'Almost there. Got a hook in. There *is* something.' Emilia leaned forwards—

Then jerked back as Plack cried out: 'Oh, my Lord! I'm there! His world – the world he dreams for us! Oh, you are blessed, my dear! Blessed! And I am reunited with him! Oh, my Lord, my Lord, your perfume surrounds me!'

But the odour that struck Emilia was the same smell she'd caught in the Cathedral. Cass's face widened with horror; the girl tried to pull her hands back, free of Plack's grip, but the man held too tight, his eyes closed in what looked like ecstasy.

'My *Lord*!' He stood, almost pulling Cass upright with him.

Then something fell as though from out of the ceiling, something large and flat and bright smashed down on Plack's head and Cass screamed and Emilia flung herself back as the object clanged heavy metal onto the table, smashing glasses and the bottle, and lay there, the letters KNIGHTSBRIDGE staring at Emilia in bold white on a blue bar that bisected a red circle.

She hadn't breath to scream. Plack had fallen back over his chair. She jerked her eyes from what the edge of the metal sign had done to his skull.

Cass opened her mouth, then covered it with her hands; her throat visibly contracted as though she would be sick.

'Well,' Emilia heard her own trembling voice say. 'That was unexpected.'

'The smell,' Cass gasped. 'He said… *his* smell. His lord. Empyreus.'

The implication hit Emilia through the madness. The smell of preserving fluid, the same as at the Cathedral – had it been Empyreus himself who'd come to her then? She didn't dare dwell on the terrifying, exhilarating possibility, but it broke part of her mind from the impossible horror before her. 'We must – what must we do?'

'Get out,' said Cass. 'Fast.'

'We can't simply—'

'You don't understand!' Cass's eyes were wide at her. 'It's the smell of *them*! The Shining Ones! Baffomet – their project baffomet is *Empyreus*!'

22

THE WIND THAT HATES

Only when Cass heard her own words aloud did it start to sink in. But she could see from Emilia's face that it might take hours for the Deaconess to accept it, and they didn't have time. The Kaybees would know right now that she knew, and they might already have started the process of communicating with the Trine, and getting the authorities to seal off the air-field, and whatever else.

Not intended for such micro instruction, the transcript had said. But to stop her getting to the magical college, the Shining Ones were bound to find a way.

'Come on!' She went for the door. She glanced at the metal sign that had killed Plack, lying on the table like a terrible gift, but too cumbersome to take. Its lettering and design were alien to Bismark, the Empyreum, everywhere she ever remembered being. But it had something to do with her – she could sense it, deep down, like tinnitus swamped by external noise.

'Thank you, Mister Plack!' she called, just before shutting the door of the room behind them. Emilia seemed mightily composed on the surface, and Cass was relieved at that. Maybe, just maybe, they could get out without drawing attention. She forced herself to not hurry along the corridor, nor through into the main room where other customers were. Most looked towards them, but without the alert curiosity of people who'd heard a loud bang and a scream: the intervening doors must have muffled the sounds.

They reached the stairs without being called back. Then the top, and the doorman was letting them out into the street, and still no one was shouting up about a murder, and they were outside.

They piled into the auto. Dinah had been joined by the pilot from two nights before. 'Drive!' Emilia called through the dividing window. 'Anywhere, for now.'

'Emilia, what happened?' said Dinah. 'You're white as a sheet. Where's Plack?'

'He had an accident. A seizure.'

'Then our plan – it's finished.'

'There's still me as backup,' Cass said.

'But you said you only *might* be able to control it.'

'We have no choice.' She had to convince them. 'They'll be trying to stop us as soon as they can.'

'You found out what this baffomet thing is?'

'Yes.'

'Not for certain, surely?' Emilia asked her. 'I understand why you think... but there might be some other explanation. It was only a smell.'

'Is anyone going to tell me anything?' said Max, as the auto edged out of the side-street and into the thoroughfare's traffic.

Emilia put a hand to her visibly damp forehead and turned to look out of the window, as if trying to root herself in normality. Cass wanted to take charge, but told herself to wait – it might work against her to seem too pushy with Emilia's friends.

'In the Cathedral,' said Emilia. 'That smell came just as the... the oppression of my thoughts lifted. But there were words. *Attend. Emergency.* If Cass was right, and it was Crome oppressing my thoughts, then the lifting happened because they called him away.'

'Oh, crap,' said Cass, suddenly realising. 'What if we didn't interrupt him – what if they pulled him away to warn him about us discovering who he is? And about me telling Tashi to get rid of him?' Forewarned, Crome would have had a chance to defend himself. And he had a gun...

'But the Lord Empyreus!' protested Emilia. 'It's too much. I had no hint of these "Shining Ones" until today, and now they're running the church, the empire?'

'What?' said Dinah and Max together.

'Yes,' said Cass. 'And maybe for hundreds of years. Not the same people, of course, but a magical organisation.'

'What *about* Empyreus?' said Max. 'Be clear, Emilia, what are you saying?'

'That he is a falsehood,' said Emilia. 'A mask, for those who would rule our lives from the shadows.'

'I cannot believe—'

'You *must*!' said Cass. 'If you don't, they'll smash us. You have to go along with us. We're in danger till we get to Jiata.'

'Jiata?' said Max.

'We need you to take us there,' said Emilia. 'And if Cass is right, all our lives depend on it. Yours too, after what we've told you.'

'But Sundara might soon be our enemy.'

'The enemy of Empyreus,' said Cass. 'Not of us. Not when we tell them.'

'You need me to help steal an air-craft,' he said. Cass wished Dinah had at least briefed him about that, given him time to adjust to it. 'This is too fast,' he said. 'Much too fast.'

'Max.' Emilia seized the pilot's hand. 'You think I don't understand? I'd like a week, a month, to think about this myself. But we *don't have time*. I know this plan goes against your instincts, your sense of duty, just as it goes against mine. But if it's true that Empyreus is other than we believed, if our whole nation has been the subject of a terrible confidence trick, then from Sundara we can unmask it, set the world on a more moral path. And in Sundara, nothing need stand in the way of our friendship.'

'Truly?' He looked like a man weighing risks against each other.

Emilia now enclosed his hand between hers. 'I'm convinced. And

I'm hopeful we can find a way to help Bastian there. I know how much you admired him. Restored, he could be the next High Prelate. A man who would fight for peace and truth.' But suddenly, her face lost its determination. She turned to Cass. 'Yet mightn't our flight prove unnecessary if I can persuade Siegfried?'

'No!' said Cass. 'He'd never listen.'

'So much depends on this. Isn't it worth the attempt? He wouldn't need to persuade the public, not at first, but if I could convince him to treat the Trine's revelations more warily…?'

'You don't change fixed ideas so quickly,' said Cass.

'Some of mine have changed in just one morning.'

'You began your change years ago. And you saw what happened in that room.'

'And Max. If we've persuaded Max…'

Have we? thought Cass. 'Listen – your brother's the one who's been using these crystals, right? The elemental ones? He even gave one to the Kymeran navy. Isn't that magic? Isn't Empyreus meant to be against magic?'

'Those crystals are blessed,' said Max. 'It's divine science, not magic.'

Cass kept her gaze fixed on Emilia's. 'What if he already knows he's really serving magicians?'

Emilia rapped on the dividing glass. 'Pauli, stop here.'

'What?' said Cass.

'I'm going to speak to Siegfried,' Emilia said. 'I have to try to convince him.'

'Em, no,' said Dinah. 'Persuade him from a distance if you can. But Cass is right. When has he ever listened to you? Why would he now?'

'Because he needs to feel himself his own man. He'd loathe the idea of being secretly manipulated. I've only to open one chink of suspicion in his faith and he'll stop at nothing to find out whether I'm right.'

'And if you don't manage to?'

'I have to try, Dinah. What if these Shining Ones hasten war to cement their hold? Thousands might die. Max, make ready your craft.

I'll join you at Lions Hill. If I fail to arrive, you must decide what to do. You'll all go to collect Orc?'

'All?' said Dinah.

'Yes,' said Emilia. 'You'll be no help to me, Di, I'm afraid, and Cass might need you. From what she was saying, it's possible her friend didn't succeed after all.'

Cass nodded agreement; she felt too sick to speak. She glanced at Max's belt and was grimly relieved to see a gun holstered there.

The car had pulled in at the kerb. Emilia opened the door.

'Don't.' Dinah grabbed her wrist. 'Don't go.'

Emilia smiled faintly. 'I was opening it for you,' she said. 'This is my car, after all.'

Cass started looking for a cab as soon as she was out. Dinah and Max joined in only half-heartedly, it seemed to her, continually glancing round at Emilia's auto until it was swamped by traffic.

The second four-seater that passed their way was free, and the driver agreed to take them to Park Crescent and then Lions Hill. Cass used the first part of the journey to bring Max up to date. At first she was unconvinced she was doing anything but feeding words into dead air, trying to persuade him to abandon ideas he'd accepted his whole life. But then Dinah reminded Max how Bastian had been a boyhood hero of his; and the prospect of helping to restore him to health and political power, and what might follow from that, seemed finally to commit him.

'I'm all in,' he said, as they turned into Park Crescent. 'Not a play I'd usually make when I'm unsure what cards I'm holding, but there you go.'

Cass couldn't even raise a smile at the joke. As the cab-horses clopped to a halt outside Crome's house, the uncertainty of what they would find within drove everything else from her thoughts. She very much hoped Tashi would answer the door, but there instead was Wetherall.

'You're expected, Miss.' He stepped back and held the door wide. Crome stood three treads up the staircase, his good hand behind his back as though concealing a gun – which, Cass supposed, he very possibly was.

'Miss Strandborn. You're late for lunch, I'm afraid. And your cousin shows no sign of improvement, I regret to say.'

Her legs felt weak. 'Where's Tashi?'

'He decided to go with his comrades after all, and chased after them. I imagine he caught up with them at the station. They might still be there, I suppose – I'm unfamiliar with the timetable for the northern routes.'

'I don't believe you.' But as soon as she said that, she thought maybe Tashi had felt himself overwhelmed by the situation, the demand she'd made of him, and decided he'd be better off with Aino and Yaggit. What if he hadn't believed her about Crome, or not enough to go through with trying to incapacitate him?

'You're welcome to search the house for him, if you wish,' said Crome. 'Perhaps you think I've hidden him in the basement?'

It sickened her to think it, but if Tashi was still here, he was most likely dead. And what good would finding his body do?

'We'll just take Orc and go.' She hated how her voice shook.

'Take him?' said Crome. 'Your cousin is much too ill to be moved. For the sake of his health, I can't allow him to be taken anywhere.'

'It's not your place to say,' said Dinah. 'She's his family.'

'And a hysterical woman,' said Crome. 'You told Wetherall so yourself.'

Cass froze inside. So she had. And maybe Tashi hadn't realised she was doing it for effect. Maybe he'd taken her at her word.

'You surely don't believe,' said Crome, 'I would place someone in my care into the hands of such a person?'

'Then place him into mine,' said Max, stepping level with Cass. 'I'm a Pilot Officer in the Empyreal Air Corps.'

Irritation spasmed across Crome's face. He pulled his hand from behind his back, but Max had his pistol already drawn and raised it before Crome could level his.

Cass's breath caught. Crome's arm stopped with the gun pointed down at the floor. But from off to the side came a soft click. Wetherall had stepped back against the wall and now held a revolver aimed at Max's head.

'You're no part of this,' Crome said to Max, his voice carrying barely a quiver. 'Whatever apprehension you act under, it cannot be a complete knowledge of the situation. There's been barely enough time for these two to tell you all their bizarre theories, let alone for you to make sense of them, let alone for you to gather the evidence to confirm them – which I suggest you really must do before you commit the capital crime of murdering a man in his own house. Now, why don't you lower that pistol, and then the three of you leave, and no real harm done?' His forehead gleamed. 'And leave me to do my best for my patient.'

'Actually—' The voice from up the stairs made Cass's heart surge – 'I think I'll go with them.'

She cupped her hands over her mouth, afraid she would scream with joy. She couldn't see him yet because of the edge of the ceiling. Crome had turned to look up the stairs.

'You're not well enough to go anywhere,' he said.

'Orc!' said Cass, pushing back the emotion that threatened to break over her. 'We've got an air-craft!'

He descended, barefoot, still in pyjamas, the jacket unbuttoned. He looked a little unsteady, but he could walk unaided. It was going to be all right. Crome had lost his excuse for keeping him; all they had to do was get Orc out without any guns going off. The Kaybees wanted Orc alive; Crome wouldn't shoot him.

Then Orc's face came into view. His expression as he met Cass's gaze sent a spike of cold iron through her heart: the sadness in it, the determination, the grief. In that moment, she could tell he was struggling not to break.

Whatever had happened, it could wait. 'We're leaving,' she said. 'Right?'

He looked confused. 'My clothes...'

'We'll get you some more. We have to leave *now*.'

He took another step down, only two stairs above Crome now. Crome studied him, his face pursed with doubt and calculation. Orc's body seemed to be trying to shrink as far as possible from the downwards-pointing gun in the man's hand.

'Wait,' he said. 'My – papers.'

Shit, thought Cass. The transcripts, and the photograph. She glanced at Crome, then back at Orc. 'Are they still there?'

More confusion. 'Why wouldn't they be?'

Because the Kaybees have probably told Crome to steal them. 'We'll do without them,' she said. 'Hurry!'

Orc looked at Crome. The man didn't move aside. There was just enough room for Orc to pass, but he didn't seem to want to try.

Come on, Orc.

'I won't act counter to your free will,' Crome told him. 'But neither will I allow your will to be manipulated when you are not in full possession of your faculties. You need time to recover. Surely you see that?'

'Orc!' urged Cass. 'If we don't get the air-craft now, we'll lose it.'

'I – I can't go to Highcloud.'

She almost laughed, he was so behind. 'Fine by me. Things have changed.'

Orc frowned a little. Cass felt almost overwhelmed at the amount she would have to explain. But that was for later. She mentally urged him on, and yes, he lowered a bare foot one stair further, his lower lip between his teeth. He would have to squeeze past Crome. Crome might grab him as a hostage.

But Crome exhaled softly and stepped back against the stair wall, and half the tension evaporated.

'As you wish,' he said, and turned to Cass. 'You're clearly used to having things your way. But I shouldn't rely on any continuance of that.'

As soon as Orc was near enough, Cass stepped forward and grabbed his hand. For a moment she thought he almost pulled back from her touch, but she shoved the thought away and gripped harder and tugged him towards the front door. Max's and Wetherall's guns both kept trained on their respective targets until the door banged shut; then, with Max keeping a wary eye on the front of the house, they all four bundled into the waiting cab. Cass sat opposite Orc. He seemed closed off, reluctant to meet her eye. She wondered if that was because of the previous evening. Probably that had lain behind his words about not going to Highcloud – no doubt he'd had the same thoughts as her about what the Conclave might uncover.

'Are you all right?' she said as the horses clattered into a trot. 'What happened?'

'I'm fine,' he said. 'I only woke up a few minutes ago. I don't remember anything else. Fragments.'

'Don't worry about last night.'

'No,' he said. 'It doesn't matter any more.'

That wasn't exactly what she'd meant. He seemed borne down by some weight, a sadness, but there was also a clarity, despite the mess he was in, his hair matted with sweat. As if he saw reality clearly again. She hadn't sensed that about him since before the college. She hoped she was right about that, and that the Mother's influence had left him. But if it hadn't, getting him off the ground would see to that. He'd just come round from an ordeal, she reminded herself. What she'd sensed as grief must be tiredness.

Then she noticed that he kept fingering his wrist. There were tiny scratch-marks there, a ring of them, a bracelet. They looked fresher than the marks of the scratches from the college cellar, or was that her imagination? She wasn't sure she wanted to ask.

Time to tell instead. 'You were right,' she said. 'Crome is the Scorpion.'

He met her gaze at that. 'Really?'

'What did you think was going on back there?'

'I wasn't sure.' His expression said he hadn't thought it mattered.

Nor did he then ask anything else.

So Cass kept talking. As the cab negotiated traffic on the way towards Lions Hill, she told him what had happened since she'd stormed out of his room. There seemed too much for one night and morning; she almost thought she must have made a mistake and run several days together. It was obvious he wasn't taking everything in, and now she'd been with him for a few minutes, she thought it wasn't tiredness she saw in him; his clarity argued against it. It had to be what had happened the evening before. If he'd only just come round, it must seem so recent.

As he turned to stare out of the window, she told herself to be patient. It was a miracle he was as together as he was.

'How do we get in?' said Dinah. 'They'll admit Max, but what about the rest of us?'

Cass glanced at Max. 'Can't we get in with you?'

'The guards at the barrier might be a problem,' he said. 'I don't know what might persuade them to admit two women and a man in his nightwear.'

'Could we hide? If there was only you in the cab…'

'They'd expect me to walk from the gate. And if your enemies have their wits about them, they'll—'

'Don't!' said Cass. 'Don't say anything they might not have thought of.' She'd already guessed one possibility: if Crome could get hold of the air-field's telephone number, he might be able to warn Max's commander of the theft attempt. And the Kaybees might know that number, or be able to discover it. She had to hope the idea wouldn't occur to them, or that Crome wouldn't seek instruction, or that the switchboard would refuse to relay the call.

'We need an official auto,' said Dinah. 'With a flag.'

'Can we get one?'

'That would take Pauli, and he's with Emilia. And it's miles back to the palace.'

Then why mention it? Cass almost snapped.

Then Orc said, 'There might be something I can try.' He turned to Max. 'That building we saw you by the other night. Would anyone be there?'

'Not usually. It's why I wait there.'

'If we could get through the fence to the back of that building, where you met the car the other night, would you be able to walk us to your craft?'

Cass frowned. *Through the fence?*

'It'd be risky,' said Max. 'You might be seen from the gate, and they'd know you hadn't been admitted. There's a stores block in the far corner that would be more use – *if* you could get through the fence. But how would you do that, without a lot of noisy sawing?'

'And we don't even have a saw,' said Cass.

'I don't know if it'd work yet.' Orc put his hand to his throat, and his face tightened in panic.

'Your stone?' Cass dug it out, handed it across. 'How would a scape help?'

He didn't look at her, just spent a lot of time seemingly finding the exact right way of hanging the crystal around his neck. 'Might be less chance of it working if I talk about it,' he said, which Cass thought nothing but a brush-off.

At the next group of shops, they bought some off-the-peg clothes for Orc, and warm coats for themselves and Emilia – Max's service papers got him immediate credit – then stood outside while Orc used the cab's interior to dress. Half an hour later, they were on the plateau of Lions Hill. As before, various vehicles had parked along the road, and a small crowd of people stood peering through the railings towards the far side of the concrete field, where the three craft were parked.

'I see that stores block,' said Orc. 'I'll walk round the fence behind it, out of your sight. You all stay here. Will there be guards? A patrol? We didn't see one the other night.'

'There's no regular patrol during daylight,' said Max. 'Astrasis keeps the contingent here to a minimum.'

Orc nodded. 'I'll be gone a while: I don't know how long. Then I'll come just into sight again. If it hasn't worked, I'll walk back and we'll have to think of something else. If it has, I'll stand around there, and you two come and join me,' he said to Cass and Dinah, 'and Max can get through the gate and collect us from round the back of that stores block. Okay?'

'Not really,' said Cass. 'Not without knowing what you're going to try. You've only just come round from some kind of coma. You might not be thinking straight. You might do something that puts us at risk.'

'We can sit here and figure out something else if you want.'

'This isn't the time to be keeping secrets. What are you planning?'

He gave her a look she couldn't even begin to read, and opened the cab door. She grabbed at his wrist as he stepped down, but he snatched it away with what sounded like a hiss of pain. 'Come and find me if you think of anything else in the meantime,' he said, and walked off.

'I'm going after him,' Cass said, but before she could step down from the cab, Max reached across and shut the door.

'Perhaps we should see,' he said.

Cass felt sick. Max couldn't have any more faith in Orc's success than herself. She suddenly doubted him, wondering if he was just playing along, delaying, so he could tell Emilia he'd done his bit and too bad it hadn't worked out.

Lack of sleep was creeping up on her. Everything was getting away from her. The thought of the air-craft had so obsessed her that when it had at last appeared over the horizon, she had fixed her gaze on it without seeing the myriad obstacles still in her path. To have recruited the Prelate's sister, to have discovered the nature of Empyreus, to have outwitted the Kaybees' agent, all were stupendous achievements. And now, to be defeated by a simple fence of iron railings…

She hadn't been able to see Orc walk along the road to the corner of the perimeter fence, but she now caught him disappearing behind the stores block. Clearly he'd lost touch with reality even further. Was his seeming clear-headedness a sign of things getting worse rather than better?

'I hope Em's all right,' said Dinah.

Max grunted: a noise of agreement that didn't commit him to further conversation.

'She's clever,' said Dinah: trying to convince herself, Cass thought. 'She won't just come out and tell Siegfried what she knows, not till she's sure he'll be receptive. If she's not convinced, she'll come straight here.'

Cass tried to breathe slowly, deeply, rather than from the top of her lungs. She thought of Orc's tendency to jig his leg when he was anxious. She wondered why she lacked the same instinct. Her fingers kept wanting to move instead, but she pressed their tips together.

Orc reappeared from behind the blockhouse. She expected him to start walking back along the fence, but he stood where he was, just within sight, hands in his pockets.

'He thinks he's done it,' she said miserably. It was one thing for him to not realise a plan was impossible, much worse that he believed he'd actually accomplished it.

'Is this it?' said Dinah. 'Should we go round?'

'Someone's got to,' said Cass, 'just to fetch him back.' She sighed. 'Okay, we'll go round. The two of us.' If he was that deluded, she might not be able to handle him alone. 'Max, stay here. No point you going through the gate if we can't get in.'

Some of the onlookers by the gate, with no other action to fix their eyes on, watched them go. There was nothing forbidden about walking the fence-line – they might just be stretching their legs – but Cass felt as if each step she took shouted with nefarious intent.

When Orc saw they were approaching, he stepped back along the fence to where the stores block screened him from the gate, to a place where the bottom of several railings had become overgrown, acting as support for some kind of white-flowered climbing plant.

'We can get through here.' His voice was jaunty but nervous. 'I think it's big enough.'

Cass stared, and the blood drained out of her.

A gap had rusted in the fence; several of the railings now began three feet above the ground, held up by the cross-braces. Around the edge of the gap, the vine with its white flowers gripped and smothered.

She struggled for speech. 'What is that?'

'Does it matter?' he said. 'Come on.'

‘No.’ Horror surged through her. She couldn’t grasp what he’d done, what might have happened to him, but nightmare hints thronged the edge of her mind.

‘Fuck’s sake, come *on*.’ He ducked through the gap.

‘We should,’ said Dinah. ‘Unless you think it’s a trap, Cass?’

No, she didn’t sense that. And it probably would be the only chance they’d get. ‘Go and stand there for a few seconds,’ she told Dinah, ‘so Max can see you.’

Once Dinah had returned to say she’d seen Max leave the cab, Cass led her on hands and knees through the gap, careful to avoid the scraps of rust littering the ground, though Orc seemed to have pushed most of them to one side. They joined Orc behind the blockhouse, and Cass stood listening to her heartbeat, hoping no guard had seen them, hoping Max was right about there being no fence patrol.

‘Some kind of manifestation?’ she asked, trying to sound casual. She remembered the Prelate saying Skalith had ‘warped’ her way into the ship.

‘You got it,’ Orc said, in a tone that didn’t invite further questions.

Several minutes passed, then a key turned in a back door of the blockhouse, and Max appeared, Emilia’s parcelled coat tucked under his arm. ‘What the hell happened there?’ he said, looking at the hole rusted in the fence.

‘I either made it myself, or I already knew about it,’ said Orc. ‘Take your pick.’

Max nodded doubtfully. ‘I’m going to lead you to my craft: the one nearest the rear fence. We’re going to pretend I’m giving you a guided tour of the field – I can’t think of anything better, and it might fool the odd maintenance man. Hopefully the guards on the barrier will stay facing away from us. Follow me briskly. Don’t run. Once we’re on board, I’ll shut up the door and we’ll have to stay there and hope no one noticed us and that Emilia will turn up.’

‘Do you have the crystal for the elemental?’ said Cass.

‘It’s fixed in place. And the starting charges in the airscrews will already be loaded. My usual engineer has to “warm up” the elemental, so I assume you'll do the same before Emilia arrives. You're sure you can call it?'

'Yes,' said Cass. No point showing doubt now.

Max led them through the blockhouse, which housed shelves and racks of parts and fitments, to the door in its front. The three air-craft rested in a staggered line abreast, their wingtips ten yards apart. A maintenance crew worked on the wheel-struts of the rightmost, but otherwise there was no one in sight. Max took a deep breath and broke cover, walking purposefully across the concrete towards his craft. Cass followed with the others. *Madness*, a voice kept telling her. And yet they'd made it this far. She pinned all her perception on the hoped-for future, the college in Jiata, the chance to at last begin to change things.

They reached the craft. Max clunked a lever and pulled down a door that folded out of the side of the hull, steps notching its inner face. At his urging, Cass scrambled up into the weirdly shaped interior with its cork-covered floor and its low metal ceiling and its strong oily smell. Once they were all in, Max used the pulley and lever to raise the door again. Daylight entered through multi-paned concave glass windows, one at the nose of the craft, one on each flank and one to the rear, each mounted with a machine-gun and with a metal seat for a gunner.

Max pulled open the ceiling hatch near the front of the craft and slid a ladder down. 'Pilot and engineer positions are up top.'

Cass followed him up. This level was more cramped than the lower. At the front, more glass canopied the pilot's seat. Levers protruded from the floor around it; dials and switches cluttered the wooden panels to either side. A gap near the pilot's feet allowed access to the nose-gunner's position.

To the rear of the hatchway, between two small portholes, the floor was inlaid with a sheet of polished black stone marked in silver: two concentric circles, the ring between them scribed with symbols, and within the inner circle a five-pointed star surrounded by other glyphs. A large yellowish stone that looked like a raw hunk of quartz was fixed by silver mountings at the tip of the star's forward-most point. Cass recognised the basic set-up from the boiler-room on *Nightfire*. But what was different here was that the ceiling, four feet above, bore the same design: a mirror-image, apart from the crystal.

She got to work. She had no idea how Thera went about summoning *Nightfire*'s elemental, but it was probably better not to be influenced by another person's methods. The basic facts she knew: her presence would allow the elemental to manifest, and the elemental was tied to the crystal. Doubt was the enemy of magic, and in those respects she had none. Nor did she doubt – she would not let herself – that she could control it. The transcripts had said she had power, even more than Orc. And this would be her first exercising of it.

She unbuttoned her coat to make herself more comfortable, and knelt. She closed her eyes and reached forward and touched the crystal. Felt it, caressed it with both mind and hands. Its nature seemed obvious to her at once. Unlike the blue stones, which heightened connection to the psychosphere – allowing their user to read the indexing more clearly – this was a million catalogue cards bound together. This was an expression of the ancient magical theory that the world was made of five elements: fire, air, earth, water, and what some called spirit, the invisible, intangible stuff that was the psychospheric medium.

And all the primitive gods of wind and air, people's belief in them and their power – these were the wider connections the crystal opened out into, sparks of sub-consciousness flying between atoms of information, linking them; she could feel it happening. The elemental had been summoned here many times. The pattern had already been established. Her mind raced down the well-marked track through the forest of thought, and found her quarry – in a moment of clarity and exhilaration she understood how to pull the secret essence of wind into the world, into this confined space, and contain it within the boundaries made for it.

It came roaring, a faceless whirling, confined, constrained – enraged. She hadn't anticipated its anger. She let go of the crystal and knelt back. Its fury at its binding alarmed her. Surely the thing was insentient – she didn't understand what it had to be emotional about. The roaring barely allowed her to think. The elemental was trying to force its way through the intangible cylindrical wall that joined the rings in floor and ceiling.

To get at her.

The air-craft lurched. Lifted.

'No!' came Max's shout.

In panic she thought it away, asserted it gone – and the elemental vanished, leaving only a faint prickling on the air. The craft creaked as it settled back on its wheels.

'Way to go, Cass!' came Orc's shout up through the hatchway.

'Damnation,' said Max. 'Only when we're ready!'

'I'm sorry,' she said, shaken.

'How in all the hells did you get it to come so quickly?' said Max. 'Well, no matter. If that's the way you do it, wait till Emilia's here. We'll just have to hope they didn't notice.'

It had hated her, Cass realised as the too-rapid experience began to sink in. Really hated her, for confining its freedom. If it had broken out, it would have torn her apart as a storm might tear apart a tree. It had been like facing an enraged tiger through cage-bars made only of thought.

'Bugger,' said Max. 'They did notice.'

Through a porthole, Cass now saw several men coming from the main building block, which sat off to the side about halfway between the craft and the gate. One wore a braided uniform and cap; the other six were soldiers with rifles.

'The colonel,' said Max. 'Is the door bolted?' he called down.

'Yes,' returned Dinah.

The men advanced to within a hundred yards of the craft. The colonel took a loudhailer from the man beside him.

'Pilot Officer Sorbring. Surrender yourself and your accomplices at once.'

No one spoke. Cass knew she might be called upon any moment to manifest the elemental again. But it would only take seconds. She didn't have to face that hate right now.

'I know you're in there, Sorbring, and without authorisation. I received a warning. I hoped it would prove false. It grieves me that you've proved it true. You surely recognise the hopelessness of your position. Whoever your engineer is, they're clearly incapable of moving you much. And as soon as I received that warning, I made a call of my own, for reinforcements. They won't be long.'

Cass now saw two men coming from the stores blockhouse, carrying between them several lengths of cable. Reaching the colonel's party, they began to hook these together.

'They'll try to tether us,' said Max. 'This is hopeless. We'll have to take off.'

'But Emilia—' said Dinah.

'We'll fly along the route to the palace, see if we can spot her auto. She'll recognise the noise of the craft. Hopefully she'll realise what's going on and follow us to somewhere we can pick her up.'

'What if they shoot?' said Orc.

'We'll survive a few rifle bullets. Stay away from the glass. Cass, get us airborne – I'll fire the airscrew starters once we're up.'

She leaned forward and touched the crystal. Again she sensed the vastness of that world, like peering down into an endless depth of sea, clear all the way down to where things lurked half-defined. And down there was the hate. Her mind resisted the necessary connections, like a child wanting to cover its eyes and hide.

'Cass?'

She'd thought everything in the psychosphere could be reduced to information, that any behaviour a thought-form exhibited was a function of the energy that had originally created it. But the elemental had hated her, and she sensed the potential for the whole field of the psychosphere to hate her, all its worlds and histories. It reminded her of her nightmares on *Nightfire*. She hadn't prepared for anything that seemed to be genuinely alive. Mister Burns had seemed a placid biddable force, but Thera had practised for months. She should have anticipated something like Skalith instead. What if the markings couldn't hold the elemental? What if their efficacy depended on her belief in them? She didn't even know how they were supposed to work!

'Cass!'

'I'm trying!'

'But you did it before!' said Max. 'We moved.' Then: 'Hell! Don't let them get those cables round the wheels.'

'How do I stop them?' called Dinah.

'Give them a burst to one side.'

'You're serious?'

'What choice is there?' Max jumped down to the lower level.

No choice, Cass told herself. *That's right, no choice.* She had to do this or be captured. But the fearful part of her wouldn't obey her instruction.

A loud rattle came from below, a faint tremor through the craft's hull.

'Got it?' said Max. 'If they try to get round, do it again.'

'It scared them, look,' came Dinah's voice.

'Of course it did,' said Max. 'They know if we're desperate enough to do something this criminally stupid, we're desperate enough to mean it.'

'Is this the reinforcements?' said Orc.

'God's teeth,' said Max. 'A land-cruiser.'

Cass glanced through the porthole. Across the air-field, a double line of perhaps fifty soldiers were jogging under the raised gate, led by a kind of auto-carriage armoured in steel plate, even its windows. From it rose what seemed a much smaller version of a warship's turret, and out of this stuck a machine-gun.

'Cass! *Now*!'

'Stop pressuring me!' She turned back to the crystal. The thought-track led her again to the elemental, but it was still writhing, thrashing through the psychospheric medium, angered by its previous capture. Perhaps she'd done wrong to just grab it. Perhaps she should have appeased it, made some kind of sacrifice – wasn't that how people were supposed to have gained the favour of ancient gods?

But what could appease this hate? What would stop the attempt making it hate her even more?

'Stand down, Cass,' said Max from below, less urgent, more bitter. 'Too late now.'

She bit down a burst of anger at herself, and looked out. The land-cruiser had drawn level with the colonel and his men.

'They won't risk damaging the craft if they can help it,' said Max. 'But if we take off, they'll probably try to bring us down, and that machine-gun could do it. And that thing's armour is too thick for our guns to get through. Our only hope now is Emilia.'

'You think they'll obey her?' said Dinah.

'They'll obey her brother. Pray she's managed to persuade him.'

'Cass?' Orc called up. 'Do you just need more time?'

'No,' she yelled, 'I need to be less shit!'

'You're not. I believe in you.'

'Oh God,' she muttered. 'Like that helps.' The whole psychosphere hated her. It held the elemental, and the Kings Behind the World, and Skalith, and her terrible dreams. Her previous instinct, to stay away from anything to do with it, had been absolutely right. How had Geist managed to persuade Orc that it was his second home?

By fucking his brain, of course.

And of course, of course, that was the answer, and it was too late. She should have got Orc to summon the elemental. He knew the psychosphere; he wouldn't have been affected by its hate. If it even hated him. Whatever the reason – whether she'd wanted to prove her rational magic, or had fixed her plans in her head before she knew Orc would recover – she'd made a mistake, and it was too late now to do anything about it. Even if Orc could control the elemental and they managed to take off, the land-cruiser's gun would bullet them out of the air.

'It's moving,' said Dinah.

'I can see that,' said Max.

'What's it doing?'

Cass looked. The land-cruiser was driving, slowly, straight towards the craft.

'Damn it!' said Max. 'If that thing blocks our flank gun, they can come and attach the tether without us being able to stop them – our other guns couldn't reach.'

'Do you think Emilia will persuade her brother?' said Orc.

'No,' said Dinah flatly.

'Then the best we can hope for is to get out of here, back through the fence,' said Orc. 'Correct?'

'I think that's significantly better than the best we can hope for,' said Max.

'We'll see. Cass, get down here.'

'What are you doing?' called Max. 'Stop!'

The sound of a bolt, of hinges. Cass scooted to the hatchway. Peering down, she saw Orc on the first step of the lowered door-stair, arms raised as though to make himself a bigger target.

'Listen!' he shouted, and the command stopped even Max, who'd risen from the flank-gunner's seat and looked about to grab him. Despite the tension and madness of the situation, Cass felt a thrill go through her. Orc's voice had a confidence and strength she hadn't heard for ages. But what was he doing?

'I have no weapon,' he called out. 'You don't have to fear me. But I know what you *do* fear. I know the dread that puts steel into your buildings and your gun barrels, that makes you concrete the ground and turn your skin to breastplates. I've seen the horror you armour yourself against. But your armour can never be enough. It only concentrates your fear around you, and that fear *gives* her the power you always feared she had – the power to take back what was always hers!'

Noise erupted. Shouts and cries came from outside: from the hatchway Cass could only see Orc in the doorway, but something had clearly happened outside because the light beyond him had dimmed. There came the sound of gunfire, but Orc didn't move.

She went to the porthole, and her breath stopped.

A thick hedge of vines had sprouted from the crumbled concrete and was still growing, writhing out of the ground – insane, impossible.

On the far side of the living wall she just caught sight of the land-cruiser enveloped, the green punctuated with red flowers. She thought she could smell blood and its aftermath, and rot and sap and thick humidity; her skin flushed with heat. Amazed, she stared. Men were running. All of them. So were the tiny people behind the distant fence.

There was a woman, in the green. Or a suggestion of one. Back, shoulders, hair; her raised arms all of grown-together vine, tangled into muscle fibres and leaf-skin—

Intuition flashed through her mind, too complex to make sense of immediately.

'Come on!' Orc shouted into the craft. 'She won't hurt us – we can get to the fence.'

Get out of here, she told herself. *Deal with it later*. It was just more Three-Eyes, more Skalith, more Red Tashi; she'd dealt with those, she could deal with this.

But the intuition came again and at the hatchway, she stopped and called, 'Wait! Stay in the craft!'

'Cass?'

'Wait! Everyone!'

Hatred, and power. No one and nothing had so completely hated her before the elemental. But she'd never had real power before. The vine raging outside drew strength from the city's fear of the goddess's power, the power of birth and death and decay. The elemental hated her because it feared her, and it feared her because it knew she had power over it.

She'd been stupid to fear its hate. That hate was the corollary of her power: inevitable and necessary.

'Cass,' came Max's voice, 'what are you—'

'Stay! For God's sake!'

She knelt quickly by the magic circles. She ignored the argument breaking out below, and the gunfire still going on outside and the eerie sound of unnaturally fast growth and the thick humid smell of moss and forest. Would it get their craft too? Was Orc *controlling* it? – no, she pushed that away for later. She grasped the crystal and threw herself into the depths, along the trail she'd already traced. She found the elemental and its roaring hate of her and seized it with her mind and pulled it through, compressing and containing it. No apology, no regret. She relished that hate. Whether it was something the creature truly felt as a separate, sentient mind, she didn't care. She controlled the thing. She might even destroy it if she wanted to. She could obliterate the numbers on the index cards that added up to its existence, and she told it that.

The space between the floor and ceiling was opaque with a howling storm of rage – and, she now knew, of fear. Up, she made it. Up. And the lurch in her stomach and the floor brought shouts of surprise from the lower level. She hoped to God everyone was still aboard.

Up, and up, directing the force of its fury. With a loud whoop, Max scrambled into the pilot's seat. Two bangs rocked the craft as he fired the starting charges in the airscrew engines. Soon came the thrum of the screws themselves, pushing against air, and Cass sensed a different movement. She glanced out of the porthole and saw the air-field below, a riot of impossible, horrible vegetation, falling behind.

'No higher!' called Max; she could barely hear him. 'Dinah! Get in the nose-gunner seat and look out for Emilia's auto. I'm heading for the palace.'

Only now did Cass notice the sweat dripping down her face. They had an air-craft. They actually had a fucking air-craft. They could get to Sundara. And there, they could do anything, learn everything.

They were going to leave Bismark behind, and everyone in it.

23

PURE

For an hour, Tashi had sat in the dark with what felt like a heavy weight on his lungs, breathing with conscious effort. At last, Crome opened the door to the laboratory and switched on the light. His good hand held a butcher's knife.

Gevurah, no, please.

'I promised you a talk, Tashi.' Crome leaned with an obviously fake casualness against a work-bench. 'And you should find it illuminating. I am about to explain the depths of my infamy, my plans, my reasons – just like the villain in a tawdry romance, you might think, who gloats over his plots for the reader's benefit before the hero dashes in to save the tied-up girl. But you'd be wrong to think that. I'm not doing this for self-aggrandisement, nor for the benefit of any observer. And there is no hero coming to rescue you. That chance has flown.'

Tashi knew the truth of that. He'd heard Cass's and Orc's voices, dim through the floor. He'd put all his will into making his body work just for one thing, to make one shout, and he'd failed. And they had gone.

'No, I'm going to explain because I'm going to set you a challenge,' Crome went on. 'And that challenge is to *not* serve me.'

He didn't understand. Crome smiled: clearly he hadn't expected him to.

'You probably think serving me is the last thing you'd do, given that I'm about to kill you – and yes, I *am* about to kill you; there's no bargaining to be done. But whether you serve me or not is all in the manner of your dying. Your challenge is to accept your death calmly. That's part of your religious training, isn't it? It's the flesh alone that fears; the spirit is assured of its ascent to the Land Beyond Sky – assuming you die on the Holy Mountain or in true service to Gevurah. Assuming Gevurah exists.

'*My* challenge is to rob you of that equanimity: to make you plead with the universe, however silently, for the continuation of your life.'

Crome was mad. There would be no mercy. The horror of it tightened, minutely, the muscles round Tashi's eyes, the ones that could still be used to blink.

'Why should that matter to me, you ask? Simple cruelty? No. I told you earlier that I had been at work on that poison for decades. I took Wetherall into my employ when he was a young man. And yet I barely look twenty. How can that be? Did you puzzle it out?'

Tashi had assumed it was some kind of glamour, like he'd thought Orc had worn on himself, like Vanessa had suggested. He wanted to answer – he wanted to talk, to try to persuade, to argue with Crome and maybe even plead, to be allowed the tiniest chance – but all he could do was move his diaphragm, his eyelids.

'Your religion teaches that the self is the gift of Gevurah,' said Crome, 'to bring you above the influence of the Witch Mother and the body. And though that is as false as all your religion, the mind-self, the identity, the "ego", as my masters call it, is indeed a very powerful thing. It fails to grasp that it's only a mask to allow interaction with other masks. It believes itself to be extremely important. After all, it can invent worlds. It can conceive of the universe entire, so it must be greater and more important than the universe. It is a man's whole past, and all he knows, and all his thoughts and ideas and hopes and dreams – whole libraries could not contain it. And being so great and important, it loathes the idea of extinction. An animal will exhaust its physical strength in fighting for survival, but it will still not bring so much energy to bear as a mind-self in danger of nothingness. A mind-self in terror of looming extinction will pull to itself the creative energy that is the stuff of the psychosphere, hoping to use this energy to bolster its life, to protect the body on which it depends, perhaps even to create for itself some new form of existence that will allow it to continue after the body is no more.

'And that energy, Tashi, can be harvested. That raw matter of creation, gathered for the victim's self-preservation, can after his death be drawn off by the magician and used for his own preservation, either to reduce the extent of injury or to forestall the effects of ageing.

'That is how I intend to make use of your death: to extend my own youth. That is how you will serve me, unless you can accept your death without terror and deny me that energy. But I don't think you will, because I have two techniques to employ. The first is the one I normally use on a victim: to make him focus on the idea of no future, of the end of his consciousness. The world will go on as before, but without you. Doesn't that bring a sickening, panicky tightness to the chest? The thought that as far as the world is concerned, there will be only a blank space where you should have been, a fading memory? That you'll have no chance to fulfil your dreams, no chance to find the love you earlier talked of serving?

'No chance to save your friends from harm?'

Crome set the knife down on the bench and pulled a thin silver case from inside his jacket. He lit a cigarette. 'And this is my second technique – see, I declare it openly to let you counter it, if you can. I use the victim's desperation to survive because of what will happen to others if he dies.'

Tashi couldn't guess what Crome was about to tell him. But he would ignore it as a trick. There was no danger to others. Orc and Cass had escaped. Aino and Yaggit would already be at the railway station. Crome couldn't hurt them. It would all be lies. He just wanted this to be over. If he could have switched off his life as Crome had switched the electric light, he would have done. He didn't care about not having a future. He wouldn't let himself think about it.

'Yes, Tashi,' Crome said after his first draw, 'you might want rather desperately to live, if you were the only one who could stop all Highcloud's novitiates being slaughtered.'

It struck him like a knife in his chest, unexpected. He wanted not to listen. But he had no choice, and in any case couldn't help wanting to know what Crome meant.

'But Anders, you might say.' Crome exhaled smoke. 'Why should they be in danger? Perhaps you think I'm merely pulling your chain, trying to get you to want to stay alive at all costs, a kind of cheat. But you see, Highcloud presents an obstacle to someone with the power to destroy it. So I'm afraid you must imagine the tragedy of Paiko's death repeated over and over, the young lives of your cohort smashed out of existence. Picture Aino, half his head torn away by a machine-gun bullet. Cank screaming from a wound in his stomach, slowly being poisoned. Nandi barely recognisable after falling to the bottom of the gorge – oh, the litany of future horror! If only you could live long enough to warn them. If only you could make up for failing to warn Paiko. Because you might have done that, Tashi. You had already met his murderer. As I said, I came back on an early train.'

Horror froze his mind, the fire of his hate made impotent.

'It was I who lured your young friend and his master to a deserted tenement and poisoned them both, well in time to come back here and meet you and give you tea, and then your fine new clothes. Befriending you was so important. That was the whole point, in the end, of all that business with meeting and conspiring with and then murdering Astolio's brainless offspring: to seal our friendship so I could pretend to search for Shoggu's soul and steer you towards suicide. Well, that didn't work, but still, a minor glitch: here we are. I've betrayed you, and I can see in your eyes that you're furious. As you must have been furious when you heard Cass's voice upstairs and couldn't cry out because I'd rendered you incapable. Yes, Tashi, don't you want to live and take your revenge?'

He did. He wanted it more than he'd ever wanted anything. And he wanted to cry because he knew this was exactly what Crome intended him to feel, and it would be all he was capable of feeling until Crome finished him.

'And not just on me.' Crome ground out his cigarette. 'It gets worse, Tashi. I'm not the only one who betrayed you. Do you recall the hopelessness you felt when I told you that the Sundaran marine who killed Shoggu had also died, and that your thirst for vengeance would have to go forever unslaked?'

Gevurah, what was this?

'Well.' A smile. 'I lied. I know who killed your master, and it wasn't a Sundaran marine.' Crome leaned forwards. 'Do you wish to know? Of course you do. It was Ranga. That's right: Ranga, whom you befriended. He shot Shoggu in the back – to protect Vanessa, the sorceress he told you he'd rejected.'

His mind was the roaring of a hot wind over a wasteland.

'Oh, Tashi, now you know that, if only you could escape and take your revenge on the person you trusted. If only you could track him down and send him where he belongs. Oh, the sweetness of a blade finding a gap between his ribs! If only you could *live*, Tashi, and not be killed by me in cold blood to satisfy my vanity! If only I were really your friend, as I made myself to be, and not the man about to commit the ultimate violation of your body, to destroy its integrity, to rob it of the means to sustain your mind. Lights out, Tashi. Forever. No more world for you, ever.'

Tashi forced all his will into moving his lips, engaging his voice. If he could blink, and breathe, he must be able to do at least this. He'd tried many times, but now, almost to his shock, a sound came strangling from his throat. 'Highcloud,' he rasped. 'Who?'

Crome looked at him, clearly surprised that he'd spoken. But not particularly worried.

'Oh, didn't I say? Not my masters, though they'd certainly have no objection to the Watchers being removed from play. No, it's Siegfried Astrasis. There's something in Highcloud's vaults that he very much wants, and he cannot get it without subduing the monastery. Yes, the man you blame for corrupting you. Him again. Another one deserving of your vengeance.'

The man he loathed would kill those he had grown up with. And now it made sense, why the Prelate had been so intent on seeing a novitiate Inspired when he'd first come to Bismark. To learn what his soldiers would be up against.

He'd thought his corruption had been to buy passage, but it was worse: it had been to aid in the destruction of his fellows.

He couldn't die. Not now. He *couldn't*.

'I imagine you're furious enough to try summoning your former demon possessors,' said Crome. 'But I wouldn't waste your energy. They were severed from you.'

It was true: he'd sensed nothing of them since Hana had returned him to consciousness, not even in the deep background of his mind. He wouldn't have called them anyway – better that Highcloud be destroyed than they be unleashed again. But anything else, any other chance, he would take – to kill Crome, Astrasis, Ranga. To soak the earth with their blood. There had to be *something*.

'That's it,' said Crome. 'I can feel the energy building. So much of it. I might get years out of you.'

The energy: could he use it, to free himself? The raw matter of creation.

There had to be a way. He was a creature of magic – not fired clay, but unfired. Mud.

And mud could be *shaped*.

But there was no Hana to shape him, no Orc and Cass to be the catalyst.

Crome had picked up his knife and a whetstone. Long dragging scraping noises grating through Tashi's ears.

But he hadn't needed Cass to be present for the Qliphoth to complete his change on the island. *'This is a place of transformation'* – their words. The very nature of the Spiral site had been altered. And wasn't his body just as much a part of the physical world? A moveable site? What if he could transform it, himself, use the depth and ferocity of his hate to draw on the power that had been behind the Qliphoth?

No – he might call something as bad as them.

Master, help me. Gevurah, help me.

But Gevurah had gone, and his master was dead.

But not dead in his mind. And Shoggu would have urged him away from vengeance and hate. *'Vengeance and justice are not the same.'* The rage that demanded revenge was a bodily emotion, belonging to the Witch Mother, not Gevurah. Not his master.

Not hate, but love. He'd wanted to serve love, the connection he'd witnessed between Orc and Cass, the love he had always wanted from Gevurah. Could there be wells of that power in the Immaterium, to free him from his paralysis and break his bonds? Or was it weak, something that only existed in snatches between realms of darkness?

Still Crome sharpened, drawing it out to deepen his terror. Still Tashi had no choice but to watch.

A thought. Orc had been trapped in stasis and had recovered – he'd heard his voice less than an hour since. Recovered, healed by Cass's love.

Healed.

He focused all his thought on his memory of Cass touching Orc. Love, healing. His body was mud. It wasn't fired; it could be reshaped. Not reshaped much, not even visibly.

Only changed so the poison was gone.

He reached out blindly with his mind, to the divine energy Crome had said surrounded him. Gevurah forgive him this magic; it was to save the monastery. Hana's brave challenge to his possessed self on the island; her arms around him; Aino's declaration that he would stand on the bridge and welcome him home. The poison was gone, he told himself, urged himself hard enough so that he couldn't doubt it. Gone. His was a different body, transformed into one that looked the same but wasn't drugged into stasis.

Something happened. He felt it as a wave of warmth spreading from his spine.

He tried to twitch a toe – and felt it move.

But his hands were still bound.

'Ready, Tashi?'

Crome looked at him. Tashi resisted the urge to attempt further movement. The energy of creation had healed him, and that energy could only belong to Gevurah. Gevurah hadn't forsaken him, even though he was mud, even though he was a creature of magic.

'You can tell if you're ready by looking two minutes into the future,' said Crome. 'If you see only endless nothing, forever, and feel acceptance – then you're prepared, and I'll have to find other sustenance. Either way, you'll die.'

The magician came forward. Tashi readied himself. What if a toe-twitch was all he could achieve?

Crome leaned over him with the knife, and Tashi whacked a foot up into the man's groin. Crome's gasp had barely left his mouth before Tashi pulled up both feet together and kicked with all his strength into Crome's ribs. Impact shocked from his feet up his legs. His chair rocked; Crome staggered and fell back to crash against the work-bench and collapse to the floor, gasping with pain and struggling to breathe.

'My eyes are vessels for the holy light of Gevurah.' Words torrented out of Tashi. 'My heart is a vessel for the holy fire of Gevurah. My lungs are vessels for the holy breath of Gevurah.' He hadn't been purified, not with the rite. But neither had the twenty-seven novitiates who'd defended Highcloud against Konstantin. 'My voice is the vessel for the holy anger of Gevurah. My limbs are vessels for the holy strength of Gevurah!'

His need was pure: to save Highcloud. His faith was as firm again as the Holy Mountain itself. The shadows of the past few days had blown away, and the summit of the peak shouted once more with light.

'I am their vessel!' he said, and again, and again, as Crome crawled to his feet, clutching his side.

The *Elohim Gibor* entered him. But not like in the arena, when they'd been called for a false purpose. His self was not pushed to one side of the fire; there was no other self than the fire. It did not take him over. It joined with him.

Crome picked up the knife.

Tashi exerted himself against the straps around his wrists. Dangerous, he knew, to express such strength through a body that wasn't wearing bindings and wasn't trained as a warrior. Or would be, if this were an ordinary human body and not something he had become.

The screws holding the straps to the chair tore loose from the wood. Tashi barely felt the effort. Crome tried to call for Wetherall, but broken ribs stifled his shout. He ran shambling from the room.

Tashi followed him out into the basement corridor, then into the old kitchen, where Astolio's sons had been shot. He arrived to see Crome, panting in pain, holding the revolver. He aimed it at Tashi's head. It shook in his grasp. 'Damn you.'

The gun cracked with a fire-flash, but Tashi was already moving; he'd reacted to the squeeze of Crome's finger on the trigger. He threw himself rolling to the floor, and as Crome lowered the gun for another shot, Tashi swept his legs round and chopped Crome's from under him. The magician fell, and at once Tashi was on top of him, pinning his gun-arm, his other hand round Crome's throat.

Crome gurgled something, staring wildly into Tashi's eyes. It might have been a plea for mercy. Judgement, Tashi knew, was the necessity. Not vengeance. The judgement of Gevurah, of that hard white peak that blazed cold in the sun. Not vengeance.

There was no pleasure in Tashi's mind, no hate, only calmness as he crushed the magician's throat until the man stopped struggling.

24

MATTERS OF STATE

Emilia had been stuck in the secretary's office for what seemed hours. A succession of staff officers had come and gone, none of them paying her any attention.

'It really is important,' she reminded Kelner.

'He is aware, Deaconess,' the secretary said, without looking up from the document he was drafting. 'Doubtless he'll see you when he is able.'

It seemed foolish now to have expected anything else. The woman who'd made the decision in the Cathedral, who'd dared the basement club and witnessed the horror without flinching from her purpose, seemed to have vanished on entering this room. She had no idea how to hasten her meeting with her brother. Nothing she could tell Kelner to pass on would achieve that result without giving away far too much.

At last Siegfried himself emerged, along with the officer who'd gone in fifteen minutes before. The two shook hands by the door to the stateroom. 'I look forward to our next meeting, Karl.'

'It will be a glorious one, your Grace. I guarantee it.'

'It is our Lord that guarantees success.'

The officer clicked his heels, bowed his head, strode off.

'Siegfried.' She stood as her brother was about to go back into the stateroom.

His glance suggested irritation that she was still there.

'Siegfried, it's urgent. You cannot guess how urgent until I tell you.'

He exhaled, and beckoned her. 'Five minutes. And get me a line to Colonel Petersen,' he added to Kelner.

Mention of the air-field commandant made Emilia nervous, but she tried to put it from her mind as she entered. The doors clicked shut behind her. The mannequin from two mornings ago was still there, dressed in its bizarre complex arrangement of black straps and with the two swords leaning against it.

Siegfried stood by their mother's full-length portrait. 'Well?'

Her mouth felt dry. 'It's about some doubts I've had as to my calling.'

He rolled his eyes. 'You said it was "urgent".'

'I know that in the past, you've had some doubts yourself.'

'Is that so?'

'After Bastian's return from Golgomera.' She lowered her voice in case Kelner had an ear to the doors. 'You talked with him about Empyreus… about his message that he approved you using the crystals. You both found it unlikely.'

His gaze might have been intended to turn her to stone. 'Bastian told you? Then he misunderstood. Or was babbling. He had the Bane, you might recall.'

'He was lucid sometimes.'

'If so, that stopped when he was found comatose in your room.'

'Siegfried, you must believe I never harmed him. I couldn't have – I love him.'

'As do I.'

'Then you would welcome revelations that might lead to his recovery?'

She hadn't intended to take so direct a path. Her heart beat harder at the risk.

'I've prayed, sister,' he said. 'Perhaps if more of us did so with conviction—'

'I've prayed too! But there hasn't been any result, has there? Empyreus busies himself with new machines and new sciences, and nothing to cure the man who…'

His head inclined a degree. 'Who…?'

But she'd stalled, unable to think how to point out Bastian's importance to the Empyrean church without hinting that Siegfried held his position only because of his brother's illness.

'If our Lord failed to help Bastian,' Siegfried said, 'it's because He punished him for expressing doubts – doubts Bastian should have begged to be forgiven, as I did. I suggest you also deal with your own doubts through prayer. Whatever they are. Now, I'm busy.'

'With preparations for war.'

'A minor action.'

'But it won't stop there, will it? Don't you realise you're being manipulated? You're being made a fool of.'

'Manipulated?'

She pushed on and took the risk. 'Empyreus isn't what he seems, Siegfried. The thoughts that come to the Trine are sent by a cabal of magicians.'

He stared at her. The telephone on his desk suddenly juddered out its harsh bell, but Siegfried ignored it. For three rings Emilia held his gaze against the instinct to shrink away from her mad assertion. Then her brother went and picked the instrument up.

'Keep him waiting,' he said a moment later. 'I – no, I said he must wait. I don't care for everyone telling me what's urgent.'

He replaced the telephone and turned back to her. 'Magicians.'

'Those responsible for the goddess attack in the Shallow Sea. They're called the Shining Ones. They've probably been behind Empyreus since the beginning.'

His gaze hardened. She saw his mind working behind it. 'Let me get this straight. They were behind the goddess-monster who destroyed *Iron Tiger*? But they also gave us the technology to build *Iron Tiger* in the first place? That's what you're saying?'

'Yes.'

'Then what is their purpose? To play chess against themselves?'

'It's to provoke war with Sundara. In which they're about to succeed.'

His eyes shifted aside; his brow furrowed. Thank God, she thought, he was actually considering this.

It didn't last. 'No,' he said. 'Sundara is a mere side-show before Golgomera, and our Lord is focused on that goal. Why else the developments in rapid forest-clearing: tracked vehicles, petroleum-driven saws? From whom did you pick up your insane idea? Or is it a product of hysteria?'

Fear gripped her at that word. She fought to stay strong. 'It's the truth, Siegfried.' She wished she sounded more convinced. 'But I can't reveal its source.'

'Was it that Watcher you were eyeing the other day? And, as I recall, you were keen to know more about that other one who passed through two or three weeks ago.' His mouth twitched in a smile. 'My foolish sister – the Watchers have a vested interest in discrediting Empyreus. They are bound by the Valkensee's ultimatum to decide whether or not to acknowledge His divinity. Clearly they have made their choice. Well, their perfidy will be short-lived.'

The menace in his tone caught her. 'What do you mean?'

'Earlier this afternoon, Empyreus contacted the Trine. Most in the Valkensee disputed the exact meaning of the revelation, but I was left in no doubt that it authorised military action.'

'What has that to do with the Watchers?'

'Not caught up yet? Against whom do you think the action was authorised?'

She gasped. 'Siegfried, no!'

'Have they dragged you so deep into their conspiracy?' he said. 'How can we go to war with Sundara and leave Highcloud at our backs to spread their denials and propaganda? The orders have already been given.'

'But the Watchers could unmask these magicians. You'll be doing their work for them. You'll be a dupe, a puppet.'

'Quiet! You've already said sufficient to have yourself committed.

It's only because you're my sister that I'm not sending you before the Council on Blasphemy. Or is it because I'm *busy*?'

He picked up the telephone. 'Get Petersen back.' He gestured Emilia away. She felt caught between escaping for the air-field, and trying to think of something that might persuade him. She still hadn't decided when, after only a short conversation, he set the instrument down.

'An air-craft stolen,' he said. 'Another damaged.'

Her heart leapt, but anxiously. What had happened that had stopped her friends waiting for her?

'Who – who could have done that?'

'Not your Watcher, by the sound of it.' He seemed distracted. Emilia's mind raced. If Max had been unable to wait, he would probably fly between the air-field and the palace, hoping to see the auto. There was nothing more to be said to Siegfried. She should accept her failure and leave. They could fly to Highcloud and warn them. Sundara would have to wait.

She was readying herself to go when a loud knock sounded. Before Siegfried could answer, the door shot open and a moustached man in a frock-coat entered, followed by a soldier with a rifle.

'Linton, what—'

'Your Grace, an astonishing communication from the Valkensee. Our Lord has revealed to the Trine again. You are in danger.'

'What?' snapped Siegfried.

'The message, your Grace, there was no doubt. All three youths spoke the same words: Prelate Astrasis in danger from an assassin.'

Emilia tensed.

'He… Empyreus mentioned me by *name*?'

'Seemingly so, your Grace.' Linton looked no less struck by the rarity. 'I humbly suggest you remain here with this man until we receive further details from the Trine. The rest of the guard are securing the palace.'

Siegfried turned to his desk and reached for the telephone.

A grunt came from the soldier. Emilia whirled to see the man crash forwards to the floor. Linton had turned to face the figure in the doorway, and now staggered back, clutching his throat, and sat heavily, gasping. Emilia's breath vanished at the speed of the attack – she backed off quickly as the boy stepped fully into the room between the two men he'd felled. He was only in his middle teens, dressed in fancy shirt and trousers. The bright gold of his eyes terrified her. And there was something unnatural about his skin, the texture, as though it were animated marble.

She stepped farther back. The boy kicked the rifle away from the soldier. It skidded across the floor, past the mannequin with its black straps and its swords.

'Wait – I know you.' Siegfried's voice trembled beneath its calm. 'You were with those others a couple of days ago.'

Emilia saw it now: he'd been in the secretary's office with Yaggit and Cass. He had to be the one Cass had named as Tashi.

'You've come to give your evidence, I assume?' said Siegfried, edging slowly round his desk. 'The enquiry was postponed on our Lord's suggestion, but I can take a deposition—'

His arm darted and he wrenched open a drawer. Tashi snapped into movement, not towards Siegfried but to the mannequin. Emilia flung herself back against the wall. Siegfried pulled out a gun just as Tashi grabbed the large sword.

She flinched at the gunshot. Another, another, another, but none hit Tashi – the boy flicked the heavy sword around as though it were a fencer's foil and bullets clanged off the blade and thudded into walls, shattered glassware; Emilia crouched down, hands over her head.

'Stop it!' she shouted.

They did. Her brother slid the spent magazine from his pistol and shoved in a new one from his desk drawer.

Tashi dipped on his knees as though about to rush. 'Don't!' yelled Emilia. 'I know Cass! Please, don't kill him.'

Siegfried had the pistol ready, but looked scared. 'You're telling him not to kill me? My thanks, but gun versus sword has only ever had one outcome.'

She could see that might not apply here. She saw in her brother's face that despite his words, he thought the same. And despite all his faults, he was her brother.

'He must die.' Tashi's voice carried a power she would never have expected from his frame, but it fitted his eyes. 'He plans to attack Highcloud.'

'I don't want that either,' she said. 'But he's already given the order. Killing him won't stop it.'

'Call it off,' the boy told Siegfried.

'Yes, do it, Siegfried.'

'And then you'll let me live?' he asked Tashi.

The boy didn't answer.

'What's your interest in Highcloud anyway?'

Tashi inhaled deeply, as though planning to breathe fire. 'I wielded this weapon before. You watched me.'

His words meant nothing to Emilia, but Siegfried looked lightning-struck. Then shock cleared his face, overtaken by a mad eagerness.

'The Zhenaii! That's a Zhenaii art, the transformation of matter! Show me how! Show me how, and I'll call off the attack – I won't need to any more.'

Tashi glanced to the doorway. Footsteps sounded outside, beyond the secretary's office; Emilia couldn't see who, but it sounded like boots. Tashi tensed to attack. Siegfried raised his gun and shot, missed as Tashi dived forwards. The boy slid over the polished floor, dragging a rug with him, and thumped against the desk. Siegfried started to lean over it when Tashi grasped the bottom of the heavy piece of furniture with his free hand and hauled upwards to tip it. Siegfried stumbled backwards and fell over his chair. The sound of boots closed. Siegfried jumped up, fired his gun wildly in Tashi's direction; Tashi snapped into a guard-stance and Siegfried ran for the door, yelling for help. In the doorway he collided with soldiers – shouting, commanding. Tashi leapt forward and sliced – but in the mass of moving bodies it was a pushed-forwards soldier his sword struck. Blood flew in an arc as Siegfried and his men crashed back into the secretary's office and the door slammed behind them.

A double-bang – two holes were punched in the doors; Emilia didn't know where the bullets ended up. Then came Siegfried's voice shouting for order.

Emilia panted a breath a second; she felt like her body was made of water. She stared at the soldier's severed arm on the floor in its uniform sleeve.

'We have ten men out here,' Siegfried's ragged voice called. 'Your swordplay can't defend against shots from two directions at once. You've no choice but to surrender. You'll be well looked after. I have no interest in harming you.'

'I heard the same from Daroguerre,' muttered Tashi.

Emilia hunkered down, slowly, wanting to be invisible. She thought the soldier who'd entered with Linton was dead. Linton himself looked like he was pretending to be so, but she could see his chest move. She prayed he wouldn't draw attention to himself.

Tashi stood a couple of paces in front and to one side of the tall panelled doors, thinking, considering.

Suddenly he sprang at them, kicked them, leapt back to the side as the doors snapped open. Bullets whizzed and thudded; Emilia threw herself down as one hit the wall a yard from her head. Then came the firework crackle of rifle bolts, and people behind the doors and to each side slammed them closed.

Astonishingly, it looked as though Tashi were planning to kick the doors again.

'Siegfried!' called Emilia. Tashi glanced round at her, but did nothing. 'Siegfried?'

No response.

'He's gone,' she told Tashi, her throat dry. 'He's left you to his men and run. You won't catch him now. Does Cass know you're here?'

'I think she believes I've left Bismark.'

'They've got an air-craft. We need to get to my auto and meet it. Warn Highcloud.'

Then she heard it – and hoped it wasn't her imagination. No, the roaring and humming loudened. She rushed to the window and the dullness of late-afternoon. She couldn't see it yet, but she knew.

'It's here! We have to—'

But the stateroom was on the first floor, and the ground floor had high ceilings: she was almost thirty feet up. She threw open the windows and stood on the balcony, overlooking the lawns and flower beds behind the palace. The air-craft came into view over the trees, its airscrews chopping. She saw Dinah's face behind the nose-gunner's glass, her hand waving frantically.

'That is an evil device,' said Tashi.

'What choice is there?' said Emilia. But she couldn't see what to do. There was no way the craft could manoeuvre to pick her up from the balcony, even with its door lowered – the wing would crash into the building.

'No!' she cried as Tashi moved past her and launched himself over the balcony railing. She looked over, horrified, in time to see him fling away his sword and hit the ground and roll. He sprang back up, ran beneath her and held out his spread arms. Her knees turned to water as she realised why.

'Jump,' he called up.

'No,' she muttered. 'No, for love of the Holy Mother, no.' She saw it might not be impossible – his strength and competence was beyond human. That almost made it worse, because it gave her an alternative to choosing safety. But safety, and what? Failure, possibly imprisonment. The Shining Ones might arrange to have her declared insane, hysterical, the diagnosis of her teens returned to haunt her.

'Hurry!'

The air-craft was coming round to land on the largest stretch of lawn. No one tried to intercept it yet, the palace's whole contingent of guards being outside the stateroom. But more would come soon, from elsewhere.

Eagle, if you can hear me, I beg you, lend me your wings.

She hitched up her skirts with shaking hands and clambered to straddle the balustrade. She got her other leg over and sat there, trying not to think of a broken back. Tashi waited below, arms ready, his expression one of calm competence. Still gripping the stone balustrade, she lowered her feet to the narrow lip on its outer edge and turned herself to face back into the room, then knelt and grasped the base of one of the balustrade's pillars.

To hell with it. Maybe with herself. She tumbled backwards.

An upwards wind buffeted her; her stomach fled; she closed her eyes and fought the instinct to try to twist and land on her feet, appalled that there was time to think, she was hurtling downwards and she could *feel* the ground coming and—

Impact shocked through her and wrenched her neck and body and she struck something else hard and rolled, bumped, stunned. There were arms round her. She thought they'd been round her as she hit the ground, but she couldn't tell; it had happened so fast.

She couldn't stand. Her body wanted her to lie there, to discover the damage. She didn't know if she couldn't move her legs or if she was just unwilling to try. She opened her eyes to grass, the palace's ground-floor windows. Then the grass moved; she moved, she was being picked up. The world span sickeningly; she saw the air-craft settling on the lawn, and Tashi carried her towards it at a run, and she was bumping, her head bumping.

Dinah stood at the top of the air-craft's steps, leaning out, extending a hand, with a look on her face that told Emilia her injuries must be bad. Tashi carried her up the steps and set her down on the cork-covered floor. She fought down the urge to be sick – and with all the force of her will, as though she had to push the instruction along every inch of her nerves, she tried to move her feet. Relief flooded her. Toes next, fingers, and hips. They worked. Whether the pain was merely bruising or fractures, she couldn't know, but at least her spine wasn't broken. She shook like she might break into pieces. She nodded and tried to smile in response to Dinah's concern. A male voice was shouting Tashi's name, frantic, over and over. She thought there might have been a gunshot. Then came the clanging of feet on the steps again and she heard Max – Max! – shout something from up above and her stomach lurched again as the craft rose into the air.

The noise of the airscrews mounted. They were moving, away from the palace, towards—

Then she remembered. 'Max,' she said. 'Tell Max – Highcloud.'

'Highcloud?' said Dinah. 'We're going to Sundara, Em. Jiata. Remember?'

'No. Highcloud's in danger. Ask Tashi.'

Dinah glanced elsewhere. 'I don't know I'd get much sense out of him. He's collapsed. Orc's looking after him.'

'Tell him, Di. Tell Max.' She tried to stand but every muscle had stiffened. 'Please.'

'Wait there.' Dinah left her. Emilia thought she could hear her voice, calling up to Max from the front gunner position, but couldn't make out their words over the sound of wind and engines and the elemental roar above.

When Dinah came back, she said, 'We're going to set down on a hill Max knows. We'll have a proper look at you then.'

'Just shock and bruising.' She hoped it was true.

'I'm amazed,' said Dinah. 'I died a hundred times watching you jump. I begged you not to, but I suppose you couldn't hear me. Or you ignored me.'

'I couldn't hear you. But there was no other way. He caught me.'

'What was he doing there?'

'Later,' said Emilia. 'Please, later for talking. Are there any blankets?' She'd started to shake harder.

'There's almost nothing on board, I'm afraid,' said Dinah. 'But we bought you a coat.'

'Thank you.' Emilia's teeth chattered. She closed her eyes. 'I flew, Di – I flew.'

'Like an eagle,' said Dinah.

She thought of the carving in the Cathedral. 'Like one made of stone, perhaps.'

25

POWER

Orc watched Cass come out of the air-craft, the last to leave. He glanced round at the hilltop they'd landed on: thirty miles west of Bismark, according to Max. A grey afternoon was turning to evening. At the hill's foot, farmhouse lights already showed.

Tashi looked shattered. He still carried his sword, but it was obvious now that he was beyond wielding it, and the ferocious gold of his eyes was gone. Emilia could barely stand or walk through stiffness, and needed Dinah's support; Max offered his too, but Dinah refused to share the burden.

'Right, what is this?' said Max. 'Highcloud's in danger?'

'Siegfried's going to attack,' said Emilia. 'The rest of the Valkensee wasn't sure, apparently, but he seemed certain Empyreus authorised it.'

'Because of this ultimatum to the Abbot?' said Orc.

'Yes. Siegfried said he doesn't want Highcloud spreading denials about Empyreus if there's war against Sundara.'

'The ultimatum was an excuse,' said Tashi. 'Crome told me there's something your brother wants, and he can't get it without attacking the monastery.'

'*Crome* told you?' said Cass.

'He taunted me with all sorts of things, before I escaped.'

'Hold on. You mean... you were *there*, when we came back?'

'Awaiting death. I couldn't move or speak, from poison. Without the *Elohim Gibor*, I wouldn't have lived.'

'Holy crap,' said Cass. 'I'm sorry,' she told Tashi. 'I should've... oh, I don't know. I'm guessing he's dead now?'

Tashi glanced down and nodded.

Orc didn't want to think about that. 'But can we believe what Crome told you? How would he know? The Shining Ones?'

'There's no doubt he had access to secret knowledge,' said Tashi. 'He also told me who killed my master. Someone you know.'

His look tightened Orc's insides.

'Who?' said Cass, her voice sounding dry.

'Ranga.'

The world pitched. '*Ranga*?' said Orc. 'But... what?'

'You knew him, did you not?'

'Yes, but... and *you* did? The *same* Ranga?'

'Isn't this getting us off track?' said Max.

'Wait,' Dinah told him. Orc was surprised at the intense look on the young woman's face, but things were moving too fast for him to give it proper thought.

'How did you know Ranga?' said Cass.

'He joined me and my master in Torrento,' said Tashi. 'I don't really know why he came with us, unless it was so he could kill us, to protect his mistress.'

'Mistress?'

'A sorceress. Vanessa.'

Orc and Cass looked blankly at each other. Then Cass said, 'His "true love"...'

'The "winner",' said Orc, and swallowed.

'What?' she said.

'The man Thera talked about, who took the big focus-stone. Remember? Civvy clothes, dark hair? Shit. Daroguerre doesn't have the big stone – Ranga does!'

'Bloody hell. Do you think he was after it all the time he was with us?'

'And he killed Shoggu?'

'He wasn't that kind of person, surely?' said Cass.

'He is evil,' said Tashi. 'He told me Orc was the magician we sought, even though he knew I wanted to kill that magician.'

'*That's* why you attacked him that time?' said Cass.

'Yes. It was Ranga who misled me.'

'And do you know where this person is now?' said Emilia – her face betraying a strange level of interest, Orc thought, considering she'd never heard of him before.

'No idea,' said Cass. 'If he's not still on the island, then maybe Torrento. But that's for later. Right now, we have to think about Highcloud.'

'Can we send a wire or something?' said Orc. 'To warn them?'

'The telegraph station at the bottom of the Petitioners Road is manned by Kurassians,' said Tashi. 'And though I have no right to demand this of you, I want to go back home.'

'You have every right to demand it of *me*,' said Emilia. 'You saved me.'

Orc closed his eyes and rubbed his temples. He too owed it to Tashi to deliver him to the home he wanted to defend. But to go there himself would be an enormous risk.

'Right,' he said. 'We'll fly there and drop Tashi off. Then on to Sundara.'

'Mightn't that be to miss an opportunity?' said Emilia. 'If we gave them the warning ourselves and the Watchers were grateful for it, they might help us.'

'No.' Orc tried not to let his tension show. 'We can't stop off at Highcloud. Or I can't. We either all agree to that, or I'm staying here.'

'Lest you forget,' said Emilia, 'this is my air-craft, effectively.'

'And it doesn't go anywhere I don't want it to,' said Cass.

'Thanks to you killing our choice of engineer.'

'Don't fight, you two!' said Dinah. 'Em, doing more than dropping

Tashi off could put Orc and Cass in a very difficult position. They both use magic.'

'It's not written on their faces, is it?' said Emilia, tight-voiced and clearly in pain. 'But very well – we'll simply drop off Tashi and fly to Sundara, and leave the world's most skilled group of diviners to their fate, even though they could have investigated the Shining Ones and who knows what else.'

'Shit,' said Cass. '*Shit!*'

The expletive silenced the hilltop.

'Emilia's right,' she said. 'I wasn't thinking straight. And we can't go about this as half-arsed as usual. We nearly lost our chance at the air-craft because we forgot about a single bloody fence. We have to think about this properly.'

Dread trickled through Orc's stomach.

'We need them,' said Cass. 'We need the Conclave to investigate Empyreus, and the Kaybees, the Shining Ones behind him. And doesn't Highcloud have an interest in that anyway? Isn't that what Yaggit was sent to Bismark for, to help that process? What if they can prove to the Kurassians who's behind Empyreus before the battle starts?'

'My brother wouldn't listen to me,' said Emilia, 'and he won't listen to the Watchers. As he said, and you've pointed out, they have an interest in discrediting Empyreus.'

'But you could only give him your word. What if the Watchers could find real proof, something objective?'

'If such a thing were possible, then yes, he might pay attention.'

'We have to make it happen,' said Cass. 'We *must*. It's the best chance we have against the Kaybees.'

'Okay,' said Orc, fighting down his queasiness. 'But what you said a few days ago still stands. Highcloud hates magicians. And how are you going to tell them about Empyreus without telling them about that séance? We can't be sure they won't guess something about us just from clapping eyes on us. And what if they investigate the air-craft and find the elemental?'

'The technology was the gift of Empyreus,' said Cass. 'That'll prove the magic connection.'

'It won't stop them knowing you use magic, will it? We can't take the risk.'

'I don't think they will trouble themselves with the air-craft,' said Tashi. 'The last time one visited, only my master was suspicious of it. Yaggit supposed it was a new technology, and the other Watchers no doubt thought the same.'

'Wait, that's a point,' said Cass. 'Yaggit. If he's there, he'll vouch for us, right? He accepted magic could be used for good purposes.'

'He cannot have reached there yet,' said Tashi.

'But if we know where he is, we can pick him up on the way.' She turned to Orc. 'Can you divine that?'

'Doubt it. It's way beyond anything I've done before.'

'The Watchers will be able to find him,' said Tashi. 'Perhaps two or three together would be enough.'

'Then here's what I think,' said Emilia. 'When we reach Highcloud, some of us, not Orc and Cass, will form an embassy to the Abbot. Dinah and I might be best – and Tashi, since he knows the place but won't be recognised. We'll warn of my brother's intention, and ask them to locate Yaggit. If possible, we'll then collect him, let him know the situation, and on our return to Highcloud, we'll plan for the Conclave to prove the truth behind Empyreus. In the meantime, they can prepare defences to hold off any attack. I'd have thought, with just that one narrow road leading to the monastery, and the gorge and the Knifebridge, that shouldn't be too difficult.'

'The novitiates will be Inspired in defence,' said Tashi. 'If forewarned, they cannot fail to bar the road.'

'From ground troops, perhaps,' said Max.

'Hopefully the Conclave will come up with the proof before the attack,' said Cass. 'Do you know when they're going to launch it?'

'The commander was in Siegfried's stateroom two hours ago,' said Emilia. 'He surely cannot reach there before tomorrow night, not by train.'

'If your brother is mounting the attack himself, he'll probably field only his guards regiment,' said Max. 'Doubly likely if the rest of the Valkensee aren't convinced. They won't have artillery, at least. But they might not need it.'

'Then we have our plan, at least,' said Emilia.

'Yup,' said Cass. 'Let's get going.'

'We can't fly to Highcloud straight away,' said Max. 'It's getting dark, and Cass hasn't been there before.'

'I have, of course,' said Tashi.

'That's not the point. During daylight, in reasonable weather, I can navigate with charts and compass, but in bad visibility we rely on the engineer being familiar with the destination and communicating that to the elemental.'

'I've never been to Sundara either,' said Cass.

'You're familiar with Torrento,' said Max. 'I was planning to get us there by dawn and fly along the coast by daylight.'

'So what are we going to do?' said Emilia. 'There won't be a moon tonight.'

'I'm sorry,' said Max. 'But I can't risk taking us into a mountainous area flying blind. If there's a significant tailwind, we could end up several miles ahead of where I think we are, with obvious results.'

'So, what?' said Cass. 'We stay here till morning? Lose all that time?'

'Not here,' said Max. 'Someone might have seen us come down. They might be heading here or reporting us even now. I think this is unworkable. If you want my opinion, we'll have to leave Highcloud to its own devices and—'

'No,' said Cass, Tashi and Emilia together.

'Right,' said Max. 'Then we'll fly north towards Thangkara for half an hour or so, and find somewhere remote to set down when it's almost dark – that'll lessen the chances of being seen. We can set off again a couple of hours before dawn. We won't reach high ground until full light.'

They began to board. Orc was about to join the others when Cass held him back. 'I need to talk to my cousin for a minute,' she told

Dinah. The airscrews, left to chop at idle, made enough noise so they wouldn't be heard from the craft's interior.

When Dinah had disappeared inside, Cass said, 'Are you all right?'

Orc saw the concern in her face, but also her weariness. 'I'm fine.' He wanted to cheer her up. 'You're doing a brilliant job with the elemental.'

'Thanks,' she said. 'It's knackering, though. I can't help thinking the normal engineers must have some trick to keep from it taking so much energy.'

'But we've only got a little way to go tonight. And tomorrow you'll be rested. You'll be okay to get to Highcloud, and then wherever Yaggit is?'

'Maybe. I think so. But what's changed, Orc? You were all for getting to Highcloud before we reached Bismark. I was the one who didn't want to.'

'That was before you started using any kind of magic.'

'No, it's not just that. Just now, you said "I" can't stop off at Highcloud. Not "we". And you looked really worried.'

He couldn't answer.

'Is it because of last night? You think they might uncover something… sordid, about our pasts? I don't think that's a danger, really – they'll be too occupied with other things.'

'No, it's not that,' he said. 'Not our pasts.'

'Then what?'

'I'm sorry. I can't tell you, not yet.'

'I meant what I said. That elemental takes us nowhere I don't want it to. If you're going to be in danger, then we can change our plan, but I need to know why.'

'We're not changing it,' said Orc. 'You're right, we need the Conclave. And the plan's good. We'll be fine.'

Dinah called from the air-craft. Orc made to move, but Cass stopped him. 'One minute!' she called back, and turned to him.

'Orc, just after we came to Bismark, you said getting up in an air-craft would free you from the Mother. Has it? Because… I don't know, you seemed pretty free anyway, after you woke. Back to normal. Clearer.

But what happened at the air-field? Where did that… stuff come from?'

'Just plants. We can manifest things, remember?'

'Not just the plants, that speech you made. And we can't just manifest. We can't create gold coins by asking – there has to be power behind it. Doesn't there?'

'There was fear there,' he said. 'I had a… dream about it. The whole city was filled with it: fear of the Witch, of nature, of their own bodies. I used it to power the manifestation, like Daroguerre did with the Mother energy on the island.'

'You called her. But this time, she didn't attack you.'

He looked down, fought to hide that he felt like crying.

'Orc, what happened when you were out cold?'

'Nothing.'

'I don't believe—'

'I can't remember!' His wrist itched, and he steeled himself against the emotional crumbling. 'I am clearer. That madness, that reality and magic merging into each other, that's gone. I think. At least, I think I'll be able to control when it happens. Maybe even use it. I'm more powerful now, Cass. That's a good thing, isn't it?'

'Depends where it came from.'

He kept quiet. He didn't want to lie, but anything near the truth might let her guess.

'Good to have you back, anyway,' she said, but her voice carried doubt. She hugged him, and he returned it, careful not to notice the warmth and firmness of her body. Even the idea of it stung his wrist like needles.

'Crazy, that about Ranga,' he said as they separated.

'We'll get the whole story from Tashi later. You think Ranga really has the big focus-stone?'

'Unless he wanted it for that sorceress.'

'Bastard. Poor Shoggu.'

'Crome could've been lying.'

'It makes too much sense,' said Cass. 'Bloody hell, I wouldn't like to be in Ranga's shoes once Tashi's done defending Highcloud. Talking of which, we really must go.'

Orc pulled the door shut once they were in. Cass disappeared up to the engineer's floor. Emilia and Dinah had taken the two bolted-down passenger seats, so Orc settled himself into a nook near the port gunner's position. The space was warmer now, the heating system run off the engines beginning to take effect. Soon the roar above grew, turned to a howl; the craft lifted off, the airscrews' noise rising in volume and pitch. Orc rubbed his wrist. His holding of Cass had only been fraternal. And he'd detected nothing more erotic in her own clasping of him. Not surprising after the disaster of the previous evening. That was how he had to think of her now, as her brother. It would make it easier. It would stop the risk of unfaithful thoughts.

'What happened when you were out cold?'

'I can't remember!'

But he could – he recalled everything, the nightmare destroyed city, the avatar Skull-face, the sinking into the marsh. And it hadn't ended there, for some time later he'd found himself lying on hard ground in unrelieved blackness, cool air about him, and unable to move. Every time he'd tried, something in himself or outside overrode it. Terrible possibilities obsessed him: that Crome's house and everything else had been a dream from which he'd now woken; or that he was dead, and this was all there would be, for ever.

But at some point, change came. Faint light flickered on tunnel walls. He shifted his head and groaned at the pain all over his skin. He was naked, and the cuts that marked the Mother's claim on him had reopened and bled. The flame approached, a brand carried in the jaws of an animal whose chestnut fur gleamed with its light. A brand lit with the sacred fire. It was weaker than he'd seen it before, and there was no reflection in water like at his Initiation, but hope rose in him.

'Otter!'

The animal stopped and took the brand from its mouth. 'No. This flame is not yours.'

Now Orc made out long, black-tipped ears. 'Hare. What are you doing here?'

'Searching.' Hare stuck the end of the brand in a crack. 'Hana's fire weakens. I seek the source, to replenish it. Like you, she has lost herself. And it is partly your fault!'

'Mine?'

Hare stood on his hind legs; dark eyes glinted in the holes of his mask. 'What did the two of you think you were doing? You treated magic with no more respect than a game. You acted on thoughtless instinct, as though in a dream, and so you have become trapped in dreams, sinking ever deeper. You should have kept each other awake! You should have taught each other who you really were! Even your sex was half a magical exercise. And yes, I am fully aware of the irony: that I, a denizen of the Otherworld, should advise that you need to be grounded in reality. But what do you think we stole the fire for? So you could have fun pissing on it? There, you've made me lose my temper.'

'Where is this?' said Orc. 'This has to be a scape, right? But I don't remember going into it. Where's Otter?'

'I don't know,' said Hare. 'You are not wearing your tattoos.'

'But we can still talk?'

'That is strange, I agree. Can you feel your body? Do you know your way back to it?'

'No,' said Orc. It worried him that the question of whether he was in the magical-mental world or the physical had not occurred to him before, not even in Magoria, the bizarre version of Bismark. The real and imaginary had merged without a join. He tried not to think what it might mean to never be able to separate them again.

'Can I come with you? Will finding the source help me? I need my real self strengthening, right? That's what you hope it can do for Hana?'

'Don't ask me questions!' said Hare. 'Decide! Identity is decision: did you not know? Why else are we in this position? You couldn't decide between Hana and Cass. You couldn't decide what to let yourself feel for either of them. You committed to nothing and no one. Even when you decided to help Tashi, you were diverted and thus failed. Every indecision weakened your own identity and increased the grip of your mythic role. It is now the strongest part of you, a costume you have put on and fastened tight. I doubt you can escape from it now. You have lost the strength to refute it.'

'Can I still come with you, though?' said Orc, his heart sinking. 'I don't want to be alone.'

'Yes, we can search together, until She has you.'

Orc looked around, expecting vegetation, some sign of imminent attack.

'She no longer needs to pursue,' said Hare. 'The weave of your self is unpicking, thread by thread. She has only to wait.'

The brand's flickering light now showed pale irregularities in the floor. Orc thought they might be buried bones protruding. He reached for one, and was about to scrape the earth away when he saw it was a stone knife – and so were the others.

'The source of the fire,' he said, to divert himself. 'It's the Smoking Mirror, right? From the story?'

'That was the form of its first container on earth.' Hare picked up the brand and sloped it across his shoulder. 'Black, glassy, reflective, and fuming with heat.'

The description reminded Orc of something – something vast, black, curved.

'We tricked it from the Mirror,' Hare said as on three legs he led Orc along the tunnel. 'And Raven passed it to humankind. So the tale goes. But what if the tale itself were a trick? Or forgotten and distorted by the time it reached the north?'

Must be some way out of this, Orc thought. He had to find the source of the fire, had to take note of Hare's words, had to commit to Cass again and again until he'd recovered himself. But just thinking about escape felt like staring up a thousand-foot cliff.

Then he realised they were in broad daylight, climbing wide stone steps. Very steep – Hare had to use seemingly all the power of his hind legs to jump each one. The sun roasted down. A mile away rose a bare hill, smooth and round, its slopes crowded with people. In the other direction stretched a city of low, simple buildings, and beyond its outskirts the fields and villages of a seemingly endless plain, threaded by the meanders of a wide river. But none of the fields was green or gold or any shade of ripening; all were bare brown, or blighted black.

Fear twisted Orc's insides as he neared the summit of the Great Ziggurat. But when he reached the top, a king already stood there: a naked man a few years older than him, his skin tawny and his ribs and hip-bones protruding. The king stared down into the square shaft-hole. The stone around it was dark with old, dried blood.

A white-robed priestess stood at the man's shoulder. She offered a knife. The king took it, but his brow furrowed. Orc's throat choked, knowing what would come. But at least it wouldn't be himself. Somehow, he had been spared.

'Is this the true story?' said Hare. 'Is this Raven now, come to pass the fire to man?'

Orc followed Hare's gaze towards the hill – what would in time become the largest of the Hollow Isles. A dot in the sky became a bird, heading their way. But it was too big to be a raven, and the wrong shape. And not black.

A man. A man with fiery wings, robed and masked in gold.

Pinions flashed in the sunlight as the man landed beside the king. He carried a golden breastplate, which he passed over the king's head. The king's hair emerged aflame with sun-fire; his eyes blazed. The breastplate settled on his shoulders, covering his torso and genitals. He stepped back from the shaft, then grabbed the priestess and slammed the blade into her chest.

Orc cried out, but the king and the Shining One and the priestess had disappeared – and so had the crowds on the hill, the city, the fields. All around was sea.

'What is this?' breathed Orc.

'You have witnessed the source of Her anger,' said Hare, 'the denial of what was promised. The waters come – hurry!' he cried, and took the brand in his mouth and bounded down the ziggurat steps. Orc turned to follow, but Hare had already vanished.

‘Hare?’ Calling in panic, he went down the steps until he reached the rising water, but saw no sign of the animath. The sea rose, beating him back step by step. It swarmed with weed, and the air was thick with the brine smell of it, and the weed writhed with currents; the dark wet backs of creatures slipped above the surface before diving again. The sea pushed Orc in retreat to the ziggurat’s plateau – where, by the shaft entrance, the knife still lay, glinting, expectant.

‘No!’ He picked it up and hurled it.

It slapped onto the mass of weed, but didn’t sink. A wind roughed up; the slipping and seething of the creatures in the weed intensified. White wave-heads frothed; water slapped against the stone, splashing him. Strange ripples in the carpet of weed carried the knife back, and a surge of water threw it onto the stone near Orc’s feet. He didn’t take it, not yet, but he sensed that he’d lost, and that now the world just waited for him to admit it. The nearby island had disappeared. Horizon to horizon, there was nothing but sea and sky and the small stone square on which he stood.

A few yards out, the weed began to move on the unsettled water, to rise in a hump, dragging with it starfish and sea-snakes and crabs and spiny fish and smooth fish and sea-cucumbers and sponges and driftwood and bones and squid and shells, all mixed in with the weed, and the weed was of all types, filmy, stringy, leaf-like. Held together with tension, with anger, and Orc knew that if he wasn’t prepared to sacrifice himself it would pull him down and drown him.

But despite the horror of what he faced, the nullness where his future should have been, the beauty of that mass of colour and movement and texture awed him. His eyes stung at a realisation – a recognition, a glimpse of a long-hidden memory that pierced both the Shroud and his heart – that it was precisely this beauty that had inspired his passion for freediving, back in his lost childhood.

‘Wait!’ He held his arms outstretched. ‘Wait.’

The tangled hump drew no nearer. The world was hushed in expectancy.

Orc came to the edge of the water. By his toes, the weed moiled with tiny creatures. The urge to walk down into that seethe of life was almost overpowering, to melt into it. He faced again the indistinct shape that had risen from the weed twenty feet away. Larger creatures now were mixed with it, flapping and disappearing and appearing again: a tuna, a large octopus, a ray. Their eyes stared without intelligence, but he sensed intelligence behind the life-mound itself.

He might have been on another planet. There were only two possible ways out, and only one possible way back.

'I agree to keep the compact.'

His words sank into the world like stones through water.

'But the *whole* compact, as it was in the beginning. A king reigned seven years before you reclaimed him. I've only ever played the role of the king at the end, the one who refused you, and so you've pursued me. I don't refuse you now. I am your willing consort. I commit to that,' he said, and felt within himself a sense of the words knotting with the fibres of his soul. 'But I have seven years before you reclaim me. That's how it was when the balance was kept – before famine, before refusal, before the Sun-King was forever parted from you.'

Tension cleared from the air. Slowly the hump flattened and dispersed back into the mat of weed, the creatures within it swimming away. But as it finally merged back, Orc thought he caught a glimpse of a face within, as though in a cloud: a human face he almost recognised, that pulled at him. A face something like Cass, but not Cass.

The sea calmed. The weed dispersed; patches of clear water appeared. Orc checked his skin: the cuts had healed. When he searched for it, he found, for the first time, the sense of his real body lying on a real bed. But he didn't need to return to it yet. He squatted down next to the water, and dipped his fingers. He didn't want to think about what he had just done, how much it had changed things, how irrevocably.

A splash jerked his gaze up. One creature remained, swimming round the breaking mats of weed. Orc caught a glossy glimpse of a wet back, then a flick of pointed tail.

'Otter!'

The animath swam towards him. He wasn't masked. He lolloped out of the water and shook his fur spiky. 'What's the guy called who comes along after the wedding and cleans up the mess, bruv? Because that's me.'

'We can talk without masks now?'

'You're the Lord of Beasts now, didn't you know?' said Otter. 'That's what you get in the north for marrying the Goddess, as well as Sun-King in these parts. I guess I should congratulate you on your nuptials. But that's a bitter, salty cake you've eaten.'

'What choice did I have?'

'To keep refusing,' said Otter. 'Desperation might've found you a way out.'

'Or she might have drowned me.'

'She might.'

'At least I get seven years now.'

'Do you?' said Otter. 'You think?'

'Yeah. What Daroguerre said: each Sun-King lasted seven years.' And his whole remembered life had only been two. To have more than three times that remaining felt plenty.

'But seven years from when?' said Otter.

Orc frowned: his animath was normally brighter than this. 'From when I became the Sun-King. From just now.'

'You're sure it wasn't earlier?' A trance-like undertone had come into Otter's voice.

'Well… the earliest it could've been was when I met the Sea Mother in the zig at Bazantin. That was only a few weeks ago.'

'But when did you become the consort of the Mother? When did the previous king die?' Otter started to shake. '*When did you become the man of the house?*' he squealed, in a horrible high-pitched voice Orc had never heard before.

'Wait,' said Orc, suddenly cold. 'You're talking about something that happened before? You're saying my father died? Otter—?'

The animath had fallen onto his side, shivering and shuddering, his fur all on end. Orc squatted beside him, scared. He was about to try touching the creature when Otter spasmed, hurled himself onto his feet, leapt into the water and disappeared.

Instinct drew Orc's attention to the previously empty horizon: there, faint with distance, stood a great black curved wall. For just a moment, Orc caught a whiff of chemicals over the salt-weed smell of the calm sea; then there came another, more homely smell and the feel of cotton against his cheek, and he opened his eyes to his room in Crome's house, dim with curtained daylight. The sea faded as quickly as a dream.

He tried to sit up, and his left hand caught on something; he winced as tiny stings bit his wrist. It was trapped against the sheet, but he couldn't see how without lifting the coverlet.

A maid sat by the door, but with her head slumped on her chest in sleep. Orc pulled back the cover with his free hand, and his breath snatched.

A vine had grown through the sheet and wound itself tightly about his wrist. Not something in his mind: he felt perfectly lucid. Many tiny white flowers bloomed along it, delicate petals suffused with tints of yellow and blue. Many tiny thorns gripped.

He calmed the impulse to struggle against it; another instinct lay beneath. Gently but firmly, he imagined the vine uncurling from his wrist, and he watched as the physical plant did the same.

He exhaled, long and slow, as he replaced the cover.

Her consort. He really was. Bound. She would know the moment he was unfaithful. There would be no getting away from her now. If he left the surface in an air-craft, she would be with him. If he travelled to the mountainous stronghold of her most implacable enemies, it would be in her hidden company.

And from what Otter had said, he couldn't know when the vegetation that manifested through him would cease to obey him and instead take his life.

PART FOUR
ANDROLOCH

26

SPIES AND SOLDIERS

Petri was grateful for the calm. Much as he'd enjoyed the mass of shouting drunkards and the smell of bodies and spilt beer in the common room the night before, the iron bands of morning-after round his forehead couldn't have stood more of the same. Now cool air came through the open doors of the Sack of Ducks, and only the sound of hooves and wheels out in the street threatened to disturb his concentration on the card game. He glanced at his opponent, seated across the table. An interesting face: half-Thangkaran, by his own account. Good structure, strong cheekbones, firm chin. Worth sketching, Petri thought. Though not in the way he sometimes drew Hana. Or probably not. He certainly wasn't in a state to entertain such thoughts right now.

'Come on,' said Ranga.

Petri checked his cards again and threw in the hand. 'By all the gods devised by man, what a pain in the arse.'

It was an oath he'd picked up from Geist months before, but Ranga showed no recognition of its brilliance, merely scooped up the pile of cards. 'Bad luck, that's all.'

'Being almost too hung-over to think isn't down to "luck".'

'No one forced you to drink anything,' said Ranga.

'It's an insult to refuse free wine where I come from – even the cheap stuff you kept buying. Why aren't you suffering?'

'Maybe I am.' Ranga shuffled. 'Got to keep things hidden in my game.'

'You're a tracker, yes? Or a fur-trader?'

Ranga raised one eyebrow, irritating Petri, who didn't have that trick. 'How'd you deduce that?'

'You said you know where Androloch is,' said Petri. 'You said we'd need your help to get there. And no one knows the Bourgoune apart from trackers and fur-traders. Simple.'

Ranga snapped each card down as he dealt. 'Maybe not so simple as you think. But I'll say no more till she comes.' He checked his pocket-watch, then looked up the staircase. 'Almost eleven. Do you think she's all right?'

Petri thought he sounded nervous. 'Worried she's avoiding you after last night?'

'I did nothing inappropriate,' said Ranga.

'Not for lack of trying.'

'Go up and see.' Ranga was still watching the stairs. 'You want breakfast, don't you?'

'Hardly. I'd puke.' Even so, Petri stood and put his cards in his pocket. He was halfway to the staircase when the sound came of a door closing above. Moments later, Hana appeared on the landing balcony.

She did look a bit rough, Petri thought, the evening's overindulgence emphasising the toll magic had taken on her a few days before. Not that it dented her attractiveness; it made her look more like someone who threw herself at life. He returned to his seat as she descended. Ranga stood, his gaze lowered, and bowed.

'Good morrow to you, Lady Vana.'

Petri suppressed a laugh.

'Hana,' she said – then frowned, as if uncertain herself.

'And she's not "Lady" anything,' offered Petri.

Ranga turned to him. 'All it takes for a woman to be a lady is for a man to think of her so.'

He'd been similarly flattering the previous evening. Petri was gratified to note Hana's wariness as she sat on the chair Ranga pulled out for her.

'We've been waiting for you before we have breakfast,' Ranga said. 'I've been looking forward to it, after two days of lumpy porridge at the Boar's Head.'

'This isn't your normal lodging?' said Hana.

'I'm staying at the Head. But Fate drew me here last night – her hand guiding me like a weaver at her loom.'

This time Petri made no attempt to stifle his snort. Ranga made no reaction, keeping his gaze on Hana – though on her shoulder, rather than her face.

'I'm sure *you* know that all people are threads in her tapestry, my Lady,' Ranga said. 'Most are dull-coloured, destined only to be worked into the scenery. But some threads are of spun gold, and those she weaves with care into her foreground figures.'

'Very poetic,' Hana said.

'Isn't the truth always?' Ranga turned his attention back to his cards. Petri glanced at Hana and rolled his eyes.

She shook her head when asked if she wanted to join the game, and took only coffee when offered breakfast, so Ranga was the only one who ate. As Petri played, determined to win at least one hand, he noticed that whereas Ranga hadn't been able to keep his eyes off Hana's face the previous night, he now seemed reluctant to look at it. Like any man, Petri thought with scorn, whose drunken attraction turned to discomfort with the morning's reality. He felt insulted on Hana's behalf, but also pleased by this fading of expected rivalry. As for Hana, she kept sneaking looks at Ranga, but her expression didn't suggest attraction so much as a desire to puzzle him out.

Seeming bored at last of winning at Sevens, Ranga suggested changing the game to Jack-Under-the-Fence, but Petri shook his head. 'Cards don't interest me,' he announced, a spur-of-the-moment decision that felt like it would stick for all time.

'Then let me settle up,' Ranga said. 'I'll find the landlord.' He pushed away his plate and headed through the door beside the bar.

'Well,' said Hana. 'He's a one.'

'One idiot,' said Petri. 'He should've thrown the first couple of games and then played me for bets.'

'And you'd have fallen for that?'

'Of course not.'

She pressed the heel of her hand against her head. 'Anyway, trying to cheat you would hardly have been helping us, would it? Isn't that what he wants to do?'

'So he claimed,' said Petri, assuming Ranga's proffered help would vanish now Hana had lost her allure in his shallow eyes. 'But if it turns out otherwise, we can do without him.'

'How much does he know about our purpose here?'

'Only what we told him last night.'

'Which was, exactly?'

He suppressed a smirk. 'Memory a little blurred?'

'Just answer the question. If you can.'

'You told him we need to find Androloch. Then he pestered us about why, until you mentioned a rescue. That seemed to confuse him, or...' Petri frowned. 'Any rate, it made an impression. He said he knew the place and how to get there.'

She nodded, slowly. 'How come he knows it, and no one else we asked has?'

'He might be some kind of fur-trader. Though he likes to paint himself as a man of mystery. And when I say "paint", I mean slapping around a big brush.'

'Still, if he does know Androloch, we'll have to hang on to him.'

Petri didn't like *have to*. 'Careful, here he comes.'

Reaching their table, Ranga met Hana's gaze tentatively, questioningly, for a moment, before his eyes shied again. 'Shall we reconvene here at three?' he said. 'I've a few arrangements to make for our journey.'

Petri frowned. It seemed Ranga hadn't gone off Hana after all, but then why the averted gaze? Was it that he no longer found her face attractive, but had switched his interest to lower down?

'As to this journey,' said Hana, 'I hope we've done nothing to encourage any expectation of payment?'

Ranga bowed. 'To serve is its own reward.'

'I'm not sure I understand.'

'Everything will become clearer soon, my Lady.'

'I don't understand that "Lady" business either. You're not mistaking me for someone else? Last night, didn't you say I reminded you of someone?'

Ranga's face quickly tightened. 'No mistake, I assure you.'

'Then who do you think I am?'

Petri caught suppressed irritation in Ranga's face, but his voice stayed pleasant. 'Could any of us claim to truly know who anyone is? We all have our masks, personal or professional, that we put on or remove to suit our company.'

'A philosopher as well as a poet,' said Petri.

Ranga smiled, seemingly missing the sarcasm. 'If so, it's because my Lady inspires me.' He turned to her. 'Since I seek no other payment, would you grant me an indulgence? I called you "Vana" earlier. Would it be objectionable to you if I carried on doing so? Just as a whim, you understand.'

She shrugged, visibly uneasy. 'I don't suppose it makes any difference what you call me.'

'Thank you, my Lady. It'll be a pleasure to have you along.'

He kissed her hand – again, without really meeting her eye – then turned and left.

'Have us along,' Petri said. 'As though he was planning to go to Androloch anyway.'

'I don't trust him,' Hana said.

'What, just because he got you drunk, tried to seduce you, and won't tell us anything about himself?'

Her withering look shifted to an uncertain, unfocused gaze at the table. 'Do you think there might be anything in what he said, about fate? Something's been niggling at me this morning. His face seems familiar. And not just from last night. Last night, I noticed he looked a bit like Tashi – Tashi as he used to be – but this morning it feels as though I've known him, actually *him*, for years.'

'Probably the drink,' said Petri. 'Or something he slipped into it.'

'Hm,' she murmured. 'I had some strange dreams. I think. I can only recall fragments. Anyway, we need to know for sure whether we can use him.'

'My fear is he's planning to use us,' said Petri. 'He knows we need his knowledge, and at some point he's going to tell us his price. I don't believe his "only want to serve" bollocks. I hate to say it, but I think that price will involve you and a lot of grunting.'

'The elegance of your speech never fails to delight.'

'How about I try a trance-drawing? Try to pick up what he's really after?'

She nodded at that. 'Good idea.'

They went up to Petri's room, where he sat on his bed with his sketchpad, and Hana took a chair by the door to ward against intrusion. As he prepared to begin, it struck Petri that he could fake it, and make a false trance-drawing of Hana naked and provocatively posed – he was practised enough – to convince her Ranga's motivation was sexual. But the idea at once felt dirty, a cheapening of his gift. There would be some other way to get rid of their new acquaintance.

So he drew his usual rows of zigzags across the page, the downward points of each row meeting the upward points of the one before, building a slanted grid whose pattern worked into his brain. All the time he held in his mind the question of what Ranga might want. He made himself a channel for the answer, pushing away all other thought, all distracting awareness of Hana's presence, her body, only feet from him and his bed.

When he'd filled the page, he flipped it to the one beneath, and gave his hand up to scribbling.

Line after line came quick, almost random, unguided by any conscious design. The picture that coalesced from those marks formed in front of his eyes, but he kept his mind blank of interpretation or judgement, gently guiding away any thoughts, never breaking his pencil's flow.

When he sensed it finished, he grounded himself back into the bed, then surveyed what he'd drawn.

Either side of the sketchbook's binding was a figure. The left page showed Geist, much as in the drawings at the college: proud, ageless. To the right was a tall woman with long, straight hair. She wore an elegant full-length dress; her hands, in front of her lower belly, held something like a crude knife. If this was Hana, it was a highly distorted vision.

'What do you think?' he asked, turning the pad towards her as she came closer. She frowned at the image of the woman, then at the opposite page.

'Did we tell Ranga about Geist?'

'Only that we hoped to rescue someone,' said Petri. 'Not even that it was a man.'

'So this can't have anything to do with your question about what Ranga wants,' she said. 'Unless he genuinely wants to help me, even without knowing what I seek. Could that be?'

'Even if he does, it might not be from good intentions,' said Petri. 'If his view of you is this distorted, so might his morals be.'

'So this woman *is* me?'

'Well, as he sees you, I assume. Not as you really are.'

She looked displeased. 'Isn't it my choice who I really am? What's that I'm holding?'

'A knife?'

She was silent a few seconds. 'No,' she said. 'I believe it's a focus-stone.'

Petri frowned. 'That size, really?'

'Not my own,' she said. 'That was the dream I had last night. More than a dream: it carried over into a hypnagogic state. When I half-woke, the lump at my wrist felt much larger than before. I knew at once it was the large stone Daroguerre had on the island. I didn't think to ask how I'd come to possess it, all I knew was that it was *right* that it should be mine. What I needed and deserved had come to me. It was a wonderful feeling of triumph.'

She sighed. 'But of course, I couldn't help myself. I tried to work out how I'd come by it. And as soon as I flexed my wrist again, the lump was the same as always: small, weak, inadequate.'

Her tone struck Petri as ungrateful. 'Geist clearly didn't think it was inadequate when he gave it to you.'

'He gave it to me to improve my link to my animath. And Hare's gone now.'

'Geist will know how to get him back.'

'If that's what I want.'

'Eh?' He thought he must have misheard.

'Hare was a dear friend,' said Hana. 'But one outgrows one's friends. Look at her, this "me" you've drawn. Now look at how I am in truth. The difference in our clothes, for one thing.'

'You couldn't run in what she's wearing.'

'Why should I run now? It's something I did as a child, because that's what children do – and I kept up the habit because of Hare, because of my friendship with an imaginary talking animal. He even called me child! But I'm a grown woman now. I aged ten years in a minute. The child in me died, but I hadn't prepared myself, hadn't grown an adult within to take her place. And now I don't know who I'm to be.

'This—' She jabbed the picture. 'This is as much a criticism as a portrayal. She has power, don't you see? The large stone symbolises it. Now contrast it with myself. How long have I been doing what others want? Training with Geist, or at the college; getting sent to the island, still living with my parents at twenty-five. And now here I am, in a town on the edge of nowhere, being toyed with by a stranger whose plans and motives are obscure.'

'Well, how about you try to find them out?' said Petri. 'I'm not the only magician here.'

'Don't you listen?' she said. 'My own stone is useless. I can't draw on my true power. How infuriating to be so taunted by one's own dreams.'

Petri held up his hands. He wasn't going to bother trying to puzzle her out in this state. Even her way of talking seemed different this morning.

'Then how about I go and ask about Ranga at the Boar's Head?' he asked. 'If he's been there a few days, he must've talked to people. At least I can find out if he's just been waiting for a damsel in distress to come along.'

Her gaze pierced him. 'In distress? Is that how you see me?'

'Figure of speech!' he protested. 'Look, anything dodgy, we'll take off on our own. We've got this far. We don't need some oily "poet".'

She nodded, to his relief. 'I'll keep that pad for a while, if that's all right?'

'Uhm, no, I need it,' said Petri, horrified that she might see the images at the back. Calm as he could, he ripped out the two pages he'd just filled, and handed them across. 'That's easier, eh?'

The beer at the Boar's Head tasted like a polecat had pissed in it – or maybe his hangover just made it seem that way – but the busy lunch-trade clientele was diverting, and he made himself popular by sketching the more distinctive-looking patrons on scraps of paper. Some customers remembered Ranga's name or description or the stories he'd told, but Petri learned nothing incriminating. After a couple of hours, lacking any other ideas, he approached the taciturn landlord and covertly offered a drawing from the back of his pad. He felt uneasy letting anyone else see it, let alone possess it, but Hana's face was turned away, so it wasn't even really her.

After a furtive perusal, the landlord slid the page between the covers of a ledger, and muttered his secrets. Ranga had indeed been there for three days. 'And just after he arrived, he paid a boy – Savin, runs errands for me sometimes – to find out if anyone knew about a place, Andro-something. The lad came in last night and whispered to him, and your Mister Samka went out just after.'

Petri walked back from the inn very satisfied with his trade. Selling the drawing had been a grubby betrayal of both art and love, but forgivable in the light of the information he'd gained, which would surely rouse Hana's suspicions. Ranga had lied – it hadn't been fate that had brought him to the Sack of Ducks, but a child spy. More damning still, he'd been asking about Androloch himself, so he clearly couldn't know the place as he'd claimed.

These thoughts were interrupted halfway along Main Street by a rumble of hooves behind. Petri glanced over his shoulder, then moved to the side of the street, as everyone else was doing.

The riders came two abreast, at a walk. The first four wore rough clothes of leather and wool, the upper parts of their heavily bearded faces shaded by wide-brimmed hats. They had rifles in holsters, but also bows, one a crossbow. Just behind them came regular cavalry: two officers, the captain barely into his twenties, then maybe thirty troopers in green jackets and peaked caps, pale breeches, boots. Their steeds were slightly smaller and coarser-haired than Petri would have expected of cavalry mounts: ponies rather than horses. At the rear came a train of laden mules and their blue-uniformed muleteers. One of these pack animals, Petri saw as it passed him, carried two wheels a yard across, another what looked like the barrel of a small field-gun.

A few excited children ran alongside, but the adult Maskarites just stared or scowled. It took a moment for Petri to realise why, and then it became obvious from the soldiers' generally pale complexions, the style of their uniforms.

'What are Empyreal troops doing here?' he asked someone next to him.

The man spat. 'Nothing good, that's a given. Half their navy's in Torrento, they say, but soldiers is new. With luck they won't stop.' He made the sign of the rose, against bad luck.

'Maybe they're for the Bourgoune,' said his wife, 'like those surveyors a while back.'

'A few men like that?' said the man. 'They'll get cut to pieces in there. They'll kick up an ants' nest, and we're the ones covered in honey.'

Along with many others, Petri followed the horsemen and their trail of dust, flies and smell. In the main square, the troop halted by the row of water troughs. Petri loitered near the edge of the square, to watch, and listened to the rumours spoken by those around him: that this was the first step of an invasion, or the Empyreum wresting control from the Republic's government. Despite what tyranny or oppression the cavalrymen might represent, Petri thought their uniforms handsome, and longed to try one on.

He was thinking up a pretext for talking to some of the men, annoyed that a few excited children were already doing so, when to his amazement Ranga came running into the square from the street that led to the Sack of Ducks, right up to the captain. At first the officer seemed ready to go for his pistol, but as Ranga spoke and gestured, he leaned down to listen. Ranga was quickly surrounded by a group made up of both the commissioned officers and two of the rough-dressed bearded men, all still mounted. He talked hurriedly, as if anxious to explain. Intrigued beyond endurance, Petri was about to cross the space himself when he heard his name spoken beside him.

It took a moment to recognise Hana, so unfamiliar were her clothes: a long, close-fitting skirt and braided jacket in dark blue, with ankle-boots and a hat seemingly chosen to match. It had to be new; he hadn't seen it in her luggage when he'd made a clandestine search.

'What's going on?' she said.

He looked her up and down. 'I could ask the same.'

'With Ranga, I mean. We were talking in the common room, when a boy came in and yelled, "They're here!" at him, and he rushed out after.'

'I've no more idea than you.' Petri felt uneasy that Hana had been talking with Ranga, and still more by the possibility that her new clothes might have been intended to impress the interloper. 'Seems he really is a man of mystery. Too much mystery. We should ditch him.'

'I'm not so sure,' Hana said, watching Ranga and the horsemen. 'Just before the boy rushed in, I had that sense again, that I'd known him longer than a day.'

'Oh, this "fate" again, the one that supposedly brought him to us?' said Petri. 'I've learned something about that.' He quickly related his discoveries at the Boar's Head, but to his disappointment, Hana showed none of the outrage he'd expected.

'Even so, he revealed something interesting,' she said. 'I challenged him about this "my Lady" business, and he said he was encouraging me to try out a role.'

'What "role"? Are those clothes part of it?'

'No, I'd already purchased them, not long after you left. He thought they suited, though.'

'Does it matter what he thinks?'

She glanced at him. 'Why, does it threaten you?'

Before he could work out his answer, a stir of movement drew his attention. The captain and one of the bearded men swung down from their saddles to join Ranga, then the captain gave orders to his lieutenant and called someone from the rear of the column to dismount and join them, a youth in a uniform that looked half-civilian.

'I demanded he explain his comment about this "role",' said Hana. 'I threatened to have no more to do with him otherwise.'

'Good.'

'He told me we couldn't part from him, because we needed him "to find Geist".'

Petri was about to say that was hardly news, when he caught the significance. 'He *named* him?'

'Correct. When I challenged him about it, he said we must have mentioned it last night. But his face showed he knew he'd given himself away. Unfortunately, the boy interrupted us before I could ask further.'

Ranga and the Kurassians were now striding across the square, towards the street that led to the Sack of Ducks. 'Look out,' muttered Petri. 'He's spotted us.'

Ranga spoke briefly to the captain, then diverted across. 'This is fortuitous,' he said when he reached them – with no trouble now looking Hana in the face, Petri noticed. The man seemed satisfied, but under strain, like a circus performer whose spinning plates had all started to wobble at once. 'My Lady, be so good as to follow us back to the inn.' He leaned closer. 'I can't explain further now, but whatever I say, go along with it. This is your best chance to achieve your aims.'

Giving them no chance to respond, he rejoined the three Kurassians.

Petri exchanged a look with Hana, but there seemed no sensible alternative. They reached the Sack of Ducks just behind Ranga and the soldiers. The rough-clad, bearded one admitted them, then firmly shut the door in the onlookers' faces.

Within, Ranga asked the innkeeper for the private dining room. A serving girl showed them all through. Ranga and the Kurassians stood behind chairs towards the far end of the long table, waiting for Hana to be seated. Petri held out the chair nearest the door for her, thinking the slight distancing from the others might prevent her getting too easily dragged into discussion, and might allow an easier escape, if necessary. He stood by the chair next to hers.

'Gentlemen,' said Ranga. 'Allow me to introduce the Lady Vana, as she will be called for the duration of this trip. My Lady, may I present Captain Franzen of the Eleventh Pioneer Cavalry, Lieutenant Rurik, who heads the troop's pathfinder detachment, and Assistant Surveyor Semplan of the Empyreal Cartographic Corps.' The three men bowed in turn.

'How do you do?' said Hana. They followed her lead in sitting. Since Ranga hadn't introduced him, Petri assumed he'd been assigned the role of a servant. Needling as that was, it would make him less visible. Indeed, the Kurassians paid him no attention, all studying Hana – blatantly in the case of bearded, rough-clothed Lieutenant Rurik, his grey eyes stabbing out from his hard-weathered face.

'I've told them only that you have an official interest in the prisoner at Androloch, my Lady,' said Ranga. 'One of the prisoners, I should say.

None of these men will ask any more. They've accepted my word that their mission and ours coincide to mutual advantage. My word as a major in the Republican Intelligence Bureau.'

Petri tried not to show shock.

'Of course,' said Hana, with a near-perfect impression of calmness.

'Indeed,' said Franzen, 'it's fortunate you were here waiting for us, Major Samka. We'd have aimed for Hallinghall otherwise. You're sure they've moved the survivors?'

'I can't reveal the source of our intelligence,' said Ranga, 'but it's rock-solid. We also have a map of the fortress.'

'Androloch is a fortress?'

'A keep and other buildings surrounded by a wall, and on three sides by a moat. But it's lightly manned and in poor repair. No drawbridge, only gates. It's more a holy site – or an unholy one. Even the clansmen shun it by choice, we understand. It's better for our purposes that the prisoners are there rather than at Hallinghall: more out of the way, less opposition.'

'It must be the place we heard of,' said Semplan, the young surveyor. 'One of the Bourgs let slip something about the "seat of true power", and the trouble started when we asked about it. They'd been quite amenable until then, thanks to our trade goods. I was the only one to escape,' he added, to Hana. 'My Lady.'

'Why would they move the captured surveyors to a holy site?' said Franzen.

Ranga's expression tightened. 'The evidence points to sacrifice.'

Semplan gasped. Petri kept himself from blurting a question as to whether Geist was also in danger.

Franzen removed his peaked cap; the light caught his white-blond hair like fire. 'That comes as no surprise. I was given to understand that this mission received encouragement from the highest level. The *very* highest.' His voice carried a fervent tremor. 'We are borne on the wings of Empyreus's own will, Major Samka. The End Times approach. All false gods must be swept away to clear the field for the final battle against Elok and the Witch. This action is part of that cleansing.'

To Petri's alarm, Hana took it upon herself to speak. 'I'd advise you not to denigrate Kymera's native traditions as "false gods", Captain. Not if you hope for the friendship of her population.'

Ranga shot her a quick frown. Franzen's pale blue eyes turned to her. 'I meant no insult. Nevertheless, I wonder which your countrymen would sooner follow: the lord of science and progress, or a dark deity that thrives on human blood? Such is the choice all men will face in the end. And all women.'

At that point, to Petri's relief, the serving girl came in with a tray of wine and proceeded to set glasses before the Kurassians and Hana. Petri tried to make sense of the revelations so far. Ranga being a secret agent explained some things, but why try to pass Hana and himself off as the same? And why hadn't Ranga prepared them for it? Out of fear they'd refuse to cooperate?

While the others were occupied watching the girl pour, he leaned close to Hana and whispered, 'We need to talk. Make some excuse.'

She shook her head. 'We might miss something.'

There was nothing Petri could do, and indeed it wasn't long before the men restarted the discussion, though at first the subject was limited to terrain and weather. Ranga seemed at pains to make sure Hana wasn't drawn into the talk. Early on, he took a tobacco tin from his pocket and produced some folded maps, and Petri leaned forward, hoping to gain at least a rough idea of where they might be headed. One map showed an overland route to Androloch that avoided clan steadings, and the other showed the fortress itself, though Ranga confessed parts of this to be speculative, especially the 'inner sanctum'. Rurik seemed mistrustful of the agent, but Captain Franzen grew ebullient at Ranga's description of the ramshackle, decaying fortress. His men had the latest spring-magazine carbines, he enthused, and the auxiliary train carried a mountain field-gun, split between four mules, and two dismantled machine-guns. He expected to face at most a few ancient muskets among the axes and spears – in any case, the clan structure of the Bourgs made it unlikely they could raise a sizable force in response.

A swift raid, and the unholy site would be destroyed and the remains of the survey team rescued, along with the prisoner the Kymeran secret service was interested in.

'Odd your people didn't contact us as we came through Torrento,' said Rurik.

'I agree.' Ranga looked troubled – though whether because he was genuinely concerned at the oversight, or because he didn't like the question, Petri couldn't tell.

An hour from dusk, the meeting wrapped up and the Kurassians left the inn. Ranga went too, but not before telling Hana and Petri that he would come for them at six the next morning, to take them to the stables to hire ponies. The column would leave at seven.

'I suppose we should be grateful you've let us know in advance this time,' said Petri.

'Oh, that,' said Ranga. 'I was just about to brief you, my Lady, when our friends showed up. Unfortunate timing. But you did splendidly. How could I have ever doubted they would accept you as the Lady Vana, when you so clearly are?'

He lightly kissed her knuckles again, gave her a bright grin that made him seem very pleased with himself, and followed after the Kurassians.

'*Splendidly*,' muttered Petri, and shut the door of the dining room. 'Did you hear what he said at the beginning? "Their mission and *ours*".'

'What of it?'

'His priority isn't the survey team – it's Geist.'

She frowned as his point struck home. 'But what could the Bureau want with Geist?'

'It won't be anything good, will it?'

'We don't have much choice but to go with him, though,' she said. 'We can't free Geist ourselves, not if the place is a fortress.'

'But what's Ranga's game?' said Petri. 'Why make out you're a fellow agent?'

'I can only assume he finds me attractive and could think of no other way to get me along.'

'He could hardly stand to look at you this morning.'

'Being a poet, he would no doubt say his eyes took time to become accustomed to the sun.'

'Oh, for—'

'I was hardly being serious,' she said. 'Nonetheless, you need to curb that tone if you're to play my servant convincingly. You must address me with respect. "My Lady" would be a start.'

'Am I to play your servant? Wouldn't you have a maid?'

'As a Bureau agent, planning to travel into the Bourgoune, I'm clearly a woman able to dress myself. Your role would be as a general…'

'Dogsbody?'

'Whatever term pleases you.'

'And should I be getting some new clothes too?' he said. 'A slave's tunic from ancient times? A peasant's smock covered in shit?'

'Do you want to help Geist or not?' she snapped. 'They're only roles we have to play until the task is done. If you're annoyed that Ranga elevated me to the nobility, ask yourself what choice he had. The Kurassians would never respect a woman otherwise.'

'You've certainly had no problem adapting to it.'

'Because I've decided to take control, you mean? Strange if that's not to your liking. It was more your doing than his.'

'Mine…?'

'That drawing you made.' Hana sat back down and toyed with her empty wine glass. 'After you left for the Boar's Head, it came to me that I had to remake myself, get myself un-lost, fill in the blank slate I'd become.' For a moment, her eyes tightened, then she shook it off. 'I realised that perhaps your drawing was neither a distortion nor a criticism, but a possibility, a call to action. I asked myself what stopped me making myself such a person, someone in control, someone with power; and the answer was "Nothing". So I invoked her.'

'*Invoked* her?'

The corner of her mouth tweaked. 'Astolio won't permit its teaching, but I've done it with Hare, many times. And with the Mother, on the island – too successfully, if anything. Invocation only requires belief and the magical connection with the energy of the idea. When I had that thought, I realised that the loss of my old sense of self might turn out to be no disaster at all, but the shedding of a redundant skin – the creation of a vacuum into which I could pull who I needed to become. And I recalled how I'd felt on waking this morning: the feeling not just that I possessed the large stone, but that it rightly belonged to me.

'So I locked myself in my room and carried out the invocation. As soon as I immersed myself in the psychosphere, I felt that ideal self as a presence, as though she were the spirit of my true power and had been watching over me. I pulled her into myself without difficulty. You should have seen Ranga's face when I came downstairs and found him there. He could see it at once. There was no unwillingness to look on my face after that, I assure you.'

Petri didn't know how to express his unease without risking her anger, and in her current mood he didn't want that. 'So the clothes are to suit this… new self.'

'Quite so. And this dress is not appropriate for a pony trek. We must find suitable riding habit, even if we have to get every seamstress and tailor to open for us. Come.'

'Yes, my Lady,' he said, without enthusiasm.

27

INTO THE BOURGOUNE

No part of Petri's sixteen years as weaver's son, backstreet grubber, sculptor's catamite and precocious magical student had necessitated horseback riding. He quickly came to the opinion that it was one of humanity's most inhuman inventions. Even padding the seat of his trousers with a spare undershirt gave little relief. An hour up the military road that led north to the edge of the Bourgoune region, he admitted defeat and got off to lead his pony on foot. The rest of the column rode on the verge, to spare their mounts' hooves, but Petri kept to the middle of the crushed stone roadway, as far as possible from the grass his piebald torturer enjoyed munching on until its fellows were far ahead.

'You'd do better to bear with riding and get yourself used to it,' said Ranga, after dropping back to him. 'You don't want to be caught out if we need to escape.'

'Escape?' said Petri. 'Does Franzen know your lack of faith in his abilities?'

'Life doesn't reward the complacent,' said Ranga. 'The Pioneer Cavalry are used to striking hard and pulling back quickly. If things go against us, they'll sabotage the heavy weapons and withdraw at speed.

The Bourgs' ponies will be slower, but they'll still catch someone on foot – or someone not in control of his mount.'

'I'd rather die by a quick spear-thrust than days of that torture.'

'My Lady told me she hasn't ridden for years,' said Ranga, looking ahead to where Hana rode on the opposite verge to the soldiers. 'Her discomfort can't be much less than yours, but she bears it stoically.'

'You're forgetting what she's missing between the hammer of her body and the anvil of the saddle,' said Petri. Then he saw a chance to probe. 'She sits well, though, wouldn't you say?'

'She does,' said Ranga, in what sounded a forcedly flat tone. 'Though I think our friends from the north don't know what to make of her riding astride like that.'

'But we do, yes?'

'Do what?'

'Know what to make of it. The strength in those thighs. What else they could grip.'

He glanced sidelong. Ranga still stared towards Hana, but his brows were taut. 'It's not fitting for a servant to talk about his mistress like that.'

'A mistress as fanciable as her, it would be unnatural not to.'

'Not from me.'

'Ah, so you're her servant too?'

'Isn't every poet the servant of grace and beauty?'

'If I were a poet, I'd be more the servant of filth and fucking.'

'You surprise me.'

Petri found that annoying, and, to his surprise, slightly hurtful. He was much more than Ranga saw, he reminded himself. 'But I meant, as far as the Kurassians are concerned. Does she work for you, or vice versa?'

Ranga's mouth firmed with distaste. 'I haven't gone into such details.'

Petri noted that. 'But they accept she *is* a lady?'

'Kurassians take matters of class very seriously,' said Ranga. 'They know I'd never dare pretend such a thing. I've told them only that she's with the Bureau in some capacity, and that I'm forbidden to say any more about her. And to be frank,' he said as he kicked his pony forwards, 'I'd rather not discuss her with you either.'

The road ended a little before noon at a garrison fort: a dismal structure overlooking a river where it flowed through a gap in the hills, marking the limit of government control. A rider had been sent ahead, and they were expected – though not welcome, from the looks on the garrison officers' faces.

At Ranga's request, Franzen had detailed two of his men to take care of Petri's and Hana's mounts as well as their own. In the stockade yard, while the ponies were being led to the troughs and Ranga was talking to Franzen, Hana drew Petri aside.

'I saw you talking to our new friend earlier.'

'Yes, we were discussing your… earthier charms.'

Her gaze hardened. 'You're obsessed with sex.'

'What lies beneath most of the world's masks if not that? And what's Ranga if not a mask?'

'And did you learn anything?'

Petri checked they couldn't be overheard: no one was within a few paces, and the activity with the ponies generated a fair amount of noise. 'Only that it's not straightforward lust with him. But I'm not sure what it is. Has he asked you anything about yourself? Your past?'

'Nothing. He's barely talked to me this morning.'

'If he was in love, he'd want to know everything about you, wouldn't he? He calls himself a poet, but has he written you anything yet? A true poet would have slipped his verses beneath the tight little crack of your door all night.'

She looked unimpressed. 'Perhaps he only has the nerve to look on me from a distance.'

'He's not some callow youth,' said Petri. 'He's probably killed people with his bare hands.'

'Does he genuinely give you that impression?'

Petri glanced at Ranga, across the yard with Franzen. 'You don't get to be a major in the secret service by pushing a pen around a desk,' he said, pretty sure of his sweeping assumptions. 'He said yesterday that masks were his line of business.'

'We need to learn the Bureau's plans for Geist,' said Hana. 'Couldn't you have asked him about that, rather than wasting time trying to divine his particular attraction to me? Whatever the Bureau intends, it's unlikely to be helpful to us.'

'Ah,' said Petri, 'but here's a thing. Does it matter what Ranga's plans are for Geist, if you can overrule them?'

'Overrule them?'

He met her puzzled gaze, savouring the moment. 'While I was "wasting time", I learned something rather interesting. Ranga hasn't told the Kurassians which of you ranks higher.'

Her eyes widened, then narrowed. 'Well done,' she said, and he felt a shiver of future possibilities.

'We must find a way to tell Franzen who *does* rank higher,' she went on. 'Once I've claimed that place for myself, Ranga won't be able to contradict me without revealing that he lied in the first place. But how? I can't discuss the Bureau's business with Franzen – I know nothing about it.'

'I'll work out something,' said Petri.

'You're playing a more useful role than I'd expected,' she said. 'I hope you're not motivated by thought of reward.'

'Geist's release is all the reward I'm after,' he said. 'Hold up, the major.'

Ranga looked almost as if he was about to salute as he reached them. 'There's going to be a conference with the garrison colonel, my Lady. To discuss our mission and so forth. All very tedious. I suggest you sit with his wife and daughters in their drawing room.'

'No,' she said. 'I'll attend, thank you.'

Ranga looked uncomfortable at this, but didn't object. Petri kept close to Hana as she went with Franzen, Rurik and the surveyor Semplan into the main building. No one challenged his presence. In the colonel's office, he sat with her a little way from the others.

From the start, there was a chill to the proceedings. The colonel clearly felt his toes being stepped on by the Empyreal force, captained as it was by someone half his age, and feared what might result from their action. The Bourgs had kept to themselves for centuries, he told them, but remained fiercely independent, resisting all assertions of Kymeran control. He worried that Franzen's bruising of their pride would lead the rival clans to join in retaliation. Franzen's questioning, however, revealed this to be pure speculation. The fort's patrols went less than ten miles into the Bourgoune, and the colonel's information came only from fur-traders returning along the road he guarded, the sole serviceable route through the hills.

'But these maps of yours must be works of utmost conjecture,' the colonel said. 'The Empyreal team were the first cartographers to enter the Bourgoune, and I'm certain the Bourgs use no such maps themselves. Where did they come from?'

Franzen looked to Ranga for a response. 'I can't reveal my source without authorisation from my higher-ups,' Ranga said. 'I'm sure you understand.'

Petri noticed Semplan's uncertain glance towards Hana, Rurik's too. His breath caught at the opportunity for Hana to position herself.

'Nevertheless,' he said, and nudged Hana's foot with his, 'I think my Lady might be able to reassure the colonel.'

'Quite so,' Hana said. 'The source must remain secret, but please be assured, their provenance is impeccable.'

Petri noticed Ranga's strained look, his desire to intercede. He prayed Hana wouldn't muck this up.

'As for retaliation, Colonel,' she went on, her voice losing its initial reticence, 'I have no fear of that. Once the Bourgs have been struck a hard blow by a force as small as ours, how will they dare attack an entire garrison? No, this raid will cow them rather than stir them up, and be the first step towards imposing law on the region. It's been absent too long. The Bourgoune is part of Kymera, after all.'

Petri sensed her tightness as she settled more heavily back into her chair. The men all looked at her, but no questions came. As they turned back to each other and the discussion resumed, Petri slowly exhaled.

Coming back out into the fort's yard afterwards, he whispered, 'Well played, my Lady.'

'This is what I meant, you see?' she returned in a low voice. 'I've put away the child. I couldn't have made any such speech, however short, just a few days ago.'

Maybe she was right, Petri thought. She did seem a different woman from the one he'd journeyed with to Maskar. If that was the power of invocation, perhaps he should get her to teach it to him.

Except that he was already on his way to who he wanted to be. And he felt troubled by what she'd said the day before, about not wanting Hare – it threatened the relationship he'd mapped out between them. He wondered if the invocation she'd performed had gone too far. But if so, it was doubtless something Geist could fix.

The road beyond the fort was nothing more than a hoof-pocked track, running through woods and scrubland as it followed the river upstream. Finding it difficult to walk his pony without getting ankle-deep in mud, Petri accepted the inevitable and mounted. For a while, he tried to ignore his bruised sit-bones and save his balls from a pounding whenever his steed trotted to catch up, until Hana stayed back with him and gave some instruction. Though it was only marginally successful, he saw her interest as a good sign, an acknowledgment that they made good partners.

After two miles, the valley road was crossed by another pony track that led onto higher ground either side, and the troop turned to the right, fording the river and then heading up a heavily pine-forested slope. Bird calls floated back, Rurik's pathfinders communicating with each other as they ranged ahead.

The weather closed in. The soldiers donned oilskins on the move, but Hana and Petri had to dismount to do so. That got them stuck at the back of the column, behind the mule carrying the field-gun barrel.

Nervous at bringing up the rear, Petri kept glancing behind, hoping not to see Bourg warriors emerging from the trees, ropes of shrunken skulls round their necks. He recalled the strange drawings he'd shown Hana at the college, and wished he'd thought to ask Astolio for a handgun.

Just after the track had stopped climbing and bent round to follow the northern slope of the hill, Hana muttered something under her breath, and Petri saw Ranga waiting for them at the trackside ahead. The major brought his pony alongside Hana's, so close their boots nudged. The track being only wide enough for two, Petri's pony was forced to the rear, something that didn't seem to distress it in the least.

'Would you fall back a little farther, my Lady?' asked Ranga. When the three of them had dropped twenty yards behind the tail-end of the column, he said in a clipped, low voice that Petri had to strain to hear over the sound of rain on oilcloth, 'I wonder if it was wise to make that speech about reclaiming the Bourgoune.'

'It seemed perfectly apposite,' Hana answered. 'It must have crossed Franzen's mind that I don't look suited to the rough and tumble of a secret agent's life. I had to suggest myself as something slightly other, a kind of political advisor or diplomat.'

'And my obvious superior?' said Ranga.

'Kurassians are ill-disposed to respect women except as housekeepers and ornaments. Making me a lady wasn't enough. Franzen will only listen to me at all if I'm someone of importance.'

'Does he need to listen to you?'

'You think I could just hang mysteriously in the background for the whole mission, without him suspecting?' Hana straightened in her saddle. 'Does it trouble you that he sees me as your superior? Is it contrary to your own view, Major?'

'No!' The vehemence of Ranga's response startled Petri. 'Not at all, my Lady. It was unexpected, that's all.'

'Then I'm glad we've had this chance to clear things up.'

'We also need to clear up our stories regarding Geist,' Petri chipped in.

'Quite so,' said Hana, with a glance and nod back at him. 'It would seem ridiculous if Franzen heard different things from us – or if I seemed in ignorance of why we want him.'

'Franzen doesn't need to hear anything from you,' said Ranga, sullen.

'He might refer to what you've told him. I must know how to respond.'

'I've told him nothing,' said Ranga. 'Only that we need to fetch Geist out.'

'And he hasn't asked for details?'

'Why should he care? He's interested in rescuing what's left of the survey team and covering himself in glory. Talk to him as little as possible, my Lady. He won't seek you out for conversation: he'd find it too awkward. There was no need for you to do what you did to raise yourself above me. Now, if you'll give me leave…?'

Without waiting for permission, he dug his heels in and sent his pony trotting up the track, forcing his way past the mule-train and up the line.

Petri lightly kicked his own pony, and to his surprise it shoved its way alongside Hana's.

'I have the measure of him now,' Hana said. 'He *is* my inferior, in every way imaginable. It feels so natural to assert myself over him, it might almost be part of the fibre of—'

She cut short, tensed.

'My Lady?'

'I had a dream last night too,' she said. 'I just glimpsed part of it.'

'About Ranga?'

'I don't recall. It doesn't matter. What matters is that he clearly understands the truth of his inferiority himself, for all that he chafes against it.'

Petri snorted a laugh. 'He's made you a queen; now he finds he doesn't like being ruled.'

'No one *made* me anything,' said Hana coldly.

All afternoon, Petri kept his eyes on Ranga, expecting to see him go up to Franzen and try to undo Hana's claim to higher rank. He wasn't sure what he could do in such a case, but the problem never arose; Ranga kept to himself.

Apart from a few words to Hana, Petri did much the same, concentrating on getting through the ride with minimal discomfort. He'd thought earlier he might use the journey to make friends with some of the cavalrymen, both for its own sake and in case it came in useful later. But every attempt at conversation fell flat. They despised him for not being able to handle a horse, he sensed; they looked down on him for being inches shorter, and younger; they mistrusted him for being some kind of spy. Annoyed, he contrived imaginary scenarios in which they ended up begging for his friendship.

The troop camped at dusk in a large, shallow dip at the outskirts of the pine forest, away from the track. The evening passed for Petri in frustration and boredom, despite having plenty to do, preparing Hana's tent and attending to her as her supposed servant. The rain had died off at sunset, but the air among the pines felt heavy with damp, not helped by the cold rations they had to eat, nor the prohibition on showing fires. Everyone had been ordered to keep noise down, and the near-silence, the chill darkness, the pathetic glimmer of low paraffin lamps, all made Petri think of the shades of the dead in the misty swamps of the underworld. He hoped that wasn't an omen of where he might end up if a Bourg war-party launched a night-attack. Franzen hadn't even ordered the machine-guns assembled.

At last, Hana retired, and Petri prepared to give up on the day and succumb to his own weariness. He went to the nearest tree for a piss, which he had trouble keeping quiet, the only other noises being the odd whicker from a horse, the mumbled curses from soldiers playing dice. About to enter his tent, he noticed a standing figure some paces distant, a touch paler than the trees behind. His heart clenched as he imagined a Bourg who'd crept past the sentries, or a ghost.

But he recognised the figure's walk and height as it approached. 'We should talk,' Ranga said, his low-voiced words somewhat slurred. 'As one "servant" to another.'

'Go ahead.'

'Not out here.'

Petri hesitated, then lifted his tent-flap. 'Go on, then.'

He had no idea what Ranga might intend – the man had no reason to seek friendship – and following him into the cramped space sped his heart with the thrill of excitement and danger, evaporating his tiredness. The only position they could occupy was lying lengthways beside each other. Petri placed the dim lamp near their heads and propped himself on an elbow. Ranga had chosen to lie staring up at the fabric slope above him, for which Petri was thankful, as it meant Ranga couldn't see his erection. His arousal surprised him and almost broke him out in nervous laughter. He imagined Ranga announcing that it had never been Hana he'd been interested in, but him. That might account for the slight smell of whisky that came off the man.

'I'd be grateful for your honesty,' said Ranga. 'Do you have any intentions towards her yourself?'

Disappointment, relief, intrigue muddled through Petri's head in the same moment. 'Of course not,' he lied. 'I'm just some hireling. Anyway, I've got girls at home. And not just girls,' he added speculatively. 'One should live as one paints, and I'm too young to specialise.'

Ranga seemed to consider this. 'You'd better keep more tight-lipped than that around the Kurassians.'

'Oh, I can keep my lips very tight when needed, believe me.' Petri was annoyed to feel his face heat up, even though he'd known damn well what he was saying. 'Anyway, why should they care? Don't they worship a golden youth with a massive lance?'

Ranga snorted a laugh. 'You have a point there. I worked in a prelate's palace for a while, and from the number of pictures of Kirrus as a young man around the place, you'd think they found the image particularly appealing.'

'In a prelate's palace, really? In Bismark?' He wished at once he hadn't sounded so gushingly impressed.

'Deep undercover,' said Ranga. 'Pretending to be a footman. I even formed a relationship with his daughter's companion.' He sighed. 'Not true love, of course. I only understood that later, when I came back to Torrento.'

Petri didn't push. With any subject, moods and secrets would reveal themselves in time; and Ranga's face, now staring intently at the underside of the canopy, suggested there was more to come.

But instead of speaking further, the agent worked a hip-flask from his pocket, and took a swig.

'Thanks,' said Petri, when offered. But though he upended the flask to his mouth, he stopped its opening with his tongue. The flask didn't hold much, and he wanted Ranga as drunk and with as few inhibitions as possible.

'Keeping things blurred helps sometimes,' said Ranga.

'Blurred?'

But Ranga looked as if he'd gone on to think about something else. 'It's not really me,' he said at last. 'This… persona. While I was waiting for the Kurassians, I made myself a mask I knew would be agreeable to them. You probably find it haughty and pompous, but that's not really how I am, and it doesn't serve any purpose with you. But it's difficult to drop.'

Petri grunted, thinking Hana had the same problem. But he still had no idea where Ranga was leading. Was the man just lonely? His mind turned again to the kinds of companionship he might offer, and whether he wanted to.

'When you were talking this morning,' said Ranga, 'about how my Lady sat her pony, I must have come across as disapproving, even prudish. But…'

'But you are a man, after all,' prompted Petri.

Ranga's brow contracted, as though he were unsure whether he'd revealed too much.

'So,' said Petri, 'my words didn't fall on stony ground.'

'The ground was sown before your words,' said Ranga.

Petri consciously relaxed his shoulders. The bones in his chest felt close to snapping. This man, almost ten years his senior, doubtless knew several ways to kill him in a moment. He had to tread carefully, but the path was irresistible.

'It's not every day that one would change places with a dumb beast,' he said. 'Or that one feels envious of a dead one.'

'A dead one?'

'The animal that got made into her saddle, of course. Which part of yourself would you choose for that honour? Groin or face?'

After a moment of what seemed shock, Ranga said, 'You really are a vulgar little shit.'

'And you really are a prude, it seems.'

Ranga seemed to have stopped breathing. Then he exhaled, slowly, and said, 'The tongue is the true instrument of passion. And what's a poet if not one skilled with it?'

Petri snorted. 'That's a bloodless way of putting it. You talk like a watercolourist. Or a virgin.'

'I'll have you know,' said Ranga, 'that on my last mission, I left a trail of sable-haired beauties moaning with satisfaction all along the Shallow Sea. But they were just rehearsals, a means to perfect my art. To give *her* that pleasure...'

'This is pointless without details,' said Petri. 'Or are you scared of tarnishing your silver tongue?'

'Some things are too sacred for words.'

'Oh, come on. What could be more sacred than kissing and licking the saddle a goddess has just dismounted from, the leather warm and damp from between her legs? Her sweat, and not just her sweat.'

Ranga closed his eyes. 'Oh, gods...'

Petri swallowed. He had no idea how far this was going, how it might break. He realised he wanted to cause Ranga to say something utterly debauched – or get hard. A quick glance told him he hadn't managed that yet. 'Shall I go on?'

'Wait,' said Ranga. 'None of this will get back?'

'You think she's the kind of person I'd talk like this with?'

'Do you ever talk about me?'

Petri almost groaned. Just when it was getting interesting. Still, this might lead to a different kind of interesting. 'You're a man of mystery, and who doesn't like a good mystery? Of course we speculate. About why you invited us along, for one thing.'

'Can't I do someone a favour without my motives being questioned?'

'If your motives are hidden, how would anyone know it's a favour?'

Ranga grunted. 'It seemed too strange to pass up, that's all – her turning up on her way to the same place. Like a nudge from fate. I wanted to help her, and it was easy to do. When I came over to your table and made that comment about her being undercover – that sowed the seed of the method.'

'And you already knew we were on our way to Androloch. That boy told you.'

Ranga frowned at the canvas. 'Yes.'

'But you didn't know then that we're after Geist too.'

'Not at that stage.' Ranga shifted. 'This isn't something I can discuss. Official secrets.'

'You haven't asked her why she wants him.'

'No,' said Ranga. 'That would be unfair, since I can't tell her the reason for my own mission.'

'Then how do you know they won't conflict?'

Ranga breathed a soft groan.

'You don't regret bringing us?'

'No. No…' Ranga rubbed his hand across his face. 'How could I? Yes, her being here makes things difficult in some ways, but to have her as a companion, albeit at a distance, it's…' He sighed. 'You wouldn't understand.'

'I understand very well.' Petri reached for his bag. A warning thought came that this would make Ranga's low opinion of him indisputable, but he ignored it, and took out his sketchpad. 'Have a look at these,' he said, opening to the back pages.

Ranga's eyes widened gratifyingly. Petri guessed Hana's wrath would be considerable if she found out. But he could always deny it was her; some of the drawings showed her face, but the likeness wasn't perfect.

'These are… these can't be drawn from life?'

'Like your maps, Major, I can't reveal the source. What do you think?'

Ranga's expression answered clearly enough, and a glance at the man's crotch told Petri he'd achieved his earlier aim. Danger shivered through him at the thoughts it provoked. Ranga took another swig from his flask.

'Borrow one, if you like,' Petri said. 'Just make sure it comes back in the same condition.'

'She's…' came Ranga's shuddering whisper – as breathless as though he'd never even imagined a naked woman before, let alone been with one. But then he closed the pad. 'No,' he said. 'I can't.'

To Petri's astonishment, tears started in the man's eyes. Ranga quickly turned his face and tensed. Petri bit his lip as an idea jumped at him.

'You're wrong if you think you've got no chance with her. She thinks you're handsome.'

After a moment's pause, Ranga said, 'Truly?'

'Of course. And you are, I should know. It's only your secrecy she doesn't like. Just act less cagey, less of this "official secrets" nonsense, and the door will open. She's worth it, from what I've heard.'

Ranga shook his head. 'Even if you're right, I can't approach her in that way.'

'Come on, be a man.'

'No, I… might be seen.'

'Why should you care what Franzen's men think?'

'Not them.'

Petri frowned. 'Who, then? Bourgs? Boars? Badgers?'

Ranga chewed his lip, then whispered, 'You really think she'd favour me?'

'Tell you what,' said Petri. 'Tomorrow, on the trek, I'll try to spot a chance for you to get together with her and talk in private.'

'My thanks,' said Ranga. 'I'll think on it.'

And on those drawings too, I bet.

When Ranga had returned to his own tent, Petri lay on his bedroll and reflected with satisfaction and self-dismay on how the unexpected conversation had turned out. Whatever Ranga had, he had it bad – Shuviana, Lady of Stars Reflected in Water, had almost drowned the idiot. Drowned him in his own tears.

He felt no guilt at using Ranga's infatuation to get the man to reveal his secrets to Hana. The more he thought about it, the less he liked Ranga's extremity of emotion. It felt like the major was making a point to him, that his supposed poet's soul was more capable of real love than his, and that annoyed him.

And with annoyance came a realisation, one that made his eyes stretch wide.

He could use Ranga's infatuation not just to learn the Bureau's plans for Geist, but further – to make Ranga discredit himself in the Kurassians' eyes, and remove any chance of him asserting himself as Hana's superior.

And if he played it right, his own credit with Hana would rise even higher, another step towards that future of love and partnership that lifted his heart to think of it.

28

LADY IN WAITING

Dreams disturbed Vana's sleep that night. In one, she was at a masquerade to which she hadn't been invited, wearing a mask whose magic imbued her with memories that let her deceive the other guests. But tendrils grew from its inner surface, insinuating themselves into her face. Keeping it on would fix it there for all time; removing it would expose her and make her a nobody once more. And she was about to meet the King...

Morning found her exhausted, and even before she mounted, her aches told her riding would be no pleasure. The mist made it even more miserable. The farther into the Bourgoune they went, the more edgy everyone became. Vana overheard that Rurik's pathfinders had encountered two cattle-drovers and had had to kill them to prevent an alarm. Twice the column diverted to avoid a steading, due to inaccuracies in Ranga's map – which reflected badly on her, since she'd vouched for it at the fort. She worried the Kurassians would demand she tell them the map's origins. But Ranga alone bore the brunt of their irritation. No one talked to her. Even Petri seemed wrapped in himself.

The mist dispersed as they came out of the hills and down to a wide bog, dry enough at summer's end to be passable with care, overhung with a silence broken only by the piping of marsh birds. The pathfinders were kept fully employed: the trail sometimes disappeared or seemed to diverge, with one branch invariably running into mire. The sun had just begun to feel almost warm when they approached a low hillock grown with gnarled pine and larch. The ground near it was less wet, and with single-file no longer necessary, Petri came alongside her.

'Ranga's drinking,' Vana said, seeing the agent take a quick pull from a hip-flask. It was the sixth time she'd observed him do so that morning.

'Last night too,' said Petri. 'I had a long chat with him before bed.'

'You should have told me that earlier. Did you learn anything?'

Petri wore a furtive little smile. 'Not why the Bureau wants Geist, no – though I think he might be more open with you about that now. But he more or less admitted his mission conflicts with ours.'

'That's hardly surprising. His orders must be to take Geist back to Torrento.'

'I got the impression the conflict was more serious,' said Petri. 'Does the government have any reason to put Geist in prison?'

The momentary thought came to Vana that Geist deserved far worse than imprisonment, but she couldn't identify its inspiration. 'Large parts of his life I know nothing about. But if they do want him for that, we need to prevent them.'

'That shouldn't be a problem, should it? Insist on interrogating Geist first, and alone. Then you can tell him the situation and develop an escape plan.'

'Yes, that's obvious.' The prospect of meeting Geist felt like a heavy swelling in her chest. 'But if I'm to do anything so drastic, I'll need to ensure Franzen truly believes me to be Ranga's superior. Yesterday's conference alone might not be enough.'

'If we're lucky,' said Petri, 'Ranga might do something to discredit himself.'

'I dislike relying on luck,' said Vana.

For some reason, the boy smirked as he turned his pony away.

On reaching the hillock, the column halted to rest and eat. The open expanse of bog had given Vana no chance to answer calls of nature, so she headed within the pines, taking Petri and posting him to make sure she wasn't disturbed. When she came out from the dense patch of trees, she found he'd been joined by Ranga, who looked agitated.

'I must talk with you,' he said. 'Alone.'

After a moment's doubt, she remembered what Petri had said, that Ranga might now be more open about Geist. She sent Petri back, but with instructions to keep an ear out for her call. After the boy had gone, Ranga made several hesitant attempts to speak, until Vana in frustration seized the initiative.

'You're worried our missions conflict,' she said. 'Is that the reason for the hip flask? You fear you cannot obey your old orders and help me as you desire?'

Ranga nodded.

'We can resolve the difference,' she said. 'But to work it out, I need to know the final pieces. Tell me what you mean to do with Geist.'

He stared at the floor of mouldering needles, sucking his teeth, then groaned. 'Geist stole something. I need to take him back for questioning.'

'And for punishment?'

His eyes searched hers with a strange intensity, as though he thought she might herself know the answer. 'Perhaps.'

'What did he steal?'

'I wasn't told,' he said, and instinct jolted Vana that there was something about her own search for Geist that Ranga mustn't know. Somehow it overlapped dangerously with this matter his Bureau chiefs had kept from him.

He looked away from her, out between the last few trees and across the bog. His face tensed in an expression that smacked of hopelessness, desperation. She noticed his hand shaking.

'I don't know if I want to obey my instructions,' he said. 'I have a bad feeling. But I can't... can't not.' He stuck his hands in his pockets. 'Have you ever been in a situation where you're not sure what's real and what isn't? Where you're afraid the most important thing in your life is a lie?'

'Ranga,' she said. 'Your spymasters are far away. I'm here. This is how you resolve the difference: by forgetting past and future, and attending to what's in front of you. By serving only me, as you said you wished to.'

She reached out and stroked his stubbled jaw.

He took hold of her wrist, levered her arm down.

'You dare?' she breathed.

His eyes twitched, but he didn't let go. 'Don't tease me, my Lady.'

She was almost surprised to realise that was exactly what she'd been doing.

'Do you like me?' He swallowed. 'I like you. Right from when we got drunk the other evening. At first I thought you were just like the others, but you're not. You're more. I think it's the real thing. It's jumped.' His voice had sped up, as though in near-panic. 'You can save me.'

She tried to ease her hand free. 'Save you?'

'I've done bad things. I've deceived people who deserved better. I've… done worse than that, even.' He glanced away. 'But I was made to. You wouldn't make me do such things, I know. At the Sack of Ducks that first night, I could see you're not that kind of person. I didn't think anything could come of it then; you were too different. But it can, I'm sure of it now. You've woken a part of me that hasn't been truly my own for years.'

He looked at the wrist he was holding. 'Something bad will happen if we find Geist, I'm sure of it. Let's leave, together. We could be good for each other. I'm clever, I could make money at anything, I just need the chance.' He met her eyes. 'You might be my only chance. I don't…' It seemed an effort. 'I don't believe her.'

Her, she noted. His Bureau superior, no doubt.

'Oh gods,' he said at her silence. 'I shouldn't have spoken. But you just have to… please.'

He raised her hand and kissed it, hard. Tears wet his cheeks. She was amazed he'd been reduced to this. The secret service must be in a poor way indeed, to send so weak a man.

'Ranga, darling.' The term surprised her, but she sensed he would respond to it, that it would tighten the snare. 'We're going to find Geist, and you're going to help me. Do you think you have a choice?'

He dropped her hand and looked at her unhappily. 'You weren't like this that first night.'

'I hadn't found myself then. You prefer me as I am now, surely?'

'Yes, of course.' He spoke like a man knowingly walking into a prison.

'You said you "like" me. That doesn't sound like a poet's choice of word.'

'Please don't press me,' he said. 'Not yet. I made a promise that I would say no more to – to a woman, until I was deserving of her.'

The extent of his delusion, that he thought he might ever deserve her, almost made her laugh. She told him to go through the trees and approach the men from another direction, to reduce any speculation about their doings. When he'd gone, she waited among the pines until Petri found her again.

'Was he bothering you?' the boy asked.

'If that possibility concerned you,' she said, 'why didn't you send him away?' Her temper rose. 'Why did you hang around with him, waiting for me to finish my necessaries? Did you advertise to everyone in the column what I'd gone to do?'

Petri looked taken aback. 'He insisted on seeing you. And I thought he'd tell you more about Geist.'

'He did,' she said. 'Or as much as he knows, I think. Geist stole something. Ranga doesn't know what.'

'Oh,' said Petri. 'And he didn't bother you? Or try to force himself on you?'

'If "force" were ever in his nature, it isn't now,' she said. 'I think he'll prove very biddable.'

'But if he does,' said Petri. 'If he presses you about his feelings, or he gets annoying, you'll let me know?'

'Are you my protector now?'

He didn't seem to know what to say to that.

'Be assured,' she said, 'I'll do whatever's necessary to remove any threat to my interests. Do you think me incapable of doing so alone, simply because I'm a woman?'

'Of course not,' he said. 'But partnership is always better than being alone, isn't it?'

She didn't bother responding to that.

Petri's words niggled her as she took her meal a little later. It was perhaps understandable that he thought she would value working together above self-sufficiency, since she'd told him how well she'd worked with Cass on the island. What she hadn't told him was how that partnership had been dissolved, against her will, once Orc had been restored, the friendship revealed as no more than a convenient alliance as far as Cass was concerned. Partnerships were not to be trusted, and it wasn't just Cass that had taught her that – there were older betrayals somewhere in her memory, though the details eluded her.

But there was part of her, still, that yearned for partnership, though she feared the vulnerability that went with it. And she was aware that her previous self might have tried another tack with Ranga, tried to tease out of him what his problem was, to win him round rather than assert dominance. For a moment, she wondered if the better response to the loss of her old self might have been to create another from scratch, rather than invoke one. Whatever else Astolio had said, his first teaching had been that all magic had its price.

But the prospect of returning to that blank, that vacuum which had followed Tashi's restoration, alarmed her more. She needed to hold on to the power she'd now acquired. It made life easier, and it made life enjoyable. Without it, the men around her would try to dominate: if not as her uncle had done, then as Astolio had.

Or Geist.

It almost frightened her to think that the very next day she would meet him again, for the first time in months, and months. It seemed almost that it would be the first time in years. And years. Was it just the passage of time that caused the faint, ticking sense that there was danger in that meeting? But Ranga had said he feared it too. Was her own sense of danger tied up with the thing Ranga mustn't know? Or was it inherent in the man they both sought?

That afternoon, as her pony plodded along the winding track across the bog, she went over all her past dealings with Geist, searching for the answer. Beneath the afternoon sun, the rhythm of her mount swayed her mind drowsily back to their first meeting at her uncle's farm. So long ago... *had* it been there, or in Torrento? Was that later? It was Lucien Daroguerre who'd first introduced them; he'd been one of her clientele. But that couldn't be true, could it? She'd only have been fifteen or so. But one packed so much in at that age. A whirlwind of travel and ideas. Initiation... yes, he'd done that to her all right. The experience of being loved, valued, worshipped, shown her true self. The first within her... the core of her... was that where Hare had come into it? It all seemed like a dream now. The railway line had just come to Torrento, the novelty of it. Of course, it turned out the Empyreum had built it to support the revolution some years later – though if the revolution hadn't yet happened, how could her parents have died in a monarchist rising? – but everything was wonderful then and they took the train to Bismark and other cities, largely with her money though she was too blind to see it then, she was so captivated by the ideas he'd shown her, developed with her, the idea that the feminine had been suppressed in the world's north and the reverse in the far south. Similar to the ideas that had sent her to the Hollow Isles; it seemed strange that she hadn't connected them before. That the world was split, at war with itself, made to be at war with itself by the powers who benefited from death, from the building of arms and the development of the industries that polluted and concentrated power in the hands of a few – and right at the top of the pyramid of power, the secret cabal he called the Kings Behind the World. What if they could be fought and their insidious influence overcome and the world set right, the balance restored? Like an image from an old memory of an ancient painting, she beheld the light in his eyes and face as he proclaimed his idealism, swept her along with him all the way to Sundara, searching, researching, through a hundred cities and a hundred incense-perfumed hotel rooms, a hundred beds in which he wrote his poetry and read it to her and then made love with her and gods yes and—

She jolted as the pony lurched, a foreleg sinking into mud. She leaned back at once and the beast backed up, righting itself.

No, that had just been a dream: the heat outside the shutters, the bed linen in the dimness, the sweat. She couldn't remember when she'd dreamed it. Recently, it must have been, but it felt so long ago.

Only snatches remained now. *You're beautiful*, he'd said, the man in her dream who was far too young to be Geist.

And she'd said something back.

And there. Somewhere in there: that was where the dangerous thing was.

29

EVE OF BATTLE

Ever since the noon halt, Petri had been careful not to let Ranga catch him alone. Now, with Hana retired for the night, he stood near his tent as if taking the air, and prepared for the culmination of his plan. The camp, again in a forest hollow, was mostly dark. A faint light shone within Franzen's command tent, in which the officers were still poring over Ranga's map of the fortress, which was now only three miles away. By skirting inhabited regions and routing through the wild lands, following little-used tracks, the column had escaped detection. The air was tense with the coming assault, planned for first light. Petri's tension arose from what would come before that.

He turned at the approach of boots on old needles.

'At bloody last,' said Ranga in a low voice. 'You've been hard to get hold of.'

'Been wanting to talk?' said Petri. 'You should've said.'

Ranga glanced behind him, his whole manner twitchy. 'When we stopped earlier, she wasn't as receptive as you led me to expect.'

Petri affected surprise. 'That's not the impression I got from her afterwards.'

'Really?' The hope in Ranga's voice was pathetic.

'We can't talk out here,' said Petri. 'My tent again?'

Once in the confined space, he noticed how rough Ranga was looking. 'I haven't slept well the last couple of nights,' the agent said, when asked. 'But that's no matter. I need your help with her. Tell me how to play it. I don't have much time. I tried to tell her how I feel, but it had no effect.'

'You probably went at it too hard,' said Petri. 'She won't throw herself at a man who declares love for her. That's not the way they do things.'

The creases in Ranga's brow filled with shadow. 'They?'

'The high-born.'

Ranga rubbed his head. 'Is she? Truly? I thought that was… uh…'

'It's a mask you gave her. But she's found it fits her too well to take it off now.'

'So she has changed her manner?' said Ranga. 'I couldn't be sure. My memory… it's got so confused lately.'

'Aren't you used to the masquerade, in your line of work?' said Petri. 'Remember at the end of the ball, the masks are removed by lovers' hands.' He wasn't sure that was true, but it sounded good. 'She uses her role as a barrier, but secretly she wants you to break through it.'

'"Secretly"? But this is something she's told you? Or is it a guess?'

'I don't guess,' said Petri. 'I *observe*. I know the tricks, even if I don't play them myself.'

'And you're always completely open, are you?'

'You can't paint what's beneath the masks of the world if you're looking through one,' said Petri. 'I've no need to disguise what I am, nor what I'm going to be – one of the greatest portrait painters of the age.'

Ranga grunted. 'And one of the most modest?'

'Modesty's just another mask,' said Petri, irritated. 'I've had a superb idea, a true original. I'll sleep with all my sitters, any age or sex. It'll give my work an unmatched insight. People will view it with amazement, and the scandal will bring crowds flocking – I'll have a reputation the world over. I even know the title of my memoir: *A Brush With Fame*. Clever, yes? The triple meaning?'

Ranga frowned. 'Triple?'

'A brush is also a fox's tail.'

It had been meant to intrigue, but he felt suddenly vulnerable, wary of even hinting at more in case it jinxed his future. Ranga didn't follow up anyway. He wasn't really interested, only in Hana. And if the dullard was going to reject his chance to turn fate in another direction, Petri wasn't going to feel guilty at what followed.

'I envy you your certainty,' Ranga said, his eyes on the groundsheet. 'I shared it, once. Now I've staked everything on a game of chancy odds, thanks to you.'

'Me?'

'Last night you drew out of me thoughts I would've kept to myself, and that made them more real even to me. And now I've spoken them aloud, I can't go back – it's all there, everything I've said, to you and to her. *She'll* be able to hear it. She probably already has.'

Before Petri could grapple the meaning from Ranga's words, the man groaned. 'And she'll know I've looked at that picture, that it stirred me. What have I *done*?'

'She won't know. I haven't told her.'

'Not *her*,' said Ranga. 'Gods, I should never have looked. But...'

'Do you want to see more?'

'No, I do not want to see more! I want... I want her. Vana. I want to know how to make her mine. She can redeem me.'

'And she will, Major,' said Petri. 'You were meant for each other.'

'That's what I feel. And hope. But I fear... Geist.'

'Fear him?'

'Something bad is looming,' said Ranga. 'To do with him. Something that will stop me and her being together. But I'm not sure what. It's like my vision is clouded.'

'She said something about a theft. To do with that?'

Ranga frowned. 'I can't see how. No, it's the meeting itself.'

Petri's breath caught at an idea. Careful, careful, he warned himself. But all the best ideas were instinctive.

'It's not because you fear they had a relationship in the past, and it might spark back into life?'

The air turned electric, though Ranga seemed frozen.

'I'm not saying they have, you understand,' Petri went on, to cover himself. 'But they knew each other a long time. And he's a very charismatic man.' It was sounding plausible even to him.

Ranga's whisper was almost too quiet to catch. 'Her *heart*.'

'What?'

'What did she say? I can't remember. *He still has it*. No, it can't be – you put that idea in my head.' Ranga pressed his fingertips against his temples. 'Why can't I *think*?'

Petri swallowed. 'Why don't you ask her about it?'

Ranga's eyes seemed almost feverish. 'Ask her?'

'Go to her tent. Have it out with her. It's hardly fair if she's been leading you on, not if she's been thinking of Geist all this time. Damn it, Major, you have a right to know.'

But Ranga shook his head. 'I can't. Not without an invitation.'

'She's been dropping invitations all day, but you haven't—'

'Quiet!' Ranga looked to be shaking. 'Tell me, did she – did Hana, and Geist – *was* there ever anything? No games, you must know. What's she said? What signs have you seen?'

The low violence now in Ranga's voice fired Petri's nerves with warning and excitement. He couldn't risk telling a lie that Ranga might accuse Hana with, but the urge to provoke further, to see what happened, was too powerful.

'He taught her for years, Major. I've worked with him myself. I know the force of his personality. If he'd wanted me, I would've given myself to him, no matter what my misgivings. And it's not credible that he wouldn't have wanted her.'

'But you don't *know* there was anything?'

'As I said. And that's why you need to ask her. Otherwise you'll have another sleepless night and be in no state for the morning. Go to her, Major – she'll be glad you think enough of her to have such worries, and glad of the chance to clear it up. And glad of company, on this eve of danger. She might be a strong woman, but she is still a woman.'

Ranga nodded firmly. 'You're right.'

He backed out of the tent. Heart speeding, ears pricked, Petri got into position himself. Soon he heard Ranga's low, indistinct words from Hana's tent, then the sound he'd been waiting for – Hana's raised voice. Not the cry of distress he'd wanted, but close enough. He raced out of his tent and across to her larger one. Ranga was nowhere to be seen – they were both inside, arguing.

He threw open the flap. Hana was still dressed, and Ranga was squatting only a couple of feet from her. Petri grabbed his collar and hauled.

'Out!'

Ranga fell back onto his arse. Though slighter, Petri had taken him by surprise, and maybe for the sake of his remaining dignity, Ranga didn't resist. When they were both out of the tent and upright, Ranga stared at him.

'What the *hell* are you doing?'

'I heard trouble,' said Petri, expecting a fight. 'Are you all right, my Lady?' he called, loud enough to be heard by others as well as her.

'But…' began Ranga, too confused to get it.

'No thanks to this idiot,' said Hana as she emerged. 'Even in the wilds, you'd think a woman would be able to retire without being molested.'

'I just wanted to talk,' said Ranga. 'I thought…'

Petri tensed, ready to lie if Ranga revealed his part in this. But Ranga clearly had too much pride to reveal he'd been talked into going to her, and clammed up.

'What's going on?' came the voice Petri had been hoping to hear. Franzen approached with Lieutenant Gessler, and Rurik, who carried a lamp. 'Why this noise?'

'A misunderstanding,' said Ranga.

'He was molesting my Lady,' said Petri. 'He dared to violate her private quarters – intending to violate her even more private quarters.'

Ranga yelled and flew at him. Petri ducked and turned, trying to cover himself, and Ranga struck his shoulder, making him stagger. Before Ranga could land another punch, Gessler pulled him off. Petri straightened, regretting that he hadn't taken the blow without flinching, which might have impressed Hana more.

'Enough!' ordered Franzen in a hoarse near-whisper. 'Is this true?' he asked Hana.

Rubbing his stinging shoulder, Petri prayed Hana would use the wits she'd shown at the fort, and recognise the opportunity – any suspicion of molesting a noblewoman must surely dent Ranga's credibility in the eyes of the class-conscious Kurassians.

'It is,' Hana said. 'He has declared inappropriate and lascivious feelings for me, entirely without encouragement.'

'That's a lie!' hissed Ranga.

'I feared for my very honour, Captain. I want him arrested.'

'No!' said Ranga. 'You—' He choked off, hate and distress bulging in his eyes. 'And you can't arrest me,' he said to Franzen. 'You've no jurisdiction over us.'

'This is an Empyreal military operation,' said Franzen. 'Only a higher Empyreal official would outrank me. I won't allow anyone to put this mission at risk.'

'It's not at risk,' said Ranga. 'I made a mistake. I misread the signs.' Petri thought he was keeping his eyes deliberately from him. 'It won't happen again. Whatever affliction I suffered from, I'm cured, believe me.'

Franzen studied him a moment, then nodded. 'Then we'll leave it at that.'

'We will not,' said Hana. 'I want him detained. As his superior, I give you full authority.'

'My superior?' said Ranga, and barked a bitter laugh. 'My *superior*? She's not even in the bloody secret service!'

Fear shot through Petri – he hadn't reckoned on Ranga giving away his own lie. 'That's bollocks!' he said, but no one paid him any attention.

'She's no one,' said Ranga, 'not even a proper lady. Just some woman I picked up in Maskar.'

'Picked up?' said Franzen. 'For what purpose?'

'Why d'you think? I fancied her. I was weak.'

'He's ranting,' said Hana. 'Why on earth would I agree to come on this expedition if I weren't who I said? Do I look like a camp follower?'

Well played, thought Petri.

'Prove it, then.' Ranga glared at her. 'Prove you're in the Bureau.'

'If Captain Franzen demands it,' said Hana. Petri hoped the nerves in her voice were too subtle to be noticed by the others. 'But I can't see why an officer and gentleman would take the side of someone like you – someone who's confessed himself willing to compromise an operation by bringing along a prostitute. Even if that was a lie.'

'And whose side should he take?' said Ranga. 'A woman who's given no evidence of her rank apart from some vague and pretty speech at that fort?'

'If you can give me such proof,' Franzen said to Hana, 'it would hasten the end of this ugliness.'

Petri dreaded Franzen asking for identity papers. His mind raced for some excuse if Hana faltered. Lost? Stolen? Could she be too secret to carry them?

'Ask her about that matter, Captain,' said Ranga. 'The one by which I proved myself to you.'

Franzen blinked once, slowly, as if to calm himself. 'Very well. My Lady, when Major Samka could give no proof of his identity in Maskar, I hinted at a matter that had been related to me when we detrained at Torrento. A member of the Empyreal naval staff briefed me about a recent event, known to few, and it occurred to me that only if Major Samka were who he claimed would he be able to expand on my hints. The same would apply to you.'

Shit. Petri's stomach sank into a pit of dread, his mind blank of ideas.

'Well, that would depend,' said Hana, her nerves more obvious now. 'Our fields of operation differ.'

'What a blatant attempt at evasion!' crowed Ranga. Petri winced.

'Silence, Major,' said Franzen. 'My Lady, if you truly hold a high rank in the Kymeran secret service, it's inconceivable that you won't have heard of this matter. It is highly significant. The words "Shallow Sea" should be enough to identify it.'

Hope caught Petri's breath.

'They are,' said Hana, and now the slight tremble in her voice was not of fear. 'You mean the loss of the dreadnought *Iron Tiger* and the heavy cruiser *Relentless* at the Hollow Isles. The magician Daroguerre manifested a monster with the aid and support of Captain Martin Seriuz. Elements of the Sundaran navy under Captain Rulanza were involved. A Watcher of Highcloud was killed. Do you require more?'

Petri glanced at Ranga's face in the light of Rurik's lamp. It would have been worth painting, that lurid expression of amazement.

'It will suffice,' said Franzen. 'It's more than I was told.'

'And you'll arrest this idiot?'

'You can't!' said Ranga. 'I gave you those maps. You'd have been lost without me. I've no idea how she knows about the Hollow Isles, but—'

'Be silent!' said Franzen, in a voice of iron and frost. 'I have neither time nor men to waste on this ridiculous internal squabble, or personal affair, or whatever it is. Whoever endangers this operation again with excessive noise, I'll have him or her gagged. All three of you will remain back from the field tomorrow until the objective is taken. Then you can deal with this "Geist", if he lives. Let him go, Gessler.'

Ranga shook the lieutenant off, turned and walked back to his tent.

'And I shall interrogate Geist alone, when the time comes,' said Hana.

'We'll see,' said Franzen. 'And pray we have no further unseemly distractions.' His expression was more of blame than sympathy.

'It was entirely Major Samka's fault,' said Petri.

Franzen turned to him. 'The Lady Vana is his superior, is she not? If I failed to control my subordinates in so grievous a manner, I should rightly be relieved of my command. But what can one expect when a woman is put in charge of anything but domestic servants?'

He and his men returned to the command tent. 'Bastard,' Hana muttered.

'But it went well for us,' said Petri. 'They won't listen to Ranga now. He lied to them and slandered you. Lucky for us he asked about the Hollow Isles.'

'Lucky?' she said. 'No, I don't think it was luck. It is part of the world's pattern that I should grind Major Samka into the dirt. He was the author of his own destruction.'

'Perhaps not the only author,' said Petri.

She frowned at him. 'What does that mean? And why did he attack you? Did he blame you?'

Petri couldn't tell whether her tone was one of admiration or criticism. But his pride in his plan wouldn't let him deny it. 'Yes, and with good reason.'

She looked unimpressed. 'I don't appreciate being made a pawn in someone else's scheme. You should have warned me.'

It struck Petri that she was right, then he remembered why he hadn't – he'd hoped rescuing her from Ranga might make her regard him in a heroic light. His admission that he'd set up the whole thing had scuppered that. 'I wasn't sure it would work.'

'Hm. Nevertheless, it was cunning.'

'Worthy of a fox, perhaps?'

She eyed him quizzically. His heart beat hard as he realised now was the time to declare himself.

'When the time's right,' he said, 'could you help persuade Geist to bond me with Fox, from those Fire Stealers you told me about? As you said, I'm cunning. And a fox has a brush, and I'm a painter! It's perfect!'

'So that's your ambition?'

'Part of it.'

'If you want to persuade Geist to regress you back to a childhood of talking animals, that's your business,' she said. 'You can wait until after he and I have talked as adults.'

Disappointment robbed him of words.

'Now, I'm retiring to bed,' she said. 'You'll stand guard outside my tent, in case that fool tries something else.'

'What, all night?'

'You goaded the snake, Petri. You had better be ready if it strikes.'

Alone in his tent, Ranga took out the revolver. He briefly imagined the satisfaction of a double murder, but his heart wasn't in it. Quite apart from the difficulty of ensuring his escape and survival, he blamed his disgrace less on Petri and Hana than on his own failings. Of course the two of them would have made some plan to get him out of the way, given that they wanted Geist too. Why hadn't he foreseen that?

Because he'd turned off the machinery of his mind and deluded himself into fantasy. And now he'd probably killed any chance with Vanessa. He'd thrown away his true love in favour of a nobody who'd put on false airs, who'd astutely adopted some of Vanessa's character, with his own stupid collusion.

The gun was a solid weight in his hand. It had felt so light when he'd picked it up at the Hollow Isles, but he'd been buoyed by victory then. He broke it open and studied the flat ends of the six cartridges. He placed a fingertip over one and shook the others out onto his bedroll. He wondered whether Vanessa were watching him now, and what she would make of him closing up the gun, like this, and spinning the cylinder, like this. Had she ever heard of this game? If so, it was unlikely she'd paid it much interest before. She didn't believe in leaving things to chance. Why should she? She had a fingertip on every pulse of government in Torrento. She was magnificent.

He almost cried aloud with horror at his ever thinking Hana an adequate substitute. Why had he ever called her Vana? He span the cylinder again and fixed on the clicking noise as though it now constituted the only meaning in the world.

Would Vanessa forgive his aberration? He could claim he'd become confused. But could he claim it was only confusion that had made him beg Hana to save him? To save him from his true love, whom he had long known, deep down, would not want him, no matter how many dangerous tasks he performed, no matter how many innocent people he killed. Long known, deep down, but only now consciously recognised. Hana's disdain had been less disguised than Vanessa's, but he'd seen the one in the other, and it had shown him the hideous truth. Both women saw him as something to use and discard.

Click-click-click-click-click-click-click-click-click-click.

He wondered if it were possible for the subconscious mind to count the clicks. He cocked the hammer. Did some part of his brain know, even now, whether the single remaining bullet sat in the chamber aligned with the barrel? He put the gun to his temple, a sting of cold steel against his skin. Was the calmness he felt because he knew he was safe? Or because he really didn't care either way? Or because he knew he wasn't yet ready to test it?

Then something occurred to him. If he were truly Vanessa's servant, he surely wouldn't even think of depriving her of the means of achieving her goal. Did the fact that he was prepared to take this risk mean he wasn't, then, truly hers? That he had a genuine choice?

Had his recognition of her disdain been the first step to freedom?

The possibility gripped him like a glimpse of land after days adrift. That first evening at the Sack of Ducks, he'd marked Hana as someone with strength and independence, regardless of her background – which he'd had no reason to suppose was anything out of the ordinary. Surely those qualities, rather than rank and power, were what attracted him? Surely they were possessed by thousands of women as much as by the wielder of true power in Torrento? Dinah, after all, hadn't been of particularly lofty birth; it was the household that had caught him. Perhaps he could get beyond that. What did it matter that his father had always scoffed that he would amount to nothing? What did it matter that his mother had called him her prince and told him he would find a princess? Where had that led him? A smelly tent deep in the bog-land wilds, toying with the idea of blowing his brains out.

But not actually doing it, he imagined Vanessa thinking.

Damn her.

He released the hammer and span the barrel again, faster and faster, so the clicks blurred into one sound and there could be no chance that any part of his brain was keeping count. He thumbed the hammer and put the gun to his temple again—

And remembered the kiss Vanessa had given him just before he'd set out for the Hollow Isles. That brief touch of her lips against his: his lips, not his cheek.

Did she feel something for him after all?

Or had she roused the memory in him, just then, so as not to lose her servant? Did she have that much power?

He saw the stark decision before him, perhaps the last he would ever make. He could believe in the kiss, and lower the gun. Or he could pull the trigger. That might kill him. But he sensed that if it did not, if the chamber beneath the hammer were empty, it would still put an end to the part of him that was Vanessa's servant. He would be free of her – to find some other love, maybe even to seek out Dinah again, or Zina at Bazantin, or one of the others. Freedom stretched before him, an unknown country.

All he had to do was pull and take the chance.

His hand shook, the tension of holding the gun there so long with his forefinger precisely brushing the trigger. His throat thickened with the need to swallow.

One chance in six that he would no longer exist. The same as rolling any given number on a die. How many times had he wanted a six in a childhood board-game and rolled a one?

The kiss, though, was six in six. It had happened for certain, along with Vanessa's promise that she would reward him. If he didn't believe that, then he was accusing her of nothing less than outright falsehood, and that horrified him.

But what of Geist and her, that looming dread? A ridiculous, offensive error, it must be. How could such a woman have lost her heart to any man who didn't love her as she deserved? No, somehow he'd picked up Hana's feelings for this Geist and confused them with his true mistress. He'd allowed himself to merge the two women, failed to keep them separate. Worse than that, he thought, as though the idea had struck him from outside – he had been played for a fool by a deliberate imposter.

He lowered the gun, and span the cylinder once more against the temptation to check what the result would have been. He set down the weapon and clasped his hands in prayer. 'My Lady, forgive my weakness, forgive me for thinking that you and that thief might have ever…' The sentence was too squalid to finish. 'Help me replace my weakness with your strength. Put forth your power and help me enact your will, so that your imposter will not succeed in thwarting us. I'll bring the thief Geist back to you, I swear.'

Reloading the other five chambers, he told himself he felt calmer. He had succeeded in recovering himself. He hadn't yet failed.

He wanted to cry.

30

REUNION

They broke camp at four and made their way towards the fortress by the light of dimmed lamps. Excitement and fear spiked Petri's mood above his exhaustion. Hana was taciturn. Ranga kept himself away.

After an hour, the column emerged from the forest and onto scrub-dotted grassland, to be met by one of Rurik's pathfinders. Just beyond, a slope led down into the valley in which the fortress lay; but they halted here, where they still couldn't be seen from the castle, and the soldiers dismounted. Orders were given in low voices. The machine-guns were taken off their mules; only the animals carrying the field-gun would go with the men on foot, down to the spot Rurik had earmarked as the best place from which to fire at the outer gates. Franzen gathered the three Kymerans together.

'You'll stay here with the mules and ponies until the objective is taken,' he said quietly. 'When that's done, accompany them to the fortress.'

'Geist must be taken alive.' It was about the only thing Hana had said that morning, and the combination of vagueness and harshness in her voice made Petri wonder if she'd slept any more than he had. 'Take no risks.'

'We'll do what's possible,' said Franzen, and left with his men.

The muleteers roped their animals and the ponies together. One machine-gun crew set up next to a bush at the beginning of the slope. Petri crouched beside them. The first grey of approaching dawn revealed the rough shape of the fortress, only a couple of lights showing in its windows. It sat just above the valley floor on a protruding shoulder of another hill that came down from the right: a large and irregular keep, with a courtyard surrounded by an outer wall, edged by a moat. The outer wall began from the keep's rear corners, meaning the keep's own rear wall formed the outer defence where it faced the upwards slope of the hill. Petri wondered why the Kurassians' plan was to head into the valley to attack through the courtyard gates, rather than blast their way through the single rear wall. He wished he'd plucked up the nerve to ask Franzen more; he hated not knowing what was going on. Downslope, the soldiers' paler breeches showed in the darkness. A small group of goats revealed themselves as grey shapes fleeing.

One of the machine-gunners told him to get back, captain's orders. Petri reckoned that when the shooting started they would be too busy to notice his return, so he obeyed and joined Hana, a little way from the animals and from Ranga. She sat staring at the ground, the light now strong enough to show the fatigue in her face.

'Are you all right?' asked Petri. 'Did you sleep?'

'My Lady,' she said, but it was barely a whisper, and she didn't look at him.

If she was going to be like that, he wouldn't bother asking again. Especially when she'd made him stay awake.

But she told him anyway. 'I slept at first, but not restfully. I was attacked.'

'Eh? I was on guard all night.'

'In a dream, of course. She tried to take my power from me. I won, but it drained me.'

'She?' He noticed Hana twining her fingers together. 'Who?'

'I don't know. She tried to rob me of the strength I've found. She called me an imposter. She had the large stone, the symbol of my power. She tried to use it like a knife, to cut away my new face, shrieking that it wasn't mine, that I would bring disaster. But I prevailed.' She shuddered.

'You think it might've been part of yourself?' said Petri.

'Nonsense.' She looked at him at last. 'Why should I want to make myself weaker?'

He swallowed, but pressed on. 'Maybe it was your old self, the one you thought was gone. Maybe she – you – thinks you went too far with that invocation. Because you don't need that power now, not with any threat from Ranga gone. And maybe, deep down, you realise it's not healthy.'

'Not healthy?'

'It's power you haven't built up yourself. It doesn't belong to you naturally.'

'Does it not?' she said. 'One cannot invoke anything alien to oneself: Astolio said so. And as for not building my own power, I always had it, but no one recognised it. I wore the docile mask I'd been given, and where did that get me? The others all went off to have their adventures and discover their big secrets – all the men, and Cass, who might as well be a man. They expected me to go back and live quietly with the Quallaces. Is that what you want me to go back to as well? Girl-child, wife, Mother, all rolled up into someone who can be easily forgotten?'

'Of course not, but—'

'And you say I no longer need power?' She closed her eyes and rubbed her head, as though in pain. 'If not for your loyalty so far, I'd think you duplicitous. You saw last night how Franzen regards me. Ranga's just waiting for his chance to reassert his position. I'll need everything I can to stand up to them. And for Geist, too.'

'Don't you think Geist would want you back to your old self?' he chanced.

'What about what *I* want? Everyone's trying to influence me, even you. You're no better than that imaginary rodent.'

Petri had had enough. And he half-needed a piss, and didn't want to be caught short after the fighting had started. 'I'm going into those trees.'

'To commune with your pet fox?'

He didn't bother answering. Passing the ponies and mules, he felt sick with the thought that Hana might now be too altered to come back. What if Geist didn't know how to retrieve her old self, or if she refused? What would be the use in having Fox if Hana still lacked Hare? He'd put together what she and Orc had got up to, and knew that given the chance, he could succeed where Orc had clearly failed: their joint-scaping and sexual passion each reinforcing the other, building a lasting partnership that would unleash astonishing abilities. The two of them under their great teacher, Geist; the first and second Fire Stealers and their instigator, Raven. They wouldn't need any of the others.

Now this Lady Vana nonsense had thrown all that into doubt.

He found his way between the outer trees and went a little way in. He'd just buttoned his fly when cold metal touched the skin beneath his ear.

'Farther in,' came Ranga's whisper. 'Quickly.'

How stupid he'd been, Petri realised, not to think Ranga would have a gun.

'You're mad,' he breathed.

'All the more reason not to risk crossing me,' said Ranga. 'Don't worry: a few questions, and our business is done. In!'

Heart pounding, Petri didn't resist the push further in among the trees. He stumbled over ground-litter, the end of Ranga's pistol now prodding between his shoulder blades.

'Enough,' said Ranga. 'Turn.'

Petri swallowed as he did so. 'They'll know you came after me.'

'I told that muleteer corporal I was following your example. Hana didn't even seem to notice.'

'They'll hear a shot.'

'What if they do? I'm not going back there anyway.'

Remembering all the reasons Ranga had for wanting revenge, Petri opted to placate him, no tricks. 'You said something about questions?'

'How did Hana know about the Hollow Isles?'

Petri hesitated, not knowing what story to tell, but then Ranga put the gun under his jaw and pushed hard.

'She was there!'

'There…?' said Ranga. 'Wait – that was *her*? With Cass?'

'What?' said Petri. 'You were there too?'

'She said a Watcher was killed. She knows about that?'

'She found his body.'

'But she doesn't know who killed him?'

'A Sundaran marine.'

Ranga grunted, nodded. His lips lost their tightness. 'Now, what do you want with Geist?'

'Just to rescue him. He's her old teacher, like I said.'

'And how did you know he's here?'

Petri's hesitation brought more pressure from the pistol barrel. His mind was blank. Any whiff of magic could be used against him and Hana.

'How?' insisted Ranga.

He tried a half-truth. 'He told me where he was going. Months ago.'

'He said he was going to Androloch?'

'Yes.'

'Try again, liar. I spoke to someone in Maskar who remembered Geist passing through. Geist had no idea where he was going, only a description of some landscape features. So how did you know he was at Androloch?'

'I… I don't know how Hana knew. You're confusing me.'

Ranga's eyes widened. 'Puristo's jugs,' he breathed. 'I've just worked it all out. No wonder she's managed to confuse me over the last couple of days. She's a bloody *magician*.'

'Rubbish,' said Petri, thinking fast against the onset of panic. 'If your Bureau found out about Androloch and Geist, why couldn't she?'

'Heh,' said Ranga. 'I don't think I'll reveal the irony in that question.'

'What, you mean you learned about it by magic too?'

Alarm froze Ranga's face. Petri realised he shouldn't have blurted that out – Ranga had assumed his comment would pass over Petri's head.

'It's the man with the gun who asks the questions,' said Ranga. 'And I'm done with them. Count yourself lucky I don't kill children.'

Petri bristled, but kept his trap shut.

'You and Hana had better get on your ponies and leave,' Ranga said. 'If I see you again, I'll tell Franzen about Hana being a magician. You might try to turn the tables and drag me in as well, but that little tin-soldier plays things by the rules. Me accusing her of magic will give him no choice but to take us all under guard to Torrento. I have powerful friends there. I'll get off, and you and Hana will be hanged. Understand, my dirty-minded friend? I'll end up with Geist anyway. Now it's time I went. After I've made sure of a head-start.'

He took some lengths of cord from his jacket pocket. Petri looked for an opportunity to break free and grab Ranga's gun as he was being tied, but no decent chance came, and he didn't want to risk a bad one. As well as being armed, Ranga was bigger and stronger than himself, and he'd become someone competent and purposeful now, no longer a lovesick dupe. To Petri's own surprise, he became aroused as Ranga bound his hands and feet, but this disappeared when he was gagged with his own filthy handkerchief.

Ranga's twig-cracking footsteps faded as he ran. Petri fought against his bonds, but in vain. He was just starting to think no one would ever come looking for him when he heard a call from back at the edge of the forest.

He made as much noise through his gag as he could. Before long, one of the muleteers freed his mouth.

'Bourgs?' the man said, hushed with fear.

Petri spat out the taste. 'Major Samka, curse him. He didn't pass you?'

'We haven't seen him since he followed you in here.'

A loud boom cracked out from down in the valley: the field-gun's first shot, the start of the assault.

'So where's he gone?' said Petri.

Ranga left the forest to the east of where the ponies and mules had been roped, then ran, crouching, into the valley. Things were going his way again, now he'd managed to shake off Hana's bewitchment. Which it had been, of course – nothing to reproach himself for, except that he should have been more alert for it. Vanessa would forgive him as long as he didn't muck up anything else. Absolutely he'd made the right choice in not pulling the trigger the previous night.

He bounded over a tussock and sent up a clattering and squawking of partridges. At the noise he threw himself to the ground, eyes turned westwards to where Franzen's men would be positioning themselves. He couldn't see them, but the light was still dim. No time for caution. He started up again and made toward the fortress's rear eastern wall, where it backed onto the upward slope of the hill's shoulder.

It had been a risk, taking the time to go after Petri, but worth it. His luck was returning. He'd gained not only a means to threaten Hana and Petri, but Geist too – because he would bet anything now that Geist was also a magician. And not just because the man had been Hana's teacher. He should have thought of it before: for Vanessa to have gone to such lengths to regain what Geist had stolen, the object had to be irreplaceable, and with her money, that surely precluded anything of purely material value. And given that she'd sought the focus-stone only to find Geist again, it had to be something even more potent than that.

To think of her with even greater power than she had now – and himself as her consort…

Out of breath, still with no sign that he'd been spotted, he reached the rear corner of the outer wall, where the moat ended. No sign of life showed in the slit-windows of the visibly crumbling guard-tower, nor on its ramparts against the greying sky. This was as he'd expected. Vanessa had mapped the castle during many hours of scrying, in much more detail than shown on the map he'd given Franzen. And although the fleshly beings moving within the structure left less of an impression, apart from Geist himself, she'd still managed to tell which parts of the castle were left mostly alone. This included the towers along the outer wall and the upper rooms to the rear of the keep.

Stumbling occasionally in the dim light, he climbed the rough slope up onto the shoulder. Goats ran from him, but none betrayed his presence by bleating. He followed the outer wall until it became the rear of the keep. There he stared up at the thick covering of ivy. With no access from any part of the courtyard, and with the upper rooms at the rear largely unused, no one had bothered to clear it. He could barely see where the windows were. Since this was a defensive wall, there were none on the ground floor, but fifteen feet up, he made out the thinning of the ivy where it grew across gaps rather than on top of stone.

He checked his revolver was secure in the holster beneath his armpit, and patted his pocket for the box of cartridges.

He climbed.

He hadn't expected to have to use this rear access, but he was glad now he'd committed Vanessa's more detailed map to memory. The ascent was hard work, however. He had to reach through the leaves for handholds and footholds. The main stems were thick and sturdy, but stuck right to the wall, and his fingers could only find purchase on the thinner stems coming off them, which sometimes snapped. The toes of his boots scrabbled for hold; his fingers ached with fatigue. He kept his thoughts from the rocky ground.

He was almost at the window when a loud blast sent his heart into his throat: the field-gun, he quickly realised. The echo rolled around the valley slopes, joined by shouts and barking and livestock noises from the courtyard at the front of the keep. He had to hurry. With their firepower, the Kurassians wouldn't take long to storm the fortress. Faster, his fingers weary almost to failure, he made it the last couple of feet, and just as a second blast came he pushed a hand desperately through the ivy stems where he judged the window to be. No resistance – Vanessa had been right about the shutters having gone. He grabbed the inner sill, then pushed his other hand after the first and widened the gap between them so he could haul himself up and shove head and shoulders through. All will and no technique, he fought his way into a damp, dark room and landed on the floor in a hard-breathing heap.

No time for rest. Through a doorway, he saw along a corridor to where faint light came up a flight of stairs from the ground floor. Voices down there roared in anger and panic, shouted instructions. Rifle-fire sounded in the distance, along with the intermittent chatter of a machine-gun. Ranga drew his revolver and steadied himself.

'Be with me, my Lady.'

He crept along to the stairs, then descended into a hall cluttered with bedding and a long table strewn with the remains of a meal, all lit by two torches and stinking of long occupation by the unwashed. Two men held ajar the large doors to the courtyard and stood looking out, ready to shut them. Across the room was the stair down to the cellars, where Vanessa was convinced the Bourgs kept prisoners.

Ranga crept down the last of the stairs, thanking the gods they didn't creak, and started across the floor.

And banged his toes on a dropped flagon.

The men turned at the clatter. Their surprise gave him a clear shot, and he took it. Luck, or his hours of practice, was with him: one bullet put each man down. For a moment, he felt stunned with potency and horror, then came the urge to run back up and get out through the window again as fast as he could.

He bit it back, left the men groaning and writhing on the floor and ran down the other stairs into a large vaulted cellar, where he tried to make sense of the wavering lamplight and the shouting. Against the wall parallel with the front of the keep, several men sat fastened to a stocks-like device – some Kurassians in tattered uniforms, some Bourgs – and in the middle of the cellar, two Bourgs with a lantern manhandled an older man in the direction of the far end, where another flight of steps led up.

Geist, it had to be.

Ranga hissed with nerves: the three were bundled together, and he couldn't shoot at the warriors without risking his prize. Unaware of him, they kept pulling Geist towards the other stairs. Ranga couldn't risk them reaching the inner sanctum. He had no wish to use the awful-sounding secret passage Vanessa had detailed.

He motioned the other captives to keep quiet, and used the cellar's supporting pillars as cover to get nearer the three.

Geist and his two captors reached the stair. It was narrow, and they went up single-file, Geist between the Bourgs. There would be only moments when all three were lined up before the first was obscured by the ceiling. From fifteen paces, Ranga sighted.

His first shot sent shrapnel exploding from the wall to the right of the lead Bourg's head. He re-cocked the hammer in panic – but the man was staggering, blood all over his face. Ranga fired again and missed as the Bourg collided with Geist, who jerked backwards into the man at the rear. All three fell to the ground, the lantern spilling a patch of lit fuel.

Ranga dashed forwards. The Bourg who'd been to the rear surged to his feet, one side of his jerkin on fire. Ranga expected him to try to put it out, but the man ignored it and started to pull an axe from his belt. Ranga aimed and fired. The bullet hit the man's left shoulder, but the warrior paid it no more attention than the flames. The next punctured his chest and put him down, but now the Bourg with the bloodied face was on his feet, roaring in pain and rage, sightlessly drawing his own weapon.

Ranga took careful aim. The gun produced only a click.

Horror froze him. He had to reload. But the Bourg's ruined eyes searching for him, the man's shouted challenges and accusations of cowardice, stopped him even trying. The madness of the Bourg, to want to still fight, even blind, terrified him. The rage, the courage, was inhuman. Superhuman.

Somehow the warrior sensed him, started towards him. Ranga panicked, raised his gun and cocked and pulled again and again, as though there might be one bullet somehow left in there to save him from this bellowing monster.

Then an axe embedded itself into the back of the Bourg's head, and the man fell.

'After six months,' said Geist, 'that was mighty satisfying.'

Ranga nodded, fighting down the urge to puke.

'Now who in Elok's trousers are you?' said Geist.

Ranga drew a hard breath, snapped himself back into his role. 'Major Samka, Republican Intelligence Bureau.'

'And that unholy racket?'

Ranga assumed he meant the fighting upstairs rather than the questions and pleas being shouted at him by the other captives, but he didn't answer at once, still trying to take in the man before him. Over six feet tall, a gaunt and drawn face with deep lines, several inches of beard and hair and not much less of eyebrows, all dark grey flecked with white. He looked tired, but his eyes burned with intelligence, suspicion. It took Ranga a moment to understand his own relief. This man had to be over sixty. Vanessa couldn't be more than thirty-five. The disparity between them shot to pieces any lingering fear. They couldn't have been involved together, not when Vanessa could have any man she chose.

'That racket is an attack by a troop of Empyreal Pioneer Cavalry,' he said, shaking the spent casings out of his gun. 'They're here to rescue those surveyors. But I'm here to rescue you, and we have to get out before they come.'

'What?' said Geist. 'Get out why?'

'Because they know about your talents.' Ranga began to reload. 'Their captain is an Empyrean fanatic. He'll have you hanged or shot or the gods know what.'

'What talents? What are you talking about?'

'Mister Geist, please—'

'That's not my name.'

'What?'

'Your intelligence must be mistaken.'

'And yours has gone completely!' said Ranga. 'We have to get out of here.' Even with the threat he held over Hana and Petri, he feared getting tangled with them. 'There's an upstairs window at the back I—'

A blast from directly above made him duck. The Kurassians had got the field-gun through the outer gates and had trained it on the doors to the keep.

'I'm going nowhere,' said Geist.

'No!' shrieked Ranga, terrified the situation was running away from him. 'You'll just get yourself killed, you stupid bastard!' He stepped back and pointed the reloaded gun. 'I demand you let me rescue you.'

'You already have,' said Geist. 'And I can't be rescued twice in one hour: my pride won't stand it. Now calm yourself. No Kurassian military man will harm me.'

'But they *know* about you,' Ranga urged. 'Why stay? Why take the risk?'

'My reasoning is my own,' said Geist. 'But be assured, your superiors will learn about your boldness. Now, I suggest we extinguish those flames and prepare ourselves in case the remaining Bourgs retreat down here. Though my bet is they'll flee to their deeper redoubt. That noise was a field-gun?'

'A small one, yes.'

'Excellent.'

Excellent why? But there was no choice but to do as Geist said. If it was Geist. No, it had to be. Lack of sleep and an impossibly fast heartbeat were turning his brain to mush. He had no idea why Geist hadn't believed in the danger. Geist couldn't know that Franzen was unaware of his magic use. Had he been wrong about him being a magician?

All was not lost, though. Even if Petri and Hana hadn't followed his order to leave, he could still expose them – though Geist recognising Hana would make things more difficult.

Under Geist's instruction – the man seemed used to being obeyed, and Ranga wasn't in a state to argue – they smothered what remained of the fire, and used storage barrels and bales to form a hasty barricade around the remnants of the survey team. They waited behind it for the battle upstairs to finish, listening on-edge to the screams and shouts, the snap and crackle of gunfire.

Then Kurassian troops came swarming down into the cellar, and Ranga declared himself and was almost shot by a jumpy private. A mania of activity followed. The survey team was released from the stocks, and several stunned-looking Bourg women and elderly men were herded down from upstairs. The surveyors and Geist and Ranga were led up into the main hall, where the bodies of several Bourg warriors were being dragged out into the yard, one of them leaving a wide blood-slick on the flagstones.

Franzen came over. 'Major Samka. I told you to remain on the hilltop.'

'I couldn't take the risk that this man might be harmed, Captain. I found another point of entry.'

'And very grateful for it I am,' said Geist. 'He came just as I was about to be hauled off to their inner redoubt. I thought at the time I was about to be killed, but now I believe they somehow knew of my identity and planned to use me as a valuable hostage.'

'Your identity? You're the man called Geist, aren't you?'

'By some. You might know of me by another name: Lieutenant-Colonel Albrecht Hollenstern, late of the forty-fifth lancers.'

Ranga stopped himself shouting *What*?

Franzen stared. 'That name is known to me,' he said after a moment. 'You'll forgive my not accepting such a claim immediately, though I can see you're of good northern blood, and about the right age.'

'These are dangerous times, Captain,' said Geist. 'You'd be foolish not to act with caution.'

'Are you saying you've been held here since your disappearance?'

'A few months only. I've been here and there since leaving the military. Mostly work of a classified type. It was such that landed me in this hole.'

Franzen called for Gessler, then took him to one side and spoke in a low voice. Gessler looked amazed at Geist, then hurried off.

'Captain,' said Geist. 'Has the redoubt been taken?'

'Not yet,' said Franzen. 'The only entrance lies down that corridor, as far as we can make out.' He indicated an opening beneath the stairs Ranga had first descended. Two soldiers stood against the wall to either side, one using a small mirror to look down it. 'I don't fear attack from that quarter, but storming it might be difficult – they've an ingenious defence. We'll consolidate before I decide. I've sent for the animals and the others to come down into the courtyard.'

'With those so-called agents?' said Ranga.

'Yes,' said Franzen. 'So-called? I thought we had this out last night.'

Ranga had no choice but to play his remaining card. It would likely bring dire consequences for Petri and Hana, but it wasn't his fault they'd ignored his warning. 'Last night, Captain, I was bewitched, as I have been for the past two days. Hence my behaviour. Hence that woman persuading me to bring her along under such a ridiculous pretext.'

'Major Samka, please—'

'It's true!

'If she's not a Bureau agent, how did she know about the Hollow Isles?'

'By the same means! Magic.'

Understanding showed on the captain's face. 'You mean you were *literally* bewitched?'

'Yes! And they've come for this man. He's in danger if he meets them. You must keep them away from him.'

'Does this make sense to you?' Franzen asked Geist.

'Possibly.' Geist turned to Ranga. 'Who are these people?'

Sweat broke from Ranga's palms as he realised that in his tiredness he'd been about to give their names. 'A woman and her supposed servant. I met them in Maskar, and they persuaded me to take them along and pretend they were also Bureau agents – by sorcery most foul, I now understand.'

'And who might they be working for?' said Franzen.

'If not themselves, I don't know.'

'I fear I do, Captain,' said Geist. 'A group of magicians who have long been my enemies. For much of my recent life I've tried to escape their detection whilst working against them. But trapped here as I have been, it could be they've identified my location and sent their agents to assassinate me. I call them the Kings Behind the World.'

Relief flooded Ranga. Geist could hardly have given a more helpful answer if he'd written it for him.

'You understand, Major,' Franzen said, 'that a suspicion of witchcraft obliges me to arrest them and take them back to Torrento.'

'You must do your duty, Captain,' said Ranga, irritated by Franzen's implication that this might still be part of a tiff that had got out of hand. 'And you'll do it best if you make sure they and this man never meet. The woman's eyes and voice hold a terrible power. What if she were to bewitch him into claiming she's a friend?'

Franzen turned to Geist. 'Is that a possibility, from what you know of these people?'

'She would have to be powerful,' said Geist.

'She is,' said Ranga. He pushed from his mind the thought that he might be signing their death warrants. 'Put hoods on them. And gag them. We have a journey of several days back to civilisation. You can't take any risks.'

A corporal presented himself and asked permission to speak. 'Sir, Lieutenant Gessler said you asked for anyone who might know anything personal of Colonel Hollenstern.' His glance flicked to Geist and back. 'My father was in the forty-fifth at the Battle of Vollund. He's often told us of Hollenstern's charge.'

'His name?' said Franzen.

'Kassin Stenk, sir.'

Franzen looked to Geist, who studied the man. 'I don't recall him.'

'He was under Captain Ralff,' said the corporal.

'Ah,' said Geist. 'Him I remember, naturally. A Laggensdorf man. Broad shoulders, broad belly. Got himself tattooed against regulations, on the arse.'

'That's right, sir! He often joked about it with his men.' The corporal saluted. 'Sir! It's an honour.'

Geist ducked his chin in a crisp nod. 'Give my regards to your father when you see him next.'

The man looked amazed with pride as he turned and left.

'I wanted to believe you, Colonel,' said Franzen. 'Your return will be a moment of national rejoicing.'

'Well, we're a way from that yet.'

'Sir,' called a soldier by the wrecked doors. 'The muleteers are here.'

Ranga itched to go and look – where they stood was at the wrong angle to see the outer gates.

'With the Kymeran agents?' said Franzen.

'Yes, sir.'

'Keep those two under guard in the courtyard. Prevent them doing anything that might be witchcraft.'

'I think perhaps I will speak to them,' said Geist.

Ranga caught hold of his sleeve, and spoke to Franzen. 'Believe me, Captain, it's too great a risk. She's been preparing for this meeting for days. You saw how she fooled me. The best thing would be to tell them the colonel is dead or was never here. Let me leave with him now.'

'I have no intention of going anywhere,' said Geist.

'But you don't know what she's capable of!'

'Against a Kymeran spy, perhaps,' said Franzen. 'The moral fibre of an Empyreal officer would surely prove more resilient.'

'And how will you judge, Captain?' said Ranga. 'If they meet, and the colonel here claims to know her, will that be because he truly does know her, or because of her magic? Making a man doubt himself is how she works!'

Franzen exhaled. 'Wait here.'

♋

Hana often seemed to miss her footing on the rough grass of the slope down towards the fortress, though whether that was just tiredness, Petri didn't know – and she shook her head to brush off any attempt he made to ask. Something seemed to have happened to her during his brief captivity in the woods: he'd returned to find her almost unresponsive. She'd paid little attention to his attempts to explain Ranga's threats, only attending to the sound of gunfire. Every noise had made her flinch as though it might mark Geist's death, whether by accident or otherwise. They still didn't know if he'd survived, nor whether Ranga had, nor what he'd done. No word had come from the fortress when the shooting had stopped, only a signal for the muleteers and others to descend.

Along with the animals and the machine-gun crew from the slope, they crossed the stone bridge over the moat, passed the second machine-gun crew now facing outwards in the ruined gateway, and entered the courtyard between the wreckage of the gates. The stink of cordite and manure hung in the still air; patches of the straw and dirt were soaked with blood. Dead hounds had been left where they'd fallen, but the bodies of about ten Bourg warriors had been dragged in front of a dilapidated-looking outbuilding. One Kurassian lay beneath his spread tunic. Four men were busy dismantling the field-gun.

Across the courtyard, a flight of steps led up to the remains of the keep's doors. Petri sensed Hana's tension, her dread.

A soldier met them. 'Wait here. The captain will come out soon.'

'And Geist?' said Hana.

The soldier avoided her eyes. 'No speaking.'

'Did he survive?' said Hana, more tightly.

The man stepped back and kept his rifle loosely aimed at them. He looked nervous. Petri felt queasy at what this avoidance of the subject might mean.

'Don't toy with us,' rasped Hana, her fists balled. '*Does he live*?'

The man only tightened his grip on his gun.

'Just a simple yes or no, then we can all relax,' said Petri, failing to hit the calm tone he'd wanted.

Boots sounded on stone. Franzen descended the steps.

'I see you won, Captain,' Petri said.

'One dead, four injured. Only three of the survey team were left alive.'

'And *Geist*?' said Hana, her voice strained almost to tearing.

'He lives.'

Petri closed his eyes with relief.

'I must see him,' said Hana. 'Alone. As I said.' Her voice shook with nerves now, its strength all on the surface. Petri feared she would crumble in some way.

'That won't be possible,' said Franzen. 'Grave accusations have been levelled against you.'

Petri's stomach sank into a pit. 'By Major Samka? Can't you see he's out for revenge for my Lady refusing him last night?'

'Why did you fail to apprise me of Geist's real identity?'

'His…?'

'This is a trick,' groaned Hana, as though at the end of her strength. 'Let me see him. You have no right.'

'I have every right,' said Franzen. 'I've been warned what might happen if I allow such a meeting.'

'At least take him a message,' said Petri. 'Please.'

Franzen eyed him impatiently. 'I'll relay a brief one, by speech.'

'Tell him that Hana Quallace and—'

'No!' cried Hana, and gave him a furious look. Then she closed her eyes and seemed almost about to faint. As Petri stepped towards her, she pulled her focus-stone from under her wristband and clutched it tight, hissing between her teeth as the pain bit.

'What's that?' said Franzen.

She stood erect at last, breathing hard, her hand clenched so hard round the stone her knuckles went white. 'CORVAN!'

She shouted it again. Franzen drew his pistol. 'Stop that! I've never harmed a woman in my life, but by God I'm prepared to now.'

'My Lady, please,' urged Petri. 'We're no use to him dead.'

She quietened, trembling all over, eyes wide and staring. Petri wondered if Geist had heard.

♋

Ranga bit back the urge to grab Geist as the man's head jerked towards the doors. Hana, that cry must have been, though it had sounded unlike her. When the call came again, he felt the command in it, even though it wasn't directed at him.

'Ignore it, Colonel, please.'

Geist stared towards the door. 'There aren't many people who would use that name.'

'They could easily have discovered it,' said Ranga. 'These "Kings of the World".'

'*Behind* the world,' muttered Geist, and looked about at the several soldiers staring at him. 'I have to go. I might no longer strictly be a colonel in the Empyreal cavalry, but I am still the man who held that rank. I will not be seen to cower in fear of a woman.'

'You heard me,' said Ranga, desperate. 'She'll appear to you in the guise of a friend.'

'Tell me her true appearance, then, so I'll know if she's changed.'

Near-panic seized Ranga. A lie would be found out if Geist talked to Franzen. 'Naturally, they chose someone who looks similar. How could I describe her in enough detail for you to be able to tell? Magic is subtle, you know that.'

Geist's eyes narrowed. 'I'm going. Come if you wish.'

Ranga had no choice. He'd just have to keep his wits about him and hope his warnings would make Geist or Hollenstern or whoever doubt Hana was who she claimed.

They went out to the top of the steps. In the courtyard, separated from the other activity, Franzen and Hana and Petri stood with a couple of soldiers on guard. Pressure sang in Ranga's ears, dulled other sound. This was it, the meeting he'd dreaded – the meeting all his efforts had failed to prevent, as though the gods themselves had put their power into bringing it about. But not even gods could stop a bullet. He drew his revolver as covertly as possible and held it down by his side.

'Corvan!' Hana's face was fixed on the man. She paid Ranga no mind at all. Even Petri only gave him an icy glance.

'Good God,' muttered Geist.

'Not really her, remember,' urged Ranga.

Geist waved him silent, and preceded him down the steps. When they were paces from the waiting group, Geist said, 'Hana?'

'No, Corvan.' Her voice came clear and strong as she stepped forwards. 'I've discarded that paper mask. Don't you recognise my true self?'

Alarm showed on Petri's face. He made to touch her but she shrugged him off.

'You resemble someone I know,' said Geist. 'Are you saying you're not that person?' He glanced at Ranga, clearly puzzled, but Ranga could say nothing to enlighten him. He had no idea what Hana intended with this.

'I have no further interest in disguise, now we've met,' she said. 'Has it really been so long since we parted, that you do not know me?'

'Remind me when you think that was.'

'You mock me!' she cried. 'You cannot have forgotten that wretched dockside, when you promised to follow me back to Torrento, and lied.'

Incredulity reshaped Geist's face. '*Vanessa…?*'

The name shocked Ranga's breath from him. What by all the gods?

'It amazes you to see me so young,' Hana said. 'But I have power now, gathered over years that have left no mark on me.'

'What—' said Franzen, but Geist put up a hand for silence.

He stepped towards her. 'Hana, what is this?'

Ranga felt frozen, unable to act. His vision tunnelled with the building horror. Was Vanessa using her power to affect Hana's words? Or had something gone terribly wrong?

'You can't deny me now, Corvan. I've proved you wrong, proved myself wrong. "I won't be beautiful forever," I said. But I shall!'

'Stop this, Hana. I don't know what's happened, but—'

'What's happened? Not age, not to me. You've grown old and I have not,' she said, ignoring Petri's attempts to hush her. 'And what do you say to that? You who cast me off because you foresaw my future, the future of all women and all men, and found it not to your liking? You, one of the deepest thinkers I've ever met, and yet with the same shallow sensibilities of all your sex. Well, have I satisfied your qualms? You won't reject me now, I think. Shall we resume our work? Our life? Our passion?'

'No!' Ranga croaked.

She turned on him. 'Silence, worm.'

The black tunnel enclosed his mind. No, he pleaded. But the veil over the story had been ripped down. Vanessa's words to Shoggu, that a magician might appear younger than his years – or *her* years. Her shut-up house, her ancient servant.

He stepped back and pulled up his gun, aimed at Geist.

'Put that down!' ordered Franzen.

'Say she's lying!' he cried. 'You and her, you never – you couldn't have.'

The man's eyes held his. 'Don't shoot, Captain. We need him for questioning.'

'Say it!' cried Ranga. 'Swear!'

But he knew. And the power behind Geist's gaze, despite weariness and age and months of captivity – this was a kind of man he himself had failed to be. He'd only ever been an overgrown adolescent, a servant – to be played with and used, and cast aside in favour of a man like this, a man of consequence, the man she'd wanted all along.

There was no way out, he saw that now. He should have listened to his doubts, should have had the guts to pull the trigger and take the chance between death and freedom. But he hadn't. He'd let her persuade him again.

He stiffened his arm, tensed for the recoil – and swung the gun towards her.

The roaring as he closed his eyes was joined by the gun's report. Someone grabbed him, then others pinned him, pulled the gun from him; breath was punched from his stomach and he folded, unable to fall with the hands grasping him. He expected to be hit further, beaten to death, and though he feared the pain he didn't much care.

But no one struck him. A voice was shouting for Hana. More than one. He raised his head and opened his eyes.

She lay on the ground, Petri and Geist crouched over her. And there was blood.

31

THE DAWNING OF THE WORLD

This doesn't look good, thought Geist, as he directed the stretcher-bearers to lay Hana next to the fireplace in the hall. Her cries and gasps lessened, but she kept shivering and her face stayed pale, her breath seething between clenched teeth. Blood soaked her riding breeches just above her knee.

Petri had been trying to communicate with and reassure her all the way from outside, holding her hand, but with no response Geist had seen. Now the boy looked up at him and said, 'She'll be all right, sir? It's only a leg wound.'

'Of course she will.' Geist faked conviction as much for Hana's benefit as Petri's. He watched the medic cut the cloth above Hana's knee and clean her wound with liquid from a small bottle. She shuddered and struggled.

'Keep her still!' the medic said. 'And press this pad against the bleeding,' he told Petri. 'No artery cut, thank God.' He manipulated the leg, and Hana cried out. 'Femur might be broken, but it doesn't seem separated. A splint should do it.'

'Can you get the bullet out?' said Petri, pressing down hard on the pad.

'Not worth trying,' said Geist. 'If it ricocheted off the bone, it might be anywhere.'

The medic grunted agreement. 'She needs a hospital, like two of the others. These stretchers are made to be dragged behind a mule, so we can get her there. Infection's the main worry. Keep pressing.' He went back to his wounded soldiers.

Geist's knees cracked as he squatted beside his student. 'Hana.' Neither the fire nor the blanket over her upper body had yet eased her shivering. 'Hana!'

'No,' she mumbled between her pained groans, her eyes still closed. 'Not that name. Not right.'

'You're Hana Quallace, remember?'

'Lies.' She twisted her head to one side. 'Masks, all masks.'

'It's Geist, Hana Freallis. Come—'

'Not her! No name.'

'Vanessa?' came Petri's cautious try.

Geist flinched inside, and Hana shuddered. 'No! Leave me alone…'

Her rejection of that name was a relief, at least. Geist glanced round to make sure no Kurassians were near enough to overhear low voices. 'Right,' he said to Petri, covering fear with brusqueness. 'What the hell's going on?'

The boy leaned closer, his sharp-featured face etched with worry. 'She did a ritual back at the college – I didn't see it, but she called on the Great Mother to save someone. And something happened and she lost herself. Hare too. Sent him away. Then a couple of days ago she invoked a new self, a stronger one. To give her the power to cope.'

The Great Mother. Of all the madness. 'But where does Vanessa come into it?'

'I don't know who that is.'

'You'd never heard the name until just now, outside?'

'No.'

'But your murderous companion had, clearly. Who is he?'

'Secret agent,' Petri said. 'A real one. We met him in Maskar. What happened to her? To Hana?'

'Possession, of a kind.' Geist spoke in a low whisper in case Hana might overhear, though she seemed almost insensible.

'You mean this Vanessa was *controlling* her?'

'Not as such, I think. Direct control would be extremely difficult, and Hana seemed to expect me to recognise her as Vanessa even still looking the same, which makes no sense if Vanessa was using her as a puppet. She mentioned masks just now: I suspect it was a particularly intense invocation, as you said. She somehow connected with Vanessa's psyche and drew it down into herself like an actor's role, probably without either of them realising exactly what was happening. Anyhow, the whys and wherefores can wait. Being shot seems to have shocked her free of it, but she hasn't regained her old self, and that's dangerous – in shamanic terms, her soul's detached. It'll weaken her will to live, and she might succumb to infection more readily.'

'Shit.'

'You said she lost Hare?'

'He dived into a swamp, carrying a flaming brand. She said she didn't even want him any more.' The boy sounded desperate. 'How do we get her soul back?'

'Let me think,' said Geist. One thing was certain: if her soul was detached in a shamanic sense, then in a shamanic sense he would have to restore it. Hare was likely the key. But to find Hare, he would have to enter the Otherworld, something he hadn't done successfully in all the six months of his captivity, and with no opportunity to practice. But at least—

He looked at Hana's arm lying outside the blanket, and felt like swearing. 'There should be a lump beneath that wristband.'

'Her stone?' said Petri. 'She dropped it outside.' He fetched it out of his pocket and handed it across, and Geist sighed with relief. Maybe there was a chance.

The medic came back to check on Hana, Franzen with him.

'Would you mind telling me what all that outside was about, Colonel?'

Geist stood to his full height. 'I'm sorry you've become caught up in it, Captain.' He let a certain annoyance into his voice in hope of deterring further questions. 'The truth will take a long time to unravel, and you have your men to see to. Let me assure you that these two are blameless, and it's Major Samka who's been working trickery here. I've been cooperating with the Kymeran secret service for some years, exposing traitors. There are some downright dangerous people involved. But even the agent Samka might be a dupe rather than an evildoer in his own right. Where is he, the cellars?'

'We'll keep him safe, don't worry,' said Franzen. 'What of his talk of magic? And those things this woman said?'

'Later,' said Geist. 'Our priority should be to get everyone back to Torrento in one piece. As to which, I need to stabilise this young lady. I have some techniques of my own that might help: ancient practices learned in my travels.'

'Ancient practices?'

'Of necessity.' Geist aimed for a matter-of-fact tone. 'I believe her enemies have worked some kind of magic on her. The Watchers of Highcloud taught me some techniques to fight it.' He hoped Franzen shared the usual Kurassian respect for the monastery. 'I'll need her taken to another room so I can work undisturbed.'

'For how long?'

'An hour, possibly. It's vital she recovers. Not just for the secret service, but for the civilised world.'

'For the—? Why?'

'All in good time, Captain. Where can we put her?'

Franzen seemed keen to pose more questions, but demurred under Geist's stare. 'The kitchens might be suitable. Through there.'

The castle's kitchens and stores, just off the hall, looked none too clean. But they were safe, the only other exit heavily barred. The fire here had almost burned down overnight, but Petri got it going again with well-seasoned wood from a stack by the hearth. After the bearers had set Hana down, Geist again tried to converse with her, but with no more response than before.

'Keep holding her hand and talking to her,' he told Petri, when they were alone again. 'And if anyone makes to come in, tell them to leave. At any event, make sure they don't see my face. I'll sit with my back to the door.'

'To do what?'

'To fetch back her soul.'

He settled himself near Hana, and began a meditation, light enough at first to keep one ear on Petri's murmurings. When satisfied the boy was doing as good a job as could be expected, Geist drew deep, slow breaths and began to clear his mind. Not easy: he was out of practice, and his thoughts kept starting down numerous paths of speculation and fear and regret, of how stupid he'd been to get trapped here, how much harm he could have prevented if he'd taken more care. It wasn't till the heat from the new logs was warming him that Geist at last felt ready, so inwardly focused that Hana's groans now barely intruded.

He took her focus-stone and passed it quickly over his face. He regretted the loss of his own crystal, the lens now in the Lamia's possession, which would have allowed him to raise his tattoo-mask by force of will alone. But Hana's stone, like all of them, had been attuned to himself before he'd passed it on, and he felt the pattern of dots spring to his skin, forming whorls and lines, right the way back to his ears and under his hairline.

Now for Raven. Now to hope that the months apart hadn't weakened the connection too much. His usual practice had always been to call the bird into his current location, but that required his lens. Since he had to travel to the Otherworld anyway, he had best call Raven there. Eyes gently closed, he brought to his mind's eye the kitchen that surrounded his physical body. In his imagination, he stood and went out into the main hall. From the guarded corridor that led to the inner redoubt, he caught a taint of evil and death, but also awareness, one that brought to mind Taslan and Felca. Of course: the Lamia would have made the twins spy on the outer castle, using his confiscated lens as an amplifier. But Geist knew the limits of their training – they would at most gain only unreliable impressions of what passed in the material world, and nothing of his mental quest.

The castle yard held echoes of the disastrous gunshot, but he guided away the anger that rose in response. He followed instinct to the northern part of the courtyard, and there he found a well.

Whether it was there in reality, he didn't know – he'd been brought unconscious into the fortress six months before, and had been too intent on Hana that morning to pay much attention to his surroundings. But it was auspicious in any case: a well-shaft symbolised intent, a sinking into the earth in search of water, the most psychic element. He descended the shaft by the handholds within it, conjuring the sensation of rough and rusted iron against his palms, easing himself ever deeper into the earth and into the borderland where his own mind joined that of the wider world. Beneath him came the unexpected chuckle of running water. His boots stepped into calf-deep cold. He waded with the tug of the underground river's flow, following twists and turns, ducking when the roof required it, until he emerged into a large cavern lit by a single hole at the apex of its craggy ceiling. He stepped onto the river's bank and fixed his eyes on that hole.

He focused his mind on the call:

Raven.

Each long second the bird failed to appear quickened his heartbeat. Had his tattoo-mask, meant to call Raven, been corrupted by the focus-stone's long association with Hare?

He cast his thoughts back to other times he'd called the bird, hoping to rekindle the bond from its enforced dormancy. That tortuous descent following Raven through the dead forest two years before, to the shore where he'd found Orc and Cass; that time a decade back when he'd discovered that Daroguerre had a living daughter; that night six months past in the College of the Inner Eye, when he'd learned of this castle and what it contained – and at last, a black speck appeared against the bright sky-patch of the ceiling hole. It grew into a large black bird flapping and soaring down, the whorls of dyed dots on the bone mask matching those on Geist's own face.

Raven alighted on the ground and folded his wings, mantled with sheens of blue and purple. 'Harr, well,' he croaked. 'You resemble my old confederate. But how can you be him? He was too clever and powerful to be kept or captured. I heard that from his own lips.'

'Don't toy with me, bird,' said Geist, covering his relief.

'It matters not, anyway,' said Raven. 'I haven't heard from him in months. I'd been planning to recruit. You'll do for now – though I don't think much of this place you've called me to. Scant scope for wings, since your only way out is one of those tunnels. Or do you fly? You don't look like a Watcher. More a peeping tom.'

Geist ignored that. 'We need to find Hare. I heard he disappeared into a swamp.'

'Harr, yes, he dived into it as frightened as if he'd seen his own shadow.'

'You saw?'

'What do I not see?'

Plenty, in Geist's experience. But the response was encouraging. Perhaps using Hana's stone would make for a stronger connection between Raven and Hare. 'Why did he enter the swamp? With what aim?'

'Mother-girl tried to destroy him, because he sought to remind her who she'd been. The flame of her self had weakened. He thought to make it burn bright again.'

'By finding fuel?'

'By returning to the flame's source: the Smoking Mirror. Foolish fur-ball! Its guardians won't be taken by surprise a second time.'

'The Sisters?'

'Lord-lady Sky-and-Earth themself,' said Raven. 'If he angers them, not even his legs will carry him clear.'

'Nor did they with the Sisters. As you well anticipated.'

'Harr, harr.' Raven spread his wings and bowed his head. 'I hear admiration, not approbation! How could I have considered any other confederate? We are too well-suited.'

Geist didn't think this was the time to defend his moral record. 'Let's go. We need to catch up.'

Raven flapped up onto his shoulder. 'The left tunnel, then. Be swift!'

The dim passage soon grew close and humid, the smell of damp vegetation followed by the sight of green algae on the walls. The floor became soft and wet, and Geist felt at the edge of his mind the presence of the Great Mother. What had Hana been thinking of, meddling with such a force? It was not only ancient, but vague, malleable, shifting: useful qualities in some circumstances, but the lack of clear boundaries made working with it very dangerous. Even the Mother's link with this quest might be enough to call her closer, he thought – and gently pushed the alarming idea of her away.

The tunnel floor turned steeply upward and became steps. The ceiling vanished, leaving in its place a dark night sky: starless and moonless, though from somewhere came just enough light to see by. Reaching the topmost step, Geist found himself on the summit of an ancient flat-topped pyramid, a step-temple. Old blood darkened the stone around a square pit in the centre. The cold of deep underground seemed to flow from it: the cold of the Mother in her death-aspect, he sensed uneasily.

'Did Hare come here?' he asked.

Raven flapped down to the stone and investigated the blood. 'Yes, he came here, with a fugitive. Here, in the place of an ancient divorce, was made a recent marriage. And it was to this place that I, in the guise of Mankind's great teacher, brought the flame that spread around the world. If that *was* me,' he cackled.

'You always did enjoy your own riddles too much,' said Geist.

'You'd prefer my silence?'

'If you're not going to speak plainly, then yes. Where did Hare go next?'

'That at least I can answer in the prosaic fashion you crave,' said

Raven. 'A trail of thought led straight from the Smoking Mirror to here – we need only retrace it. And the substance of thought shall be our road. Fly with me.'

'Fly?'

Raven hopped to the edge of the level and took off to swoop down the steps. Geist turned, intending to follow, and swore. A sea had risen up the stair – not of water, but what seemed a layer of dense fog. Raven skimmed the surface out toward the horizon, barely visible in the darkness. Geist stepped down to the edge of the fog-sea and probed with his foot. In frustration he felt tempted to assert that the stuff was dry land, but he held back. Rejecting its true nature, whatever that might be, risked inhibiting genuine revelation.

The strange fog turned out to act like dry land anyway – of a sort. His foot sank little more than ankle deep. Each step forwards felt disconcertingly like missing a stair in the dark: slightly too long a drop before meeting resistance, even though he never sank any lower. And the resistance, when it came each time, was peculiar; he experienced it as the substance turning from vapour to solidity in response to the touch of his boot.

His footsteps passed, tens, then hundreds. Raven had disappeared ahead, and there was nothing but the featureless fog-sea Geist walked and the featureless dark sky. His previous mind-taste of the Mother, whether in her vegetative or death aspects, had faded behind; but all around was the sense of something related to her, though larger and more diffuse, the same power that turned the fog solid. Something even older than the Mother, if that were possible. His stomach felt tight with the sense of unfathomable depth, though whether of distance beneath his feet or of something else, he couldn't tell. He'd never experienced anywhere so alien, nor felt himself such an intruder.

An intruder, the strange thought came, who was also returning.

At last he saw Raven wheeling stiff-winged above a dot on the ground. This grew as Geist approached until it revealed the V-shape of long ears seen from behind. Hare stared away into the distance, holding the brand sloped across his shoulder, its flame almost dead.

'Hail, Hare,' said Geist, stopping a few paces behind the creature. 'Lithe leaper, dark-eyed darter, lord of the form in the field.'

'Greeting to you, Wanderer.' Hare didn't turn. 'If not to him who accompanies you.'

'Oh, it wounds!' called Raven from above. 'Is there anything more hurtful than the disdain of a pie filling?'

Geist ignored the bird. 'Where are we, Hare? Why stop in this place?'

'I await the dawn.'

'But the Smoking Mirror isn't here.'

'It will come.'

'With the sunrise?'

'It is not one day's dawning I await, but that of Time itself.'

'Enough babbling!' cried Raven – and swooped on the other animath.

'Stop that!' said Geist in shock. But Raven kept up his assault, beating at Hare with his wings, stabbing with his bill, dodging the kicks of the squealing animal. Hare had dropped the brand – Geist grabbed it, seeing that contact with the strange ground was extinguishing its guttering flame.

Hare broke free from beneath Raven and ran, leaving scraps of fur floating down. Raven pursued him for thirty yards, then returned and landed a couple of paces from Geist.

'What the hell was that about?'

'His work was done,' said Raven. 'His presence now interferes.'

Geist fought to maintain evenness in his thoughts and words. 'He needs to retrieve the flame of Hana's self.'

'If you think that wise, then call him back,' said Raven.

'Why wouldn't it be wise?'

But Raven set to preening his wing-feathers.

Damn the bird, thought Geist. But he would be better off working it out himself anyway. Relying too heavily on Raven would unbalance their relationship.

He turned his mind to the question, hoping months of reduced mental activity hadn't left it too weak for the task. If Hare brought the rekindled flame to Hana, what might happen? He had assumed it would be the same as at her Initiation, since the situation was roughly comparable. Initiation relied on the subject having a weak sense of self, either naturally or because it had been degraded. During Hana's Initiation, Hare had restored her self-sense with the sacred fire. On the face of it, a repetition might not only repeat the effect, but might strengthen the relationship between Hana and Hare, and thus her ability when scaping.

Why then did Raven seem to think otherwise? Geist watched the bird's preening. The bird who had so gleefully and inexplicably driven Hare away.

As Hana had done, going by Petri's report.

Was that the issue, that Hana's rejection of Hare might prevent a repeat of the effects of Initiation? Was that a reason not to try, when he had no other options?

Or was it – almost the opposite, yes – in a flash of instinct, he understood.

Hana might become a greater shaman than before, but at a terrible price.

Rational thought confirmed his intuition. Hana's Initiated self had been a rebuilding around the idea that Hare was the new core of her, a papering over the crack of the self-loss she'd previously suffered. But that self-loss hadn't been as extensive as this one. With Hana's soul detached to its current extent, patching it up with the same façade might be a disastrous failure – might leave only Hare, and nothing of Hana at all. She might be left totally mad.

No, it wasn't her animath she needed to reattach with, but the human world, her real self before she'd first become detached from it. And he knew when that must have been. No wonder she'd come to desire power. No wonder, too, that she'd become interested in the figure of the Mother.

'Stop trying to beautify yourself,' he said to Raven. 'I know what

I have to do: restore the sense of self she had before her parents were killed, so she can grow from that.'

'Ah,' said Raven. 'You've slowed, but you got there in the end.'

The brand Geist held now barely smouldered. 'Where's the flame to come from?'

'Dawn approaches.' But instead of looking to the horizon, Raven turned his eyes skyward. Geist followed with his own gaze, sensing something was about to happen but with no instinct as to what.

Fire tore apart the cloud-base. A roaring pillar of flame struck the fog-ground and turned it to glass, and descending upon it came what at first seemed a globe, then a gleaming black statue of a stern-faced man, then a disc. It set down on the glass desert, extinguishing the pillar of fire beneath, and sat there smoking, or steaming.

Cautiously, Geist approached, Raven walking beside him. The Smoking Mirror, if such it was, had quickly cooled, but Geist sensed heat within. Though he hadn't seen it change, it now took the form of a great black curved wall, possibly that of a circular enclosure. It stretched so far overhead, he couldn't tell if its visible limit was the wall's top, or merely the place where it bent out of sight towards the apex of some peak or dome.

'How do I reach the flame?' said Geist.

'The sacred fire is deep within,' answered Raven. 'But the wall is still hot enough. We are present at the very beginning, the stroke that begins Time itself.'

Symbols, thought Geist. But of what?

He closed to within a few paces, where the wall's heat was just bearable. He shivered with the sense that the cosmos was about to break open and disgorge some dreadful understanding upon him, an understanding for which he'd searched his whole life but now feared to find. He caught his reflection in the glassy mirror surface of the wall, and for a moment saw himself as being made of the strange gas-solid substance the ground had formerly been. Glancing away, he saw the same was true for Raven.

Unease threatened to break him out of the soulscape. He stepped forward and pressed the end of the dying brand against the black wall.

'No!' came Hare's cry. 'That must be my task, or the child will be lost!'

'It's the child in her that must be discarded,' said Geist. The brand glowed, spurted into flame. He willed it brighter.

'You will fail her and yourself.' Hare ventured closer. 'Don't take her friend from her. She has no others now.'

Raven cawed at him. 'Flee, fur-brain. That's what you do best, even if you can't do it well enough.'

Hare hissed. 'And where were you when the Sisters chased me?'

Raven hop-flapped towards him. Hare shrank back, then hissed again. 'Black feather, black heart. Your lies turned me against the Goddess, and she won't have me back. I'm forever running. And now you would rob me of my only companion! Did we Fire Stealers improve the world? No! Better you had never freed the first man and woman! Better the fire had never come! Better all had been left one.'

Hare ran at another part of the wall, pivoted on his front paws, and kicked it.

'You have the brand, confederate,' Raven said to Geist. 'Pointless to remain.'

As Hare kept up a relentless hind-footed attack against the wall, Geist turned away, and with Raven once more on his shoulder, began to retrace his steps. Across the strange world-floor he trod, the dull thuds of Hare's foot-strikes slowly fading, then up the temple's steps, then down and into the tunnel and to the great cave, where he and Raven parted, with expressions of gratitude on one side and insults on the other. Maintaining awareness that he held the brand, he came along the underground river, up the handholds in the well and back through the castle to the kitchen, where Petri sat with Hana.

This would be the most difficult part, he knew, to operate in the soulscape and the material world at once, especially without the lens designed to enable exactly that. He visualised himself settling back into the same space as his physical body occupied in reality, and slitted his real-world eyes to a narrow crack, balancing his awareness between the two worlds.

He breathed deep in preparation for the delicate task: to bring Hana back to before her moment of powerlessness, but without shocking her once again with its extremity. Whatever the risk, he had to take it. He would lose her anyway if he delayed.

'Hana Freallis,' he said aloud. He sensed Petri's alertness at the first words he'd spoken in almost an hour. 'Hana Freallis!' She turned her pain-drawn face away from him, but didn't otherwise respond.

He closed his hand harder round the focus-stone. *Her* focus-stone. He concentrated on what the flame represented, of where he had journeyed to fetch it. He held the brand to Hana's temple and visualised the fire flowing into her head as he spoke. Her own self, her real self: not the current absence, not the in-between of her Initiated self, not the lost girl he'd arranged to be sent to her uncle.

He leaned closer. 'Hana! You must wake up. Your mother's just left for the market at Pellam.'

She cried out in shock. Her upper body jerked upright on her arms.

'Hold her,' snapped Geist. Petri pressed down on her shoulders.

She cried out, struggling. 'No! I've got to fetch her back. Get off me!'

'Keep hold,' said Geist. 'She might try to get up.'

'Let me go after her! Something bad's going to happen. Ma!' she screamed. 'Ma! Ma!'

Petri was having a hard job keeping her still. Geist added his weight, pinning an arm and her hips; he couldn't risk more injury to her leg.

'You're with them!' she cried. 'You *want* her dead!'

'No!' said Geist, stung with the damage her suspicion might wreak. He made his voice both forceful and calm. 'Don't dwell on what you couldn't stop, dwell on what you can. That mentality, the drive towards war and domination that allowed it to happen: *that* is our enemy. That fight is where you must exert your power, Hana.'

She'd gone still, staring up at the ceiling, her eyes taut with pain. Geist took the chance to will his tattoo-mask to sink beneath his skin. He'd broken from the soulscape rather than returned with care, but he couldn't worry about that now. More important was that Hana was back, as far as he could tell. She hadn't rejected her name this time.

Petri eased up. Firelight swam on his sweat-damp face. 'Will she be all right?'

'Hana?' said Geist. 'How do you feel?'

She looked at him now, eyes hard and edged with tears. 'You bastard.'

'You're in a lot of pain, I understand.'

She turned away. 'Not just that.'

'I did what I had to, to get you back.' Now for the test. 'Who do you feel yourself to be, Hana? I know it's a difficult question.'

She hissed a breath. 'Someone who's woken up to the mistakes she's made.'

'It wasn't a mistake. There was nothing you could have done—'

'Not that,' she said. 'You. My biggest mistake was you. Ever letting you get me involved.'

'You can't mean that,' said Petri.

'Quiet,' Geist told him, though he hoped the boy was right, and that this was a temporary response to hurt. 'You've had a hard time, Hana, I know.'

'And whose – *shit*.' She gasped with the pain. 'Whose fault was that?'

'I'm sorry, I was careless to get trapped here. You were brave to come for me.'

'Not that. Before. Everything.'

'Hana, this doesn't sound like you.' A horrible suspicion gripped him. 'Vanessa's gone, hasn't she?'

'I don't know who that is,' she said. 'I thought they were my memories, but they weren't. They've faded now, but... you.' She groaned. 'All about you. Everything always was. You're a spider at the heart of a web, and I'm not the only fly who got caught. Now I'm cutting myself free.'

Damn it. He wanted to explore this further, to remove what he suspected were the last traces of Vanessa's hate still poisoning her mind. But he couldn't risk antagonising her and making her worse. She was tired and in pain and had suffered a shock. He could try to put her mind right later, if it didn't happen by itself.

'Don't distress yourself. Just rest.' He looked at Petri. 'Tell the medic we've done what we can.'

He just hoped it would be enough.

32

FIRE OF YOUTH

As soon as the medic came, Geist pocketed Hana's stone and took Petri back out into the hall, where the smell of cigarettes now masked everything else. A door had been taken off its hinges from somewhere and placed as a barricade across the corridor leading to the redoubt; a crack had been left down one side, allowing a soldier to aim his carbine.

'What happened?' whispered Petri, as Geist looked around for Franzen. 'Did you get Hare back to her?'

'Not yet,' muttered Geist. 'That'll have to wait. She's stabilised at least, which means she's no longer my main concern.'

'Then what is?'

'Ah, there. Captain!' The officer came over to him. 'I've cleared the effects of the mind-control,' said Geist. 'Your men can look after her now.'

'Very good,' said Franzen. 'We'll leave within the half-hour.'

'There's still the redoubt.'

'We've achieved our objective, Colonel.'

Geist heard a subtle but troubling difference in how Franzen voiced his supposed rank. The last hour had given the man too much time to think. ‘There can’t be many Bourgs left in there,’ Geist said. ‘And they hold something I need.’

‘That being…?’

‘Two children.’

‘Children?’

‘They hold the key to a monarchist plot,’ lied Geist. ‘That’s only part of a wider story, but it’s all I may tell you at present. It’s vital we rescue them and take them with us.’

He was treading a tightrope. He might say too much to be credible, or too little to convince the man. Either side risked a long fall.

‘I don’t like it,’ Franzen said. ‘We’ve been questioning some of the Bourgs about what happened to the other surveyors. One of them admitted the men were sacrificed – to some kind of queen, who keeps herself hidden even from her own people. What do you know about that?’

‘I’ve never seen her,’ said Geist. ‘But she exists.’

‘This is a place of evil, Colonel.’

‘I’m well aware.’

‘Our prisoners say this queen controls the Bourgoune by sorcery and fear, that she’s done so for hundreds of years, that she’s the one responsible for the Bourgs largely withdrawing from contact with the outside world, even hostile contact.’

‘Hundreds of years, Captain? You know that’s impossible.’ It wasn’t, strictly, but he didn’t think it could be true in the Lamia’s case. ‘She probably keeps herself concealed to hide the fact that she’s a succession of different women.’

‘Supposition,’ said Franzen. ‘It’s all supposition – we have no idea what she can do. What more likely place for Elok and the Witch to spread their influence than out here in this God-forsaken wilderness? One prisoner claimed this queen can send dreams to the clan chiefs. She might have already called for reinforcements. With the wounded on stretchers, we can’t make the same speed. If there’s a chance more Bourgs are on their way, we have to move at once.’

'It might only take a quick assault, Captain. You said they've rigged up a defence?'

'At the end of that corridor we've screened off. The doorway into the redoubt is to the right, and the floor in front of it is effectively a drawbridge over a pit of spikes, hinged also to the right. They've raised that to cover the doorway, meaning we can't get at it directly, and not without exposing ourselves to attack – there's a loophole in the end wall.'

Geist had never been to the end of the corridor, but when being led to the schoolroom he'd noticed the loophole at the end, and the strange wooden floor. 'Couldn't we fire your field-gun down there? Breach the end wall?'

'Even if we could ensure the crew's safety, a shell could bring the whole fortress down.'

'And from outside? Hole the external wall?'

'It's only a six-pounder,' said Franzen, voice harder. 'It might take more shells than we carry – and if ever you got through those three feet of stone, you'd still risk causing a collapse.'

Geist exhaled. Clearly the man had made up his mind.

'Sir,' said Petri. 'What about what you said at the Sack of Ducks?'

Franzen turned to the youth.

'You said you were carried on the wings of Empyreus's own will,' said Petri. 'This is a holy mission. Would you want to turn back with the evil not destroyed?'

Franzen clearly felt irked at having his own words turned against him. 'I now believe Empyreus intended this mission mainly as reconnaissance. My report will recommend returning with overwhelming force and conducting a thorough purge. We'll leave in half an hour.'

He walked off. 'The idea of magic has unnerved him,' muttered Geist. 'Well, that's buggering awkward. I need those children, and there might not be another chance.'

'Who are they?' said Petri.

'You remember when we did those sessions at the college? They're who I was trying to locate.'

'They're not… you're not going to make them animals?'

Geist froze inside. But the boy couldn't suspect the serpents; it must be something he'd picked up from Hana. 'Align them with Fire Stealer animaths, you mean? Why do you ask?'

'Not Fox at least. If he's free, I'm your man.'

Geist stared at him, unsure what to make of this sudden swerve.

'I'm cunning and resourceful. Hana will tell you. And I use a brush.'

Geist snorted. 'If you're so resourceful, persuade Franzen.'

'That's not a fair test,' said Petri. 'He's pissed off with me for being part of the whole Ranga mess. Anyway, can't we manage without him? You said there can't be many Bourgs back there, and I'm sure he'll leave us with a couple of guns – you're a colonel in his army, aren't you? Or were.'

He left a pause for an answer. Geist filled it with a grunt.

'All we need,' said Petri, 'is some plan to sneak past the Bourgs' defences. Maybe there's another way in.'

'The sneaking will be difficult,' said Geist. 'I have a feeling we're being observed. You haven't sensed the same?'

'There's a feeling of… I'm not sure. I've had it since I've been here.'

'The twins. The Lamia, this "queen", had me train them to be her eyes, and she's using them now to keep a watch on what happens out here. I felt it when I soulscaped. There won't be any sneaking. Not unless I can baffle their scrying somehow. Damn it, if I'd been in there, I might've been able to get them out in the confusion, my lens too. I'm starting to wish that bloody agent Samka hadn't rescued me.'

Petri frowned. 'It was Ranga who rescued you?'

'A few minutes before Franzen's men got there. Why?'

The boy nodded. 'Yes, I didn't see him go in with the others. How did he get in before them?'

'He said something about an upstairs window at the back. No idea how he knew it was there; that whole side's swamped with ivy. Unless they've cleared it since I came.'

Petri was frowning hard. 'I wonder...' he said in a low voice. 'Ranga never said where his maps came from. I assumed the Bureau, but maybe not. Franzen said Ranga couldn't show him any papers. He knew about the Hollow Isles, but that's because he was there, and maybe not on Bureau business. And Rurik asked why they weren't told there was a Kymeran agent waiting for them in Maskar. This Vanessa, she's a magician?'

'I think she must be now,' Geist said heavily.

'Then if Ranga works for her,' said Petri, 'she could've picked up that Franzen's men were on their way, and told Ranga to join them. The bastard's probably not an agent at all.'

Geist grasped it. 'You think it was Vanessa made his maps, through scrying?'

'And maybe she didn't put every detail on them,' said Petri. 'Hence Ranga knowing about that window.'

'Plausible,' said Geist. 'But how does that help us?'

'Because... do you think there might be a secret way into the redoubt? As an escape route in case of siege? If so, Ranga might know about it.'

Geist was impressed. 'Good thinking. Go and worm it out of him.'

'It needs to be you, sir,' said Petri. 'You cut an impressive figure. He thinks I'm a child.'

But the idea of talking with Ranga filled Geist with unease. The young man had seen Vanessa recently, knew of her world and something of her past thirty years. Faced with such a source of information, curiosity would gnaw at him, perhaps irresistibly; and he didn't want to know the things Ranga might tell him. From Hana's words, Vanessa hadn't aged, and Geist knew what that meant, and what it meant that she'd done it for him. Gods above, below and everywhere, if she had the scrying power to draw maps, she was probably observing him now.

'Sir?' said Petri. 'Just awe him into submission.'

'Wait.' Something was trying to occur to him, to do with Vanessa, her learning of the fortress's secrets by magical means...

He had it.

'Come!' He made for the doors, Petri following. 'What fills the moat?'

'Uh, water?'

'But no stream comes down the hillside behind the fortress.' Outside the keep, the company was busy with preparations for departure, Franzen talking to soldiers in the gateway, men dismantling the machine-guns.

Petri followed him down the steps. 'So… an underground spring?'

'Precisely.' Geist walked across to the well, where soldiers were drawing water. They let him through. His heart raced as he looked into the well, and found his theory confirmed: metal rungs led down into darkness.

'Quiet, please!'

The men stilled. Geist leaned over the well, but there was still too much noise elsewhere in the courtyard to tell if water ran in its depths.

He steered Petri away again, beyond the soldiers' earshot. 'I saw those handholds in my soulscape journey earlier. And there was a stream at the bottom. I bet that's the secret passage to the redoubt.'

The boy's eyes widened. 'Franzen could send men down there.'

'I don't think he will. No, your previous idea was better: stay here ourselves and use guns to overpower the few Bourgs left. Now I think about it, I don't want to risk Franzen and the twins coming into contact. If he believed me about their importance to a monarchist rising, he might want to take them for questioning.' He saw Hana being stretchered out of the keep and over towards the mules. 'Go and see if you can get Ranga to confirm about the well.'

'Yes, sir!' The boy saluted, badly, and ran off.

When Hana's stretcher had been attached as a travois to the mule, Geist approached her. She looked marginally more comfortable, and a ruck in her blanket showed her leg splinted. Her obvious vulnerability made him realise Franzen was right: the Kurassians couldn't afford to delay their departure.

'You're in good hands, I see.' He squatted beside her, lowering his voice so as not to be heard by the muleteer at the animal's head. 'I won't be coming with you, at least at first. I might not see you again until you've recovered. Then I'll find you and we can make a clean start, a fresh Initiation.'

'No.' Her voice was lucid, but hard. 'I've had my fill of magic. Leave me alone.'

'Still this?' He knew he should let it lie, but she was trying his patience. 'Think of all your journeys with Hare, your joy at first discovering him. Could you really give up your friend?'

'If I live, I'll make real friends. Ordinary friends.' She met his gaze only briefly. 'Isn't that what people do? Isn't that what I've been lacking all these years?'

'But who wants "ordinary friends", Hana? We're part of a great work. It's true I haven't told you enough about that. I should have been more open about our plans.'

'*Your* plans,' she retorted. 'Your silence, your lies. You made me a target without warning me. No, I'll stay my real self. For as long as I have left.'

'Hana, you're needed. We're in a war.'

'I don't give a damn.'

Urgency gripped him. 'You don't have a choice.'

'I'll have nothing more to do with magic.'

'That won't keep you out of it,' he said, voice lowered further. 'This war might take place in the psychosphere, but it will change the world of every man, woman and child. On one hand, equality and freedom – on the other, the absolute subjugation of nature, the absolute primacy of gold. They truly exist, Hana – the Kings Behind the World.'

'I know. I met one.'

'*Met* one…?'

'Probably signed my own death warrant. I'm so weak now, they could do to me what they did to Jorik. Are you going to guard me against that?'

His stomach felt twisted. 'Jorik as in Ferman's brother? Tell me what's happened.'

'Too tired,' she said. 'Astolio met the Shining One too. He's seen their city, deep in the psychosphere. A city of gold and glass.'

'A *city*? What do you mean?' A dreadful possibility occurred to him. 'Is he on their side?'

'No. But he doesn't trust you. He thinks you were planning some trickery with Orc and Cass.'

His breath caught. 'He knows about them? And you do?'

She grunted a laugh. 'Yes, I know a great deal about Orc. A lot's been going on. I told Petri most of what happened, with the Shining One too.' She winced at some spasm of pain. 'He wants Fox.'

'I know.'

'But there is already a Fox, I assume. You made them all, didn't you?'

He saw no purpose in denying it. 'The girl who had Fox died.'

'Oh, what a surprise.'

'In an accident, Hana. And yes, Petri might be a suitable replacement.'

'Except he's too sure of who he is, of who he wants to be. Ironic, isn't it?' Her voice had weakened. 'Wanting to be Fox is part of his sense of self, but that sense of self will keep it from him. Unless you break him. But he hasn't got any parents to be killed.' She closed her eyes.

'I had nothing to do with that.'

'I didn't say you had. Leave me.'

'Where are Orc and Cass now? Just tell me that.'

'They headed for Highcloud. To find answers.'

'About their memories?'

'Everything. Their pasts, you, the animaths. Their… talent.'

He didn't like the particular weight she'd given that last word. 'You mean their psychic ability?'

'You don't know?' A frown tensed her brow. 'We thought you would. I swore to keep it secret. Didn't tell Petri. You'll have to ask them yourself.'

'Give me a clue, at least.'

So quiet he could barely make it out, she whispered, 'Zhenaii.'

'Hana, this is too serious for a joke.'

A half-smile, and she rested her head to one side. 'Maybe you've bitten off more than you can chew, Geist. But you've taken your last bite out of me.'

He pushed himself straight and started back towards the keep. He felt, suddenly, unutterably weary. More than he could chew. Events out in the wider world had run far ahead of him during his captivity; a race had started, and he'd missed the flag – and he was too old to be an athlete. There was no knowing if he would ever be able to coax Hana back, even assuming she survived her injury. Orc was over a thousand miles away. He'd sensed no psychic activity from Emilia for years, and had read she'd been appointed to a religious post. He'd lost sight of Thera.

And Vanessa. In the background of all this, Vanessa. He'd assumed he'd left his past behind, but all he'd done was plough it ahead of him, like a sweeper pushing an ever-growing pile of rubbish that had now grown too heavy to move. If Vanessa had truly remained young, then she had accepted the teachings he himself had refused. So that was the legacy of his grand plan, his beautiful idea, the idea that had inspired and fired them both through that heady, golden year half a long life ago. His lover had become a murderess, and out of a misguided obsession with him.

Gods, better he had never been born.

'Sir?'

He focused with effort. Petri stood before him.

'I talked with Ranga. He wanted to make some kind of deal, to stay with us when the soldiers leave. He's worried about what'll happen in Torrento. But don't worry, we won't have to. When I said we knew where the secret entrance was, his face gave it away.'

'Doesn't matter,' Geist said. 'We're leaving with the others.'

'What?' Petri looked past him. 'Because of Hana? She'll come around. How can she not? What you're doing is important.'

'You don't even know what that is.'

'I don't need to, not yet. I've heard enough about those Shining Shits to want to fight them.'

The passion in the boy's face reminded Geist too much of Vanessa, back in those early days. Someone who believed in him, as he'd once believed in himself. 'You don't want to be following me. I turn people into killers. And I'm worn out.'

'Don't talk like that,' Petri said. 'You're still vital. My first lover was fifty, and he had everything working.'

Geist wasn't sure what he was supposed to do with that information. 'It's over. It was over twice as long ago as you've been alive.' Holy hells, that was depressing. 'I tried to keep the fire going, but it was only to push back the darkness I'd made myself. It's all ashes now.'

'Horse shit,' said the boy. 'So you've got a few years on you, so what? Being sixteen doesn't have much going for it either. You want fire, I've got it. I *believe* in you. Who else could've got Hana's soul back? Who else would've worked out where the tunnel was? If this has to do with that Vanessa, best thing for you is to let Ranga piss off and stay here without him, and forget her.'

I need to believe in you, his ridiculously young face said, *because there's nothing else*. Nevertheless, Geist thought, the boy's idea had something to it. He studied him with more attention, filled with a terrible sense of being on the edge of a bargain, of accepting Petri's belief in him as a sustaining force. And yes, his work was important, and who else was going to do it? He rested a hand on the boy's shoulder, felt the heat of young blood through his palm. A follower, a disciple. How long since he'd had a willing one of those, rather than a student he'd tricked or coaxed?

'Very well,' he said. 'Consider yourself a shaman in training.'

Petri's face glowed. Yes, thought Geist, that passion would do him well. It would fuel him as hers had. And if he was repeating an old mistake, well, he'd hardly be the first to do so.

'I won't let you down,' said Petri. 'And we'll get Hana back. The three of us – we won't need the others. Raven, Fox, Hare, that's all. So we're not leaving now?'

'No, we're not.' Geist felt mentally re-energised, better able to marshal his thoughts. 'The twins have genuine talent, and I want them.

And I need my crystal back. But we must have some soldiers here, at least. The twins will be spying on what goes on, I'm sure of it. They might not get much detail, and I very much doubt they can pick up speech, but they'll know if all the Kurassians leave, and if one of us then goes down the well, they might know that, and prepare for it. We have to keep the troops here at least until I can baffle the twins' scrying.'

'Baffle it? You can do that?'

'I think so: I know them and I know my lens, and I'll have a connection through Hana's focus-stone. Once the twins are psychically blind, you'll have to use the secret entrance and... well, probably shoot everything in sight. Apart from them, of course.'

The boy's lips tightened for a couple of seconds, and Geist wondered if he'd pushed him too far. Then he nodded. 'All right.'

'Ever fired a gun before?'

'Yes.' A tiny spasm twitched the corners of his mouth. 'I mean, not really.'

'Well, it's not difficult.' Geist saw Franzen come away from the gate, and made for him. 'Ah, Captain!'

'Five minutes left, Colonel. I've had a pony prepared for you.'

Geist pushed aside his weariness, steeled his voice with all Hollenstern's character and history – for why had he appropriated it, if not for a moment like this? 'My thanks, but I shan't be needing it yet. I'm staying.'

'I'd strongly advise against that.'

'Your military history should tell you I'm known for impetuous decisions.'

Franzen's eyes narrowed. 'The Kurassian army has changed since the Islands War.'

'Not to me, Captain. Not in what it stands for. Risk, and glory: that's the lancers' way, of course. You on the other hand must command your troop as you see fit.' Others had paused to witness the exchange. 'I need only another hour or two.'

'Impossible,' said Franzen. 'I have the wounded to think of.'

'Then just a few men. Enough to deter an egress from the redoubt.'

'Permission to speak, sir.' A soldier presented himself before Franzen: Geist recognised the corporal from before, whose father had served under Captain Ralff. 'I volunteer to stay with the colonel.'

'I didn't ask for volunteers,' said Franzen, but he seemed aware of the unvoiced eagerness of others to throw their hats into the same ring. 'Very well – you and half your section remain here for not more than one hour, and then promptly catch us up. No unnecessary risk. If after an hour he refuses to leave this place, you will join us anyway. Clear?'

'Sir!'

'I suggest you place one lookout at the high-point of that road out of the valley, and remain in readiness to escape if Bourg reinforcements are spotted. Now, choose your five men. Colonel, I'll leave you a rifle.'

'And Samka's revolver? I assume you won't be returning it to him.'

'As you wish. Gessler, let's get under way.'

Geist watched them leave. Ranga had been brought out and placed on a pony, which had been roped to the one in front. He looked broken. Again curiosity pricked Geist, the urge to ask the young man what he knew of Vanessa before it was too late. He tore his gaze from him and focused on Hana, on her travois. He hoped for a look of reconciliation, but she kept her eyes closed.

When the main body of Franzen's force was gone, Geist deployed Corporal Stenk and his five men: one to act as lookout as Franzen had suggested, one to stay with the mounts, one to stand guard on the Bourg prisoners roped in the cellars, and three to guard the corridor leading to the redoubt and act as a reserve.

'Are any of you familiar with the Thangkaran blessing?' he asked the latter three, as they halted before the removed door blocking the corridor. The soldiers expressed ignorance, but not, he thought with relief, suspicion. 'It's a prayer taught me by the holy Watchers of Highcloud, calling for God's protection against sorcery. I'll go into the kitchen to perform it, and when I think it's worked, this lad here,' he clapped Petri on the shoulder, 'will sneak into the redoubt by a secret entrance and rescue the children. In the meantime, keep your watch and don't disturb me unless absolutely necessary.'

'You've clearly lived an interesting life since you left the lancers, sir,' said Stenk.

'Ah,' said Geist, tapping the side of his nose. 'Does one ever truly leave the lancers?'

True in his case, he thought as he led Petri into the kitchen. He'd never been discharged from the forty-fifth. Just as he'd never been more than a trooper.

'How many bullets?' he asked as soon as he'd closed the door behind them.

Petri looked in the box Gessler had handed over. 'Twelve, plus those in the gun.'

'Very well, there'll be no practising.'

'I expect it's easy enough, as you said.'

'Once I give you the nod that I've managed to baffle their scrying,' said Geist, 'go down the well and see what you can do.'

'What if an hour's up and I'm still down there? I don't have a pocket watch.'

'I won't leave, don't worry,' said Geist. 'If I've baffled the twins, they'll have no reason to think the soldiers have gone, and my guess is they'll stay holed up in there and wait for other Bourgs to turn up – which I'm sure won't be for a while.'

'And what if you think you've baffled their scrying but you haven't, and they see what I'm doing?'

'I thought you believed in me?'

'I do. Of course. But—'

'No glory was ever won by doing something safe,' said Geist, and saw the boy's face both brighten and harden at the word *glory*. 'You'll be a perfect match for brave Fox, I know.'

'He was important, wasn't he?' said Petri. 'The others, all they had to do was run, but he had to use his cunning to get the brand in the first place. That's why he was first.'

'Yes, he was first,' said Geist. *And first to be torn apart*, came the uncomfortable thought, as he settled down to meditate.

33

THE POOL OF THE LAMIA

Silent, Petri hunkered and watched the firelight dance on Geist's lined and tattooed face. It made it look like a mask from a primitive dawn age, and the hidden knowledge implied by this roused in him an overwhelming need to be part of the man's secrets and his plans.

Geist had told him to think of himself as a shaman in training. But that bond of promise felt too thin for security. Would Geist still want him if Hana couldn't be talked around, or if she died? He'd have been happier if Geist had shown any interest in his impulsive confession that he'd had a fifty-year-old lover. He was coming to understand the power he'd had over the sculptor, his patron, both tormentor and tormented – youth itself. And Geist was in thrall to that power too, perhaps even more than the sculptor had been. As far as Petri could tell from the confrontation outside the keep, Geist hadn't rejected Vanessa when she was old, but merely because he'd realised she was doomed to age.

And his own youth, to which he'd never attached any particular value: that too would fade.

He snapped alert. Geist nodded his head and gestured towards the door, the agreed sign that the twins' scrying had been blocked. Petri took a deep breath, and stood.

Glory, here I come.

He opened the door to the hall just wide enough to sneak through. Stenk and the others looked at him but didn't speak. He went out into the courtyard, with its bodies lined up by the wall, and its blood, and its gathering flies. Rungs led down into the well, as Geist had said. He eased himself over the edge of the dank shaft and lowered himself rung over rung, crusted metal biting his palms. The well wasn't deep, and the sound of water quickly grew louder. He'd descended only twice his height when his boot filled with a shock of cold.

It took a while of probing and peering to work out the situation. Two tunnels led from the well-shaft, one in the direction of the keep and one away. A shallow stream ran out of the former, over a lip and down a fall of a few inches into the well-shaft, and out again towards the wall and the moat. But the shaft itself was deeper, bored down through the streambed to make the well. After some effort, his foot getting ever colder, Petri manoeuvred himself into the mouth of the inflow tunnel. The water here was only inches deep. The tunnel seemed to be a natural stream that had been banked and roofed over with large blocks of stone; the roof must have then been filled in on top so as not to show from the courtyard.

Now his eyes had adjusted, he saw a faint lightening of the darkness some way ahead. He groped walls and ceiling and streambed to find his way, soaking the ends of his sleeves as well as his boots. Twenty yards seemed to take as many minutes. Against the dim light ahead grew a hard black edge. The tunnel bent, he realised, and the source of the feeble illumination lay beyond the turn.

He paused, and with his splashing no longer adding to the noise, he heard a voice: a woman or young boy, singing. He listened hard, but made out no words, only a melody with a narrow range of notes.

He wrestled the pistol out of its holster, advanced to where the tunnel kinked, and peered round. Not far ahead, the roof disappeared into an open space: a water-filled, natural-walled cave not five yards across that must be open to the sky, though from here he couldn't see that high. On the far side of the pool, a narrow waterfall tumbled from a cleft in the rock – and not far from its splashing, a woman stood submerged to her chest.

Amazed, he gripped the rock he peered round. She was alone, and – from what he could see, with the water just above her breasts – naked. Her eyes had the static focus of trance. Now he made out her chant-like song, repeated over and over.

Speak my peril, valley stream;
Waken warriors to my plight
Throughout the land, let chieftains' dreams
Lead them here by sun or moonlight
To deliver vengeful slaughter,
Reddening your faithful water

The queen, could this be? If so, she was younger than he'd expected. Maybe some kind of servant or priestess. At the left side of the cave, a short run of stone steps led from the water to a closed door in the natural rock. A passage into the redoubt, he guessed. He should make for it. But he felt reluctant to disturb the scene. The waterfall pool, the naked woman, her song, possessed a magic unlike anything he'd encountered. Geist couldn't have expected this, or he would have warned him. He should go back and tell him. But he felt reluctance. To share this secret would diminish it.

The singing stopped. The woman's eyes lost their inwardness and fixed on him. Petri almost ducked back, but that would give her a chance to escape up into the redoubt and warn the remaining warriors. Gun in hand, he plunged forwards and started to edge round the side of the pool that led to the steps, hoping the water there wouldn't be too deep. It came only to his knees, but the footing was uneven. The woman sank deeper, to her throat, as she backed away to the pool's far side. Her wary gaze never left him; his rarely left her, apart from quick glances to get the layout of the place. The natural cave-rock ended not far above the waterfall; beyond it, dressed stone walls continued upwards, windowless, to the overcast sky. An interior courtyard or light-well of the keep, built to enclose this space.

Her space. She was submerged now almost to her eyes. Their expression unnerved him, their focus on him, their anger and fear at his intrusion.

'I won't hurt you,' he said.

She sank completely. He could barely make out her shape beneath the surface, five yards away. She must have thought he'd lied, and that he'd stopped so he could shoot her.

He made to carry on towards the steps and the door – then his feet were yanked from under him and he fell backwards with a yell and crashed into a detonation of cold. His back and shoulders banged against the pool edge, his head plunged under. Something quickly bound his ankles – he dropped the gun and tried to grasp the rope, but it had gone – then at once he felt it round his upper body, constricting his arms against his chest before he could pull them free. His head broke the surface, and he gasped at air. The rope round his chest held him, supported him, as his feet found the bottom of the pool, letting him stand neck-deep.

The rope felt wrong. It shifted its grip on him. Felt warm.

The woman's head rose from the water an arm's reach from him, her eyes bright above her taut smile. After her face came her long dark hair, her shoulders, her breasts with their dark nipples, her smooth belly. And below her navel – scales.

Scales, a muscular lengthening where her hips should have been. Scales after scales, all a deep glazed green shot through with blues.

Petri stared. The world had burst the bounds of its possibilities.

The Lamia lowered herself back into the water, as far as her chest, keeping herself taller than him. 'You spoke truly. You won't hurt me.'

'Please,' he said, finding his voice at last. 'Don't – don't kill me.'

'Why should I not?' she said. 'Death is useful to me. A slow death, especially, one that allows full contemplation of the void that grows closer with each cracked rib, then each ruptured organ. There are too few soldiers left to risk looking for you, I think. We can take our time.'

Petri fought to expand his chest, but the rope – her *tail* – was right round his ribs. 'But you need me alive!' he gabbled, his mind working desperately. 'Franzen, the captain, he'll come back, with a hundred field-guns. A thorough purge, he said. I can help you!'

'You came to rob me,' she said, calm, irrefutable. 'Geist sent you to steal my twins, which he craves – the twins who would be my protection, my warning eyes. Why should I give the words of a captured thief any credence? Or do you deny that was your intent?'

His first instinct was to do just that. But his second told him it wouldn't save him anyway, and from somewhere came a last-ditch sense of pride, of being an artist who served the truth. If these were to be his last words, they wouldn't be a lie. 'It's true—'

The squeeze came, fast, before he could say more. He cried out at the snapping in his chest. He expected worse to follow, but the crushing pressure relented, a little.

'Do you wish to recant,' she said, 'before I punish you further?'

It took him a while to gather speech through the mounting pain of his cracked rib. But it didn't get as bad as he'd feared. She was expert in this, he realised. 'Yes, I came to steal,' he said, forcing the words out, 'but I didn't know what I'd find down here.' It was a desperate, perhaps futile throw of the dice, but it was also true. 'I never guessed the world might hold someone like you.'

'Someone like me? What do you think that to be?'

'Magnificent. Unique. Ah!' he cried, as the pressure built again.

'Many have sought to defer their ending,' she said, 'but never before with flattery.'

'It's not flattery,' he said. 'I'm an artist. It's my job to find what lies beneath the masks of the world. As soon as I saw you, here, I knew the world is all a mask, and you're what lies beneath it. You are my life's purpose – it would be cruel to take it from me! And senseless for you to die when Franzen returns. You'd be the most glorious subject ever to inspire a man. All who saw your portrait would fall to the ground in awe.'

'You chose the wrong compliment, little man,' she said. 'I *despise* art. You wonder what I am? I *am* art. I am the arrogance of artists made flesh. I am not some secret truth of the world – I illustrate its oldest commonplace, that men of power use others for their own gratification. Even my killing you is not so tawdry.'

The coil constricted. Pain burst in Petri's chest, but at the same time a realisation burst in his mind. 'Manifestation!'

She held him no tighter, no looser. 'What do you know of that?'

'Magic…' He frantically tried to recall what Hana had told him of Daroguerre's goddess creation. 'A magician made you.'

Her eyes flared anger. The coil tightened again.

'*Changed* you!' he screamed, as his wits pieced together what she'd said.

'You are swinging wildly in hope of striking the truth. So you have heard rumours of what was once possible.'

'Still is,' he gasped. 'I know of someone who was changed. Transformed. Twice.'

'You lie. The crystal skull was shattered. Even Geist only possessed a small piece. If he were powerful enough to manifest creations, he would hardly have allowed himself to be captured.'

'Not Geist.' Then her mention of the crystal skull clicked with old stories. 'You're *Zhenaii*.'

Her eyes showed the truth of it. 'The last of them. So you have my secret. Now I shall make it a true secret once more.'

'Don't! I can get you to safety. A magical college, in Kymera. They'll worship you.'

'*Worship* me? It was a school of magicians that made me thus!'

'No, they'll hold you in honour.' He grasped at the chink of possibility, sought to widen it. 'Because of the knowledge they'll never have otherwise. And because – you're beautiful.'

Despite the pain, he felt a passionate pride in having spoken that. He stared into her eyes, wanting to erase the scepticism he saw there.

'Then you wish to kiss me,' she said.

Gods, he suddenly did. From her words sprang a fervent desire to achieve this previously unguessed possibility, to be the lover of this secret, ageless serpent-goddess. 'Yes,' he said, and tried to lean towards her, to struggle his arms free. Her coil held him at bay.

'Not yet,' she said. 'But I am minded to believe you. Indeed, your confession of wanting to steal the twins might have saved us both, for it confirms the strength of Geist's desire for them, and that might guarantee my safety.'

'*I* guarantee it.'

'One must never rely on one defence alone,' she said. 'How would you bring me to this college? Where is it?'

The coil had relaxed until it was holding him up, nothing more. Petri took in welcome air. 'Several hours from the Kymeran coast, right out in the wilds. We'll think of something.'

'Return to Geist, then. He must cease blocking the twins' scrying, and dismiss any remaining soldiers. I will then send out my last three men, by the way you came in. They will believe themselves to be making a surprise attack. You and Geist will kill them.'

'Kill... your men?' He couldn't have heard right.

'Their loyalty will waver if they think I am abandoning my people. Kill them, and I shall then lead the twins out. But be sure to tell Geist that I know why he came to steal the twins from me. He seeks to use their power. And I have knowledge pertaining to that, which he cannot acquire elsewhere. One male twin, one female – I know how our rulers tried to use them, at the end, and I beheld the consequence. Tell him I shall portion out this knowledge, and not until I feel truly safe from harm will he have all of it. Understand? Now repeat it.'

He did, with effort, still shivering and in pain as he was, and at last she nodded and the coil slipped from him. In moments the tip of her tail emerged from the water, wrapped around the revolver. 'You will need this,' she said, and he took it in his hand, which was shaking not only with cold, but with amazed relief at his survival.

'Th-thank you,' he said. 'How – how shall I call you?'

'My name was once Karminaya,' the Lamia said. 'Perhaps it might be again. Now, leave.'

Stenk regarded him critically as he walked dripping and shivering through the hall. 'No luck, eh?' In the kitchen, Geist was still in trance. A slight shift of his head acknowledged Petri's entrance.

Petri closed the door firmly and stood with his back to the fire. It took several breaths to compose himself to speak, to overcome his reluctance to tell Geist anything. He wanted to keep Karminaya secret, but of course that wouldn't work, so at last, in measured tones, he related what had happened, without hinting at any desire for her. Though Geist continued to meditate, excitement tensed the man's face until he abandoned his trance altogether.

'Zhenaii,' he said, standing. 'By all the gods ever faked, I'd never have guessed. I envy you, Petri, discovering that.'

'You can envy me pissing myself too. Lucky it was underwater.'

'And you're certain what she said, about twins? That the Zhenaii used them for magical purposes, and that she knows how?' Geist paced across the kitchen flagstones, his tattoos already fading. 'It's too tempting. A trick?'

'I don't think so,' Petri said. 'She seems to believe her knowledge will keep her safe, and judging by your reaction, she's right. And she knows the Kurassians will come back. Where else can she run?'

Geist nodded. 'Stenk's hour must be almost up. When he takes his men off, wait by the well with your gun. I'll stay by the corridor in case it is a trick: those are the only two exits from the redoubt.'

'I said, she clearly doesn't mean to trick us. Anyway, the gun got wet.'

'It's not a flintlock,' said Geist. 'Water won't have penetrated the cartridges. With any luck.'

'But I've never used one. Wouldn't it be better for you to stand by the well?'

'Why the reluctance? You'd have shot them if you'd met them down there, wouldn't you?'

He supposed so. But the idea, which had previously seemed an unpleasant if heroic possibility, now repelled him. 'I don't want to kill anyone.'

'That's precious. Have you ever seen a chicken coop after a fox has been at it? He kills even beyond necessity.'

'But I'm an artist.'

'And you'll never be a great one if you don't sink yourself in life.'

'Don't throw that at me! I've always known it.'

'Just as you'll never be a great shaman, if you're not careful,' said Geist. 'This will help you, unsettle your sense of yourself. It's the same experience that had that effect on me, and when I was younger than you are.'

Petri breathed deep, shivering harder despite the fire at his back.

'Anyway,' said Geist. 'If all three of her men come out along that corridor at a rush, it will take an expert rifleman to put them down in time. Shooting them in the well will be like fish in a barrel.'

Petri hunkered, stared between his splayed knees. He said nothing more. After a few minutes, a gentle knock came on the door. Geist called for whoever it was to enter.

Stenk. 'The hour's up, sir, and a bit.'

'I understand, Corporal,' said Geist. 'Gather your men and go.'

'I'd be happier if you came too, sir. You won't gain anything here on your own.'

'We have guns and ammunition. Leave the two ponies. We might well catch you up.'

'Sir—'

'Captain Franzen gave you your orders, Corporal. I wouldn't think much of an Empyreal trooper who failed to obey his commanding officer.'

Stenk nodded, saluted. 'Best of luck, sir.'

He'd left the door ajar. Through the gap, Petri heard the men organising. Hooves sounded, faint from the courtyard, fading. When quiet descended, Geist took up his carbine, checked it. 'Get to the well.'

It had been hours since his meagre breakfast, but Petri felt as though everything he'd eaten in the past day had returned to his stomach, waiting to be thrown up. He sat a few feet from the well, aiming the cocked gun just above the stonework, ready to shoot any man's head as soon as it appeared above the edge. That would be one down, which would leave two, with five bullets. No problem.

The problem was that killing felt too big a thing to enter into suddenly. His idea of who he was had been shaken up in only the past hour; all the pieces had come down in a different pattern, and he hadn't had time to figure out where taking a life might fit, even an enemy's. Nor was he sure if his desire to be Karminaya's lover had eclipsed his ambition to follow Geist and become joined with Fox. He felt it had – he couldn't stop thinking about her. Maybe it would be possible to achieve both.

Perhaps the problem was that he was being *told* to kill. He resented having no choice when it was something likely to be so crucial. But he would have chosen to kill in her defence. Did this count as—

He yelled as a surprise hand gripped the lip of the well. It jerked back.

He jumped up. Stupid, stupid, but he'd been expecting a head and now he'd given himself away. He had to act, fast. He darted round the well, to come at it from the other side. Gun ready, he looked over the edge, but could hardly see. No, there was movement, not up by the top of the rungs, but down. He aimed, saw how much his hand was shaking but fired anyway. Flash-bang-kick, a spark somewhere down in the well-shaft, but not where he'd been aiming. Shouts, more movement. He re-cocked the hammer, aimed again into darkness.

Nothing. No movement, as his vision adjusted, no noise but the water's soft chatter.

The men had gone, doubtless retreated into the stream tunnel that led under the keep. Petri's heart banged against his ribs. Should he go after them? Would they have gone all the way back to the pool, or might they be waiting just inside the stream-tunnel, so they could put a spear up his arse as he climbed down? Could he climb one-handed, the gun aimed below all the time?

No – his thoughts calmed at a realisation. All he had to do was guard against them emerging from the tunnel down there. After Karminaya came out, Geist could go down via the redoubt and kill the men from behind. Or just block that door by the pool, and the well-shaft too. The Bourgs would then be trapped.

He watched, from the side away from the keep, and waited. There came no sign of movement. No man so much as peered round. They must have gone back to the pool. Dared he risk going to talk to Geist? He leaned into the well, straining for any sound of voices.

The shock of a gunshot almost tipped him in. A grunt came from behind – he jerked up and turned to see a Bourg warrior slump to the ground halfway between him and the outer gates. The man had been in front of two others, who now started forwards. A second shot echoed from stonework; another warrior went down. The third, older and heavier, went into a crouch and looked towards the doorway to the keep. The man's face twisted, and another shot dropped him like a sack of meat.

Petri's legs were fire and water. He'd moved round to the well's far side without even realising. Geist walked down the keep's steps, to the Bourgs, all of whom were soaked wet and darkening the courtyard with water and now blood. Two still moved, groaned. Geist put another bullet into each, the shots echoing. 'Nice to have the chance to say goodbye, Ulnur.' He turned to Petri. 'Come.'

'What happened?' He wondered what he'd done with the revolver, then found he still held it. 'How did they—?'

'They followed the tunnel to the moat. Didn't you think of that?'

Shame stung him.

'Seems age has its use, then,' said Geist. 'When it brings wisdom.'

Petri nodded, badly shaken. The nearest Bourg had been only ten paces away, and he'd heard nothing. Might never have heard anything again. Two held naked swords, the third a spear. 'You let them get pretty close.'

'Couldn't risk any of them making it back out the gate,' said Geist.

'Maybe I left it longer than I needed, though. Didn't realise how quickly this thing reloads. Marvellous.'

On ropey legs, Petri followed Geist into the hall. They removed the heavy door from across the entrance to the redoubt corridor. Petri wondered if Karminaya had heard the shots, or if the twins' scrying had witnessed his ineptness. He was furious with himself for not having thought of the tunnel to the moat. Some fox.

Clanking sounded at the end of the corridor, and the right-hand wall slowly lowered, held by a single chain on its farther side – like a drawbridge, hinged at its base – to rest over the pit. Through the doorway walked two children, aged twelve or thereabouts; behind them, a hand on a shoulder of each twin, came the Lamia. Petri's throat tightened as the glory of her tail followed, fifteen feet of it, pushing her along with the rhythmic fluidity of a snake. He glanced at Geist. The man, too, was intent on her, amazed by her – would also want her, Petri felt horribly certain.

Preceded by her child-magicians, the Lamia entered the hall. The light glowed in her skin and on the curves of her breasts, and flashed in her green-glazed scales like sun through overlapping leaves. Pride stiffened her bearing, but hesitation shadowed her eyes. About her narrow waist was belted a long knife.

'Madam,' said Geist.

'My men?'

'Dead, as you commanded,' Petri jumped in, wishing now it had been himself who'd done the deed.

To his relief, Geist didn't clarify the matter. 'Good morning, children,' he said.

They looked at his knees, sullen, scared.

'You have something for your teacher?' Karminaya said.

The boy reached into a pocket of his filthy jerkin and brought out a blue crystal lens in a leather surround, the one Petri had seen Geist wear at the college. Geist grasped it as though fearing it might be snatched away again.

'Don't be afraid, children,' he said. 'I'll take good care of you.'

'And of you,' Petri added to Karminaya.

'We'll move shortly,' said Geist.

'Your young friend talked about a college,' the Lamia said.

'Temporarily, perhaps,' said Geist. 'But now I've seen the truth of you, I think we should move farther. Empyreal influence will only grow in Kymera, and the college itself might be at risk. Its mother institution will be safer: the Mystic Heart, in Jiata.'

Petri bit back a protest. Was Geist planning to leave him behind with Astolio and take Karminaya out of his reach?

Suspicion tightened her eyes. 'I have no pleasant memories of Sundara.'

'Nevertheless,' said Geist, 'I believe it to be your best chance, and my best chance to pursue my work.'

'Your work with these children?'

'I'm led to believe you know things that might be useful to me.'

'And I'll share none of it until I judge myself safe. But I do not bluff, Geist. You will want to be wise to what happened to the Zhenaii when they attempted to harness similar forces.'

'Meaning what? The Cataclysm? You're telling me that had something to do with twins?'

'I am telling nothing. Not for certain.'

'Then do so. Give me some token that what you say is true.'

'Not of that matter.'

'And how do I know you'll ever judge yourself "safe"?' said Geist. 'You might string it out for ever. I must be sure journeying with you will be worth the risk. I need a down-payment.'

'You are free to go your own way,' she said, 'and we shall go ours. It was your friend who offered me sanctuary at this college, not you.'

Geist snorted. 'You think he'll follow you over me? He'd have to give up too much.'

'I think he can guess what he might gain.'

'Stop this, please,' said Petri, though excited that they seemed almost to be fighting over him. 'We're all going together.'

'I'm not willing to risk everything for what might be a ruse,' said Geist, still looking at Karminaya. 'The Zhenaii's destruction was always supposed to have been a consequence of their manifestations. Nothing to do with twins. Seems to me this is a desperate attempt to bargain, to keep yourself from justice. Well might you fear that. I know of your crimes; you made me listen to them – to intimidate me, I'd guess. But it's clear now what else you gained from the terrified deaths of those men. Your longevity declares it. Where did you learn that skill? That of harvesting the energy the desperate dying draw to themselves?'

'I had to survive,' she said. 'You would have done the same.'

'Not true. I was offered those same secrets, and I refused them. Again, who taught you?'

'A magician of Zhena,' she said. 'The same one who instigated my change.'

'Which he did why?'

'For purposes of ritual theatre. And the character I portrayed could not be seen to age, so he taught me the secrets he himself had learned. I fed first upon the death-panic of slaves and criminals, and then, after we'd fled the Cataclysm, upon the magician himself.'

Petri shivered, knowing now what she'd intended in the pool.

'And where did he learn those secrets?' asked Geist.

'The hidden masters he called the Luminous Ones,' she replied. 'Ah, you try to flatten your expression, but I see this interests you too. If you refused their arts, then you are their enemy. And I know something of them. Rumours, whispers. For they were behind how the twins were used in Zhena. And there, if you like, is your "down-payment".'

Geist's eyes had narrowed. '*They* were behind how the twins were used?'

'Have I not said so?'

'The Kings Behind the World?' said Petri.

'Their predecessors, perhaps,' said Geist. 'The current ones surely can't date from that time.'

But he looked shaken, Petri thought, by the possibility he'd voiced.

'Very well,' said Geist. 'I grant you know enough for me to take the risk. Just one more thing. Have you heard of a city of gold and glass? Or a gate of gold?'

'I have given you enough for now.'

'Just whether you've heard of either, that's all.'

'The bargain's been kept,' said Petri.

Geist shot him a tight glare, then grunted. 'We're wasting time. I'm going to scry out a safe route from here. Don't disturb me.' He went into the kitchen.

When the door had shut, Karminaya said, 'Are the servants all dead?'

'No,' said Petri, uneasy at being alone with her again, despite the thrill of it. 'In the cellars.'

'Leave food and water within reach of them. They will be freed before long. How shall we travel? There should be a wagon in the courtyard.'

He'd seen it. 'But wouldn't that leave tracks?'

'How should I be concealed otherwise?' she said.

'I don't know what Geist plans.' He wanted to come up with his own idea, but such a logistical problem was beyond his experience, and the near-intoxication of her presence made it difficult to think. 'I'm sure he'll tell us when he's worked out the route.'

'Do you trust him?'

'Geist?' He didn't answer.

'What is his interest in that city he asked of?'

'The gold one? No idea. Have you heard of it?'

'Could I tell you without telling him also?'

He grasped her meaning. 'Yes, absolutely.'

'Do you still think me beautiful, now the light is stronger?'

Her undertone of urgency surprised him, but only increased his eagerness to affirm it, despite the irritating presence of the twins. 'More so than ever.'

'Those few men I allowed into my presence, they felt only fear and horror. Do you not fear me?'

'Yes, in a way,' he said: honesty had served him well with her so far. 'It excites me.'

One corner of her mouth formed a smile. 'We must handle this with care. There will be no need for you to choose one of us over the other, not in seeming. Doling out this information that Geist wants carries risk to me, and must be subtly done. That's why I shall only do it through you. You shall judge how he reacts to each scrap, and tell me.'

Petri nodded, pleased and relieved at the implications of her plan – if he was indispensable as a go-between, Geist could hardly leave him behind when he went to Sundara.

Karminaya gently shook a shoulder of each twin in turn. 'Now, Taslan, Felca, we shall soon begin a long journey. But first we must go out into the courtyard, and the dead lie there. You must be prepared.'

'I am,' said the boy, Taslan.

'There's no such a thing as ghosts,' said Felca. 'Nothing lives after death.'

'Will our power still grow, in this new place we're going?' said Taslan.

'It will,' Karminaya said. Petri thought she sounded almost afraid. 'Perhaps even more swiftly.'

34

THE FINDING

Geist had been focused on concealing his agitation, and as soon as he shut the kitchen door behind him and was free of that pressure, he wondered if it wouldn't be better to wait – to get out of the castle to safety first, and interrogate Raven later. Hadn't Petri talked about the Lamia sending magically for help? But if the serpent-queen worked through dreams, as Franzen had heard, her summons would probably have been sent too late in the morning to draw a response. And waiting would only agitate him further. The answers he sought were too important.

He eased himself into position, wiped the grime from his crystal lens, and for the first time in months strapped it over his left eye. The world blurred a little, and acquired the old-familiar blue overlay. It took all his self-training to quieten his whirl of thoughts and breathe himself into a relaxed state. Only then did he awaken his tattoo-mask and call Raven.

With a heavy beat of wings, the great black bird landed in front of him: fully part of his visual reality once again, thanks to his lens. Every detail of every feather, the iridescence of his back, the glint of light on his beak and talons and mask, was perfect.

‘Third time you’ve called me today,’ said Raven. ‘It must be the last. And I hope it’s for something more than flapping around a pair of wretched brats to distract them. Have you any idea how tiring it is to hover, for a bird so majestic? I’m a soarer, a wheeler, I fly high and cast my keen eye over where and why. Make me your bluebottle again, and our acquaintance ends.’

‘I need to talk to you,’ said Geist. ‘Test your memory.’

‘When the halls of one’s memory hold everything ever said and done, they can take a while to search.’

‘We’ll try, anyway,’ said Geist. ‘Recall a time, two years ago, when I was on my expedition into the Dead Lands.’

‘Harr, and what a success that was!’

Geist ignored that. The crucial thing was to connect with the past as vividly as possible, to bring it back to life, and the best way he knew was to relive it through words. ‘Recall those days after we passed the village of Tar Ellen: the last place people still lived, as far as I knew. Dead forests either side of the road, and the road itself deserted. But I had to be prepared for enemies – I couldn’t know whether the Kings knew of my expedition, despite my shroud. So each morning, I sent you to scout ahead for potential dangers.’

‘Asked me to.’

‘Three nights after Tar Ellen, I made camp in an abandoned farm. The next morning, I sent you off to scout, and you returned with a reading.’

‘*A key, cast up, awaits he who would unlock the gate of gold*,’ intoned Raven. ‘Well do I remember the greed that lit your eyes.’

‘Not true,’ growled Geist. ‘I never thought you meant wealth.’

‘There are other kinds of greed than for money,’ said Raven. ‘And you were keen enough to be led to it. A long way.’

‘Yes,’ said Geist. ‘A long way from the road…’

… through the forest of crumbling pines, Raven leading him down the slope, gliding from dead tree to dead tree. An eerie, lifeless silence broken only by the slither of his boots in drifts of mouldering needles, the creak and shift of his mule's tack and baggage, his muttered curses at his aching knees and the sweat that itched in his beard and beneath his lens-patch.

Whatever the 'key' was, it had better be worth it.

By the time two hours had passed since leaving the road, Geist's tattoo-mask was a constant effort to maintain, and Raven was beginning to fade. Then the ground levelled out, and the last trees appeared ahead, rotted bars over a window of sea. Geist cracked across the deadwood litter to where forest gave way to shore – a shallow beach stretched left and right, the end of a south-facing inlet, with a natural barricade of storm-raised driftwood fencing him from the sand. Raven waited on a tine of a weathered root-plate. Geist tugged his hat-brim against the bright sky and peered beyond the driftwood, a hundred yards to the water's edge.

He drew breath between his teeth.

'Something cast up, at least.'

The motionless forms on the strandline looked like bodies, but apart from the pale blotches of heads and hands, they were glossy black, and their feet seemed strangely extended.

'This "key". Something they're carrying?'

'One way to find out,' said Raven. 'Never fear, they can't hurt you if they've been rotting in the sea for a week.'

The bird had an evil streak sometimes. 'It's definitely them we're here for?'

'I'm only here because you are.'

Geist grunted. 'And I'm here because you led me.'

'Then who's to blame?' said Raven. 'Both of us, or neither?'

'Blame for what?' said Geist.

'Harr,' said Raven. 'We won't know that until you've done it.'

Geist didn't dignify that with a response. He was about to hitch his mule to a stump when movement caught his eye. He ducked into a crouch. Out from the dead forest farther along the shore walked a figure, dressed like him in a pale dust-coat and wide-brimmed hat.

'Who the hell...?'

'You might find out if he spots that mule,' said Raven.

Irritated that he'd had to be told, Geist moved the animal back among the trees and tethered it, before drawing his rifle from its long holster on the mule's flank. Back behind the driftwood, he knelt and loaded a cartridge, the greased bolt moving more freely than his fingers.

The man, walking with a stiff, awkward gait, was halfway to the bodies. His presence here couldn't be chance, Geist thought. They were miles from the road, which in any case now led nowhere but desert. Had that stranger come here following a reading similar to Raven's? Might he also have occult abilities?

His palms felt damp on the stock of his gun. He couldn't risk losing whatever the 'key' was. Safer to shoot first. But if the man were innocent, perhaps even a potential ally...

'When I bade you search ahead for dangers,' he murmured, 'you told me there were none. Does that mean he's not an enemy?'

'Did I complete my search?' said Raven. 'Or did my reading so intrigue you that you forgot everything else?'

'Damn,' muttered Geist, then, 'Hell!' – the man had pulled a revolver. Geist butted his rifle against his shoulder.

But the man didn't fire at him, seemed not even to have noticed him. He reached the first of the bodies, locked his arm straight, and took aim at its head.

Geist's heart clenched. The two were *alive*?

'Hold, there!' He pushed himself standing.

The slowness with which the stranger turned, his gun now pointed at the sand, seemed almost mocking.

'Declare yourself,' called Geist. 'Who are you?'

His heart thumped in the silence that followed. He repeated the question, louder. The mule shifted, Raven croaked. But the man didn't speak, didn't move.

'And those two?' said Geist. 'Why—'

The revolver jerked up. Geist twitched, the rifle banged and bucked, his shot went wild.

A bullet ripped the air past him. The man had dropped to a crouch.

Geist ducked to one knee, fumbling to eject and reload, cursing his mistake. Two more shots barked from the revolver. The mule was skittering, hawing; Raven had flown off. Geist shoved the bolt home, hands sweating. The man's fourth bullet sent a spray of rotted wood from the pine next to him.

Geist raised the rifle just as the man turned to aim again at the stranded figure. Breath stilled, he sighted, squeezed. The stranger's head snapped back in a puff of red as he dropped, limbs out-flung.

The smell of cordite faded. Geist shakily chambered another cartridge. After collecting himself, he clambered over the driftwood barrier and set out across the beach, glancing back along the edge of the skeletal forest in case the man hadn't come alone.

By the time he'd reached the three sprawled bodies, Raven was perched on the gunman's head. Geist hoped the bird would leave be; the damage done by the bullet was enough. He couldn't guess how the stranger had hoped to match a rifle at a hundred yards, nor why he'd wanted to kill two washed-up… whatever-they-were.

Boy and girl both looked just about full-grown, their breathing steady, no sign of distress from water intake. They appeared simply asleep, which, given the gunfire, was as strange as their clothing, and that was some of the strangest Geist had ever seen. Glass-fronted masks covered their eyes and noses; duck-paddles lengthened their feet; their bodies were sheathed in single-piece outfits of a slippery-looking substance that resembled dolphin skin. The girl's stretched with the slow movements of her chest.

'Tight fit.' Raven's jet eye glinted in the hole of his mask. 'Eh?'

'Quiet, bird.' Geist thought better of touching the girl's outfit, and examined the boy's arm instead. The stuff had some give in it, but was like no gum or rubber he'd encountered. 'What have we here?'

'Trouble, that's for sure.'

'They don't look like they're carrying anything. This "key", could it be inside their clothes?'

'Harr, harr – yes, why not take a look? Ladies first.'

Geist rejected the suggestion, not merely for reasons of propriety. The outfits were so close-fitting and pliable, nothing could be concealed beneath. Could the 'key' be knowledge they held? No, the gunman wouldn't then have tried to kill them, assuming he'd been seeking the same. Perhaps their equipment was of an experimental substance, itself a valuable secret.

A moan shook him from his thoughts. He straightened up and stepped back. The boy groped a hand across his face and pulled off his strange mask. His blue-green eyes met Geist's and turned wide.

'Easy, there.' Geist tried to smile. 'I'm a friend.'

The boy gave no sign of comprehension. He glanced left and jolted at the sight of the gunman's corpse. Then he looked to his other side and cried out. On hands and knees he scrambled to the girl, tore off her mask and shook her, crying 'Breathe!' over and over, desperate.

'She is breathing,' Geist told him. 'I checked.'

The boy stopped as the girl made a noise. Moving around him, Geist got his first clear view of the girl's face, her mask now off.

He froze in shock.

'Her face, and the boy's,' he said softly to Raven now. 'Almost the same face, but one male, one female. As soon as I saw them together, I thought they might be twins.'

'*Might* be? Harr!'

'Thought they *were*, then. And of course your "gate of gold" made sense at once, for what could that be referring to if not my plan?'

'I didn't call them twins,' said Raven. 'Why seek guidance from the wise if you just distort their words into your own?'

'You didn't say they *weren't*,' said Geist. 'Many times, in the months that followed, we tried to find out. Always, the shroud around them baffled us. The identity and purpose of the gunman too.'

'Obscurity reigned,' agreed Raven.

'For a while, I remained convinced,' said Geist, translating his earlier thought-processes into speech, testing their sense. 'I thought maybe they'd been shrouded to hide that relationship. I took that as confirmation that I was on the right lines, that mixed-sex twins possessed mythical potency and might be used to heal the Great Divorce.'

'But you started to have doubts.'

'It seemed so visibly apparent that they were twins,' said Geist. 'Why should anyone expend such magical effort to conceal something so obvious? Besides, when we think of twins, we think of identical ones. Non-identical, they're no more alike than any other brother and sister: Taslan and Felca show that. Yet here were two, non-identical but uncannily similar.'

'Perplexity,' said Raven.

'So I asked myself, what if they'd been *chosen* to look alike, selected from who knows how many, so that someone – myself, presumably – would think they were twins? And what if they were then shrouded to hide not that they were, but that they weren't? As a decoy, perhaps, to divert me from my expedition?'

'Of course!' crowed Raven. 'Because you posed such a threat to the Kings Behind the World, they must go to any lengths to divert you!'

'Even allowing your objection, if the Kings were behind Orc and Cass, who sent the gunman? And if the Kings had sent the gunman, who caused Orc and Cass to be washed up?'

'A juicy mystery,' said Raven. 'As always was, and doubtless ever shall be. And if you've only called me here to reminisce over old times—'

'No, I haven't,' said Geist. 'I've gone over all this not just to reminisce, but to bring the past into present clarity and add it to everything that has happened since.' He drew a deep breath. 'The mystery cannot be left any longer. It must be answered.'

'Why trouble yourself?' said Raven. 'Finding these young Bourgs has removed the need. They are undeniably twins, with some magical ability, and you only need one pair: a boy for Saeraf, a girl for Chthonis. Or the other way round.'

'Nonetheless, I need to know, perhaps now more than ever. And there might now be new pathways to that information.' Geist focused on bringing his thoughts into coherent words rather than letting them rattle off in speculation, for he had reached the heart of it. 'The Lamia said that brother-and-sister twins were used by the Zhenaii: the only people who knew the secrets of manifestation. The inference is clear: twins had something to do with manifestation. And Hana told me Orc had a magical talent, one so remarkable she wouldn't name it.'

'Arr,' came Raven's soft croak. 'You think…'

'She also said the Kings Behind the World had a city in the psychosphere, a city of gold and glass.' He shivered as though at a thread of cold air. 'My friend – my oldest friend, in both senses – I ask again. What is the "gate of gold" of which the Strandborns are the key?'

'It is given to me at times to speak prophecy,' said Raven. 'It ruins the mystique to explain it in prosaic terms.'

'Do the Kings intend to use Orc and Cass to manifest this city?' A whole city – the grandeur and madness of the scheme would barely fit in his imagination. 'Is that what they tried thousands of years ago? Is that what destroyed the Zhenaii?'

Raven's bone mask grew suddenly brighter, its tattoos sharper still. Geist tensed: this was exactly what had happened when Raven had given him the gate of gold reading two years before.

He was shocked when Raven croaked out a peal of harsh laughter.

'Wrong, wrong, wrong!' cried the bird. 'How could they do that without tearing down the barrier between thought and matter? And if this cabal, whose existence you cannot even prove, if they can break that barrier, why have they not already? Why place Orc and Cass for you to find? Why the strange gear? Why the gunman? Nothing about your idea makes sense.'

Geist had hardly dared hope for a full revelation, but Raven's dismissive attitude perturbed him. But he wasn't going to dismiss his main idea, that he might have critically underestimated the Strandborns' importance.

'Hana said they've gone to Highcloud. If they are linked with the Zhenaii art of manifestation, and the Watchers find out…'

'There, I agree,' said Raven. 'Your pair will be in grave danger. And twin or not, the male subject remains a part of your plan. Otter is the only swimming Fire Stealer, and one of Chthonis's elements is water.'

'Then fly to Orc. Bring me news of him.'

'And feast on his eyeballs if it's too late.' Raven spread his wings, made an exaggerated sweeping bow, then flapped heavily up to a window ledge, and was gone.

Geist remained seated. Again, the thought came to him that he didn't have time for this now, that he should get the others away from the castle. But he needed to know if Orc was safe. It might not take long. He kept himself in near-trance, his mind on Raven's quest, his focus strengthening the bird's flight northwards.

A gunshot startled him.

Damn it. If that had been Petri practising with his revolver, he'd wring his neck. If not—

'Master Geist!' came Taslan's voice from the main hall. 'Quick!'

He grabbed his carbine and pushed to his feet. Taslan was alone in the hall, by the door. The boy disappeared outside. Geist followed to see Petri crouching by the broken courtyard gates, the Lamia and Felca huddled against the wall nearby. Taslan ran to join them; Geist jogged to join Petri.

As soon as he reached him, he saw the reason for the shot, and swore loudly. Four Bourg riders were spread out either side of the track that led out of the valley towards Hallinghall: not advancing, but milling about. Two hundred yards away, perhaps.

'You'd never have hit from here,' snapped Geist.

'Didn't want them getting any closer,' said Petri. 'What do we do?'

Geist raised his gun, braced himself against the stonework, and let off a shot at the man with the biggest pony. With its shorter barrel and poor sighting, the carbine wasn't as accurate as his old rifle, and all that came of it was noise. The ponies skittered, the riders seeming uncertain what to do.

'Scouts, I'd guess,' said Geist. 'If they leave, we'll make a run for it. If they attack, we'll try to bring them all down.' If Petri had let them all get to within close range, he might have stood a chance.

'They're going!' the boy said.

The riders had turned and now raced their ponies back up to the crest of the track. 'Right,' said Geist. 'Get ready to move.'

But the Bourgs weren't as stupid as he'd hoped. Two disappeared beyond the crest, but two reined in their mounts and stayed against the skyline, waiting. Watching.

'Keep an eye on the Lamia,' Geist muttered to Petri.

'Karminaya.'

Geist bit his teeth together at that. 'If she sees the situation's going against us, she might pretend we slaughtered her men and captured her. And don't think you'll get out of this alive just because she's made eyes at you. Someone who's lasted three thousand years has forgotten what loyalty and friendship means.'

'What do we do?'

'I don't know. I'd have a damn sight better chance of working it out if I was allowed to think.'

But his thoughts were all of self-recrimination. He should have got them out to the woods at once, not wasted time quizzing Raven about Orc. His delay might end up killing them.

'Could we hide in the tunnel?' said Petri. 'They won't know about it. We can get out at nightfall.'

'They'd find it. They'd know we hadn't left – they'd search everywhere for us.'

'Then what?'

'I don't know! I don't know…'

Despair threatened to paralyse him. The one clear course of action was to prepare a defence. He and Petri dragged the wagon from its outbuilding and across the gateway. Then he got Petri practising loading the carbine's spare magazine, so he would never be disarmed until he ran out of cartridges. The Bourg warrior class had atrophied during their centuries of isolation, having been restricted to clan squabbles and hunting game. If fewer than twenty men came, he might be able to defeat them. If more… well, a spear was still a spear.

At last, there was no more to be done but wait. And wait they did:

him, and Petri, and the Lamia and the twins – and up at the crest of the Hallinghall track, the two Bourg riders sat their grazing ponies. Waiting, as hour stretched into hour and the bright patch behind the clouds climbed to its noon height, and then began its slow fall. Geist hoped the undisciplined Bourgs were taking time to muster, and none would arrive before nightfall. As soon as darkness came, they could escape under its cover, perhaps through the back window Ranga had used. Tough on the Lamia if she couldn't climb down the ivy. Her information was less valuable than the twins, or his own life.

The agonising building of this hope was dashed when the two riders were joined by two more. Then another ten, and another, until no fewer than fifty mounted warriors were spread along the high ground that overlooked the castle.

'Buggering bollocks.' It briefly occurred to Geist that he might be allowed to live if he surrendered, that he might return to his role as teacher of the twins. Go back to that hell, go back to waiting for rescue – or more likely, being buried in the rubble of an artillery barrage when Franzen returned for his 'purge'.

The Bourg warriors began to ride down the slope. Geist wiped his palm on his trousers and drew back the firing bolt. He glanced at the Lamia, one hand on a shoulder of each child again, huddled against the wall and out of sight of the warriors she had earlier summoned. If it came to it, the last bullet he fired would go into her heart.

No, the second-last.

Are you watching this, Vanessa? Is this giving you any joy?

He knew it would not. What place for joy had there been in the world since they'd parted, since his betrayal of her and of his own ideals? Before that last bullet, he would shout her name and that he was sorry. For all the good it would do.

But before that, he had others to use as best he could.

Finger on trigger, he waited.

PART FIVE
KRITI

35

THE COURT OF WELCOME

Emilia peered over Max's head, watching through the many glass panes of the air-craft's nose as their destination drew nearer. She'd seen drawings and even some photographs of Highcloud, though none from this astonishing aerial perspective. The newer, red-roofed monastery sat on a relatively level shelf of the Holy Mountain's lower slopes, perched on the western lip of the gorge that plunged eighty feet down to the Oar-stream; higher up, on the eastern side, lay the half-destroyed remains of the old monastery. Spanning the gorge about a hundred yards in from its opening onto the cliff-like mountainside was the inches-wide Knifebridge, on which the novitiates famously stood to welcome and warn visitors. But none stood there now.

'How defensible is it, do you think?' she asked Max.

'From ground troops, not bad,' he said. 'Even against firearms, they could probably hold it where the road turns at right-angles into the gorge, or they could stop anyone getting into that trench that runs up from the gorge alongside the building.'

'The Spiral Path.'

'Yes. But mountain troops could scale those cliffs from lower down on the road, and get onto the slopes below the old ruin. And if he brings his air-craft, its firepower could wipe out the novitiates waiting in the gorge, or on the cliff-top, or anywhere.'

Emilia felt sick. Some of the novitiates were barely into their teens.

'They'd have no way to retaliate,' said Max. 'Their only chance for survival would be to stay in the monastery, but then they'd cede the whole ground, and your brother's men could set up machine-guns to cover every exit. It looks pretty hopeless.'

'But we have an air-craft too.'

'But no trained gunners. And not enough ammunition to waste practising.'

She'd been afraid he would say something like that. 'Do you think he will bring it?'

'He'd be mad not to.'

'Then we can't afford a battle,' she said. 'We'll have to resolve the situation before it comes to that.' She pointed to a stretch of level ground west of the newer monastery building. 'That must be what Tashi called the ball-pitch, where Siegfried's craft landed when he came.'

'I see it,' said Max. 'Miss Strandborn!' he shouted, loud enough to jar Emilia's nerves. 'Forward neutral, maintain height. I'll guide us in with the airscrews. I'll let you know when to set us down.'

When the building was lost to sight from the pilot's position, Emilia clambered to the lower deck and went to the machine-gun port where Dinah sat. Max called further instructions to Cass, counting out the slow descent. The trench of the Spiral Path separated the ball-pitch from the monastery's western wall, and over a bridge from a gateway came twenty or thirty shaven-headed monks of all ages – none of them Watchers, by the lack of yellow scarves.

The craft grounded; the combined roar of the airscrew engines and the elemental died. Tashi already stood by the door, visibly tense. Emilia and Dinah went to join him. Orc rose from where he'd been sitting.

'Is it still the same plan, then?' said Emilia. 'Tashi, Dinah and I go. Tashi?'

The boy's throat moved. 'Don't call me by name. Not here.'

We haven't left the air-craft yet. He was clearly in a state. If the

Watchers picked up on it, tension might result. 'Maybe you should stay here for now. Shall we take Max?' she asked Dinah.

'Why?' she said. 'You outrank everyone else here.' Dinah clanged the bolt across and pushed the door. It lowered, letting in cool mountain air, revealing the group of monks ten yards distant: silent, motionless, staring. 'Come on, Em. Assert yourself for once.'

Not wanting to argue, nor to disappoint Dinah, Emilia forced her unsteady legs to carry her down the steps. She shrank inside a little at the group facing her. The only congregations this size she'd addressed had been entirely women, and there were no women here – none in Highcloud at all, she'd read, save the nursemaids to the youngest boys. It now struck her how ludicrous had been her former ambition of having the monastery teach her their version of trance-flight. But the near-hostility in the monks' gazes would surely change once they'd learned the reason for their unexpected arrival.

When she stood on the hard-packed earth of the ball-pitch, a stout monk took a step forwards and declared across the ten paces of ground: 'I am Keeper of the Western Gate, assistant to his Holiness the Abbot Taropat. He will receive you in the Court of Welcome.'

Dinah at her shoulder, Emilia walked to him. The Keeper's expression showed increasing unease as they approached, and when they reached him, he said, 'Why have some remained on the craft?'

'The Lady Emilia is a high-born official of the Church,' said Dinah. 'She's quite capable of speaking for us all.'

'Dinah, please.' She hoped the Keeper wouldn't take offence.

'You must all come,' he said. 'It is not permitted for anyone to come to this ground who has not been granted prior leave. The Abbot must absolve you all. He will speak with none of you on any other matter until this is done.'

Emilia sighed inwardly; Empyreal protocol could be similarly petty. The plan had been clear, to avoid exposing Orc and Cass to any possible scrutiny until friendly relations had been established with the Abbot; but arguing risked antagonism. Better, she thought, to make it seem they had nothing to hide. The risk should be small.

She walked with Dinah back to the craft. Tashi met her at the doorway.

'Did you hear that?' she said, climbing the first two steps. 'It has to be all of us.'

'Why?' he asked, nerves clear in his voice.

'Something about needing to be absolved for coming here without the Abbot's permission. Does that make sense to you? Is it a rule?'

He thought a moment, then nodded. 'It might be now. There is no lawful route here except up the Spiral Path and through the monastery. There was no possibility before the air-craft, so no rule was needed. They must have made it after your brother's visit.'

Another problem Siegfried had made for her.

'I'll tell the others.' Tashi climbed to the engineer deck. After some discussion, from which she caught the tension if not the words, he clambered back down. Max and the Strandborns followed. Cass looked exhausted, Orc troubled.

'Can't Tashi and Max go and pretend it's all of us?' he said. 'Me and Cass can hide here.'

'And if they find out?' said Emilia. 'We'll be off to a very bad start. We mustn't give them a reason to mistrust us. As bearers of bad news, we're unlikely to be welcomed with enthusiasm as it is.'

'And it is right that we must be absolved,' said Tashi. 'We must obey the monastery rule.'

Cass sighed. 'Come on, then. Hopefully they can't tell anything about us just from looking. They'll have other things to think about anyway. But no one mention the elemental, or Empyreus – not yet. We need Yaggit to vouch for us before we say anything about magic, or that séance.'

'Understood,' said Emilia. 'You and Orc say as little as possible. If you want, you can come back here as soon as you're absolved. Make out you're feeling peaky.'

Max came out last, shutting the door behind him. The Keeper nodded curtly and turned back to the monastery. The other monks parted, and the Keeper led Emilia's group towards the gate in Highcloud's western wall. The monastery grew before her, its interior dark, the mass of its stone seeming to hold the weight of the Holy Mountain itself.

They'd just reached the bridge across the trench when Tashi halted, breathing louder. Emilia turned; before she could ask if anything was wrong, he bent over and groaned out a thin stream of vomit.

All stood still. No one spoke. Emilia's sympathy was blunted by a fear that the monks might somehow intuit why the boy felt so unsettled.

'That's quite common after one first travels by air, unfortunately,' said Max. His smooth, polished voice made Emilia grateful he was there.

When Tashi had straightened again, pale-faced but showing no other sign of distress, they crossed over into the monastery. Dimness enclosed them. Elusive smells haunted the stone-cooled air – some kind of cooking, damp, animals or their pelts – all unchanged, perhaps, for hundreds of years, as though they'd circulated here since the monastery had been built. The sense of entering a very different world from her own prickled on Emilia's skin.

The Keeper led them round the corners of a broad corridor, to a double door thrown wide, and through into what Emilia assumed must be the Court of Welcome. Welcome indeed, the opening into brightness. A broad expanse of sky overhung the square space, the edges of which were sheltered by a cloister supported by carved wooden pillars. At the far end, on a low dais, stood a small bespectacled man Emilia took for the Abbot. Either side of him were three yellow-scarved monks, and with each Watcher a youth in grey, a short sword at his belt. As she followed the Keeper into the centre of the court, Emilia saw that six other Watchers and their novitiates, all boys aged between twelve and twenty, occupied the shadows of the cloisters to left and right – and behind her, three either side of the door through which they'd entered. Two dozen men, two dozen youths.

Naturally it was meant to be somewhat intimidating, since she and her group had committed an infraction. But the stern atmosphere didn't have the feel of mere ritual. She wished Tashi felt able to declare himself. He stared at one of the sloping red-tiled cloister roofs, as if steeling himself not to look at these people he had known for years but who no longer knew him.

'His Holiness the Abbot Taropat,' said the Keeper, before withdrawing.

'Please announce yourselves,' the Abbot said.

'Holiness,' Emilia began, trying to adopt her crisp, confident official voice, as though she were the guest speaker at a meeting of the League for Women's Health. 'I am Lady Emilia Astrasis, Deaconess of the Chapel of the Holy Mother, she who as Arris Entarna was once well-received here.' But her voice sounded like a squeak to her ears – these were men, learned old men and young warriors, and they looked at her with the eyes of the Valkensee and an officer cadet corps. 'Our apologies for the impropriety of our arrival, but on hearing our message you'll surely agree that we had no choice but to come without notice.'

The Abbot studied her. 'Tell me, then.'

She took a breath. 'My brother, Prelate Siegfried Astrasis, plans an attack on this monastery. Perhaps even within the day. I know this will come as a shock...'

She had readied herself for loud disbelief, but there came none. These people really did have an iron grip on their emotions; she had to admire it, whatever Dinah or Cass might think.

The Abbot slid his spectacles a little towards the end of his nose. 'Your message comes as no shock at all.'

'You already know?' The Watchers must have detected it. But then why no sign of preparation?

From a fold of his robe, the Abbot took a piece of paper. A foreboding she couldn't identify chilled Emilia's nerves.

'This telegram was delivered by Empyreal courier during the night,' said the Abbot. 'I quote: "Six criminals will come to you in a stolen air-craft, claiming forces under my control intend an attack. Their intention is to foment mistrust between us and thus aid the Witch."'

She couldn't breathe. Dismayed mutterings and whispers came from her companions, but none spoke aloud: they were waiting for her. She tried to scrabble her wits together.

'Holiness,' she began, 'you must see that's precisely the message my brother *would* send, when he realised the danger of our warning you.' Yet she hadn't anticipated it – the gulf of her error yawned before her, and perhaps others of which she wasn't yet aware. 'I understand a holy man like yourself might not be able to appreciate such deviousness, but—'

The Abbot raised his palm. 'There are none more devious than magicians, and they have long been our field of study. Do you aid the forces of the Witch Mother?'

'No! I am Deaconess of the Church!'

Her answer fell flat against the flagstones and pillars. She felt the sudden urge to make Max take over, to thrust him forwards with his height and masculinity and uniform against this old man she hadn't the power to defeat. She couldn't think what to say except a repeated denial, but her word would mean nothing here against a prelate's, against her brother's.

'It continues.' The Abbot turned back to the telegram. '"If proof of their perfidy be needed, witness events at the Empyreal air-field at five this afternoon."'

Orc hissed under his breath. A soft groan escaped Emilia.

'I convened a Conclave early this morning,' said the Abbot, 'and had the Watchers investigate. What they reported viewing I can barely bring myself to repeat.'

No, thought Emilia, *No*...

'And did you see *why* it happened?' said Cass.

The tall Watcher next to the Abbot made an arm signal. The novitiates drew their short swords. Emilia gasped and drew closer to the others, but the youths made no move, merely kept their weapons held out.

'Any attempt at sorcery will be met with utmost force,' the chief Watcher said.

Sick fear had drained Emilia of blood, of voice, of every thought.

'Yaggit,' said Cass. 'He'll vouch for us.'

'You know him?' said the Abbot.

'Or *of* him,' said the chief Watcher. 'Their divination has told them he is not here, and so they claim friendship with him.'

'Wait, Rukhan,' said the Abbot. 'If they are to be condemned, let it be by their own lies.'

'It's not a lie,' said Cass, sounding like her vocal cords were near snapping. 'He was in Bismark looking for evidence about Empyreus, but he got a train back. He might not be far away by now. You can find out, right? We can bring him here.'

Rukhan scoffed. 'What better way to escape justice than by appearing to leave here to collect one of our own?'

'Give us a chance!' said Cass. 'We came here to help you. This prelate's going to attack you, and *we're* the ones you treat as your enemy?'

Because we're women, thought Emilia. Even without the air-field, their words would have meant nothing. They should have made Max their spokesman, but it was too late now, and in any case a glance showed him at a loss.

'You expect us to heed your warning?' said Rukhan. 'Why should Astrasis attack us? We have not yet refused his ultimatum.'

'That's not the reason,' said Cass. 'That's just a cover. You have something he wants.'

Rukhan made no attempt to conceal his incredulity. 'And what might that be?'

Cass turned to Tashi. 'Now would be a good time to remember.'

'I told you before.' His voice came like a cracked bell. 'Crome did not say.'

With all hope now gone, Emilia saw her fate as though a court had decreed it. The hysteria Siegfried would accuse her of rose from her belly. Her brother would come to claim her, and she would spend the rest of her life in an asylum, her womb removed. Had he not threatened her with incarceration at their last meeting?

Their last meeting…

Something was trying to break into her thoughts. What her brother wanted: she had the sudden conviction that it was there in her mind already.

'Let us put an end to this nonsense,' Rukhan said. 'Never mind that the Prelate wants them – the Empyreal charter gives us jurisdiction over magicians.'

Panic had her in its claws. Something to do with that last meeting, but it was part of a muddle of so much happening and she would never separate it out in time.

'We should put them to trial immediately,' another Watcher said.

'Novitiates,' said Rukhan, 'seize them.'

Help, came her desperate thought – and as though in answer, a sound pierced the voices around her and jolted her heart: the high, distant call of a bird of prey. Whether it was in reality the cry of a lammager or even a mind-phantasm, she seized it, focused herself. Despite the loss of her stone and years of absence, Eagle had come; her animath was watching over her.

And Eagle's eyes saw everything. And saw—

'Wait!' she cried, and thrust out her hand. The court stilled in surprise. She looked at Tashi. 'Siegfried gave us the reason. Don't you remember – he said if he could learn the secrets of Zhenaii manifestation, he wouldn't need to attack.'

'He did,' said Tashi.

'That's what he wants,' she told the Abbot.

The novitiates hadn't moved, looked uncertain.

'You're claiming one of the highest Prelates of the Empyrean church is a *magician*?' said Rukhan. A murmur went round the cloisters.

'I'm saying he wants those secrets.' Her heart raced with this confrontation with power, and how much hung on her need to persuade them. But she had heard Eagle; she must draw on Eagle's heart as she had on her eyes. She'd had the courage to let go of the balcony. She had flown.

The Abbot's voice came more measured than it had been. 'Why should he think such secrets are here?'

She turned to Tashi. 'You said it's something in the vaults?'

'Yes,' was his flat response.

Emilia firmly met the Abbot's gaze. 'And I believe you know what that would be.'

'I cannot credit this.'

'She tries to turn us against the Empyreum,' said Rukhan. 'What could be more pleasing to the Witch Mother than for us to throw ourselves on Kurassian bayonets? This one learned her cunning from King Serpent. Silence her.'

'I will NOT be silenced!'

Her own shout, a cry from outside her familiar self, shocked her – but it gave her the moment she needed. She briefly closed her eyes and sought Eagle within her, and as though from a great height, she glimpsed the landscape of connections.

'Tell me, Holiness,' she said, pushing into her voice all the authority and confidence she could borrow, 'why did Konstantin not destroy Highcloud?'

'He was repulsed by the twenty-seven novitiates, Inspired by the *Elohim Gibor*.' The Abbot's voice had a strange tension. 'Is this no longer known in Bismark?'

'It is. And so is the fact that he later returned, and with a much larger force.'

She sensed Tashi stiffen. 'He did?' Similar confusion marked the novitiates' faces, but not their masters'.

'But he didn't press his second attack,' she went on. 'Your predecessor came out to meet him, and after their parley, Konstantin withdrew. The Watchers were afterwards granted the charter to hunt out and defeat magicians, and were given aid to build the new monastery. Is that not strange, Holiness? Konstantin had come to Highcloud seeking an easy source of loot, treasure built up from centuries of donations. So why, after his second visit, did he instead become its benefactor?'

No one offered an answer. But their faces betrayed that they knew one.

'My brother was obsessed with Konstantin,' she went on. 'I recall him reading every book he could find about the emperor, old tomes whose source he wouldn't tell me and which he kept locked up. I think I can now guess the direction of his studies. Did the abbot of the time reveal to the emperor something the monastery was guarding? Something so important, so *dangerous*, that Konstantin agreed to fund Highcloud so it could keep anyone else from possessing it?'

There came no answer, and Emilia saw behind the Abbot's eyes the struggle to hide the truth without committing the grievous sin of lying. But it didn't come fast enough, and as if in realisation that silence had already signified agreement, he said in a weak voice, 'Konstantin swore never to divulge its existence.'

'It seems he didn't keep that promise.'

'So there is such a thing?' said Cass. 'Something that contains all the secrets of the Zhenaii? Their history? Is it a book?'

'Whatever it is, it's what my brother wants.' Emilia held the Abbot's gaze. 'All the evidence points to it.'

The Abbot studied the telegram, as though trying to puzzle it out. 'This is beyond us.'

'How can it be?' said Emilia. 'Who can find truth if not the famed Watchers of Highcloud?'

'And what truth have we already witnessed?' demanded Rukhan. 'You have not denied the events at the air-field, yet you ask us to trust you?'

'My Lady had no part in that,' said Max. 'She wasn't even there. As for me, it took me completely by surprise.'

'It was me,' said Orc. 'No one else.'

'Shut up,' said Cass. 'We're in this together.'

'Yes, together,' said the Abbot. 'All this talk is fruitless. The six of you will be handed to the Prelate when he arrives at ten o'clock tomorrow.'

'Holiness, no!' said Emilia. 'Whatever you think of us, you can't trust him either.'

But her brother carried the weight of the Empyreum, and as the Abbot's eyes shifted downwards and his expression sagged, Emilia realised with despair that the old man and his monastery wouldn't dare cross that force, not without absolute proof, maybe not even then.

'We have no quarrel with him,' said the Abbot. 'Not yet.'

'No quarrel?' Tashi's unexpected voice came strong and clear, taut with anger. He stepped forwards. 'Set your Conclave to examine what happened in Bismark the day after *that man* left with one of your Watchers and his novitiate. Then you'll learn how he forced the Watcher to Inspire the novitiate in exchange for transport – so he could witness the power of the *Elohim Gibor* and know what his army would face.'

'He did what?' said a Watcher.

'How do you know this?' asked the Abbot.

'I was there,' said Tashi, his voice increasingly strained. 'And I know the Watcher only made such a bargain because he had no other way of investigating the return of Zhenaii magic – because you refused to support him, believing there was no danger. And now a new danger has arisen, or a part of the same one, and again you will ignore it because you fear it too much. Do not make the same mistake you made then. If you had listened and sent more Watchers with – with my late master, things would have turned out very differently, not least – not least for me.'

A taut hush had fallen over the court.

'*Your*... master?'

Tashi's head jerked in a nod. Everyone's eyes were on him, but his own gaze was fixed hard on the Abbot. Emilia's heart clenched as she saw the tears running down the boy's face, the muscles in that face locked into rigidity. 'We must speak,' he said, his voice trembling with the effort of maintaining its flatness. 'In private.'

Glancing around at the Watchers and novitiates, Emilia saw Tashi's revelation had passed none of them by.

The Abbot swayed, staggered. Amid gasps, Rukhan moved to steady him.

'I think we must,' said the Abbot weakly. 'Come.' After taking a moment to recover his balance, he left through a small door behind the dais. Tashi unsteadily followed, Rukhan and his novitiate going through after.

'Well, that very nearly went all to shit,' muttered Orc when they were gone.

'What do we do now?' said Max.

'Wait, I assume.' Emilia felt drained; she wondered if she would be able to remain standing. 'If he's going to tell him everything, we might be here a while.' And what might happen then, she had no idea. She felt oppressed by the scrutiny of the Watchers and novitiates: she sensed them on edge for anything untoward, shocked by what had already been revealed.

'What about Empyreus?' whispered Cass. 'Do we say anything about that yet?'

'Wait till we find out what Tashi's told them,' said Orc. 'I don't know if there's any chance of us getting Yaggit now. Even if we can, who knows if he'll be able to convince this lot? What happened at the air-field might even turn him against us.'

'Surely not,' said Cass. 'He already knows about manifestation – and he was there in the college's cellar.'

'The Mother energy attacked me in the cellar,' said Orc. 'At the air-field, it…' His exhalation turned into a groan. 'Cass, if they do investigate us, they might find out something I haven't told you. I need you to be ready for it.'

She looked worried. 'What do you mean?'

Orc motioned her a short distance, halfway between the group and the cloister where their guards stood. Emilia pushed down her curiosity and turned to the others.

'Dinah, Max,' she said, 'I'm so sorry. I've landed you in the most dreadful danger.'

'We all agreed to come,' said Max. 'And you couldn't have known your brother would send that telegram.'

'With hindsight, it seems laughably obvious.'

'We'll get through it,' said Max. 'None of *us* is a magician,' he whispered. 'We can claim bewitchment.'

'We'll do no such thing.' Dinah linked her elbow with Emilia's.

'I felt so weak after he accused us,' Emilia said. 'My mind wouldn't work. I thought, away from Siegfried, I'd be less afraid, but—'

'These men are just as bad,' said Dinah. 'It dates from before Empyreus. It's stronger here than anywhere.'

Emilia nodded. She sensed Tamfang beyond the monastery walls almost as a giant living presence. The dreadful thought came to her that if Arris Entarna had indeed conceived her child on the Holy Mountain, it might have been through being raped by a spear of ice.

'But it's not all-powerful,' she whispered to Dinah, too low even for Max to hear – she felt guilty at excluding him, but he knew nothing of that part of her history. 'I felt Eagle, briefly. She gave me the strength to speak. But now it hardly seems real.'

'We'll get your stone,' Dinah replied, and patted Emilia's arm. 'Till we do, I'll stand in for her.'

Just then a call of, 'Hann!' came from one of the Watchers, and Emilia turned. A novitiate approached: the tallest, and one of the oldest, with a lean but well-proportioned face. His master called him back again, louder, but the young man ignored it.

'Is it truly him?' he said in a low voice. 'The one who claims to be Tashi?'

'Why would you believe us, whatever we say?' cut in Dinah. 'Aren't we witches?'

'Dinah, please,' said Emilia, and to the youth: 'Two of our party witnessed his transformation.'

'He said "late master". So Shoggu is dead? Then why come back, after everything?'

'To warn his comrades. Don't you value loyalty here?'

'We hardly needed warning,' Hann said. 'Ever since the Prelate came, we've felt King Serpent's coils tightening round this place.' He lowered his voice further and spoke quickly. 'If I help you escape, will you take me with you? And teach me the lower world and how to live there?'

'Hann!' called the Watcher. 'Your braving them impresses no one. Return before you are put on punishment.'

'You want to leave?' Emilia whispered.

'I'll be sent away at twenty-one anyway. Shouldn't loyalty run both ways?' His nostrils widened slightly. 'So it's true – women do smell different.'

'Stand away from her!' said Max.

'I meant no insult.' He stepped back. 'I'll seek an opening,' he muttered with a serious, intense look, then turned and strode back to his glowering master with the jauntiness of one who'd won a dare.

'Did he mean all that?' said Dinah. 'Or was he toying with us?'

Emilia didn't know. All was so uncertain, it seemed hardly worth saying anything. She glanced at the Strandborns, squatting where they talked as though the strength of their legs had given out. Cass looked stricken, Orc grim and set-faced. Some personal issue between them, she assumed, and felt a little irritated. It was hard to believe that anything personal could seem other than trivial, next to what had now befallen their whole party.

36

LAST GOODBYE

Cass stared at the ground in front of her, at the flagstones over which she wanted to puke. On top of everything else, this. She tried to find a way to shrink what Orc had told her, to make it something she could cope with. To push down the thing within her that wanted to fly at him with teeth and claws.

'This… it's not *marriage*. It's something that happened in your head.' It felt like explaining to a child. 'And it can unhappen in your head.'

'There's no way out of it,' he said, 'even if I wanted one.'

Even if… 'Stop talking like she can overhear you. You said before, she can't exist here.'

'Unless I've brought her with me.'

Then tell yourself you didn't! she wanted to scream. But the cloisters, the eyes she sensed on her, kept her voice quiet. 'Are you even looking for a way out?'

He said nothing. By his own logic, if he even let disloyal thoughts into his mind, the goddess might punish or even kill him. But she didn't think that was all of it.

'It's clever, I have to say.' She hated that she sounded barely in control of her own voice. 'You've made it so no one can even try to help you get out of it. Because you don't want to. Hana wasn't enough, because she was only human, and she rejected you. So you went one better: someone who'll never let you go, who'll kill you if you try to leave her. To get away from me.'

'That's not it.'

'No? On the island, you refused to believe anything could stop us being together if we only found out the truth. Then a photograph falls out of a chimney, and suddenly you're so terrified of your Voice of God you throw up a wall between us. If we're no good for each other, that's something we have to decide for ourselves. I'm not having it decided by fucking *magic*.'

'So what should I have done on top of that ziggurat? You'd rather I was lost for ever?'

She sagged. She risked looking at him, but got only the top of his head, his hair. A flash of memory came, of how she'd touched his hair that time on that beach, before Geist's insidious question had changed everything. The sense of loss made shit of her insides.

'At least…' She had to focus. 'If the monks pick up on it, deny it. She'll let you do that, won't she? She'll let you tell a white lie to escape her worst enemies?'

'I don't know,' he mumbled: hiding something, she felt sure. 'Look, I'm sorry it's all come out this way. Really I am.' He stood up straight.

'Orc,' she said, rising too. 'Remember what we said as we left the island? You promised to be more in the world, less in your head. How does this fit with that?'

'But She is the world, in a way.' As if that answered anything, he turned and walked back to the others, where he stood with his hands in his coat pockets, toeing the courtyard dirt. Emilia and everyone else seemed to know not to ask him any questions.

Cass didn't move from her spot, unsure what to do, what her emotional state would let her do or make her do. Minutes dragged by. The tense calmness of the courtyard seemed to deny the cataclysm of Orc's revelation. Could it be that it wasn't as big as she'd felt, that she couldn't trust her judgement? It had all happened in Orc's mind, and only in his mind. Maybe her wrung-out heart was fooling her, and this was something that could be easily solved, if only she wasn't so tired. Or perhaps she needed to be *more* tired – maybe there was a place on the far side of exhaustion where her human self would be burned away and she would become a being of infinite capability: a sword shaped from a blunt rod by hours of violent pounding.

Like Tashi's red form. No answer lay there.

After a while, monks entered the court with chairs, and a table with a pottery water jug and cups. Cass hoped this was a good sign. A monk set her chair near where she stood, which saved her having to join Orc and the others. After perhaps half an hour, a young monk with an officious air came through the Abbot's door and fetched two more of the Watchers. Those remaining, and their novitiates, by now looked bored as well as wary. At last, a good hour after leaving, Tashi returned with the two Watchers who'd gone out last, but not with Rukhan or the Abbot. As he walked to Emilia's group, who rose nervously to their feet, Tashi glanced across at Cass with a puzzled expression. She sighed, pushed herself off her chair, and joined them.

'The Abbot is keeping an open mind,' he said quietly.

'About what?' said Emilia. 'What did you tell him?'

'What happened to me. But none of your secrets, and nothing of the Shining Ones. He won't commit to anything before speaking to Yaggit, and then he'll judge what the next Conclave will investigate. But he won't allow that next Conclave until eight tomorrow.'

'But that's only two hours before Siegfried arrives!' said Emilia.

'The Watchers must have a whole day's rest between Conclaves to lower the risk of dark-flight. It is a rule.'

'Back up a bit,' said Cass, feeling the first hope she had for ages. 'You said "before speaking to Yaggit"? So they know where he is?'

Tashi nodded. 'The three Watchers conducted flight and sensed him in a village down in the valley – he must have made good speed by train.'

'Thank God,' said Cass. 'How long will it take him to get here?'

‘Ordinarily, many hours. But…’Tashi turned as Rukhan approached, in his hand a piece of paper.

‘This is a map to the village where we have located Yaggit.’ He offered it to Max. ‘You are the craft’s operator?’

‘So you’re letting us fly down to get him?’ said Max.

‘We need Yaggit returned with all speed. But as for “us”, no, only you.’

Cass seized the chance. Even better than getting Yaggit back would be to escape this mess altogether. ‘It needs all of us to fly it.’

Rukhan turned a narrowed stare on her. ‘You insult my intelligence: only four of you were present at its theft. In any case, some of you were particularly demanded by the Prelate, and until we have the truth of the matter, those three will stay here.’

‘It does need her, though,’ said Orc, a weird strain to his voice. ‘She’s the engineer.’

Cass wondered if she’d been one of those ‘demanded by the Prelate’. But it seemed not, for Rukhan said, ‘Very well. You and the officer, come.’

‘I need to speak to her first,’ said Orc.

‘On their return.’

‘No, those machines are dangerous. I have to talk to her in case they don’t make it.’

What? thought Cass. He hadn’t expressed any worry before their previous take-offs.

The chief Watcher looked about to forbid it, but Tashi said, ‘Please allow them, Master Rukhan, for my master’s sake.’

Annoyance, but also perhaps guilt, showed in his face. ‘A minute, then.’

Orc gestured her to one side again.

‘What now?’ she said. ‘What was that bollocks about not making it?’

‘You’re not going to make it.’ His eyes were serious, his voice hushed. ‘I mean you’re not coming back.’

‘What?’

'Don't argue, there isn't time. It's too dangerous to come back here.'

'You're insane,' she said in a hoarse whisper. 'I'm not going to *leave* you.'

He gripped her arm. 'Even if they get proof about the Prelate, or Empyreus, who says they'll let us go? They know too much about us already, and they can find out more. You were right: the monster Tashi became, the fanatic witch-hater, it's from *this* place, *this* mountain. Can't you feel it? You think Yaggit will persuade them to ignore our magic, even if he doesn't change his mind when he gets back here?'

She shook her head, struggling to get her thoughts round his argument. 'We need to all get out.'

'That's not possible, though, is it?'

'I can't just...'

'Emilia will be okay, she's the Prelate's family. Max'll understand that. Get to Sundara, like you planned. Find your name. There's an island called Kriti somewhere – the photograph was taken there. You can give me all the answers when we meet up again. Yes?'

His eyes told her he didn't think they would.

'You've had your minute,' came Rukhan's voice.

'Cass, *go*. I can't say goodbye properly, I – ah!' he winced, and rubbed at his wrist. 'Please don't make this hurt more than it does already.'

Confusion buffeted her. Somewhere in the whirl of her mind was the suspicion that he was using this as a chance to get her away – not just to get her to safety, but because his goddess wanted her gone. But did that invalidate everything he'd said? She needed somewhere to think, to clear her head. And the air-craft was as good as anywhere. She was the one who controlled Windbags, as she'd named the elemental: she could come back if she chose.

As she turned from Orc, Rukhan said, 'Beware, everyone – they might have roused up some brew of emotion.'

'What the *fuck*?'

'She's just upset,' said Emilia, sounding as if she was trying to mask the same. 'The strain of flying here. I think Dinah had better go too, as a back-up. Just to be safe.'

'What?' said Dinah.

'I'll be fine,' Emilia told her, with a weak smile. 'Believe me.'

Something in Emilia's face told Cass that she'd guessed Orc's plan. Or had their group cooked it up together when she'd been sitting apart? No, they couldn't have: Dinah looked puzzled and distraught. Emilia stepped right next to Max and whispered something to him, a few lines that clearly took him aback. His face struggled to conceal hurt.

'What's happening here?' said Rukhan. 'Is this other woman truly needed?'

'Cass's strength might not hold out,' said Emilia. 'You can see how overwrought she is.'

'If you're suspicious,' said Orc, 'why doesn't one of your warriors go along as a guard?'

Cass's brows clenched in surprise.

'I volunteer!' The tallest novitiate stepped forwards, the one who'd had some kind of exchange with Emilia and the others earlier. 'I have no fear of them. I have already shown that.'

Cass felt she might shatter with confusion. Why would Orc scupper his own idea by suggesting a guard? Had he changed his mind?

'Very well, Hann,' said Rukhan. 'Be alert for trickery. Now come, you four. We cannot know if Yaggit will remain where we sensed him.'

As Cass started to follow Rukhan, Tashi touched her arm. 'You were arguing,' he said in a low voice. 'Fighting.'

'So what?'

'It will damage your love.'

'Our *what*?'

'I saw it in Bismark, that last time. It saved him.'

She suppressed what might have been the most hideous laugh ever. 'No, Tashi. What saved him was some stupid thing he did to himself, in a *dream*.'

He looked shocked, but she had neither time nor energy to work out what was going on in his religious-nutcase head, nor correct whatever misunderstanding he suffered from. She glanced once at Orc, then left after the others.

They walked to the air-craft under guard. Max and Dinah seemed subdued, as though they really were leaving for good, as though having a novitiate with them would make no difference. If they were relying on Max's pistol to negate Hann's threat, that proved short-lived, as Max was made to fetch it from the air-craft and hand it to Rukhan. There was discussion about removing the craft's machine-guns from their mounts, but Rukhan accepted it would take too much time and the guns posed no threat to Hann in the confined space.

'Whatever you do, don't let him onto the upper deck,' Cass whispered to Dinah when she could snatch a moment to do so. 'If he asks about the noise from Windbags, make something up.'

'Does it matter now?' whispered Dinah. 'If we're not coming back, who's he going to tell?'

'Not coming back? Going to persuade *him*, are you?'

'Are you stupid? He *wants* to leave.'

Cass gasped, both at Dinah's angry tone and the shock of pieces clicking together. Of course: when Hann had talked to Emilia and the others, something Rukhan hadn't witnessed. And Emilia must have told Orc – Orc had used Hann not only to placate the chief Watcher, but to guarantee his own plan.

For a moment she had the urge to throw open the air-craft door and shout to Rukhan not to let them leave, or that they would need more guards. But what would that mean for Dinah, for Max? Maybe this really was their only way to escape disaster. It wasn't just herself she had to think of. Nor Orc.

She shut her mind to him. She climbed to the upper deck, amazed that her muscles still worked, that the rungs didn't give way in this world that felt like it was all falling apart. Max was out on the left wing by the airscrew, cranking round the starting-charge cylinder to line up the fresh cartridge. She waited while he did the other screw and returned.

'What do we reckon?' he said softly, clambering back into his seat. 'Are we really bound for Sundara?'

'You're fine with that?'

'By no means "fine".' He closed the canopy. 'But speaking frankly, Emilia said she couldn't bear to have me suffer for her having used me. It seems it was only my ability to fly that inspired her heart. I've always feared it might be so, and I don't believe her words were purely out of concern for my safety. I've gambled and lost. The best that awaits me now is a strange country with whom my old comrades might soon be at war.'

Not the words of a man in love, Cass thought. Maybe love didn't exist any more. She felt sorry for Tashi: at least he'd tried to believe in it, by the sound of things, in some crackbrained way. 'Let's go to that village first anyway, tell Yaggit the situation. If he hurries back here, he might still be in time to help Orc and Emilia.'

'Won't our passenger object? He'll hardly welcome running across another monk and one of the colleagues he's deserting.'

'He can hide in the craft; he won't have to meet them. We'll make something up for Yaggit about why we can't take him and Aino back.'

'Very well. Power up the elemental when ready.'

The thought of having to face all that hate again drained what little energy Cass had left. But she did it. She sent her mind into the psychosphere and conjured Windbags, whose jocular name did nothing to mask its staggering age and potency and its desire to shred her mind and flesh. The craft lurched from the ground, and she felt grateful that she was so focused on her work she barely had space to think she might never see Orc again.

37

THE PLACE OF THE FATHER

When a couple of hours had passed since the departing air-craft had overflown the Court of Welcome, Orc began to accept that Cass had heeded his urging, or at least that Hann had prevented her from refusing to do so. By four hours, it seemed a certainty. Tashi had been taken off to talk again with the Abbot; Orc and Emilia's turn would come afterwards. In the meantime, they'd been placed in the Hall of Conclave, a large chamber taking up the smaller top floor of the monastery's main block, with narrow windows looking out in all four directions. Almost thirty identical tables or platforms stood against the walls, each three feet square and four off the ground, and each covered with a rug. About ten of these platforms were occupied by the novitiates tasked to watch them.

The waiting was a tedious business. Each time he and Emilia tried to talk to each other, one of the novitiates barked at them for silence – in case they called up a mass of killer vegetation, Orc assumed. Emilia had just whispered him a question about Otter – they'd talked a little about their animaths the previous night, but not nearly enough – when the double doors to the hall opened and Tashi entered with Rukhan's novitiate, a young man of about Orc's own age. The latter joined his comrades. Tashi came to the centre of the room.

'I guess we're allowed to speak to *you*,' Orc said. He'd meant it as a joke, but the look on Tashi's face made him regret the attempt at humour.

'They have finished with me,' Tashi said quietly. 'Shikar will take you to the Abbot. But I have to ask you something first. Cass told me you saved yourself, in a dream. That it wasn't the love between you.'

Orc felt as if he'd missed half a conversation. 'Not sure I get your meaning.'

'What is there now that means anything?' said Tashi. 'I offered you my service. You refused. Then I hoped to serve the ideal of love, but it was an illusion.'

'Is that what she said?'

'What other certainties are left? I don't even know if I'll be a novitiate again. The Abbot says the question is "complex", and will have to wait till everything else is settled. They won't even look to see what's happened to Shoggu's soul, or if they can help him. Perhaps they're like Crome and don't even truly believe it exists. Doubt and compromise have risen from the lower world like a flood. How to escape it, except by climbing?'

'If you must talk to them,' said Shikar, 'speak so we can all hear.'

Tashi turned. 'And how many goddess-monsters have you destroyed, Shikar, that you think you still outrank me?'

'So you entangled yourself in the mess of the lower world,' said Shikar. 'If your tale was correct, tomorrow we'll defend the monastery, as did the first twenty-seven. That is the purest service.'

'The monastery was founded to guard against Zhenaii magic,' said Tashi. 'But what does it matter? None of you are worth listening to. Only Aino.' He turned to Orc. 'What can be keeping them? You said the air-craft might not make it. Can that be true?'

Orc and Emilia shared glances. 'They aren't coming back,' Orc whispered. 'I had to get Cass out.'

'And the others,' said Emilia.

'It would be too dangerous for them, after what the Abbot said.'

'But… Hann is with them,' said Tashi, shocked.

'He wanted to leave too,' said Emilia. 'He came and talked to us when you were with Rukhan.'

Tashi closed his eyes.

'If he hadn't gone with them, Cass wouldn't have got away,' said Orc. 'And her safety's more important to me than anything. If you need something to believe, try that.'

Tashi nodded. 'I did want to see Aino again, but I had a feeling I might not. You must tell the Abbot now, about everything. He will need time to gather his courage.'

Orc glanced at Emilia, who nodded. 'Okay.'

Tashi turned and walked from the chamber. The novitiate called Shikar motioned to another boy, who followed Tashi out.

'Come with me,' Shikar said to Orc and Emilia. With two other novitiates, he escorted them through the maze of the building to the Abbot's audience chamber. The Abbot sat behind his desk, elbows on its surface as though he lacked the strength to hold himself upright. Rukhan stood beside him. The novitiates stationed themselves.

The Abbot asked at first about the failure of the air-craft to return. Despite the temptation to suggest possible mechanical problems, Orc braced himself and told the truth. Rukhan's verbal fury hit him like a wall of fire, but he stood his ground. All he gave as explanation was that if the Watchers hadn't showed such hostility on their arrival, he wouldn't have needed to play the trick.

Rukhan went to stand at one of the windows that looked south over the lower world. The Abbot spoke: 'So you have deprived yourself of the Watcher you thought might have vouched for you. Or was it always that you knew he would not?'

'Holiness,' said Emilia, 'my brother will arrive tomorrow at ten. By then, the Conclave must verify that he means to attack. You must base your plans on what they say. Our guilt or innocence has no bearing on it.'

'Unless you have altered Records to reflect what you wish it to.' Rukhan turned, voice taut with suppressed anger. 'After the trickery you've just confessed, we would be mad not to expect further falsehood.'

'If we're capable of changing Records,' said Orc, 'we would've hidden what happened at the air-field, wouldn't we?'

'Unless you left that unchanged to give the impression you could not change them, and so perpetrate the greater deceit—'

'Oh, for God's sake—'

'Rukhan,' said the Abbot. 'If these two are capable of changing Records such that the Conclave cannot tell, then we were always lost. I do not believe them so capable, and their trickery with the air-craft is understandable in the circumstances.' He took off his spectacles and rubbed the lenses, his naked eyes amid folded skin looking more tired than before. 'We must, then, plan what to do in the event of Tashi being proved correct. What he said is right: we cannot hide our heads and hope the storm will pass over us.'

'Twenty-four Inspired novitiates will still be a match for the Prelate's "storm",' said Rukhan.

'You can't rely on that,' said Emilia. 'Siegfried might shoot the novitiates from his air-craft before his men occupy the plateau. I wouldn't be surprised if he's hoping to find them all lined up on the Knifebridge to greet him.'

A ball of sickness tried to punch its way up Orc's throat. He hadn't thought of that.

'Gevurah,' said Rukhan. 'You cannot accuse your brother of such an intent!'

'You have to plan for it.'

'And yet every visitor – every *permitted* visitor – has been greeted by the novitiates standing the Knifebridge. To do otherwise would be an insult. He mentioned it in his telegram.'

'Indeed, he did so,' said the Abbot. 'On his last visit there was some lack of discipline. He expressed a hope of seeing better this time.'

'I bet he did,' growled Orc.

'And if he does not come with hostile intent,' said Rukhan, 'the insult could drive a wedge between us and the Empyreum.'

'Hostile intent will have been proven or otherwise by then,' said the

Abbot. 'And if Tashi's claims are verified, then what?' he asked Emilia. 'You think the novitiates should simply hide from him?'

'Wait in concealment, yes.'

'Better they die on the bridge with honour,' growled Rukhan, 'than sully themselves with cowardice.'

Orc glanced at Shikar's expressionless face.

'Rukhan,' said the Abbot, 'I will not allow that.'

'The foundation of this monastery is the bravery of those youths,' said Rukhan, 'their pure courage in the face of death, their willingness to sacrifice. I could accept concealment with the aim of ambushing a force equipped with firearms, but not with the aim of avoiding harm. And neither would they.'

'There is no hope in fighting,' said Emilia. 'What you gain by keeping the novitiates hidden is the chance to parley. Without the threat of armed resistance, Siegfried will have no reason to use force. Instead, I'm sure he'll want to talk to you about surrender, and probably about where the novitiates are hiding. And when he does, you can turn him from an enemy to an ally, as happened with Konstantin.'

The Abbot looked confused. 'But Konstantin agreed that the Orb of Archive should remain hidden. You claim your brother wishes to acquire it.'

Orc frowned, sure he'd heard the name *Orb of Archive* before. But no one had called it that in the Court of Welcome.

'I believe so,' said Emilia.

'We cannot allow that. There is no basis for parley.'

'But I believe his desire for this "Orb" has been brought about through manipulation,' said Emilia. 'Prove this to him, and I'm sure he will turn against his manipulators, who are also your chief enemies, did you but know it.' Her voice sounded more nervous as she was coming to what Orc knew would be the big revelation.

'Our chief enemies?' said the Abbot.

'Those magicians who wear Empyreus as a mask to direct the Kurassian empire.'

The Thangkarans stared at her as if cast in stone.

'You had better expand on that,' said the Abbot at last.

'This is a trap,' said Rukhan. 'They know it is exactly what we wish to hear, that worship of Empyreus is false.'

'But it fits what we always believed to be true, and could not prove,' said the Abbot. 'Lady Emilia, please tell us more.'

'I know little. We call them the Shining Ones, but what their true name is, we have no idea. They keep themselves well hidden. But this must be the second goal of the Conclave, to prove this claim. I know my brother. He needs to think himself his own man; he will not stand to have been made the secret tool of others. I tried to convince him yesterday, but he didn't believe me. Prove our claim about Empyreus, and Siegfried will have no reason to attack you. He will ally with you to expose the magicians – it will be in his own interest, as he will no longer be constrained to follow the rules of the God-Head and will gain more power for himself.'

Like we need that, thought Orc. But first things first.

'If he were coming because of the ultimatum about the divinity of Empyreus, that would make sense,' said the Abbot. 'But how does it fit with your claim that he wishes to gain the Orb of Archive?'

'Empyreus must have subtly driven him to that goal over the years, and once Siegfried realises his path is not his own, why would he continue it?'

'You think these "Shining Ones" wish your brother to gain this power?'

'It makes sense,' said Orc. 'Did Tashi tell you about Daroguerre, who manifested Skalith? We know the Shining Ones were behind him – we found records of secret conversations. But maybe they don't have all the power the Zhenaii did. Maybe they want the Prelate to gain that knowledge for their own use.'

The two monks were silent, thinking. Then Rukhan faced Orc and said, 'Answer me this. I take it you do not deny that the Witch Mother is your mistress?'

Orc's stomach plummeted. But he was the Sun-King. He pulled himself erect. 'I serve the Goddess, yes.'

Rukhan's nostrils flared minutely. 'And how do you serve her here? You cannot be ignorant of the risk you ran in coming here, even had the Prelate not sent his telegram. And with so great a risk, I cannot believe that exposure of these rival magicians was your sole objective. It might have served your unholy mistress to drive a wedge between us and the Empyreum, but how could it serve her for us to persuade the Prelate? Why does the Witch Mother's servant seek to save us from destruction, when our destruction would surely have been in her interest?'

'Why does she have to be the one to gain something?' said Orc. 'I'm my own person as well. I count Tashi a friend, and this is his home. And these magicians have made my life hell. You think I wanted to be able to manifest? It's almost got me killed a couple of times. The only reason I can do it is because the Shining Ones changed me somehow. That's how they work. They use people however they like, and they'll use the whole world too – and that's why the Goddess gains if we expose them, because they're worse for her than you are. You might have a warped view of nature, but I can't see that you want to destroy it.'

'And they do? To destroy it?'

'They act like it. The north coast of the Shallow Sea is turning to desert, and that's down to them.' Or so Geist had thought. 'And they seem to feed on death, somehow – they talked about gaining some kind of energy when those two Empyreal warships went down. And now it looks like they're trying to get a war going between the Empyreum and Sundara – who knows how many will die in that? We're like insects to them. Whatever their aim is, it's not good for any of us.'

'But if they changed you, as you say,' said Rukhan, 'how do you know so little about them?'

'Because that happened before the Shroud,' said Orc. 'They've hidden all my memories from me, from before two years ago.'

'As indeed they hide their own activities, Shoggu believed,' said the Abbot. 'Would that I'd listened to him.'

'I confess,' said Rukhan, 'that although I would feel happier discounting this boy-magician's claims, there is order to the tapestry these threads weave. Several times in the centuries since the advent of

Empyreus, the Conclave has sought to probe the matter of his divinity. Always it was met with obfuscation too strong to penetrate, and many instances of dark-flight resulted. I recall Tashi's story of when Shoggu fell into dark-flight when seeking the warship *Nightfire*. Tashi suspected the magician Daroguerre, but perhaps that too was the work of these Shining Ones, if Daroguerre was under their patronage.'

'It begins to seem that Empyreus is precisely what these two claim,' said the Abbot.

'But can we act on the knowledge?' said Rukhan. 'We failed to penetrate the mystery of Empyreus when we had our full twenty-seven. What hope with fewer?'

'There's still a shield around this monastery, to stop scrying?' asked Orc.

'There is,' said Rukhan. 'Why?'

'So they won't know what I'm about to suggest.' He took a breath. 'Go through me.'

'What?'

'Going for Empyreus directly is too obvious. They must have a fortified barrier round him, and that's why it's always defeated you. But I don't believe they're actually more powerful than you – just better organised and more knowledgeable. There are only thirteen of these Shining Ones, half your number, and not all of them seem to be active. In those transcripts I mentioned, they admitted they couldn't properly get through your shield, and they couldn't get through the one around a college we stayed in. I think you should try to break through the Shroud around my memories. They made it strong enough to defeat me and my old teacher, but I don't think they'd have made it strong enough to defeat the Conclave. It would've been a waste of energy: they couldn't know I'd ever come here. They might be trying to build it up now, if they've thought of it, but that would take time. It's your best bet. The Shroud is the back door to them. Get through it, connect with them, and you can uncover their secrets.'

'An interesting possibility,' said the Abbot. 'But what proof could we get that might satisfy the Prelate? He knows we have always considered the worship of Empyreus an error.'

'But he also knows you hold untruth to be a grievous sin,' said Emilia.

'He might believe we do not know ourselves to lie, that any findings of the Conclave are the result of our prejudice. In his place, I would argue so.'

Orc sucked his teeth, thinking. 'What about those three boys Empyreus sends messages to, the Trine?' He really hoped the Shining Ones weren't able to hear this. 'If you focus on tapping the psychic channel the Shining Ones use for those messages, couldn't you send one to the Trine yourselves?'

'Even if that were possible,' said Rukhan, 'what message? Have Empyreus declare his own falsehood?'

'No,' said Emilia. 'The Trine would never even record something so clearly mistaken. But the idea is a good one, if we can find a suitable wording. Then, when you are parleying with Siegfried, you can tell him what we've done, and suggest he fly down to the telegraph station, to contact Bismark and confirm your story. I predict he'll be curious enough to at least investigate.'

'How about something like, "Someone high up in the Empyreum is not who he seems"?' said Orc. 'Only us and him would know it meant Empyreus. The Trine and the Valkensee would take it at face value.'

'Yes, that's good,' said Emilia. 'It's not watertight, but I think it stands a better chance than anything else.'

The Abbot drew in a long breath through his nostrils, then let out an even longer one. 'Would that we had a month, a year, to consider this. Would that I had thirty fewer years sitting in my bones. We must discuss this with the other Watchers. You will speak with them all later. They will want to question you, so they can prepare for the morning's Conclave as best they can.'

'Can the Conclave not be earlier than eight o'clock?' said Emilia.

'The twenty-four hour rule exists for a reason,' said the Abbot. 'And if dark-flight is indeed the result of magical defences by these Shining

Ones, all the more reason to lower its risk. I concede that with your brother arriving at ten, time will be tight, but the two hours should be enough.'

He gestured to the three novitiates, who led Orc and Emilia from the chamber. They were taken to a room off the main refectory, where they were fed and at last allowed to talk freely. After about an hour, they were summoned back to the Hall of Conclave, and made to stand in the centre of a semicircle of Watchers for questioning. The Watchers, prepared by the Abbot and their chief, wanted to know as much as Orc and Emilia could tell them about the Shining Ones. Orc held nothing back regarding the transcripts, though he couldn't recall everything he'd read in them. To his relief, they didn't press him for details about his relationship with the Goddess.

Towards the end, as dusk was falling, the Abbot revealed that he had earlier sent two of his monks down to the valley, to check for evidence of military activity. Though there had been ample time to make the journey, they had not yet returned. Kurassian hostility was no longer merely a possibility, but a likelihood.

'Then shouldn't the Orb be moved, or even destroyed?' asked one Watcher.

'Alas, it seems impervious to harm,' said the Abbot. 'No doubt because it was made with the Zhenaii power of manifestation. As for moving it, the old vaults are still more secure than any part of this newer building, and High Place is where I shall send the novitiates, if you confirm the Prelate's intent. They will then be in the right place to defy him, if he proves impossible to persuade.'

Orc and Emilia were separated, Emilia being taken to lodge with the nursemaids to the infant boys, and Orc up to High Place, whose habitable parts were still used by the Watchers. Shikar and two younger novitiates led him to an unused monk's cell, where he settled on a mattress away from the door, hoping to sleep. Shikar sat by the door-curtain with his lantern; the two younger ones stationed themselves in the corridor outside, where they chatted in low voices.

It grew cold, but Shikar made no move to light the fire-pit. Orc wrapped himself in the blankets he could find, trying to ignore the musty odours. There were a few personal effects in the room and others visible past a curtain in an adjoining alcove, which he guessed meant the cell was normally inhabited. It presumably belonged to Yaggit, Murun or Shoggu. Probably not the first, since Yaggit was still alive. Logically it would be the second, since Tashi would have told the Abbot that neither Murun nor his novitiate would ever be returning. But his instinct was otherwise. Murun and Paiko had fallen in the pure service of the monastery: their cell would be kept clean, not soiled with the presence of a servant of the Goddess.

'This was Shoggu and Tashi's cell,' he said.

Shikar's suspicious look confirmed his guess.

'Where you are now, is that where Tashi slept?'

'That was before.'

'Shouldn't he be here?' said Orc. 'If this was his room, maybe he wants to sleep here.'

'It is his no longer.'

'So he can't be made a novitiate again? Even if it's what he most wants?'

'*You* care what happens to him?' scoffed Shikar. 'His fate is your doing. You distort and warp things. You belong to the Witch Mother. Now quiet. No more talking.'

Orc sank into thought. He couldn't see why Tashi would want to go back to living with such people, but it wasn't his business. The fact was that all Tashi wanted was his normal body back and his master and his home and his routine – and he deserved all that, for the near-impossible courage he'd shown in playing the dreadful hand he'd been dealt. It made Orc flinch to think how badly he'd failed the boy who'd offered him his service that night in Bismark. All his promises at the college, and at Crome's house, had turned to nothing. Tashi wasn't the easiest person to help, so prickly and difficult and with his strange way of looking at things, but if there had been a way to help him, they should have done it.

And maybe it wasn't too late. Cass would be far away by now and heading for safety, and it was time to switch his priorities. The fate of Shoggu's soul still clearly worried Tashi, and it sounded like the Abbot wasn't prepared to help. But maybe he could make good on his earlier promise. His marriage had arrested his uncontrolled slide into madness. Perhaps now he could approach the Otherworld without risk.

There was no point thinking up some pretext for Shikar to leave – the edgy novitiate hadn't even let him piss in private. It would have to be done in full view. Trying to call up his tattoo-mask would likely give Shikar an excuse to put a sword through him, but from what Otter had said after his 'nuptials', he might not need the mask any more. The Little Death, too, he might be able to work without. The Goddess was the Serpent Mandala, in some sense; his marriage effectively superseded his Initiation.

He near-closed his eyes and carefully reached under his shirt to grasp his focus-stone. The Little Death had been necessary because he'd never been good at meditation. But the earliest forms of the Goddess reached back to before language, and as he relaxed his mind, he found it easier now to still its distracting chatter. He drew on Geist's old lessons, observed the thoughts that arose, gently guided them away until his mind was empty of words and pictures and his awareness was all on the breath.

After ten minutes, he was disturbed by the arrival of another novitiate. 'Nandi,' said Shikar. 'Is anything wrong?'

'Thought you might want some company,' said the newcomer, kneeling. 'And some help, just in case.'

'Yes, good,' said Shikar. 'Watch him closely. Gevurah knows what he'll try.'

'They say he had to rant for a while before the air-field abomination,' said Nandi. 'As soon as he starts that, we'll deal with him.'

Shikar drew three inches of blade. 'I don't trust his quietness.'

'You told me to be quiet,' muttered Orc.

'Then shut up!' ordered Shikar. 'Do you think someone ought to be kept ready for Inspiration?' he asked Nandi.

'All our masters are busy,' said the other youth. 'And don't worry, the Witch Mother has no power here. If we guard so well against even her subtlest corruptions, how will she corrupt physical matter? She could only do so in Bismark because the Kurassians lack mental discipline.'

Maybe so, thought Orc. He'd barely sensed the Goddess's presence since his arrival at Highcloud, and Nandi's words suggested why. Even if he had brought her with him, she was weak here, having power only over those who believed it. Even though the Kurassians wanted to separate themselves from her, they knew and feared that even in the city, they were in her domain – it was that belief that had enabled Orc to raise her at the air-field. But Highcloud held itself above the lower world, its inhabitants convinced of their discipline's effectiveness.

She didn't belong here, and neither did he. At his back he felt the obligation, the psychic force built up through hundreds of previous Sun-Kings, to declare himself for her, to act as her warrior and her prophet at every opportunity. But the Sun-Kings of the past had lived surrounded by those who believed in her, in the country of her strength. His own circumstances made him feel horribly vulnerable.

He tried to clear his mind of those thoughts while the two novitiates talked about the Prelate's possible attack, and when they'd fallen silent, he resumed meditation. This time, he maintained an awareness that it was Shoggu's pallet on which he sat, Shoggu's blankets wrapped around him in musty-smelling warmth. He steeped his thoughts in the idea of the dead monk – who he'd never met, but had helped bury – and reached his mind towards the Mandala, in which all was one.

When he was ready, he mentally called, *Otter*.

The bottom of the door-curtain both moved and stayed still, two realities as one through his near-closed eyes. The half-solid presence of his animath, unmasked again, crept in and round the novitiates.

'Crowded in here, bruv. Take a wander?'

Orc shut his eyes now, wholly entering the world of imagination. The novitiates paid him no attention as Otter led him out into the corridor. The two younger boys were playing a game with counters.

Farther along, a breach in the wall, made by cannon-shot during Konstantin's first assault, let them out onto open ground.

'Didn't want to say it in front of your friends, but this is a hard, cruel home they've got,' said Otter. 'That stream down there is like being punched with icicles. And no fish! Your new missus isn't much for this place, I'm guessing.'

'I think you guess right. But listen, I need to find Shoggu's soul. Or at least learn where it ended up.'

'That didn't go too well in that basement.'

'No,' agreed Orc. 'And I can't use Eel again. But I can approach the Serpent Mandala safely now, yes? Sparrow said I could if I was the Goddess's consort.'

'All I know is I'm meant to keep people away from that snaky craziness, not egg them on to flirt with it. It's how we met!'

'I know.'

'I pulled you back from it.'

'But things change. Like we don't have to use masks any more.'

'Which is good, I'll grant,' said Otter. 'Masks are only ever made to conceal. But if you start off towards those dancing snakes, you'll have to leave me behind. And that'd be cruel hard.'

'But if not the Mandala, how can I find Shoggu's soul?'

Otter looked over to the right. 'Maybe ask that guy.'

And old, shaven-headed man in the yellow scarf of a Watcher stood on a rise twenty paces away, staring out over the downwards slope. He turned at Orc's approach. Orc had never seen Tashi's master's face, and indeed it wasn't clear now, but he sensed the connection with the pallet he physically occupied.

'Shoggu?'

The monk bowed his head.

'I mean, the real Shoggu? His actual soul? Not a ghost made up of memories of him?'

'How could I, or you, prove one thing or the other?' said the Watcher.

Good point. He'd been stupid not to think of that and explain it to Tashi, right at the start. But that didn't absolve him of his promise.

'Tashi asked me to pass on a message.' Crome's house seemed weeks ago. 'He asked if you could come to him in dreams. If you could be his guide.'

'I am no longer the guide he requires,' said Shoggu. 'You must help him.'

'I thought I was, by finding you. What else should I do?'

'Not fail him as all his other fathers have failed him.'

Not this again. 'He just looks a bit like me. I can't be his father, I'm barely older than him.'

'And I am too much older,' said Shoggu, 'and in truth can never have fathered any child. But responsibility falls where it falls. I failed him by being too old and too weak. You failed him by refusing his offer of service. The Lord Gevurah failed him by His absence.'

The silence afterwards seemed to suggest a missing fourth in the list. Orc sensed he was connecting with things Shoggu had given much thought to, sitting or lying on his pallet, perhaps in wakeful nights observing Tashi asleep across the cell.

'What about his real father?' A shiver crossed his shoulders, as though he'd struck a nerve in the psychosphere. 'Who were his parents?'

'They lived in the lower world.'

'So how did he come here? Did they give him up for adoption? Did they die?'

Cold shocked up Orc's arm as Shoggu grabbed his wrist. The dead Watcher's face swam before him. 'I...' Shoggu gasped. 'I was sent, when the Abbot of the time learned of the child. The ability valuable in a novitiate often runs true. And his birth-father was one of the most able ever to serve Highcloud.'

'His dad was from here?'

Shoggu let go of him, turned away and began to walk along the edge of the old monastery wall.

'Where are you going?' asked Orc, following.

'To where secrets are buried.'

At Orc's feet, Otter huffed a laugh. 'Bad luck if you've had enough of secrets, bruv.'

They came to the top of a flight of steps leading into the ground. At the bottom was a strong-looking metal-faced door.

'The vaults?' said Orc.

'Wait,' said Shoggu. The door opened, and a figure emerged, a tall novitiate aged about twenty. He shut the door behind him and climbed the steps, anger bristling in a face that Orc thought he recognised.

Ranga?

No, he realised in a moment, though there was a similarity. Then his attention fixed on an object clenched in the novitiate's fist, like a stone carrot that protruded either side of his grip.

'What's that spike thing he's holding?' But the figure had faded before reaching the top of the steps.

'Now I understand,' said Shoggu. 'He kept it hidden from me, but that must have been the source of my nightmares.'

Something pricked Orc's memory – to do with reading a book, or some papers – but nothing more came. 'Is this important for Tashi? About his father? I assume this isn't something he knows already?'

'I failed him in that, as in so much else,' said Shoggu. 'I wanted him to build the life I had stolen from him. But his courage was too great to let him run into safety.' He turned to Orc. 'And so he has returned here. This is the place of the father. For him, and for you.'

Orc didn't like the switch in focus. 'My father's dead, far as I know. And I'm fine with that. I don't need another.'

'You have one nonetheless.'

'If you mean your god, he isn't mine.'

'Is that what you think?' said Shoggu, and faded to nothing.

'Great...'

'These monks have to be enigmatic,' said Otter. 'It's in their terms of service.'

'We were meant to be talking about Tashi's dad. Why did he have to start on about mine?'

'Why indeed?' said Otter. 'Maybe he thinks yours is important, and not just to you.'

Orc didn't like the sound of that. 'So when he said "this is the place of the father", did he mean I can connect with the truth about mine here?' He hadn't given any thought to it since the day before. 'Or you can?'

'I don't know anything about your sire. Wouldn't know where to start.'

'You were the one who told me he died. If my seven years started then, I ought to know when that was.'

'Ah, that,' said Otter. 'I recall saying it, but I can't get back to the inspiring of it.'

'Maybe it was a mistake, then,' said Orc, hopeful. 'It doesn't seem fair otherwise. It should be seven years from when I agreed to be Sun-King. That's how it worked in ancient times.'

'You want more life, bruv. Understandable in one so young. But maybe there were factors at work you're not aware of.'

'Like what?'

'I can't tell now!' said Otter. 'What I spoke back then was prophecy. And you won't get anything like that from me here. Too far from the source. If you're after rare fish, you need to hunt in their home waters.'

'The source? Meaning what?'

'Whatever made my brain-whiskers twitch back then, it came from behind the black wall.'

'That big round one? The one the Shroud turned into in my scape on the island?'

'How should I know about that? You went along on that jaunt without me.'

'But when you told me about my dad, it was because of that wall?' He'd glimpsed it after his marriage. 'It was near there. I saw it.'

'Near in thought, yes,' said Otter. 'If you tried to walk it, you'd be a while.'

Orc looked out over the lower world. *Her* world. 'I need to know how much time I have. What if my dad died almost seven years ago? I won't have a chance to work out how to use her power against the Kaybees. Or how to relate to her, person to person.' He recalled the face he'd glimpsed as the sea-life dispersed, and at Crome's house. The face that had something of Cass in it, but wasn't Cass.

'You want to reduce the dancy snakes and all existence to a *person*?'

'Eventually, sure.'

'Heesh,' exhaled Otter. 'You wouldn't be the first to try.'

'But first, I want to help Tashi. After this thing's over, I'll ask if he wants to find his real parents, and if he does, we'll help him, yes?' He looked around for the doorway Tashi's father had come from, the door to the vaults, but couldn't find it again. The voices of Shikar and Nandi began to intrude, discussing the possibility of battle, and the way in which they would each prefer to die.

38

ELEMENTS

From the moment they lifted off from Highcloud, Cass's tired mind was wholly focused on Windbags and Max's instructions, with no spare energy to think about anything else. After perhaps twenty minutes, the craft underwent a sequence of direction changes so abrupt she wondered if they'd become lost, and then Max guided her to ground, the portholes showing a narrow rocky valley with a stream running through it. As soon as he declared they were down safely, Cass dismissed the elemental and sagged with weariness.

Max switched off the airscrews and dropped down to the lower level. Cass struggled after and followed him to join the others, who had already disembarked.

Hann, appearing a little ill, leaned against the hull as though mistrusting his balance. 'Why have we come down so soon?' he asked Max. 'I thought—' He stopped, uncertain.

'Why the surprise?' said Dinah. 'Aren't you here to make sure we find your colleagues?'

'Don't tease him,' said Cass, and addressed Hann. 'We're going to tell Yaggit the situation, that's all. And then you want to carry on out of here, correct?'

'Isn't that your plan too?' he said, suspicious. 'Isn't that what you were arranging?'

'It's what Em and Orc arranged *for* us,' said Dinah. 'For our safety.'

'They were right,' said Hann. 'We all risk death if we go back there. And I've risked it often enough on the Knifebridge. If anyone is having second thoughts, I'd rather fight you than hundreds of soldiers.'

'You're not worried about leaving your comrades?' said Cass. Max and Dinah looked at her, as if to puzzle out her motivation. 'I'm just interested.'

'My master often tells me how lucky I was to pass my Rite of Acceptance,' said Hann, 'how my mind ranges beyond what he calls its "proper course". If it comes to a fight, who knows if the Lords of Holy Battle will inhabit me? I think they won't. I'll be left like a calf among warring bulls. I came to the monastery too late. I was nine. It's not my real home, and I won't be slaughtered for it. And what will talking to Yaggit achieve? They won't be able to get to the monastery, not through those men.'

'Men?' said Cass.

'A military camp near the foot of the Petitioners Road,' said Max. 'Astrasis's guards regiment, I assume.'

'Hundreds of soldiers,' said Hann.

'Hence us setting down here,' said Max. 'I had to give the impression we were flying on, then I doubled us back at low level. We're five miles or so from the village. Any closer, and we'd risk being seen.'

'What do we do?' said Dinah.

'Fuck it.' Cass sat on the fold-down stair. 'Are we really going to just leave them there? Orc and Emilia?'

'Yes,' said Hann.

'It is what they wanted,' said Max. 'Could we help them if we *were* there?'

'No,' said Hann.

'That was Orc's argument,' said Cass. 'He even said Yaggit wouldn't be able to help him. But can that really be true?' She hissed between her teeth. 'What I know for sure is that if he dies, I'm going to be furious with him for the rest of my life. And that's something I can do without.'

'Fury is an emotion,' said Hann. 'You can be trained to calm it. Even as a woman.'

'What if we pick up Yaggit and Aino and fly them up to the monastery, at least?' said Dinah. 'We can drop them there, and see how things are from the craft. We could take straight off again if necessary. How could they stop us?'

'An Inspired novitiate with a *clathma* could immobilise this craft in moments,' said Hann.

'And how long would it take to Inspire one?' said Cass. 'I bet it's not instant.'

His resentful face confirmed it.

'Settled, then,' said Dinah. 'Five miles to the village: a couple of hours?' She buttoned her coat. 'We can be back before dark and nip straight back to Highcloud.'

'No,' said Hann. 'I know what'll happen. You lack any resolve. Sentiment will rout sense. You'll go back to Highcloud and stay, and we'll all die. Get back in the craft. Now.'

No one moved.

'I had an agreement with your Deaconess. If I aided your escape, you'd take me with you. Rukhan wouldn't have let your craft leave without me.'

His sword scraped as he drew it.

Shit, thought Cass. She backed up the steps, trying to think what might be in the air-craft that would help.

'Hann, put up that weapon,' said Dinah, with what Cass thought incredible coolness.

'I told you all to get back in the craft!' He pointed the sword's tip towards Max. He was only a lunge away, Cass was scared to see.

'You did,' said Max. 'And we haven't. What now?'

'This isn't right! You played me false.' He glanced between Max and Dinah, as if judging which of them could be seized as hostage.

'Hann,' said Cass, struggling to sound calm. 'You wanted to get to the lower world. We've brought you here. You're free. Go.' *Please, just go.*

'You don't understand!' he said. 'I need someone to show me how to live down here. Our masters don't prepare us. They throw us out at twenty-one, and Gevurah abandons us. We hear of some who return when they tire of misery and climb the mountain in secret and never come down again. That's not going to happen to me.'

Max reached into his inside jacket pocket. 'Not a weapon!' he said as Hann took a half-step towards him. 'Take this money: it should be enough to keep you going for a while.'

'I don't know how to use money!'

'Then learn,' said Max. 'What choice is there? If you kill or injure one of us, do you think we'll meekly obey you afterwards? Cass and I are both needed to fly the craft. How will you keep us from turning the tables on you? Will you never need to sleep?'

The boy considered this, his face growing increasingly fraught. 'Give it me, then, if you're so determined to die. I'll take my chances.'

Max tossed the wad of notes at Hann's feet. The novitiate grabbed them, tore off his red headband and threw it down, and turned and ran up the slope to the east.

Cass breathed freely at last, her legs weak with relief. 'How were you two so calm about all that?'

'I judged him more scared than dangerous,' said Max. They watched Hann vanish over the crest. 'We'd better get going.'

'Shouldn't we leave a guard on the craft?' said Dinah.

'Who, though?' said Cass.

'You,' she said. 'You need to rest, anyone can see that. And Max told Hann a fib, didn't he? You don't need him. Perhaps you can't do such fine manoeuvring alone, but the elemental can move side-to-side as well as up and down.'

'It's a good point,' said Max. 'If soldiers discover the craft, you at least stand a chance of getting it away. I suggest you watch from that ridge. It looks to give a good view over the approaches from the west.'

Cass nodded and tried to ignore her dread.

* * *

She climbed the ridge, about a quarter-mile from the craft, and watched Max and Dinah make their way downslope towards distant trees that presumably marked the village.

There was no food. That morning, before setting off for Highcloud, they'd eaten what they'd haggled from a remote farmstead. There hadn't been enough even then, but they'd expected to reach other habitation by tonight. She could last that long, at least.

But lack of food and lack of movement worsened the cold. Shivering even in her coat, teeth chattering, she walked around, hugging herself and stamping her feet. Eventually she had to give up her watch position on the ridge, with its bone-chill fingers of wind, and return to the craft. But the cold seeped through the hull to its interior, her clothes, her skin. She muttered to Max and Dinah, willing them to hurry back, to bring Yaggit and Aino and food: hot food, somehow kept warm. Cloud hid the sun, and time passed unmeasured. All she knew was that it was still daylight. Until, gradually, it wasn't, and a sickening worry grew to fill her empty stomach. She braved the ridge once more, stayed there for half an hour as dusk encroached. Then, barely able to see where she put her feet, she made her way back to the dark hull and, with effort, pulled the door up behind her and battered away the urge to cry.

It got colder still, and still no Max, and still no Dinah. She shivered so hard she wondered if she would survive the night. She should never have come here. She should have just said no, told Orc and his concern and his goddess to fuck off. He'd foxed her because at bottom she'd been afraid of staying. And it hadn't even saved her; instead it had brought her to where she was doomed to shiver to death, and serve her right for being so gutless.

No, that was crap. She had guts, and she had brains. She had to use them now.

It was hard to think when she was so cold, but her life might depend on it. She needed fire. There was petroleum fuel in the tanks, probably somewhere in the wings near the airscrew engines; but she couldn't access it and had no means of lighting it. There was cordite in the starting charges; but even if that wasn't too dangerous, she had no means of getting it out without tools, and even if the tools were somewhere on board, it was too dark to find them.

If only the craft were somehow powered by a fire elemental, like *Nightfire*. She remembered the roasting heat of the ship's rearmost boiler room as though it were the greatest bliss.

No, that wasn't helping. She shook the diversion from her mind—

And glimpsed an idea.

She hardly dared probe it, afraid scrutiny might crumble it to dust. When she'd first summoned Windbags, she'd intuited the idea of a whole block of index-cards fused together, a mass of psychosphere connections that facilitated the elemental's conjuring. Who'd fused that block of cards in the first place? What if the fact that the crystal summoned an air elemental wasn't down to anything inherent in the stone itself, but was down to the connections in the cards to which the stone was linked? She'd seen no difference between the air-craft's crystal and *Nightfire*'s.

Index-card references could be obscured – the Shroud around her memories proved it. Could they also be overwritten?

Oh, God, this was just fantasy. The implications would be enormous.

But what if it were true?

She groped her way up to the engineer deck, and in near-total darkness felt her way to the crystal, and settled there with her hand on it. She kept her mind quiet, and made no thought towards calling or summoning anything. Instead, she envisaged a cabinet of cards, flicking through them, thousands upon thousands. It was the first time she'd tried this literal imagining of Ferman's metaphor. She visualised the connections, a blur of catalogue numbers. This was all it was: data. In the same way that magicians and shamans used Otherworld entities to collate and interpret uncountable atoms of knowledge, she would use this much safer metaphor of card and ink.

Deeper and deeper. Information. She had the sense this was something she'd once been good at. Manipulating information. Deeper and deeper.

In her mind's eye, she came across a card with a picture on it.

The image moved. Her sense of the picture was so fragile, she hardly dared breathe. Across a featureless plain walked a man made of crystal, his body all shades of oranges and reds and browns and greens, his head blue, the jaw of his stern face edged with a beard as hard as the rest of him. She had the strangest feeling that he had some connection with her.

The crystal man walked, and the landscape never changed, never gained definition. He was searching, Cass realised. Just as the image faded, she saw him raise a crystal hand, and in response a large round hill rose up from the distant plain. *The Hollow Isles*, she thought, not knowing if that was important.

What was important were the crystals. The blue focus-stones, and the elemental stones. His head, and his body.

Did that bizarre metaphor of the crystal man hold value for her? Perhaps. It made sense that the blue focus-stones, which connected with the mental psychosphere, came from the man's head. And if the earth-coloured crystals were elemental stones, related to what made up the physical world, then it made sense that they came from his body.

But it made no sense to differentiate between different parts of that body. Why should a crystal from part of an arm be related to fire, but one from a leg to water, or a rib to earth? Her intuition was that she'd been right, that the type of elemental was a product of the index cards, not the crystal itself.

She called up her most vivid memory of *Nightfire*'s Mister Burns.

Her life might depend on her making this work.

It was only an hour later that she stopped shivering. Hunger was also easier to bear now she was warm. The flickering light gave even the craft's interior a homely feel, and the small elemental's shifting shape fascinated her, with its suggestion of faces of flame.

Her creation.

In its way, it was a greater achievement than first calling Windbags.

She might in time be able to do almost anything, re-index the psychosphere wholesale: scour out Orc's jealous goddess, free him. Maybe wipe out the evidence of the air-field, all that. Trap the Kaybees behind a shield of her own making.

But there was no one to tell, to show. At the moment, it was just a way to avoid freezing.

Her focus was broken by a noise somewhere in the craft.

'Dinah? Max?' She turned, but no light showed in the hatchway to the lower deck.

The sound came again: the creak of the metal ladder. A head—

Hann—

She scooted round to the other side of the elemental's glyph-circle. The disruption let the thing free and plunged the craft into darkness.

'What do you want?' Her voice came out sharp with fear, Esteban's attempted assault on her on the island fresh in her mind.

'I mean no harm,' Hann said. 'I saw firelight. I'm cold.'

If he came at her, she could try to call the elemental again as he crossed the circle. It would probably be Windbags – it had taken half an hour of careful searching to find a route to the fire elemental – but raging air would injure him just as readily.

'You should be miles away,' she said. 'There's nothing here for you. When the others come, we're going back to Highcloud.'

'I know,' he said. 'So am I.'

'You've changed your mind?'

In the silence that followed she held her breath to listen, thinking he might be making his way towards her. Esteban had overpowered her struggles with ease, and Hann was a trained warrior.

The darkness spoke. He hadn't moved. 'It was seeing those soldiers down below. I couldn't stop wondering which of those ants would be the one to kill Nandi, or Genku.' He paused. 'That's all.'

His words made her swallow. She felt herself in his place. 'I understand,' she said. 'In the end, we have less choice than we think.'

'We have the choice,' he said. 'But Gevurah reminds us of our true road.'

Or something does. Always. 'I don't know much about your Lords of Holy Battle,' she said, 'but I'm sure they won't refuse to come to someone who made the decision you just did.'

At first there was no response, and she wondered if he'd thought her attempt at sympathy inappropriate. If so, fuck him. Then the darkness cracked in a series of horrible half-choked sobs, which sounded to her like the cries of babies being strangled at birth.

When he'd overcome his emotion, she rasped, 'Go.'

'Hn?'

'You won't make enough difference.' But that was what Orc had said to her. 'Go and learn the lower world. Become someone's lover. Don't be one of those who crawl back to die in the snow. You don't need training, just courage and wits, and you've got those.'

'No.' Even that one word seemed to come with difficulty. 'Please, don't say any more. I won't come near you. I'll stay here. It's warm enough.'

Cass hung her head. She couldn't take on another burden, she just couldn't. To save him felt as crushing a weight as saving the world. She didn't even know him. It was too much. People died all the time, even children, and there was nothing to say he *would* die, nothing to say there would even be a battle. She was losing perspective.

The silence was unbearable. 'Hann?'

'We shouldn't talk.' His voice came unsteady. 'We must not – where it could lead – I must remain pure.'

'What, you think I meant…? Don't be stupid.'

Silence returned. Stretched. It felt like it was mocking them, mocking the way they let it drag on even though they were both afraid, the way they shared this fear but let themselves be separated. Cass swallowed the saliva that had pooled in her mouth. 'Tell me about Tashi.'

'What has he not told you himself?'

'We haven't talked much,' she said, and the memory of why that was pricked the backs of her eyes. 'To be honest, I haven't always been fair to him…'

It loomed over her, the last few days: the grief and the misery, this darkness, this hunger. 'God, Hann—' And he had a name, this boy who was scared he was going to be killed. Her diaphragm pushed, making her breath spasm. Her throat closed up. 'This is so stupid. I don't even know you.'

She put her face in her hands and broke down in sobbing, too weary to fight it. The horror and sadness pushed to get out of her, but there was always more to replace it, and there always would be. As her tears began to exhaust themselves, she sensed him crawling cautiously but not with stealth along the deck. If she was going to tell him to back off, it had to be now.

'Wait,' she said.

He stopped. 'I didn't know how to help. Do you still want me to talk about Tashi?'

'No,' she said. 'Talk about you.'

'What do—'

'Just talk, Hann. Make me laugh.'

'I don't know what would make a woman laugh.'

'You really think we're so different?'

'I've spent the last few years rather hoping so.'

She felt a moment of shock, of awareness, and then she laughed. She laughed harder than she knew the joke deserved, but she couldn't help it. Encouraged, Hann started to talk, and from initial awkwardness his voice relaxed, as though he'd forgotten that the next morning might be his last, and Cass laughed at his stories about his fellow novitiates and their pranks and accidents, as though she might have only a day left in which to laugh about anything. With each pause, it seemed Hann's voice started again from a few inches nearer, until he was just the other side of the glyph-circle, and at no point had she asked him to stay back.

'It's getting cold again,' she said, when his stories seemed to have run dry. 'I can't summon the elemental, not if I'm to sleep.'

She waited, heart thumping, for him to think. 'I could keep you warm,' he said, nerves clear in his voice.

She almost rolled her eyes. But he was brave as well as nervous, and handsome enough, and something reminded her a little of—

Recognition broke a laugh from her.

'What is it?' he said.

'Uniforms,' she said. 'What is it about uniforms?'

'Uhm… sorry?'

'Nothing.' She knew now she was going to. Damn it, damn everything. Maybe it could even save him, and it wasn't much of a cost, and she wanted to know what it was like and for the finding out to not be weighted with world-shattering significance. Easy, Orc had said. Nice.

'Let's warm each other.' She scooted across to find him in the dark.

His arms around her were tentative at first, but firmed up as she burrowed into the heat of his hold. Slightly crushing. She didn't expect much: this would be his first time, and any experience of her own that might be useful was locked behind the Shroud. The important thing was to stick a finger up to the world and its battles and its dying. And not get pregnant.

In the end, the reality of sex wasn't far from what she'd expected. Hann was warm at least, and considerate, and his muscles were firm, and they laughed a bit. And now, perhaps, she didn't have to fear for him, and she could sleep. Except she didn't, and neither did he. It felt in that silence as if no one in the world would ever sleep again: all would lie dead still in wakeful thought, waiting for who knew what.

As the mist beyond the porthole greyed with dawn, they sat by the fire elemental, which Cass had roused again to a size small enough to not need her full focus. She sensed Hann working up to something. When he said he had to go outside for a while, she guessed it wasn't just to relieve himself.

'To pray?'

He hesitated, then said, 'To purify myself. I'll use the stream.'

It was what she'd planned for, but too baldly stated. 'I'm not some *disease.*'

'No, of course not,' he said in alarm. 'The body isn't inherently evil, not even… well, that. But you must understand, the Lords of Holy Battle can't come to me as I now am.'

'You're right,' she said. 'And scrubbing yourself in a stream isn't going to change that. What we've done, that changes you forever. You understand? You're a lower-worlder now. Didn't you like it? Don't you want to do it again? At some point?'

He kept his gaze on where the elemental had been. It had gone.

'Nothing in the body is evil,' he said. 'But the flesh acts as a conduit for the influence of the Witch Mother, and that influence mustn't override the will. Her influence is never so subtle as when it comes in wanting comfort.'

'Highcloud's teachings. You said it wasn't your real home.'

'It's the only one I know.'

She pressed her lip between her teeth. 'People make new homes. They won't have you now, the Lords of Battle. You'll never be sure. And you know what happens if you call them in and there's a trace of doubt in you? That's what turned Tashi into a monster.'

He stood.

'Don't!' she said as he made his way to the ladder. 'What's wrong with you people? Why does everyone want to *die?*'

It maddened her that what she'd done for him might prove pointless in the face of his religious bloody-mindedness. She feared for him again. Hadn't he enjoyed her enough to be changed? It hadn't been bad, as such, despite the false starts and the lubrication issue and the clumsy finishing by hand. At least he'd got an orgasm out of it. As for her, she tried not to compare it with her time in bed with Orc at the college. But she couldn't help it, and the difference in type of experience annoyed her even more, the sense that without her being aware of it, Orc had been there last night in the back of her mind, a shadow.

Hann. Hana. She chilled at the coincidence, then told her mind to shut up and got to work on recalling the elemental.

Hann returned half an hour later, wet and shivering, wearing only his breechcloth and the headband he must have retrieved from outside, carrying the rest of his uniform. No fat covered the muscles of his torso at all; he looked like a biological machine. A bit more weight would suit him well. She wanted to feel his arm muscles again.

'Did it work?' she said as he crouched on the other side of the fire, and was relieved to see doubt in his face and hear doubt in his silence. 'Why don't you go out and hunt something?' she added. She'd meant it as a joke, based on him looking like a near-naked primitive, but the time for jokes was apparently over.

Hunger dragged on. Dressed again, Hann kept urging her to take the craft back to Highcloud at once, but he had no authority and seemed to know it. They wouldn't move, Cass told him, until Max and Dinah returned. They wouldn't abandon them.

Not like she'd abandoned Orc, it seemed. But she was still tired and famished, and this at least gave her something she could grasp. Going back might not even help Orc. But staying away would help Hann, whether he wanted to be helped or not.

The Prelate was due to reach Highcloud at ten. From everything she'd seen of the Kurassians, he would be bang on time; and if he was going to attack, she imagined he would do it right away.

If she could hold out till then, she might at least save someone.

39

CONCLAVE

Orc found the Hall of Conclave bustling with preparations when Shikar and Nandi led him in. Incense fumed the air; Watchers draped in their strange feather mantles stood talking in low but animated voices; lesser monks were pushing the wooden table-platforms into a tight circle around the fire-pit. Emilia was already there, with two younger novitiates as a guard, but Tashi was not.

Just as Orc joined her, Rukhan came over, sour-faced. 'What did you say to Tashi in here yesterday?'

'Nothing much,' said Orc. 'He said you wouldn't make him a novitiate again.'

'And you used that to turn him against us?'

'Of course not!' said Emilia.

'Why are you asking?' said Orc.

'Just after dawn, he slipped his guard and cannot now be found. Do you know why? Was it because he knew his accusations against Prelate Astrasis to be false?'

No, it's because he came home a hero and you treated him like shit, Orc didn't say. The boy's absence disturbed him; there was no margin in the plan for things to go wrong.

'I can't say why he would have absconded,' said Emilia. 'But I have no doubt about his story. You don't need his presence to check its veracity, do you?'

'Connecting with the events he described would be far easier, and take less time and energy, if he were here,' said Rukhan. 'And until we have proof of your brother's hostile intent, I cannot sanction withdrawing the novitiates from the Knifebridge. It would be too grave an insult.'

Emilia looked desperate. 'But Tashi must know that. Where can he be?'

'We have ordered a search,' said Rukhan.

The Abbot had come over. 'You may leave now,' he said to the novitiates. 'Ready yourself to stand the bridge—'

'Holiness, no!' said Emilia.

'Allow me to finish,' he told her, and turned back to the youths. 'Remember: bind yourselves and wear your ceremonials over the top. If we divine that the Prelate plans to attack, I will send a message, and you will conceal yourselves in the covered parts of High Place and hold yourselves ready. If there is no such indication, you will stand as normal, and make sure your discipline is better than last time.'

'It shall be, Holiness!' said Shikar, and the novitiates left.

'Shall we wait to see if Tashi can be found?' the Abbot asked Rukhan.

'Each minute gives us less time for the Empyreus proof.'

'Hold on.' Orc turned to Emilia. 'You said yesterday your brother talked about the attack when you confronted him in his room.' He faced Rukhan. 'Can't you witness that instead?'

'Yes,' said Emilia. 'Surely?'

Rukhan nodded hesitantly. 'The connection will be weaker; she is not one of our own. But it is better than delay.'

Orc exhaled. One disaster averted; only a hundred more things that needed to go exactly to plan.

The Abbot called forward a large monk named Thu, who held what Orc assumed to be Max's pistol. 'Guard these two,' the Abbot said, and he and Rukhan went to organise the Watchers. A younger monk was going round with portable steps, and each Watcher climbed up onto his platform and settled cross-legged on the rugs there.

'I hope the others are all right,' Orc muttered to Emilia.

'They might be almost at Torrento by now,' she replied. 'I wish Tashi were here, and not just because I don't wish to be the centre of such scrutiny. What did he say yesterday, something about climbing? What could he have meant by that?'

Orc had no idea.

Preparations over, the Abbot seated himself on a high chair to the rear of the Watchers and gestured Emilia within the circle, then asked her to present herself to the seated Watchers in turn. In silence, each took Emilia's right hand with one of his, and placed two fingers of his other hand on her forehead. When Emilia had gone round the whole circle, the Abbot directed her to sit on a chair near the central fire-pit.

Heads bowed and eyes closed, the Watchers stretched out their arms to either side, spreading their feather mantles with them, to rest their hands on the shoulders of their neighbours.

'The Watchers will now prepare to link minds in the Immaterium,' said the Abbot. 'You outsiders will remain silent. And make no interference with your own thoughts. That will not be tolerated.'

The preparation felt to Orc interminable, but he made no show of boredom, nothing that might attract attention or disapproval. It seemed a good half-hour before one of the Watchers said, 'I fly with you, Tudrin, Memburan, Liw.' Another made a similar declaration, with more names, and then another, and eventually the first again, with even more names, until Orc guessed each Watcher had intoned a list of all his colleagues. When that was done, they said in unison: 'We soar the high airs on lammager wings, borne on Gevurah's will. Our eyes pierce to the heart of truth.'

Silence restored, the air felt tense with their attention. Occasionally one would mutter, but Orc suspected that this was only to make their mind-voices more real, and that they were aware of each other's projected thoughts. If so, it was a joint-scape of amazing ability. He wondered what Hana would make of it, or if Geist had ever contemplated such a thing. Perhaps, if Geist truly had planned for his students to joint-scape eventually, the idea had come from witnessing this.

The muttering grew, until Rukhan spoke in a heavy voice halfway to trance. 'It is true. He intends an attack.'

Orc's shoulders sagged. He'd feared the Shining Ones might have guessed their plan and hidden the conversation from Records. That they hadn't done this suggested they also didn't know the plan to go through the Shroud.

'Janik,' said the Abbot. 'Tell the novitiates to fall back to High Place as arranged. Rukhan? You are ready to continue?'

'There is no time for rest.'

'Young lady,' said the Abbot, 'please remove yourself from the circle. Young man, replace her.'

Orc swapped with Emilia and made the same circuit of the Watchers she had. The contact of their fingertips on his forehead tingled each time. With some Watchers it was an almost painful prickling, with some a soothing warmth. It made him feel exposed, as though they might be seeking out all his secrets. When done, he sat by the incense-smoking fire-pit, as the Watchers re-formed the circle with their outstretched arms and sank into the same meditation as before.

This took less time than it had with Emilia. After the Watchers had announced their flight with each other, Orc's sense of being the focus of attention became palpable: tiny needles of scrutiny over his skin and through his mind. Revealing the Shroud and making himself the centre of investigation had been dangerous, however necessary. Even without searching for it, the Watchers might discover his true relationship with the Goddess. And if they did break through the Shroud, then not only the Shining Ones' secrets might be revealed.

Murmuring began.

'Speak your findings aloud,' said the Abbot.

'The Witch Boy told true,' said a Watcher. 'There is deliberate obfuscation of his past.'

'Two years ago,' said another.

'Woven with skill,' came a third voice to Orc's rear. 'It will take time to unpick.'

Damn, thought Orc.

'Delve deeper into the past,' said Rukhan. 'It might weaken in his early life.'

There was no speech for several more minutes, then a Watcher said, 'It ends.'

Orc tensed on his chair.

'This "shroud" obscures a period of three months only.'

'I concur.'

More silence. Orc could hardly breathe, waiting for what would come next. A part of his life – of his life, and Cass's – he had no memory of. Even though he'd had to let Cass go, and now belonged to the Goddess, anticipation tightened every fibre of him.

'I cannot find him,' said the voice behind Orc.

'Nor I,' said another.

Agreement rippled.

'What?' muttered Orc.

'The shroud conceals the three months before you woke on that shore,' said Rukhan. 'Prior to that, Records does not hold you.'

'But... you must've missed something. Maybe I was just a long way from that beach?'

'We would still find you,' said Rukhan. 'Unless there were another, earlier barrier, too subtle to be detected. But that would make these magicians vastly more powerful than you led us to believe.'

Orc's brow tensed in bafflement. 'Well, can you pierce those three months?'

'The shroud is so tight-woven,' said a Watcher, 'that if it were cloth, no threads would be visible.'

'We could spend hours just seeking a mind-hold on which to fix our focus,' said another.

An idea jumped Orc. 'The wall. Look for a wall.'

'In what sense?' said Rukhan.

'A huge black one. Like around some massive enclosure.'

'The connection?'

'It's something to do with the Shroud, a… like a symbol of it. I saw it once, in a trance-flight.' He struggled to recall details from his powerful scape on the island. 'There was writing on it. Words, or a name. Gai-Eng.'

'That chimes in my memory,' said a Watcher, leading to murmurs of agreement. 'But where…'

The air prickled with attention.

'I have it,' said another. 'A volume in our library: *Legendarium of the Sundaran Coast*.'

'Can you quote the passage?' said the Abbot.

Orc sensed the Watchers joining focus. The one who'd named the volume spoke. 'Something like this: "In the beginning was a wondrous creature named Gai-Eng, which contained all within itself, mother and father, male and female. From it came the knowledge that awakened the gods." That is all I can find.'

'The source?' said the Abbot.

'Part of an old folk-tale, obscure. Shall we seek it?'

'Unnecessary,' said another Watcher. 'I detect a thought-path leading from those words.'

'Aye, into the far distance,' said yet another, his voice querulous.

'A long way, or a long time.'

'A vast desert…'

'A pillar stands there.'

'Of fire and smoke.'

'We must clear the smoke.'

The air thrummed with focus. At last a Watcher said, 'It thins…'

'Behold!'

'A black dome.'

'I also see it.'

More Watchers affirmed. Orc gripped the edge of his chair with one hand; his other slid into his shirt and grasped his focus-stone.

'The dome is top of a half-buried sphere,' said a Watcher.

'Both physical, and also mental, made of will and—'

'It is being strengthened.'

'They seek to deny us.'

'Concentrate.'

'There is a peculiar odour.'

Orc caught it too, faintly – the chemical whiff from Crome's before his fall into Magoria, the one Cass had likened to a hospital.

Push harder, he mentally urged the Watchers. He grasped his focus-stone and half-closed his eyes, wanting to add his mind to theirs, despite the Abbot's command to not interfere.

'Resistance weakens,' said one Watcher. 'We are stronger.'

The air felt ready to snap. Orc called to memory the black wall in his island scape, the words or names he'd uncovered on it. In his mind's eye, the black surface curved away to either side and overhead. He sensed where the Watchers were concentrating their force. He sensed the resistance, the mustering of opposition. The resistance had to fail.

The photograph: his one tangible connection to his past. And the Shining Ones knew of it; their skull-faced avatar had spoken of it. Him and Cass, an island named Kriti in the background. His mind was a spear-point, the Watchers the force that drove it. With his need for truth he rammed the black wall, and again, harder, and *again*—

It shattered.

Cass thought the deadline had to be drawing near, when Hann, on watch on the ridge, came down to report figures approaching through the thinning mist. Cass went out and stood beside him, to greet them.

Four figures, she saw when they were still some way off. Detail resolved from murk. Beneath a cloak, Aino was dressed in his complex armour of black leather straps. His master looked exhausted.

'What are you doing here?' Max asked Hann.

'I knew it couldn't be true!' said Aino.

'It was true,' said Hann. 'I have changed my mind. I hope that can be an end of it.'

'Almost,' said Max, and held out his hand. Cass thought it was for them to shake, but his palm was uppermost. Hann, clearly understanding, reached into his pocket and returned Max the banknotes.

Cass turned to Dinah. 'What the hell happened to you?'

'A misunderstanding.'

'A fiasco,' said Max. 'The villagers thought we were Empyreal agents looking to capture Yaggit, and we couldn't persuade them otherwise. These two were off trying to find a way through to the Petitioners Road. A boy from the village had to track them down and bring them back. That didn't happen till this morning.'

'At least tell me you brought food,' said Cass.

Max unslung a bag off his back.

'I can't believe we are to fly,' said Aino, staring wide-eyed at the craft. 'You'll want to examine its workings, master.'

'Later, perhaps,' said Yaggit. 'The priority now must be to return. We are surely too late for the Conclave, but we must try to reach the monastery before the Prelate.'

'And find Tashi,' said Aino, and passed Cass to climb up into the craft.

'Yes, we'd better get moving,' said Max.

Cass nodded tightly. Now came the deceit. She couldn't openly go against the previous day's decision to return to Highcloud. But to miss any battle, she could pretend to fail at calling an air elemental, at least until it was too late.

She chewed her way through a few mouthfuls of bread and cheese and went up to the engineer's station. She stared at the glyph-ring as if she'd never seen it before, or wished she hadn't.

And maybe no pretence would be necessary. Using the stone for the fire elemental might have changed it, made it useless for calling Windbags. In fact – clever, this – merely introducing doubt into her mind might scupper her attempt, because doubt was the enemy of magic.

Was that really what she wanted?

'Gevurah reminds us of our true road.'

But there was no Gevurah. She only had her own conscience, and she'd fought it to an impasse. Go back to help Orc and Emilia, and risk the two boys, one of whom had held her through long hours of darkness. Or save them from the possibility of battle and death, and risk Orc. She guessed Orc wouldn't be killed; the Prelate's telegram had asked for him. Perhaps she could even save Hann and rescue Orc later. Win both ways.

Fantasy.

'Cass?' Max had done his thing with the starting charges out on the wings and was now in the pilot's seat. 'Any problem?'

'It might take a moment.' Or an hour, two hours. But delay would make her decision for her, and she needed to make it herself.

It suddenly annoyed her that others had their sources of advice, even if they were imaginary – Orc had Otter, Hana Hare, Hann his god. When had she ever had anyone she could trust to ask for advice? Her only 'teacher' had been a manipulative bastard intent on turning her or Orc into a nutcase, and not caring which.

But maybe, she thought, she could have something like an animath too, a way of seeking advice from her inner self. She'd sensed a connection with that crystal man. It would still be part of herself, after all; she wouldn't be handing the decision to another. And though he was probably some kind of Otherworld entity, contacting him needn't pull her towards madness, not so long as she didn't fall into the trap of believing him to independently exist.

She calmed her mind as best she could and rested her hand on the crystal. Again, the cabinet of index cards; she found the same pattern through them as before, the coded route, the network of connections from her previous time.

Again, she found him, on his endless walk across the featureless plain. She maintained a background awareness that he was part of her own mental workings, just enough not to break her out of it. But God, he seemed real. *Who are you?* she wondered.

At that thought, the crystal man turned to face her, as if, from the time of his own existence – immeasurably deep in the past, she sensed – he had become aware of her.

'Which way?' she said in her mind. 'Take Hann to safety, or go back to Orc?'

In that featureless landscape, she sensed a rousing of tension, as of distant thunder.

She repeated her question – and a voice came back at her, though the blue crystal jaws did not move.

Keep away from him. I forbid you to be with him.

She hadn't expected anything like that. The word *forbid* unpleasantly reminded her of the last evening at Crome's house, before she'd fled into the street. 'Who? Orc?'

You're not to be alone with that boy. Understand?

'You need to tell me why.'

The anger beat at her. *This is not for discussion. You'll do as I say.*

Her own anger fought up in response, like an old fury rekindled. She pulled out, disturbed. 'Fuck that.' No one was going to order her like that, not even part of her own mind. Her decision seemed suddenly so clear, like confusing debris had been shunted out of her path. Hann would have to take his chances, impure or not. Going back was what he wanted to do, in any case. It wasn't her business to save anyone who didn't want to be saved.

Not even a lover. Well, okay, the sex had just been sex. It had lost her any moral high ground, but she didn't want that anyway. Orc and she were on the same level now, and if that was the moral low ground, they could sink into it together. And she could forgive Orc for Hana, forgive Tashi for looking like them both. Everybody won.

Except the people about to die, which might include her.

Orc plunged into endless and ageless space, like hanging in deep water, an ocean of information that made his head feel light. The Watchers swarmed around him, then their disparate mental presences knitted again and shifted and excluded him, throwing up a shield as though following some plan they hadn't told him. He sensed the Shining Ones too, their dismay, their frantic attempts to repel the invaders.

The battle of wills moved elsewhere, a psychic lightning-war in the mental distance. Every time he headed towards it, it moved. He had no experience of this kind of soulscape. Images flashed: a great hall lit with a thousand candles; a withered-looking head in a golden cage. Occasional muttering came from the Watchers in the physical world, but they were otherwise silent, focused.

Maybe he should pull out. According to the Abbot's instructions, he shouldn't even be here. But the Watchers wouldn't have broken through the black wall without him, and he resented the thought that they might want him to slink off.

Their breathing got louder. A groan came from Rukhan.

'Are you able to report?' said the Abbot.

'Identified route to the Trine,' Rukhan half-mumbled. 'But resistance strong. Counter-attack. They are fewer, but their power, their skill… this is their domain.'

It struck Orc then that he might be able to divert some of the Kaybees' defences. The secrets the Shroud had been created to screen must be here somewhere, and they wouldn't want him to find them. If even one of the Kaybees had to switch their energies to stopping him, it would increase the Watchers' chances.

And if they couldn't stop him, the secrets would be his.

His father's death, for a start. If he could find out how long ago, he'd know how much of his seven years remained.

He cast his mind's net out into the darkness – and there: a silvery fish of thought, the idea of 'father'. As soon as he fixed on it, it seemed to grow in significance – powerfully so, as if this whole place had been built to house it. Its gravity pulled him. The realisation struck him that there was no sense of the Goddess here at all, that she was *Outside* and this was *Inside*, but there was no time to explore that: he rushed as though down an increasingly strong river current, towards that idea of *father*, and as he drew nearer, he began to feel it almost as a presence.

An immense raised tomb of black stone unveiled before his mind's eye, and upon it lay a carved figure. From the base of the tomb, lines and pipes of metal or ceramic led in all directions across what seemed a vast plain of glass.

He urged himself closer. There would be a date there.

Unless – a thought from nowhere – this 'father' wasn't *his*...

A chill washed through him, though he couldn't place the source of his dread. A sudden conviction – that he'd been foolish to come here, that he'd been warned against this – slipped through him as a power stirred in the mind-space, like something rousing itself from the mud of millennial sleep in dark ocean depths.

Whatever was entombed here wasn't dead.

You.

Hostility flayed him, its psychic taint far stronger now than in the college, than in Crome's house. The Voice of God – this was where it lived. The tomb-figure clarified: its face stern and bearded, its eyes deep set, the features possessing distant familiarity.

You.

The power beat on his mind like heat, like scrutiny from a vast spirit of black fire. Instinct screamed at him to scour the tomb from his mind and get out. But now he sensed the attention of the Kaybees, their panic. His plan had worked, he was drawing some of them away from the battle. He steeled himself to resist his fear, to give the Watchers a chance.

'When did my father die?'

That weakling, that idiot, that thief. *I rejoiced when it happened.*

Puzzled, he pressed harder. 'When did it happen?'

When is this? How long has it been?

'Who are you, if you're not him?'

You thought I *was him? You thought* I *spawned a shit like you?*

Not the words of any god Orc would have expected. The presence grew even stronger, and so did his awareness of the Kaybees. Confusion rattled him, the fear that he'd gone dangerously into something beyond even his guesses. He pushed against it. 'Why did you scratch out my face in the photograph?'

After what you made happen? My beautiful, clever daughter! And now you're trying to marry your own mother and keep her from me too, you perverted fuck.

'Your…?'

I'll scratch out more than your face. I'll gouge out your heart, your liver, every memory of you. I'll make it so you never existed, I'll—

GET OUT. A different voice crashed into his mind, along with the image of Skull-face. *Get out or you'll die. Everyone will die!*

The avatar's conviction shattered doubt, loosened his hold. He sensed the Kaybees around him, several of them, their attempts to limit damage, to effect repairs in the midst of a growing maelstrom. A psychic push came, a pain stabbed through his head; he cried out and broke from the scape.

The air in the Hall of Conclave was a taut wire. He hadn't exited properly. Something had come out with him, or was still with him. The hatred.

'Holiness,' came Rukhan's voice. 'The resistance weakened. We implanted the message.'

Yes! thought Orc, as an excited murmur came from the non-Watchers around the room. But still the hatred, still the growing power. He sensed it trying to focus on him.

'Then return,' said the Abbot.

'Hold,' said a Watcher. 'I sense a presence come amongst us. It feels as though—'

Oh shit.

'It is Lord Gevurah!' cried another.

'Wait,' said Orc, but his voice was lost.

'We have cracked open this nest of magicians and exposed it to His wrath!'

'Call down His judgement!' said Rukhan. 'Exterminate them utterly!'

'I don't think that's Gevurah,' said Orc, but his warning made no impact on the eager cries. He rose from his seat, skin thrumming with the mounting vibration. 'Fuck,' he said, 'stop it, stop it!'

Pressure spiked, a shockwave from all directions. Watchers cried out in pain, letting go of each other's shoulders. Several slumped on their platforms, their hands in spasm – two fell to the floor and lay senseless.

'Orc!' shrieked Emilia, as an iron taste came in the air.

A cracking sound tore through the chamber and he looked up and something large hung right above him. Instinct hurled him aside; screams and cries came from all around and the sound of wood splintering – a giant black sword had smashed his chair, its point embedded in the floor. It toppled, slowly, the Watcher beneath its path scrambling out, and Orc was moving, he threw himself between two platforms and barged between the ordinary monks standing agog. He tried to get to the door but his arm was grabbed and then his collar; a seam in his shirt ripped. The big monk Thu had him round the chest now. Shouted orders came above the cries and din. 'Let me go, let me go!' he yelled, pulling hard as he could and panicking that there would come another sword, forming above him right this second – then he sensed that the power had gone out of the air, the vibration, the hate. It was just air, and people, human people confused with fright and trying to restore calm.

He breathed, making himself take more air into his constricted lungs. 'Okay, okay,' he gasped at Thu, who loosened his hold a little, and he realised how hard he was shaking.

If Emilia hadn't shouted his name…

Don't think.

The Voice of God was gone – maybe the Kaybees had regained control. Ten or so Watchers were slumped in what he assumed was dark-flight. Others were trying to help them. Orc glanced round for Emilia and found her, scared-looking, to one side.

Rukhan yelled for silence, then said, 'Fetch the herbs of recall! And their novitiates.'

'Not the novitiates!' said the Abbot. 'The Prelate is due in minutes. We must help them without. Is this truly dark-flight? How so many? What happened?'

'A trick,' said Rukhan. 'We thought Gevurah had come amongst us to punish the Shining Ones. In our eagerness we lost the discipline of our defences and their attack broke upon us.'

'But it wasn't Gevurah?'

'Something roused by the Witch Boy.'

'I didn't trick you!' said Orc. 'I never said it was Gevurah.'

Rukhan ignored him. 'The herbs!' he shouted at the monk he'd ordered last time, who scurried from the room.

Thu let Orc go, apart from a hand on his collar. Orc still shook, and from more than the sword attack. That hate, but more than the hate. *My beautiful, clever daughter.* But not his own father, so she couldn't be his sister, and yet – *After what you made happen.* That hate, the hate of a presence so powerful the monks had mistaken it for God – all that hate because of something he'd done. It made no sense, no sense that a god and he and Cass should be tied up like that. It made no sense, but deep down he felt the truth of it.

After what you made happen.

No, it couldn't be true. How could that presence have been a human father? It must have been a soulscape thing, a tapping into connection with a force in the psychosphere.

'Orc?' Emilia had come over. 'They did it.'

'I know,' he said, trembling less now. 'Was that the easy part, or the hard?'

The monk who'd been sent out returned. Herbs were thrown into the small fire-pit, their scent infusing the air at once. All the Watchers unaffected by dark-flight were aiding their afflicted fellows, but only one of these had so far responded. Again Rukhan demanded that the novitiates of those still in dark-flight be brought over to help, and this time the Abbot did not give an instant refusal.

'I suppose if we bring some here, they are still in concealment,' he said. 'Very well: summon those novitiates whose masters have succumbed. And quickly – they must not be out in the open when the Prelate's craft arrives.'

'Holiness!' called one of the monks at the windows overlooking the gorge. 'Too late!'

40

APOTHEOSIS

The Hall of Conclave stilled, apart from the muttering of the Watchers in dark-flight, and even that seemed subdued. Through the eastern windows came the increasing drone of engines, then the noise passed over the monastery building, monks craning their necks as though to track the air-craft through the ceiling. The engine sound increased through the northern and western windows, and replacing it through the eastern ones came the noise of booted feet running on the Petitioners Road along the bottom of the gorge.

'So here it is,' said Rukhan. 'We have given up control of the plateau.'

'As was the plan,' said the Abbot heavily. 'And you delivered the message to the Empyreal Trine? There is no doubt?'

'None in my mind.'

'Then come, we must meet our "guest".'

'Who shall?' said Rukhan. 'It was to have been all the Watchers. But nine are incapacitated, and the rest must stay and aid them.'

'All those capable must come,' said the Abbot. 'We must present as strong and united a face as possible. The fact that some of our number have succumbed to dark-flight will surely prove we encountered an evil force.'

'Let us hope Astrasis is persuaded swiftly, then,' said Rukhan.

'You won't need us, right?' said Orc, as the Abbot and the Watchers approached. 'Me and Emilia, we'll stay here.'

'No, you'll both come,' said Rukhan. 'His telegram asked for you and Tashi explicitly. To defy him more than necessary will not gain us his ear.'

'More than necessary?' said Emilia, her voice brittle. 'And if you can persuade him to ally with you, will you give me back to him anyway?'

Rukhan gestured to Thu, who pushed the end of Max's pistol into Orc's back. 'Detail can wait for when the frame is clearer.'

Orc felt sick to his stomach again, scared for both Emilia and himself. He'd assumed he would be hidden from the Prelate until the alliance had been formed. But he saw that from Rukhan's position, it made sense to at least appear willing to surrender them.

As they descended the stairs, they were met by monks coming up from the lower floors, asking what they should do. The Abbot told them simply to clear his path. They arrived at the Western Gate to find it shut, monks crowding to peer through the viewing port. The Abbot ordered the gate opened, and as the gap was heaved wider, there came the sound of many running feet from the trench of the Spiral Path that ran beneath the bridge. The revealed ball-pitch, beyond the first thirty yards or so, was busy with Empyreal troops who had already gained the level ground. At that thirty-yard arc, soldiers stood with rifles aimed, and three machine-gun crews had their weapons trained on the gate.

'Show no fear,' said the Abbot tightly, and led the way out across the bridge. Orc no longer felt the pistol at his back, but there seemed little choice but to follow. His legs felt about to give way, as if anticipating the burst of fire that would kill him. Commanding the scene from two hundred feet above the north-western corner of the ball-pitch hung the Prelate's air-craft, like a mechanical version of the gryphon painted on its wings. The creature's muted roar sounded from its idling engines, and it had unsheathed its claws – a soldier with a long rifle sat at its open door, and machine-guns at nose and flank were trained on the monastery group as they crossed the bridge over the still-bustling trench and walked onto the ball-pitch.

'Hold!' An Empyreal officer stepped forwards; fifteen yards now separated the Abbot from the arc of men.

'I am the Abbot Taropat.' Even if he'd spoken with the voice of a bull, it would have seemed too weak before what he faced. As it was, he spoke with the voice of an old man trying to cover nerves. 'I must talk with Prelate Astrasis, alone.'

'First give up your novitiates,' said the officer.

'They will not attack,' said the Abbot. 'It is to avoid any conflict that I must meet with his Grace.'

'You were sensible not to resist us. But his Grace will not alight until the novitiates are accounted for. Once they're disarmed and restrained, so they present no threat even if possessed by their demons—'

'*Demons*?' said Rukhan.

'One attacked his Grace in his palace,' said the officer. 'How can they be other than demons to attack a Prelate of the Church? Now surrender them!'

The soldiers looked jumpy, Orc thought, as if they feared the Inspired novitiates might charge out from the building at any moment.

'The information I have for him will change everything,' said the Abbot. 'He must come down to speak with us.'

'Impossible.'

'Maybe you could go up in his craft?' said Orc. 'He'd feel safe then.'

The Abbot looked terrified at the idea. The officer pointed at Orc. 'Him you must surrender too. He's dangerous.'

Orc stiffened with dread, but Rukhan said, 'He presents no danger here. Do you suppose any form of the Witch Mother could manifest in this place? And were he to make any attempt to manifest her, do you think we would not pull him down ourselves?'

To Orc's relief, the conviction and controlled outrage in Rukhan's voice seemed to persuade the officer – though Orc guessed the Watcher had spoken from genuine affront rather than from wanting to save him. As the discussion moved to whether the Abbot was willing to enter the air-craft, Orc tried to judge whether the Kurassians' fear of the Goddess might give him an opening to draw on her power. A quick assessment told him Rukhan's words matched the reality. Even with the Kurassians' presence and belief, he still couldn't sense her. And even if their fear were stronger, it wouldn't enrich the thin mountain soil, steeped in millennia of her denial. In his joint-scape with Hana, he'd only been able to fertilise the mountainside by shedding more blood than he possessed.

He was on his own.

At last, following the urging of Rukhan and Emilia, the Abbot agreed. The officer sent a sergeant to find out if his Holiness's going aloft was acceptable. The man jogged the two hundred yards to the corner of the ball-pitch beneath the stationary craft, which then descended ponderously to a few feet from the ground, and after a brief exchange, he waved the Abbot across. The officer sent four riflemen with him. Only when this group reached the sergeant did the craft fully land. The Abbot was clumsily hustled on board, and was barely off the steps and into the hull when the craft lofted once more.

'Siegfried's terrified of the novitiates,' muttered Emilia. 'Though having seen Tashi attack him, I'm not surprised.'

Orc's stomach hurt. The Abbot had to succeed. Surely the Prelate wouldn't risk a battle with novitiates who terrified him so much? He tried to persuade himself that Emilia had been right earlier, that her brother would hate the Kaybees for having manipulated him. He tried to put from his mind the fact that even if the Abbot succeeded, his own safety wasn't guaranteed. *Witch Boy*, Rukhan had called him, and the Prelate's opinion would hardly differ.

He closed his eyes and tried to breathe steadily.

'Why is this taking so long?' said Rukhan. 'We need to help the Watchers in dark-flight.'

Soldiers continued to arrive up the Spiral Path and organise on the ball-pitch. None made any attempt to enter the monastery, but about fifty formed up into a group that went marching along the track round the corner, towards High Place. Orc guessed all the Watchers were wondering the same as him: what would happen if the soldiers tried to enter the ruins and discovered the novitiates there.

Come on, come on…

At last, the craft descended and disgorged the Abbot, then lifted off again. Orc studied the Abbot as he was escorted back, trying to glean clues from his posture, his stride, his face. The first was stooped, the second halting, the third seemed a mask of despair. The soldiers rejoined their comrades and officer, leaving the Abbot to walk the last fifteen yards alone.

'What happened?' Emilia's question mixed with several others.

The Abbot raised a silencing hand. 'I told him of our proof.'

'What did he say?' said Rukhan. 'Will he confirm it?'

'He did not dismiss it, and yes, he said he will send a telegram.'

'Thank God,' said Emilia, and Orc exhaled his tension; he didn't understand why the Abbot hadn't seemed more happy. Queasiness from the air-craft?

Then he glanced at the machine, which had resumed its commanding station high above the corner of the ball-pitch. 'But he's not moving.'

'No.' The Abbot sighed, and lowered his voice to a softness only just audible above the background noise. 'He said my claim does not affect his primary mission. As we surmised, he seeks the Orb of Archive.'

'But only because of the Shining Ones' manipulation,' said Rukhan, his voice also muted.

'He claims otherwise, that Empyreus gave no guidance on the matter. He wants it because the Sundarans used manifestation, and he needs to understand the mechanism.'

'No, that can't be the reason,' said Emilia. 'He was interested in Konstantin years ago.'

Orc had only half his attention on the conversation. Again, hearing the name Orb of Archive had pricked his memory, but this time more urgently.

'Nevertheless, he demands we hand it over,' said the Abbot. 'He will confirm our claim about Empyreus only when he has possession of the Orb.'

'We cannot agree,' said Rukhan.

'I know,' said the Abbot.

'Why can't he confirm the Empyreus proof first? How does understanding any threat from Sundara compare with that revelation?'

'You think I didn't argue the same?' said the Abbot. 'But he was adamant. He has allowed us half an hour to agree to surrender the novitiates and the Orb.'

Fuck. Orc glanced round at the monastery. He had no doubt they would be stopped from re-entering if they tried it. 'What happens when that passes?'

'He might have some of us shot,' said Rukhan.

'He wouldn't!' said Emilia. 'You're Watchers of Highcloud. None of his men would agree.'

'You forget, Tashi attacked him: Tashi possessed by a "demon", as your brother has persuaded his men. He has already begun the work of turning his soldiers against us.'

Orc felt certain he would be first in the firing line. Dry-mouthed, he tried to put together an argument that there was no point refusing the Prelate's demands, not when the man had enough firepower to kill the novitiates anyway, and probably explosives to blow open the vaults.

The vaults…

Something sparked. '*That must have been the source of my nightmares.*'

'What?' said Emilia.

He hadn't realised he'd spoken aloud. He gripped his forehead, trying to work free the connection with the Orb, sensing its importance. 'Shoggu said it, in a scape I did last night. We saw a novitiate take something from the vaults.'

'The Orb?' she said.

'No, a kind of spike. Shoggu said it gave him nightmares.'

'What relevance is this?' said Rukhan.

'I don't know. Something to do with the Orb of Archive, I think.' Again, the prickling.

'Shoggu mentioned the Orb?' said Emilia.

'No, but it's linked, I'm sure of it.' If only he could have space to think, or to scape.

'Who was this novitiate?' said the Abbot.

'Beware, Holiness,' said Rukhan. 'This could be a trick.'

'In these circumstances, I'll take the risk. Who was he?'

'Tashi's father,' said Orc. Emilia gasped.

'That is suggestive,' said the Abbot. 'Anik was indeed connected with the Orb.'

'A novitiate?' said Rukhan. 'How?'

The Abbot didn't answer him, but spoke again to Orc. 'And he was holding a spike?'

'Yes. And Shoggu said—'

It leapt to his mind: words on a page of the transcripts he'd barely noticed at the time. *This is the one who was exposed to the stolen key of the Orb of Archive?*

He bent towards the Abbot. 'Is any part of the Orb missing?'

'It seemed whole when I saw it,' the Abbot said. 'But that was only once, at my investiture. Its box is otherwise kept locked.'

'I think you'll find there's a section that can be taken out, and it's gone. The Kaybees called it the key. Tashi's father took it.'

'Hm,' said the Abbot. 'He might well have believed himself to have cause.'

'What cause?' said Rukhan. 'What happened?'

'That is a history I was charged to keep to myself,' said the Abbot.

'Forget why,' said Orc. 'See what this means? Even if you give him the Orb, Astrasis can't use it without the key. And as soon as you give it to him, he'll check out your Empyreus proof, and that'll take priority, like you said. Then we just have to make sure he doesn't get the key – and how will he find out where it is? We're not going to tell him. And the Shining Ones aren't, either – he'll be their enemy by then.'

'And if you're wrong,' said Rukhan, 'and it does have power without this "key"?'

'Or if he already possesses it?' said the Abbot.

'Come up with another idea, then. I'm all ears.'

The Abbot turned to his chief Watcher. 'What do you think?'

'The story is credible,' Rukhan said. 'Shoggu travelled with Anik for some time. And being near part of the Orb might indeed account for his dreams of Zhenaii magic.'

The Abbot nodded. 'I am persuaded, at least far enough.'

'But the idea of handing the Orb across sickens soul, mind, and body,' said Rukhan. 'To give away what this monastery was founded to guard…'

'We all feel the same,' said the Abbot. 'But we are on a sinking island. Dare we set foot in the swamp of compromise in hope of finding firmer ground beyond?'

'Or do we fight,' said Rukhan, 'in the certainty that dying here will gain us the Land Beyond Sky? I know what the novitiates would say.'

'Why would they?' said Emilia, shocked. 'They have their whole lives ahead of them.'

'Their priority is not to attain dotage,' said Rukhan. 'Many after graduating either seek the mountain right away, or return to do so.'

'Seek the mountain…?'

'Where do you think Tashi went?'

Orc glanced towards Tamfang, its lower slopes disappearing into patchy cloud.

'You claimed not to know where,' said Emilia faintly.

'It is obvious,' said Rukhan. 'The weight of his witch-created body became too much. He has gone to rid himself of it, and seek redemption in hope of attaining his true and eternal home. Holiness, when the alternative is to betray the long guardianship for which this monastery was founded, can we do otherwise?'

'And what happens,' said Emilia, in a low and dangerous voice, 'when your wonderful sacrifice lets my brother step over your dead bodies and take what he came for? You're needed to unmask Empyreus – isn't that what God would want? But instead, you plan to serve only your integrity. I've never heard anything so selfish.'

Rukhan visibly bristled, but the Abbot gave a bitter chuckle. 'She has you there. Indeed, this is one time when pragmatism best serves Lord Gevurah. We shall venture the swamp.'

'Which is the realm of the Witch Mother.' Rukhan eyed Orc and Emilia. 'And which we enter at the bidding of these two.'

'The young man's idea gained us the Empyreus proof.'

'And sent nine of our number into dark-flight,' said Rukhan. 'Following the advice of such as these will never bring unalloyed good.'

'Then let us at least avoid unalloyed bad,' said the Abbot. He faced the officer across the fifteen-yard gap, and raised his voice above the drone of the air-craft's engines. 'You may tell his Grace I agree to his demands.'

Orc and Emilia walked with the others up the track towards High Place, guarded by riflemen front and rear, the Prelate's craft keeping slow pace overhead.

'Do you think it's true?' said Emilia. 'About Tashi?'

'Hope not,' said Orc, wishing he could say something less obvious, less meaningless. But soon they were approaching their destination, and Tashi was driven from his thoughts. Their group was halted fifty yards down the gentle slope from High Place – all except the Abbot and two other Watchers, who were escorted to the ruin to make contact with the concealed novitiates. Orc shivered in the breeze, looking round at the many soldiers busy or stationed across the area. The engine drone overhead lent a disturbing vibration to the scene. After a few minutes' talk between the Abbot and someone Orc couldn't see, the novitiates emerged in a line, unarmed and in their leather bindings. Their downturned faces spoke of confusion and betrayal; Shikar's glowed with fury. A guard of soldiers marched them fifty yards, where an officer ordered them to halt, face right, and kneel with hands behind heads. A rifleman was stationed behind each youth. An order to fire would wipe out the entire cadre in a second.

With the novitiates neutralised, the Abbot, his companions and escort entered the ruin. None of those around Orc spoke. When the party emerged, the two Watchers carried between them a dark wooden box bound in metal.

The Abbot and the box-bearers returned to the other Watchers. Under the direction of an officer, soldiers cleared a space nearby, and the air-craft descended to earth like a sky-god deigning to visit. The Prelate came down the steps in full dress uniform, followed by his adjutant and a boyish-faced man in a tweed suit and hat. 'Ex-Trine,' muttered Emilia. 'But not the elemental's engineer, I think.' After a hard look towards the kneeling novitiates barely thirty yards away, as if to convince himself they now posed no threat, the Prelate led the other two across to the Highcloud group.

'Open it.'

The Abbot took an intricate key from within his robe, unlocked the box still held by the two Watchers, and lifted the lid.

Suddenly came commotion, a raised boy's voice speaking quickly. Orc looked towards the novitiates. There was a shout, a soldier had his rifle raised—

Orc didn't look away in time.

The gunshot faded. The hammering of Orc's heart didn't. He'd glimpsed the effect the rifle bullet had had on the boy's skull. That wouldn't fade either.

'He was trying to Inspire himself, sir!' called the officer commanding the novitiates' guard.

'Good work, Lieutenant,' said the Prelate, his voice frighteningly composed. 'Carry on.'

Orc tried to breathe himself down. He'd seen people shot dead before, right in front of him, but this was far worse than Pettor or Esteban. The novitiate had died wanting to defend everything he valued, and right in front of his friends and comrades. Died, Orc knew, trying to stop something *he* had set in motion.

'Genku has gained the Land Beyond Sky,' murmured Rukhan.

The Prelate wiped his hands on his jacket. He reached into the box and lifted out an obviously heavy sphere, nine inches across, wrapped in chamois leather. Still shocked from the gunshot, Orc strained to look closer as the Prelate discarded the leather. The Zhenaii Orb was near-black, and not glassy and shiny as Orc had expected, but with a dull sheen. Faint threads of silver and blue caught the light.

'It was wise of you to relinquish this, Holiness,' the Prelate said, turning the Orb in his hands with effort. 'This will enable us – wait.' He clutched it against his chest with one hand and with the other felt around in the box still held open before him. Orc swallowed.

'What is this?' The Prelate showed the Abbot one side of the sphere, where there was an inch-square hole. 'A section is missing.' He turned to the sergeant who'd accompanied the Abbot into the vault. 'Was there any interference with this?'

'None, sir.'

Astrasis now faced the Abbot. 'Well?'

'That is as it was when I took it under my guardianship,' the Abbot said, clearly struggling to steady his voice.

'Konstantin described it as a perfect sphere.'

'So I assumed it to be,' said the Abbot. 'That hole is only visible from one side, clearly.'

'Your answers reek of evasion.' The Prelate handed the Orb to the tweed-suited man, who supported it with one hand and stroked it with the other.

'It feels inert,' came the verdict.

The Prelate breathed in slowly, then out. 'Is a piece missing?' he demanded of the Abbot, his voice pitched almost too soft to hear above the idling air-screws. 'I repeat: *is a piece missing*?'

The Abbot seemed frozen, unable to speak. Orc saw in the old man's face a fright that came from not knowing how to make his next move in a dangerous game. *Lie*, thought Orc, *for God's sake*. He couldn't see how anyone, no matter how holy, could hold truth so absolutely necessary. A novitiate had been *killed*, for fuck's sake.

But the Abbot didn't speak. No one did.

'An eloquent silence,' said the Prelate. 'In one way, it speaks in your favour. Your inability to lie now, when it would clearly benefit you, suggests your earlier claim was truthful. We might yet become allies in that matter. But not if you keep this from me.'

'Siegfried,' said Emilia, her voice betraying her nerves. 'Surely you can see how dangerous that thing is, to yourself and Kurassia as much as your enemies. Think what happened to the Zhenaii – the sea rose a hundred feet, never to go down again. Think what that means – either all that water was made from nothing, or the sea-bed was changed – either way, that's far more power than Daroguerre used to manifest his goddess-demon. And the Zhenaii clearly couldn't control it, or they wouldn't have suffered their fate. How do you hope to? Put that aside for the moment. Attend to the more urgent matter. Be the statesman I know you can be.'

Astrasis looked at her with contempt. 'What statesman would take instruction from his younger sister? But don't worry, I have no intention of flooding a continent.'

'And what makes you think the Orb would obey you?'

'My intent at present is merely to comprehend the weapon Sundara has used against us. That you seek to dissuade me speaks volumes as to your loyalty.'

'I don't believe you,' said Emilia. 'You were studying Konstantin years ago.'

'Captain Kline,' Astrasis said to the officer who'd guarded them outside the monastery. 'Tell me: in between his Holiness's return from my air-craft and his acceding to my demands, did my sister seem material to any discussion that might have led him to this deceit?'

'I couldn't make out the talk, sir,' said Kline. 'But if any seemed instrumental, it looked to be the young man there.'

For the first time, Orc found the Prelate's gaze fully upon him. 'I wondered when we might detect the hand of the Witch in this,' Astrasis said. 'You shame yourself, Holiness, by agreeing to any scheme that has her mark on it – and have no doubt, it is her hand behind this. Through her slave here, she hopes to prevent me destroying her stronghold in Golgomera. By withholding the missing piece from me, you are serving her.'

‘I am not withholding any such piece.’

‘Knowledge of it, then. Does he have you under some kind of threat?’ He gave the Orb to the tweed-suited man and drew his pistol, armed it. ‘You needn’t fear him.’

Orc stepped back. What was going on?

‘However terrible his mistress – and even she will fall eventually – he is only human.’

The Prelate raised the gun. Orc couldn’t get his mind to work. Astrasis wanted to take him back: the telegram had said so. This couldn’t be serious. Emilia was saying something.

He stumbled back before he’d registered the sound of the gunshot. The loud crack came again and this time he felt it in his chest and fell back to the ground. He couldn’t breathe. He’d been shot, really shot. Emilia’s cry and others sounded muffled, from a mile away. He had to get up, get help, but his legs wouldn’t work. There was blood in his mouth, wetness inside his coat. Pain began. Panic surged at the realisation of what was happening, but just as it came, it was swamped by a sense of outrage that welled up from deeper than his own self.

His life was the Goddess’s to take, no one else. He needed to express that, to explain. Another bullet cracked into him. The wrongness and violation filled him with anger, every nerve and fibre and blood vessel. Things were happening inside him. Tendrils snaked between vessels and muscle strands, mending, knitting. His breathing cleared of fluid but brought a new taste, acid and fresh.

He pushed himself to his feet amid gasps and cries.

No more gunshots. The Watchers and Emilia had backed away. Everyone stared, wide-eyed: soldiers, novitiates. The Prelate’s arm had dropped.

Something broke from each corner of Orc’s mouth and grew, curved round to touch his cheeks, sprouted leaves. He felt sick but it was a very wrong-feeling kind of sick, because something had altered his stomach.

‘So you truly are her warrior and her prophet.’ The Prelate’s voice trembled behind its assertiveness. ‘I should have killed you in Bismark.’ He darted a look at the nearest soldiers. ‘Finish him.’

'No!' cried Emilia, and tried to move forwards, but one of the Watchers grabbed her. The soldiers raised their rifles. Orc was about to plead with them, when something else pushed past that. Realisation: not merely knowledge but the understanding and making of reality. In a moment, faster than the pressure of a finger on a trigger, he saw in the men's scared faces what his altered body had changed in their minds. Even in this place so far removed from the Goddess's world, these soldiers now believed in her power here, *gave* her power here.

And as for the thinness of the soil – oh yes, his sudden, horrific understanding – she had other material to grow from.

A mass of slithering burst from the first soldier's abdomen. His comrades turned, faces and eyes stretched wide, and contagion tore through them. Man after man, officer after private erupted in hysterias of vegetation, muscle and tendon and entrails entwined with the vine-stems, scraps of skin in the pale leaves along with bits of fabric and kit, wet slipping sounds cutting short screams and cries. Exultation filled Orc, dampening his horror; he needed to avenge, to punish, to stamp the Goddess on this place that had denied her.

He swung towards the Prelate. The ex-Trine exploded in body-vegetation, but Astrasis had grabbed the Orb from him and now fled towards the air-craft. Orc focused, aimed power, willed that uniform of red cloth and gold braid to bloom into the Goddess's deadly glory.

Nothing happened. He sensed interference. Some force was protecting the man.

A howl of anger sent the vines surging from the nearest corpses, creepers twisting together into heavy green cables, snaking fast towards the air-craft. Orc was blind to all else. He had no thought to spare for Emilia or the Watchers; his whole brain was bent on the Prelate's death. The man reached the craft barely ahead of the vines; a crewman leaned out and hauled him up the steps and in, just as the craft lifted off. Its nose machine-gun opened fire. Bullets hissed through the air to Orc's left, but the craft was rotating in the pilot's panic and the arc of fire swung off.

He sent the vine-cables twining together into a trunk, thick enough to support its weight: higher and higher, seeking the fleeing craft, twenty feet up, forty.

Too high. He couldn't bolster it enough. The trunk's searching tip swayed to one side. Exhaustion broke the strength of his knees and he sank to the ground as the fifty-foot vine-cluster toppled. All around him was vegetation. He couldn't see anyone over it, only the air-craft now dominating the sky again, safe from the Goddess's power. Gunfire came from somewhere beyond the mass of plant-life; he couldn't tell who was shooting at who, had no energy to wonder. Pain returned with full force. One of the air-craft's flank machine-guns was firing towards where the novitiates had been. He tried one more burst of hate, but nothing happened. Even movement was beyond him. He stared at the nose of the craft, knowing that any moment its gun would—

There were *two* air-craft.

He screwed his eyes narrower, needing to make sense of his coming death. Higher and farther than the first craft was its near-copy, but it couldn't be double vision because they were different sizes, different angles.

The nose machine-gun fired – but only the one mounted on the second, farther craft. And not at him, but at the top of the first. He couldn't see the place where the bullets struck, but dim recollection of the layout told him it had to be somewhere near where the elemental was – and the engineer who controlled it.

The Prelate's craft began to drop. Engines suddenly revving high, it turned downslope, falling. It disappeared from Orc's view behind the man-high forest of vines. There came the sound of tearing, smashing, drowning the now-faded rifle fire.

The other craft lowered, neared. Another sky-god, another Saeraf setting himself above Chthonis, another abomination against the Goddess. Instinct told Orc this one was an even greater threat than the first. He had to destroy it, had to stop the machines multiplying before the world was covered with them.

Renewed power flooded him, flooded out of him. Every creeper and vine from the mass of transformed corpses swarmed together into one trunk and grew, ever thicker, ever taller, knitted into a single column of rapidly hardening creeper that speared itself skywards like a shout of power. And this time there was enough force behind it, all the Goddess's strength, pain stabbing through his altered viscera as her energy was diverted to counter this threat; and that was right, that was how it had to be. Higher and higher the trunk mounted from its ever-thickening base. At two hundred feet the tree thrust out branches in all directions, the fastest-growing towards the craft, which veered aside.

Someone grabbed his arm. 'Orc, no!' shouted the voice named Emilia. 'It's Max! And Cass!'

He pushed her off. The air-craft had to be destroyed. Its occupant shouldn't have come back, should have stayed away, hundreds of miles, thousands.

The branches swarmed outwards and upwards, snaking crazily, smaller branches and twigs splitting off into a dense covering thick with red flowers – a one-tree canopy for the whole mountainside, blotting out the sky. Its roots would burrow through rock, bring down buildings. The air-craft seemed uncertain what to do, whether to flee or try to evade. Its indecision would be its destruction.

'For God's sake, didn't you hear me? It's *them*!'

The hand grabbed him again. He lashed out and struck her, and she fell back with a cry. But the diversion had cost him, and the energy of the branches was lost. The air-craft started to move away.

'No!' yelled Emilia.

He couldn't regain impetus, couldn't channel enough power for the tree to catch up with the machine. It had exhausted him. He'd failed.

'What were you *doing*?' demanded Emilia.

He turned towards her, and saw that on the ground that had been behind him, there was no vegetation. The Watchers' discipline had saved them, letting them flee. Another failure. Gunfire still came from somewhere, but it was farther away, sporadic.

‘Think clearly, for God’s sake,’ she said. ‘Soldiers are coming up from the monastery. We need Max and Cass, it’s our only chance. Were you trying to drive them away again, to save them? They’re not the ones in trouble – *we* are.’

Trying to drive them away again. But no distance would be far enough. He doubled over in pain, trying to breathe through it, rasping, gurgling with the obstruction of the things growing from his mouth.

‘Thank God!’ said Emilia. ‘They’re coming back.’

And he didn’t have the strength to power the tree any more; the effort would end him, and the Goddess didn’t want him dead.

But she was ever resourceful, and another possibility germinated. If the Saeraf-craft abomination was coming to pick him up, then it would land, and nearby. If he husbanded his strength before then, he might have enough for one surge of power, to send the vines to grab the machine as it set down, to crush it into misshapen metal, destroy its unnatural lines, bleed out its earth-robbed fuel.

The engine drone mounted. He didn’t look up at the approaching craft, didn’t want to divert his energy from building strength for that surge of violence. But there was something he needed to think of, to push his own thoughts into consciousness alongside those inspired by the Goddess.

To destroy the Saeraf-craft.

It would kill—

Kill Cass.

The clarity was a momentary shock, but quickly replaced by the obviousness of it. Cass was as much of a threat as the craft, more so. Her death was necessary. The world was a constant turning over of life. Many had already died that day. He would die too, before very long, even if he survived this.

Cass, though. He couldn’t seem to work out the reasons her death was needed, why she threatened everything. Something in his tired, pain-filled thoughts struggled to assert itself. Her freckled face, her sunburned nose, her clear eyes that always opened up onto her heart, with their accusation and pain and annoyance and joy and—

He couldn't. *Couldn't.*

But she had come back to take him from the Goddess – that was why. That was a crime, a violation of sacred law every bit as great as killing him would have been. She couldn't be trusted.

And neither could he, not now it seemed likely she wasn't his sister. He was too weak. He still treasured the memories of that night in the college, how it had felt to wildly rut against her, the energy of her response. His own weakness meant she must be removed forever. That was why he'd sent her away. That she'd refused to stay away was her own bad judgement.

'Come on, Max, come *on*...' said Emilia.

The sound told him the craft was approaching low under the canopy. He didn't look up. He needed to give the impression of total exhaustion, so Emilia wouldn't suspect what was coming. He would have to kill Emilia too, straight afterwards, because he was now so bodily weak she might be able to finish him in revenge for Max. He began to prepare for the vegetative violence he would unleash as soon as the craft left the sky-father's realm and touched ground.

A worm of opposition struggled to find his mind. He didn't want to hurt Cass – how could he even think he did?

But he was too weak to counter the force behind all life on the planet. Too weak to resist the girl with the human heat between her legs, too weak to stick to the vow of his sacred marriage.

Overhead now, the craft's engines shifted in pitch as it manoeuvred to land.

His sacred marriage. Now he understood the flaw. He had sworn to be the Goddess's willing consort, but hadn't explicitly forsaken all others, and until he did, she would fear all rivals. And her power was building, beyond his ability to deny it. He had to act now. He sought for a form of words, and into his mind stabbed Hana's speech to him in the college cellar before Tashi's transformation, the raw power he'd felt behind it.

It would be his model.

I renounce all desire for Cass or any other woman, he asserted, the words in his mind clear and strong with the knowledge that this was the only way to save her. *She is not mine. I am not hers. I give her back to herself, without regret, without hesitation.* And now the final nails, struck by a hammer made of all his psychic strength: *I want no part of her.*

It exhausted him. And as if something inside had torn with no hope of mending, sobs choked up from his ruined chest and he started to cry. All the urge to violence fled from him, and into the gap that was left rushed the awareness of all the violence he had unleashed, all the people he had killed when he had never killed anyone before, never wanted to. The horror of it, now stripped of the shielding of the Goddess's righteous anger, brought howls of anguish bubbling up from whatever his lungs had become. He fought them down because they hurt too much.

You are mine, he sensed the words rise from the depths. *Mine alone at last, my beautiful boy…*

The air-craft set down. Emilia helped him to stand. He could hardly do so; he felt all wrong inside, pain everywhere, like thorned creepers coiled around his viscera. He didn't think the Goddess could keep him alive much longer, not when he left her domain – there were bullets still inside him, and the skin of his shaking hands had a green tint, and he couldn't breathe properly with the growths sticking from his mouth.

But at least Cass could now live.

The craft's door was already open, Hann in his grey uniform leaning out, arm outstretched. 'They're getting close!' he called, looking downhill towards the monastery. Orc kept his gaze from the novitiate's face as he was hauled in. He collapsed on the floor, avoiding the eyes of anyone. Darting glances showed him Dinah throwing her arms round Emilia, and he saw Aino and Yaggit there – Aino was shouting about Tashi, where was Tashi, but Orc couldn't hear Emilia's reply.

Then Aino cried out, Dinah too, and Orc saw Hann was gone from the doorway. Aino made for the door, and Yaggit shouted to forbid him; the boy halted, and Orc risked a look at his face and saw agony. There came the sound of things striking the machine's skin very hard. Glass cracked. Distant-sounding Max called out, then Dinah and

Emilia crashed the door closed and the air-craft lurched off the ground, the speed of its lift pressing Orc against the floor.

'We have to find Tashi!' cried Aino over the roar. 'We have to help him! And Hann!'

'Highcloud is lost, beloved one,' said Yaggit.

Lost, thought Orc. Highcloud, the Orb, probably his own life, Tashi's too. Now that everything else was over, that last struck him properly for the first time since Rukhan had talked about the boy's fate. Slipping towards blackness, he almost cried out at the sudden, terrifying sense of his failure. He'd promised Cass he would be more in the world. What was the world but people? What was Tashi but a person who'd needed and deserved more than his feeble attempts to help? Now the boy who'd saved everyone from a monstrous evil had gone alone to die on a cold mountainside because no one had tried hard enough, because no one had taken on the task of loving him.

He fought the approaching faint, tried to push himself up. He wanted to shout out what had happened to Tashi, that Aino was right, they had to help him, that it might not be too late. But his arms and his voice lacked any strength. He barely felt his head hit the floor.

41

THE MAKING OF THE WORLD

'Beloved one. Attend.'

The voice had been saying that for some time. Tashi wanted to raise his head, but his body, lying in thin snow, made no response to the sluggish command of his will. He'd stopped feeling cold now, stopped feeling anything. Hours of climbing, up past the last straggly trees, up into the first snows, had wasted him. Five skeletal bodies, he'd seen; but the last had been two hours ago. He'd made it perhaps higher than anyone. But he was still nowhere near the peak, and he had no strength now even to answer the voice that might be the one he'd searched for.

He had to. Had to. He'd managed to keep his Qliphoth-shaped body from running amok. He'd drawn his fortitude then from the sight of the Mountain, and here he was on its actual slopes.

With an effort that felt like it might bleed out the last of his life, he lifted his head and worked his arm enough to push his chest up. The world was white and grey with breeze-blown shreds of cloud. He searched with numbed eyes for the source of the voice.

Lord Gevurah?

Nothing but snow and mist, the cold air bitter in his nostrils. The voice had been imagination, conjured from his mind by the influence of his flesh, trying to rouse him enough to save him. He should have known it would be so. The power that had let him escape from Crome hadn't come from Gevurah at all, but had been some trick of magic, his own isolated self. He thought of trying to call on it again – perhaps it would allow him to reach the very peak, so that he would know for sure.

But he did already know for sure. And there was no extremity of need this time, no one he had to warn. Highcloud had taken his warning and rejected him.

'Dear heart. Look to me.'

He blinked, slowly, thinking he could pinpoint now the direction of the voice. He couldn't work his mouth.

Where are you?

In front of him, a little up the slope, a human shape began to form.

Master?

'No, dear heart.' The voice came from the figure. 'I am not your master.' And indeed, the outline was wrong. 'But I wish to help you.'

He couldn't make out any detail. Was this Gevurah? Or one of His servants? Or was it still a trick of his dying mind?

My master's soul. Did it reach the Land Beyond Sky?

'There is no "soul", dear heart.' It was the same as Crome had said. 'No soul, no God, not even any Witch Mother, not really. These are all masks for something deeper. If you accept death now, you will not find God. But if you let us help you to live, you will be allowed to find what lies beyond God.'

Beyond Gevurah? The impossibility confused him.

'You have searched so hard for truth. Let us now show it to you.'

His vision swam. Before him, the vague shape became what seemed to be a human being and a fiery serpent sharing the same space. As Tashi stared, trying to make it out, the cloud or mist rolled back, and he found himself looking up the glittering snow-shining slope to the high peak of Tamfang, the Holy Mountain, its summit not as distant as he'd believed.

He found he could stand, though stiff and numbed, feeling disconnected from his body. 'You are King Serpent.' Though he didn't know how King Serpent could be on the Holy Mountain, not unless the world were more broken than he'd thought.

'If I really were King Serpent, would I not appear in disguise?' spoke the figure. 'Your cultural devil was made a serpent out of fear of Chthonis, but also because Saeraf is the esoteric God, too inhuman for the masses and thus rejected in favour of a human mask. Behold.'

The figure faded. Behind where it had stood, there formed a line of golden warriors armed with swords: the *Elohim Gibor*, they had to be. He thought one had the face of Shikar, another of Nandi: all his fellow novitiates were there. Then they disappeared, and something began to form farther up the slope, but still some way down from the peak: a massive figure, enthroned, his face lacking detail but for his sternness.

Gevurah. But even as he tried to articulate his limbs to run towards the figure, it too faded. At the very peak of the mountain, there hovered in the high airs a great winged serpent of red and gold, bright feathers flashing in the sun. It looked made of jewels and sparks. Tashi's instinct was to refuse the idea that this serpent was somehow beyond Gevurah, but a counter instinct told him that this was right. He had never found Gevurah. All his life, all his teaching, had been based on a falsehood. Was this magnificence what he had truly sought?

And then the winged serpent, too, faded, and the sun faded, and far beyond the mountain's peak, far beyond even the distance to the sun, he saw a great light. But such a light! It almost made him weep with loss that he could not reach it.

The figure that was both man and fire-serpent re-formed. 'You see, dear heart? Gods behind gods, layers of increasing truth, all leading up to En Sof Aur, the Light Beyond the Mountain, and beyond which there is nothing.'

'The Land Beyond Sky.'

'That is a so-vague reflection of the true divine. Not that it is located beyond this peak in particular.'

Other figures appeared, like the first, an arc of them.

'Who are you?' asked Tashi.

'We are seraphim,' said the one who had spoken before, 'the fiery serpents who serve the true divine, which is love. And we know that you also wish to serve love.'

'I was deceived. What I wanted to serve was false.'

'With Orc and Cass, yes, it was false. Their version of love is confused. Your pure conception of it reached out to it, mistaking it for a kindred spirit. We can show you the real thing, for it is what we all serve. It is the longing for oneness, to heal the severed world.'

'Are you what they called the Shining Ones? The Kings Behind the World?'

'You have to see that everything is distorted. You know better than anyone that the lower world is all confusion. And even Highcloud is the lower world to us.'

That made sense. But they hadn't answered his question.

'You are wondering if you can trust us,' said the foremost seraph. 'If we had intended deceit, would we not have shown you things more in keeping with your wishes, rather than give you this hard lesson? Would we not have shown you this…?'

And there in front of the lead seraph was Shoggu, as solid as the mountain itself. Tears sprang to Tashi's eyes as his master smiled. He tried to speak but his throat wouldn't work.

He gasped, his heart pushing out with longing as Shoggu disappeared.

'Alas, Tashi, that was but a memory,' said the seraph. 'But we could have used it to manipulate you, had we so desired. Everything that ever happened, that has ever been spoken, ever been thought, is recorded by the world. This you were taught but did not realise its implication. For these records, occasionally glimpsed, are what gave rise to the consoling belief in the survival of the individual soul. It has no other truth. I know this is hard, but you have had to learn some hard truths already. That is why we believe you can learn these and help us.'

'Help you how?'

'We cannot form physical bodies – not yet. We need your help to build a better world. You heard the magician Daroguerre claim that he plans to build a new world. In truth, many desire to do so – especially now, for the idea is energised in the psychosphere, more so than for millennia. For the sake of love, Tashi, it must be ours that succeeds. We have been working on it so very long.'

'Heed this lesson,' said the next seraph. 'Once, long ages ago, there was a world that was very wicked. It was too complicated, and unguided. None had sufficient power to direct its progress, and so it made none. It spiralled into chaos, and had to be wiped clean, of life, of form, even of memory.'

The figure scribed a circle in the air before him. Somehow the shape remained in the air after its finger withdrew, a line of glowing light.

'A clean circle was left,' the seraph said. 'But now, see.'

Its finger touched the topmost point of the glowing circle, and a dot appeared on it, which protruded both above and below the line.

'Look closer. It is the Ouroboros.'

Tashi saw that the dot was in fact a serpent's head, and the whole glowing line its body.

'It bites its own tail,' he said.

'It is the first stage of existence,' said the seraph. 'Unity: the oneness that suffices unto itself. Yet behold, it now makes the fundamental cosmic error. It does not realise its oneness. The Ouroboros believes it bites the tail of another; it believes its tail to be bitten by the head of another. And so there is "other". One becomes two.'

And suddenly, there were two heads, two snakes, each taking half the circle. They writhed and fought, each not letting go, twisting into many different shapes. At last they formed a double spiral, and hung there.

'This is the form of life,' said the seraph. 'This is the form of the Serpent Mandala, the paradox that is both One and Not-One, the foundation of the world as humankind struggled up from primitivism. But now, watch! The Great Divorce.'

The serpents released each other's tails. One grew fiery wings and gold scales and rose above the other. It screamed down at the lower one, which writhed and coiled beneath, slippery and wet.

'Saeraf, which you saw earlier, and Chthonis, esoteric symbol of the lower world. Their sundering was a necessary ill. It brought pain, but also potential. It allowed the development of conscious ego structures. Now that has happened, we must reunite them, restoring oneness without losing what we have gained. Restore oneness to a world with ego structures, which you call your God-given self.'

'I don't understand.' But he felt it a beautiful idea, to restore oneness. It fitted the glimpse of the light they'd shown him, the one with the name that had sounded like Soulflower.

'You will understand in time,' said the seraph. 'All you need to grasp at present is that the resulting world will be beautiful. You who have glimpsed the power of love, who have yearned for it, will have a role in bringing it to all. The love you wanted from Gevurah, from your master, from Aino, from Sergeant Rasmuss, will be everyone's to enjoy.'

'How do you want me to help?'

'You must let us into you.'

'Possession?'

'We understand you have been tormented by it in the past. But you have also achieved great things: think back to your escape from Crome. Surely you do not take us for Qliphoth? You sensed the truth of what we showed you, of En Sof Aur?'

He had. And Soulflower couldn't have been false, could it? From what Orc and Cass had said, the Shining Ones were evil. But could he trust the Strandborns' opinions, when their love had been false and confused?

'Why do you need to possess me?'

'We need a physical body to spread our message,' the seraph said. 'We need to speak through you, on occasion, and it would not be possible to relate to you what to say: the delay would make our words seem incoherent, and in any case communication would not be perfect. It is largely so clear at the moment because of our joint focus, but also because you are dying, and your threatened ego is gathering to you the energy you used before, which makes certain magic possible.'

'It won't be long before you are beyond our help,' said the original seraph. 'And if your life were to end, there would be no Land Beyond Sky. It is not possible to enter En Sof Aur. We must bring its glory down to Earth. That is what love is.'

He thought he'd been resigned to die if he hadn't found Gevurah, or even if he had. But he didn't want to miss out on further understanding of what he'd seen. And Shoggu had told him that trust never required apology.

'Will you help us, Tashi? Will you help love?'

He checked his heart, and said, 'Yes.'

'Thank you,' said the seraph. 'Let yourself be displaced. Your past experiences will make it easier. Please do so quickly, so we can repair the cold-damage to your body.'

He recalled how it had felt, in the arena in Bismark, in the Torrento hotel room, to have his self pushed to one side. He felt the mental pressure of the seraph, and he let it happen. To not resist, to surrender, felt the most beautiful experience, like falling gently asleep without worry or care.

'I'm in,' came the voice of the seraph, now clearly male. 'Working to stabilise.'

'How much damage is there?' said the female voice of the second.

'I think he's saveable. Increasing energy. Heat infusion. Wow, that was easy.'

'Good response?' came a third voice. 'Need any help?'

'Don't think so. Hold on. Tissue repair progressing well too. He's... my god, he's more or less human modelling clay. The biological structures are almost completely transformable.'

'Of course,' said the female voice. 'He's a manifestation. Don't push it too hard, though. We don't want to break him.'

Tashi realised he was feeling less sleepy, but was still on the ground.

He'd never stood up at all. His eyes opened, truly this time, to cloud and mist. He couldn't move any part of his body. But he felt the warm surge through his blood, through muscles and skin he realised had become numbed with cold. They began to hurt.

'Aargh, that's not pleasant at all.'

'What isn't?'

'Pain. I'm going to try dampening it.'

'Sensory mechanisms are working, then?'

'Seem very good. And the pain's going now.'

Tashi felt that too.

'Let's get him up.'

He stood, with no will of his own, and brushed off snow that was melting to water. He felt the movements of his body, but had no control over them.

He directed a thought. *If you like, I can move by myself until you're ready to speak through me.*

No response. He moved without self-direction, striding down the snow-covered slope, retracing the wavering line of his footprints.

He tried harder. *Can you hear me?*

'How's the muscle control?'

'Near perfect. Much better than Bruce.'

'Bruce?'

'Our man on the beach?'

'Oh, God, you and your pet names.'

Please, answer me!

'Talking of assassins, aren't we running a risk of being mistaken for one after what happened in Bismark? Shouldn't we change his appearance?'

'We don't know what effect further transformations will have on his physical integrity. He won't be much use if he turns to gloop.'

'Ha! I quite fancy rampaging around as a blob. But yes, understood. We'd better think of something, though.'

Please, please, answer me…

'A code word, perhaps,' said the female voice. 'Actually, "pet names" has given me an idea. We'll have a dig.'

'Sure. We have a while yet.'

'They won't be going anywhere.'

Please...

A passenger in his own body, he descended the mountainside. The chatter in his head became less frequent, then stopped altogether. Still occasionally he tried to make contact. There must have been some mistake, some error in their taking control. Or perhaps there was something vitally important they had to accomplish right away, and they couldn't spare the attention necessary to talk with him or let him have any self-direction. It would need refining. Maybe the effort they'd put into saving his life had spent something.

The snow-cover thinned. The cloud and mist too, until the air cleared. He passed between the thin spruce trees and came within sight of both the main monastery and the ruin of High Place. From the ground to the south and east of the latter grew something extraordinary, a vast tree with a flattened canopy.

What happened? he asked, but not now expecting a reply. Beyond the tree and off to one side, the dull light glinted on an air-craft, half-crumpled and with a wing ripped off.

The Prelate's, it had to be. So the attack had happened. He couldn't account for the tree – he hoped the voices might mention it – but his unease at the sight was nothing next to his hope that Astrasis had been killed.

But even if so, his forces clearly hadn't been defeated. Tents had been set up farther downslope near the edge of the cliff, and grey-uniformed figures were moving everywhere, hundreds of them. The implications scared him: what had happened to the novitiates, to their masters? But the fear felt detached. At some point in the descent, he realised, he'd lost all contact with his body. The fear he now felt, and the disturbance at his realisation, was a thing of mind alone: nothing from his gut, from his skin, from his spine. *It is the flesh that fears*, he'd always been taught, and now he had no connection with his flesh. He wondered if that should be welcomed, but it felt wrong.

The female voice broke into his awareness. 'Sneezle-bear.'

'*Sneezle-bear*?' scoffed his occupier.

'From when he had the flu. As far as we know, he's told no one.'

'I am not the least surprised.'

'How's our boy doing?'

'I'm refining control all the time. What's happening in the wider world?'

'Nothing to worry you for now.'

'Come on, don't keep me in the dark.'

'Might I remind you that you volunteered? No benefit without cost.'

'Is that envy I detect?'

'Over and out.'

He carried on down to behind High Place, the red-flowered tree looming closer all the time. Skirting the ruin, he came upon three Kurassian soldiers smoking cigarettes.

His hands raised. 'Comrades!' came his voice. The soldiers dropped their cigarettes and swung rifles off shoulders, fumbling in surprise.

'Halt!'

'It's one of those bastards!'

'No, he's not Thangkaran, look.'

He faced the dark mouths of three barrels. 'I need to see Prelate Siegfried Astrasis.'

'You'll see our sergeant first.'

From the sound of it, then, the Prelate had survived. Tashi wondered why his occupier needed to see him. He remembered talk of an assassin. Was his body about to be used to kill Astrasis? He couldn't see how he could survive an attempt on the Prelate's life. But that didn't matter. If anyone was the enemy of love, it was that man.

The soldiers told him to keep his hands high and not speak. Two of them took him down the slope of the hill towards the tents, giving the space beneath the tree canopy a wide berth, as though they feared what might drop from its branches. Tashi both wanted to look at it and feared that his eyes would turn that way. It struck him as a towering and spreading presence of evil. Around the base of the trunk was an area of vegetation with an unsettling look; he was glad his gaze mostly kept away from it. He wondered what could have happened, but his mouth didn't ask, and the seraphim didn't speak with each other about it. Once past the base of the trunk, he saw that some distance down the hillside lay a row of what could only be bodies covered by blankets. The fear, the abstract bodiless fear, grew stronger. He'd departed the monastery that morning feeling no connection left with the place, feeling that he had no choice but to climb. He had pushed from his mind everything that an attack would mean, not expecting to return. But he realised now that Highcloud had never stopped being home.

The soldiers took him to a sergeant, who said, 'Who the hell are you?'

'Someone Prelate Astrasis will want to speak to,' said Tashi's mouth. 'Be so kind as to inform him that it concerns codename Sneezle-bear. His Grace will know what I mean.'

The sergeant looked at him in baffled irritation, then went to talk to an officer, who entered the largest tent.

'Let us know if you need advice,' came the female voice.

'I can handle it,' said Tashi's controller.

'Of course.' The female seraph sounded nervous. 'But given how critical this is...'

The Prelate emerged. Terrible bruises covered the right side of his face, and his eye had a patch over it; his left arm was in a sling, the wrist heavily bandaged. Welcome injuries, as far as Tashi was concerned, and fewer than the man deserved. But his fury and hatred, like his earlier fear, felt strangely detached.

'Your Grace!' his voice called, as he raised his arms higher. 'Be not alarmed! I present no danger!'

'You'll understand my reluctance to credit any such assurance.' The Prelate's voice and breathing betrayed pain. 'Keep your guns trained on him,' he told his men.

'Much has changed since our last encounter in your stateroom,' spoke Tashi, 'in ways I can only discuss in private. I have already given you a token that I am not who I was. Our talk will be to your great advantage. I consent to be bound if that will facilitate a meeting.'

The Prelate's single eye stared at him, narrowed, for several seconds, then he nodded. 'Sergeant, tie his hands and hobble him.'

This was done. Under the Prelate's direction, Tashi was led into the tent. The Prelate dismissed the medic in there, and the sergeant. 'Be alert for my call,' he told them, and when they'd gone he sat heavily in a camp-chair, a pistol in his good hand.

Tashi mentally readied himself for whatever the seraphim would do. He hadn't needed a catalyst at Crome's, and assumed he could now be infused with the same strength, perhaps enough to break his bonds. No doubt all this talk was to lull the Prelate into complacency, and though he hated his voice being employed to be pleasant to such a man, he saw sense in it.

'Speak,' said Astrasis.

'You should prepare yourself for some unusual revelations.'

'I doubt anything you tell me can be more strange than this morning's events. I'm astonished I'm not already insane.'

'Nonsense,' came Tashi's voice. 'You possess a robust mind in terms of accepting the supernatural, not least because of your research into the elementals. And after all, you have long planned something that would give many of your citizens an attack of the vapours.'

The Prelate's eye hardened with suspicion. 'Which is?'

'To put right a great and long-standing loss.'

'How can you know of that?'

'True, you have never spoken of it. But there have been hints enough. As you might have guessed by now, I who speak through this boy have replaced the force that caused him to attack you in your palace. You have lost an enemy and gained a friend.'

'A "friend" who keeps his identity from me?'

'A friend who saved you from becoming human clematis.'

That seemed to catch him out. Tashi wondered what the voice was referring to. 'I was too strong to be caught like that,' the Prelate said.

‘Believe that if you wish.’

‘I do. Not least because if you are who I suspect, you have no reason to want to save me.’

‘Because you know too much? You will soon have no reason to expose us.’

The Prelate exhaled. ‘Thank God for the morphine, or I think I truly would now be insane. You are who I think?’

‘We have hoped for the chance of a meeting for some time.’

‘You have the advantage of me, then. It was only two days ago that I first heard of your cabal of magicians.’

‘*Magicians*?’ Tashi’s voice growled. ‘We descended to the Earth on wings of fire, long before Kadmon left Eden. If you must give us a name, let it be “angels”.’

If that had been intended to impress the Prelate, it clearly failed. ‘Whatever you are, you enslaved my country to a falsehood. And made me a puppet.’

‘We have given your empire the means to rule the world.’

‘To what benefit of yours?’

‘Careful,’ said the female.

‘Our aims align with your own,’ came Tashi’s voice; ‘the destruction of the Witch Golgometh. The means by which the Empyreum achieves this has always been left open. But the Zhenaii Orb of Archive is one possibility. And we would not object to other uses to which you might put it.’

Tashi’s thoughts whirled. He’d never heard of the thing, but its name sounded like a warning.

‘There is a piece missing,’ said the Prelate.

‘We know. Some years ago, a Watcher greedy for forbidden knowledge tried to Inspire a novitiate with the Orb’s secrets. The novitiate was expelled, but he contrived to steal away the key of the Orb. We know where it is.’

‘And it will grant the power to conquer Golgomera? To destroy the Witch and build a cathedral to the Holy Mother?’ The Prelate’s voice lowered. ‘The true, and *restored*, Holy Mother?’

'It will. But you must first acquire more power, become High Prelate as your father was. And we can also help you in that. We can relate to you the secrets of your rivals, for nothing can be hidden from us. Did we not know what your mother called you when you were ill?'

'That must go no further. And you mustn't speak of her again.'

'Fear not. We have no interest in embarrassing you, nor in letting anyone know your true desire.'

'Objective.'

'As you wish.'

Astrasis turned his head slightly, hand covering his eyes and most of his face, as if he were struggling with thought or emotion. Surely, thought Tashi, now would be the time for his occupiers to infuse his body with strength. Surely if they served love, they could not let this man live.

Break the ropes! Attack him!

'Your Grace,' said his voice, when the Prelate had recovered himself. 'If you could release me.'

Yes!

'Your mouth is free,' Astrasis said. 'That's sufficient for you to advise me.'

'Naturally, some doubt still lingers from when this boy attacked you in your stateroom. But if you cannot trust us, you are useless as an ally.'

'Even if I trust your intentions, your vehicle has good reason to attack me. How can I know your control over him can't be broken? How can *you* know?'

'A fair question. But you must understand this boy's relationship with his body. Being raised here, he was never allowed to identify with it. It was only a tool. He has undergone possession several times, each of which has weakened his connection with his physical self. Most important of all, his last two physical forms have been abhorrent to him, and he has disassociated himself from his material nature. I have previous experience of taking control of another. Even with the subject being willing, it was difficult before. This boy was so easy, it was a joke.'

'Interesting.' Astrasis eyed him. 'But we cannot test your assertion without great risk. Say I removed your bonds, but kept hold of this pistol; your failure to attack me would not prove your control. He might hold himself in reserve until presented with a better chance.'

'True,' said Tashi's voice. 'But I believe one novitiate was taken alive?'

Only one? What happened to the others? Please, tell me!

'Yes,' said Astrasis, 'one who failed to Inspire himself.'

'Have him brought.'

None of Tashi's pleading to be told what had happened led to anything. But when Hann was led in after a minute, gagged and with hands bound and feet hobbled like his own, hope rose in him. Only now did he realise how demoralised he'd felt at the older novitiate's desertion. But that feeling now left him – Hann had realised where his duty lay. Even if he hadn't been able to Inspire himself, the dried blood caking one side of his head spoke of a willingness to fight. Hann's scared eyes met Tashi's and blazed with questions, with hope in return, with warning.

'Release my guest here,' Astrasis said. The men removed Tashi's bonds. 'Now leave.'

'First make him kneel,' said Tashi's mouth. 'Then no one is to enter, under any circumstances.'

The men looked at the Prelate, who nodded.

A ploy, Tashi thought, his excitement mounting. There were now two novitiates alone with the Prelate. Yes, the man had a pistol, but if Hann could be freed, there would be a chance – even if they both died in the process, it would be worth it. He didn't know why his occupier had asked for Hann to be made to kneel, maybe to put the Prelate off his guard; but such a position would hardly impede Hann if he could achieve Inspiration, and whatever the reason he hadn't done so during the battle, this opportunity must compel the *Elohim Gibor* to enter him even without the full ritual. If the gag was removed and Hann quickly called the Lords of Battle, he might become strong enough to break his bonds.

His controller made him pick up one of the lengths of rope that had been used to bind him, and moved him round behind Hann. Hann's questioning eyes followed him as far as they could, until Tashi was at his rear. Hann sounded like he was trying to speak Tashi's name. But Tashi's hands didn't remove the gag. Instead they put the rope around Hann's neck – to act as the choke-collar, clearly, since Hann for some reason wasn't in his bindings.

No, the breath-restriction needs to come last.

He pulled.

No, not yet!

But could it work? Could Inspiration come from the last element of the ritual alone, if the need was desperate? The *Elohim Gibor* had come to the first twenty-seven with no ritual at all.

The noises from Hann's throat weren't the words of the ritual. He was struggling, trying to wriggle free. Tashi's hands pulled the collar tighter. Too tight, he knew. He willed his hands to ease their grip, shouted in his mind that they were doing this wrong – he strove with the will that had been strong enough to halt his Qliphoth armour-shell – but still his hands pulled and pulled too tight, even after Hann had gone still, even long after he had gone still. Tashi's hands released the rope, and the older boy crumpled to the ground, silent, unmoving.

Tashi's eyes were fixed on him. He couldn't look away. Couldn't even blink. He didn't react. Couldn't react. There was nothing. No tears, no faster heartbeat, no sickness in his gut, no breathing hard, no way to howl, no way to express the pain and horror that was the entirety of his being, a flat, cold waste. He wanted to look away, willed himself and willed himself to look away; he willed his mind to oblivion. But there was no relief, just the merciless face of Hann's murder.

'Enough staring,' said the female.

'Just testing the control limits,' came the mind-words of his occupier. 'No sense from him at all.'

Tashi's body turned. His eyes met the Prelate's. The man looked faintly sickened. Tashi's arm extended, hand open.

'Think what's at stake, your Grace,' came his voice. 'Only we can make the Orb serve you, but you must trust us.'

Astrasis visibly steeled himself and handed Tashi his pistol.

SHOOT HIM, Tashi screamed in his mind, *SHOOT HIM SHOOT HIM SHOOT HIM SHOOT HIM SHOOT HIM*, as if Hann's murder might possibly have been part of the plan, a terrible but necessary sacrifice. *SHOOT HIM SHOOT HIM.*

His body made no move to. He strove to regain control of just his hand, to aim, to fire. He might as well have willed the sun from the sky.

His hand, after weighing the pistol, handed it back to the Prelate.

The bodiless pain carried on, an endless jarring squeal.

'Your courage is commendable,' he was made to tell the Prelate in a voice that couldn't coexist with the screaming inside him. 'It will be necessary in the days ahead.'

'I'll do anything to get her back and set her in her rightful place.'

'We understand. Now we'll leave you to your recovery.'

Tashi walked out of the tent, and nodded to the sergeant, who went in. He walked to the edge of the rough cliff above the Petitioners Road, and stood looking out over the hazy lower world as if contemplating a newly conquered realm. If he'd been able to grasp a moment's control, he would have hurled himself off.

'Excellent work,' came the female voice. 'Though staring at Hann was cruel.'

'After all we've done – all we're *going* to do – you're worried about that?' said his occupier. 'This little shit killed Scorpion. I was fond of Scorpion.'

It would hardly sink in, the enormity of it, of what his hands had been made to do, and of the realisation that his trials with the Qliphoth had served only to make him the tool of those who had replaced them: these people who were more evil than the offspring of sin. That such a thing was possible of human beings threatened him with utter despair.

Trust, his master had said, never required apology, even if misplaced. That his greatest mistake had come through heeding his master felt a grief too great to bear – and with no heart to break, he felt his mind might break instead.

Had Soulflower been nothing but a trick?

Could he trust his instinct that it had not? Or would that, too, be a terrible error?

And if it truly existed, could he find it again?

But what would be the point, he asked himself, as his body began a wandering examination of the Empyreal camp. Even if Soulflower was the power of love, of oneness, it would not punish or destroy evil. It had no will of its own. It was the power he had thought belonged only to Gevurah, but there was no Gevurah to wield it in judgement. There was no one.

The thought came as a stab of both light and pain.

No one but himself.

This wasn't like his Qliphoth ordeal. This time, his mind was free, not occupied with his body. And what inspired him was not false, like the Holy Mountain, but an eternal truth. He would not renounce his faith in Soulflower. He would find it again, and use it.

He, the most powerless soul alive, would put on the mantle of God.

42

WITCH BOY

The jolt of landing bumped Orc awake into pain worse than when he'd fallen unconscious. He struggled to make sense of the voices around him.

'We have to go back!' That was Aino. 'Help Tashi.'

'He's already gone,' said Emilia. 'I'm sorry.'

The noise of the elemental died, though the engines kept idling. In the relative quiet, Aino's question came querulous. 'What do you mean?'

'According to Rukhan, he climbed the mountain,' said Emilia.

'What? And you *let* him?'

'We weren't there.'

'But why? Why would he do that?'

Orc struggled to sit up. At his groan of pain, they all looked at him. Emilia made a step towards him, but only one.

He knew talking would be difficult, and so it was. 'They wouldn't let him be a novitiate again.' His speech slurred with the growths from his mouth.

Anger and upset blazed in Aino's face. 'Then we'll fly up onto the Mountain. He might still live.'

The ladder creaked. Orc's gaze shied as Cass's face came into view. All he caught was her obvious exhaustion.

'Shit, what *happened* to him?' she gasped. 'What are those in his mouth? How do we…?'

'I don't know if we can,' said Emilia. 'He was shot—'

'*Shot*?'

'And then this happened. Whatever it is, it might be the only thing keeping him alive.'

'Oh, my god…'

'Cass,' said Aino, 'we must fly onto the Mountain. We *must* find Tashi.'

She ignored him. 'Orc, how bad are you?' she asked in a trembling voice. She came and knelt beside him. He still couldn't meet her eyes.

'Been better.'

'This is her, isn't it? And that tree and everything was her too?'

'Cass!' insisted Aino.

'We'd never find him,' said Emilia. 'I'm sorry, but he could be anywhere on those slopes, and they're covered in cloud. Orc needs our help. Whatever Tashi did, he chose to do it. Orc didn't choose to be shot.'

'But look at him! He'd be better off dead.'

'Oh, for—' began Cass. Then, 'Wait, where's Hann?'

'I'm sorry, Cass,' came Dinah's voice. 'He jumped out. To fight.'

'No!' cried Cass. 'What the hell for? What good could he do?'

'There were soldiers coming closer,' said Dinah. 'Maybe he thought…'

'Oh, fuck…'

'Please,' said Orc, gathering the strength to speak again. 'Will someone tell me what happened? Where are we now?'

'A valley,' said Emilia, 'about fifteen minutes from Highcloud. As for what happened, after the vegetation began…' Her voice became tighter. 'Most of the soldiers ran. The novitiates Inspired themselves. Some attacked the fleeing soldiers and took their rifles and carried the fight to the ones farther away.'

'Used their *rifles*?' said Aino.

'They seemed to know how. But some novitiates didn't fight; they ran across to where we were and grabbed the Watchers and ran off with them.'

'What?' said Orc.

'Pig-a-back. Behind the ruin. It all happened so quickly. You were focused on Siegfried.'

'They would have taken them to safety, I think,' said Yaggit, the first he'd spoken. 'There's a secret path off the mountain.'

'It was chaos,' said Emilia. 'Then Cass and Max shot down Siegfried's craft.'

Orc glanced at her. Her face gave away nothing of her feelings.

'I don't think he's dead,' said Dinah. 'I've already told Em, I saw someone in a fancy uniform coming out of the wreck.'

'The only reason I hope he's not,' said Emilia, 'is he might still follow up the Empyreus proof, despite what's happened.'

'He also has the Orb,' said Orc.

'Not the Orb of Archive?' said Yaggit. 'Surely?'

'There's a lot to tell,' said Emilia.

'But not yet!' protested Aino. 'If the other air-craft was destroyed, then there is no threat. If we dominate the sky, we dominate the ground. We must go back there and defeat the soldiers, then find Tashi. Why are we here talking?'

'There were too many,' said Max from over by the craft's nose. 'The novitiates who chose to fight couldn't have won, not with all those men pouring up from the monastery. I'm afraid we have to assume they're dead. We'd never free Highcloud with one air-craft.'

'Then we go up on the Mountain,' said Aino.

Before anyone could repeat their objections, Orc said, 'I agree.'

'Don't be stupid,' said Cass. 'We need to get you help.'

'Help how? From where?' Pain ripped through him again; he could almost feel the internal bleeding. 'Find him… least he has a chance.'

She stood. 'You're not thinking straight. And we're wasting time.'

'Does no one else agree?' pleaded Aino. 'Are you all going to leave him?' He looked around at them, at his master and Emilia and Cass and Dinah and Max. None of them spoke. 'Then please,' he said, 'take me to the Mountain. I'll search for him myself.'

'No, beloved one,' said Yaggit. 'It is not your time.'

'He'll die!'

'He'll gain the Land Beyond Sky, if he is not already there. No one deserves it better.'

'You don't believe that!' said Aino, his face tracked with tears. 'You don't think he deserved to stay a novitiate after he changed. You would have refused him along with the Abbot!'

'Beloved one, you are letting emotion dominate.'

'Yes, master,' Aino bit back, a colder voice than Orc had ever heard from him. 'It is the influence of my body. It must be taught.' He stood and drew his short sword. The others gasped or cried out – Orc feared he might be the target, but Aino turned away and dropped to one knee. The boy quickly transferred the sword to his left hand, trapped its point against the deck with his foot, brought its hilt down hard like a butcher's guillotine to cut something on the ground before him.

He stifled a cry. It had all happened so quickly; Orc hadn't seen, but Yaggit clearly had, and with a yell of horror grappled with his novitiate, pulling him away from the sword, which he'd dropped on the blood-slicked deck. Yaggit called for bandages, and suddenly people were in commotion, more people than the craft was made to comfortably hold, and Aino's breathing seethed with shock. A wave of sickness washed over Orc at the sight of the two bloodied fingers lying there; he closed his eyes as the blank swamped him.

He woke from howling dark dreams to find a coat laid over him, and the only sound that of a distant crow. The air smelled faintly of farming, and was warmer on his face than before. They must have moved.

'How're you feeling?' came Cass's voice.

He tried to push the coat off and gasped at the clawing of his insides. He wasn't going to be able to get up. All he could do was lie still and breathe shallowly so it didn't hurt too much.

'Orc?'

He steeled himself to meet her gaze. She looked even more exhausted than before. He couldn't guess how long he'd been asleep. The door was open, he realised now, and there was no one else in the craft.

'Where are the others?' he slurred round a mouthful of saliva. 'Where are we?'

'Em, Di and Max have gone to see if they can find a farm and buy food,' said Cass, studying his face. 'We're somewhere in the south of Kurassia, so Max's money should be good. I wanted to try to get farther tonight, but...' She released a groan. 'I just couldn't. I was worried I'd lose Windbags and we'd fall out of the sky. Tomorrow, though. Tomorrow we should be able to get there.'

'Where?'

'Astolio's college. They might be able to help you there. We thought a normal doctor would be too dangerous, and probably useless anyway.'

'Good call.' It would have put Cass and the others in danger too.

'Just hang in there,' she said. 'I reckon we're over halfway.'

The whole night, he had to last, and most of the next day. It was too much, even if the college knew how to help. But he wasn't going to say so.

'Aino okay?'

She winced. 'He wouldn't say why he did it. Him and Yaggit left, I think to try finding the rest of the survivors. We bandaged up his fingers. Yaggit seemed to know what he was doing there. Em told us all about the Orb and everything. I had an idea about that, actually,' she went on, as if talking about something else would make his condition go away. 'Maybe, if we could get hold of it ourselves, it could tell us whatever connection we have with the Zhenaii, explain those dreams I had on *Nightfire*. If it's the Orb of Archive, maybe it holds their whole history, not just their magical secrets.'

It made sense. But they would have to get it first, and the key, and he didn't have the strength to work his mouth around that argument, so he just let out a soft grunt. His eyes had closed again. It would be a monumental struggle to open them.

'Shit, stay with me,' came Cass's voice, shaky now. 'You'll be okay, right? Till we get to the college?'

Even swallowing was an effort. 'I'll try.'

'Why doesn't that bitch fix you properly? She's kept you going, why can't she heal you?'

He had to attempt an answer. 'Only so much power, maybe.'

'Only so much power? Did you see the size of that fucking tree?'

'I meant…' But he couldn't organise his instinct into words: that it was the primitive vegetative aspect of the Goddess the Kurassians had feared, and so that was the aspect that had worked through him, and the finer points of biology were probably beyond her. But that was all guesswork, and it wasn't worth the effort it would take to articulate.

'And can't she do anything she wants anyway?' said Cass. 'Isn't that how Hana brought Tashi back, by becoming the Mother?' She gasped. 'Holy shit,' she said – a whisper, as though anything louder might frighten off whatever thought she'd had.

'Hn?'

'Why didn't I think of it before? Transform yourself by manifestation!'

It hadn't occurred to him either. The idea almost paralysed his pain-fogged brain, the chances and risks, the unknowns of it. But it made him come round, a little. The existence of this chink of a possibility raised the last energy from his near-dry well.

'I can't become the Mother like Hana did.' He spoke carefully around the growths in his mouth. 'And I don't know anatomy well enough to properly restore myself. My insides are all messed up, and I don't know how they should go.'

'Stop thinking of problems!'

'I'm not, just figuring it out. Everything—' He coughed, and Cass groaned at the mix of blood and sap he spat out. 'Everything is held in the Serpent Mandala. Everything about me. The Goddess – the complete Goddess, not the plant-thing – she knows every atom of my proper body.' The implication shivered through him. 'I can't transform myself. I need to go in there and ask *her* to do it.'

To encounter the Goddess as herself: he didn't feel ready. But now that he had no choice, the possibility thrilled as well as scared him.

'You mean go into the Mandala?' said Cass. 'Is that safe?'

He didn't give her the straight *no*. 'What else is there?'

She breathed out. 'Okay, how do I help? Same as at Crome's place?'

'No, don't leave. I'm not sure. Just keep holding my hand. Keep thinking who I am. And close your eyes. Hana said it might work better if no one's looking.'

She nodded. 'I need to pee first.'

While she was outside, Orc tried to ready himself mentally for what he was about to do. Even if this kept him alive, it might still be the end of his self. Sparrow had told him many magicians' minds had been wrecked by getting too close to the Mandala, and he'd sensed the danger every time he'd approached it when calling Otter. The first time, at his Initiation, it had almost destroyed him, and there would be no Otter to pull him back now; his animath couldn't follow where he was going.

But in his scape on the island, Sparrow had also said he might be able to approach the Mandala and survive without being dissolved, because of his identity as the Goddess's consort. It was true that Sparrow had been speaking Daroguerre's words, but the magician had told the truth when it suited him. And it had felt instinctively right at the time; the mistake was that he hadn't truly been her consort then. Now he was.

Still, it couldn't be denied: he was pinning his survival on the possibility that the magician who'd wanted to trash his mind had nonetheless spoken the truth.

When Cass returned, she knelt on the floor beside him and took his hand.

He held her eyes a short while, and realised that he truly did see her now only as a friend, rather than with desire. It felt peaceful, but also a loss. 'Ready?' he said.

'Uh-hn.'

'If I make it back—'

'None of that "if" crap. Doubt is the enemy of magic, right?'

He settled as comfortably as he could, slipped his focus-stone over his head and grasped it tight in his free hand, and began to clear his mind. As at High Place, he was more successful in this than ever before his marriage. Gradually the pain receded, and after perhaps half an hour, when finally ready, he took himself directly back to the Great Ziggurat.

Water softly lapped against its summit. Out to the horizon, blue sea reflected warm sky. He listened to the water for some time, then turned to the shaft: the route of sacrifice, by which the Sun-King finally met the Goddess. The stone grille was gone.

He shed his clothes and squatted naked beside the shaft, his toes gripping the edge. He shifted his weight and tipped himself in.

Down he swam, and down, as the light faded into dim green between the weed-covered walls of the shaft, and soon the stone was no more, and he was swimming between great, close-pressed columns of kelp, glimpsing shy fish and seals between them. Farther down, the kelp stems closed in, knotting together with tree roots until his dive became ever more twisting. His skin brushed slippery fronds, scraped against bark.

Too deep for an otter. He'd committed himself to being beyond his animath's help, even if he panicked and wished for it.

Ahead he sensed the dance of the serpents before their separation, the beautiful, dangerous, dissolving oneness. There was no difference in size now between the kelp stems and the tree roots, and all was alive and moving, with scales visible in the deep green dimness. He fell between the coils that seethed and writhed – impossible that there were only two serpents – falling towards its core as though he were stone-weighted. The scaled bodies thrashed around him but never touched him; he plummeted through a tunnel whose walls were moving snakes, greys and purples and reds and greens, patterns of stripes and diamonds. He couldn't remember how he'd come here, nor from where. He had a vague feeling that there had been pain, but now even the possibility of his body began to seem unreal, as though he'd only ever been a mind, falling forever towards its peaceful, finally accepted dissolution.

And yes, he did accept it now. All the times he'd ever called Otter to save him had been a mistake. Otter had been a ruse of Geist's, to stop him achieving what Geist himself had always feared to accept. How had he not seen that this was best? The universe had existed in Oneness before, and longed to return to it, but the artificial construction of the mind-self prevented it. Now he would discard his self, and nothing would prevent it. Even if his consort identity did allow him to survive the Goddess-Mandala with his mind-self intact, he would refuse to let that construct get in the way of full connection, completion, Oneness.

He plummeted. Not far now. The tunnel began to lose definition.

From somewhere distant came the squeeze of a hand. It pricked his mind, the same hand that had pulled him back once before. But that was when he'd feared the Mother, and he no longer did.

The hand wanted to remind him of himself. To re-mind him, re-self him. But the self was pain. His life, everyone's life, was proof of that. The mountain-top god of the self was the many-headed serpent monster that had begged him not to look at its shame, the shame of self-awareness. The god to which Tashi had been in agonising thrall.

Tashi.

The one he'd failed to help.

And suddenly, as sharp and clean as a needle, he saw that he was about to fail again, in the same way. Dissolution of his self would free him from pain, but millions of others would still suffer. All the heads of that degraded serpent.

He had to accept pain, to help others. That was what a true shaman did.

His hand grasped the other's hand. His mind grasped the bright knife named *Orc*.

The snake-tunnel vanished. He shot out into a vast space filled with stars. Before him was a milk-white globe. He fell towards it, ever-faster but with no sense of movement. As the globe filled his vision, he saw features on its surface, features that made up the suggestion of a woman's face that was not Cass's but reminded him of her: the same face he'd seen at Crome's house, and in the mat of sea-life at his marriage.

He aimed his thought at the ever-nearing features. He was about to meet the Goddess in her human form, and she would know his.

Great Goddess, he spoke with his mind. *Mother of All. Somewhere, at some time, you gave birth to me.*

The globe's surface was now all he could see. The face filled his vision, getting less distinct as he fell meteor-fast. In the centre of her forehead was a black dot.

I am part of you, though a separate part. You know me.

The dot approached at terrifying speed. He was going to fall right into it.

Mother, let me know my true self so I can help others.

It was a dome. A black dome. It rushed to fill his vision. He couldn't close his eyes.

Across it was written in giant metal letters GAIA ENGINEERING INC.

He smashed through it and down into blackness.

He came to as though from a long, deep sleep, but behind another's eyes, another's ears. He was lying in bed, on his side, covers up to his armpit. Someone was stroking his bare shoulder. Conflicted feelings, vaguely sensed: annoyance at the presence, enjoyment of the touch.

'You're coming, and that's that,' said a woman's voice. 'You're not old enough to stay here for a week by yourself.'

'I am, if you give me the chance. Anyway, why isn't Dad staying home this time?'

'The only reason he's never come before was work commitments. This year, he doesn't have any the second week, so you can both come and join us then. You'll like it. It's by the sea.'

'Dad doesn't want to go.'

'He said that?'

'He doesn't like John.'

'Don't be silly. John's a wonderful man, when you get to know him. Julia wouldn't have married him otherwise. They're expecting us all to be there and we will all be there. Your moping isn't going to change that.'

He came round again, as though he'd fallen back to sleep in that bed, but clearly he hadn't slept all the time between because he was now in a moving vehicle, still behind the other's senses. The strange auto halted outside the gates of a white house whose walls were bright and warm with sun. A man in his forties stood there, eyes deep-set in his stern face, his jaw fringed with beard. He came to the open window on the far side of the vehicle, the driver's. 'Pavel,' the bearded man said, holding out his hand, and the driver leaned through the window to shake it. 'Glad you could make one of our little gatherings, at last.'

'Thanks, John.' Pavel sounded nervous. 'It's the first year I've been able to get away.'

'Of course, of course.' The bearded man smiled thinly and looked past the driver. 'Good to see your boy, too. Come on out, Kasperi, let's see how tall you are.'

Kasperi got out of the passenger door – reluctance, nerves – and walked round the front of the vehicle. John's eyes were almost at his own level.

'The terrible two have gone shopping in town together,' said John. 'Drinks on the terrace? Leave the luggage.'

Kasperi followed, hands in pockets, as the two men walked up the winding path to the house and round its side to the terrace. Weird-looking statues bordered the rear garden, catching Kasperi's attention, provoking unease. But through a gap in dark-green trees, a sea sparkled joyously.

'And here's the other member of our merry troupe, not on her phone for once,' John said. 'Caroline?'

And Kasperi turned his head and the girl—

And everything blurred into her and changed, and the sun was full on them and they were up to their necks in the sea, sitting against a stretch of old wall whose submerged parts were heavily grown with bladder-wrack that moved in the soft swell of low tide, caressing skin, squidgy at their backs. Out in the sheltered bay, boats bobbed; along the curve of the beach, children built sandcastles.

Kasperi picked a frond, popped one of the air-sacs. '*Fucus vesiculosus*,' he announced, 'is the taxonomic name. It was once used to treat a disease of the thyroid gland, when it swells because of lack of iodine.'

'And I thought it was just nature's bubble-wrap,' said Caroline. 'How d'you know that?'

'I'm going to be a marine biologist. It's our job to know such things.'

'"Our job to know such things",' she repeated with a slight smile, mimicking the sound of him.

Embarrassment, but pleasure. 'What about you? What will it be your job to know?'

'Dad wants me to help him with his esoteric bullshit, but I'm going to code. I seem to be good at that. Not as interesting as seaweed, I know.'

She'd sounded mischievous, a little sarcastic. 'You know giant kelp?' he said. '*Macrocystis*. It grows many metres tall off the Pacific coast of North America. One day I'm going to go there and freedive in it.'

'You can freedive?'

'Only to beginning level. My father made me promise no deeper than ten metres for now, but I've been to fifteen. I could teach you?'

'I think my dad would make me promise ten centimetres,' Caroline said. 'What's it like?'

'When you're neutrally buoyant down there, just hanging in the water, it's beautiful.'

She watched him. 'I think that's the first time I've heard a boy use that word.'

'Beautiful? Did I use it right?'

'Perfectly. The boys I know, they'd think it was soft.'

'But they must call you beautiful?'

Her smile seemed to trap the sun on the water. 'Charmer! "Cute", sometimes.'

'English boys are idiots, then.'

'Are they,' she said. 'C'mon, back to the beach, I'm cold.'

She stood up, adjusted the fit of the tiny shorts that sucked wet to her backside. In a panic of caught breath, Kasperi eye-grabbed as much of her as he could as she bent her knees and flung herself forward into the sea—

And it was later, much later, maybe years later, and the world had darkened in the meantime, but now there was music and a hubbub of excitement. He stood in a crowded place with many tables and chairs and a floor cleared for dancing, everything lit with a few electric lights. The man with the deep-set eyes and stern beard, John, stood halfway across the room, sharing a smile with the woman whose hands he held, the woman who looked a little like Caroline, and who Kasperi knew very well – unease sensed faintly, trouble. The two kissed, and he looked away and found Caroline, on her way back from the crowded bar. He watched her stare at John and the woman. Then she turned and met his gaze. Held it. No trace of smile to match the laughter of those around her, only a bleeding of pain. She set her drink on the nearest table, so clumsily it fell over, and turned and pushed through people towards the open front of the building.

He forced his way after her. The building's front was strung with lamps, their light reaching across the road to the beach, just far enough for him to catch sight of her running across the sand. He chased her across the thumping surface lit by the falling, waxing moon. Spray flung up as she hit the water. She angled farther out, towards the horizon, each step plunging. He called her name, and she slowed, but didn't face him. His shoes filled as he charged in after her, and still the music from the hired restaurant came faintly – *Just help yourself to my lips* – as he stopped behind her, thigh-deep.

'It's okay, Caz.' He touched her shoulder. 'It doesn't have to affect us.'

She grabbed the hand he'd put on her shoulder and turned to face him, what he could see of her face a ruin of grief. 'Of course it fucking affects us! It's why they're doing it.'

'They just want to be happy.'

'Yeah, and what would make them happier than breaking us up?'

'Caz—'

'No, you listen. You're happy with it, are you? Going back to lies, everything being secret? You're not bothered? Because if you're not, just say so.'

'Wasn't it kind of fun, when it was secret?'

'I don't want it to be a secret. I love you. I don't want to hide it. We haven't done anything wrong.'

'I know. And I hate it too – I just wanted to make you less upset, but that's gutless. We can't scrub out how we feel. I love you, more than anything.'

'Then help me.'

She clutched him in desperation, and he clutched her in desperation, and she dragged him down so they sank to their knees, the water at their chests.

'How can we stop them?' she said. 'Pull the electrics?'

'Maybe there's another way,' he said. 'How about we do it first?'

'What?'

He took her hands under the water, pressed them between his. 'Marry before they do. Right here and now. Then they can't nullify it. They'll have to let us be.'

'Marry how? It won't be legal.'

'Your dad doesn't care about that. This ceremony of theirs isn't legal either, but it means more to them than the official one next week.'

'You're right,' she said. 'Make his belief in magic work against him for once. Quick. We've only got minutes.'

'I'll go first.' His voice shook. 'I, Kasperi Oscar Heikkinen, take you, Caroline Jessica Jackson, to be my wife, witnessed by moon and sea and stars. To be my wife forever, and let nothing separate us, and if anyone tries, let the moon and sea and stars destroy them.'

She repeated him with the names changed. A moment of silence passed, the weightiest, densest moment ever, before she said, 'They heard. They witnessed it. I could tell.'

He drew breath. 'You may kiss the groom.'

Their mouths locked, and she dragged him down and under the surface, and their airless kiss carried on. And something shifted and time shifted and there was no mouth, but the airlessness continued, and the weight built, and the pressure, as though he was sinking, not two feet under but many, many times that.

Deep in the sea, the dark…

He'd lost sense of when this was. He'd lost contact with Caz, and with Kasperi; he was behind no one's eyes now. Blackness surrounded him, pressed right through him. No self, no him, no nothing. Terror gripped him, a mind-shredding violence of it, a buffeting horror of the endless and nameless. He struggled against it, his mind straining for release, for escape, up, and up, but this time there could be no help—

A hand in his. He squeezed it hard, and knew whose it was – and knew that she knew who he was. She knew.

'You back?' she said, into the restored calmness.

'Think so.'

'I'm going to look.'

A moment later she gave a short scream and her hand broke from his. He flashed open his eyes to her staring at him, hands cupped over her nose, wide eyes wet at their lower lids.

It hadn't worked. Shit. But the pain had gone. He checked the feel of his body and found no discomfort.

'Kas—' she hoarse-whispered. 'Kasp—'

Surprise robbed him of voice for a moment. No taste of sap now, he realised, no sense of plants on his face. He sat up. No pain.

'Kasperi?' he said. 'Is that what—'

'Yes! That's it!'

'How did you…?'

'Your face,' she said weakly. 'You came back!' She threw herself at him, arms round him, kissed him full on the lips. No stabbing in his wrist, no bracelet of thorns. But nor did he feel anything at her kiss except regret and a hope that she would make it short.

She pulled away, troubled, perhaps at his lack of reaction. The silence that followed was too much.

'Your name's Caroline,' he said. 'Caz.'

'Caz!' Excitement lit her again. 'Of course. So I almost had the right name all along.' She wiped her eye. 'You got through the Shroud! Will all our memories come back now?'

'I don't think it'll work like that. I guess going straight to the Goddess bypassed it, but I don't know if I can do it again. I almost lost myself. If I didn't happen to have the right train of thought…'

'But did you find out – you know, *that*? What we were?'

'I saw some of my old self's memories, but I couldn't get his thoughts.'

'But you got our names,' she said. 'Our surnames too?'

He hated that he lacked the courage. But he couldn't lie outright, not to her. 'That doesn't prove anything. If we had the same father, say, but different mothers.'

'Did we? Is that likely?'

'Like I said, it was all confusing.' He wanted to get her off this subject. 'I found our middle names, though. Yours is Jessica, mine's Oscar.'

'Oscar! So that's why it came to me at the ziggurat? But I thought it was from a link to your wetsuit. Why would you choose a suit that went with your middle name?'

'Maybe there wasn't one that sounded like Kasperi,' he said – and immediately, a needle of instinct warned him of his mistake, and that he had to cover it. 'Or maybe our suits had nothing to do with our names after all.'

But her eyes were already wide. 'Hold on,' she said. 'Just a second. O-R-C-A. C-A-R-O. Kass-pri. Pi-cass. Do you see?'

He'd already seen. 'That's a bit of a stretch, isn't it?'

'No. There's something I'm still missing, but my heart tells me the idea's right. We didn't choose our suits for our *own* names, we chose them for each other's.' She breathed deep, and he dreaded what was coming. 'And why would we do that? Only one reason.'

He'd lost. He had to get it over with. 'Yes.'

'So we could wear each other. We were lovers.'

'Hm.' He couldn't tell her they'd gone even further than that. He never would.

She made a sound that might have been a word, or might not, and buried her face in her hands and burst into tears. He made no move to comfort her. This wasn't distress, but relief, the end of two years of uncertainty and anguish. Except it wouldn't be, and she didn't yet know that. He closed his eyes, his heart filled with cold lead.

'My god,' she said at last. 'Why didn't you say?'

'Because it can't change anything. Not now.'

'What, your goddess? We'll see about that. I've learnt a few things.'

'Cass – Caz – listen. She would've brought down your air-craft – that's what the tree was about. Her power was out of control, because you were a threat, to me and her. So I had to… change how I felt about you. Like Hana did to me at the college, before she restored Tashi.'

He wanted to brave her face, but couldn't. After a dry silence, she said, 'And it worked?'

'We can be good friends, though. The best friends.'

She said nothing.

'And it means we can focus on what's more important,' he said, to fill the space between them. 'Remember when we left the island, we agreed to focus not on us but what was going on around us? You said it again, at Highcloud. Well, we messed that up, didn't we? We should've been all about helping Tashi, but this thing between us took over. But now we can draw a line under it. We have to focus on the world, on the Kaybees, on uncovering their plan and fighting it.'

'*Fighting* it?' she scoffed. 'Oh, sure. Why do you think they changed your face?'

'Changed?'

'Yes! That's how I almost got your name, when I recognised your real face. They made you look more like me, to keep us apart. It's obvious.'

He ran a hand across his features. They felt the same, but he knew she wouldn't lie, not about that.

'They *want* us not to be together,' she said. 'And now they must be dancing for joy. Bloody hell, Orc, you talk about fighting against them, but when have you ever fought *for* anything? For *us*? You said the Goddess tried to bring down our air-craft, but she was acting through you.' She shook her head. 'Kasperi didn't come back just now, only his face. You're still the weakest person I've met. I need some air.'

She quickly stood, almost stumbling. The steps creaked under her feet.

He didn't know whether he should follow her. He suspected not. He felt empty inside, as though she'd ripped the guts out of him and spread them out on a table with neatly written cards to caption all his faults.

But all the same, he'd been right to say this was bigger than them. They had to direct all their energies towards those that threatened the wider world. They had to fight the Kaybees, and they had to get the key to the Orb of Archive before Astrasis could. And doing that as lovers wouldn't have worked anyway; they would have squabbled, got jealous, focused on themselves and each other again. And this way, he could bring the Goddess's power into play. Even if he was weak, *She* most certainly was not.

When Cass hadn't reappeared after several minutes, he got to his feet and moved around. His legs were a little shaky, but otherwise he felt newly made. He went to the door. There was no sign of Cass in the field, a hillside pasture that had recently been cleared of sheep, judging by the short grass and the dried dung. The hilltop screened them on one side, and woodland on the others; he guessed the trees fifty yards to the east was where Cass – the girl he'd married, in some lost time and place – had gone to think.

He went carefully down the steps and along to the window of the machine-gun port. His reflection was different, though still recognisable. Red now tinted his dark-blond hair; his skin was a little paler and his features more pronounced, with a slight pointedness to his eyes. Less like Cass, but still not wholly unlike her. It felt a spear of cold, dirty iron all through him, the extent of the Kaybees' manipulation of his life, the theft of what might have been.

And what could they possibly have gained from it?

He lay on a patch of grass free of sheep-dung, gazed up at the gentle clouds that almost covered the sky, and tried to make sense of everything, to pull it together into a theory: the Voice of God, the 'beautiful, clever daughter' he'd apparently caused something terrible to happen to; his visions, his memories. But nothing worked. The woman he'd seen at the wedding ceremony, the one about to marry Cass's father John – why should she be the face of the Goddess? If she was Cass's mother, as the resemblance suggested, why was she only then marrying Cass's father? Was John not Cass's father after all? Or had they been living together unmarried? But in either case, why would their marriage have broken up his and Cass's own relationship?

Had his supposed memories been distorted, to include images from his previous visions? Or the other way round? And if visions or memories were being manipulated, then was it by a deeper part of his own mind, or an outside force?

He growled at himself. Again, he was becoming self-focused. Unless it helped to fight the Kaybees, he had to stop this. Fighting them, on his own account but more importantly on behalf of the Goddess, was what his life was about now. If he was weak, it was because he hadn't fully committed himself to the battle.

And it now seemed he might have more time to accomplish that than he'd feared. He reckoned he'd been fourteen or so when he and Cass had met, and his father had still been alive then. Even if Pavel had died right after, that would take him to twenty-one, and instinct told him he wasn't quite there yet. And maybe Pavel had died not long before the wedding ceremony: perhaps that was the sense of darkness he'd sensed hanging over it. What had they been then? Sixteen?

Had he already taught Cass to freedive?

'No...' He sat up and curled over and buried his face in his knees. Why had his memories been about her? Surely he could have restored himself just as well by remembering something unrelated? Why would the Goddess have wanted to show him marrying Cass? For all time, or so he'd said. Was his newer wife mocking him?

What an unholy fuck-up. He wondered if Otter might have any advice to give him, but he was too psychically exhausted to scape and find out.

An hour later, as dusk was falling, the Bismark trio returned. After they'd got over the surprise of his recovery, and Orc had sketched out an explanation for his altered face, they told their own tale of spotting wood-smoke and finding a track to a farm, where Max's money had bought them food and beer and some horse-blankets.

'I don't think we were followed back,' Max said. 'But we'll have to keep a watch tonight.'

'Not Cass, though,' said Emilia. 'She needs to sleep. If anyone comes, we'll just have to keep them out of the craft and take off as quick as she can manage it.'

'She might need someone to talk to, as well,' said Orc. 'Someone who isn't me.' He knew difficulties might arise from her telling the Kurassians about his relationship with the Goddess, but that couldn't be helped. If she needed to unload her heart, so be it.

Cass came back not long after. She said little over their meal except that she was tired, and cut off any attempt to discuss what they would do in the morning. No one pressed the point.

The women slept upstairs; Orc shared the main deck with Max. All but Cass took turns at the watch. In the grey dawn, they gathered to share breakfast on a blanket laid out beside the craft. To Orc, Cass looked barely less tired than the evening before.

'Where to, then?' said Emilia. 'There's no rush to get to this college of yours any more.'

'Sundara gets my vote,' said Orc. 'The big college in Jiata, the one linked to Hana's. We'll be safe from Astrasis if he does decide to come after us, and the shield will keep the Kaybees off our backs while we work out how to tackle them. And we need to convince the Sundarans about Empyreus.'

'Are we sure we are in danger from Siegfried, though?' said Emilia. 'He might still follow up the Empyreus proof, and then we'd be throwing away a chance to work together. Not an altogether enticing prospect, but needs must.'

'Once we're safe in Sundara, we can find out how things lie with your brother,' said Orc. 'Assuming Dinah's right, and he's still alive. Till then, we can't take the risk. The Kaybees might find a way to convince him the proof was fake.'

'But the Trine should have received it, nonetheless,' said Dinah. 'It might still be something we can use in the future. Em? You all right?'

She was looking troubled. 'We shouldn't be discussing our plans till we know we can't be overheard,' she said. 'I've had an idea, but I'll keep it to myself for now. You said the college we were heading for yesterday has a shield too? Would it not be best to make for there anyway, even if we no longer need their help?'

'Hm,' said Orc. 'Yeah, I guess that does make sense. And Hana should be there, or at her parents' close by. Maybe we can find out something with a joint-scape. We'll have three of the Fire Stealers then. I know you don't have your stone—'

'Yes, about that—' said Dinah, but Emilia cut her off:

'Later. But if the Shining Ones are listening to us now, they'll know we're heading there. Assuming they still control the Empyreum, they could send troops – or Siegfried's other air-craft, the one you damaged in Bismark, if it's been repaired.'

'The transcripts said project baffomet wasn't suitable for "micro instruction",' said Orc. 'And they seemed very reluctant to use Empyreus that way. I think going straight there so we can plan more openly is our best bet. Caz? Think we can get there today?'

'I don't know, Orc,' she said. 'I've no idea how far it is. I can get Windbags moving us in the right direction, but that's as much as I know. And we're out of starting charges, correct?' she asked Max.

'Used the last ones yesterday,' he said. 'But from what I've seen of your ability, we should still make a good rate.'

'Okay,' she said. 'And I agree we should go there first. Someone needs to tell Astolio and Nadora about their sons, if they don't already know.'

Orc's stomach sank as he realised he'd completely forgotten about them.

'Better get going,' said Cass as she stood. 'I need to visit the woods.'

They all did. Orc went last, after helping to clear away the remains of breakfast. Ten yards into the trees, he scraped out a pit with the end of a fallen branch, and used that, cleaning himself afterwards with leaves.

He didn't return to the field straight away. He had a niggling sense of a realisation waiting, just beyond his awareness or past the edge of his vision, for him to come across it – something about what had changed in himself. He thought of scaping and calling Otter, as this felt like Otherworld stuff; but he also sensed it was related to the Goddess, and that wasn't Otter's area.

He wandered slowly through the wood, its spacious quiet punctuated by occasional bird-calls and the scrabble of squirrel-claws on bark. It felt as if he recognised it from a dream, and perhaps in that dream he had arranged to meet someone here – or was it that he was dreaming now, and the truth was trying to push through from outside? Each boot-crack of a twig seemed both as ordinary as could be, and as though it might trigger a shift in the whole world. The way an oak branch passed in front of another as he walked beneath them, the depth of it, struck him as forcefully as if he'd never witnessed it before; the leaves' russets and golds felt a message he might decode if only his mind could wake in the right way. The smells of rot and fungus hung damp and elusive in the cool air, the long-ago scent of summer's gentle fall into autumn.

He froze, stock still, as a dizziness of understanding swayed through him.

Geist had forcibly Initiated him into the mysteries of the Otherworld, and ever since, he'd felt divided, torn between the worlds of magic and reality. But here, the two were one: this was both the world of magic, every bit as much as the soulscape, *and* the world of reality. How had he not seen that it had been flipped around, that it was the city, not nature, that belonged to the psychosphere, the world of ideas?

The beauty of it flooded him. He wasn't divided between two worlds at all – they had always been one and the same. The Goddess had given him back his old self, healed into wholeness. He sensed there was more he should understand; he turned this way and that, as if the secret language that could define this new world might be hanging in the air, waiting for him to pluck like a ripe fruit or a harp-string.

'Where are you?' he whispered, as though She might come walking towards him in human form, a form whose lover he could truly be. 'Teach me,' he breathed. 'Show me what it means to be your consort. Let me love you. Let me live for you before I die for you.'

He folded his hand around his focus-stone and tried to relax his mind. His sense of Her grew stronger, but no more defined: She was everywhere, but in no one place more than another. Fear struck him that it would always be this way, that he would never know Her any better than he did now.

The sound of flapping made him whirl round. *Kronk*, came the deep-throated call of the large midnight-black bird on the tree branch.

Orc stared. It was too solid to be an Otherworld entity. The bird wore no mask, but that might mean nothing now. He grasped his focus-stone harder.

'Raven?'

'Harr,' came the answer. 'You know me, then. And I know you, though as Lord of Beasts you don't impress. Where's your beard? Those few bits of stubble hardly warrant the name. And where are your antlers? Is your phallus primed and loaded?'

Lord of Beasts? Otter had used that term. 'Why are you here?'

'To check on your well-being. That's what he asked of me. You seem hale enough. I'll tell him so.'

'Geist, you mean?' He gasped. 'He asked you? So you know where he is?'

'Harr,' said Raven. 'Is he here, is he there? He's not all there, that much is plain.'

It seemed too clear a sign to ignore. 'Can you show us?'

'If you can keep up,' said Raven, and launched into the air, flapping towards a gap in the woodland canopy.

Orc tore his focus-stone pendant over his head and grasped the crystal hard. He pelted to the edge of the wood and across the field to the air-craft, exulting in a body that once again worked. He hurtled panting up the steps and into the hull, relieved to hear Windbags already roaring. 'We have to go, now!' he called as he heaved the door closed. Ignoring Dinah and Emilia, he climbed the ladder enough to stick his head through the hatch. 'I saw Raven,' he told Cass's hunched-over form. 'We can follow him to Geist.'

'Oh, God,' groaned Cass. 'That's all we need.'

'But he can help, surely?' called Emilia from below. 'And I have a lot to talk to him about.'

'Fine,' said Cass. 'So do I. Call out the directions, then. I'll get us up.'

Orc sat himself in the nose-gunner's position. Luckily the craft was already facing south, the direction in which the distant dot of Raven was heading. Orc willed the bird to stay in sight. The craft lifted off, moved forwards.

'Ten degrees right,' he called up to Max.

'Not much I can do till we pick up speed,' came the reply. 'Then the flaps and rudder will start working.'

Orc worried Raven might drift out of sight to one side before that, but even without airscrews the craft quickly gained speed. It tilted as Max worked the controls and lined up with the black dot. 'Right, right... back left a bit,' Orc called, as woodland and farmland fell away beneath him, tens of feet, then hundreds. Still their speed built, until the elemental's roar was drowned out by the wind against the nose and Max called back to Cass to take it steady: the craft had only been tested to one hundred and fifty knots.

For all their speed, they never gained on Raven. Sometimes Orc lost sight of Geist's animath, but a squeeze of his focus-stone and a moment to open his mind always brought the bird back. Rural country zipped beneath them. They overflew farms and villages, where people looked and pointed, and once a town. Orc hoped the insignia on the wings would prevent reports to the authorities, or they'd make an easy trail to follow.

After an hour or so, the land began to grow more wild. They passed over high moorland dotted with clumps of pine; herds of deer panicked at their approach. They climbed over a range of mountains: not high enough for snow, but the air still grew cold. Luckily the weather was clear and kind, and they only caught the edges of a couple of clouds. On the far side of the range, a layer of overcast limited their altitude to a thousand feet above the moorland and forest, which stretched as far as Orc could see. They passed over no more than a few isolated settlements. He saw no metalled roads.

Raven began to descend.

'Slow!' Orc called back. 'I think we're here.' Nerves attacked him at the prospect.

Wind resistance quickly rubbed off their speed. They came over the lip of a valley. On a descending shoulder of a hill stood an old castle; near the gate in its courtyard wall milled warriors from a story of olden times: men armed with spears and bows, mounted on ponies. At the sight of the air-craft, the horsemen turned their faces to the sky; many drew up in confusion. Then they bolted every which way, the various groups gradually finding a common heading up the track out of the valley.

They overflew the castle. Two hundred feet below, the courtyard's gateway was blocked by a wagon. Several bodies lay about, but Orc saw living figures too, staring up at them. The one with the rifle had to be Geist, and there was a boy in his teens, and two slightly younger children, and...

'What the hell is that?' he muttered. Some kind of disguise or illusion, it had to be.

'Okay!' he said. 'I'll guide us down. We'll come in just in front of the gates.' He hoped the horsemen wouldn't regain their nerve.

'Dinah!' called Max. 'Get ready on the starboard gun.'

Emilia counted Cass down. Orc shoved the door open even before the craft was settled. As soon as they'd properly landed, thirty yards from the castle wall, he jumped down and ran towards the entrance. Halfway across the bridge that spanned the moat-ditch, a gruff voice he recognised called from behind the wagon that blocked it.

'Hold, there! Who are you?'

Orc stood straight, heart almost bursting. 'Not forgotten my name, surely? You were the one who gave it to me.'

'Elok's stinking trousers!' Crawling between the wagon's wheels, clutching a rifle, came Geist. He clambered stiffly to his feet, dirt all down his front. Teacher and student eyed each other. Orc thought Geist's cheeks more sunken, his face more lined. But there was a fire in his eyes.

'Speak of the devil, they say,' said Geist. 'Though legend makes him out to be more prompt when you do.'

'Had a long way to come,' said Orc. 'We followed Raven back here.'

'Lucky I sent him to check on your health.'

'Lucky I thought you'd want to see for yourself.'

'Hm,' said Geist. 'Well, you look fine. More than fine: a real sight for sore eyes. Changed a little, though, it seems to me.'

'A lot has,' said Orc. 'But you're still menacing me with a rifle, just like the first time we met.'

Geist grunted, pointing his gun down to the ground. 'And this time you're saving me, I suppose you'd say. That's one of the new Empyreal air-craft, is it? Borrowed?'

'Something like that.'

'Can it take five more?'

'No problem. Cass is the best elemental operator around.'

'What a day,' muttered Geist. 'If my brain doesn't burst from this, I'll be amazed. Petri!' he called behind him. 'Get that wagon moved!'

He turned back to Orc. 'We'll find somewhere isolated, then we'll talk. And plan. I'm already thinking an Empyreal air-craft might be enough to persuade a certain captain to give up a prisoner or two.'

'Plans should probably wait till Astolio's college,' said Orc as the wagon's wheels creaked. 'The Kings Behind the World? We've learned a lot about them.'

'Likewise.' Geist turned back to the gate. 'Look, you'd better brace yourself.'

Through the gap came the teenager Orc had seen from the air, who he now vaguely recognised as being from the college, and the two children, and then the woman who was naked above the waist – and who below the waist was, genuinely, no disguise, no illusion, a snake. A giant snake. He stared in amazement, horror, fascination.

And then a surge of delight filled him, purely at the absurdity and unexpectedness of the world – the broad world in which he'd now found his place. He only held back from laughter because it would be impolite.

Even if he didn't have much time left to him, by the Goddess, it was going to be interesting.

43

PATIENT J

Nadia tried to infuse her walk with a sense of confidence as she approached Simeonov across the roof-garden of Hephaestus Tower, at the far end of which he stood theatrically backed by the lights of the city's tallest buildings. More theatrically still, he affected the costume in which he'd talked to Hana Quallace: the heavily embroidered cloth-of-gold robes, the mask with the brightness behind its eye-holes. Ostentatious beyond belief, but she had to humour him.

'Dragomir,' she said.

'Oh, now, call me "A",' he replied. But perhaps sensing her struggle for a response that expressed anything of her feelings without insulting him, he waved a hand to get her out of an answer and replaced his appearance with that of a trim, imposing man in his sixties – possibly even something like his original self, she thought – wearing a pin-striped suit.

'Tell me, then,' he said. 'How did it go with Vanessa?'

'Exceedingly well. Her despair was easy to turn to anger. Though timing was touch and go – I only broke through just as she was about to hurl the stone into the depths.'

'Close shave.'

She sensed disapproval, and aimed for greater positivity. 'But I'm going to enjoy being her handler, I think. The sense of engagement is like having a favourite character in a novel. I actually like that she has independence, that I have to persuade her rather than control her.'

'So you wouldn't prefer Hollander's role? He seems to find Tashi rewarding.'

'Well, he would, with full sensory input.'

'Not envious, Nadia? We others won't have long to wait now. But we'll have to keep an eye on Hollander. It'll serve us ill if he spends all his time making the boy stuff his own face, and others' orifices.'

'Perhaps we should give him a little more credit,' Nadia said, though pleased Simeonov's opinion of him seemed so low.

'Talking of influence,' Simeonov said, 'Stanwyck is convinced Kasperi is now experiencing the animaths without masks.'

'What?' she said. 'How?'

'It might have come from an identification with the Lord of Beasts.'

'He's the Sun-King, not the Lord of Beasts! How did that happen? The Sun-King is agrarian. The role has no connection with animals.'

'Both are the consorts of the Goddess. And Kasperi has a northern influence from Geist and the Fire Stealers story.'

'Yet another problem from that marriage fiasco.'

'Well, it saved his life at Highcloud,' said Simeonov. 'Also, his decision to be loyal to it throws up a barrier between him and Caroline. That's useful, for now.'

'It opened a channel to the Serpent Mandala.'

'A fluke. Future occurrences can be inhibited.'

'It got him back his *face*, for fuck's sake.'

Simeonov raised an eyebrow at her language, though she'd heard him use much worse. 'Manipulating his appearance had served its purpose anyway. It inhibited them. His marriage now fulfils that role.'

'And if Caroline tries to recode the Goddess out of existence – and succeeds?'

'I doubt she can. She might not even want to reclaim her teenage "husband" – not for now, anyway. But just in case, I'll think of a way to stop her without damaging anything else, until the time comes.'

'There've been too many close calls,' she said. 'My nerves are worn ragged. It's only luck he didn't learn more at the Conclave. Only luck he didn't die.'

'There I agree. I didn't enjoy it.'

'Oh, come now, Drago, it was a rush,' came a voice. Nadia turned, and for a moment of panic saw diseased skin stretched over a skull, a breath-mask, tubes, wires, plexiglass. Then order re-established itself, and the newcomer wore robes and the ibis head of Thoth. Tsegaye, she guessed, from his voice and feel. She tried to dispel the glimpse of his true appearance, along with the knowledge that her own must be similar.

'A rush,' said Simeonov, who seemed not to have shared it. 'The point of all that preparation was to avoid rushing.'

'We always knew this would be a plate-spinning exercise,' said Tsegaye, his bill clattering bizarrely.

'Not a whole dinner service.'

'I quite enjoy it,' Tsegaye said. 'Problem-solving on the fly. Speed-chess.'

'If there were less at stake,' said Simeonov, 'I might agree with you.'

'It's passed, Drago. The Conclave alone had the power to breach the barrier, and it's a spent force.'

'Yes, fine. We dodged a bullet. And dear old Patient J seems to be settling down after his little... episode.'

Even the use of the initial jangled Nadia's nerves. She glanced across to the black pyramid dominating the city centre, twice as high as the tallest skyscrapers. Its gloss reflected the lights lower down, while towards the apex its surface possessed only a sheen from the underlit clouds. No sign or sense of activity, to her relief. The human magma chamber was quiet.

'Might he be affected if they start using their real names?' she said.

'He always used the full version himself,' said Simeonov. 'Kasperi seems minded to call her Caz, and she seems minded to keep calling him Orc. But we'll monitor.'

'But should *we* be using them?'

'Hm, that's worth thinking about. Perhaps we should take their example.'

'And what happens,' she said, alarmed at the number of things Simeonov hadn't yet given proper thought to, 'if we have another college episode before the proper time, and they do call out each other's real names? Even the short forms? His anger might be too great to suppress.'

'Shit, you're right,' said Tsegaye. 'Could be enough to flick the big reset switch.'

'Reset?' she said. 'We won't have the energy to start again. We'll be fucked.'

'We'll give him some thought too,' said Simeonov. 'We have time.'

'We hope,' said Nadia.

'Maybe set up a cult with the aim of keeping him suppressed?' suggested Tsegaye. 'An anti-Gevurah?'

'And anti-Chokmah,' said Simeonov. 'And anti-Kefer.'

'Another plate to keep spinning,' said Nadia.

'And I always hated circuses,' said Simeonov.

'Yet here you are,' said Tsegaye, 'running the biggest there's ever been. The chief of thirteen ringmasters.'

Simeonov smiled, albeit tight and thin. 'And who are the clowns, I wonder?'

'Well, I can name the tragic one,' said Tsegaye. 'All the more amusing because he takes himself so seriously.'

'Mister Geist,' said Nadia, 'prepare to meet Mister Custard Pie.'

For the first time in she didn't know how long, Simeonov's teeth showed in a grin. 'Spot on.'

GLOSSARY OF CHARACTERS, PLACES, TERMS

(Characters are listed by first or last name depending on which usage is more common in the text)

Aino: novitiate of Highcloud
Androloch: fortress in the Bourgoune, seat of the Lamia
Anik: former novitiate of Highcloud, with whom Shoggu travelled from Thangkara to Torrento before becoming a Watcher
Animath: shamanic power animal or spirit guide, such as any of the Fire Stealers
Arris Entarna: mother of Wilhelm Kirrus, later called the Holy Mother of Empyreus
Astolio: master of the College of the Inner Eye
Astrasis: aristocratic Empyreal family; see Siegfried, Emilia and Bastian
Bane: affliction often suffered by those who attempt to penetrate the interior of Golgomera
Bastian Astrasis: now-comatose explorer, brother of Siegfried and Emilia
Bazantin: town on the Kymeran coast
Bismark: capital city of Kurassia and the Empyreum
Bourg: inhabitant of the Bourgoune
Bourgoune: region of north-western Kymera

Cank: novitiate of Highcloud

Carnega: harbour town on the Kymeran shore of the Shallow Sea

Cass Strandborn: freediver, approximately nineteen years old. Named by Geist after the word 'Picasso' on her wetsuit. Ostensibly cousin to Orc.

Chthonis: one of the two serpents of the Mandala, associated with water and earth, matter, dissolution, the female, the unconscious

City of Gold and Glass: according to Astolio, the abode of the Shining Ones deep within the psychosphere

Clairaudioscope: device for listening to voices recorded in the psychosphere

Clathma: Thangkaran two-handed sword used by novitiates of Highcloud when under the influence of Inspiration

Commonwealth: trading empire around the north and east of the Southern Ocean, centred on Sundara

Crome, Anders: resident of Bismark

Daroguerre, Lucien: Kymeran magician, ostensibly part of a conspiracy with elements of the Sundaran Navy to manifest a goddess and drive the Empyreum out of Kymera

Dinah Strevin: companion to Emilia Astrasis

Dreadnought: largest class of Empyreal warship

Dughra: a Thangkaran short sword used by a novitiate

Eagle: one of the Fire Stealers

Eel: creature of the Otherworld, source of knowledge, an aspect of Chthonis

Elohim Gibor: angelic warriors, servants of Gevurah, called during Inspiration

Elok: devil figure in Kurassian religion

Emilia Astrasis: Deaconess of the Holy Mother, sister of Siegfried and Bastian

Empyrean Church: Kurassian state religion dedicated to the worship of Empyreus

Empyreum: the Kurassian Empire

Empyreus: formerly Wilhelm Kirrus, held by the Empyreum to be Son of God
Eve: in Thangkaran and Empyrean religious teaching, the first woman
Felca: one of twin children under the protection of the Lamia
Ferman Quallace: Kurassian émigré to Kymera, psychic researcher, adoptive father of Hana
Fire Stealers: in myth, six animals (Fox, Hare, Otter, Sparrow and Eagle, under the instruction of Raven) responsible for passing the sacred fire to humankind
Focus-stone: crystal that enhances connection with the psychosphere
Fox: one of the Fire Stealers
Freediver: one who goes deep underwater by holding their breath
Geist: adventurer and shaman who discovered Orc and Cass washed up on a beach, and who initiated Orc into shamanism. Former teacher of Hana Quallace, and possibly others. His animath is Raven.
Genku: novitiate of Highcloud
Gevurah: Thangkaran name for God
Goddess, the: general term encompassing the many aspects of female deity, such as the Mother
Golgomera: large and mostly undeveloped continent in the south
Golgometh: Witch-goddess supposedly resident in Golgomera
Hall of Wisdom: chamber holding the head of Empyreus
Hana Quallace: Kymeran shaman in her mid-twenties, formerly a student of Geist. Her animath is Hare.
Hann: novitiate of Highcloud
Hare: one of the Fire Stealers, animath of Hana Quallace
High Place: old part of Highcloud monastery, mostly ruined in an attack by the Kurassian Emperor Konstantin
Highcloud: Thangkaran monastery on the lower slopes of Tamfang
Hollow Isles: cluster of three small islands in the Shallow Sea
Holy Mother: name given to Arris Entarna after her son Wilhelm Kirrus was renamed Empyreus

Immaterium: term used by the Watchers of Highcloud for the psychosphere

Inspiration: process by which a novitiate of Highcloud becomes possessed by the *Elohim Gibor*

Iron Tiger: Empyreal dreadnought destroyed by Skalith on the orders of Daroguerre at the Hollow Isles

Jiata: capital city of Sundara

Jorik Quallace: brother of Ferman, clairaudioscope inventor

Kadmon: in Thangkaran and Empyrean religious teaching, the first man

Kaybees: term used by Orc and Cass for the Kings Behind the World (from KBs)

King Serpent: devil figure in Thangkaran religion

Kings Behind the World: secretive and seemingly long-lived organisation of magicians

Kirrus, Wilhelm: see Wilhelm Kirrus

Konstantin: Kurassian emperor, pre-Empyreum

Kurassia: chief country of the Empyreum

Kymera: country to the south of Kurassia

Lamia: ruler of the Bourgoune

Lammager: bone-breaker vulture, holy bird of Thangkara

Land Beyond Sky: in Thangkaran religious teaching, destination of the righteous dead

Lions Hill: site of the Bismark air-field

Lords of Holy Battle: the *Elohim Gibor*

Mandala: shortened term for the Serpent Mandala

Manifestation: the practice of altering or creating physical matter by magical means, an art reputed to have been used by the ancient Zhenaii before they were destroyed

Maskar: town in Kymera near the Bourgoune

Mister Burns: fire elemental used to help power the warship *Nightfire*

Mother, the: primeval aspect of the Goddess

Murun: Watcher of Highcloud

Nadora: wife of Astolio, mistress of the College of the Inner Eye

Nandi: novitiate of Highcloud
Navel, the: sacred site at the highest point of the Hollow Isles, situated above a large cave
Nightfire: experimental warship in the Kymeran Navy
Novitiate: boy between the age of twelve and twenty assigned to protect a Watcher of Highcloud
Orc Strandborn: freediver and shaman, approximately nineteen years old. Named by Geist after the word 'Orca' on his wetsuit. Ostensibly cousin to Cass. His animath is Otter.
Otherworld: broadly, the shamanic term for the psychosphere
Otter: one of the Fire Stealers, animath of Orc Strandborn
Paiko: novitiate of Highcloud
Park Crescent: residential street in Bismark in which Anders Crome resides
Petri: esoteric student at the College of the Inner Eye
Plack, Simonis: occultist, ex-Trine
Psychosphere: non-material aspect of the world, comprised of the accumulation of mental, emotional and psychic energies, which can be manipulated as thought-forms or used for divination, etc.
Purakash: grandmaster of an esoteric institution in Jiata, Astolio's superior
Qliphoth: in Thangkaran religious teaching, demons, the offspring of sin
Ranga Samka: half-Thangkaran adventurer, previously 'manager' of Orc and Cass during their search of the sunken ziggurats
Raven: one of the Fire Stealers, animath of Geist
Records: aspect of the psychosphere in which the world's memories are held
Riaz: eldest son of Astolio and Nadora
Rukhan: Chief Watcher of Highcloud
Sack of Ducks: inn located in Maskar
Saeraf: one of the two serpents of the Mandala, associated with air and fire, thought, definition, the male, the conscious
Saguna: large harbour town in Kymera

Sallo: household servant of Ferman and Stefanie Quallace
Sattrano: second son of Astolio and Nadora
Scape: short for soulscape, in the sense of a shamanic journey
Serpent Mandala: symbolic form of the core of the psychosphere, seen as two serpents dancing, being Saeraf and Chthonis before they take their separate identities. Mastery of it is believed to confer immense knowledge and power.
Shallow Sea: near-landlocked body of water between Kymera and the northern coast of Golgomera
Shikar: novitiate of Highcloud
Shining Ones: the Kings Behind the World
Shoggu: Watcher of Highcloud
Shroud: term for a barrier obscuring part of the psychosphere, especially *the* Shroud, which blocks Orc's and Cass's memories
Siegfried Astrasis: prelate of the Empyreum, brother of Bastian and Emilia
Sink: in Thangkaran religious teaching, the site in Golgomera that leads to the Witch Mother's hell
Skalith: ancient dark goddess of the ziggurat-builders
Sorrell: youngest son of Astolio and Nadora
Soulscape: state of psychic interaction between a shaman and the Otherworld, also term for a shamanic journey
Sparrow: one of the Fire Stealers
Stefanie Quallace: Kurassian émigré to Kymera, psychic researcher, adoptive mother of Hana
Sundara: large country to the east of Kurassia and Kymera, centre of the Commonwealth
Sun-King: in the ancient ziggurat-building culture, the sacrificial consort of the Goddess
Tamfang: the Holy Mountain in Thangkara
Taropat: Abbot of Highcloud
Tashi: sixteen-year-old novitiate of Highcloud monastery
Taslan: one of twin children under the protection of the Lamia
Thangkara: country in the Empyreum, to the north of Kurassia

Thera Malchis: psychic engineer of the warship *Nightfire*
Three Eyes: a guardian of the sacred fire, enemy of the Fire Stealers
Torrento: capital city and chief port of Kymera
Tree of Death: site of Wilhelm Kirrus's sacrificial death in Golgomera
Trine: trio of adolescent boys trained to receive psychic messages from Empyreus, the means by which he guides the activities and technological progress of the Empyreum
Ulnur: Bourg warrior, guardian of Taslan and Felca
Valkensee: lower chamber of government in the Empyreum
Vanessa: sorceress of Torrento, possessor of a large focus-stone given her by Ranga Samka
Watcher: one of twenty-seven monks of Highcloud monastery tasked with protecting the world from magicians
Wilhelm Kirrus: Kurassian War leader, later renamed Empyreus
Windbags: an air elemental
Witch Mother: Thangkaran term for the Goddess
Witch, the: Kurassian term for the Goddess, specifically identified as Golgometh
Yaggit: Watcher of Highcloud
Zhena: land of the Zhenaii in ancient times, south of Sundara
Zhenaii: ancient people reputed to have possessed the art of manifestation, later destroyed by a flood
Ziggurat: ancient pyramidal step-temple, most of which now lie underwater

Acknowledgements

Once again I'm indebted to Jane Middleton and Jeff Richards of the Blockies writing group, who helped nursed this book from its conception; to Sam Primeau, Dave Thompson and Pete Long of the wonderful *SFF Chronicles* community; and the Tri-Angels: Juliana Spink Mills, Liz Powell and Regina Yau, all for their help and advice. Special mention must go to Chris Van Meter, who went far beyond the call of friendship in critiquing this large tome despite the bad eyestrain it caused him. Thanks to Anna Dickinson for recommending to me Karl Theweleit's excellent study of the proto-fascist Freikorps, *Male Fantasies*, which was instrumental in helping me focus the Bismark section of the story, and to Emma Barnes of Snowbooks for her hard work and belief.

The Fire Stealers sequence continues in THE MANDALA PRAXIS Read a taster...

The jungle air fumed with an overabundance of fertility and its inevitable counterpart, decay. For all Geist's experience of being in the wilderness for weeks at a time, he longed now — ridiculous — to hear some comforting human sound from the university buildings. But there were only bird-calls, the hum of insects, the chatter of a distant macaque.

Orc stopped against a near-wall of vegetation. The trees grew unfeasibly close together: Geist didn't understand how each could get enough light.

'I only found a way through yesterday,' Orc said. 'Tell me if you can't manage it.'

The boy got belly to the ground and wriggled through a gap where the host-victim of a strangling fig had rotted away. Geist set his hat down, half-convinced he'd never see it again. The next ten minutes were a twisting torture, following the dirty soles of buckskin boots, often having to shout for Orc to wait. At last they reached an opening where a tree had died, the ground littered with rotted wood and crawling with millipedes. Geist stood with difficulty — and saw her.

Ten feet up on the nearest teak, the bark had fallen away to reveal a face grown from the sapwood. The tree beyond showed something similar, still mostly bark-covered but more extensive, an upper body with a suggestion of breasts and shoulders. Turning, Geist was amazed to see many of the trees had some suggestion of the same form and face.

And it was a face he recognised. From fifty years in the past came the memory of the glimpse at the forest edge as he'd struggled through the snow, fleeing for his life from the friends of the man he'd killed.

He swallowed emotion. 'What the hell is this?'